D0209142

Reader's Digest

Reader's Digest

VOLUME 2 1997
THE READER'S DIGEST ASSOCIATION, INC.
PLEASANTVILLE, NEW YORK

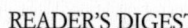

READER'S DIGEST

Editor-in-Chief, Books & Home Entertainment: Barbara J. Morgan
Editor, U.S. Condensed Books: Tanis H. Erdmann

The volumes in this series are published every two to three months at Pleasantville, N.Y.

FIRST EDITION: Volume 230

CONTENTS

THE THIRD TWIN

KEN FOLLETT

Twins.

One, a violent criminal.

The other, a kind, thoughtful man.

Two different people. Yet both are living proof of an insidious cold war experiment.

And now that experiment is about to spring frighteningly to life.

———

"Provocative, well-paced and sensational. . . . Shines with the authenticity that's Follett's trademark."

—*Publishers Weekly*

Sunday

A HEAT wave lay over Baltimore like a shroud. The leafy suburbs were cooled by a hundred thousand lawn sprinklers, but the affluent inhabitants stayed inside with the air-conditioning on full blast. On North Avenue listless hookers hugged the shade, and the kids on the street corners dealt dope out of the pockets of baggy shorts. It was late September, but fall seemed a long way off.

A rusty white Datsun, the broken lens of one headlight fixed in place with an X of electrician's tape, cruised through a working-class neighborhood north of downtown. The driver was a handsome man of twenty-two, wearing cutoff jeans, a clean white T-shirt, and a red baseball cap with the word SECURITY on the front. On the car's passenger seat was an open binder. He glanced at it occasionally, memorizing a page of technical terms for a test tomorrow. Learning was easy for him, and he would know the material after a few minutes.

At a stoplight a blond woman in a Porsche convertible pulled alongside him. He grinned at her and said, "Nice car!" She looked away, but he thought he saw the hint of a smile at the corners of her mouth. "Race you to the next light," he said. She laughed, then put the stick shift into first and tore away like a rocket.

He shrugged. He was only practicing.

He drove by the wooded campus of Jones Falls University, a much swankier college than the one he attended. As he passed the imposing gateway, a group of eight or ten women jogged by in running clothes—tight shorts, Nikes, sweaty T-shirts. They were a field-hockey team in training, he guessed.

The women turned into the campus, and suddenly he was overwhelmed, swamped by a fantasy so powerful and thrilling that he could hardly see to drive. He imagined them in the locker room—the plump one soaping herself in the shower, the redhead toweling her long hair—when something happened to terrify them. Suddenly they were all in a panic, wide-eyed with dread, screaming and crying, on the edge of hysteria. They ran this way and that, crashing into one another.

He pulled over to the side of the road. He was breathing hard, his heart hammering. This was the best fantasy he had ever had. But a little piece of it was missing. What were they frightened of? He hunted about in his fertile imagination for the answer and gasped with desire when it came to him: a fire. The place was ablaze, and the women were terrified. They coughed and choked on the smoke as they milled about, half naked and frenzied. And he was there watching. Walking around, he would select his main victim: a pretty girl with a vulnerable look. He stared straight ahead, seeing the scene like a movie projected onto the inside of the Datsun's windshield.

After a while he calmed down. He knew he should drive on, but the fantasy was too wonderful. It would be dangerous—he would go to jail for years if he were caught—but danger had never stopped him doing anything in his life. "I want it," he murmured, and he turned the car around and drove through the gateway, into the campus of red brick buildings.

MRS. Ferrami said, "I want to go home."

Her daughter Jeannie said, "Don't you worry, Mom. We're going to get you out of here sooner than you think."

Jeannie's younger sister, Patty, shot Jeannie a look that said, "How do you think we're going to do that?"

The Bella Vista Sunset Home was all Mom's health insurance would pay for, and it was tawdry. The room contained two high hospital beds, two closets, a couch, and a TV. The walls were painted mushroom brown, and the flooring was plastic tile. The window had bars, but no curtains; it looked out onto a gas station.

"I want to go home," Mom repeated.

Patty said, "But Mom, you can't take care of yourself anymore."

Jeannie bit her lip. Looking at her mother, she wanted to cry. Mom had strong features: black eyebrows, dark eyes, a straight nose, a wide mouth, and a strong chin. The pattern was repeated in Jeannie and Patty, although Mom was small and they were both tall, like Daddy. All three were as strong-minded as their looks suggested: Formidable described the Ferrami women. But Mom would never be formidable again. She had Alzheimer's.

She was not yet sixty. Jeannie, who was twenty-nine, and Patty, twenty-six, had hoped she could take care of herself for a few more years. That hope had been shattered this morning at five o'clock, when a Washington cop had called to say he had found Mom walking along 18th Street in a grubby nightdress, crying and saying she could not remember where she lived.

Jeannie had got in her car and had driven to Washington, an hour from Baltimore, on a Sunday morning. She picked Mom up from the precinct house, took her home, got her dressed, then called Patty. Together the sisters made arrangements for Mom to check into Bella Vista, in the town of Columbia, Maryland, between Washington and Baltimore.

"I don't like this place," Mom said.

Jeannie said, "We don't either, but right now it's all we can afford." She intended to sound reasonable, but it came out harsh.

Patty shot her a reproving look and said, "Come on, Mom, we've lived in worse places."

It was true. After their father went to jail the second time, the two girls and Mom had lived in one room with a hot plate on the dresser and a sink in the corridor. Those were the welfare years. But Mom had been a lioness in adversity. As soon as both Jeannie and Patty were in school, she got a job as a hairdresser and moved them to a small apartment in Adams Morgan, a respectable working-class neighborhood.

She would fix French toast for breakfast and send Jeannie and Patty to school in clean dresses, then do her hair and her face—you had to look smart, working in a salon—and always leave a spotless kitchen with a plate of cookies out for the girls. Mom had always been so capable, so reliable; it was heartbreaking to see the forgetful, complaining woman on the bed.

Now she frowned, as if puzzled, and said, "Jeannie, why do you have a ring in your nose?"

Jeannie touched the delicate silver band and gave a wan smile. "Mom, I had my nostril pierced when I was a kid. Don't you remember how mad you got about it?"

"I forget things," Mom said.

"I sure remember," said Patty. "I thought it was the greatest thing ever. But I was eleven and you were fourteen, Jeannie, and to me everything you did was bold and stylish and clever."

"Maybe it was," Jeannie said with mock vanity.

Patty giggled, and suddenly the mood was lighter. It was a good moment to leave. "I'd better go," Jeannie said, standing up.

"Me too," said Patty. "I have to make dinner."

They both kissed their mother and then moved toward the door. Jeannie felt she was abandoning her. Nobody here loved her. She wanted to say, "Tomorrow I'll bring you breakfast and stay with you all day." But it was impossible. She had a busy week at work. Guilt flooded her.

The moment they were outside the door, Patty burst into tears. Jeannie felt like crying too. She put an arm around her sister's shoulders as they walked along the antiseptic corridor.

"I wish I could have her at home with me, but I can't," Patty said woefully.

She was married to a carpenter called Zip. They lived in a small row house with two bedrooms. The second bedroom was shared by Patty's three boys. There was nowhere to put a grandma.

Jeannie was single. As an assistant professor in the psychology department at Jones Falls University, she earned thirty thousand dollars a year—a lot less than Patty's husband, she guessed—and she had just taken out her first mortgage and bought a two-room apartment. One room was a living room with a kitchen nook, the other a bedroom with a closet, and a tiny bathroom. If she gave Mom her bed, she would have to sleep on the couch every night, and there was no one at home during the day. "I can't take her either," she said.

Patty showed anger through her tears. "So why did you tell her we would get her out of there? We can't!"

They stepped out into the torrid heat. Jeannie said, "Tomorrow I'll get a bank loan. We'll put her in a better place."

"But how will you ever pay it back?" said Patty practically.

Jeannie had only just started as assistant professor. It would be three years before she was considered for promotion. As they neared the parking lot, Jeannie said desperately, "Okay, I'll sell my car."

She loved her car. It was a twenty-year-old Mercedes 230C, a red two-door sedan with black leather seats. She had bought it eight years ago, before it became chic to own an old Mercedes. "It's probably worth double what I paid for it," she said.

"But you'd have to buy another car," Patty said.

"You're right." Jeannie sighed. "Well, I can do some private tutoring. Can you spare anything?"

Patty looked away. "Zip will kill me for saying this, but we might be able to chip in seventy-five or eighty a week."

Jeannie began to feel more cheerful. "Let's ask around, see if anyone knows of a nice place."

"Okay." Patty turned to her car, a big old Ford station wagon, the back full of brightly colored kiddie junk: a tricycle, a folded-down stroller, a toy truck with a broken wheel.

Jeannie said, "Give the boys a big kiss from me." She got her keys out, hesitated, then hugged Patty. "I love you, Sis."

"Love you too."

Jeannie got in her car and drove away. She felt jangled and restless, full of unresolved feelings about Mom. She remembered that she was supposed to play tennis at six, then go for beer and pizza with a group from the psychology department at Jones Falls. Her first thought was to cancel. But she would play tennis, she decided; the vigorous exercise would make her feel better. Afterward she would go out for an hour or so, then have an early night.

But it did not work out that way.

HER tennis opponent was Jack Budgen, the university's head librarian. He had once played at Wimbledon, and though he was now bald and fifty, he was still fit and the old craft was there. Jeannie had never been to Wimbledon. The height of her tennis career had been a place on the U.S. Olympic team while she was an undergraduate. But she was stronger and faster than Jack.

They played on one of the red clay tennis courts on the Jones Falls campus. They were evenly matched, and the game attracted a small crowd. Out of habit Jeannie always played in crisp white shorts and a white polo shirt. Her long dark hair was curly and unmanageable, so she tucked it up inside a cap.

Jeannie's serve was dynamite, and her two-handed crosscourt backhand smash was a killer. On a normal day she could beat Jack, but today her concentration was shot. They won a set each; then the third went in his favor when he returned a perfect lob that sailed over her head.

Jeannie stood looking at the ball, hands on hips, furious with herself. She calmed her feelings and put a smile on her face. "Beautiful shot!" she called. She walked to the net and shook his hand, and there was a ragged round of applause from the spectators.

A young man approached her. "Hey, that was a great game," he said with a broad smile.

Jeannie took him in at a glance. He was a hunk—tall and athletic, with curly fair hair cut short and nice blue eyes—and he was coming on to her for all he was worth. She was not in the mood. "Thanks," she said curtly.

He smiled again, a confident, relaxed smile that said most girls were happy when he talked to them. "You know, I play a little tennis myself, and I was thinking—"

"If you only play a *little* tennis, you're probably not in my league," she said, and she brushed past him.

Behind her she heard him say in a good-humored tone, "Should I assume that a romantic dinner followed by a night of passion is out of the question, then?"

She could not help smiling, if only at his persistence, and she had been ruder than necessary. She turned her head and said over her shoulder, "Yes. But thanks for the offer."

As Jeannie headed for the locker room, she ran into Lisa Hoxton. Lisa was the first real friend she had made since arriving at Jones Falls a month ago. She was a technician in the psychology laboratory. Like Jeannie, she came from a poor background and was a little intimidated by the hauteur of Jones Falls. They had taken to one another instantly.

"A *kid* just tried to pick me up," Jeannie said with a smile. "He looked like Brad Pitt, but taller."

"Did you tell him you had a friend more his age?" Lisa asked. She was twenty-four.

"No." Jeannie glanced over her shoulder. "Keep walking, in case he follows me."

"How could that be bad? You might have given him my phone number at least," Lisa said, and giggled. "So, are you coming out for beer tonight?"

"Yeah. Just for an hour or so. I have to shower first."

"Me too." Lisa was in shorts and running shoes. "I've been training with the hockey team. Why only for an hour?"

"I've had a heavy day. I had to put my mom into a home."

"Oh, Jeannie, I'm sorry."

Jeannie told her the story as they entered the gymnasium and went down the stairs to the basement. In the locker room Jeannie caught sight of their reflection in the mirror. They were so different in appearance that they almost looked like a comedy act. Lisa was a little below average height, and Jeannie was almost six feet. Lisa was blond and curvy, whereas Jeannie was dark and muscular. Lisa had a pretty face, with a scatter of freckles across a pert little nose and a mouth like a bow. Most people described Jeannie as striking, but nobody ever called her pretty.

As they climbed out of their sweaty sport clothes, Lisa said, "What about your father? You didn't mention him."

Jeannie sighed. It was the question she had learned to dread. For years she had lied, saying Daddy was dead, or had disappeared, or had remarried and gone to work in Saudi Arabia. Lately, however, she had been telling the truth. "My father's in jail," she said.

"Oh, my gosh. I shouldn't have asked."

"It's okay. He's been in jail most of my life. He's a burglar. This is his third term."

"How long is his sentence?"

"I don't remember. It doesn't matter."

They went to the showers. Jeannie took her time washing her hair. She was working in conditioner when she heard strange noises. She stopped and listened. It sounded like squeals of fright. A chill of anxiety passed through her, making her shiver. Suddenly she felt very vulnerable. She hesitated, then quickly rinsed her hair before stepping out of the shower to see what was going on.

She smelled burning as soon as she got out from under the water. She could see thick clouds of smoke close to the ceiling. It seemed to be coming through the ventilators. There was a fire.

She felt afraid. She had never been in a fire.

The more coolheaded women were snatching up their bags and heading for the door. Others were getting hysterical, shouting, and running here and there pointlessly. Some jerk of a security man, with a spotted handkerchief tied over his nose and mouth, was walking up and down, shoving people and yelling orders.

Jeannie knew she should not stay to get dressed, but she could not bring herself to walk out of the building naked. She found her locker, stepped into her jeans, and pulled her T-shirt over her head. It took only a few seconds, but in that time the room emptied of people and filled with fumes. I know where the door is, she told herself. Just keep calm. Holding her breath, she walked quickly past the lockers to the exit.

The corridor was thick with smoke, and her eyes began to water, so that she was almost blind. She kept one shaky hand on the wall as she rushed along the passage, still holding her breath. She thought she might bump into other women, but they all seemed to have got out. When there was no more wall, she knew the stairs had to be straight ahead. She crossed the small basement lobby and crashed into the Coke machine.

With a groan she sucked in air. It was mostly smoke, and it made her cough convulsively. She staggered back along the wall, eyes streaming. She knew she had found the staircase when she tripped over the bottom step, and she scrambled up the stairs on hands and knees.

The smoke thinned suddenly when she reached the ground-floor lobby. The building doors were open. A security guard stood just outside, beckoning her and yelling, "Come on!" Coughing and choking, she staggered out into the blessed fresh air.

She stood on the steps for two or three minutes, bent double, gulping air. She heard the whoop of an emergency vehicle in the distance and looked around for Lisa but could not see her.

Surely she could not still be inside. Still feeling shaky, Jeannie moved through the crowd, scanning the faces. Lisa was not in the crowd. With mounting anxiety Jeannie returned to the security guard at the door.

"I think my girlfriend may be in there," she said.

"I ain't going after her," he said quickly. "That's their job." He pointed to a fire truck coming down the road.

Jeannie watched, impatient and helpless, as the firemen got out of the truck and put on breathing apparatus. They seemed to move so slowly that she wanted to scream, "Hurry, hurry!" Another fire truck arrived, then a white police cruiser.

As the firemen dragged a hose into the building, an officer buttonholed the lobby guard and said, "Where did it start?"

"Women's locker room," the guard said. "In the basement."

"How many exits are there from the basement?"

"Only one. The staircase up to the main lobby, right here."

A maintenance man standing nearby contradicted him. "There's a ladder in the pool machine room that leads up to an access hatch at the back of the building."

Jeannie caught the officer's attention and said, "I think my friend may be inside there still. A woman, short, blond."

"If she's there, we'll find her."

For a moment Jeannie felt reassured. Then she realized he had not promised to find her alive.

The security man who had been in the locker room was nowhere to be seen. Jeannie said to the fire officer, "There was another guard down there. I don't see him anywhere. Tall guy."

The lobby guard said, "Ain't no other security personnel here."

"Well, he had a hat with 'Security' written on it, and he was telling people to evacuate the building."

"I don't care what he had on his hat—"

"Oh, for Pete's sake, stop arguing," Jeannie snapped. "Maybe I imagined him, but if not, his life could be in danger!"

The fire officer said, "Keep calm. We'll find everyone. Thank you for your cooperation." He walked off.

Jeannie felt the fire officer had dismissed her as a hysterical woman because she had yelled at the guard. She clenched her fists, distraught. Think, think! Where else could Lisa be?

She decided to make a tour of the gymnasium in case Lisa was sitting on the ground somewhere, catching her breath. She ran around the side of the building, passing through a yard full of giant garbage cans. At the back she saw a tall figure jogging along the footpath, heading away. She thought it might be the missing security guard, but he disappeared around the corner before she could be sure.

She continued around the building, passing by the running track. Coming full circle, she arrived at the front of the gym. The crowd was bigger, and there were more fire engines and police cars, but she still could not see Lisa. It seemed almost certain she was still in the burning building. A sense of doom crept over Jeannie, and she fought it. You can't let this happen!

Jeannie remembered the maintenance man saying there was another entrance to the basement. She returned to the back of the building.

She saw it immediately. The hatch was set into the ground close to the building. The steel trapdoor was open, leaning against the wall. Jeannie knelt by the square hole to look inside.

A ladder led down to a dirty room lit by fluorescent tubes. There were wisps of smoke in the air, but not thick clouds: It must be closed off from the rest of the basement.

"Is anybody there?" she called. "Hello?"

There was no reply.

She hesitated. The thought of reentering the building made her legs weak. But Lisa might be down there, hurt and unable to move, or just passed out. She had to look.

She steeled her nerve and put a foot on the ladder. She went down quickly to the concrete floor. The smell of smoke was strong, but she could breathe normally.

She saw Lisa right away, and the sight made her gasp.

She was lying on her side, curled up in the fetal position. A smear of blood was on her thigh. She was not moving.

"Lisa!" Jeannie shouted. She made her way across the room and knelt beside her friend. "Lisa?"

Lisa opened her eyes.

"Thank God," Jeannie said. "I thought you were dead."

Slowly Lisa sat up. She would not look at Jeannie. Her lips were bruised. "He . . . he raped me," she said.

Jeannie's relief at finding her alive was replaced by a sick feeling of horror that gripped her heart. "Here?"

Lisa nodded. "He said this was the way out."

Jeannie closed her eyes. Tears came, and she held them back fiercely. "Who was he?"

"A security guy."

"With a spotted handkerchief over his face?"

"He took it off." Lisa turned away. "He kept smiling."

"He was no security guard," Jeannie said. She had seen him jogging away just minutes ago. A wave of rage swept over her. She wanted to chase after him and strangle him.

She heard loud noises—men shouting, heavy footsteps, and the rush of water. The firemen were operating their hoses. "Listen, we're in danger here," she said urgently. "We have to get out."

Lisa began to move to her feet. Jeannie led her to the ladder on the wall, then made her go up first. As Jeannie followed, the door crashed open and a fireman entered in a cloud of smoke. Water swirled around his boots. "We're getting out this way," Jeannie yelled to him. Then she went up the ladder after Lisa.

A moment later they were outside in the fresh air. Jeannie felt weak with relief. But now Lisa needed help. Jeannie put an arm around her shoulders and led her to the front of the building.

Jeannie felt she was getting the nightmare under control. She steered Lisa to the emergency vehicles parked across the road. Three cops standing by a cruiser looked up. Jeannie spoke to them. "This woman's name is Lisa Hoxton. She's been raped."

BERRINGTON Jones looked at his two oldest friends. "I can't believe the three of us," he said. "We're being offered sixty million *each*—and we're talking about turning the offer down!"

Preston Barck said, "We were never in it for the money."

Senator Jim Proust said, "I still don't understand. If I own one third of a company worth a hundred and eighty million dollars, how come I'm driving a three-year-old Crown Victoria?"

The three men had a small private biotechnology company, Genetico Inc. Preston ran the day-to-day business; Jim was in politics, and Berrington was an academic. But the takeover was Berrington's baby. On a plane to San Francisco he had met the CEO of Landsmann, a German pharmaceuticals conglomerate, and had got the man interested in making a bid. Now he had to persuade his partners to accept the offer.

They were in the den of Berrington's house in Roland Park, an affluent suburb of Baltimore. There was little in the room—a laptop computer, a photograph of his ex-wife and their son, and a pile of new copies of his latest book, *To Inherit the Future: How Genetic Engineering Will Transform America*. A TV with the sound turned down was showing the Emmy ceremonies.

Preston Barck, a thin, earnest man, was one of the most outstanding scientists of his generation. "The clinics have always made money," he said. Genetico owned three fertility clinics that specialized in in vitro conception—test-tube babies—a procedure made possible by Preston's pioneering research in the '70s. "Fertility is the biggest growth area in American medicine."

Jim Proust was a bald, suntanned man, with a big nose and heavy spectacles. He and Berrington had been friends for twenty-five years. "How come we never saw any money?" Jim asked.

"We always spent it on research." Genetico had its own labs and also gave research contracts to universities. Berrington handled the company's links with the academic world.

Berrington said in an exasperated tone, "I don't know why you two can't see that this is our big chance."

Preston said, "You're just impatient."

"Impatient?" Berrington said irritably. "You bet I'm impatient! I'll be sixty in two weeks. We're all getting old. We don't have much time left!"

Jim said, "He's right, Preston. Don't you remember how it was when we were young men? We looked around and saw America going to hell: civil rights for Negroes, Mexicans flooding in, kids smoking pot and dodging the draft. And boy, look what's happened since then! We never imagined that a third of all babies would be born to mothers on Medicaid. And we're the only people with the guts to face up to the problem—us and a few like-minded individuals."

They did not change, Berrington thought. Preston was ever cautious and fearful, Jim bombastically sure of himself. And Berrington was accustomed to his role as the moderator.

Now he said, "Where are we with the takeover, Preston?"

"We're very close," Preston said. "Landsmann wants to announce it at a press conference one week from tomorrow."

"A week from tomorrow?" Berrington said with excitement.

Preston shook his head. "I have to tell you, I still have doubts. We've been going through disclosure. We have to open our books to Landsmann's accountants and tell them about anything that might affect future profits, such as pending lawsuits."

"We don't have any of those, I take it," Jim said.

Preston gave him an ominous look. "We all know this company has secrets."

There was a moment of silence in the room. Then Jim said, "That's a long way in the past."

"So what? The evidence of what we did is out there walking around."

"But there's no way Landsmann can find out about it—especially in a week."

"We have to take that risk," Berrington said firmly. "The capital we'll get from Landsmann will enable us to accelerate our research program. In a few years we'll be able to offer affluent white Americans who come to our clinics a genetically engineered perfect baby."

"But how much difference will it make?" Preston asked. "The poor will continue to breed faster than the rich."

"You're forgetting Jim's political platform," Berrington replied.

Jim said, "A flat income tax rate of ten percent and compulsory contraceptive injections for women on welfare."

"Think of it, Preston," Berrington said. "Perfect babies for the middle classes and sterilization for the poor. We could start to put America right again. It's what we always aimed for."

"Jim can propose his political platform," Preston said, "but that doesn't mean it's going to happen."

"That's where Landsmann comes in," Jim said. "The cash we'll get will give us a shot at the biggest prize of all."

"What do you mean?" Preston looked puzzled, but Berrington knew what was coming, and he smiled.

"The White House," Jim said. "I'm going to run for President."

A FEW MINUTES BEFORE MIDNIGHT Steve Logan parked his rusty old Datsun on Lexington Street in the Hollins Market neighborhood of Baltimore. He went to law school in Washington, D.C., but he was going to spend the night with his cousin Ricky Menzies, who was studying medicine at the University of Maryland. Ricky's home was one room in a big old house tenanted by students.

Ricky was the greatest hell-raiser Steve knew. He loved to party, and his friends were the same. Steve had been looking forward to spending the evening with Ricky. But the trouble with hell-raisers was that they were unreliable. At the last minute Ricky had got a hot date, and Steve spent the evening alone.

He got out of the car, carrying a small sports bag with fresh clothes for tomorrow. The night was warm. He locked the car and walked to the corner. A bunch of youngsters, all black, were hanging out by a video store, smoking cigarettes. Steve was not nervous, although he was white. He looked as if he belonged here, with his old car and his faded blue jeans, and anyway he was a couple of inches taller than the biggest of them. As he passed, one of them said quietly, "Wanna buy some blow, wanna buy some rock?" Steve shook his head without pausing in his stride.

At that moment his cousin came along. Ricky said, "I see you've already made friends in the neighborhood."

Steve laughed as they reached Ricky's house and went in. The place smelled of cheese, or maybe it was stale milk. They edged around the bicycles chained up in the hallway and went up the stairs to Ricky's small room.

Steve sat on the sagging couch. "How was your date?"

"I wouldn't be home this early if she was as crazy for me as I was led to believe. How about you?"

"I looked around the Jones Falls campus. Pretty classy. I met a girl too." Remembering, Steve brightened. "I saw her playing tennis. She was terrific—tall, muscular, fit. A serve like it was fired out of a bazooka, I swear."

"I never heard of anyone falling for a girl because of her tennis game." Ricky grinned. "Is she a looker?"

"She's got this really strong face." Steve could see it now. "Dark brown eyes, black eyebrows, masses of dark hair. And this delicate little nose ring."

"No kidding. What's her name?"

"I don't know." Steve smiled ruefully. "She gave me the brush-off. I'll probably never see her again in my life."

"So what did you do after she gave you the brush-off?"

"Went to a bar and had a couple beers and a hamburger."

"That reminds me—I'm hungry. Want something to eat?"

"What have you got?"

Ricky opened a cupboard. "Rice Krispies or Count Chocula."

"Oh, boy, Count Chocula sounds great."

Ricky put bowls and milk on the table, and they both tucked in.

When they had finished, they got ready for bed. Steve lay on the couch; Ricky took the bed. Before they went to sleep, Ricky said, "So what are you going to do at Jones Falls?"

"They asked me to be part of a study. I have to have psychological tests. They said I was a special case and they would explain everything when I get there."

"What made you say yes? Sounds like kind of a waste of time."

Steve had a special reason, but he was not going to tell Ricky. "Curiosity, I guess. I mean, don't you wonder about yourself? Like what kind of person am I really, and what do I want in life?"

"I want to be a hotshot surgeon and make a million bucks a year doing breast implants. I guess I'm a simple soul."

"Don't you ask yourself what's it all for?"

Ricky laughed. "No, Steve, I don't. But you do. You were always a thinker. Even when we were kids, you used to wonder about God and stuff. And I never knew anyone score so high in tests without breaking a sweat."

That was true. Steve had always been a quick study, effortlessly coming out at the top of the class. But there was another reason he was curious about his own psychology. Ricky did not know about it. Nobody at law school knew. Only his parents knew.

Steve had almost killed someone.

He had been fifteen at the time—already tall but thin. He was captain of the basketball team. That year Hillsfield High made it to the city championship semifinal. They played against a team of ruthless street fighters from a Washington slum school. One opponent, a boy called Tip Hendricks, fouled Steve all through the game. And every time he did it, he would grin. It drove Steve wild. He played badly, and the team lost.

By the worst of bad luck Steve ran into Tip in the parking lot, where the buses were waiting to take the teams back to their schools. Steve ignored him, but Tip flicked his cigarette butt at Steve, and it landed on his jacket.

That jacket meant a lot to Steve. He had saved up his earnings from working Saturdays at McDonald's to buy it. It was a beautiful soft leather, the color of butter, and now it had a burn mark right on the chest. It was ruined. So Steve hit him.

Tip fought back fiercely, kicking and butting, but Steve's rage numbed him and he hardly felt the blows. Tip's face was covered in blood by the time his eye caught a bus driver's tool kit, and he picked up a tire iron. He hit Steve across the face with it twice, and Steve's rage became blind. He got the iron away from Tip, and he could remember nothing after that, until he was standing over Tip's body with the bloodstained iron bar in his hand and someone else was saying, "Jeez, I think he's dead."

Tip was not dead. But Steve had wanted to kill him, had *tried* to kill him. Steve had used the tire iron savagely.

He was sentenced to six months in prison, but the sentence was suspended. Because he had been a juvenile at the time of the fight, his criminal record could not be disclosed, so it did not prevent his getting into law school. Mom and Dad now thought of it as a nightmare that was over. But Steve had doubts. He knew it was only good luck and the resilience of the human body that had saved him from a murder trial. Tip Hendricks was a human being, and Steve had almost killed him for a jacket. As he listened to Ricky's untroubled breathing across the room, he lay awake on the couch and thought, What am I?

Monday

LISA said, "Did you ever meet a man you wanted to marry?"

They were sitting at the table in Lisa's apartment drinking coffee. Lisa was going to take the day off, but Jeannie was dressed for work in a navy skirt and white cotton blouse. It was an important day, and she was jumpy with tension. The first of her subjects was coming to the lab for a day of tests.

However, she did not want to leave until the last possible moment. Lisa was still very fragile. She'd been upset by the invasive questions the police asked about the rape last night, and she wouldn't stay at the hospital long enough for tests. Jeannie had driven Lisa home, stopping first at her own apartment to pick up some clothes for work the next day, and then stayed overnight with her friend. She figured the best thing she could do was sit and talk to Lisa, help her get on the road back to normality.

"Yeah, one," Jeannie said in answer to the question. "There was one guy I wanted to marry. His name was Will Temple. He was an anthropologist. Still is." Jeannie could see him now, a big man with a fair beard, in blue jeans and a fisherman's sweater.

"What was he like?" Lisa said.

"He was great." Jeannie sighed. "He made me laugh, he took care of me when I was sick, and he ironed his own shirts."

"What went wrong?"

It hurt Jeannie to remember. "He left me for Georgina Tinkerton Ross." She added, "Of the Pittsburgh Tinkerton Rosses. She was perfect. Strawberry blonde, hourglass figure."

"When did all this happen?"

"Will and I lived together when I was doing my doctorate." It had been the happiest time she could remember. "He moved out while I was writing my article on whether criminality is genetic. When Berrington offered me a job at Jones Falls, I jumped at it."

"Men are creeps."

The entry phone sounded, startling them both. Lisa jumped up, bumping the table. A porcelain vase fell to the floor and shattered, and Lisa said, "Damn it." She was still right on the edge.

"I'll pick up the pieces," Jeannie said in a soothing voice. "You see who's at the door."

Lisa picked up the handset. A troubled frown crossed her face as she studied the monitor. "All right, I guess," she said dubiously, and she pressed the button to open the building door.

"Who is it?" Jeannie asked.

"A detective from the sex-crimes unit."

The last thing Lisa needed now was more intrusive questions, Jeannie thought as she swept shards of porcelain into her hand.

The detective was a stocky black woman of about forty, smartly dressed, carrying a briefcase. "I'm Sergeant Michelle Delaware," she said. "They call me Mish."

Jeannie wondered what was in the briefcase. Detectives usually carried guns, not papers. "I'm Dr. Jean Ferrami," Jeannie said. "This is Lisa Hoxton."

The detective said, "Ms. Hoxton, I want to say how sorry I am about what happened to you yesterday. My unit deals with one rape a day on average, and every single one is a terrible trauma for the victim. I know you're hurting, and I understand."

"I'm trying to put it behind me," Lisa said, but tears came to her eyes and betrayed her.

The detective sat at the kitchen table and took a card from her purse. "Here's the number of a volunteer center for victims of rape," she said. "Sooner or later every victim needs counseling."

Lisa took the card but said, "All I want is to forget it."

Mish nodded. "Take my advice. Put the card in a drawer. There will probably come a time when you're ready to seek help."

"Would you like some coffee?" Jeannie asked Mish.

"I'd love a cup."

"I'll make some fresh." Jeannie got up and filled the coffeemaker.

Mish said, "Do you two work together?"

"Yes," Jeannie replied. "We study twins. We measure their similarities and differences and try to figure out how much is inherited and how much is due to the way they were raised."

"What's your role in this, Lisa?"

"My job is to find twins for the scientists to study. I start with the birth records. Then, to track down the twins, we use a CD-ROM that has every American phone book on it. We can also use driving license registries and credit reference agencies."

"Do you always find the twins?"

"Goodness, no. We track down about ninety percent of ten-year-olds but only fifty percent of eighty-year-olds. Older people are more likely to have moved, changed their names, or died."

Mish looked at Jeannie. "And then you study them."

Jeannie said, "I specialize in identical twins who have been raised apart. They're much more difficult to find." She brought the coffeepot to the table and poured a cup for Mish. If this detective was planning to pressure Lisa into talking about the rape, she was taking her time about it.

Mish sipped her coffee, then said, "The fire yesterday was no accident. I've talked to the fire chief. Someone set fire to a storage room next to the locker room. Now, rapists are not really interested in sex; it's fear that turns them on. So I think the fire was all part of this creep's fantasy." She turned to Lisa. "Am I right in thinking you had never seen this man before?"

"I think I saw him about an hour earlier," Lisa replied. "When I was out running with the field-hockey team, a car slowed down and the guy stared at us. I have a feeling it was him."

"What kind of a car?"

"It was old. White with a lot of rust. Maybe a Datsun."

Jeannie expected Mish to write that down, but she went on talking. "The impression I get is of an intelligent and completely ruthless pervert who will do whatever it takes to get his kicks. And most rapists are serial rapists." Mish looked hard at Lisa. "The man who

raped you will put another woman through the same torture—
unless we catch him first."

"Oh, my God," Lisa said.

Jeannie could see where Mish was heading. She was determined
not to let Mish bully Lisa into helping with the investigation. But it
was hard to object to the things she was saying.

"We need a sample of his DNA," the detective said. "I'd like you
to go to Mercy Hospital, which is a designated sexual assault center.
You'll see a nurse examiner, who's specially trained in dealing with
evidence."

Mish opened her briefcase. Inside was a laptop computer. She
lifted the lid and switched it on. "We have a program called E-FIT,
for Electronic Facial Identification Technique. We like acronyms."
She gave a wry smile. "It enables us to put together a likeness of the
perpetrator." She looked expectantly at Lisa.

Lisa looked at Jeannie. "What do you think?"

"Think about yourself," Jeannie said. "Do what makes you feel
comfortable."

Mish said to Lisa, "There's no pressure on you. But I want to
catch this rapist. And without you I don't stand a chance."

Lisa hesitated, then said, "Okay."

Mish said, "To begin, we'll get a rough approximation of his face.
Then we'll refine the details. I need you to concentrate hard, then
give me a general description. Take your time."

Lisa closed her eyes. "He's a white man about my age. Short hair,
no particular color. Light eyes, blue. Straight nose."

Mish was operating a mouse. In the top-right-hand corner of the
screen was a face divided into eight sections. As Lisa named features, Mish would click on a section of the face, pulling down a
menu, then check items on the menu based on Lisa's comments:
hair short, eyes light, nose straight.

Lisa went on. "A square chin, no beard or mustache . . ."

Mish clicked again, and an entire face came on the screen. She
turned the computer so that Lisa could see the screen. "Now we're
going to change the face bit by bit. First I'll show you a whole series

of different foreheads and hairlines. Just say yes, no, or maybe. Ready?"

Mish clicked the mouse. The face on the screen changed, and suddenly the forehead had a receding hairline.

"No," Lisa said.

She clicked again. This time the haircut was wavy, and Lisa said, "That's more like it. But I think he had a part."

The next was curly. "Better still," Lisa said. "But too dark."

Jeannie was fascinated, but this would take time; she had work to do. "I've got to go," she said. "Are you okay, Lisa?"

"I'm fine," Lisa said, and Jeannie could tell it was the truth.

"I'll call you," Jeannie said to her friend.

Lisa hugged Jeannie. "Thank you for staying with me."

Mish held out her hand, and Jeannie shook it.

"Good luck," Jeannie said. "I hope you catch him."

STEVE parked in the large student parking lot of the Jones Falls campus. It was a few minutes before ten o'clock, and the campus was thronged with students in light summer clothes on their way to classes. As he walked across the campus, he looked out for the tennis player. The chances of seeing her were slender, he knew, but he could not help staring at every tall dark-haired woman.

The Ruth W. Acorn Psychology Building, known as Nut House, was a modern four-story structure in the same red brick as the older college buildings. He gave his name in the lobby and was directed to the laboratory.

In the next three hours Steve underwent more tests than he imagined possible. He was weighed, measured, and fingerprinted. Scientists and technicians photographed his ears, tested the strength of his grip, and assessed his startle reflex. He answered questions about his leisure-time interests, his religious beliefs, and his job aspirations. He had to state if he could repair a doorbell, if he considered himself well groomed, and if he would spank his children. But no one told him why he had been selected for the study.

He was not the only subject. Also around the lab were two

middle-aged men wearing cowboy boots, blue jeans, and western shirts. Steve realized they were twins, dressed the same.

He learned that their names were Benny and Arnold. "Do you guys always dress the same?" Steve asked.

They looked at each other; then Benny said, "Don't know. We just met."

"You're twins, and you just met?"

"We were both adopted as babies—by different families."

"And you accidentally dressed the same?"

"Looks like it, don't it?"

Arnold added, "And we're both carpenters, and we both smoke Camel Lights, and we both have two kids—a boy and a girl."

"Wow," Steve said.

The door opened behind Steve, and someone said, "Hello, Dr. Ferrami."

Steve turned and saw the tennis player.

Her muscular body was hidden beneath a knee-length white laboratory coat, but she moved like an athlete as she walked into the room. She still had the air of focused concentration that had been so impressive on the tennis court. He stared at her, hardly able to believe his luck.

Dr. Ferrami began to introduce herself. When she shook Steve's hand, she did a double-take. "So you're Steve Logan," she said.

"You play a great game of tennis," he said.

"I lost, though." She sat down. Her thick, dark hair swung loosely around her shoulders, and Steve noticed in the unforgiving light of the laboratory that she had one or two gray hairs.

She thanked the three of them for giving up their time in the service of scientific inquiry. After a few more platitudes she sent the cowboys away to begin their afternoon tests.

She sat close to Steve, and he had the feeling she was embarrassed. She said, "You're wondering what this is all about."

"Was I picked because I've always done so well in school?"

"No," she said. "True, you score very high on all intellectual tests. In fact, your IQ is off the scale. But our project here is to ask how much of people's makeup is predetermined by their genetic inheritance." Her awkwardness vanished as she warmed to her subject. "Is it DNA that decides whether we're intelligent, aggressive, romantic, athletic? Or is it our upbringing? If both have an influence, how do they interact?"

"An ancient controversy," Steve said. He had taken a philosophy course at college, and he recalled the catchphrase that summed up the argument: nature or nurture?

She nodded, and her long hair moved heavily, like the ocean. Steve wondered how it felt to the touch. "We're trying to resolve the question in a strictly scientific way," she said. "You see, identical twins have the same genes—exactly the same. We study twins who are brought up apart, measuring how similar they are."

Steve was wondering how this affected him. He was also wondering how old Dr. Ferrami was. Seeing her run around the tennis court yesterday, with her hair hidden in a cap, he assumed she was his age; now he could tell she was nearer thirty.

She went on. "If environment was more important, twins raised apart would be quite different. In fact, we find the opposite. Identical twins resemble one another regardless of who raised them."

"Like Benny and Arnold?"

"Exactly. You saw how alike they are. That's typical."

"But you still haven't explained my involvement," he said.

She looked awkward again. "It's a little difficult," she said.

Suddenly Steve realized. "You think I have a twin that I don't know about?" he asked incredulously.

"I can't think of any gradual way to tell you," Dr. Ferrami said with evident chagrin. "Yes, we do."

"Wow." He felt dazed. It was hard to take in.

"I'm really sorry. Normally people know they're twins before they come to us. However, I've pioneered a new way of recruiting subjects for this study, and you're the first."

"I always wanted a brother," Steve said. He was an only child, born when his parents were in their late thirties. "Is it a brother?"

"Yes. You're identical."

"An identical twin brother," Steve murmured. "But how could it happen without my knowledge?"

She looked mortified.

"Wait a minute. I can work it out," Steve said. "I could be adopted." It was an even more shocking thought. Mom and Dad might not be his parents. "Or my twin could have been adopted."

"Yes."

"Or both, like Benny and Arnold."

"Or both," she repeated solemnly. She was gazing intently at him with those dark eyes. Despite the turmoil in his mind, he could not help thinking how lovely she was.

Steve said painfully, "I just can't believe Mom and Dad would have kept adoption a secret from me. It's not their style."

"Tell me about your parents."

He knew she was making him talk to help him work through the shock. He collected his thoughts. "Mom's kind of exceptional. You've heard of her—her name's Lorraine Logan."

"The lonely-hearts columnist?"

"Right. Syndicated in newspapers, author of six best sellers about women's health. Rich and famous, and she deserves it."

"Why do you say that?"

"She really cares about the people who write to her. She answers thousands of letters. They basically want her to wave a magic wand—make unwanted pregnancies vanish, get their kids off drugs, turn abusive men into kindly and supportive husbands. She gives them the information they need and tells them it's their decision what to do, not to let anyone bully them. It's a good philosophy."

"And your father?"

"Dad's in the military, works at the Pentagon. He's a colonel. He does public relations, writes speeches for generals."

"A disciplinarian?"

Steve smiled. "He has a highly developed sense of duty, but he's not a violent man."

"But did you require discipline?"

Steve laughed. "I was the naughtiest boy in class all through school. Constantly breaking the rules. Running in the hallway. Wearing red socks. Chewing gum in class."

"Why did you break all the rules?"

He shook his head. "I just couldn't be obedient. I did what I wanted. The rules seemed stupid, and I got bored. But I always got good grades. I don't understand myself. Am I a weirdo?"

"Everybody's weird in their own way."

"I guess so. Why do you wear the nose ring?"

Jeannie raised her dark eyebrows, as if to say, "I ask the questions around here." But she answered him just the same. "I guess because I feel that total respectability is deadly dull."

Steve smiled. I like this woman, he thought. Then his mind switched back to what she had told him. "What makes you so sure I have a twin?"

"I've developed a computer program that searches medical records and other databases for pairs. Identical twins have similar brain waves, electrocardiograms, fingerprints, and teeth. I scanned a database of dental X rays held by a medical insurance company, and found someone whose teeth measurements are the same as yours."

"So who is he?"

"His name is Dennis Pinker, and he's in Richmond, Virginia. I'm going to see him tomorrow. I'll do tests on him and take a blood sample to compare his DNA with yours. Then we'll know for sure."

Steve frowned. "Do you have a particular area that you're interested in within the field of genetics?"

"Yes. My specialty is criminality and whether it's inherited."

Steve nodded. "I get it. What did he do?"

"Pardon me?"

"What did Dennis Pinker do? You're going to visit him instead of asking him to come here, so obviously he's incarcerated."

She colored faintly. "Yes, you're right," she said.

"What's he in jail for?"

She hesitated. "Murder."

"Jeez!" He looked away from her, trying to take it in. "Not only do I have an identical twin brother, but he's a murderer."

"I'm sorry," she said. "I've handled this badly. You're the first subject like this I've studied. And you're very important to me."

"How so?"

"The question is whether criminality is inherited. I published a paper that identified four inherited traits that lead to criminal behavior: impulsiveness, daring, aggression, and hyperactivity. But my big theory is that certain ways of raising children counteract those traits. To prove that, I have to find pairs of identical twins raised apart, one of whom is a criminal and the other a law-abiding citizen. You and Dennis are perfect: He's in jail, and you—forgive me— you're the ideal all-American boy. To tell you the truth, I'm so excited about it I can hardly sit still."

Steve was restless too. What she had told him was disturbing. If he had the same DNA as a murderer, what did that make him?

The door opened behind Steve, and Dr. Ferrami looked up. "Hi, Berry," she said. "Steve, I'd like you to meet Professor Berrington Jones, the head of the twins study here at J.F.U."

The professor was a short man in his late fifties, handsome with sleek silver hair. Steve had seen him on TV a few times, talking about how America was going all to hell. Steve did not like his views, but he stood up politely and held out his hand to shake.

Berrington Jones started as if he had seen a ghost. "Good Lord!" he said, and his face turned pale.

Dr. Ferrami said, "Berry, what is it?"

The professor said nothing for a moment. Then he seemed to collect his wits. "I'm sorry. It's nothing," he said, but he still seemed shaken to the core. "It's just that I suddenly thought of something I've forgotten. Please excuse me." He went to the door, muttering, "My apologies. Forgive me." He went out.

Steve looked at Dr. Ferrami. She shrugged and spread her hands. "Beats the heck out of me," she said.

BERRINGTON sat at his desk breathing hard.

He had a corner office, but otherwise his room was monastic: white walls, utilitarian file cabinets. Academics were not expected to have lavish offices. The screen saver on his computer showed a slowly revolving strand of DNA twisted in the famous double-helix shape. Over the desk were photographs of himself with Newt Gingrich and Rush Limbaugh. The window overlooked the tennis court.

Berrington rubbed his eyes and swore.

He had persuaded Jeannie Ferrami to come here. Her paper on criminality had broken new ground by focusing on components of the criminal personality. The question was crucial to the Genetico project. He wanted her to continue her work under his wing, and he had arranged for her research to be financed by Genetico. With his help she could do great things.

Berrington was completely smitten. Jeannie was as stunning physically as she was intellectually. He was torn between a fatherly need to guide her and a powerful urge to seduce her. And now this!

When he had caught his breath, he called Preston Barck. Preston was his oldest friend. They had met at Harvard in the '60s, when Berrington was doing his doctorate in psychology and Preston was an outstanding young embryologist. Over the years the friendship had proved more robust than either of their marriages.

Right now Preston would be at Genetico's headquarters, north of the city. Preston's secretary said he was in a meeting, and Berrington told her to connect him anyway.

"Good morning, Berry. What's up?"

"Who else is there?"

"I'm with Lee Ho, an accountant from Landsmann. We're going over the final details of Genetico's disclosure statement."

"Get him out of there."

Preston's voice faded as he moved the phone away from his face. "Lee, this is going to take a while. I'll catch up with you later." There was a pause, and he spoke into the mouthpiece again. Now his voice was peevish. "That was Michael Madigan's right-hand man I just threw out. Madigan is the head of Landsmann, in case you've forgotten. If you're still keen on this takeover—"

Berrington interrupted him. "Steven Logan is here."

There was a moment of stunned silence. "At Jones Falls?"

"Right here in the psychology building. He's a subject undergoing tests in the laboratory."

Preston's voice went up an octave. "How did *that* happen?"

"I don't know. I just ran into him. He's in our twins study."

"Twins?" Preston yelled. "*Twins?* Who's the other twin?"

"I don't know yet. Look, something like this was sure to happen sooner or later."

"But now of all times! We'll have to pull out of the deal."

"No, we won't. We just have to control the situation."

"Who brought Logan into the university?"

"The new associate professor we just hired, Dr. Ferrami. I assume she recruited Steven. I'll check."

"That's the key to it, Berry." Preston was calming down now and focusing. "Find out how he was recruited. Then we can begin to assess how much danger we're in. Call me right back, okay?"

"Sure." Berrington hung up.

He dialed Jeannie's internal number. She picked up right away. He lowered his voice. "Jeannie, it's Berry," he said. "Would you mind stepping into my office?"

As he waited, he tried not to think about her body. Women had always been his weakness. No other vice tempted him. He drank in moderation, never gambled. He had loved his wife, Vivvie, but he had not been able to resist temptation, and she had eventually left him because of his fooling around. When he thought of Jeannie, he imagined her running her fingers through his hair and saying, "You've been so good to me. How can I ever thank you?"

She knocked at the door and came in. Berrington drew out a chair for her, then pulled his own chair around next to hers. His first task was to offer Jeannie some plausible explanation for his behavior on meeting Steven Logan.

He gave her his most disarming grin. "I want to apologize for my weird behavior," he said. "I've been downloading files from the University of Sydney, Australia." He gestured at his computer. "Just as you were about to introduce me to that young man, I realized I'd forgotten to hang up the phone line. I felt foolish."

She seemed to accept the explanation. "I'm relieved," she said candidly. "I thought I'd done something to offend you."

So far, so good. He went on smoothly, "You've certainly got off to a flying start. You've only been here four weeks, and your project is well under way. Tell me, have any problems come up?"

"Recruitment is my biggest problem," Jeannie said. "Because our subjects are volunteers, most are like Steve Logan—respectable middle-class Americans who believe that the good citizen has a duty to support scientific inquiry. On the other hand, it's not possible to find out about criminality by studying law-abiding families. So it was crucial to solve the recruitment problem."

"And have you?"

"I think so." She explained how she'd searched through medical insurance databases for the kind of data used to determine whether twins are identical or fraternal: brain waves, electrocardiograms, and so on.

"That's remarkable," Berrington said. "Simple, but ingenious." But for him personally, it was a catastrophe. He looked at her and tried to hide his dismay. This was worse than he had feared.

Berrington clutched at a straw. "Finding similar entries in a database is not as easy as it sounds. I believe it's quite a problem in software design. So what did you do?"

"I wrote my own software. When I was in graduate school, I worked with my professor on neural-network-type software for pattern recognition."

Could she be that smart? "You did? How does it work?"

"The pairs we're looking for are similar, but not absolutely identical. For example, X rays of identical teeth, taken by different technicians on different machinery, are not exactly the same. But the human eye can see that they're the same, and when the X rays are scanned and digitized and stored electronically, a computer equipped with fuzzy logic can recognize them as a pair."

"And your program works?"

"It seems to. I tried it out on a database of dental records held by a large medical insurance company. It produced several hundred pairs. I eliminated all the pairs with the same surname, and all the married women, since most of them have taken the husband's name. The remainder are twins with no apparent reason for having different surnames. Twins raised apart."

Berrington was torn between admiration of Jeannie and fear of what she could find out. "How many were left?"

"Three pairs—a disappointment. I was hoping for more. Fortunately, one pair are just what I was looking for: Steven Logan is a law-abiding citizen, and Dennis Pinker is a murderer."

So Jeannie had found Dennis. She's dangerous, Berrington thought. She could ruin everything—the takeover, Jim's political career, Genetico, even Berrington's academic reputation. Fear made him angry. How could everything he had ever worked for be threatened by his own protégée?

He looked at his watch. "I'm running out of time," he said, "but I'd love to discuss this some more. Are you free for dinner tonight?"

He saw her hesitate. But he was her mentor; it was hard for her to refuse him.

"Sure," she said, standing up.

"Then I'll pick you up at eight?"

"Fine."

As she shut the door, Berrington shook his head to clear his mind of her long, long legs. Then he called Preston again.

"It's worse than we thought," he said without preamble. "She's written a computer program that searches medical databases for matched pairs. First time she tried it out, she found Steven and Dennis. We've got to tell Jim."

Preston swore. "I still think we'll have to pull out of the Landsmann deal in the end."

"I don't agree," Berrington said. "She's pretty bright, but one girl isn't going to uncover the whole story in a week."

However, as he hung up, he wondered if he should be so sure.

JEANNIE entered her office, thinking anxiously of the next stage of her project. She was hoping to use her software to scan the FBI's fingerprint file. It was the perfect source. Many of the twenty-two million people on file had been suspected or convicted of crimes. If her program worked, it should yield hundreds of twins, including several raised-apart twins. It could mean a quantum leap forward. But first she had to get the Bureau's permission.

Her best friend at school had been Ghita Sumra, a math wizard of Asian Indian descent who now had a top job managing information technology for the FBI in Washington. Ghita had already agreed to ask her employers to cooperate with Jeannie. She had promised a decision by the end of the week, but now Jeannie wanted to hurry her. She dialed her number.

Ghita's voice still held a hint of the Indian subcontinent in its softness of tone. "Hey, Jeannie, how was your weekend?"

"Awful," Jeannie said. "I had to put my mom in a home."

"I'm sorry to hear that. How do you feel about it?"

"Bad," she said. "She's in a cheap place for now, but I'm going to do some private tutoring to get the money for something better." She paused. "Ghita, did you talk to your boss about my proposal?"

"As a matter of fact, I did."

Jeannie held her breath.

"Your search engine is faster by far than anything we've got. They're talking about licensing the software program from you."

"Wow. Maybe I won't need to do private tutoring after all."

Ghita laughed. "Before you open the champagne, let's make sure the program actually works. We'll run it at night for minimal interference with normal use of the database. Can you upload the program to me by modem?"

Ghita read out an E-mail address, and Jeannie wrote it down. "I'll send you the results the same way."

"Thanks, Ghita." They hung up.

Jeannie clicked her mouse on America Online and accessed the Internet. As her search program was uploading to the FBI, there was a knock at her door and Steve Logan came in.

"How are you doing?" she asked him.

He closed the door behind him with his heel. "All finished," he

said. "I've undergone all the tests that can be devised by the inge-
nuity of humankind."

"Then you're free to go home."

"I was thinking of staying in Baltimore for the evening. As a matter of fact, I wondered if you'd care to have dinner with me."

She was taken by surprise.

He went on. "I'd like to know more about your research."

"Oh. Well, unfortunately, I have a dinner engagement already."

He looked very disappointed. "Do you think I'm too young?"

Then it struck her. "I didn't know you meant a date."

He was embarrassed. "You're kind of slow to catch on."

"I'm sorry." She *was* being slow. He had come on to her yesterday on the tennis court. But she had spent all day thinking of him
as a subject for study. However, now that she thought about it, he
was too young to take her out. He was twenty-two, a student; she
was seven years older. It was a big gap.

Jeannie's computer made a doorbell sound to tell her that the
program had finished uploading. "I'm through for the day," she
said to him. "Would you like to have a drink in the faculty club?"

He brightened immediately. "Sure. Am I dressed okay?"

He was wearing khakis and a blue linen shirt. "You'll be better
dressed than most of the professors there," she said, smiling. She
exited the program and turned her computer off.

"I called my mom," he said. "Told her about your theory."

"Was she mad?"

"She laughed. Said I wasn't adopted nor did I have a twin."

"Strange." It was a relief to Jeannie that the Logan family was
taking all this so calmly. On the other hand, it made her worry that
perhaps Steve and Dennis were not twins after all.

"You know . . ." She hesitated. Then she plunged on. "There is
another possible way you and Dennis could be twins."

"Babies switched at the hospital," he said.

He was very quick. This morning she had noticed more than
once how fast he worked things out. "That's right," she said. "It's
the old staple of romance writers. But it's not impossible."

"Is there a book on this twin stuff?" he said.

"Yeah. I have one at home."

"Where do you live?"

"Close by."

"You could take me home for that drink."

She hesitated. This one is the normal twin, she reminded herself, not the psychopath. She shrugged. "Why not? Let's go."

It was five o'clock, and the day was beginning to cool as they left Nut House. Steve whistled when he saw the red Mercedes.

"What a neat car! My car's in the parking lot. I'll come up behind you and flash my lights."

Jeannie got into her car and started it. A few minutes later she saw headlights in her rearview mirror. As she drove off the campus, she noticed a police cruiser tuck in behind Steve's car. She checked her speedometer and slowed down to thirty.

Steve stayed on her tail all the way home. She pulled up outside her house, and he parked right behind her.

As in many old Baltimore streets, there was a row stoop, a communal front porch that ran the length of the row. She crossed the stoop, getting out her keys.

Two cops exploded out of the patrol car, guns in their hands. Jeannie's heart stopped as they yelled, "Police! Freeze!"

Jeannie and Steve both raised their hands.

The policemen approached them as cautiously as if they were ticking bombs. Jeannie said, "What the heck is going on?"

They did not reply. They kept their guns pointed at Steve. With a swift, practiced motion one of them handcuffed him. "You're under arrest," the cop said.

Jeannie tried again. "What's he supposed to have done?"

A light blue Dodge Colt screeched to a halt behind the police cruiser, and two people got out. One was Mish Delaware, the detective from the sex-crimes unit. She looked at Steve.

"It's him," she said. "This guy raped Lisa Hoxton."

"He did?" Jeannie said incredulously. *Jeez. I was about to take him into my apartment.*

"Rape?" Steve said.

"The patrolman spotted his tan Datsun leaving the campus," Mish said, and handed Jeannie a piece of paper. It was a flyer bearing a computer-generated black-and-white picture of a man. Jeannie stared. It did look something like Steve Logan.

"It might be him and it might not," Jeannie said.

"What are you doing with him?"

"He's a subject. We've been doing tests on him at the lab. I can't believe he's the guy!"

Mish said to Steve, "Can you account for your movements yesterday between seven and eight p.m.?"

"I was at J.F.U.," he said. "I watched the tennis for a while. Then I spent a couple of hours at a bar in Charles Village."

It sounded lame even to Jeannie. Maybe Steve was the rapist, she thought with dismay. But if he was, her entire theory was shot.

Mish said, "Can anyone corroborate what you say?"

"Well, I spoke to Dr. Ferrami, although at that point I didn't actually know who she was."

Mish turned to Jeannie, who said, "It was after my tennis game, a few minutes before the fire broke out."

"So you can't tell us where he was during the rape."

"No, but I can tell you that I've spent all day giving this man psychological tests, and he doesn't have the profile of a rapist."

Mish looked scornful. "That's not evidence."

"Nor is this." Jeannie balled up the flyer and dropped it.

Mish jerked her head at the cops. "Let's go."

Steve spoke in a clear, calm voice. "Wait a minute." He turned to Jeannie. "I didn't do this. I never would do anything of the kind."

She believed him. She asked herself why. Was it just that she needed him to be innocent for her theory? No. She had tests to show that he had none of the characteristics associated with criminals. But there was something else—her intuition. She felt safe with him. He gave out no wrong signals. He liked women, and he respected her. Steve Logan was not a rapist.

She said, "Do you want me to call someone? Your parents?"

"No," he said decisively. "They'd worry. And it will all be over in a few hours. I'll tell them then."

"Let's go," Mish said impatiently.

"What's the hurry?" Jeannie snapped. "You have some other innocent people to arrest?"

Mish glared at her. "Do you have anything more to say to me?"

"What happens next?"

"There'll be a lineup. We'll let Lisa Hoxton decide whether this is the man that raped her. Okay, Dr. Ferrami?"

"That's just fine," Jeannie said.

BERRINGTON ordered champagne.

Champagne meant romance. On previous occasions when Jeannie and Berrington had met socially, he had been charming rather than amorous. Was he now going to make a pass at her? Jeannie wondered. It made her uneasy. This man was her boss.

She did not tell him about Steve. She was on the point of doing so several times during dinner, but something held her back. If Steve did turn out to be a criminal, her theory would start to look shaky. But she felt sure it was all an appalling mistake.

She had talked to Lisa. "They've arrested Steve Logan!" she had said. Lisa was horrified to think that the man had spent the entire day at Nut House, her place of work, and that Jeannie had been on the point of taking him into her home. Jeannie had explained that she was sure Steve was not the perpetrator. Later she realized she probably should not have made the call: It might be construed as interfering with a witness. Not that it would make any difference. Lisa would look at a row of men, and she would see the man who raped her or she would not.

Jeannie had also spoken to her mother. Patty had been there today with her three sons, and Mom talked animatedly about the boys. Mercifully, she seemed to have forgotten that it was only yesterday she moved into Bella Vista.

"How was the sea bass?" Berrington said now.

"Delicious. Very delicate."

He smoothed his eyebrows with the tip of his right index finger. For some reason the gesture struck her as self-congratulatory. "Now I'm going to ask you a question, and you have to answer honestly." He smiled so that she would not take him too seriously. "Do you like dessert?"

"Yes. Do you take me for the kind of woman who would pretend about a thing like that?"

He shook his head. "There's not much you do pretend about."

"Not enough, probably. I have been called tactless."

"Is that your worst failing?"

"I could probably do better if I thought about it. What's yours?"

Berrington answered without hesitation. "Falling in love."

"That's a failing?"

"It is if you do it too often. Maybe I should write to Lorraine Logan and ask her advice."

Jeannie laughed, but she did not want the conversation to get onto Steve.

She dipped a spoon into her mango sorbet. This was definitely not a business dinner. She glanced up at Berrington, delicately eating caramelized apples. The guy was smart, and she respected him for his scientific work. All the same, she did not feel any warmth of affection for him. The best course might be to pretend to interpret his attention as kindly and paternal. That way she might avoid spurning him outright and maybe ruining her career.

When Berrington had paid the bill, they went down to the parking garage and got in his silver Lincoln Town Car. He drove along the harborside and got onto the Jones Falls Expressway.

"There's the city jail," he said, pointing to a fortresslike building occupying a city block. "The scum of the earth are in there."

Steve might be in there, Jeannie thought.

As he pulled up to the curb outside her house, she said firmly, "Well, Berry, thank you for a charming evening." Would he shake hands, she wondered, or try to kiss her?

But he did neither. "I need to make a call," he said. "May I use your phone?"

She could hardly say, "Heck, no. Stop by a pay phone." It looked as if she was going to have to deal with a determined pass. "Of course," she said, suppressing a sigh. "Come on up."

She led the way in through the front door to a tiny lobby with two more doors. One led to the ground-floor apartment, occupied by Mr. Oliver, a retired stevedore. The other, Jeannie's door, opened onto the staircase up to her second-floor apartment.

She frowned, puzzled. Her door was open.

She led the way up the stairs. A light was on up there. That was curious; she had left before dark.

The staircase led directly into her living room. She stepped inside and screamed.

He was standing at her refrigerator with a bottle of vodka in his hand. He was scruffy and unshaven, and he seemed a little drunk.

Behind her Berrington said, "What's going on?"

"You need better security in here, Jeannie," the intruder said. "I picked your locks in about ten seconds."

Jeannie said, shocked, "When did you get out of jail, Daddy?"

THE lineup room was on the same floor as the cells.

In the anteroom were six other men of about Steve's age and build. He guessed they were cops. They did not speak to him and avoided his gaze. He wanted to say, "Hey, guys, I'm on your side. I'm not a rapist. I'm innocent."

They all had to take off their wristwatches and jewelry and put on white paper coveralls. While they were getting ready, a young man in a suit came in and said, "Which of you is the suspect, please?"

"That's me," Steve said.

"I'm Lew Tanner, the public defender. I'm here to make sure the lineup is run correctly. Do you have any questions?"

"How long will it take me to get out of here?" Steve said.

"Assuming you're not picked out, a couple of hours."

"Two hours!" Steve said indignantly.

"I'm afraid so. I'll ask them to handle your discharge as fast as possible," Lew said. "Anything else?"

"No, thanks."

"Okay." He went out.

A turnkey ushered the seven men through a door onto a stage. There was a backdrop with a graduated scale that showed their height, and there were positions numbered one to ten. A powerful light shone on them, and a screen divided the stage from the rest of the room. The men could not see through the screen, but they could hear what was going on beyond it.

For a while there was nothing but footsteps and occasional low voices, all male. Then Steve heard the unmistakable sound of a woman's steps. After a moment a man's voice spoke.

"Standing before you are seven people. They will be known to you by number only. If you would like them to turn around or face sideways, then they will do that as a group. Do you recognize any one of them who has done anything to you or in your presence?"

There was silence. Steve's nerves were wound up as tight as guitar strings, even though he was sure she would not pick him out.

A low female voice said, "He had a hat on. A baseball cap."

Steve heard anxiety and tension in her voice but also determination. There was no hint of falseness. He felt better.

"Dave, see if we have seven baseball caps in that closet."

There was a pause. Eventually a detective came onto the stage from the side and handed a baseball cap to each man in the lineup. They all put them on, and the detective left.

From the other side of the screen came the sound of a woman crying. The male voice repeated some of the words used earlier. "Do you recognize any one of them who has done anything to you or in your presence? If so, call out their number."

"Number four," she said with a sob in her voice.

Steve turned and looked at the backdrop. He was number four.

"No!" he shouted. "This can't be right. It wasn't me!"

The other men in the lineup were already leaving the stage.

"There's something wrong here," Steve yelled.

The turnkey appeared. "It's all over, son. Let's go." He took Steve's arm in a grip that felt like a steel clamp.

Steve felt as if he had been bludgeoned from behind. His shoulders slumped, and he was seized by helpless fury. "How did this happen?" he said. "How did this happen?"

BERRINGTON said, "Daddy?"

Jeannie wanted to bite off her tongue. She felt mortified. Her father's face had been bruised, and he had several days' growth of beard. His clothes were dirty, and he had a faint but disgusting smell. She felt so ashamed she could hardly look at Berrington.

"This is Professor Berrington Jones," she said. "Berry, meet my father, Pete Ferrami."

Berrington was gracious. "Good to meet you, Mr. Ferrami," he said, shaking his hand. "Your daughter is a very special woman."

"Ain't that the truth," Daddy said with a pleased grin.

"Well, Berry, now you know the family secret," she said resignedly. "Daddy was sent to jail on the day I graduated from Princeton. He's been incarcerated for the last eight years." She wanted to get rid of Berrington fast now. "If you want to make that call, you can use the phone in the bedroom."

"Uh, it'll keep," he said.

Thank goodness for that, she thought.

"Good night." He shook hands awkwardly and went out.

Jeannie turned to her father. "What happened?"

"I got time off for good behavior. I'm free. And naturally, the first thing I wanted was to see my little girl."

"Right after you went on a three-day drunk." She felt a familiar rage rise inside her. "Give me that bottle," she said.

Reluctantly he handed her the vodka, and she put it back in the freezer. She put water in the coffeemaker and turned it on.

"You look older," he said. "I see a little gray in your hair."

"Gee, thanks." She put out mugs, cream, and sugar.

"Your mother went gray early too."

"I always thought you were the cause of that."

"I went to her place," he said in a tone of mild indignation. "She doesn't live there anymore."

"She's in Bella Vista now."

"That's what the neighbor told me—Mrs. Mendoza. I don't like to think of your mother in a place like that."

"Then take her out of there!" Jeannie said. "Get yourself a job and start taking care of her."

"You know I can't do that, honey. I never could."

Jeannie's anger turned into sadness. She swallowed hard and changed the subject. "What are you going to do now, Daddy? Do you have any plans?"

"I'll look around for a while."

He meant he would scout for a place to rob. Jeannie said nothing. Daddy was a thief, and she could not change him.

He coughed. "Maybe you could let me have a few bucks to get me started."

That made her mad again. "I'll tell you what," she said in a tight voice. "I'll make you eggs and toast. You can sleep on my couch. But I'm not giving you cash. I'm desperately trying to find the money to pay for Mom to stay someplace where they'll treat her like a human being. I don't have a dollar to spare."

"Okay, sweetie," he said with a martyred air. "I understand."

She looked at him. In the end, when the turmoil of shame and anger and pity died down, all she felt was longing. She yearned for a father who would be a father, loving and supportive and stable. And she knew she would never, ever have her wish.

The phone rang.

It was Lisa, sounding upset. "Jeannie, it was him! I picked him out of the lineup. Steven Logan."

"He's the rapist?" Jeannie said incredulously. "Are you sure?"

"There's no doubt, Jeannie," Lisa said. "It was horrible seeing his face again. I didn't say anything at first. But when the detective made them all put on baseball caps, I knew for sure."

"Lisa, it can't be him," Jeannie said. "His tests are all wrong."

"This spoils your theory, doesn't it?" Lisa sounded annoyed. "You wanted one twin to be good and the other bad."

"That's not the reason I'm saying it can't be him." Jeannie

sighed. "Well, maybe it is. I don't know anymore. Are you okay?"

"Yes, I'm fine now that he's locked up. I'm going to bed. I'm exhausted. I just wanted to tell you. How was your evening?"

"So-so. I'll tell you all about it tomorrow."

"I still want to fly down to Richmond with you tomorrow."

Jeannie had planned to take Lisa to help her interview Dennis Pinker. "Do you feel up to it? Dennis Pinker will probably be Steve Logan's double."

"I know. I can handle it. I'll call you early."

"Okay. Good night."

Jeannie sat down. Could Steve's engaging nature be no more than a mask? I must be a bad judge of character if that's so, she thought. Maybe a bad scientist too. Perhaps all identical twins will turn out to be identically criminal.

She sighed. Her own criminal ancestry sat beside her.

BERRINGTON Jones drove home slowly. He felt disappointed, no closer to solving the problem of Jeannie's project and what it might uncover. He frowned as he parked and went inside.

He checked his answering machine. There was one message.

"Professor, this is Sergeant Delaware from the sex-crimes unit calling on Monday night. As you are Ms. Hoxton's employer and the rape took place on campus, I thought I should tell you we have arrested a man this evening. His name is Steven Logan."

"Good Lord!" Berrington burst out.

"The victim picked him out at the lineup," the voice went on, "so I'm sure a DNA test will confirm that he is the man. Please pass this information on to any others who are appropriate. Thank you."

"No!" Berrington sat down heavily. "No."

He began to weep. He buried his head in his hands and stayed that way for some time.

When at last the tears dried up, he lifted the phone and dialed a number he knew by heart. A young man answered. "Hello?"

"This is me," Berrington said.

"Hey, how are you?"

"Desolate."

"Oh." The tone was guilty.

If Berrington had any doubts, that note in the voice swept them away. "I'm calling about Sunday night. You damn fool, you went to the campus, didn't you? You did it again."

The young man sighed. "How did you know?"

"At first I didn't suspect—I thought you'd left town. Then they arrested someone who looks like you. So you're off the hook."

"Wow! What a break. Listen . . . you wouldn't say anything. To the police, or anything."

"No, not a word," Berrington said with a heavy heart.

Tuesday

THE city of Richmond had an air of lost grandeur, and Jeannie thought Dennis Pinker's parents fit right in. Charlotte Pinker, a red-head in a whispering silk dress, had the aura of a great Virginia lady even though she lived in a frame house on a narrow lot.

Jeannie guessed she was probably near sixty. Her husband, whom she referred to as the Major, had the careless grooming and unhurried air of a man long retired. He winked roguishly at Jeannie and Lisa and said, "Would you girls like a cocktail?"

His wife spoke a little too loudly, as if she were addressing a meeting. "For mercy's sake, Major, this is no party. These ladies are here to *study* us. It's because our son is a murderer."

She called him "our son," Jeannie noted, but that did not mean a lot. He might still have been adopted. She was desperate to ask about Dennis Pinker's parentage, but it was a delicate question.

Charlotte and the Major had filled out questionnaires in advance, and now they had to be interviewed for about an hour each. Lisa took the Major into the kitchen, and Jeannie interviewed Charlotte.

When she asked Charlotte if any other family members had ever been in trouble with the law, Charlotte turned her imperious gaze on Jeannie and drawled, "The men in my family have always been terribly violent. We are hot-blooded."

That suggested that Dennis was not adopted or that his adoption was not acknowledged. The question had to be asked. Jeannie said, "Mrs. Pinker, is there any chance Dennis has a twin?"

"No." The response was flat—no indignation, no bluster.

"You're sure."

Charlotte laughed. "My dear, that's one thing a mother could hardly make a mistake about. I carried that boy in my womb."

Jeannie's spirits fell. Charlotte Pinker would lie more readily than Lorraine Logan, Jeannie judged, but all the same it was worrying that they should both deny their sons were twins. She felt pessimistic as she and Lisa took their leave of the Pinkers.

Their rented Ford Aspire was parked outside. As they pulled onto the highway, heading for the prison, Lisa said, "It really bothers me that you think I picked the wrong guy in the lineup."

"It bothers me too," Jeannie said. "I know you wouldn't have done it if you didn't feel sure."

"How can you be so certain I'm wrong?"

"I'm not certain about anything. I just have a strong feeling about Steve Logan. Are you offended?"

Lisa sighed. "I ought to be, but I like you too much to be mad."

Jeannie reached across and squeezed Lisa's hand. "Thanks."

There was a long silence as they drove ten miles out of town. They pulled off the interstate at a sign marked GREENWOOD PENITENTIARY and parked the car in the shade of a tree in the visitors lot.

"Are you ready for this?" Jeannie said.

Lisa nodded grimly. "I'm ready."

The main gate opened to let out a delivery truck, and Jeannie and Lisa walked in unchallenged. They were expected. A guard checked their identification, then escorted them into the office of the warden, John Temoigne. He wore a short-sleeved shirt and a tie, and there were cigar butts in his ashtray.

Jeannie shook his hand. "I'm Dr. Jean Ferrami from Jones Falls University, and this is my assistant, Ms. Hoxton. I explained our work when I wrote to you, Warden, but if you have any questions, I'd be glad to answer them."

"Do you know the details of Pinker's crime?" said Temoigne.

"I believe he killed a woman in a cinema."

"You're close. It was at the old Eldorado movie theater down in Greensburg. They were all watching some horror movie. Pinker got into the basement and turned off the electric power. Then, while everyone was panicking in the dark, he ran around molesting girls. One woman tried to resist him, and he strangled her."

Jeannie exchanged a startled look with Lisa. It was so similar to what had happened at J.F.U. on Sunday. A diversion had created confusion and panic, and given the perpetrator his opportunity. If Steve Logan was Dennis's identical twin, it seemed they had committed very similar crimes.

Temoigne went on. "Normally you would interview the prisoner through a grille. You've asked to be in the same room with him, and I have orders from above to let you. All the same, I urge you to think again. He is a violent and dangerous criminal."

Jeannie felt a tremor of anxiety, but she stayed outwardly cool. "I appreciate your concern, Warden. But we have to carry out certain procedures, such as taking a blood sample and photographing the subject, which can't be done through bars. Furthermore, we feel it would compromise our results to have an artificial barrier between us and the subject."

He shrugged. "Well, I guess I'll walk you to the cellblock."

They left the office and crossed a baked-earth yard to a two-story concrete blockhouse. A guard opened an iron gate, and Temoigne said, "Robinson here will take care of you from now on."

"Thank you, Warden," Jeannie said.

Robinson was a reassuringly tall black man of about thirty. He had a pistol in a buttoned holster and an intimidating-looking nightstick. He showed them into a small gray-tiled interview room with a table and chairs. There was no window.

Robinson said, "Pinker will be here in a minute." Jeannie and Lisa sat down.

A moment later the door opened.

BERRINGTON Jones met with Jim Proust and Preston Barck at the Monocle, a power-lunch venue close to the Senate office buildings in Washington. He had bad news for them, and he got it out of the way as soon as they had ordered. "Jeannie Ferrami is in Richmond today seeing Dennis Pinker."

Jim scowled. "Why on earth didn't you stop her?"

As always, Jim's overbearing manner irritated Berrington. "What was I supposed to do? Tie her down?"

Preston said nervously, "Let's keep our voices down, fellas. We knew this might happen sometime. I say we take the initiative and confess everything right away."

"Confess?" Jim said incredulously. "Are we supposed to have done something wrong?"

"It's the way people might see it—"

"Let me remind you that when the CIA produced the report that started all this, 'New Developments in Soviet Science,' President Nixon himself said it was the most alarming news to come out of Moscow since the Soviets split the atom. Don't you remember how scary that was back then?"

Berrington certainly remembered. The Soviets had a breeding program for human beings, the CIA had said. They were planning to turn out perfect scientists, perfect athletes, and perfect soldiers. The President had ordered the creation of a parallel program to find a way to breed perfect American soldiers. Jim Proust had been given the job of making it happen.

He had come immediately to Berrington for help. A few years earlier Berrington had gone to work at Fort Detrick, in Maryland, studying fatigue in soldiers. By the early '70s he was the world's leading expert in the heritability of soldierly characteristics, such as aggression and stamina. Meanwhile, Preston, at Harvard, had made a series of breakthroughs in understanding human fertilization.

Berrington had talked him into leaving the university and becoming part of the great experiment with him and Proust.

It had been Berrington's proudest moment. "I also remember how exciting it was," he said. "We were at the leading edge of science, we were setting America right, and our *President* had asked us to do this job for him."

Preston toyed with his salad. "Times have changed. Men have gone to jail for doing what the President told them."

"What was wrong with it?" Jim said testily.

"We went undercover," Preston said.

Jim flushed. "We transferred it into the private sector."

That was sophistry, Berrington thought, though he did not say so. Preston had set up Genetico as a private corporation, and Jim gave it enough military contracts to make it financially viable. After a while the fertility clinics became so lucrative that Genetico's profits paid for research without help from the military. Berrington moved back into the academic world, and Jim went from the army to the CIA and then into the Senate.

Preston said, "I'm not saying we were wrong—although some of the things we did in the early days were against the law."

Berrington did not want the two of them to take up polarized positions. He intervened, saying calmly, "But we were smart enough to see the possibilities of genetic engineering."

"Nobody had even heard the *words* back then," Jim growled as he cut into his steak.

Berrington nodded. "Jim's right, Preston. We should be proud. We set ourselves the task of finding out whether traits such as intelligence and aggression are genetic. Then we identified the genes responsible, and finally, we engineered them into test-tube embryos—and we're on the brink of success!"

His two friends were so predictable, Berrington thought amiably; Jim had blustered, and Preston had whined. Now they might be calm enough to take a cool look at the situation. "That brings us back to Jeannie Ferrami," Berrington said. "In a year or two she may tell us how to make people aggressive without turning them into criminals. The pieces of the jigsaw are falling into place. The Landsmann takeover offers us the chance to accelerate the program and get Jim into the White House too."

"That's all very well," said Preston. "But what should we do?"

Berrington swallowed some fish. "The first thing to realize is that we do not have a crisis here; we just have a *problem,*" he said. "And the problem is Jeannie Ferrami. We have to stop her learning anything more, at least before next Monday, when we sign the takeover documents. Leave it in my hands. I'll deal with her."

Preston was not satisfied. "How?"

"I think her use of medical databases raises ethical questions. I believe I can force her to stop."

"What's this girl like?" Jim said.

"About thirty. Tall, very athletic. Dark hair, ring in her nose, drives an old red Mercedes. Clever, feisty, and stubborn."

Jim nodded thoughtfully. "We still have many friends in intelligence. It wouldn't be difficult to make her vanish."

Preston looked scared. "No violence, Jim, for heaven's sake."

A waiter cleared away their plates, and they fell silent until he had gone. Berrington knew he had to tell them what he had learned last night from Sergeant Delaware. With a heavy heart he said, "There's something else. On Sunday night a girl was raped in the J.F.U. gym. The police have arrested Steve Logan."

Jim said, "Did he do it?"

"No."

"Do you know who did?"

Berrington looked him in the eye. "Yes, Jim, I do."

Preston swore.

Jim said, "Maybe we should make the *boys* vanish."

Berrington felt his throat tighten up. He leaned over the table, jabbing his finger at Jim's face. "Don't ever say that again!"

Preston hissed, "Knock it off, you two. People will see!"

Berrington was not through. He grabbed Jim's lapel. "We brought those boys into the world. Good or bad, they're our responsibility. If one of them is even hurt, so help me—"

"All right, all right," Jim said.

A waiter appeared. Berrington, muttering, let go of Jim.

Preston said to the waiter, "Bring me the check, please."

JEANNIE stared at the door of the room as it slowly opened.

The man who walked in was Steven Logan's double. Beside her she heard Lisa gasp.

The system worked, Jeannie thought triumphantly. She was vindicated. The two young men were as alike as her two hands.

The curly fair hair was cut the same way: short, with a part. Dennis Pinker rolled his sleeves the same neat way Steve did. Dennis closed the door behind him with his heel, the way Steve had when he had walked into Jeannie's office. As he sat down, he gave her an engaging smile just like Steve's. She could hardly believe it.

Here it was, the same genetic material transformed into two completely different individuals—one a charming college boy, the other a psychopath. But was the difference merely superficial?

Jeannie was calm. With Robinson, the tall prison guard, standing next to her with a nightstick and a gun, she was perfectly safe.

"Are you okay?" she murmured to Lisa.

Lisa was pale, but she said grimly, "I'm fine."

Like his parents, Dennis had filled out several forms in advance. Now Lisa began the more complex questionnaires. As they worked, Jeannie compared Dennis with Steve. The similarities were astonishing: interests and hobbies, tastes, physical skills—all were the same. Dennis even had the same high IQ as Steve.

The big difference between Dennis and Steve was in their socialization. Steve Logan was a man with above-average social skills— comfortable meeting strangers, prepared to accept legitimate authority, happy to be part of a team. Dennis had the interpersonal skills of a three-year-old. He grabbed anything he wanted, he had trouble sharing, and if he could not get his way, he became violent. Steve had grown up, but Dennis never had.

As she watched and listened, Jeannie realized there was another difference. She was afraid of Dennis. There was menace in the air all around him. She had the sense he would do anything that came into his head, regardless of the consequences. Steve had not given her that feeling for one moment.

Jeannie photographed Dennis and took close-ups of both ears. In identical twins the ears were normally highly similar, especially the attachment of the earlobes. When they were almost done, Lisa took a blood sample, something she had been trained to do. She routinely sealed the vial and signed the seal, then left to put it in the cool box in the car.

Jeannie completed the last set of questions on her own. "Thank you, Mr. Pinker." She began hurriedly to tidy up her papers.

Robinson said, "Dr. Ferrami, I'll take you out."

The three of them left the room together. Outside the door Dennis smiled at Jeannie, a long, intimate smile, as if they were lovers who had spent the afternoon together. Then he was taken back to his cell. Jeannie watched him go with immense relief, tinged with revulsion.

Robinson walked her to the main gate. She crossed the parking lot to the car, where Lisa was waiting, thinking, I'll be glad to drive out of this place. She had a sample of Dennis's DNA. That was the most important thing.

AFTER lunch Berrington went to a quiet neighborhood bar and ordered a martini.

He focused his mind on Jeannie Ferrami. She had to be stopped immediately, today or tomorrow, before she learned enough to ruin them all.

Her weak point was her use of medical databases without the permission of the patients. It was the kind of thing the newspapers could make into a scandal, regardless of whether anyone's privacy was genuinely invaded. And universities were terrified of scandal; it played havoc with their fund-raising. He would plant the idea with a reporter at *The New York Times*.

Most journalists knew Berrington; he was a minor celebrity. All the same, this would be a dangerous strategy. There was a chance they would begin by investigating Jeannie and finish up investigating him. But he could think of no other way.

He drained his glass and went to a pay phone.

LISA and Jeannie drove to the Richmond-Williamsburg airport, where they caught the plane back to Baltimore.

The key to the mystery must lie with the hospital where Dennis and Steve were born, Jeannie mused as they took off. Somehow identical twin brothers had ended up with different mothers.

She looked through the papers in her case and checked the birth information on the two subjects. Steve's birthday was August 25. To her horror she found that Dennis's birthday was September 7—almost two weeks later.

"There must be a mistake," she said. "I don't know why I didn't check this before." She showed Lisa the documents. "Do our forms ask which hospital the subject was born in?"

"I believe that's one question we didn't include," Lisa said.

"It must have been a military hospital in this case. Colonel Logan is in the army, and presumably the Major was a soldier at the time Dennis was born."

"We'll check."

Jeannie was impatient. "I'd like to call right away. Is there a phone on this plane?"

Lisa frowned. "Are you thinking of calling Steve's mother?"

Jeannie heard the note of disapproval. "Yes. Why shouldn't I?"

"Does she know he's in jail?"

"Good point. I don't know. Darn. Maybe I'll go see him in jail. Anyway, I can call the Pinkers." She waved at a passing stewardess. "Is there a phone on the plane?"

"No, I'm sorry," the stewardess said.

As soon as they landed, Jeannie went to a pay phone and called the Pinkers in Richmond. The line was busy. She waited five minutes, then tried again; but she got the same infuriating tone. "I'll try later," she said.

Lisa's car was in the parking lot. As they drove into the city, Jeannie said, "Could I ask you a great big favor? Start the DNA extraction tonight?"

Lisa's face fell. "Oh, Jeannie, we've been out all day. I have to shop for dinner—"

"I know. And I have to visit the jail. Let's meet at the lab later, say at nine o'clock? If we start tonight, we could have a result by the day after tomorrow."

Lisa looked dubious. "Okay."

Jeannie got out at her apartment and then got right into her own car to drive downtown. She put her car in a parking garage and walked to police headquarters.

In a swanky lobby with marble benches she told the police receptionist she was here to see Steven Logan, who was in custody. She expected to have to argue, but after a few minutes' wait a young woman in uniform took her up in the elevator.

She was shown into a room the size of a closet. It was featureless except for a small window set into the wall at face level and a sound panel beneath it. The window looked into a similar booth.

She stared through the window. After five minutes Steve was brought in, handcuffed and his feet chained together. He came to the glass and peered through. When he recognized her, he smiled broadly. "This is a pleasant surprise!" he said.

Despite his cheerful manner, he looked terrible—strained and tired. "How are things?" she said.

"A little rough."

Jeannie's heart went out to him. She could not believe he was the man who had raped Lisa. She said, "I saw your twin today. There's no doubt. He's your double."

"Maybe *he* raped Lisa Hoxton."

Jeannie shook her head. "He's locked up."

"Do you think he might have escaped from jail, then returned? To establish an alibi?"

"Too fanciful. If Dennis got out of jail, nothing would induce him to go back."

"I guess you're right," Steve said gloomily.

"I have a couple of questions. First, when is your birthday?"

"August twenty-fifth."

That was what Jeannie had written down. Maybe she had Dennis's date wrong. "And do you know where you were born?"

"Yes. Dad was stationed at Fort Lee, Virginia, at the time, and I was born in the army hospital there."

"Are you sure?"

"Certain. Mom wrote about it in her book *Having a Baby*." He narrowed his eyes in a look that was becoming familiar. It meant he was figuring out her thinking. "Where was Dennis born?"

"I don't know yet. I'm going to check. I'll call his mother as soon as I get to my office. Have you spoken to your parents yet?"

"No."

"Would you like me to call them?"

"No! Please. I don't want them to know until I can tell them I've been cleared."

Jeannie shrugged. It was his decision.

"Jeannie . . . what's he like?"

"Dennis? Superficially, he's like you. It could have *been* you."

"Jeez." Steve looked deeply uncomfortable.

"The big difference is his behavior. He doesn't know how to relate to the rest of the human race."

The door opened behind her, and the young woman police officer looked in. "Time's up, Dr. Ferrami."

"Okay," she said. "Steve, Lisa Hoxton is not the kind of person who would make a wild accusation. All the same, I want you to know that I don't believe you did it."

For a moment she thought he was going to cry. "Thank you," he said gruffly. "I can't tell you how much it means to me."

"Call me when you get out." She gave him what she hoped was an encouraging smile. "Good luck." She turned away and left.

The policewoman walked Jeannie to the lobby. Night was falling as she returned to the parking garage. She flicked on the headlights of the old Mercedes and got onto the Jones Falls Expressway. Heading north, she drove fast, eager to get to the university.

LISA'S WHITE HONDA WAS already parked outside Nut House. As Jeannie went inside, Lisa was just turning on the lights in the lab. The box with Dennis Pinker's blood sample was on a bench.

Jeannie's office was right across the corridor. She unlocked her door by passing her plastic card through the card reader and went in. From her desk she called the Pinker house in Richmond.

Charlotte answered. "How is my son?" she said.

"He's in good health," Jeannie replied. She tried to think of something positive to say. "He was very cooperative."

"He always had beautiful manners," Charlotte said in the southern drawl she used for her most outrageous utterances.

"Mrs. Pinker, may I double-check his birthday with you?"

"He was born on the seventh of September. We were at Fort Bragg, in North Carolina, at the time. The Major was training conscripts for Vietnam," Charlotte went on proudly. "The army medical command has a big hospital at Bragg. That's where Dennis came into the world."

The mystery was as deep as ever. "Mrs. Pinker, I want to thank you again for your kind cooperation."

She returned to the lab and said to Lisa, "Apparently, Steven and Dennis were born thirteen days apart and in different states. I just don't understand it."

Lisa opened a fresh box of test tubes. "Well, there's one incontrovertible test. If they have the same DNA, they're identical twins no matter what." She took out two of the little glass tubes. Each had a lid at the top and a conical bottom. She opened a pack of labels, wrote "Dennis Pinker" on one and "Steven Logan" on another, then labeled the tubes and placed them in a rack.

She broke the seal on Dennis's blood and put a single drop in one test tube. Then she took a vial of Steve's blood out of the refrigerator and did the same. Using a precision-calibrated pipette—a pipe with a bulb at one end—she added a tiny measured quantity of chloroform to each test tube. With a fresh pipette she added a similarly exact amount of phenol.

She closed both test tubes and put them in the Whirlimixer to agitate them for a few seconds. The chloroform would dissolve the fats, and the phenol would disrupt the proteins, but the long, coiled molecules of deoxyribonucleic acid would remain intact.

Lisa put the tubes back in the rack. "That's all we can do for now," she said. The DNA could be drawn off with a pipette for the next stage of the test. But that would have to wait for the morning.

Wednesday

BERRINGTON Jones sat in his office and thought of all the things that could go wrong with his plan. The editors of *The New York Times* might decide not to follow up the story. They might make some inquiries and realize there was nothing wrong with what Jeannie was doing. Or they could simply move too slowly and start looking into it next week, when it would be too late.

He looked out the window and watched four youngsters on the tennis court while he waited for the phone to ring.

He did not have to wait long.

At nine thirty the president of Jones Falls University, Maurice Obell, called. "We've got a problem," he said.

Berrington tensed. "What's up, Maurice?"

"Woman on *The New York Times* just called. Says someone in your department is invading people's privacy. A Dr. Ferrami."

Thank the Lord, Berrington thought. He made his voice solemn. "I was afraid of something like this," he said. "I'll be right over."

He left his office and walked across campus to Hillside Hall, the university's administration building, where the president had his office. Berrington nodded pleasantly to Dr. Obell's secretary and said, "He's expecting me."

Maurice was sitting facing the bay window overlooking the lawn. A short, barrel-chested man, he often wore a harassed air. To keep

J.F.U. going, he had to raise ten million dollars a year from bene-
factors, and consequently he dreaded bad publicity.

He turned his chair around to his desk. "They're working on a
big article on scientific ethics, she says. Berry, I can't have Jones
Falls heading that article with an example of unethical science. Our
donors would have a cow. We've got to do something."

"Who's the reporter?"

Maurice consulted a scratch pad. "Naomi Freelander. She's the
ethics editor. Yesterday the paper got a tip-off about Ferrami."

"I wonder where the tip came from?" Berrington said.

"There are some disloyal fools around." Maurice sighed. "Say it's
not true, Berry. Tell me she doesn't invade people's privacy."

Berrington crossed his legs, trying to appear relaxed when he was
in fact wired taut. This was where he had to walk a tightrope. "I
don't believe she does anything wrong," he said. "She scans medical
databases and finds twins. It's very clever—"

"Is she looking at medical records without permission?"

Berrington pretended to be reluctant. "Well . . . sort of."

"Then she'll have to stop. Get her in here now, Berry."

Berrington picked up Maurice's phone and called Jeannie's office.
"Can I see you right away?" he said to her. "I'm in Dr. Obell's
office."

Jeannie gave a sigh, then said, "I'll be right over."

The next few minutes would be crucial. Berrington had to keep
Maurice firm without seeming hostile to Jeannie. He also needed a
fallback plan in case Jeannie defended herself well.

Struck by inspiration, he said, "We might rough out a press statement while we're waiting for her."

"That's a good idea."

Berrington pulled over a pad and began scribbling. He wrote that
Jones Falls University admitted mistakes had been made. The university apologized to those whose privacy had been invaded. And
it promised that the program had been discontinued as of today.

He handed his work to Maurice's secretary and asked her to put
it through her word processor right away.

Jeannie arrived wearing a baggy emerald-green T-shirt and tight black jeans. She looked kind of cute to Berrington, but to the university president she would appear the kind of irresponsible junior academic who might get J.F.U. into trouble.

Maurice invited her to sit down and told her about the call from the newspaper. His manner was stiff.

"This is ludicrous," Jeannie said with irritation.

"But you do access medical databases," Maurice said.

"I don't look at the databases; the computer does. No human being sees medical records. My program produces names and addresses. We do nothing further without asking permission of the subject. We don't even tell them they're twins until after they've agreed to be part of our study. So whose privacy is invaded?"

Berrington pretended to back her. "I told you, Maurice," he said. "The *Times* has it all wrong."

"But I have to think of the university's reputation."

Jeannie said, "Believe me, my work is going to enhance that reputation. I've figured out how to study the genetics of criminality. When we publish the results, it will be a sensation."

"She's right," Berrington put in. It was true. Her study would have been fascinating. It was heartbreaking to destroy it. But he had no choice.

Maurice shook his head. "It's my job to protect the university from scandal."

Jeannie said, "It's also your job to defend academic freedom. If a university is going to buckle under pressure, what hope is there?" Berrington was exultant. She was digging her own grave. Maurice was antagonized by every word.

Then Jeannie seemed to realize what she was doing, for she suddenly changed tack. "On the other hand, none of us wants bad publicity for the university," she said in a milder voice. "I quite understand your concern, Dr. Obell." Jeannie hesitated. "But for my research I need identical twins, raised apart, at least one of whom is a criminal. My computer program locates people who don't even know they're twins. There's no other way to do it."

"I hadn't realized," Maurice said.

The tone was becoming perilously amicable. Then Maurice's secretary came in and handed him the press release Berrington had drafted. Maurice showed it to Jeannie, saying, "We need to issue something like this today if we're to kill this story off."

She read it quickly, and her anger returned. "But no mistakes have been made! No one's privacy has been invaded."

Berrington concealed his satisfaction. "Jeannie, Dr. Obell feels we have to put out a firm statement."

"You can't say the use of my computer program has been discontinued!" she stormed. "That would be tantamount to canceling my entire project!"

Maurice's face hardened. "I can't have *The New York Times* saying that Jones Falls scientists invade people's privacy," he said. "It would cost us millions in lost donations."

"Find a middle way," Jeannie pleaded. "Say you're looking into the problem. Set up a committee."

Oh, no, Berrington thought. That was dangerously sensible. This would be a good time to bring the meeting to a close. "Let me make a proposal here. We have two separate problems. One is to find a way to progress Jeannie's research without bringing scandal upon the university. That's something Jeannie and I have to discuss. The second question is how the university presents this to the world. That's a matter for you and me to talk about, Maurice."

Maurice looked relieved. "Very sensible," he said.

Berrington said, "Thank you for joining us, Jeannie."

She realized she was being dismissed. She got up with a puzzled frown. She knew she had been outmaneuvered, but she could not quite figure out how. "All right." She hesitated, then went out.

"Difficult woman," Maurice said.

Berrington looked down in an attitude of humility. "I feel at fault here, Maurice. I hired Jeannie Ferrami. Of course, I had no idea that she would devise this method of work, but all the same it's my responsibility, and I have to get you out of it."

"What do you propose?"

"I can't ask you not to release that press statement. I don't have the right. You can't put one research project above the welfare of the entire university. I realize that." He looked up.

Maurice hesitated. "I appreciate that, Berry. But what will you do about Jeannie?"

Berrington relaxed. "She's my problem. Leave her to me."

STEVE Logan dropped off to sleep in the early hours of Wednesday morning.

The jail was quiet, and his cellmate was snoring. Steve had tried to stay awake, rehearsing his bail-application speech, but he kept slipping into a dream in which the judge smiled benignly on him and said, "Let this man go free." Sitting on the floor of the cell, with his back to the wall, he nodded off.

He was in a profound sleep when he was jerked awake by the sound of his cell door opening and the voice of the turnkey.

The man said, "Time to pull you out of there, boy. These gentlemen have come to take you to court." He got three other men out of cells and chained them all together with Steve. Then two cops took them to a bus.

They drove through the city for fifteen or twenty minutes, then entered a garage door in a court building. They got off the bus and went down into the basement. There were eight barred pens around a central open area. All four prisoners were put in a pen that already had six men in it. Their chains were removed and dumped on a table in the middle of the room.

Over the next hour another thirty or more prisoners arrived.

Steve figured it was about midday when they began taking prisoners out of the cells. He was in the second batch. Ten men were chained together; then they went up to the court.

The courtroom was like a chapel. There was a green carpet on the floor and nine rows of blond wood benches like pews.

In the back row sat Steve's mother and father.

He gasped with shock. Dad wore his colonel's uniform, with his hat under his arm. He sat straight-backed, his expression rigidly blank, taut with suppressed emotion. Mom sat beside him, small and plump, her pretty round face puffy with crying.

Steve wished he could fall through the floor. He stopped walking, holding up the line of prisoners, and stared in dumb agony at his parents, until the turnkey gave him a shove and he stumbled forward to the front bench.

His father stood up then and came forward. A man in blue jeans spoke officiously to him. "Yes, sir?"

"I'm Steven Logan's father. I'd like to speak to him," Dad said in an authoritative voice. "May I know who you are?"

"David Purdy, pretrial investigator. I called you this morning."

So that was how Mom and Dad found out, Steve realized. He should have guessed an investigator would call his parents. He winced at the thought. What had the investigator said? "Steven Logan is in custody in Baltimore, accused of rape. Are you his mother?"

Purdy said, "You can speak to your son. Go ahead."

Dad nodded curtly. He edged along the bench behind the prisoners and sat behind Steve. He put his hand on Steve's shoulder. Tears came to Steve's eyes. "Dad, I didn't do this," he said.

"I know, Steve," his father said.

His simple faith was too much for Steve, and he started to cry. Once he began, he could not stop.

After a while Dad said, "We wanted to get you a lawyer, but there wasn't time. We only just made it here."

Steve nodded. He would be his own lawyer if he could just get himself under control.

The judge came in. She was an attractive woman of about fifty, very small and neat. She wore a black robe and carried a can of Diet Coke, which she put on the desk when she sat down. Steve tried to read her face. Was she cruel or benign?

She looked at the row of prisoners and said, "Good afternoon. This is your bail review. Have you all received your statement of charges?" They all had. She went on to recite a script about what their rights were and how to get a lawyer.

After that was done, she said, "When named, please raise your right hand. Ian Thompson." A prisoner raised his hand. She read out the charges and the penalties he faced. Thompson had apparently burglarized three houses in the swanky Roland Park neighborhood. He had a heroin habit and a criminal record. Steve would not have released such a man onto the streets.

However, the judge set his bail at twenty-five thousand dollars. Steve felt encouraged. The accused normally had to put up only ten percent of the bail in cash, so that seemed lenient.

The judge looked at her sheet. "Steven Charles Logan."

Steve raised his hand. *Please let me out of here. Please.*

"You are charged with rape in the first degree, which carries a possible penalty of life imprisonment."

Behind him Steve heard his mother gasp.

The pretrial investigator stood up. He recited Steve's age, address, and occupation, and said that he had no criminal record.

Then Steve said, "May I speak, Your Honor?"

"Yes, but remember that it may not be in your interest."

He stood up. "I'm innocent, Your Honor, but it seems I may bear a resemblance to the rapist. If you grant me bail, I'll promise not to approach the victim, if you want to make that a condition of bail."

"I certainly would."

He wanted to plead with her for his freedom, but all the eloquent speeches he had composed in his cell now vanished from his mind. Feeling frustrated, he sat down.

The judge looked at Steve. "Mr. Logan, was the woman known to you before the alleged crime took place?"

"I've never met her," Steve said.

"Had you ever *seen* Lisa Hoxton before?"

"I can't tell. I don't know what she looks like."

The judge seemed to reflect on that for a few seconds. Steve felt as if he were hanging onto a ledge by his fingertips.

At last she spoke. "Bail is granted in the sum of two hundred thousand dollars."

Relief washed over Steve like a tidal wave, and his whole body relaxed. He felt Dad grasp his shoulder again. He reached up with his manacled hands and touched his father's bony fingers.

It would be another hour or two before he was free, he knew, but now he was sure of freedom. He wanted a hot bath and clean clothes and his wristwatch back. And he realized, to his surprise, that what he wanted most of all was to call Jeannie Ferrami.

JEANNIE was in a bilious mood as she returned to her office. Maurice Obell was a coward. And Berrington was too weak to defend her effectively.

Her computer search engine was her greatest achievement. She had taken three years to develop it. If her search engine was no good, she felt, she herself would be worthless.

Jeannie made some coffee. She was just about to pour a cup when the phone rang. She picked it up.

"Naomi Freelander from *The New York Times* here."

Jeannie hesitated. "I'm not sure I should talk to you."

"Dr. Ferrami, I believe you've stopped using medical databases for your research."

"No, I haven't stopped. Your phone call to the president has started some discussions, but no decisions have been made."

"I have a fax here from the president's office. In it the university apologizes to people whose privacy has been invaded, and assures them that the program has been discontinued."

Jeannie was aghast. "They sent out that release?"

"You didn't know? It seems they've canceled your program."

"They can't just do that."

"Are you telling me you're going to continue in defiance of the university authorities?"

Jeannie realized she had to be careful talking to the press, and calmed herself down. "Look," she said in a reasonable voice, "have you found anyone who's complained about my program?"

"No."

"Then wouldn't you do better to find a case of invasion of privacy that someone really cares about? Wouldn't that make a better story?"

"I'll be the judge of that," Freelander said.

Jeannie sighed. Gritting her teeth, she tried to end the conversation on a friendly note. "Well, good luck. Good-bye."

She walked along the corridor to the office of the secretary to all the professors. "Hi, Julie. Can I see Berry?"

"He left for the day, but he asked me to fix an appointment for you tomorrow. Nine thirty?"

Damn. He was avoiding her. "I'll be here."

She made her way to the lab. Lisa was at the bench, checking the concentration of Steve's and Dennis's DNA in the test tubes.

"How are you?" Jeannie asked.

"I'm fine."

Jeannie looked hard at Lisa's face. She was still in denial; that was obvious. Her expression was impassive as she concentrated on her work, but the strain showed underneath.

Jeannie told the story of the *Times* reporter while Lisa worked. She mixed the DNA samples with an enzyme called a restriction endonuclease. This enzyme cut the long molecule of DNA into thousands of shorter fragments. The process of fragmentation took several hours and could not be hurried.

Lisa was shocked by the story Jeannie told, but not quite as sympathetic as Jeannie expected. Perhaps that was because she had suffered a devastating trauma just three days earlier, and Jeannie's crisis seemed minor by comparison. "If you have to drop your project," Lisa said, "what would you study instead?"

"I've no idea," Jeannie replied. "I can't imagine."

She returned to her office and called the Bella Vista Sunset Home. With all that was going on, she had been lax about talking to her mother. "May I speak to Mrs. Ferrami, please," she said.

The reply was abrupt. "They're having lunch."

Jeannie hesitated. "Okay. Would you please tell her that her daughter Jeannie called, and I'll try again later."

"Yeah."

Jeannie had the feeling that the woman was not writing this down. "That's J-e-a-n-n-i-e," she said. "Her daughter."

"Yeah, okay."

Jeannie hung up. She had to get her mother out of there.

She checked her watch. It was just after noon, but it seemed pointless to work when her project might be canceled. Feeling angry and helpless, she decided to quit for the day.

She turned off her computer, locked her office, and left the building. She still had her red Mercedes. She got in and stroked the steering wheel with a pleasant sense of familiarity.

Feeling better, she drove home. "Daddy, I'm home," she called as she went upstairs. When she entered the living room, she sensed that something was wrong. The TV had been moved. Maybe he had taken it into the bedroom. She looked in the next room; he was not there. She returned to the living room. "Oh, no," she said. "Daddy, you didn't!" Her stereo had disappeared, and the computer was gone from her desk. "No, I don't believe it!"

The phone rang, and she picked it up automatically.

"It's Steve Logan," the voice said. "How are you?"

"This is the most terrible day of my life," Jeannie said, and she began to cry.

BERRINGTON Jones had a plastic card that would open any door in Nut House. All the same, he had never used his master key. Snooping was undignified—not his style, only for emergencies.

This was an emergency.

The university had ordered Jeannie to stop using her computer search program and had announced to the world that it was discontinued. But how could he be sure it was true? The thought nagged him that she might already be searching another database. And there was no telling what she might find.

So he had returned to his office and now sat at his desk as the warm dusk gathered over the red brick of the campus buildings. He was tapping a plastic card against his computer mouse and getting ready to do something that went against his instincts.

He checked his watch. The lab would be closed now. Most of his colleagues had left for the day, heading for their suburban homes or for the bar of the faculty club. This was as good a moment as any.

He walked along the hall to Jeannie's door. There was no one around. He swiped his card through the card reader, stepped inside, switched on the lights, and closed the door.

It was the smallest office in the building, a narrow room with a small window. However, Jeannie had livened it up with two wooden chairs painted bright red, a palm in a pot, and a reproduction of a Picasso etching, a bullfight in vivid yellow and orange.

He sat down at her desk and switched on her computer. While it was booting up, he went through her drawers. The top one contained ballpoints and scratch pads. The next drawer contained a hand mirror and a hairbrush; the last, a pocket dictionary and a paperback called *A Thousand Acres*. No secrets so far.

Her menu came up on screen. He picked up her mouse and clicked on Calendar. Her appointments were predictable: lectures and classes, lab time, dates for drinks and movies. There was no entry that said, "Scan medical files." Her to-do list was equally mundane: "Buy vitamins. Call Ghita. Lisa birthday gift."

He exited Calendar and began to look through her files. Using the FIND feature, he searched her entire directory for the word "database." It came up several times, but none of the references told him where she planned to use her search engine next. "Come on," he said aloud. "There has to be something, for heaven's sake."

He checked that her modem was switched on, then clicked on America Online and accessed her mailbox. Her terminal was programmed to give her password automatically. She had three pieces of mail. He downloaded them all. The first was a notice about increased prices for using the Internet. The second came from a friend at the University of Minnesota. Berrington binned it and opened the third letter. It electrified him.

> You'll be relieved to know that I'm running your scan on our fingerprint file tonight. Call me. Ghita.

It was from the FBI.

"This will kill us," Berrington whispered.

STEVE LOGAN HUNG up the phone.

He had showered and shaved and dressed in clean clothes, and he was full of his mother's lasagna. He had slept all the way from Baltimore to Washington in the back of his father's car, and although that hardly made up for the days in jail, he felt fine.

Now that he knew how much trouble Jeannie was in, he was more eager than ever to see her. She had told him, when he called, how her father had robbed her and the university president had betrayed her. He wanted to put his arms around her and tell her everything would be all right.

He also wanted to know more about the mystery of his origins. He had not told his parents about that. It was too bizarre and troubling. But he needed to talk to Jeannie about it.

He picked up the phone again to call her back; then he changed his mind. She would say she did not want company. Depressed people usually felt that way. Maybe he should just show up.

He went into the kitchen. Mom was scrubbing the lasagna dish with a wire brush. Dad had gone to his office for an hour. "Mom," he said, "this is going to sound a little strange, but . . ."

"You're going to see a girl," she said.

Steve smiled. "How did you know?"

"I'm your mother; I'm telepathic. What's her name?"

"Jeannie Ferrami. *Dr.* Ferrami. She's a scientist."

"What's she like?"

"Well, she's kind of striking. She's tall and very fit—she's a tennis player—with a lot of dark hair, and dark eyes. She's forceful and laughs a lot, but mainly she's just"—he sought for a word—"this *presence.* . . ." He trailed off.

For a moment his mother just stared at him. Then she said, "Oh, boy, you've got it bad."

"You're right. I'm crazy about her."

His mother smiled fondly. "Go on. I hope she deserves you."

Steve's car was parked outside; his mother had driven it back to Washington. Now he got on I-95 back to Baltimore. As he drove, he pictured Jeannie sitting next to him on a couch, laughing, and saying, "I'm so glad you came over. You've made me feel much better."

He stopped at a strip mall in the Mount Washington neighborhood and bought a seafood pizza, a ten-dollar bottle of chardonnay, a container of Ben & Jerry's ice cream, and ten yellow carnations. *The Wall Street Journal* caught his eye with a headline about Genetico Inc. That was the company that funded Jeannie's research, he recalled. It seemed they were about to be taken over by a German conglomerate. He bought the paper.

His delightful fantasies were clouded by the worrying thought that Jeannie might have left her apartment since he had talked to her. But he was pleased to see a red Mercedes 230C parked near her house; she must be in.

He pressed the entry-phone bell and stared at the speaker. There was a crackling noise, and his heart leaped. An irritable voice said, "Who is it?"

"It's Steve Logan. I came to cheer you up."

There was a pause. "Steve, I don't feel like having visitors."

"At least let me give you these flowers."

She did not reply. She was scared, he thought, and he felt bitterly disappointed. She'd said she believed he was innocent, but that was when he was behind bars. Now he was on her doorstep. "You haven't changed your mind about me, have you?" he said.

The buzzer sounded, and the door opened.

She was a woman who could not resist a challenge, he thought.

He stepped into a tiny lobby with two more doors. One stood open and led to a flight of stairs. At the top stood Jeannie in a bright green T-shirt.

"I guess you'd better come up," she said.

It was not the most enthusiastic of welcomes, but he smiled and went up the stairs carrying his gifts in a paper sack. She showed him into a little living room with a kitchen nook. She liked black and white with splashes of color, he noted. She had a black-upholstered couch with orange cushions, an electric-blue clock on a white wall, and a white kitchen counter with red coffee mugs.

He put his sack on the counter. "Look," he said, "you need

something to eat to make you feel better." He took out the pizza. "And a glass of wine. Then, to give yourself a special treat, you can eat this ice cream right out of the carton. And after the food and drink is gone, you'll still have the flowers. See?"

She stared at him as if he were a man from Mars.

He added, "And anyway, I figured you needed someone to tell you that you're a wonderful, special person."

Her eyes filled with tears. "I never cry!" she said.

He put his hands on her shoulders. Tentatively he drew her to him. She did not resist. She was nearly as tall as he. She rested her head on his shoulder, and her body shook with sobs. He stroked her hair. "It's going to be all right," he said.

She remained slumped in his arms for a long, delicious moment. He felt the warmth of her body, and he wondered whether to kiss her. Then the moment passed, and she moved away.

"Thanks," she said. "I needed a shoulder to cry on."

"All part of the service," he said facetiously.

She opened a cupboard and took out plates. "I feel better already," she said. "Let's eat."

He perched on a stool at her kitchen counter. She cut the pizza and took the cork out of the wine. He enjoyed watching her move around her home. There was a fluid physical grace about her that gave him an awestruck sensation.

"You're resilient," she commented. "Last time I saw you, you looked awful. And it was only twenty-four hours ago."

"I'll be okay, as long as I never have to go back inside that jail." He put the thought out of his mind. He was not going back; the DNA test results would eliminate him as a suspect.

They started to eat. Jeannie was thoughtfully silent for a while; then she said, "I really messed up today. I can see it now. I needed to keep the whole crisis low-key. Instead I came on too strong."

Steve showed her *The Wall Street Journal.* "This may explain why your department is oversensitive about bad publicity at the moment. Your sponsor is about to be taken over."

She looked at the first paragraph. "A hundred and eighty million dollars. Wow." She read on while chewing a slice of pizza. When she finished the article, she shook her head. "Your theory is interesting, but I don't buy it. It was Maurice Obell who seemed to be against me, not Berrington. Anyway, I'm not that important. I represent a tiny fraction of the research Genetico sponsors. Even if my work did invade people's privacy, that wouldn't be enough of a scandal to threaten a multimillion-dollar takeover."

Steve picked up a framed photograph of a woman with a baby. She looked a bit like Jeannie with straight hair. "Your sister?"

"Yes. Patty. She has three kids now—all boys."

"I don't have any brothers or sisters," he said. Then he remembered. "Unless you count Dennis Pinker." Jeannie's face changed, and he said, "You're looking at me like a specimen."

"I'm sorry. Want to try the ice cream?"

"You bet."

She put the tub on the table and got out two spoons. That pleased him. Eating out of the same container was one step closer to kissing. She ate with relish.

He swallowed a spoonful of ice cream and said, "I'm so glad you believe in me. Not many women would have let me in tonight, especially believing I have the same genes as Dennis Pinker."

"I hesitated," she said. "But you proved me right."

"How?"

Jeannie gestured toward the remains of their dinner. "If Pinker is attracted to a woman, he pulls a knife. You bring pizza."

Steve laughed.

"It may sound funny," she said, "but it's a world of difference."

"There's something you ought to know about me," Steve said.

She put down her spoon. "What?"

"I almost killed someone once."

"How?"

He told her the story of the fight with Tip Hendricks. "That's why I'm so bothered by this stuff about my origins," he said. "I can't tell you how disturbing it is to be told that Mom and Dad may not be my parents. What if my real father is a killer?"

"You were in a schoolboy fight that got out of hand," Jeannie said. "That doesn't make you a psychopath. A big strong kid like you might clash with the law once, whereas Dennis will be in and out of jail until someone kills him."

"How old are you, Jeannie?"

"You didn't like me calling you a kid, did you? I'm twenty-nine."

"I'm twenty-two. Do I seem like a kid to you?"

"Listen, I don't know. A man of thirty probably wouldn't impulsively drive here from Washington just to bring me pizza."

"Are you sorry I did it?"

"No." She touched his hand. "I'm real glad."

He still did not know where he was with her. But she had cried on his shoulder. You don't use a kid for that, he thought.

"When will you know about my genes?" he said.

She looked at her watch. "The blotting is probably done. Lisa will make the film in the morning."

"Can't we look at the results now? I can't wait to find out if I have the same DNA as Dennis Pinker."

"I guess we could," Jeannie said. "I'm pretty curious myself."

BERRINGTON was afraid to talk on the phone about Jeannie and the FBI fingerprint file. So many phone calls were monitored nowadays. The last thing he needed was some CIA eavesdropper wondering why Senator Jim Proust was so interested in an FBI file. So he got in his silver Lincoln Town Car and drove at ninety miles an hour on the Baltimore–Washington Parkway.

It was late, but Jim was waiting for him at his office in Washington. "What couldn't you tell me on the phone?" he said.

"She's about to run her computer program on the FBI's fingerprint file."

Jim went pale. "Who's her contact at the Bureau?"

Berrington handed him the printout he had made of Jeannie's E-mail.

Jim studied it. "I never heard of anyone called Ghita Sumra," he said. "She can't be high up."

"Who *do* you know at the FBI?" Berrington said impatiently.

"David Creane worked for me in the diplomatic directorate, and now he's moved over to the Bureau. He doesn't run the fingerprint division, but he's a powerful guy."

"Can he stop this Ghita woman?"

"I don't know. I'll ask, okay?"

"Okay, Jim. Pick up the damn phone and ask him."

JEANNIE switched on the lights in the psychology lab, and Steve followed her in. "The genetic language has four letters," she said. "A, C, G, and T. Adenine, cytosine, guanine, and thymine. They're the chemical compounds attached to the central strands of the DNA molecule. They form words and sentences, such as 'Put five toes on each foot.' "

"But everyone's DNA must say 'Put five toes on each foot.' "

"Good point. We even have a lot in common with the animals, because they're made of the same proteins as we are."

"So how do you tell my DNA from Dennis's?"

"Between the words there are bits that don't mean anything—they're gibberish. They're like repeated spaces in a sentence. They're oligonucleotides, but everyone calls them oligos. Now where you have thirty-one oligos between five and toes, I might have two hundred and eighty-seven."

"How do you compare my oligos with Dennis's?" Steve asked.

She showed him a rectangular plate. "We cover this plate with a gel, make slots all across the top, and drop samples of your DNA and Dennis's into the slots. Then we put the plate in here." On the bench was a small glass tank. "We pass an electric current through the gel. This causes the fragments of DNA to ooze through the gel in straight lines. Small fragments move faster than big ones. So your fragment, with thirty-one oligos, will finish up ahead of mine with two hundred and eighty-seven."

"How can you see how far they've moved?"

"Chemicals called probes attach themselves to specific oligos." Jeannie showed him a piece of rag like a dishcloth. "We take a nylon membrane soaked in a probe solution and lay it on the gel so it blots up the fragments. Probes are also luminous, so they'll mark a photographic film." She looked in another tank. "Lisa has already laid the nylon on the film. The pattern has been formed. All we need to do is fix the film."

Steve tried to see the image on the film as she washed and rinsed it. But all he could see was a ladderlike pattern on the clear plastic. Finally she shook it dry, then pegged it to a light box.

Steve peered at it. The film was streaked from top to bottom with straight lines about a quarter of an inch wide, like gray tracks. The tracks were numbered along the bottom, one to eighteen. Within the tracks were neat black marks, like hyphens.

Jeannie said, "The black marks show you how far along the tracks your fragments traveled."

"But there are two black marks in each track."

"That's because you have two strands of DNA, one from your father and one from your mother."

"Of course. The double helix."

"Right. And your parents had different oligos." She consulted a sheet of notes, then looked up. "Track three is your blood." His two black marks were about an inch apart, halfway down the film. "Track four is a control. It's probably my blood or Lisa's. The marks should be in a completely different position."

"They are." The two marks were very close together, right at the bottom of the film near the numbers.

"Track five is Dennis Pinker. Are the marks in the same position as yours or different?"

"The same," Steve said. "They match exactly."

She looked at him. "Steve," she said, "you're twins."

He did not want to believe it. "Any chance of a mistake?"

"We normally test four different fragments," Jeannie said. "That reduces the chance of a mistake to one in a hundred million. Lisa will do three more. But I know what they're going to say."

"I guess I do too." Steve sighed. "I'd better start believing this. Where the heck did I come from?"

Jeannie looked thoughtful. "Something you said has been on my mind: 'I don't have any brothers or sisters.' But from what you've said about your parents, they seem like the kind of people who might have wanted a houseful of kids—three or four."

"You're right," Steve said. "But Mom had trouble conceiving. She was thirty-three, and she had been married for ten years when I came along. She wrote a book about it—*What to Do When You Can't Get Pregnant*. It was her first best seller."

"Charlotte Pinker was thirty-nine when Dennis was born," Jeannie said. "I bet they had subfertility problems too. Did your mother have any kind of special treatment?"

"I never read the book. Shall I call her? It's time I told them about this mystery, anyway."

Jeannie pointed to a desk. "Use Lisa's phone."

He dialed his home. His mother answered. "Hi, Mom."

"Was your friend pleased to see you?" she asked.

"Not at first. She thinks I'm too young." Steve looked at Jeannie. "But I'm still with her."

"Is she listening?"

"Yes. Mom, we're in the laboratory, and we have kind of a puzzle. My DNA appears to be the same as that of another subject she's studying, a guy called Dennis Pinker."

"It can't be the same. You'd have to be identical twins."

"And that would only be possible if I'd been adopted."

"Steve, you weren't adopted. And you weren't one of twins."

"Well, did you have any special fertility treatment?"

"Yes, I did. The doctor referred me to a place in Philadelphia that a number of officers' wives had been to. It was called the Aventine Clinic. I had hormone treatment."

Steve repeated that to Jeannie, and she scribbled on a pad.

Mom went on. "The treatment worked, and there you are, the fruit of that effort, pestering a beautiful woman in Baltimore when you should be here in D.C. taking care of your mother."

Steve laughed. "Thanks, Mom. I'll be home soon. Bye."

Jeannie said, "I'm going to call Charlotte Pinker right away." She flipped through Lisa's Rolodex, then picked up the phone. She was soon speaking to Dennis Pinker's mother.

Jeannie's face lit up with excitement. "In Philadelphia? Yes, I've heard of it. . . . Hormone treatment. That's very interesting. . . . Thank you again. Good-bye." She cradled the handset. "Bingo," she said to Steve. "Charlotte went to the same clinic."

Steve was riveted. "Records," he said. "The clinic must have records. There might be clues there."

Jeannie frowned thoughtfully. "I have a release signed by Charlotte Pinker—we ask everyone we interview to sign one—and it gives us permission to look at medical records. Could you get your mother to sign one tonight and fax it to me at J.F.U.?"

"Sure."

She got the clinic's number from Philadelphia information and dialed. Then she said, "Good evening. Is that the Aventine Clinic? . . . Do you have a night manager on duty?"

There was a long pause. She tapped her pencil impatiently. Steve watched adoringly; this could go on all night.

"Good evening, Mr. Ringwood. This is Dr. Ferrami from the psychology department at Jones Falls University. Two of my research subjects attended your clinic twenty-three years ago, and it would be helpful to me to look at their records. I have releases from them. . . . That's very helpful. Would tomorrow, say two p.m., be okay? . . . Thank you very much. Good-bye."

"Fertility clinic," Steve said thoughtfully. "Didn't I read in that *Wall Street Journal* piece that Genetico owns fertility clinics?"

Jeannie stared at him, openmouthed. "Of course it does."

"I wonder if there's any connection? If there is, then . . ."

"Then Berrington Jones may know a lot more about you and Dennis than he's letting on," said Jeannie.

IT HAD been a pig of a day, but it had ended all right, Berrington thought as he stepped out of the shower.

When he had walked into the house after driving back from Washington, the phone had been ringing. Jim Proust had confirmed that David Creane would stop the FBI cooperating with Jeannie. He had promised to make the necessary phone calls tonight.

Berrington toweled himself dry and put on a blue-and-white-striped bathrobe. The housekeeper had the evening off, but a casserole was in the refrigerator. He put it in the oven to warm and poured a glass of Scotch. As he took the first sip, the phone rang.

It was his ex-wife, Vivvie. "*The Wall Street Journal* says you're going to be rich," she said.

He pictured her, a slender blonde of sixty years, sitting on the terrace of her California house, watching the sun go down over the Pacific Ocean. "I suppose you want to come back to me."

"I thought about it, Berry. For at least ten seconds. Then I realized a hundred and eighty million dollars wasn't enough."

That made him laugh.

"Seriously, Berry, I'm pleased for you."

He knew she was sincere. She had plenty of money of her own. After leaving him, she had gone into real estate. "Thank you."

"What will you do with the money? Leave it to the boy?"

Their son was studying to be a certified public accountant. "He won't need it; he'll make a fortune as an accountant. I might give some of it to Jim Proust. He's going to run for President."

"What'll you get in return? Do you want to be the U.S. ambassador in Paris?"

"No, but I'd consider Surgeon General."

"Berry, I gotta go. My date just rang the doorbell. See you sooner, Montezuma." It was an old family joke.

He gave her the response. "In a flash, succotash."

He found it a little depressing that Vivvie was going out for the evening with a date, while he was sitting at home alone with his whiskey. He still missed her, thirteen years after the divorce. They had had fun together in the good times.

Just as he was taking his casserole out of the oven, the phone rang again. This time it was Preston Barck. He sounded shaken. "I just heard from Dick Minsky in Philadelphia," he said. "Jeannie Ferrami has made an appointment to go to the clinic tomorrow."

Berrington sat down heavily. "How on earth did she get onto the clinic?"

"I don't know. Dick wasn't there; the night manager took the call. But apparently she said she wanted to check some medical records. Said she'd be there at two p.m. Thank heaven Dick happened to call in about something else and the night manager mentioned it."

Dick Minsky had been one of the first people Genetico had hired back in the '70s. He had been the mailroom boy then; now he was general manager of the clinics. He knew that the company's past held secrets. Discretion was automatic with him.

"What did you tell Dick to do?"

"Cancel the appointment, of course. If she shows up anyway, turn her away. Tell her she can't see the records."

Berrington shook his head. "Not good enough. It will just make her more curious about the files. I think we're going to have to shred all the record cards from the '70s."

There was a moment of silence. "Berry, those records are unique. Scientifically, they're priceless."

"You think I don't know that?" Berrington snapped. Then he sighed. He felt as bad as Preston did. He had fondly imagined that one day, years in the future, someone would write the story of their pioneering experiments, and their brilliance would be revealed to the world. It broke his heart to see the evidence wiped out, but it was inevitable now. "While the records exist, they're a threat to us. They have to be destroyed right away."

"What'll we tell the staff?"

"I don't know, Preston. So long as they start shredding first thing in the morning, I don't care what you tell them."

"Okay. I'll get back to Dick. Bye."

Berrington dialed Jim Proust's home number. His wife answered and put Jim on. "I'm in bed, Berry. What is it now?"

He told Jim what Preston had reported and the action they had decided on.

"It's not enough," Jim said. "Ferrami has to be scared off."

Berrington felt a spasm of irritation. "Jim, for heaven's sake—"

"I know this brings out the wimp in you, Berry, but it has to be done."

"Forget it. I have a better idea. I'm going to have her fired. Then she'll have no facilities to pursue her investigation and no reason to stick to it. Besides, she'll be too busy looking for another job."

"Maybe you're right."

Berrington was suspicious. Jim was agreeing too readily. "You're not planning to do something on your own, are you?"

Jim evaded the question. "Can you do that, get her fired?"

"Sure. I've been in the academic world for most of the last forty years. I know how to work the machinery."

"Okay."

Berrington frowned. "We're together on this, right, Jim?"

"Right. Good night."

Berrington hung up. His dinner was cold. He dumped it in the trash and went to bed. He lay awake thinking about Jeannie Ferrami.

IT WAS a hot night in Philadelphia. In the tenement building all the doors and windows were open. The sounds of the street floated up to an apartment on the top floor: car horns, laughter, snatches of music. On a cheap pine desk a phone was ringing.

He picked it up.

A voice like a bark said, "This is Jim."

"Hey, Uncle Jim, how are you?"

"I'm worried about you. I know what happened Sunday night."

He hesitated. "They've arrested someone for that."

"But his girlfriend thinks he's innocent," Jim said, "and she's coming to Philadelphia tomorrow."

"What for?"

"I'm not sure. But I think she's a danger. You may want to do something about her. It's up to you."

"How would I find her?"

"Do you know the Aventine Clinic on Chestnut? She'll be there at two p.m."

"How will I know her?"

"Tall, dark hair, pierced nostril, about thirty. She'll probably be driving an old red Mercedes. Now, the other guy is out on bail."

He frowned. "So what?"

"So if she should meet with an accident after she's been seen with you . . ."

"I get it. They'll assume it was him." He laughed. "You always were mean-thinking, Uncle Jim. Bye. And thanks."

Thursday

JEANNIE woke up to the insistent ring of her phone. It was her friend Ghita from the FBI. "What's going on?" Ghita said without preamble. "My boss just called me and told me to have nothing to do with you. Then there's this *New York Times* article headed 'Gene Research Ethics: Doubts, Fears and a Squabble.' "

"No!" said Jeannie. "Does this mean you can't run my scan?"

"I did the scan last night and sent it to you by E-mail. But Jeannie, you have to destroy that list or I'll lose my job."

"But I can't destroy it! Not if it proves me right."

"Jeannie, I got into this by doing you a favor. You have to get me out of it."

Jeannie felt despairing. "Ghita, I can't."

"Then there's nothing more to say," Ghita said, and hung up.

Did I just lose one of my oldest friends? Jeannie wondered.

Feeling miserable, she took a quick shower and threw on clothes. Then she stopped to think. She was going into battle: She'd better dress for it. She made up her face carefully. She put on a black suit with a gray blouse, sheer stockings, and patent-leather pumps.

She studied herself in a full-length mirror. "Kill, Jeannie. Kill," she murmured. Then she went out.

JEANNIE THOUGHT ABOUT STEVE Logan as she drove to J.F.U. She had called him a big strong kid, but in fact he was more mature than some men ever got to be. She had cried on his shoulder, so she must trust him at some deep level. She had liked the way he smelled, sort of like tobacco before it is lit.

Steve was the only good thing on her horizon. She was in bad trouble. She could not resign from her post at J.F.U. now. After the *Times* had made her famous for causing trouble, she would find it hard to get another scientific job. Her only hope was to press on stubbornly, using the FBI data, and produce convincing scientific results.

It was nine o'clock when she walked into Nut House. As soon as she stepped into her office, she knew someone had been there. Her computer keyboard was at the wrong angle, and the mouse had been left in the middle of the pad, whereas she always tucked it neatly up against the keyboard. Who had been here? And why?

An envelope had been slipped under her door. It contained a release signed by Lorraine Logan and faxed to Nut House by Steve. She took Charlotte Pinker's release out of a file and put both in her briefcase to take with her to the Aventine Clinic.

She sat at her desk and retrieved her E-mail. There was only one message—the results of the FBI scan. She downloaded the list of names and addresses with profound relief. She could hardly wait to see if there were any more anomalies like Steve and Dennis.

She was about to look at the names on the list when the phone rang. It was the president. "Maurice Obell here. I think we had better discuss this report in *The New York Times,* don't you?"

Jeannie's stomach tightened. Here we go, she thought apprehensively. It begins. "Of course," she said. "I'll be right there."

She copied the FBI results onto a floppy disk. She thought for a moment, then labeled it SHOPPING.LST. No doubt it was an unnecessary precaution, but it made her feel better. She slipped the floppy into the box containing her backup files and went out.

As she crossed the campus, she was glad she had worn the black suit: It made her look older and more authoritative. Her high heels clacked on the flagstones as she approached Hillside Hall. She was ushered straight into the president's lavish office.

Berrington Jones was sitting there, a copy of the *Times* in his hand. She smiled at him, glad to have an ally. He nodded rather coolly and said, "Good morning, Jeannie."

Maurice Obell was behind his big desk. He said abruptly, "The university simply cannot tolerate this, Dr. Ferrami."

He did not ask her to sit, but she selected a chair, moved it, sat down, and crossed her legs. "It was a pity you told the press so quickly that you had canceled my project," she said as coolly as she could. "However, I do think we should stop bickering."

Berrington answered her. "It's too late for that," he said.

"I'm sure it's not," she said. She wondered why Berrington had said that, but she kept her eyes on the president. "We must be able to find a compromise that would allow me to continue my work and yet preserve the university's dignity."

Obell frowned and said, "I don't quite see how—"

"This is all a waste of time," Berrington said impatiently.

Jeannie choked back a rejoinder. Why was he being like this? Did he *want* her to stop doing her research and get into trouble and be discredited? It began to seem that way.

"We have already decided the university's course of action," Berrington added.

She realized she had mistaken the power structure in the room. Berrington was the boss here, not Obell. Berrington was the conduit for Genetico's research millions, which Obell needed. Berrington had nothing to fear from Obell; rather the reverse.

Berrington had now dropped the pretense. "We didn't call you in here to ask your opinion," he said. "We called you in to fire you."

Jeannie was stunned. "What do you mean?" she said stupidly.

"I mean you're fired," Berrington said. He smoothed his eyebrows with his finger, a sign that he was pleased with himself.

She felt as if she had been punched. "No," she said. She was bewildered by how fast they had acted. She tried to collect her thoughts. "You can't fire me."

Maurice Obell pushed a folder with termination information in it across his desk. "I think that's all," he said.

Jeannie stood up, still shocked. "I can't believe it's come to this," she said. She took the folder and left the room.

She returned to Nut House. As she approached her room, she noticed with irritation that the cleaners had left a black plastic garbage bag right outside her office. She would call them immediately. But when she swiped her card through the card reader, her door did not open. She was about to walk to reception and call maintenance when a dreadful thought occurred to her.

She looked inside the black bag. The first thing she saw was her canvas briefcase. Also in the sack was the Kleenex box from her drawer, a framed photograph, and her hairbrush.

They had cleared out her desk and locked her out.

She was devastated. They had taken away her science, her work. She did not know what to do with herself, where to go. For eleven years she had been a scientist—as an undergraduate, graduate student, and assistant professor. Now, suddenly, she was nothing.

As her spirits sank from despondency to black despair, she remembered the disk with the FBI data. She rummaged through the plastic sack, but there were no floppy disks. Her results, the backbone of her defense, were locked inside the room.

There was no point standing at the locked door. She picked up the plastic bag and checked her watch. She was due at the Aventine Clinic in Philadelphia at two p.m. She had to leave soon.

DRIVING to Philadelphia, Jeannie found herself thinking about Steve Logan.

She had kissed him good-bye last night in the visitors parking lot on the Jones Falls campus. She found herself regretting that the kiss had been so fleeting. His lips were full and dry, his skin warm. What the heck, she thought. When I see him next, I'm going to kiss him again, and this time I'll kiss him good.

She threaded the Mercedes through the crowded center of Philadelphia. The Aventine Clinic was in University City, west of the

Schuylkill River, a neighborhood of college buildings and student apartments. The clinic itself was a pleasant low-rise '50s building surrounded by trees. Jeannie parked and went inside.

A chirpy receptionist asked Jeannie to take a seat in the waiting area, and she picked up a glossy brochure about Genetico Inc. She held it open on her lap without reading it; instead she tapped her feet impatiently on the carpeted floor.

A man emerged from the back of the lobby and said, "Dr. Ferrami," in a loud voice. He was an anxiously jolly man of about fifty, with a monkish fringe of ginger hair. "Dick Minsky. I'm a colleague of Mr. Ringwood's. How do you do." Dick had a nervous tic that made him blink violently.

They shook hands, and he walked her up a staircase. "What's led to your inquiry, may I ask?"

"A medical mystery," she explained. "Two women have sons who appear to be identical twins, yet they seem to be unrelated. The only connection I've been able to find is that both women were treated here before getting pregnant."

"Is that so?" he said as if he were not really listening. Jeannie was surprised; she had expected him to be intrigued.

They entered a corner office. "All our records can be accessed by computer," he said. He sat at a terminal, and Jeannie sat opposite him. "Now, the patients we're interested in are . . . ?"

"Charlotte Pinker and Lorraine Logan." She handed over the release forms.

"This won't take a minute." He began to key in the names. Then he frowned. "That's odd. We have no record of either name." He spun his screen around so that Jeannie could see it. "When do you think these patients attended the clinic?"

"Approximately twenty-three years ago," she said, uneasy.

He looked at her. "Oh, dear," he said, and he blinked hard. "I'm afraid you've made a wasted journey. We shred old record cards after twenty years, unless of course the patient has been readmitted, in which case the record is transferred to the computer."

It was a sickening disappointment. She said bitterly, "How strange that Mr. Ringwood didn't tell me this when I called last night."

"He really should have. It's hard to understand." Seeming regretful, he said, "I'm afraid there's no more I can do for you." He stood up. "And now I've run out of time."

Jeannie got up and preceded him down the stairs to the lobby. "Good day to you," he said stiffly.

"Good-bye," she said. But outside the door she hesitated. She felt combative. She was tempted to snoop around a bit.

The parking lot was full of doctors' cars—late-model Cadillacs and BMWs. She strolled around one side of the building. A man was sweeping up litter with a noisy blower. There was nothing remarkable or even interesting there. She retraced her steps.

Through the glass door at the front she saw Dick Minsky, still in the lobby, talking to the chirpy receptionist. He watched anxiously as Jeannie walked by.

Circling the building in the other direction, she came to a garbage dump. Three men were loading trash onto a truck. Something struck her. The men were lifting huge plastic sacks effortlessly as if they weighed very little. What would a clinic be throwing away that was bulky but light? Shredded paper?

She heard Dick Minsky's voice. He was coming around the corner of the building, accompanied by a security guard.

She walked quickly to a stack of sacks.

Dick Minsky shouted, "Hey!"

The garbage men stared as she ripped a hole in one sack, reached inside, and pulled out a handful of the contents. She was holding a sheaf of strips of thin brown card. When she looked closely at them, she could see they had been written on. These were shredded clinic record cards.

They had destroyed their records *this morning*—only hours after she had called.

She dropped the shreds on the ground and walked away. She stood in front of Dick Minsky, hands on hips. "You've got a shameful secret here, haven't you?" she yelled. "Something you're trying to hide by destroying these records."

He was completely terrified. "Of course not," he managed. "And by the way, the suggestion is offensive."

"Of course it is," she said. She pointed at him with the rolled-up Genetico brochure she was still carrying. "But this investigation is very important to me. You'd better believe that."

"Please leave," he said.

The guard took her by the elbow.

"I'm leaving," she said. "No need to hold me."

The guard released her, and she walked away. She had been right. The solution to the mystery was connected with this place. But where did that get her?

She went to her car but did not get in. It was two thirty, and she had had no lunch. Across the street was a café that looked cheap and clean. She crossed the road and went inside.

The café was quiet but for a few students finishing lunch. She ordered coffee and a salad. While she was waiting, she opened the brochure she had picked up in the clinic. She read:

> The Aventine Clinic was founded in 1972 by Genetico Inc. as a pioneering center for research and development of human in vitro fertilization—the creation of what the newspapers call "test-tube babies."

And suddenly it was all clear.

Test-tube babies. In vitro fertilization. That was the link. Jeannie saw it all.

The clinic had pioneered in vitro fertilization, the process by which sperm from the father and an egg from the mother are brought together in the laboratory, and the resulting embryo is then implanted in the woman's womb.

Identical twins occur when an embryo splits in half in the womb. That might have happened in the test tube. Then the twins could have been implanted in two different women. Bingo.

The waitress brought Jeannie's coffee and salad; she was too excited to eat.

Both Lorraine Logan and Charlotte Pinker said they had been

given hormone therapy. It seemed the clinic had lied to them about their treatment. But Jeannie realized something worse. The embryo that split might have been the biological child of Lorraine and Charles, or of Charlotte and the Major—but not both. One of them had been implanted with another couple's child.

Jeannie's heart filled with horror and loathing as she realized they could *both* have been given the babies of total strangers.

She wondered why Genetico had deceived its patients in this appalling way. Whatever their motive for lying, Jeannie now understood why her investigation scared Genetico so badly. Impregnating a woman with an alien embryo, without her knowledge, was about as unethical as could be imagined.

She took a sip of coffee. She did not yet have all the answers, but she had solved the central puzzle.

Looking up, she was astonished to see Steve walk into the café.

She blinked and stared. He was wearing khakis and a blue button-down, and he closed the door behind him with his heel.

She smiled broadly and stood up to greet him. "Steve!" she said delightedly. Remembering her resolution, she threw her arms around him and kissed him on the lips. He smelled different today, less tobacco and more spice. He hugged and kissed her back.

She released him. "What are you doing here? I can't believe it. You must have followed me. No, no. You decided to meet me."

"I just felt like talking to you." He smoothed his eyebrow with the tip of his index finger. Something about the action bothered her, but she pushed it to the back of her mind.

"You go in for big surprises."

Suddenly he seemed edgy. "I do?"

"You're a little strange today. What's on your mind?"

"Listen, there's something I want to show you," he said. "Can we get out of here?"

"Sure." She put some money on the table and met him outside by her red Mercedes. They got in, and Jeannie fastened her seat belt, but he did not. As soon as she pulled away, he edged close to her on the seat, lifted her hair, and started kissing her neck.

She liked it, but she felt embarrassed and said, "I think we may be a little too old to do this in a car."

"Okay." He stopped and faced forward, but he left his arm draped around her shoulders. He said, "Take the expressway." Following the signs, she turned onto Schuylkill Avenue. The hand over her shoulder dropped even lower on her blouse.

She felt uncomfortable. "Steve, I like you," she said, "but you're going a little too fast for me." She shoved him away with her right hand. *And I imagined this boy was mature!*

She drove down the ramp and eased onto the southbound expressway. "What do you want to show me anyway?" she said, trying to distract him.

"This," he said.

Next thing she knew, she was struck a mighty blow on the face.

She screamed and jerked sideways. An air horn blared as her car swung across the next lane of the expressway, in front of a Mack truck. The bones of her face burned with agony. Fighting to ignore the pain, she regained control of the car.

She realized with astonishment that he had punched her.

Out of the corner of her eye she saw him draw back his fist for another blow. Without thinking, she stepped on the brake.

He was thrown forward, and his punch missed her. His head banged the windshield. Tires screeched in protest as cars and trucks swerved around the Mercedes, horns blaring. Jeannie was terrified; at any moment another vehicle could slam into them. But he seemed to have no fear. He put his hand on her skirt.

She tried to push him away, but he was all over her. Surely Steve would not try to rape her right there on the expressway? To her left, traffic was flashing by at sixty miles an hour. As she struggled, her foot came off the brake and the car crept forward. To keep him off-balance, she put her foot on the accelerator and floored it.

The car took off with a lurch. Brakes squealed as a Greyhound bus narrowly missed her fender. Steve was thrown back in his seat, but a few seconds later his hands were all over her again as she tried to drive. She was frantic. She swung the car hard to the left, throwing him up against the passenger door. He just laughed as he was thrown around, and then he came back at her.

She hit him with her right elbow and her fist, but she could not put any power into the blows while she was at the wheel.

She saw that she was passing an off-ramp. At the last moment she swung the steering wheel; the Mercedes went up on two wheels, and Steve fell against her helplessly. An ancient Cadillac swerved to avoid her; then she heard the thud of cars crashing behind her. Her nearside wheels came down and hit the tarmac with a bone-shuddering thump.

She accelerated down the off-ramp. As soon as the car was stable, Steve grabbed her upper leg. She wriggled, trying to stop him. She glanced at his face. He was smiling, his eyes wide.

There were no cars ahead or behind her on this deserted street. Ahead a light turned red. If she stopped, she was done for. She accelerated wildly toward the light.

An ambulance came from the left, swinging in front of her. She braked hard and swerved to miss it, thinking crazily, If I crash now, at least help is at hand.

Suddenly Steve withdrew his hands. She had a moment of blessed relief. Then he grabbed the transmission lever and pushed it into neutral with his left hand and jerked the steering wheel with his right. The car slowed down and mounted the curb.

Jeannie took both hands off the wheel, put them on Steve's chest, and shoved him away with all her might. He was flung backward. She put the car in drive and stamped on the accelerator, but Jeannie knew that she could not fight him off much longer. Just then the car rounded a bend, and the cityscape changed abruptly.

There was a busy street, a hospital with people standing outside, a line of taxicabs, and a sidewalk stall selling Chinese food. "Yes!" Jeannie shouted triumphantly. She stamped on the brake. Fishtailing, the car screeched to a halt in the middle of the road.

Steve opened his door, got out, and ran.

"Thank God," Jeannie breathed.

She sat there panting. He was gone. The nightmare was over.

One of the cabdrivers came over and put his head inside the passenger door. "What the heck was that all about, lady?"

She shook her head. "I sure wish I knew," she said.

STEVE sat on a low wall near Jeannie's house waiting for her. It was hot, but he took advantage of the shade of a big maple tree.

He was worried and desperate. This afternoon his parents' lawyer had talked to Sergeant Mish Delaware of the sex-crimes unit in Baltimore. She had the results of the DNA test. The DNA from traces of sperm in Lisa Hoxton's body exactly matched the DNA in Steve's blood. He was devastated. He had been sure the DNA test would end this agony.

There had to be an explanation. And the only person who could figure it out was Jeannie Ferrami.

The sun dipped behind the row of houses on the other side of the street. Toward six o'clock the red Mercedes eased into a parking slot fifty yards away. Jeannie got out. At first she did not see Steve. She opened the trunk and took out a large plastic garbage bag. Then she came along the sidewalk toward him. She was dressed in a black skirted suit, but she looked disheveled, and there was a weariness in her walk that touched his heart. She was still gorgeous, though, and he watched her with longing in his heart.

As she got near him, he stood up, smiling, and stepped forward.

She glanced at him, met his eye, and a look of horror came over her face. She opened her mouth and screamed.

He stopped dead. Aghast, he said, "Jeannie, what is it?"

"Get away from me!" she yelled. "Don't you touch me!"

Nonplussed, Steve held his hands up in a defensive gesture. "Sure, sure, anything you say. What's gotten into you?"

Jeannie's neighbor came out the front door they shared. He was an old black man wearing a checked shirt and a tie. "Is everything all right?" he said. "I thought I heard someone cry out."

"It was me, Mr. Oliver," Jeannie said in a shaky voice. "This jerk attacked me in my car in Philadelphia this afternoon."

"Attacked you?" Steve said incredulously. "No, I didn't."

"You did. Two hours ago."

Mr. Oliver intervened. "This young gentleman been sitting on that wall for nigh on two hours, Jeannie. He ain't been to Philadelphia this afternoon."

Steve noticed that one side of Jeannie's face was slightly swollen and reddish. *Someone* had attacked her. He yearned to put his arms around her and comfort her. It made her fear of him even more distressing.

Her face changed. The look of terror went. She spoke to the neighbor. "He got here two hours ago?"

The man nodded. "If he was in Philadelphia two hours ago, he must have come here on the Concorde."

She looked at Steve. "It must have been Dennis."

He walked toward her. She did not step back. He reached out and touched her swollen cheek. "Poor Jeannie," he said.

"I thought it was you," she said, and tears came to her eyes.

He folded her in his arms. Slowly he felt her body lose its stiffness, and she leaned on him trustingly. He stroked her head and closed his eyes, thinking how lean and strong her body was. I'll bet Dennis has some bruises too, he thought. I hope so.

Mr. Oliver coughed. "You youngsters like a cup of coffee?"

Jeannie detached herself from Steve. "No, thanks," she said. "I just want to get out of these clothes."

Tension was written on her face, but she looked even more bewitching. I'm falling in love with this woman, Steve thought. I want to watch TV with her, and go to the supermarket with her, and give her NyQuil on a spoon when she has a cold. I want her to ask me what time I will be home.

He wondered if he had the nerve to tell her that.

She crossed the porch to her door. Steve hesitated, but she turned on the doorstep. "Come on," she said.

He followed her up the stairs and entered the living room behind her. She dropped the plastic bag on the rug. She looked blankly at Steve for a moment, then said, "I have to take a shower."

She left the room. Steve sat on her black couch and waited. A

moment later he heard water running. After a long shower she
returned in a big fuchsia-pink terry cloth robe.

She sat on the couch beside him and said, "You must think I'm
out of my mind."

"No, but I think you're probably in shock after what happened
to you in Philadelphia. Would you like a drink?"

She shook her head. "What I really want is some jasmine tea."

"Let me make it." He got up and went behind the kitchen
counter. "Why are you carrying a garbage bag around?"

"I was fired today. There was an article in *The New York Times*
saying that my use of databases violates people's privacy. But I think
Berrington Jones was just using that as an excuse to get rid of me."

He burned with indignation. "You and I are both having an
unbelievably bad week." He was going to tell her about the DNA
test, but she picked up the phone.

"I need the number of Greenwood Penitentiary, near Richmond,
Virginia," she said to an operator. As Steve filled the kettle, she
dialed again. "Good evening, Warden. Dr. Ferrami. . . . I'm fine.
This may sound like a silly question, but is Dennis Pinker still in
jail? . . . You're sure? You saw him with your own eyes? . . .
Thank you. . . . And you take care of yourself too. Bye." She
looked up at Steve. "Dennis is still in jail. The warden spoke to him
an hour ago."

Steve put tea into the pot and found two cups. "Jeannie, the cops
have the result of their DNA test."

She went very still. "And . . . ?"

"Someone who has my DNA raped Lisa Hoxton. The same guy
attacked you in Philadelphia today. *And it wasn't Dennis Pinker.*"

Their eyes locked, and Jeannie said, "There are three of you."

"Jeez." He felt despairing. "How could this happen?"

"Wait," she said excitedly. "You don't know what I discovered
this afternoon before I ran into your double." She looked concerned. "Steve, you're going to find it shocking."

"I don't care. I just want to understand."

She reached into the plastic garbage bag and took out a glossy brochure folded open to the first page. "Look at this." She handed it to him, and he read the opening paragraph.

Steve said, "You think Dennis and I are test-tube babies?"

"Yes. And identical twins could be conceived in the laboratory and then implanted in different women."

Steve had a strange nauseated feeling. "But did the sperm and egg come from Mom and Dad or from the Pinkers?"

"I don't know."

His mind leaped ahead. "Maybe they didn't come from my parents *or* the Pinkers. I could be the child of total strangers."

"Steve, none of this takes away the fact that your mom and dad loved you and raised you and would give their lives for you."

With a shaky hand he poured tea into two cups. He sat beside Jeannie on the couch. "How does all this explain the third twin?"

"If there were twins in the test tube, there could have been triplets. It's the same process: One of the embryos split again. It happens in nature, so I guess it can happen in the laboratory."

Steve felt as if he were spinning through the air. "I need to be able to prove your theory of the third twin. The only way of doing that is to find him." A thought struck him. "Could your computer search engine be used? I mean, if one search threw up me and Dennis, another search might throw up me and the third, or Dennis and the third, or all three of us."

"Yes." She was not as thrilled as she ought to be.

"Can you do it?"

"After this bad publicity I'm going to have trouble getting anyone to let me use their database." She paused. "But there is one possibility. I've already run a sweep of the FBI fingerprint file."

Steve's spirits rocketed. "Dennis is sure to be in their files. If the third one has ever had his prints taken, the sweep will have picked him up. This is great!"

"But the results are on a floppy disk in my office."

"Oh, no! And you've been locked out. All right, so I'll bust down the door. Let's go there now."

"You could end up back in jail. There must be an easier way."

He tried to read her mind and failed. She was looking at him. He stared right back, gazing into her dark eyes.

Then she leaned over and kissed him lightly. "Steve, you're the real thing," she said.

It was a quick kiss, but it was electric. He felt great. He was not sure what she meant by "the real thing," but it must be good.

Meanwhile, Jeannie picked up the phone. She had a lot of work to do.

Friday

WHEN Jeannie woke up, her face throbbed gently where she had been punched. She felt it was astonishing that she could have spent part of last evening with a man who looked exactly like her attacker. But now she could be even more sure of Steve.

Her mood darkened as she went into the shower. As she washed her hair, she brooded over how hard she had struggled over the last ten years. She had worked like a robot to get where she was today— all because she wanted to be a scientist and help the human race understand itself better. And now because of Berrington Jones she had lost it all.

She toweled her hair, then sat on the couch drinking coffee. Her father had stolen her TV, so she could not even watch that to take her mind off her misery. She would have pigged out on chocolate if she had any. Shopping? She would probably burst into tears in the fitting room, and anyway, she was now even more broke than before.

At around two o'clock the phone rang. It was Steve, calling to see how she was doing. He was also reporting on a meeting he'd had with his lawyer. "I'm at the law office now," he told her. "We want you to take legal action against Jones Falls for recovery of your FBI list. My family will pay the costs. They think it will be worth it for the chance of finding the third twin. This is important to me."

Jeannie hesitated, then sighed. She remembered how he had worried about her. "Steve, of course I'll help you. What do I have to do?"

"Nothing. The lawyer will go to court if you give permission."

She began to think again. "Isn't it a little dangerous? I mean, I presume J.F.U. will have to be notified of our application. Then Berrington will get to the FBI list before we do."

"We can apply for access to your office without specifying what we're looking for."

"They might just wipe everything off my computer and disks."

Steve said, "What we need is a burglar."

"Oh, my gosh," Jeannie said.

"What?"

Daddy. "I just had an idea. Call me later." Jeannie hung up.

Daddy could get into her office. And he owed her. Oh, boy, did he owe her. But where was he? She started by calling her sister.

JEANNIE'S father was sitting on the couch in Patty's untidy living room, with a cup of coffee in his lap, watching *General Hospital* and eating a slice of carrot cake.

When she walked in and saw him, Jeannie lost it. "How could you do it?" she screamed. "How could you rob me?"

He jumped to his feet, spilling his coffee and cake.

Patty followed Jeannie in. "Please don't make a scene," she said.

Daddy said, "I'm sorry, Jeannie. I'm ashamed."

Patty got on her knees and started mopping up the coffee.

"You know I'm broke," Jeannie said. "I'm trying to raise enough money to pay for a decent nursing home for my mother—your wife! And still you could steal my TV! I just don't get it."

"All right, I'll tell you why I did it," Daddy said with sudden force. "Because I've lost my nerve." Tears came to his eyes. "I robbed my own daughter because I'm too old and scared of the cops to rob anyone else. So now you know."

Jeannie's anger evaporated. "Oh, Daddy, I'm sorry. Sit down."

"I don't deserve you girls. I know that," Daddy said as he sat down again. "After I sold all your things, Jeannie, I wanted to kill myself, I swear. But I had a few drinks and got into a poker game, and by the morning I was broke again."

"So you came to see Patty," Jeannie said.

"I won't do it to you, Patty. I'm going straight."

"You better!" Patty said.

Jeannie said, "But not yet."

They both looked at her. Patty said nervously, "What are you talking about, Jeannie?"

"You have to do one more burglary job, Daddy. For me. Tonight."

IT WAS getting dark as they entered the Jones Falls campus. "Pity we don't have a more anonymous car," her father said as Jeannie parked in the student lot. He got out of the red Mercedes, carrying a battered briefcase. In his checked shirt and rumpled pants, with untidy hair and worn shoes, he looked just like a professor.

Jeannie felt strange. She herself had never done anything more illegal than driving at seventy miles an hour. Now she was about to break into a building. It felt like crossing an important line.

Jeannie and her father walked past the tennis court, where two women were playing under floodlights. She nodded toward the psychology building. "That's the place," she said. "Nut House."

"Keep walking at the same speed," he said. "How do we get around the back?"

"I'll show you." A footpath across a lawn led past the far side of Nut House. Jeannie followed it, then turned off to a paved yard at the back of the building.

Her father ran a professional eye over the rear elevation. "What's that door?" he said, pointing.

"I think it's a fire door."

He nodded. "It probably has a crossbar at waist level, the kind that opens the door if you push against it. That's where we'll go in."

Jeannie remembered a sign on the inside of it that read THIS DOOR IS ALARMED. "You'll set off an alarm," she said.

"No, I won't." He looked around. "Okay. Let's go to work."

He put his briefcase down and took out a small black plastic box with a dial. Pressing a button, he ran the box all around the door frame, watching the dial. The needle jumped in the top-right-hand corner.

He returned the box to the briefcase and took out a similar instrument, plus a roll of electrician's tape. He taped the instrument to the door's top-right-hand corner and threw a switch. There was a low hum. "That should confuse the alarm," he said.

He took out a long piece of wire that had once been a shirt hanger. He twisted it, then inserted the hooked end into the crack of the door. He wiggled it for a few seconds, then pulled.

The door came open. The alarm did not sound.

He picked up his briefcase. "Okay, Jeannie, lead the way."

She ran up the fire stairs and hurried along the corridor to her office. He was right behind her. She pointed to the door.

He took yet another electronic instrument out of his briefcase. This one had a metal plate the size of a charge card attached to it by wires. He inserted the plate into the card reader and switched on the instrument. "It tries every possible combination," he said.

She was amazed by how easily he had entered a building that had such up-to-date security. "How long will this take?"

"Any second now."

A moment later the door gently swung open. He grinned. "Won't you step inside?" he said proudly.

She went in and turned on the light. Her computer was still on the desk. She flipped through her box of backup disks frenziedly. SHOPPING.LST was there. "Thank goodness," she said, and switched on the computer.

"What are you doing?" Daddy said.

"I want to read the file. I don't have a computer at home, Daddy. It was stolen."

He missed the irony. "Hurry up, then."

The screen flickered, and she clicked on word processing. She slid the floppy into the disk drive and switched on her printer.

The alarms went off all at once.

The noise was deafening. "What happened?" Jeannie yelled.

Her father was white with fear. "That emitter must have failed, or maybe someone took it off the door. Run, Jeannie!"

She wanted to snatch the disk out of the computer and bolt, but she forced herself to think coolly. If she were caught now and the disk taken from her, she would have lost everything. "Just a few more seconds. I just have to print this. Wait for me!"

He was shaking. "I can't, Jeannie, I can't. I'm sorry!" He snatched up his briefcase and ran.

Jeannie felt pity for her father, but she could not stop now. She highlighted the FBI file and clicked on PRINT. Nothing happened. Her printer was still warming up. She cursed.

She went to the window. Two security guards were entering the front of the building. She stared at her ink-jet printer. "Come *on*."

At last it ticked and whirred. She sprung the floppy out of the disk drive and slipped it into the pocket of her jacket. The printer regurgitated four sheets of paper. Heart pounding, Jeannie snatched up the pages and scanned the thirty or so pairs of names for either Steven Logan or Dennis Pinker.

Both were there. And they were linked with a third: Wayne Stattner. There was a New York City address and phone number.

"Yes!" Jeannie shouted exultantly.

She stared at the name. *Wayne Stattner.* This was the man who had raped Lisa right here in the gym and attacked Jeannie in Philadelphia. She whispered vengefully, "We're going to get you."

She stuffed the papers into her pocket and switched off the lights. She stood by the door as she heard voices in the corridor.

A man shouted, "I'm sure there was a light on in one of these."

Another voice replied, "We better check each one."

Jeannie glanced around. There was nowhere to hide.

She opened the door a crack. At the far end of the corridor, light streamed out of an open door. The guards came out, killed the light, and went into the next room, which was the laboratory. It would take them a minute or two to search that. Could she slip past unseen and make it to the stairwell?

Jeannie stepped out and closed the door behind her with a shaky hand. She walked along the corridor, passing the lab. She could not resist the temptation to glance inside. Both guards had their backs to her; one was looking inside a stationery closet, and the other was staring curiously at a row of DNA test films on a light box. They did not see her.

Almost there. Every nerve strained, she walked on to the end of the corridor and opened the door. She went light-footed down the stairs and then ran like the wind all the way to the parking lot.

Her father was waiting beside her car. She unlocked it, and they both got in. She tore out of the parking lot with her lights off.

"I'm sorry, Jeannie," he said. "It's no use. I've lost it. I'll never rob again."

"That's good news," she said. "And I got what I wanted!"

"I wish I could be a good father to you. I guess it's too late."

She drove out of the campus into the street and turned on her headlights. "It's not too late, Daddy. Really it's not."

"Maybe. I tried for you anyway, didn't I?"

"You tried, and you succeeded! I couldn't have done it alone."

"Yeah, I guess you're right."

She drove home fast. As soon as they got inside her apartment, she picked up the phone and called the number on the printout.

A man answered. She said, "May I speak to Wayne Stattner?"

"Yeah, Wayne speaking. Who's this?"

It sounded just like Steve's voice. She said, "Mr. Stattner, I'm with a market research firm that has chosen you to receive—"

He swore at her and hung up.

"It's him," Jeannie said to her father. "I'm calling the cops."

She dialed the sex-crimes unit. It was nine o'clock, but by good luck Mish Delaware was still in the building. Jeannie explained about Wayne Stattner, and after some convincing, the sergeant agreed to go with Jeannie to New York in the morning.

Saturday

THEY caught the USAir flight to New York at 6:40 a.m.

Jeannie was full of hope. This might be the end of the nightmare for Steve. She had called him last night to bring him up to date, and he had been ecstatic. She had promised to call him as soon as she had more news.

Mish was maintaining a kind of tolerant skepticism. She found it hard to believe Jeannie's story, but she had to check it out.

Jeannie's data did not reveal why Stattner's fingerprints were on file with the FBI, but Mish had checked overnight. Three years ago the distraught parents of a missing fourteen-year-old girl had tracked her down to Stattner's New York apartment. They had accused him of kidnapping. He had denied it, saying she had not been coerced. The girl herself had said she was in love with him. Wayne had been only nineteen; in the end, there had been no prosecution.

Jeannie and Mish arrived at La Guardia a few minutes after eight o'clock and took a battered yellow New York taxi into the city. Wayne Stattner's address turned out to be a downtown loft building just south of Houston Street. It was a sunny Saturday morning, and there were young people on the streets shopping for bagels and drinking cappuccino in sidewalk cafés.

A detective from the First Precinct was waiting outside the building. He grumpily introduced himself as Herb Reitz. Jeannie guessed that baby-sitting out-of-town detectives was a chore.

They went into the building and took a slow freight elevator to the top. "One apartment on each floor," Herb said. "This is an affluent suspect. What did he do?"

"Rape," Mish said.

The elevator stopped. The door opened directly onto another

door, and Mish rang a bell. There was a long silence. She rang again.

At last a voice came from within, demanding, "Who is it?"

It was him. The voice made Jeannie go cold with horror.

Herb said, "The police, that's who it is. Now open the door."

The tone changed. "Okay. Just a minute."

The door was opened by a tousled, barefoot young man in a black terry cloth bathrobe. Jeannie stared, feeling disoriented.

He was Steve's double—except that he had black hair.

Herb said, "Wayne Stattner?"

"Yes."

He must have dyed it, she thought.

"I'm Detective Herb Reitz from the First Precinct."

Wayne glanced at Mish and Jeannie. Jeannie saw no flicker of recognition in his face. "Won't you all come in?"

They stepped into a big high-ceilinged loft. Black velvet curtains were drawn across the windows, and the place was lit by low lamps. On one wall was a Nazi flag. A collection of whips stood in an umbrella stand. An oil painting of a woman being crucified rested on an easel. Jeannie shuddered with disgust. This was the home of a sadist.

"What do you do for a living, Mr. Stattner?" Herb said.

"I own two nightclubs here in New York," he said. "Frankly, that's why I'm always keen to cooperate with the police. I have to keep my hands spotlessly clean for business purposes."

Herb clicked his fingers. "Of course. Wayne Stattner. I read about you in *New York* magazine. 'Manhattan's Young Millionaires.' "

"Won't you sit down?"

Jeannie headed for a seat, then saw it was an electric chair of the type used for executions. She grimaced and sat elsewhere.

Herb said, "This is Sergeant Michelle Delaware of the Baltimore City Police."

"Baltimore?" said Wayne, showing surprise. He seemed to be a good actor. "They have crime in Baltimore?"

Jeannie said, "Your hair's dyed, isn't it?"

Mish flashed her a look of annoyance. Jeannie was supposed to observe, not interrogate the suspect. However, Wayne did not mind the question. "Smart of you to notice."

I was right, Jeannie thought jubilantly. "When did you dye it?"

"When I was fifteen," he said.

Liar. Your hair was fair on Sunday, when you raped Lisa.

He said, "What's this all about? I love mysteries."

Mish said briskly, "We need to know where you were last Sunday evening at eight o'clock."

"That's easy," he said. "I was in California."

"Can anyone corroborate that?"

He laughed. "About a hundred million people, I guess."

Jeannie was beginning to get a bad feeling about this. He couldn't have a real alibi. He *had* to be the rapist.

Mish said, "What do you mean?"

"I was at the Emmys."

How could Wayne have been there? Jeannie wondered.

"I didn't win anything, of course," he added. "I'm not in that business. But Salina Jones, an old friend, won best actress in a comedy, and I kissed her on both cheeks as she came off the stage with her trophy. It was a beautiful moment, caught by the television cameras. And there's a photo in this week's *People*."

He pointed to a magazine lying on the carpet. With a sinking heart Jeannie picked it up. There was Wayne in a tuxedo, kissing Salina as she grasped her Emmy. His hair was black. The caption read "New York nightclub impresario Wayne Stattner congratulates old flame Salina Jones on her Emmy in Hollywood Sunday night." It was about as impregnable as an alibi could be.

Mish said, "Well, Mr. Stattner, we don't need to take up any more of your time."

"What did you think I might have done?" he asked.

"We're investigating a rape that took place Sunday night."

"Wasn't me," Wayne said. "All my victims are volunteers." He gave Mish a long, suggestive look. She turned away.

Jeannie was desolate. But her brain was still working, and as they got up to leave, she said, "May I ask you something?"

"Sure," said Wayne, ever obliging.

"Around the time you were born, your father was in the military, am I right?"

"Yes, he was at Fort Bragg. How did you know?"

"Do you know if your mother had difficulty conceiving?"

"These are funny questions for a cop."

Mish said, "Dr. Ferrami is a scientist at Jones Falls University. Her research is closely connected with this case."

Jeannie said, "Did your mother ever say anything about having fertility treatment?"

"Not to me. And we can't ask her now. She's dead."

"I'm sorry to hear that. How about your father?"

He shrugged. "You could call him. He lives in Miami. I'll give you the number." He scribbled it on a page of *People* magazine and tore off the corner.

Herb said, "Thank you for your cooperation, Mr. Stattner."

"Any time."

As they went down in the elevator, Jeannie shook her head. She said disconsolately, "I can't believe he's innocent."

Mish said, "He's guilty as hell, honey, but not of this one."

STEVE sat in the big kitchen of his parents' home in Georgetown, watching his mother making meat loaf, waiting for Jeannie to call.

Mom was chopping onions. She had been dazed and astonished when first told what had been done to her at the Aventine Clinic. Last night Steve had sat up late with Mom and Dad, talking over their strange history. Mom had gotten angry then. The notion of doctors experimenting on patients without permission was just the kind of thing to make her mad.

Surprisingly, Dad was calmer. He had been tirelessly rational, going over Jeannie's logic, concluding in the end that she was probably right. However, reacting calmly was part of Dad's code. Right now he was out in the yard placidly watering a flower bed, but inside he might be boiling.

Mom started frying onions, and the smell made Steve's mouth

water. "Meat loaf with mashed potatoes and ketchup," he said. "One of the great meals."

She smiled. "When you were five, you wanted it every day."

She prepared the ground beef and wiped her hands. "I've been thinking about this stuff all night, and you know something? I'm glad they did that to me in the Aventine Clinic. If they hadn't experimented on me, I wouldn't have you." She put her arm around him. "Beside that, nothing else matters."

The phone rang then. Steve snatched it up. "Hello?"

"This is Jeannie."

"What happened?" he said breathlessly. "Was he there?"

"Yes. And he's your double, except he dyes his hair black. Wayne's mother is dead, but I just spoke with his father, and he confirmed that she was treated at the Aventine Clinic."

It was good news, but she sounded dispirited. Steve's elation was checked. "You don't seem as pleased as you ought to be."

She told him about Wayne and his alibi. Steve could see why she was so down. Her discovery of Wayne had gotten them no further.

"Then who raped Lisa?" he asked.

"Do you remember what Sherlock Holmes says? 'When you have eliminated the impossible, whatever remains—*however improbable*—must be the truth.' Or maybe it was Hercule Poirot."

His heart went cold. "What's the truth?"

"There are four twins."

"*Quadruplets?* Jeannie, this is getting crazy."

"Not quadruplets. I can't believe this embryo divided into four by *accident*. It had to be deliberate. You've heard of cloning. Genetico must have been working in secret on it."

"You're saying I'm a clone."

"You have to be. I'm sorry, Steve. I keep giving you shattering news. It's a good thing you have the parents you have."

Steve was silent. One of my clones is a murderer, and another is a rapist. Where does that leave me?

Jeannie said, "The clone idea also explains why you all have different birthdays. The embryos were kept in the laboratory for varying periods before they were implanted in the women's wombs."

Why did this happen to me? Why aren't I like everyone else?

"They're closing the flight," Jeannie said. "I have to go."

"I want to see you. Will you drive down from Baltimore?"

"Okay, I will. Bye, Steve."

He hung up the phone. "You got that," he said to his mother.

"She thinks there must be four of you, and you're clones."

"If we're clones, I must be like them."

"No. You're different because you're mine."

"But I'm not." He saw the spasm of pain cross his mother's face, but he was hurting too. "I'm the child of two complete strangers selected by Genetico research scientists."

"You must be different from the others, Steve," she said. "You *behave* differently."

"But is my nature different? Or have I just learned to hide it? Did you make me what I am? Or did Genetico?"

"I don't know, my son," said Mom. "I just don't know."

JEANNIE studied Steve's father. Charles was dark-haired, his expression dour and his manner rigidly precise. Although it was Saturday and he had been gardening, he wore neatly pressed pants and a short-sleeved shirt with a collar. He did not look like Steve in any way. The only thing Steve might have gotten from him was a taste for conservative clothes—he favored khakis and button-downs.

Steve had not yet come home, and Charles speculated that he might have dropped by his law school library to read up on rape trials. Steve's mother was lying down. Charles made fresh lemonade, and he and Jeannie went out on the patio of the house.

Jeannie needed Charles's help to find the fourth clone. But she was not sure he would be willing.

He passed her a tall, cold glass. They sipped their lemonade; then he said, "Jeannie, what is this all about?"

She put down her glass. "Berrington and Proust were both in the military before they set up Genetico," she said. "I suspect the company was originally a cover for a military project."

"But what interest could the army have in women's fertility problems?"

"Think of this. Steve and his doubles are tall, strong, fit, and handsome. They're also very smart, although their propensity to violence gets in the way of their achievements." She added casually, "I wonder if the army was trying to breed the perfect soldier."

It was no more than an idle speculation, but it electrified the career soldier. "Good Lord," he said.

"What?"

"There was a rumor back in the '70s that went all around the military. The Russians had a breeding program, people said. They were making perfect soldiers, perfect athletes, everything. Some people said we should be doing the same."

"So that's it!" Jeannie felt that at last she was beginning to understand. "They picked a healthy, aggressive, intelligent, blond-haired man and woman and got them to donate the sperm and egg to form the embryo. But what they were really interested in was *duplicating* the perfect soldier. The crucial part of the experiment was the division of the embryo and the implanting into host mothers." She frowned. "I wonder what happened next."

"I can answer that," Charles said. "Watergate. All those crazy secret schemes were canceled after that."

"But Genetico went legitimate. And its profits financed the research into genetic engineering that it's been doing ever since. My own project is probably part of their grand scheme."

"Which is what?"

"A breed of perfect Americans. A master race." Jeannie shrugged. "It's an old idea, but it's possible now with modern genetics."

"So why would they sell the company? It doesn't make sense."

"Maybe it does. The money will finance Proust's run at the presidency. If they get into the White House, they can do all the research they want—and put their ideas into practice."

Charles sighed. "And all this means I'm not Steve's father."

"Don't say that."

He opened his billfold and took out a photo. "I have to tell you something, Jeannie. I never suspected any of this stuff about clones, but I've often looked at Steve and wondered if there was anything at all of me in him."

"Can't you see it?" she said. "There's no physical resemblance. But Steve has a profound sense of duty. None of the other clones could give a darn about duty. He got it from you!"

Charles still looked grim. "There's bad in him. I know it."

She touched his arm. "Listen to me. Steve was what I call a wild child—disobedient, impulsive, fearless. So were Dennis Pinker and Wayne Stattner. Dennis is a murderer and Wayne a sadist. But Steve isn't like them, and you're the reason why. Only the most dedicated of parents can bring up such children to be normal human beings. Steve *is* normal."

"I pray you're right." Charles started to replace the photo.

Jeannie forestalled him. "May I see it?"

She studied the picture. It had been taken quite recently. Steve was wearing a blue-checked shirt and was grinning shyly at the camera. "I don't have a photo of him," Jeannie said regretfully.

"Have that one. I have a million photos of Steve."

"Thanks. I really appreciate it."

"You seem very fond of him."

"I love him, Charles. When I think he might be sent to jail, I want to offer to go instead of him."

Charles gave a wry smile. "So do I."

Jeannie felt self-conscious. She had not meant to say all this to Steve's father. She had not really known it herself; it had just come out, and then she had realized it was true.

She gave him a calculating look. It was time to ask him. "There is something you could do, you know."

"Tell me what it is."

She leaned forward in her chair. "Genetico experimented on soldiers' wives. Therefore all of the clones were probably born in army hospitals. The babies must have had army medical records twenty-two years ago. Those records may still exist. Do you think you could get access?"

"What exactly do you need to do?" he said.

"I have to load my program into the army computer, then let it search all the files. There's no way to know how long it could take."

Charles frowned. "If we're caught, it's the end of my career."

"Will you do it?" Jeannie said impatiently.

"Hell, yes."

STEVE was thrilled to see Jeannie sitting on the patio drinking lemonade and talking earnestly to his father as if they were old friends. He crossed the lawn from the garage, smiling, and kissed her lips softly. "You two look like conspirators," he said.

Jeannie explained what they were planning, and Steve allowed himself to feel hopeful again.

Dad said to Jeannie, "I'll need help loading your program."

"I'll come with you," Steve said. "I'm sure I could load it."

Dad looked at Jeannie, and she nodded. "If there are any glitches, you can call me from the data center and I'll talk you through it."

Charles Logan went into the kitchen and brought out the phone. He dialed a number. "Don, this is Charlie. Who won the golf? . . . Listen, I need a favor. I want to check my son's medical records from way back. . . . Yeah, he's got some kind of rare condition, and there may be a clue in his early history. Would you arrange security clearance for me to go into the command data center?"

There was a long pause. Steve could not read his father's face. At last he said, "Thanks, Don. I really appreciate it. We'll be there in fifteen minutes. . . . Thanks again." He hung up.

Jeannie had a disk containing her search program in a small plastic box. She handed it to Steve and said, "Good luck."

THEY got in the Lincoln Mark VIII and drove to the Pentagon. They parked in the biggest parking lot in the world, then went up a flight of steps to a second-floor entrance. Steve showed his identification at a security checkpoint and was signed in as a visitor and given a pass to stick to his shirtfront.

On a Saturday evening the corridors were deserted. They went up a staircase and around to another security point. They turned several more corners and came to a pair of glass doors. Beyond the doors a dozen or so young soldiers were sitting in front of computer screens. A guard checked Steve's identification yet again, then let them in.

The room was carpeted and quiet, windowless and softly lit. A woman about fifty, overweight and in lieutenant's uniform, introduced herself as Caroline Gambol. She was expecting them.

Dad told her, "We have authorization to search the records of babies born in military hospitals around twenty-two years ago."

Lieutenant Gambol nodded and sat at a terminal. Then, looking at Steve, she said, "I'll be glad to load that for you."

Steve shrugged and handed the woman the floppy disk. After a few minutes she looked up. "Who wrote this software?"

"A professor at Jones Falls," Steve said.

"It's very clever," she said. "I've never seen anything quite like it." Then she said, "I'll begin the search," and pressed ENTER.

THE FBI contact had told Jim Proust and Berrington about Jeannie's visit to Wayne Stattner in New York. They decided they had to watch her, and Berrington had reluctantly agreed to trail her for the rest of the day.

A hunch made him follow Colonel Logan's black Lincoln Mark VIII from the driveway of the Georgetown house. He was not sure whether Jeannie was in the car or not.

He found it relatively easy to track Logan through the Washington traffic. He stayed two cars behind, as in the gumshoe movies. They drove around the Lincoln Memorial, then crossed the Potomac by Arlington Bridge. They took Washington Boulevard, and Berrington realized their destination must be the Pentagon.

He followed the car down the off-ramp into the Pentagon's parking lot and found a spot in the next aisle. Steve and his father got out of the car and headed for the building. Berrington realized that Jeannie must have stayed behind at the house.

He found a pay phone and called Jim Proust. "I'm at the Penta-gon. I followed Jeannie to the Logan house, then trailed Steve Logan and his father here. I'm worried, Jim."

"What's at the Pentagon that could harm us?" Proust said. "The army has no record of what we did. I'm sure of that."

"Isn't there some way you can find out what they're doing?"

"I guess. If I don't have friends at the Pentagon, I don't have them anywhere. I'll make some calls. Stay in touch."

Seething with impatience, Berrington went back to his car.

STEVE waited in a fever of anticipation. The search had finished. There was a list of names and addresses in pairs on the screen. Jean-nie's program had worked. But were the clones on the list?

He controlled his eagerness. The first priority was to make a copy of the list. He found a box of new diskettes in a drawer and slid one into the disk drive. He copied the list, ejected the disk and slid it into the back pocket of his jeans.

Only then did he begin to scroll down the names; there seemed to be several pages. It would be easier to scan a piece of paper. He called Lieutenant Gambol. "Can I print from this terminal?"

"Sure," she said. "You can use that laser printer."

Steve stood over the printer, watching avidly as the pages came out. He was hoping to see his own name alongside three others: Dennis Pinker, Wayne Stattner, and the man who had raped Lisa Hoxton. His father watched over his shoulder.

The name Steven Logan appeared halfway down the second page. Dad spotted it at the same time. "There you are," he said.

But something was wrong. Along with Steven Logan, Dennis Pinker, and Wayne Stattner were Henry Irwin King, Per Ericson, Murray Claud, Harvey John Jones, and George Dassault. Steve's elation turned to bafflement as he counted.

"There are eight names." Then he saw it. "That's how many Genetico made," he said. "Eight of us."

"Eight clones?" Dad said in amazement. "Eight?"

"I wonder how the search found them," Steve said. He looked

at the last sheet out of the printer. At the foot it said, "Common characteristic: Electrocardiogram."

"That's right, I remember," Dad said. "You had an electrocardiogram when you were a week old. I never knew why."

"We all did. And identical twins have similar hearts."

"I still can't believe it," Dad said. "There are eight boys in the world exactly like you."

"Look at these addresses," Steve said. "All army bases."

"Doesn't the program pull out any other information?"

"No. That's how come it doesn't invade people's privacy."

"The heck with privacy," Dad said. "I'm going to pull these people's full medical histories, see if we get any clues."

"I could use a cup of coffee," Steve said. "I'll be right back."

He left the data center with a nod to the guard at the door. The rest area around the corner had a coffeemaker and machines selling soda and candy. He ate two Snickers bars and drank a cup of coffee, then headed back to the data center.

He stopped outside the glass doors. Several new people were inside, including a general and two military policemen. The general was arguing with Dad. Their body language made Steve wary. He stepped into the room and stood by the door. Instinct told him not to draw attention to himself.

He heard the general say, "I have my orders, Colonel Logan, and you're under arrest."

Dad was saying angrily, "You don't have the right!"

The general shouted, "Don't you lecture me, Colonel."

Steve had the floppy disk with the list of names right in his pocket. Dad was in trouble, but he could look after himself. Steve should just get out of there with the information.

He turned and went out through the glass doors. He walked briskly, trying to look as if he knew where he was going. He felt like a fugitive. He turned a couple of corners and walked through a security checkpoint.

Behind him he heard the voice of Caroline Gambol. "Mr. Logan! One moment, please."

He glanced back over his shoulder. Lieutenant Gambol was running along the corridor behind him, red-faced and puffing.

Heart racing, Steve darted around a corner and found a staircase. He ran down the steps to the next floor.

Hurrying along a wide corridor, he heard her voice again. "Mr. Logan! The general wishes to see you!"

Steve found a staircase and went up. That ought to slow the pudgy lieutenant. On the next floor he hurried around two corners, then went down again. There was no further sign of Lieutenant Gambol. He had shaken her off, he thought with relief.

He was pretty sure he was on the exit level. The next corridor looked familiar: This was the way he had come in. He came to the security checkpoint where he had entered. He was almost free.

Steve walked toward the entrance. Behind him he suddenly heard someone shout, "Stop, or I'll shoot!"

He turned. The guard he had seen earlier was there. The guard had drawn a pistol and was pointing it at him.

Steve felt his muscles seize up as he stared down the barrel. With an effort he shook off his paralysis. "You won't shoot me," he said. "It would be murder."

He turned and walked to the door. The distance was only three or four yards, but it felt as if it took years.

As he put his hand on the door, a shot rang out.

The thought flashed through Steve's mind: He fired over my head. But he did not look back. He flew through the door and ran down the long flight of steps. Night had fallen while he was inside, and the parking lot was lit by streetlamps. He heard shouting behind him, then another shot. He reached the bottom of the stairway and veered off the footpath into the bushes.

He emerged onto a road and kept running. He came to a row of bus stops. He slowed to a walk. A bus was pulling up at one of the stops. Two soldiers got off, and a woman civilian got on. Steve boarded right behind her.

The bus pulled away. It drove out of the parking lot and onto the expressway, leaving the Pentagon behind.

IN A COUPLE OF HOURS JEANNIE had come to like Lorraine Logan enormously.

She was heavier than she seemed in the photograph that appeared with her lonely-hearts column. She smiled a lot. To take Jeannie's mind and her own off their worries, she talked of the problems people wrote to her about: domineering in-laws, bosses with wandering hands. Whatever the subject, Lorraine managed to say something that made Jeannie think, How come I never saw it that way before?

They sat on the patio as the day cooled, waiting anxiously for Steve and his father to return. They heard a car outside, and Lorraine got up and went to the corner of the house to look out into the street. "Steve's come home in a taxicab," she said, puzzled.

Before Jeannie could respond, he appeared on the patio. "Where's your father?" Lorraine asked him.

"Dad got arrested."

Jeannie said, "Oh, Lord. Why?"

"I'm not sure. I think the Genetico people somehow found out what we were up to and pulled some strings. But I got away."

Lorraine said suspiciously, "Stevie, there's something you aren't telling me."

"A guard fired two shots."

His mother gave a small scream.

"I think he was aiming over my head. Anyway, I'm fine."

Jeannie's mouth went dry. The thought of bullets being fired at Steve horrified her. He might have died!

"The sweep worked, though." Steve took a diskette from his back pocket. "Here's the list. And wait till you hear what's on it. There aren't four clones. There are eight."

Jeannie's jaw dropped. "Eight of you?"

"We found eight identical electrocardiograms."

Genetico had split the embryo seven times and implanted eight unknowing women with the children of strangers. The arrogance was unbelievable. This was what Berrington was so desperate to conceal, Jeannie thought. When this news was made public, Genetico would be disgraced. And Steve would be cleared.

"You did it!" she said. Then a snag occurred to her. "But which of the eight committed the rape?"

"We'll have to find out," Steve said. "And that won't be easy. The addresses we have are almost certainly out of date."

"We can try to track them down. That's Lisa's specialty." Jeannie stood up. "I'd better get back to Baltimore. This is going to take most of the night."

Steve said, "I'll walk you to your car."

Jeannie said good-bye to Lorraine, who hugged her warmly.

Outside, Steve handed her the diskette. "Take care of that," he said. "There's no copy, and we won't get another chance."

"Don't worry. It's my future too." She kissed him hard.

"Oh, boy," he said after a while. "Could we do a lot of this quite soon?"

"Yes. But be careful. I don't want to lose you."

He smiled. "I love it that you're worried about me."

Jeannie kissed him again, then got in the car and pulled away. She drove fast and got home in under an hour. There she called Lisa, and they agreed to meet in the lab at midnight.

Sunday

As JEANNIE walked into the lab, she thought it weird to be there in the middle of the night. The antiseptic white decor, the bright lights, and the silent machines all around made her think of a morgue.

She also thought they might get a visit from security sooner or later. "If a security guard comes to check on us, I'm going to hide in the stationery closet," she told Lisa.

"I hope we get enough warning of his approach," Lisa said nervously as she booted up her computer.

Jeannie started the coffee machine, then put Steve's floppy disk into Lisa's computer and printed the Pentagon results. There were the names of the eight babies whose electrocardiograms were as similar as if they had all come from one person. Eight tiny hearts beating exactly the same way. Somehow Berrington had arranged for the army hospitals to give these babies this test.

"Let's start with Henry King," Jeannie suggested. "Full name Henry Irwin King."

On her desk Lisa had two CD-ROM drives, one on top of the other. "We have every residential phone in the United States on two disks," she said, "and software that enables us to search both disks at the same time." She typed "Henry I. King" and clicked on the Retrieve icon. A list appeared on the screen. "We have seventeen Henry I. Kings. What's his last known address?"

Jeannie consulted her printout. "Fort Devens, Massachusetts."

"Okay. We have four Henry I. Kings in Boston."

"Let's call them."

"You do realize it's one o'clock in the morning. People won't talk to us at this time of night."

"Sure they will," Jeannie said with bravado. She just was not prepared to wait until morning. "We'll say we're from the police, tracking down a serial killer. Give me the first number."

After the first phone call, where a sleepy but outraged middle-aged voice demanded that she put her lieutenant on, Jeannie wasn't quite so sure of herself. "I hope it's not going to be a night of conversations like that."

Lisa had already hung up from her call. "Mine was Jamaican and had the accent to prove it," she said.

Bracing herself, Jeannie dialed again. The third Henry King had not yet gone to bed; there was music in the background and other voices in the room. "Yeah, who's this?" he said.

He sounded about the right age, and Jeannie felt hopeful. She did her impersonation of a cop, but he was suspicious. "How do I know you're the police?"

He sounded just like Steve, and Jeannie's heart missed a beat. She decided to brazen it out. "Would you like to call me back here at police headquarters?" she offered recklessly.

There was a pause. "No, forget it," he said. "I'm Henry King. They call me Hank. What do you want?"

"Could I first check your date and place of birth?"

"I was born in Fort Devens exactly twenty-two years ago. Saturday was my birthday as a matter of fact."

It was him! Jeannie tried to keep the excitement out of her voice as she said, "When did you last travel outside the state?"

"Let me see. That was August. I went to New York."

"What were you doing last Sunday?"

"I was working. I'm a graduate student at M.I.T., but I have a Sunday job tending bar at the Blue Note Café in Cambridge."

Jeannie scribbled a note. "Thank you, Mr. King. Would you just give me that phone number so I can confirm your alibi?"

She drew the conversation to a close, hung up, and blew out her cheeks, drained by the effort of deception. "Whew! Found him," she told Lisa. "But he seems to have an alibi. He says he was working at a bar in Cambridge." She looked at her scratch pad. "The Blue Note. I guess a bar should still be open on a Saturday night."

Jeannie dialed the number. "This is Detective Susan Farber of the Boston police. Let me speak to the manager, please."

"This is the manager. What's wrong?" The voice sounded worried.

"Do you have an employee named Henry King?"

"Hank. Yeah."

"When did you last see him?"

"Lemme see. Last Sunday. He worked the four-to-midnight shift."

"Would you swear to that if necessary, sir?"

"Sure, why not? Whatever it is, Hank didn't do it."

After Jeannie hung up, she said disappointedly, "Alibi stands up."

"Don't be downhearted," Lisa said. "We've done well to eliminate such a common name so quickly. Let's try Per Ericson. There won't be so many of them."

The Pentagon list said Per Ericson had been born in Fort Rucker, but twenty-two years later none were in Alabama.

Jeannie and Lisa began to work their way through all the Per Ericsons in the United States—thirty-three listings.

As Jeannie was hanging up from her sixth fruitless call, she heard Lisa say, "Oh, I'm terribly sorry. Please forgive this intrusion, Mrs. Ericson. Good-bye." She hung up, looking crushed. "He's the one all right," she said. "But he died last winter. That was his mother. She burst into tears when I asked for him."

"How did he die?" Jeannie wondered.

"He was a ski champion apparently, and he broke his neck trying something risky."

A daredevil without fear. "That sounds like our man."

It had not occurred to Jeannie that not all eight might be alive. Now she realized that there may well have been more than eight implants. Even nowadays, when the technique was well established, many implants failed to "take." Genetico might have experimented on fifteen or twenty women, or even more.

They were not so lucky with the next name. There were seven George Dassaults in the United States, but three of them did not answer their phones. There was nothing to do but try again later.

There was another snag. "I guess there's no guarantee that the man we're after is on the CD-ROM of addresses," Jeannie said.

"That's true. His number could be unlisted."

Murray Claud was another unusual name, and they tracked him down quickly. Murray Claud, Sr., told Jeannie in a voice full of bitterness and bewilderment that his son had been jailed in Athens three years ago, after a knife fight in a taverna, and would not be released until January. "That boy could have been anything," he said. "Astronaut. Movie star. President. He has brains, charm, and good looks. And he threw it all away."

She understood the father's pain. He thought he was responsible. She promised herself she would call him again one day.

They left the hardest name—Harvey Jones—until last.

Jeannie was daunted to find there were almost a million Joneses in America, and H. was a common initial. He had been born at Walter Reed Hospital in Washington, D.C., so Jeannie and Lisa began by calling every Harvey Jones and H. Jones in the Washington phone book. They accumulated only a long list of maybes.

Jeannie's eyes were getting bleary, and she was feeling jumpy from too much coffee and no sleep. At four a.m. she and Lisa began on the Philadelphia Joneses.

At four thirty Jeannie found him.

The phone rang four times; then there was the click of an answering machine. "You've reached Harvey Jones's place," the message said, and the hairs on the back of her neck stood up. It was like listening to Steve's voice. "I can't come to the phone right now, so please leave a message."

Jeannie hung up and checked the address. It was an apartment on Spruce Street, in University City, not far from the Aventine Clinic. She noticed her hands were shaking. It was because she wanted to get him by the throat.

She picked up the phone and called police headquarters.

BERRINGTON Jones remained in the Pentagon parking lot watching Colonel Logan's black Lincoln Mark VIII until midnight. Then he called Proust and learned that Logan had been arrested but that his son, Steve, had escaped.

"What were they doing in the Pentagon?" he asked Jim.

"They were in the data center. I'm trying to find out what they were up to. See if you can track down the girl."

When Berrington returned to the Logan house, Jeannie's red Mercedes had gone. He drove back to Baltimore and cruised up and down her street, but the car was not there either.

It was getting light out when he pulled up outside his house in Roland Park. He went inside and lay on the bed, exhausted.

Proust called at eight. He had spent half the night at the Pentagon with a friend who was a general, questioning the data center personnel under the pretext of investigating a security breach. Colonel Logan, who was still under arrest, would not say anything except "I want a lawyer." However, the results of Jeannie's sweep were on the computer terminal Steve had been using. "I guess you must have ordered electrocardiograms on all the babies," Jim said.

Berrington had forgotten, but now it came back. "Yes, we did."

"Logan found them. All eight."

It was the worst possible news. "Does Preston know?"

"Yes. He says we're finished, but he always says that."

"This time he could be right," Berrington said.

Jim's voice took on its parade-ground tone. "You may be ready to wimp out, Berry, but I'm not," he grated. "If we can keep the lid on this until the press conference tomorrow, the takeover will go through. After that we'll have a hundred and eighty million dollars, and that buys a lot of silence."

Berrington wanted to believe him. "What should we do next?"

"Is there any way we can check to see if Jeannie Ferrami's tracked down the boys yet?" Jim wondered.

"I could call them and find out if they've heard from her."

"You'd have to be discreet."

"You aggravate me, Jim. Of course I'll be discreet." Berrington hung up with a bang and then got out his address book.

MISH Delaware refused point-blank to drive to Philadelphia and interview Harvey Jones. "We did that yesterday, honey," she said when Jeannie finally got her on the phone Sunday morning.

"But you *know* I'm right!" Jeannie protested. "I was right about Wayne Stattner—he *was* a double for Steve."

"Except for his hair. And he had an alibi. I'll call the Philadelphia police, and I'll fax them the E-FIT picture. They'll go and check whether Harvey Jones resembles the picture and ask if he can account for his movements last Sunday afternoon."

Jeannie banged the phone down in a fury. She sure didn't feel like sitting around waiting. She thought about Harvey Jones. If he *was* in Baltimore last Sunday, why? To see a girlfriend? Perhaps, but the likeliest explanation was that his parents lived there. He was probably in the city now, eating his mother's pot roast or watching a football game on TV with his father.

How many Jones families were there in Baltimore—a thousand?

She knew one: her former boss, Professor Berrington Jones—
Oh, my God. Jones.

She was shocked. *Harvey Jones could be Berrington's son.*

She suddenly remembered the little gesture Harvey had made in the coffee shop in Philadelphia. He had smoothed his eyebrows with the tip of his index finger. At the time, she could not recall who else did it. But now she remembered. *Berrington* smoothed his eyebrows with the tip of his index finger. Harvey had learned it from his father as an expression of self-satisfaction.

Harvey could be at Berrington's house right now.

PRESTON Barck and Jim Proust arrived at Berrington's house around midday and sat in the den drinking beer. None of them had slept much, and they looked and felt wasted.

"Jeannie has talked to Hank King, and to Per Ericson's mother," Berrington reported despondently. "She'll track them all down before long."

Jim said, "Let's be realistic. What can she do by tomorrow?"

Preston Barck was suicidal. "I'll tell you what I'd do in her place," he said. "If I could get hold of two or three of the boys, I'd take them to New York and go on *Good Morning America.*"

"Heaven forbid," Berrington said.

A car drew up outside. Jim looked out the window and said, "Rusty old Datsun."

Preston said, "I'm beginning to like Jim's original idea. Make them all vanish."

"I won't have any killing!" Berrington shouted.

"Don't yell, Berry," Jim said with surprising mildness. "I realize there are limits. But I have another idea."

The other two stared at him.

Jim said, "We have to know what Jeannie Ferrami's intentions are. We know one person who could easily win her confidence and find out exactly what's on her mind."

Berrington felt his anger rise. "I know what you're thinking—"

"Here he comes now," Jim said.

There was a footstep in the hall, and Berrington's son came in.

"Hi, Dad!" he said. "Hey, Uncle Jim. Uncle Preston."

Berrington looked at him with a mixture of pride and sorrow. The boy looked adorable in navy-blue corduroy pants and a sky-blue cotton sweater. He picked up my dress sense anyway, Berrington thought.

He said, "We have to talk, Harvey. Jim, why don't you and Preston go into the drawing room."

Preston and Jim left. Berrington got up and hugged Harvey. "I love you, son," he said. "Even though you're wicked."

"Am I wicked?"

"What you did to that poor girl in the basement of the gym was one of the most wicked things a man can do."

Harvey shrugged.

Dear Lord, I failed to instill in him any sense of right and wrong, Berrington thought. But it was too late now for regrets. "Sit down and listen," he said. Harvey sat.

"Your mother and I tried for years to have a baby, but there were problems," Berrington said. "At the time, Preston was working on in vitro fertilization, where the sperm and the egg are brought together in the laboratory and then the embryo implanted in the womb."

"Are you saying I was a test-tube baby?"

"This is secret. You must never tell anyone. And there's more to it than that. Preston split one live embryo, forming twins."

"That's the guy who's been arrested for the rape?"

"He split it more than once," Berrington said.

Harvey nodded. All of them had the same quick intelligence. "How many?" he said.

"Eight."

"Wow. And I guess the sperm didn't come from you."

"No. An army lieutenant from Fort Bragg—tall, strong, fit, intelligent, aggressive, and good-looking. The mother was a civilian typist from West Point, similarly well favored."

A wounded grin twisted the boy's handsome face. "My real parents. Why are you telling me now?"

"Steve Logan, one of your doubles, was a subject for study in my department. I had a heck of a shock when I saw him, as you may imagine. Then the police arrested him for the rape of Lisa Hoxton. But a professor, Jeannie Ferrami, got suspicious. She wants to prove Logan's innocence. And she probably wants to expose the whole story of the clones and ruin me."

"She's the woman I met in Philadelphia."

Berrington was mystified. "You've met her?"

"Uncle Jim called me and told me to give her a scare."

Berrington was enraged. "I'm going to tear his head off—"

"Calm down, Dad. Nothing happened. I went for a ride in her car. She's cute in her way."

Berrington controlled himself with an effort. "Let's talk about what we have to do. We need to know her intentions, and we can't think of any way to get to her—but one."

Harvey nodded. "You want me to go talk to her, pretending to be Steve Logan."

"Yes."

He grinned. "Sounds like fun. Want me to go right away?"

"Yes, please. I hate to ask you to do this."

"Relax, Dad. But what if the real Steve is there?"

"He drives up from Washington. Check the cars in the street. He has a Datsun like yours; that's another reason the police were so sure he was the perpetrator."

"No kidding!"

"You're like identical twins; you make the same choices. If his car is there, call me, and we'll think of some way to get him out."

"Okay." Harvey stood up. "What's the girl's address?"

Berrington scribbled on a card and handed it over. "Be careful."

"Sure. See you sooner, Montezuma."

Berrington forced a smile. "In a flash, succotash."

JEANNIE called police headquarters again. Mish wasn't there, but she left an urgent message asking her to call.

Next Jeannie called Steve's house, but there was no reply. She guessed he and Lorraine were with their lawyer, trying to get Charles freed. She was disappointed; she wanted to tell Steve the good news about Harvey.

The thrill of having discovered Harvey soon wore off, though, and she felt depressed. Her thoughts returned to a future with no money, no job, and no way to help her mother.

To cheer herself up, she made brunch. She scrambled three eggs and ate them with toast and coffee. As she was putting the dishes in the dishwasher, the doorbell rang.

She lifted the handset. "Hello?"

"Jeannie? It's Steve."

"Come on in!" she said happily.

He came in wearing a cotton sweater the color of his eyes. She kissed him and hugged him hard. Today he smelled different again: He had used some kind of aftershave with an herbal fragrance. He tasted different too, sort of like he had been drinking tea.

After a while she broke away. "I have so much to tell you!"

He sat on the couch while she went to the refrigerator. "Wine, beer, coffee?"

"Wine sounds good."

"Do you think it will be okay?"

What did she mean by okay? "I don't know," he said.

"How long ago did we open it?"

Okay, they shared a bottle of wine but didn't finish it, so she replaced the cork, and now she's wondering whether it has oxidized. But she wants me to decide. "Let's see. What day was it?" he asked.

"It was Wednesday. That's four days."

Harvey could not even see whether it was red or white. "Just pour a glass, and we'll try it," he said.

She poured some wine into a glass and handed it to him.

He tasted it. "It's drinkable," he said.

She leaned over the back of the sofa. "Let me taste." She kissed his lips. "You're right," she said. "It's drinkable." Laughing, she filled his glass and poured some for herself.

He was beginning to enjoy himself.

She sat beside him and put her head on his shoulder. "I'm so glad you're here," she said.

With a huge effort of will he said, "We need to talk seriously."

"You're right." She sat up. "Is your father still under arrest?"

Jeez, what do I say to that? "No, you first," he said. "You said you had so much to tell me."

"Okay. Number one, I know who raped Lisa. His name is Harvey Jones, and he lives in Philadelphia."

Harvey struggled to keep his expression impassive. *I never thought anyone would track me down!* "You've done amazingly well," he said. *Steve would be thrilled by this news; it lets him off the hook.* "I don't know how to thank you."

She went on. "But you haven't heard the best part. Who else do we know called Jones?"

Do I say, "Berrington?" "It's a common name," he said.

"Berrington! I think Harvey has been brought up as his son!"

"Incredible!" he said. What do I do next? Maybe Dad would have some ideas. I need an excuse to make a phone call.

She took his hand. "You still haven't told me what happened to your dad. Did you get him released?"

"Why don't I phone home and get the latest news?"

His father had mentioned that Steve Logan lived in Washington. Harvey held the cradle down with a finger while he tapped three random digits, to represent an area code. Then he released it and dialed his father's home.

Berrington answered, and Harvey said, "Hi, Mom."

His father got it immediately. "You're with Jeannie?"

"Yes. I called to find out whether Dad got out of jail yet."

"The military police still have Colonel Logan under arrest."

"That's too bad. I was hoping he might have been released."

Hesitantly Dad said, "Can you tell me . . . anything?"

"Jeannie has worked wonders, Mom. She's discovered the real rapist." Harvey tried hard to put a pleased tone into his voice. "His name's Harvey Jones. And he was brought up as Berrington's son."

"Jeez! At least we're forewarned. What about Genetico? Does

she have any plans to publicize what she's found out about us?"

"I don't know yet."

"Make sure you find out. That's important too."

"Okay. Well, I hope Dad gets out soon. Call me here if you get any news, okay? Just ask for Steve." He laughed, as if he had made a joke.

"Jeannie might recognize my voice," Berrington said. "But I could get Preston to make the call."

"Exactly. Bye." Harvey hung up.

Jeannie bounced up out of the couch. She said, "I ought to call police headquarters again. Maybe they didn't understand how urgent this is."

He realized he was going to have to kill her.

"Kiss me again first," he said.

JEANNIE slid into his arms, leaning against the kitchen counter. She opened her mouth to his kiss, and he stroked her side.

But somehow she did not feel as good as she expected to. She tried to relax and enjoy the moment she had been looking forward to. Some doubt nagged at her, however.

He sensed her unease. He said, "You're not comfortable. Let's sit on the couch again." Taking her agreement for granted, he sat down. She followed. He smoothed his eyebrows with the tip of his index finger and reached for her.

She flinched away. *No! It can't be!*

"You . . . you did that thing with your eyebrow."

"What thing?" he said.

She sprang up from the couch. "You creep!" she screamed. "How dare you? Get out of my place!"

He tried to keep up the façade. "What's going on?"

"I know who you are. You're Harvey!"

He gave up his act. "How did you know?"

"You touched your eyebrow, just like Berrington."

"Well, what does it matter?" he said, standing up. "If we're so alike, you could pretend I'm Steve."

"Get out of here!"

He stepped toward her, smiling. In a flash he grabbed her, lifted her, and threw her on the floor.

She screamed, "Help! Mr. Oliver! Help!"

Harvey snatched up a dishcloth from the counter and stuffed it roughly into her mouth. He held her wrists so that she could not pull the cloth out. She tried to push it out with her tongue, but it was too big. Had her neighbor heard her scream? Mr. Oliver was old, and he turned up his TV loud.

The phone rang.

Harvey grabbed the waist of her jeans. She wriggled away from him. He slapped her face so hard she saw stars. While she was dazed, he let go of her wrists and went for her jeans again.

Jeannie snatched the cloth out of her mouth and screamed, "Help me. Help!"

Harvey covered her mouth with his big hand, muffling her yells, and fell on her, knocking the wind out of her. For a few moments she was helpless, struggling to breathe.

The phone was still ringing. Then the doorbell rang too.

Jeannie opened her mouth. Harvey's fingers slid between her teeth. She bit down hard, as hard as she could. Warm blood spurted into her mouth, and she heard him cry out.

The doorbell rang again, long and insistently. Harvey jerked his hand away, and Jeannie yelled again, "Help! Help!"

There was a loud bang from downstairs, then a crash and the sound of wood splintering. Harvey scrambled to his feet, clutching his hand. He swung around, turning his back on Jeannie.

Steve burst in.

Steve and Harvey stared at one another in astonishment for a frozen moment.

They were exactly the same. What would happen if they fought? They were equal in height, weight, strength, and fitness. A fight could go on forever.

Jeannie rolled over and stood up. On impulse she picked up a pan from the kitchen nook. Imagining that she was hitting a crosscourt ground shot with her famous doublehanded backhand, she shifted her weight to her front foot, locked her wrists, and swung the heavy pan with all her might.

She hit the back of Harvey's head with a thud. He sank to his knees, swaying. Then his eyes rolled up, and he crashed to the floor.

Steve said, "Boy, am I glad you didn't hit the wrong twin."

Jeannie started to shake. She dropped the pan and sat on a kitchen stool. Steve put his arms around her.

The phone was still ringing.

STEVE said, "Who is he?"

"Harvey Jones," Jeannie answered. "Berrington Jones's son."

Steve was amazed. "Well, I'll be damned."

Jeannie stared at the unconscious figure. "What should we do?"

"For a start, why don't we answer the phone?"

Jeannie picked it up. It was Lisa. "It almost happened to me," Jeannie said without preamble. "The same guy."

"Oh, no! I can't believe it! Shall I come right over?"

"Thanks. I'd like that."

Jeannie hung up. She ached all over from having been thrown to the floor, and she could still taste Harvey's blood. She poured a glass of water and rinsed her mouth.

There was a footstep on the stairs, and Mr. Oliver put his head around the door. "What happened here?" he said. He looked from Harvey on the floor to Steve. "Well, I'll be. This must be that guy in Philadelphia. They got to be twins!"

Steve said, "Let's tie him up. Do you have any cord, Jeannie?"

Mr. Oliver said, "I have some electric cable." He went out.

Jeannie hugged Steve gratefully. She felt as if she had awakened from a nightmare. "I thought he was you," she said.

"We need to make up a secret code. Then you'll know it's me."

"Okay, let's do it," Jeannie said. "When you approached me on the tennis court last Sunday, you said, 'I play a little tennis myself.'"

"And you modestly said, 'If you only play a *little* tennis, you're probably not in my league.'"

"That's the code. If one of us says the first line, the other has to say the second."

Mr. Oliver came back with his toolbox and some cable. He rolled Harvey over and tied his hands and feet. Then he stuffed the dishcloth in his mouth. "This guy won't cause you no more trouble. Now, I got some loose timber in the yard. I could fix the front door so we can lock it tonight."

Jeannie felt profoundly grateful to him. "Thank you."

"Don't mention it. This is the most interesting thing that's happened to me since World War Two." He picked up his toolbox and went downstairs.

Jeannie collected her thoughts. "Tomorrow Genetico will be sold for a hundred and eighty million dollars, and Jim Proust will be on the presidential trail. Meanwhile, I've got no job, and my reputation is shot. But I could turn both situations around."

"How are you going to do that?" Steve said.

"Well, what if we gate-crash the press conference tomorrow."

"Yes!" he said. "Then maybe the people from Landsmann will decide not to sign the papers, and the takeover will be canceled."

"I'll have a press release ready to give out," Jeannie said. "Then you'll come in with Harvey."

Steve frowned. "What does that prove?"

"Because you two are identical twins, you'll have the kind of dramatic impact that should cause the press to start asking questions. Once they learn that you have different mothers, they'll know there's a mystery to be uncovered, just as I did."

"Three would be better than two, though," Steve said.

"We could invite them all and hope at least one will show up."

Lisa's voice came from downstairs, greeting Mr. Oliver, who was repairing the door. A moment later she came in, looked at Steve and Harvey, and said, "My gosh, it's true."

Steve stood up. "I'm the one you picked out of the lineup," he said. "But he's the one who attacked you."

Jeannie swiftly brought Lisa up to date with the day's developments and the plan for disrupting the press conference. "We were just saying we could feel more confident if one of the other clones was going to be there."

Steve said, "Could they even get here on time?"

"We could check flights on CompuServe," Lisa said. "I have my PowerBook in the trunk of my car. I'll get it."

A few minutes later she returned, and they got to work. Jeannie wrote the press release while Lisa accessed WorldSpan Travelshopper and checked flights. Steve made some calls and found out that the press conference was scheduled at the Stouffer Hotel. He reserved a room.

As he hung up, Lisa said, "There are three early flights that would get Hank King here from Boston on time." She listed them.

"Book a seat on the nine forty-five," Jeannie said.

Steve passed Lisa his credit card, and she tapped in the details.

Jeannie said, "I still don't know how to persuade him to come."

"If he's a student working in a bar, he needs money," Steve said. "Let me try something."

He dialed and asked for Hank. A minute later a voice just like Steve's own came on the line. "Yeah, who's this?"

"Hi, Hank. I'm Steve Logan. We have something in common."

"Are you selling something?"

"Your mother and mine both received treatment at a place called the Aventine Clinic before we were born. You can check that with her. To cut a long story short, I'm suing the clinic for ten million dollars, and I'd like you to join in the suit with me."

There was a thoughtful pause. "I don't know if you're for real or not, buddy, but I don't have the money for a lawsuit."

"I'll pay all the legal costs," Steve said. "I don't want your money."

"You better write me with the details—"

"That's the problem. I need you to be here in Baltimore, at the Stouffer Hotel, tomorrow at noon. I'm holding a press conference ahead of my lawsuit, and I want you to appear."

"Who wants to go to Baltimore? Like, it's not Honolulu."

Get serious, jerk. "You have a reservation out of Logan at nine forty-five. Your ticket is paid for. Just pick it up at the airport."

"You're offering to split ten million dollars with me?"

"Oh, no. You get your own ten million."

Hank said, "You're beginning to sound a little more convincing. I'll think about it after I get off work tonight."

"Call me at the hotel," Steve said, but Hank had hung up.

Jeannie and Lisa were staring at him.

"We'll just have to see if he shows up," Lisa said.

"What about Wayne Stattner?" Steve asked. "Do you have a number?"

A few moments later he dialed and got an answering machine. "Hi, Wayne. My name is Steve Logan, and you may notice that my voice sounds exactly like yours. That's because—believe it or not—we are identical. I'm six feet two, a hundred and ninety pounds, and I look exactly like you except for hair color. Now here's the kicker: We're not twins. There are several of us. And we're meeting tomorrow at the Stouffer Hotel in Baltimore at noon. This is weird, Wayne, but I swear it's true. Call me or Dr. Jean Ferrami at the hotel, or just show up. It will be interesting." He hung up and looked at Jeannie. "What do you think?"

She shrugged. "He may be intrigued. On the other hand, I wouldn't take a plane on the strength of a phone message like that."

The phone rang, and Steve picked it up automatically. "Hello?"

"Can I speak to Steve?" The voice was unfamiliar.

"This is Steve."

"This is Uncle Preston. I'm putting your dad on."

Steve frowned, mystified. A moment later another voice came on the line. "Is anyone with you? Is she listening?"

Suddenly Steve understood. "Hold on a moment," he said. He covered the mouthpiece. "This is Berrington Jones!" he said to Jeannie. "And he thinks I'm Harvey. What do I do?"

Jeannie spread her hands in bewilderment. "Improvise."

"Gee, thanks." Steve put the phone to his ear. "Uh, yeah."

"What's going on? You've been there hours. Have you found out what Jeannie's planning to do?"

"Uh . . . yes, I have."

"Then get back here and tell us! We're all in bad trouble!"

"Okay."

"Now, when you hang up, say it was your parents' lawyer calling to say you're needed back in D.C. in a hurry. Okay?"

"Okay. I'll be there as fast as I can."

Berrington hung up, and Steve's shoulders slumped with relief. "I think I fooled him."

Jeannie said, "What did he say?"

"It seems Harvey was sent here to find out what your intentions are. They're worried about what you might do."

"*They*? Who?"

"Berrington and someone called Uncle Preston."

"Preston Barck, president of Genetico. So why did they call?"

"Impatience. Berrington got fed up with waiting. He told me to get back to his house as fast as I can."

Jeannie looked worried. "This is very bad. When Harvey doesn't show up, Berrington will know something's wrong."

Steve said, "Then Harvey must go home."

Jeannie shook her head. "He'll tell them everything."

"Not if I go in his place."

Jeannie stared at him, aghast. "Steve, it's so hazardous. You don't know anything about their life."

"If Harvey could fool you, I guess I could fool Berrington. I'll tell them I have to return home to Philadelphia, and I'll be back with you by midnight."

"But Berrington is Harvey's *father*. It's impossible."

Steve knew she was right. "Do you have a better idea?"

Jeannie thought for a long moment; then she said, "No."

STEVE put on Harvey's blue corduroy pants and light blue sweater and drove Harvey's Datsun to Roland Park. It was dark by the time he reached Berrington's house. He parked and sat for a moment. He had to get this right.

What mood is Harvey in? he asked himself. He's been summoned peremptorily by his father. I think he's in a bad mood.

He sighed. He got out of the car and went to the front door.

There were several keys on Harvey's key ring. Before Steve could find the right one, Berrington opened the door. "What are you standing there for?" he said irritably. "Get in here. Go in the den."

Steve stepped inside. *Where is the den?* He fought down a wave of panic. The house was a suburban ranch-style split-level, built in the '70s. To his left, through an arch, he could see a living room with formal furniture. Straight ahead was a passage with several doors off it, which he guessed led to bedrooms. On his right were two closed doors. One of them was probably the den—but which?

Steve picked a door at random.

He had chosen the wrong door. This was a bathroom.

Berrington looked at him with an irritated frown. Steve hesitated, then remembered he was supposed to be in a bad temper. "I can use this first, can't I?" he snapped. He went in.

It was a guest bathroom, with just a toilet and a sink. He leaned on the sink and looked in the mirror. "You have to be crazy," he said to his reflection.

He flushed the toilet, washed his hands, and went out.

He could hear male voices from farther inside the house. He opened the door next to the bathroom—this was the den. He stepped inside, closed the door, and took a swift look around. There was a desk, a wood file cabinet, lots of bookshelves, a TV. On the desk was a photograph of an attractive blond woman of about forty, wearing clothes about twenty years out of date, holding a baby. *Berrington's ex-wife? My "mother"?* He opened desk drawers, glancing inside. There was a bottle of Scotch in the bottom drawer, almost as if concealed.

As he closed the drawer, the door opened and Berrington came in, followed by two men. Steve recognized Senator Proust. He presumed the quiet black-haired man was "Uncle" Preston Barck.

Steve remembered to be bad-tempered. "You needn't have dragged me back here in such a hurry."

Berrington adopted a conciliatory tone. "We just finished supper," he said. "You want something?"

Steve's stomach was knotted with tension, but Harvey would surely have wanted supper, so he pretended to soften. He said, "Sure. I'll have something."

Berrington shouted, "Marianne!" After a moment the housekeeper appeared. "Bring Harvey some supper on a tray."

Steve watched her go, noting that she went through the living room on her way to the kitchen.

Proust said, "Well, my boy, what did you learn?"

Steve had invented a fictional plan of action. "You can relax—for the moment at least," Steve said. "Jeannie Ferrami intends to take legal action against Jones Falls University for wrongful dismissal. She will cite the existence of the clones during that proceeding. Until then she has no plans for publicity."

The three men looked relieved. Proust said, "A wrongful dismissal suit. That will take at least a year. We have plenty of time to do what we need to do."

Berrington said, "What about the Lisa Hoxton case?"

"Jeannie thinks I did it, but she has no proof."

Berrington nodded. "That's good, but you still need a lawyer. You know what we'll do. Stay here tonight—it's too late to drive back to Philadelphia. You'll come to the press conference with me in the morning, and afterward we'll go see our attorney."

Don't panic. Think! If I stayed here, I would know exactly what these three creeps are up to. Nothing much can happen while I'm asleep. I could sneak a call to Jeannie to let her know what's going on. "Okay," he said.

Barck said suspiciously, "It didn't occur to the girl to try and sabotage the takeover of Genetico?"

"She's smart, but she's not business-minded," Steve said.

Marianne came in with a tray: sliced chicken, a salad, bread, and a Budweiser. Steve smiled at her. "Thank you," he said.

She gave him a startled look, and Steve realized Harvey probably did not say thank you too much. He caught the eye of Preston Barck, who was frowning. *Careful! Don't spoil it now. All you have to do is get through the next hour or so until bedtime.*

He started to eat. Berrington went out to use the bathroom.

"I need a Scotch," Proust said.

Steve said, "Try the bottom drawer of the desk. That's where Dad usually keeps it."

Proust opened the drawer. "Well done, boy!" he said.

"I've known about that hiding place since I was twelve years old," Steve said. "That was when I started stealing it."

Proust roared with laughter. Steve stole a glance at Barck. The wary look had gone from his face, and he was smiling.

Mr. Oliver produced an enormous pistol he had kept from World War II. "Took it off a German prisoner," he said. He sat on Jeannie's couch, pointing the gun at Harvey on the floor.

Lisa was on the phone with George Dassault, who turned out to be an actor in a play off-Broadway.

"He'll come tomorrow!" Lisa said excitedly after she hung up. " 'I'll do anything for publicity,' he told me. I said I'd meet him at the airport."

"That's wonderful," Jeannie said.

"We'll have three clones. It will look incredible on TV."

"Now we have to get Harvey into the hotel." Jeannie looked at him still lying bound and gagged on the floor. "I have some ideas," she said. "Mr. Oliver, can you retie him so he can walk, but not very fast?"

"Sure." He began retying Harvey's bonds.

"I want to dress him up," Jeannie said, and went into her bedroom.

"You go ahead," Mr. Oliver said, standing back after getting the groggy Harvey to his feet. "I'll just stand by with my gun to keep him cooperative."

When Jeannie returned, she nervously wrapped a long sarong around Harvey's waist and draped a wraparound shawl over his shoulders, covering the bonds on his ankles and wrists. Next she tied a handkerchief across his mouth so the dishcloth could not fall out. Finally, she put on an old Nancy Reagan Halloween mask to hide the gag. "He's been to a costume party, and he's drunk," she said.

"That's pretty good," Mr. Oliver said.

The phone rang. It was Mish Delaware.

Jeannie had forgotten about her. It was hours since she had been desperate to contact her. "Hi," Jeannie said.

"You were right," the detective said. "Harvey Jones did it. The Philadelphia police went to his apartment. He wasn't there, but a neighbor let them in. They found the security hat and realized it was the one in the description. I'm ready to arrest him, but I don't know where he is. Do you?"

Jeannie looked at him, a six-foot-two Nancy Reagan. "No idea," she said. "But I can tell you where he'll be at noon tomorrow. Regency Room, Stouffer Hotel, at a press conference."

As soon as Steve had finished eating, he stood up and said, "I need to turn in." He wanted to be safe from discovery.

The party broke up. Proust swallowed the rest of his Scotch, and Berrington walked the two guests to their cars.

Steve saw an opportunity to call Jeannie. Thinking she would probably have gone to the hotel by now, he snatched up the phone and called information. Come on, come on! At last he got through and asked for the number of the hotel. Frantically he dialed. "I'd like to speak to Dr. Jean Ferrami," he said.

Berrington came back into the den just as Steve heard her voice. "Hello?"

"Hi, Linda. This is Harvey," he said. "I've decided to stay over at my dad's place; it's a little late for a long drive."

"For heaven's sake, Steve, are you okay?"

"Nothing I can't handle. How was your day, honey?"

"Mr. Oliver and I got Harvey into the hotel. George Dassault has promised to come, so we should have three."

"Good. I'm going to bed now. See you tomorrow, honey."

"Hey, good luck."

"You too. Good night."

Berrington winked. "Hot babe?"

"Warm," Steve said with a grin. "Good night, Dad."

Berrington put his arm around Steve's shoulders. "Good night, son," he said. "Don't worry. We'll come through all this."

He really loves his rotten son, Steve thought, and for a moment he felt irrationally guilty for deceiving a fond father.

Then he realized he did not know where his bedroom was.

He left the den and took a few steps along the passage. At the end of it were two doors on opposite sides—Harvey's room and the maid's, presumably. Steve had to make a choice. He glanced back. Berrington was watching him. "Night, Dad," he said.

"Good night."

Left or right? No way to tell. Pick one at random.

Steve opened the door on his right.

Football shirt on the back of a chair, Snoop Doggy Dog CD on the bed, *Playboy* on the desk. A boy's room. Thank goodness.

He stepped inside and closed the door behind him with his heel. He slumped against the door, weak with relief.

After a moment he undressed and got into bed. He turned out the light and lay awake listening. For a while he heard footsteps, doors closing and taps running. Then the place was quiet.

Monday

THROUGH the night Jeannie and Mr. Oliver had taken shifts, one guarding Harvey while the other lay down, but neither of them got much rest. Only Harvey slept.

In the morning they took turns in the bathroom. Jeannie dressed in the clothes she had brought with her—a white blouse and black skirt—so that she could be taken for a waitress.

They ordered breakfast from room service. Mr. Oliver signed the check at the door, saying, "My wife's undressed. I'll take the trolley from here." Harvey lay trussed up on the bed.

Jeannie waited anxiously for Steve to call. What had happened to him? He had spent the night at Berrington's house. Was he keeping up the pretense?

Lisa arrived at nine o'clock with a pile of copies of the press release, then left for the airport to meet George Dassault and any other clones who might show. None of the three had called.

Steve called at nine thirty. "I have to be quick," he said. "Berrington's in the bathroom. Everything's all right. I'm coming to the press conference with him."

"He doesn't suspect anything?"

"No—although I've had some tense moments. Gotta go."

"Steve?"

"Make it fast!"

"I love you." To heck with playing hard to get, she thought.

At ten Jeannie went on a scouting expedition to check out the Regency Room. A publicist was already there, assembling a backdrop with the Genetico logo for the benefit of the TV cameras. Jeannie took a swift look around, then returned to her room.

Lisa called from the airport. "Bad news," she said. "The New York flight is late."

"Oh, no!" Jeannie said. "Any sign of either Wayne or Hank?"

"No."

"How late is George's plane?"

"It's expected at eleven thirty."

"You might still get here."

"If I drive like the wind."

AT ELEVEN o'clock Berrington emerged from his bedroom, pulling on his suit coat. He was wearing a blue chalk stripe over a white shirt with French cuffs, old-fashioned but effective. Steve had showered and put on a shirt and tweed sport coat. It all fit perfectly, of course.

They got into the silver Lincoln, and Berrington drove fast, heading downtown. To Steve's relief he did not talk much on the journey. They parked the car in the hotel garage and went up in the elevator.

As they headed for the Regency Room, a smartly coiffed public relations woman intercepted them. She showed them into a small VIP room, where drinks were laid out.

There were six or seven people in the room already, including Proust and Barck. With Proust was a muscular man in a black suit who looked like a bodyguard. Berrington introduced Steve to Michael Madigan, head of Landsmann's North American operations.

Berrington nervously gulped a glass of white wine. Steve looked at the watch he had taken from Harvey's wrist. It was five to twelve.

Just a few more minutes, Steve thought. And then I'll have a martini.

The publicity woman clapped her hands for attention. She said, "Gentlemen, everyone but the platform party should take their seats in the conference room, please."

Berrington turned to Steve and said, "See you sooner, Montezuma." He looked expectant.

"Sure," Steve said.

Berrington grinned. "*Sure?* Give me the rest of it!"

Steve went cold. It seemed to be a catchphrase, like "See you later, alligator," but a private one. Obviously there was a reply, but it wasn't "In a while, crocodile." Steve cursed inwardly. He needed to keep up the pretense just a few more seconds!

Berrington frowned in puzzlement, staring at him. "You can't have forgotten it." Steve saw suspicion dawn in his eyes.

"Of course I haven't," Steve replied quickly—too quickly, for then he realized that he had committed himself.

Senator Proust was listening now. Berrington said, "So give me the rest of it." Steve saw him cut his eyes to Proust's bodyguard, and the man tensed visibly.

In desperation Steve said, "In an hour, Eisenhower."

There was a moment's silence. Then Berrington said, "That's a good one!" and laughed.

Steve relaxed. That must be the game: You had to make up a new response every time. To hide his relief, he turned away.

"Showtime, everybody," said the publicist.

"This way," Proust said to Steve. "You don't want to walk out onto the stage." He opened a door, and Steve stepped through.

He found himself in a bathroom. Turning, he said, "No, this—"

Proust's bodyguard was right behind him. Before Steve knew what was happening, the man had him in a painful half nelson. "Make a noise, and I'll break your arms," he said.

BERRINGTON stepped into the bathroom behind the bodyguard. Jim Proust followed him and closed the door. The bodyguard held the boy tightly.

Berrington's blood was boiling. "You young punk," he hissed. "Which one are you?"

Jim said, "Berry, what the hell is going on?"

"This isn't Harvey," he said. "This is one of the others, probably the Logan boy. He must have been impersonating Harvey since yesterday. Harvey himself must be locked away somewhere."

Jim paled. "That means that what he told us about Jeannie Ferrami's intentions was a blind!"

Berrington nodded grimly. "She's probably planning some kind of protest at the press conference."

"Not in front of all the cameras! We've got to stop her!"

"She might have checked into the hotel." Berrington snatched up the phone beside the toilet. "This is Professor Jones in the Regency Room," he said to an operator in his most authoritative voice. "We're waiting for Dr. Ferrami. What room is she in?"

"I'm sorry. We're not allowed to give out room numbers, sir." Then she added, "Would you like me to connect you?"

"Yes, sure." He heard the ringing tone. After a wait, it was answered by a man who sounded elderly. Improvising, Berrington said, "Your laundry is ready, Mr. Blenkinsop."

"I didn't give out no laundry."

"Oh, sorry, sir. What room are you in?" He held his breath.

"Eight twenty-one."

"I wanted eight twelve. My apologies." Berrington hung up. "They're in room eight twenty-one," he said excitedly.

Proust said, "The press conference is about to start."

"We may be too late." Berrington hesitated. He said to Jim, "You go onstage with Madigan and Preston. I'll do my best to find Harvey and stop Jeannie Ferrami."

"Okay."

Berrington looked at Steve. "I'd be happier if I could take your security man with me. But we can't let Steve loose."

The bodyguard said, "No problem, sir. I can cuff him to a pipe."

Berrington and Proust returned to the VIP room. Madigan looked curiously at them. "Something wrong, gentlemen?"

Proust said, "A minor security question, Mike. Berrington is going to handle it while we go ahead with our announcement."

Berrington said, "A woman I fired last week is in the hotel. She may pull some kind of stunt. I'm going to head her off."

That was enough for Madigan. "Okay, let's get on with it."

Madigan, Barck, and Proust went into the conference room. The bodyguard came out of the bathroom. He and Berrington hurried to the elevator.

They went to the eighth floor and ran to room 821. Berrington rapped on the door. A man's voice called, "Who is it?"

Berrington said, "Housekeeping. I need to check your bathroom."

"I'm busy right now. Come back in an hour."

Berrington looked at the bodyguard. "Kick in this door."

The man looked pleased. Then he kicked.

The frame cracked and splintered, but the door held. There was the sound of rapid footsteps from inside. He kicked it again, and it flew open. He rushed inside, and Berrington followed.

They were brought up short by the sight of an elderly black man pointing a huge antiquated pistol at them.

"Stick up your hands, or I'll shoot you both dead," the man said. "After the way you bust in here, ain't no jury in Baltimore going to convict me for killing you."

Berrington raised his hands.

Suddenly a figure catapulted off the bed. It was Harvey, with his wrists tied together and some kind of gag over his mouth. The old man swung the gun toward him. Berrington was terrified that his son was about to be shot. He cried out, "No!"

The old man moved a fraction of a second too late. Harvey's bound arms knocked the pistol out of his hands. The bodyguard snatched it up from the carpet and pointed it at the old man.

Berrington breathed again. The old man raised his arms in the air.

The bodyguard picked up the room phone. "Hotel security?" he said. "There's a guest here with a gun."

Berrington looked around. There was no sign of Jeannie.

JEANNIE emerged from the elevator carrying a tray of tea she had ordered from room service. Her heart was beating like a drum. Walking at a brisk, waitressy pace, she entered the Regency Room.

Two women with checklists sat behind tables. A hotel security guard stood near, chatting with them. Jeannie forced herself to smile at the guard as she headed for the inner door.

"Hey!" he said. "They have plenty of beverages in there."

"This is jasmine tea, a special request."

"Who for?"

She thought fast. "Senator Proust." She smiled again, opened the door, and walked into the conference room.

At the far end three men in suits were sitting behind a table on a dais. One of the men was making a formal speech. The audience consisted of about forty people with notebooks, miniature tape recorders, and handheld television cameras.

Jeannie walked to the front. Standing beside the dais was the publicist Jeannie had seen earlier assembling the backdrop. She looked curiously at Jeannie but did not stop her, assuming that someone had ordered something from room service.

The men on the dais had name cards in front of them. Jeannie recognized Senator Jim Proust on the right. On the left was Preston Barck. The man who was speaking was Michael Madigan.

She smiled and put down the tray in front of Madigan. He looked mildly surprised and stopped his speech. Jeannie turned to the audience. "I have a special announcement."

STEVE was sitting on the bathroom floor with his left hand cuffed to the washbasin pipe, feeling desperate. He had to warn Jeannie that Berrington had found them out.

The pipe was attached at its top end to the drain of the basin. It turned in an S curve, then disappeared into the wall. Contorting his body, Steve got his foot on the pipe, drew it back, and kicked. The entire fitting shuddered. He kicked again. The mortar around the pipe fell away, but the pipe was strong.

Frustrated, he grasped the pipe with both hands and shook it frenziedly. Once again everything trembled, but nothing broke.

He tapped the underside of the sink. It was made of some kind of artificial marble, quite strong. He looked at the place where the pipe connected with the drain. If he could break that seal, he might be able to pull the pipe out.

He drew back his foot and started kicking again.

JEANNIE said, "Twenty-three years ago Genetico carried out illegal and irresponsible experiments on eight American women. All the women were wives of army officers." She searched the audience for Steve. Where on earth was he?

The publicity woman said in a shaky voice, "This is a private function. Please leave immediately."

Jeannie ignored her. "The women went to Genetico's clinic in Philadelphia to have hormone treatment for subfertility." She let her anger show. "Without permission they were impregnated with embryos from total strangers."

There was a buzz of comment from the assembled journalists.

Jeannie raised her voice. "Preston Barck, supposedly a responsible scientist, was so obsessed with his pioneering work in cloning that he divided an embryo seven times and implanted identical embryos in eight unsuspecting women."

Jeannie spotted Mish Delaware sitting at the back, watching. But Berrington was not in the room. That was worrying.

On the platform Preston Barck stood up. "Ladies and gentlemen, I apologize. We were warned there might be a disturbance."

Jeannie plowed on. "The three perpetrators of this outrage— Preston Barck, Senator Jim Proust, and Professor Berrington Jones—have been prepared to go to any lengths to cover it up, as I know from bitter experience."

The publicist was speaking into a hotel phone. Jeannie heard her say, "Get security in here right away, please."

Jeannie had been carrying a sheaf of copies of the press release that she had written, and she began to pass them around. "Those eight alien embryos were born, and seven of them are alive today. You'll know them because they all look alike."

A glance at the platform showed Proust with a face like thunder and Preston Barck looking as if he wanted to die. About now Mr. Oliver was supposed to walk in with Harvey, Steve, and possibly George Dassault. But there was no sign of any of them.

Jeannie went on speaking. "I study twins, and the puzzle of twins who had different mothers was what first started me investigating this shameful story."

The door at the back of the room burst open. Jeannie looked up, hoping to see one of the clones. But it was Berrington who rushed in. Breathlessly he said, "Ladies and gentlemen, this lady is suffering from a nervous breakdown and has been dismissed from her job. She was a researcher on a project funded by Genetico and bears the company a grudge. Hotel security has arrested an accomplice of hers on another floor. Please bear with us while they escort this person from the building."

Jeannie was knocked for a loop. Something had gone terribly wrong. What had happened to Steve? And Mr. Oliver and Harvey?

A uniformed security guard strode into the room. In desperation Jeannie turned to Michael Madigan. He had a frosty look on his face. "Mr. Madigan," she said. "Don't you think you should check out this story before you sign any legal papers? Suppose I'm right.

Imagine how much money those eight women could sue you for!"

Madigan said mildly, "I'm not in the habit of making business decisions based on tip-offs from nutcases."

The journalists laughed, and Berrington began to look more confident. The security guard approached Jeannie. She said to the
audience, "I was hoping to show you two or three of the clones. But
they haven't showed up."

The reporters laughed again, and Jeannie realized she had become a joke. It was all over.

The guard took her firmly by the arm and pushed her toward the
door. She passed Berrington and saw him smile. She felt tears come
to her eyes, but she swallowed them and held her head high.

Behind her she heard the publicist say, "Mr. Madigan, if you
would care to resume your remarks."

As Jeannie and the guard reached the door, it opened and Lisa
came in. Jeannie gasped when she saw that right behind her was
one of the clones.

It must be George Dassault. He had come! But one was not
enough. If only Steve would show up, or Mr. Oliver with Harvey!

Then with blinding joy she saw a second clone walk in. It must
be Hank King. "Look!" she yelled. "Look here!"

As she spoke, a third clone walked in. The black hair told her it
was Wayne Stattner. "See!" she yelled. "They're identical!"

All the cameras swung away from the platform and pointed at the
newcomers. Lights flashed as photographers snapped photos.

"I told you," Jeannie said triumphantly. "Now ask them about
their parents. Their mothers have never met. Go on. Ask them!"

Several reporters leaped up and approached the three clones,
eager to question them. In the background she heard Berrington
raise his voice over the buzz of the reporters. "Ladies and gentlemen, your attention, please." He began by sounding angry but soon
became petulant. "We *would* like to continue with the press conference!" It was no good. The pack had scented a real story.

Out of the corner of her eye Jeannie saw Senator Proust slip quietly out of the room. She looked around. Where was Steve?

STEVE GAVE ONE MORE KICK, and the pipe sprang away from the washbasin in a shower of marble chips. Heaving on the pipe, he pulled it from the sink and slipped the handcuff through the gap. Freed, he got to his feet.

He put his left hand in his pocket to conceal the handcuff that dangled from his wrist; then he left the bathroom.

The VIP room was empty. He stepped out into the corridor and saw a door marked REGENCY ROOM. Farther along the corridor, waiting for the elevator, was one of his doubles.

Who was it? The man was rubbing his wrists, as if they were sore. He had a red mark across both cheeks that looked as if it might have been made by a tight gag. This was Harvey, who had spent the night tied up.

He looked up and caught Steve's eye. They stared at one another; it was like looking into a mirror. Steve tried to look beyond Harvey's appearance and see the cancer inside that made him evil. But all he saw was a man just like himself, who had walked down the same road and taken a different turn.

He tore his eyes away and went into the Regency Room.

It was pandemonium. Jeannie and Lisa were in the center of a crowd of cameramen. He saw one—no two—*three* clones with them. He pushed through to her. "Jeannie!" he said.

She looked up at him, her face blank.

"It's Steve!" he said.

Mish Delaware was beside her. Steve said to Mish, "If you're looking for Harvey, he's outside, waiting for the elevator."

Mish said to Jeannie, "Can you tell which one this is?"

"Sure." Jeannie looked at him. "I play a little tennis myself."

He grinned. "If you only play a *little* tennis, you're probably not in my league."

She threw her arms around him. He smiled and bent to her face, and they kissed.

The cameras swung around to them. A sea of flashguns glittered, and that was the picture on the front page of newspapers all over the world the following morning.

Next June

FOREST Lawns was like a genteel old-fashioned hotel. It had flowered wallpaper, and it smelled of potpourri, not disinfectant. The staff called Jeannie's mother "Mrs. Ferrami," not "Maria" or "dear." Mom had a little suite, with a small parlor for visitors.

"This is my husband, Mom," Jeannie said, and Steve gave his most charming smile and shook her hand.

"What a nice-looking boy," Mom said.

Jeannie said, "Daddy came to our wedding."

"How is your father?"

"He's good. He started his own security firm. It's doing well."

"I haven't seen him for twenty years."

"Yes, you have, Mom. He visits you. But you forget." Jeannie changed the subject. "You look well." Her mother was wearing a pretty cotton shirtwaist with a candy stripe. Her hair was permed, and her nails were manicured. "Do you like it here?"

Mom began to look worried. "How will we pay for it?"

"I have a new job, Mom. I can afford it."

"What job is that?"

"I'm director of genetics research for a big company called Landsmann." Michael Madigan had offered Jeannie the job after someone explained her search engine to him. The salary was three times what she had been making at Jones Falls. Even more exciting was the work, which was at the leading edge of genetics research.

"That's nice," Mom said. "Oh, before I forget. There was a picture of you in the newspaper. I saved it." She delved into her handbag and brought out a folded clipping.

Jeannie had seen it before, but she studied it as if it were new to her. It showed her at the congressional inquiry into the experiments at the Aventine Clinic. The inquiry had not yet produced its report, but there was not much doubt what it would say. The questioning of Jim Proust, televised nationwide, had been a public humiliation such as had never been seen before. Proust had blustered and shouted and lied, and with every word his guilt had become plainer. When it was over, he had resigned as a Senator.

Berrington Jones had been dismissed from Jones Falls University. Jeannie had heard he had moved to California, where he was living on a small allowance from his ex-wife.

Preston Barck had resigned as president of Genetico, which had been liquidated to pay compensation to the eight mothers of the clones. A small sum had been set aside to pay for counseling to help the clones deal with their troubled history.

And Harvey Jones was serving five years for arson and rape.

Mom said, "The paper says you had to *testify*. You weren't in any kind of trouble, were you?"

Jeannie exchanged a smile with Steve. "For a week back in September I was kind of in trouble, Mom. But it worked out all right in the end."

"That's good."

Jeannie stood up. "We have to go now. It's our honeymoon. We have a plane to catch."

"Where are you going?"

"A little resort in the Caribbean. People say it's the most beautiful place in the whole world."

Steve shook Mom's hand, and Jeannie kissed her good-bye.

"Have a good rest, honey," Mom said. "You deserve it."

Small Town Girl

LaVyrle Spencer

"One-way traffic crawlin' round
  the small-town square,
Eighteen years've passed since
  she's been there,
Been around the world, now
  she's coming back,
Wider-eyed and noting what
  this small town lacks.

Can't return.
Too much learned."

Chapter One

*T*HE black Nissan 300ZX with the smoked windows looked completely out of place in Wintergreen, Missouri, population 1713. Heads turned as it downshifted and growled its way around the town square behind Conn Hendrickson's lumbering Sinclair fuel oil truck and Miss Elsie Bullard's 1978 Buick sedan, whose speedometer hadn't seen fifty since she drove it off the showroom floor. On the open road Miss Elsie cruised at forty-five. In town she preferred a genteel fifteen.

The Z came up short behind her, its stereo booming through the closed windows. The brakes shrieked and its rear end vaulted, drawing attention to the Tennessee vanity plates.

MAC, it said.

And MAC said it all.

Four old men stood out in front of Wiley's Bakery with coffee on their breath, sucking toothpicks, following the car with their eyes.

"There she is."

"Showin' off some, too."

"Shoo-ey. 'At's some car she's herdin'."

"What's she doin' here anyways? She don't come back often."

"Her momma's havin' her other hip surgeried. Come back to help her out awhile's what I heard."

The traffic around the town square moved one way, and on this lazy Tuesday in April, Miss Elsie putt-putted around four sides of the square at the speed of a candle melting, searching for just the right place to park. The Z followed a scant yard off her bumper.

Inside her sports car Tess McPhail interrupted her singing and said aloud, "Move it, Miss Elsie!"

For the last five hours she'd been listening to her own voice on a rough cut off the upcoming album she'd been recording in Nashville for the past several weeks. Her producer, Jack Greaves, had handed the tape to her on her way out of the studio yesterday and said, "Give it a listen on your way up to Missouri, then call me and let me know what you think."

The tape continued playing as Tess impatiently tapped the leather steering wheel with a long persimmon fingernail. Miss Elsie finally reached the corner, turned left, and got out of Tess's way while Tess laid on the gas and burned her way up Sycamore, muttering, "Lord o' mercy, small towns."

This one hadn't changed since she'd left it eighteen years ago. Same tired storefronts, same old World War II veterans watching the traffic and waiting for the next parade, same aging houses along Sycamore. There was Mrs. Mabry's house. She had taught geometry and could never instill the tiniest flicker of interest in Tess, who had drifted her way through any class that wasn't related to music, insisting she wouldn't need it—not when she was going to be a big country-western singer after she graduated.

Tess reran the tape of "Tarnished Gold" one last time, listening with a critical ear. Overall, she liked it—liked it a lot—with the exception of one single harmony note that continued to bother her.

She passed Judy and Ed's house, on Thirteenth Street. The garage door was up, but Tess gave the place little more than a hard-edged glance. Sister Judy and her damned peremptory summons.

"Mama's got to have surgery on her other hip, and this time *you're* taking care of her," Judy had said.

What would Judy know about the demands of a major career? All she'd ever done was run a beauty shop. Why, she hadn't a glimmer of what it meant to be pulled away from your work midway through recording an album that a record label was planning to release on a date that had been set more than a year ago.

But Judy was jealous—always had been—and throwing her weight around was how she got even.

Then there was Tess's middle sister, Renee, whose daughter, Rachel, was getting married in a few weeks. It was understandable that Renee had plenty to do before the wedding, but couldn't they have scheduled it and the surgery a little further apart? After all, Mom had known she needed this second hip replacement ever since she'd had the first one, two years ago.

Tess turned onto Monroe Street, and memories rolled back while she traveled the six-block stretch she had walked to elementary school every day for seven years. She pulled up at the curb in front of her mother's house, killed the engine, and got out of the car—a size-seven woman in jeans, oversize sunglasses, cowboy boots, and dangly Indian earrings made of silver and turquoise, with hair the color of an Irish setter and fair, freckly skin.

Her heart sank as she studied the house. How could her mother have let it get so shabby? The post–World War II bungalow was made of red brick, but the white wood trim was peeling and the front steps were listing badly. The sidewalk was pitted, and dandelions spangled the yard.

What does Mom do with all the money I send her?

Tess reached into the car, shouldered an enormous gray soft leather bag, slammed the door, then headed for the house. As she approached, her mother appeared in the doorway, beaming. "I thought I heard a car door." She flung open the screen door and both of her arms. "Tess, honey, you're here!"

"Hey, Mama." Tess vaulted up the three steps and scooped her mother up hard. They rocked together while the door sprang shut and nudged them inside a tiny vestibule. Mary McPhail was half a head shorter and forty-five pounds heavier than her daughter, with a round face and metal-rimmed glasses. When Tess pulled back to see her, there were tears in Mary's eyes.

"You sure you should be up walkin' around, Mama?"

"Course I should. How else can I hug my daughter hello? Take them glasses off so's I can see what my little girl looks like."

Tess smiled and removed her sunglasses. "It's just me." She held her hands out at her sides.

"Just you. That's for sure—just you, who I haven't seen for nine whole months." Mary shook her finger under Tess's nose.

"I know. I'm sorry, Mama. It's been crazy, as usual."

"Your hair is different." Mary held her in place by both elbows, giving her the once-over. Tess's hair was cut in a shag that fell in disheveled layers well below the neck of her T-shirt in back, while in front it just covered her ears. "And land, girl, you're so skinny. Don't they feed you down there in Nashville?"

"I work at keeping thin, Mama, you know that, so please don't start pushing food on me already, okay?"

Mary turned away and hobbled into the house. "Well, I should think—making the kind of money you do—that you could eat a little better."

Tess resisted rolling her eyes and followed Mary inside. They went through a shallow living room with bumpy stucco walls and well-used furniture, dominated by an upright piano. There were three archways off the opposite wall—the center one led upstairs, the right one to the bathroom and Mary's bedroom, the left one to the kitchen, at the rear of the house. Mary stumped through the left one, still talking.

"I thought country singers wore big hair."

"That's old, Mama. Things're changing in country."

"But you flattened all them pretty, natural curls right out of it."

Her mother's own hair could use some styling, Tess thought, studying a pinwheel of exposed skull on the back of her head. More important, however, was the pained gait with which she moved, using whatever furniture or walls were available for support.

"Are you *sure* you should be walking, Mama?"

"They'll have me off my feet plenty after the operation's over. Long as I can hobble around, I'm going to."

She was a squat, squarish woman of seventy-four, wearing an old slacks set made of polyester knit that had begun to pill. Tess wondered about the stylish silk trouser outfit she'd had shipped from Nordstrom last fall when she'd been on tour in Seattle.

"The kitchen looks the same," she remarked while Mary turned on the water and began filling a coffeemaker.

"It's old, but I like it this way."

The kitchen had white metal cupboards with brown Formica tops that were so worn they looked white in places. The walls were papered in a ghastly orange floral, and the two windows hung with orange floral tiebacks. Beside the stove was a homemade pecan pie loaded with about three hundred calories per slice.

Tess's eyes moved no further. "Oh, Mama, you didn't."

Mary turned around and saw what Tess was ogling. "Course I did. I couldn't let my little girl come home and not find her favorites."

What was it about being called her little girl that touched a nerve in Tess? She was thirty-six. Her face and name were as familiar to most Americans as those of the President, and her income topped his many times over. But her mother insisted on referring to Tess as her little girl. The few times that Tess had corrected her, saying, "I'm not your little girl anymore," Mary looked baffled and hurt. So Tess let it pass this time.

"Are you making that coffee for me?" she asked.

"Can't have pecan pie without coffee."

"I really don't drink coffee much anymore, Mama, and I really shouldn't eat the pie either."

Mary glanced over her shoulder. Her exuberance faded, and she slowly shut off the water. She glanced down dubiously at the half-filled pot, then turned on the tap and resumed filling it. "I'll go ahead and cook some for myself, then."

"Do you have any fruit, Mom? I eat a lot of fruit now, and I could sure use a piece. I haven't eaten since breakfast."

"I've got some canned peaches." Mary opened a lower cupboard door and attempted to lean over stiffly.

"That'll be great, but I can get 'em. I came home to take care of you, not the other way around."

The peaches were packed in syrup, but Tess took a fork and began eating them straight from the can as she wandered around the kitchen. Mary opened the refrigerator and said, "I made your favorite hot dish—hamburger and Tater Tots. I could put it in the oven now, but"—she checked the wall clock—"it's only four o'clock, so maybe we ought to wait a while and—"

"The peaches are fine for now, Mama. I know you don't usually eat till six."

She watched the concern fade from Mary's face once she was reassured the danger of altering the supper hour had passed. Tater Tot hot dish had been Tess's favorite when she was twelve years old. These days beef was a once-a-week meat and deep-fried Tater Tots never passed her lips. Not when she had a collection of custom-made concert clothes in size seven that cost upward of a thousand dollars apiece. She took the can of peaches to the kitchen table and sat down. In the middle of the table a potted plant sat on the worst-looking plastic doily Tess had ever seen. It had been white once but was now as yellow and curled as an old fish scale.

Mary poured herself a cup of coffee and sat, too. She glanced at Tess's oversize white T-shirt, which was silk-screened with four faces and a logo.

"What's that, then, 'Southern Smoke'?" she asked.

Tess glanced down at her chest. "Oh, that's the name of a band. I've been sort of dating one of the guitar players. This one. See?" Tess spread the shirt and pointed to a bearded face.

Mary squinted. "What's his name?"

"Burt Sheer."

"Burt Sheer, huh? How long you been seein' him?"

"Oh, just a couple of months."

"Is it serious?"

"In this business?" Tess laughed. "It better not be. With his schedule on the road, plus me gone all over, singing a hundred and fifty concerts a year, I've seen him exactly four times."

"Oh."

Tess watched the gleam of hope fade from her mother's eyes. Mary would never accept the fact that her youngest daughter had chosen a career over marriage and children. To Mary McPhail that was tantamount to squandering your life.

"Mama, I really should call my record producer. It'll just take me a minute."

She called, using her credit card, from the wall phone at the end of the kitchen cabinets and reached Jack Greaves at the studio, where she knew he'd be working.

"Mac, good to hear from you," Jack said. "You at your mother's?"

"Yes, sir. Got here safe and sound. Hey, I listened to 'Tarnished Gold' all the way down, and the harmony on the word 'mistaken' still bothers me. I think it's got to be an E flat instead of an E. Can you get Carla back in there to record it again? . . . She still having trouble with her voice? . . . Well, ask her, will you? . . . Thanks, Jack. Then FedEx it to me as soon as you've got it, okay? I won't be here tomorrow—tomorrow's the surgery—but I'll call you from the hospital. . . . Sure. Thanks, Jack. Bye."

Her mother wore an astonished expression. "You'd record something again just because of a single word?"

"It's done all the time. Sometimes we record an entire harmony track and never use it at all."

Tess put away her peaches in the fridge and dropped her fork into the sink. Through the window above it she had a clear view of Mrs. Kronek's backyard. The block was bisected by an unpaved alley, and the two lots were laid out like mirror images, one on each side. Houses, sidewalks, and gardens matched as perfectly as spots on a butterfly's wings. The garages sat snugged up against the alley so tightly that their doors were perpendicular to it. While Tess was looking out, the garage door across the alley began to rise; then a car nosed up the alley and pulled into Mrs. Kronek's garage. A moment later a tall man in a business suit emerged, carrying a briefcase. He went up the sidewalk to Mrs. Kronek's back door.

"Who's that?" Tess asked.

Mary stood up and took a look. "Why, that's Kenny Kronek—you remember him."

"Kenny Kronek?" Tess watched him climb the steps and enter the glassed-in back porch. He was tall and lean and dark-haired, and he glanced over before the door slammed behind him. "You mean that dork who used to get the nosebleeds all the time?"

"Tess, shame on you. Kenny Kronek is a nice boy."

"Oh, Mama, that's what you always said because he was Lucille's boy and she was your best friend. But you know as well as I do that he was a dork of the highest magnitude. Why, he couldn't walk a chalk line without tripping on it. And all those pimples! I can still smell the acne medication on him."

"Kenny took care of his mother till her dying day, and not every nice person in this world is coordinated, Tess. Besides that, he's a real good father and he takes real good care of the property since Lucille died."

"You mean somebody actually *married* him?"

"Well, of course somebody married him. A girl he met in college—Stephanie. But they're divorced now."

"No wonder," Tess mumbled, turning away from the window.

"Tess," her mother scolded with a gentle glower.

"Well, he was always . . . looking at me. You know what I mean?" She faked a shudder. "He was such a creep."

"Oh, Tess, come on."

"Well, it's true. The only class we were ever in together was choir, and when we went to the choir festival in St. Louis, Kenny came over and sat with me on the bus, and I couldn't get rid of him. There he sat, blushing so hard I thought he was going to have a nosebleed right on the spot. And then he tries to hold my hand! I swear, all my friends teased me so bad I thought I'd die."

Mary picked up her coffee cup and carried it to the sink. Quietly she suggested, "Why don't you get your bags out of the car and park it back by the garage. It's probably better if you don't leave it on the street overnight, an expensive thing like that."

Tess knew when she was being chastised, and it put a knot in her chest. What was it about her mother's displeasure that weighed heavier than that of others?

She drove around the south end of the block and headed up the alley past sheds and garages where she used to play hide-and-seek and kick the can when she was little. The yards were green and old enough that their lot lines had become obscured by trees and bushes that had seeded themselves. But here in Wintergreen, just above the bootheel of Missouri, where neighbors truly were neighbors and had been for twenty and thirty years, nobody cared about lines of demarcation.

Mary's garage needed painting. Surprisingly, however, it had a new door. Nosing the car up to it and getting out, Tess glanced at the place across the alley. Everything painted, no junk anywhere. Good for Saint Kenny, she thought sarcastically, grabbing her duffel bag and heading for the house. On the way through the backyard she noticed that her mother had somehow managed to put in a garden, no matter how it must have hurt her hip to get down on her hands and knees to plant it.

The back stoop was three steps high, with a black iron handrail. Inside was a small landing, with the basement door straight ahead and the kitchen up a single step to the right. As Tess bumped through the kitchen with her bag, she said, "Hey, Mama, you shouldn't have put in that garden this year with your hip so bad."

Tess was in the living room rounding the center arch toward the stairs when Mary called back, "Oh, I didn't put it in. Kenny did it for me. And did you see my new garage door? He installed that for me, too."

The nerd installed the garage door, too? What was he after?

The upper story of the house was laid out shotgun style, its ceiling shaped like the roofline, with a window at either end. The girls had called it the barracks when they were growing up, sleeping in a row on three single beds. The stairs emerged onto one end of the expanse, with a sturdy homemade railing. Straight ahead, at the top of the steps, was a window giving a bird's-eye view of Saint Kenny's yard. Tess whisked past it, executed a U-turn around the handrail, and dropped her duffel on the farthest bed. They had earned their distance from the stairs by birth order: closest to the stairs and the downstairs bathroom was the oldest, Judy; middle bed was Renee's; and way over at the farthest end was Tess's, because she was the baby. She had always hated being referred to as the baby and felt a ripple of smug satisfaction at being the one who went off and did the best.

She stood looking around, then wandered to the dressing table, where she had first written in her diary that she wanted to be a singer, where she had learned to put on makeup, and had sat staring out at the street with puckered mouth when she'd been sent to her room as punishment. For what? Times when she'd needed it, she supposed.

Down below, her mother was calling, "Tess? Should I put the hot dish in now?"

Tess called, "I'll do it, Mama. Just let me hang up some clothes first, okay?"

"Well . . . okay," Mary replied with doubt, then added, "but it's ten after five already, and it really should bake for a full hour."

Tess couldn't help shaking her head. The normal schedule of a professional musician meant rising near noon, doing studio work from about two till nine, with a caterer bringing food in around eight. On concert nights it meant performing between eight and eleven and eating supper around midnight.

But Tess dutifully hollered down, "I'll be right there."

Her mother had already put the hot dish in the oven, but she let Tess set the table. Mary's suggested accompaniments to the fat-filled Tater Tot hot dish were coffee, with cream and sugar, of course, and pecan pie with whipped cream—the real kind.

But when the main dish was hot and bubbling, it looked so tempting Tess dug into it like a soldier after a foot march. Mary smiled in satisfaction, watching her. Tess was eating a bite of pie when someone tapped on the back door and opened it without waiting for an answer.

"Mary?" he said, and stepped into the tiny back entry, no longer wearing a business suit but a red windbreaker, and hefting a forty-pound sack of pellet salt on his left shoulder.

"Oh, Kenny, it's you," Mary said, going joyful in an instant.

"I brought your softener salt," he said, opening the basement door. "I'll take it right down."

"Oh, thanks a million, Kenny."

His footsteps thumped down. There was a pause while he slit open the bag; then the salt rattled into the plastic softener vat and he came back up. When he closed the basement door and stepped into the kitchen, Tess fixed her eyes on her plate. She needn't have worried, for he gave her not so much as a glance. He stopped beside Mary's chair, looking directly down on her. "There. All filled. Anything else you need while I'm here?"

"I don't think so. Kenny, you remember Tess, don't you?"

He gave Tess a nod. It was brusque enough to be rude, and accompanied by not so much as a single word of greeting.

While Tess went on eating her pie, he said to Mary, "So, you've got that walker all polished up for tomorrow?"

"Yes, sir, I'm all set."

"Scared?" he inquired with an easy casualness.

"Not much. Been through it before, so I know what to expect."

"So you don't need anything?"

"No. Tess is taking me to the hospital in the morning. That is, if I can get in that little car of hers. I don't know what it's called, but it cost more than this house. Did you see it, Kenny?"

What could Kenny do but answer? "Yeah, Mary, I sure did."

When he turned to level his impersonal gaze on Tess, what could she do but acknowledge him? "Hello, Kenny," she said colorlessly.

"Tess," he said so coolly she wished he hadn't spoken at all. The pimples were gone. He wasn't a bad-looking man—brown-eyed, dark-haired. But so cold to Tess. After their requisite hello Tess escaped from the table, ostensibly to get the coffeepot but actually to hide her mortification at being ignored. Tess McPhail, whose appearance on a stage made fans scream and chant. Tess McPhail, snubbed by that nerd Kenny Kronek.

"I'll be thinking of you in the morning," he said quietly to Mary, "and I'll be up to see you as soon as you're feeling up to it. Casey says to tell you hi and good luck. Now, you be good, and no dancing till the doctor tells you to, okay?"

Mary laughed. "Oh, my dancing days aren't over yet, Kenny."

He laughed, too. "Good luck, Mary," he said quietly. The kitchen was small. He turned to leave and found Tess in his way, the coffeepot clutched in her right hand. "Excuse me," he said, and moved around her as if she were a stranger on an elevator.

Chapter Two

♪ ♥ ♪ ♥ ♪

TESS McPhail was unaccustomed to being treated like a tree stump. The moment Kenny left, she slammed the coffeepot on the burner, spun to the table, and began throwing dishes into stacks. "Well!" she exploded, marching to the sink and whacking the dishes down. "When did *he* become the man of the house?"

"Now, Tess, don't be ungrateful. There are lots of times when one of the kids can't get over here to help me, and Kenny is more than willing. I don't know what I'd do without him."

"I could see that."

"Why, Tess, what are you so upset about?"

"I'm not upset. But he comes right in here like he owns the place. And who's Casey?"

"His daughter, and stop throwing my dishes around. They've been here since your dad was alive, so please take some care."

"I suppose she walks in here without knocking, too."

"What are you getting all worked up about? He's my neighbor. I knew his mother for forty years." Then the truth hit Mary. "Tess, I think you're upset because he didn't pay any attention to you."

"Oh, Mother, really. Give me a little credit."

"I give you all the credit in the world when you deserve it, but not when you criticize Kenny."

"He was rude."

"Can you blame him? You just got done telling me how awful you used to treat him."

Tess made no reply. She turned on the tap, filled the sink with soapy water, and began washing the dishes, a job she abhorred.

"All right. But the man is a complete boor."

Her mother found a dish towel hanging inside a cupboard door and picked up a wet plate. "I don't want to argue with you, Tess. You never thought much of Kenny; I don't expect that to change now. But he *has* been good to me."

Tess took the towel and plate out of her mother's hands. "I'll do the dishes. You go do whatever you want to—lie down and rest, read, get your things ready for tomorrow."

Mary glanced toward the living room. "Well, the nurse gave me some special soap to take a bath with tonight."

"Go ahead, take your bath while I clean up the kitchen."

When Mary was gone, Tess gripped both ends of the dish towel and snapped it into a straight line. Four weeks, she thought. I'll be crazy before two. A moment later the tub could be heard running in the bathroom. Tess continued cleaning up the kitchen, trying to ignore the house across the alley. She had dim memories of playing in it with Kenny when they were both toddlers. More clearly she remembered balking at going there to play when they were older. She was nearly finished washing dishes when the front door opened and a familiar female voice called, "Tess, you here?"

Renee. Tess's heart gladdened. She waited for Renee to appear in the kitchen doorway, and momentarily she did—a tall, dark-haired woman with a face like a Walt Disney drawing of a princess.

"You are here!" Renee rejoiced, opening her arms.

"Hi, you creep."

Renee laughed, got Tess in a hug, and rocked her like a bowling pin. "What do you mean?"

"You know what I mean, ordering me to come home and take care of Mama. I'm so mad at you I could choke you."

Renee found it amusing. "Well, if that's what it took to get you home, I guess we did the right thing."

"You probably got me in a heap of trouble, you know that?"

"Oh, come on," Renee disparaged.

"I've got a record contract, and I'm supposed to be in a studio recording right now. Do you know that I had to cancel seven appearances because of this?"

"And what do you think we had to cancel the last time Mama had surgery?"

They were no longer hugging, but leaning back, taking each other's measure.

"But it's easier for you," Tess reasoned. "You live here."

"Try that argument on Judy and see how far it gets you."

"Ha! I won't have too much to say to Judy after the way she talked to me."

"She's disgusted with you, too. Has been for the last ten years because you never come home."

"What do you mean I never come home? I come home."

"Sure. Once a year or so when your schedule permits. Honey pie, families deserve more than that."

"But you don't understand."

Renee said simply, "It's your turn, Tess, and you know it."

They were at a stalemate. Tess returned to the sink, pulled the plug, and let the water drain, then turned and gestured toward the bathroom, whispering, "She's gonna drive me nuts."

Renee, too, kept her voice lowered. "It's only for four weeks; then I can help her once the wedding's over."

"But I don't live like this anymore, eating Tater Tot hot dish and pecan pie, for heaven's sake."

"For the next four weeks you do." Renee looked straight into Tess's amber eyes. "She's your mother. She loves you. It's how she shows it. And how in the world would she know what you eat anymore? You're never around."

Apparently, this was going to be a repeated refrain during Tess's time back home. She had difficulty stifling a retort, for her family hadn't the vaguest idea of the immensity of the commitments she made and how many people were affected by them.

"Is she in bed already?" Renee asked.

"No. She's taking a bath."

"Well, I'll go tap on the door and say hi and good-bye. I gotta get home. Just wanted to stop by and see if you got here okay."

Renee went through the living room into a small hall alcove, where she tapped on the bathroom door with her car key.

"Mama? Hi, it's Renee, but I can't stay. Gotta get home and feed my family, but Judy and I'll be there in the morning before they wheel you in, okay?"

"Okay, dear. Thanks for stopping by."

"Anything you need?"

"Nothing I can think of. But if there is, Tess can get it for me."

"Okay, then, see you in the morning."

When Renee came back through the living room, Tess was there with her hands in the pockets of her jeans. Renee pecked her on the cheek. "See you in the morning, bright and early. She tell you she's got to be there by six? Her surgery's at six thirty."

"Don't worry, she'll be there."

"Okay, just asking."

Tess followed her sister and stood in the front vestibule watching her drive off in a blue van. Evening had fallen, and the street was quiet. Tess stood feeling disgruntled and misplaced, wishing she were in the studio in Nashville, where she belonged.

Her mother came out of the bathroom dressed in a flowered cotton nightie. The way she was moving, Tess could tell she was in pain.

"Mom, what can I do for you?"

"Get me a bed pillow, and I'll stretch out on the sofa; then sit down and let's talk."

It took some time to get Mary reasonably comfortable on the sofa. When she was, she said, "Now tell me about the places you've been lately."

Tess began giving highlights of the last couple months, but after only a few minutes Mary's eyes grew heavy. Tess finally said, "Mama, you're tired. Let me help you to bed."

Mary murmured, "Mmm . . . guess you're right, honey."

Her mother's bedroom had changed no more than the rest of the house. The furniture was the same, and the carpet hadn't been replaced in all the years Tess could remember. On the chest of drawers her parents' wedding picture shared the space with the same wooden key-and-change holder that had held flotsam from the pockets of the daddy she barely remembered. He had died in an accident while driving a U.S. mail truck when she was six. The three girls' portraits on the wall were the same ones that had been taken when they were all in elementary school.

What's wrong with me, Tess thought, that so little of this evokes nostalgia? Instead, it raised a mild revulsion for the stifling change-lessness of her mother's life. How could she have lived all these years without replacing the carpet, let alone the man? But she'd always said, "One man was enough for me. He was the only one I ever wanted."

With a heavy sadness in her heart for all that her mother had missed, Tess bent to draw up the covers when Mary lay down.

"Mom, how come you never married again after Daddy died?"

"I didn't want to. I had you girls, then the grandchildren. I know it's hard for you to understand, but I was happy. I am happy."

Mary reached up and took Tess's face in both hands. "I know you came home against your will, dear. I'm sorry that Judy and Renee made you."

"No, Mom, I didn't, honest."

"Sure you did. But you know what I think? I think that the life you lead is wearing you out. That's why I let the girls force you into coming home, 'cause I think you needed it worse than I did. Now, you make sure you get plenty of sleep yourself. We have to get up by four thirty to be there by six, and that comes awful early. Now give me a kiss and turn out the lamp."

After settling her mother for the night, Tess felt a pang of disillusionment. I'm not ready for this reversal of roles, she thought, as if I've become the mother and she's become the child. She wandered restlessly around the living room, glancing at the piano, compressing one key soundlessly, wishing she could sit down and play. But Mary needed sleep, and the piano would keep her awake. Tess missed work already, missed the vital pulse of nonstop activity that marked her days.

She went to stare out the window over the kitchen sink at the house across the alley. It was all lit up, upstairs and down. Another car was parked on the apron, and she wondered whose it was. What did she care? The way the houses were situated, she'd be spending the next four weeks watching all the comings and goings over there, but what Kenny Kronek did with his time was of absolutely no interest to her.

Irritated, she headed upstairs to get her pajamas, then went back down to take a bath. In the bathroom the water pipes seemed to sing like a boiling teakettle, so she ran them at a dribble to keep from waking Mary while the tub filled.

Once in the water she lay back, closed her eyes, and thought about the album in progress. She had eight solid songs on tape, but ten were requisite. Two more songs for this album. Finding good material—that was the key to success in this business. Tess planned to spend some time at the piano writing while she was here. It was the perfect time, when her duties caring for Mary would leave her ample time to compose. Maybe she'd write about coming back home and what it was like.

An opening line came into her head, and she hummed it.

One-way traffic crawlin' round a small-town square.

She hummed the melody four times, then sang the words softly. It entered the world in four-four time, in major chords, as an upbeat ballad.

She thought of a second line.

Eighteen years've passed since she's been there.

And a third.

Been around the world, now she's coming back.

Tess opened her eyes and sat up to soap her washcloth, humming the verse and trying to come up with a last line. None pleased her, but by the time she dried and powdered and put on her silk pajamas, she had the first three lines pegged and was impatient to get upstairs and write them down.

She sat at her old dressing table and got the words on paper, wishing she could go down to the piano and pick out the chords she heard in her head. Unlike most country singers, she had never played guitar. Piano was the instrument on which all three McPhail girls had been given lessons. But often Tess envied the band members who could pick up their instruments on a bus or in a motel room and play, sing, or compose wherever they were.

At eleven o'clock she crawled into her old bed and turned out the light. At midnight she was still awake, energized by the song, kept awake further by the mattress that was far from comfortable. The last time she looked at her clock it was one thirty-eight.

TESS awakened with a start when her mother called up the stairs, "Tess? Time to get up, dear. It's five after five already."

"Okay, I'm awake," she croaked, and sat up unsteadily. "Hey, Mama?" she called, shuffling to the railing. "Where we going again?"

"To Poplar Bluff." Wintergreen was too small to have a hospital of its own. "Thirty minutes' drive, same as always."

With little time for morning ablutions Tess managed with only a quick splash and a smear of lipstick before dragging on jeans, cowboy boots, and a white sweatshirt with the word BOSS plastered across the front in huge black letters. She spared time to hook on her earrings—she felt naked without earrings, but her hair was hopeless. In the end, she rubber-banded it and pulled the tail through the hole of a bill cap. Boy, did she look bad. But surgery schedules wouldn't wait, and her mother was hovering outside the bathroom door with her purse handle over her wrist.

Tess told her, "I'll take your suitcase out and put it in the car; then I'll come back to help you down the back steps. Now, you wait for me, okay?"

She returned to the house to find Mary in the kitchen with her hand on the light switch, surveying the room as if afraid she might never see it again. A single word uttered last night by Kenny Kronek came back to Tess. "Scared?" he'd asked. At the time Tess had so much resented his presence that she'd disregarded the conversation. Now, watching Mary's hesitation, Tess realized she hadn't bothered wondering if her mother was scared to face this second surgery. It appeared she was.

"Come on, Mama," she urged gently. "We'd better go. I'll take care of everything, don't worry."

They left the house with the sun bending their long shadows against the back steps. Watching her mother painfully negotiating the three steps, Tess felt pity and the greatest wave of love since she'd arrived home. She took her mother's arm and helped her along the narrow back sidewalk toward the alley.

As they passed the newly planted garden, Mary said, "You'll water the garden, won't you, Tess?"

"Sure I will."

"If you don't know where anything is, just ask Kenny. The yard's going to need mowing before I get back, but maybe you can get Judy's boy to do it. Otherwise, sometimes if Kenny sees it needs doing, he just comes over and does it without asking."

For Pete's sake! Fat chance she'd ask that man anything.

They reached the Nissan ZX, and Tess opened the passenger door, but it was apparent from Mary's first effort that getting into the car was going to be too painful for her. The seat was low-slung and would require her to bend too far.

"Mom"—Tess glanced at the closed garage door—"can you wait while I get your car out? I think we'd better take it instead."

"I think so, too."

Tess ran back to the house and got the keys, but before getting Mary's car out of the garage, she had to move her own. She maneuvered it backward into the alley, left the engine running, and got out.

Mary said, "Use the activator on my key chain. I've got a new automatic garage-door opener."

"You do? Wow. Way to go, Mom."

"Kenny installed it for me."

Tess's exuberance soured. Saint Kenny again.

The new garage door rolled up smoothly, and Tess backed out her mother's sensible five-year-old Ford Tempo, got out to transfer Mary's suitcase, and found her mother smiling at Kenny himself, who'd come walking over from across the alley. He was dressed in gray sweats and moccasins and hadn't shaved yet. He didn't seem to care. Tess stood beside her mother's car, ignored.

"Morning, Mary," Kenny said pleasantly. "Saw you out here, so I came to see you off. Got everything?"

"My suitcase is still in Tess's car. We were going to take hers, but mine is roomier."

"Want me to get it?"

"Well, sure, if you don't mind. She's trying to shuffle both of these cars here."

He went to the Z, opened the passenger door, and extracted the suitcase from the cramped space behind the seats. He took it to Mary's car, opened the back door, and shoved it inside, then opened the front door for Mary and helped her get in.

"Careful, now," he said while she gingerly fitted herself inside.

He slammed the door and, for the first time that morning, looked over the roof of the car at Tess, his expression deliberately flat. She waited to see if he'd greet her in any way at all, but he did not, only let his eyes drop to the word BOSS on her chest. Finally he stepped back and waited for her to get in and back the car up.

Tess threw herself into the driver's seat and slammed the door so hard her eardrums popped. Flinging an arm along the top of the seat, she shot backward only to discover that she had not backed her own car far enough out of the way. Exasperated, she rammed the Ford into park and threw her door open.

"I'll get it," he said, and headed for the Z.

"Don't bother," she shouted.

He ignored her and got into the forty-thousand-dollar black bullet—every man's dream car—leaving her sputtering with anger.

The Z moved backward and waited. All she could do was pull ahead to make room for him.

Mary said innocently, "That Kenny is so thoughtful."

Tess rolled down her window and waited, seething, while he veered her car into the slot before the garage and got out. He sauntered over, dropped the keys into her outstretched hand, and said, "Nice car."

She retracted her arm like a sprung window shade and took off up the alley. She made a left turn onto Peach Street, and her mother said, "You shouldn't be so rude to Kenny, Tess."

"He was rude to me. And nobody touches my car. Nobody!"

"Why, Tess, he was just being helpful."

"He didn't even ask me. He just . . . just got in as if it were somebody's old junker. Nobody but me has ever driven that car. I don't even let valets park it." Tess realized she was yelling, but she was unable to stop herself.

After a perplexed pause Mary mumbled, "Well, I just . . ." Her voice trailed off as she turned her face to the side window.

I shouldn't have yelled at her, Tess thought, especially not today. But apologies had never come easy to Tess, and this one stayed locked in her mind. "Aw, just forget it, Mom, okay?"

They drove on for a while. Outside, the sun sat smack in the middle of Highway 160, forcing Tess to slip on her sunglasses. Things here looked the same as always. This was a poor county—Ripley. Seemed as if half the residents of Ripley County lived in trailer houses. But the land was pretty—red clay earth, green grass, dogwoods, rolling Ozark foothills, and horse farms. They passed fields where biscuit-colored cows grazed, and a farm where goats stood on the tin roof of their shelter. Farther along they rumbled over the Little Black River, which ran full and brilliant as it was struck by the morning sun.

While they rode, Tess let the beautiful morning do what her absent apology should have done—take the edge off the tension in the car.

When she pulled up beneath the porte cochere of Doctors Hospital, Tess got out of the car. "Stay here, Mom. I'll get a wheelchair."

She headed into the brown brick building. A stocky brown-haired woman looked up from behind the reception desk in the hospital. Her name tag said MARLA.

"Good morning. I need a wheelchair for my mother. She's having surgery today."

The woman gaped. "You're—you're Tess McPhail, aren't you?"

"Yes, I am."

"Oh, my gosh. I love your music!"

"Thanks. Any chance of getting a wheelchair?"

"Oh, of course."

Marla nearly broke her legs hurtling around the desk. As Tess strode toward the entrance, Marla followed with the chair, her adulating eyes wide.

Marla and Tess accompanied her mother inside and saw her through the necessary paperwork. When registration was complete, Marla passed a paper over the counter and said, "Could I have your autograph, Mac? It's okay if I call you Mac, isn't it?"

Tess quickly signed, flashed a generic smile, and reminded her, "Mother's surgery is set for six thirty. Shouldn't we get going?"

In the surgery wing Mary was taken away to get prepped. Tess, meanwhile, was directed to a family lounge. The room was empty when she walked in. On a wall bracket a television with its sound turned off flickered through some morning newscast. A small sink shared a wall alcove with an electric coffeemaker. Tess dropped her big gray bag on a chair and headed straight for it.

The coffee was steaming and fragrant. She filled a Styrofoam cup and lifted it to her lips. Turning, she encountered her sister Judy in the doorway.

The cup lowered slowly while the two sisters stared at each other, and Tess remained where she was.

Judy offered no spontaneous exuberance, as Renee had. Instead, she let her purse strap slip from her shoulder and said, "I see you got her here on time."

"Well, that's a nice greeting."

"Too early in the morning for nice greetings." Judy went to the coffeemaker and filled a Styrofoam cup for herself. Watching her, Tess thought, She's gained weight again. She was shaped like a hogshead and covered her mammoth curves with oversize tops. She owned a beauty shop, so her hair was always dyed and styled, but the truth was, Judy was a very unattractive woman. Smiling, her eyes seemed to get lost above her cheeks; unsmiling, she looked jowly. Her mouth was too small to be pretty. For years Tess had held the conviction that the reason she and Judy didn't get along was because Judy was jealous.

As the older sister turned with a cup of coffee in her hand, the contrast between the two women pointed out this likelihood. Even as thrown together as Tess was this morning, she was cute and thin in her skinny jeans. With nothing but lipstick for makeup, her features broadcast the photogenic quality that had put her on the covers of dozens of magazines—milky skin with a hint of freckles, almond eyes with auburn lashes, and pretty lips.

Judy said, "The truth is, I really didn't think you'd come."

"The truth is, I didn't like how I was asked."

"I suppose nobody you work with gives you orders."

"You don't know the first thing about the people I work with or how we operate. You just make assumptions."

"That's right. And I assumed you'd do like you've been doing since you left Wintergreen, which is to leave every bit of Mother's care up to Renee and me."

"You could have asked, Judy."

"And what would you have said? That you had to go on tour in Texas or whatever else is so almighty important that everything in the world should revolve around your schedule?"

"Judy, could we just . . ." Tess raised both hands as if pushing open a heavy plate-glass door. "Could we just shelve this and try to get along while I'm here? And the next time you need something from me, don't call and issue an imperial order. Just try asking. I'm all grown-up now, and I don't take orders from you, okay?"

"Well, you did this time, didn't you, Mac?"

Nobody in the family called her Mac. To them she had remained Tess, while Mac had become her professional nickname. It was the one her fans had coined, the one that was printed on the shirts she sold at concerts, the one the nation recognized as they recognized only a select group of other entertainers who'd gone by single names: Elvis, Sting, Prince—Mac.

The word was still reverberating in the room when Renee showed up in the doorway. "Hey, you two, here you are! They want us down the hall before they take Mama in. Come on."

Tess got up and took off like a shot.

"What's wrong with her?" Renee asked Judy.

"Same as always. Thinks she's too good for the rest of us."

"Judy, do you have to be at her all the time? She just got here, for heaven's sake."

In the hall Mary was lying on a gurney. By turns her children kissed her. Then they watched the gurney roll away and stood motionless, three sisters in the middle of a hospital corridor experiencing some tempering of the discord among them as their concern was funneled toward the mother they all loved. She was the source of so many of their mutual childhood memories, the provider of sustenance and love that had been ever present in their lives. And for those few seconds while they stood watching her being rolled away into the care of strangers, the trio bonded.

The doors swung shut behind the gurney, and the squishy-soled white shoes and blue scrubs disappeared. Renee sighed and turned to the others. "What do you say to a hot cup of coffee in the cafeteria?" Taking their elbows, she forced them to walk with her. "Come on, now, you two, stop your squabbling."

Throughout the entire time in the cafeteria Judy said nothing. Her silent antipathy was a felt thing that colored the feelings among the three sisters as they ate their breakfast.

Renee ordered oatmeal.

Tess ate half a grapefruit and a dry toasted muffin.

Judy had two doughnuts and a cup of hot chocolate.

Chapter Three

*T*ESS found it difficult to stay awake when they finally returned to the family lounge. She was on the davenport nodding off when a male voice said, "Ladies? I'm Dr. Palmer."

She stretched to her feet as he entered the lounge, wearing blue scrubs, and shook hands all around.

"Our local star," he said, releasing Tess's hand. "It's nice to meet you." To all of them he said, "Your mother's doing fine. The surgery went very well, and we didn't find anything unusual. I understand one of you will be taking care of her for a while."

"Yes, me," Tess said.

"We'll want to get her standing tomorrow and walking the day after. It's best to start using the hip right away. She'll be getting physical therapy here, and you'll be helping her with therapy at home. The therapist will give you some instructions."

"When can she go home?"

"She'll be discharged in five or six days, depending on how well she's progressing."

"When can we see her?"

"They're just taking her up to her room. Give her time to get settled—ten minutes or so—then you can go right up."

When the girls went in to visit Mary, they found her dozing with the head of her bed propped up. She opened her eyes and smiled wanly. Renee went to the bedside. "It's all done now. The doctor said it went just fine."

Mary nodded weakly. She had oxygen prongs in her nose, an IV drip in her hand, and a catheter trailing from under the sheets. "So tired," she murmured, and her eyes drifted closed.

A nurse came in, smiled, and began taking her pulse. After writing it on a chart, she said, "She's going to sleep for a while. We can call you when she wakes up if you'd rather wait in the lounge."

So they returned to the lounge to sip more coffee and pass the hours taking turns checking on their mother. They were still in the lounge late that afternoon when a teenage girl stuck her head around the doorway.

"Hi, everyone. How's it goin'?"

Judy looked up from her magazine. "Oh, hi, Casey."

Renee said, "Well, Casey, what are you doing here?"

"I was out riding my horse near here. How's Mary doin'?" She was cuter than a bug's ear, with a loose blond French braid, a messy straw cowboy hat, a faded shirt, and blue jeans with enormous holes in the knees. When she advanced into the room, the smell of horses came with her.

"Pretty well, actually. The surgery went perfectly, and she's been resting a lot," Renee said.

"Well, hey, sounds good!" She extended her hand to Tess. "I don't believe we've ever met. I'm Casey Kronek. I live across the alley from your mom."

"Hello, Casey. I'm Tess."

"I know. Heck, everybody knows. I told my dad soon as I found out you were coming home, 'Hey, I gotta meet her.' Your mom's one fine old babe. She's always been like a grandma to me." Abruptly she turned to Judy. "So, is Tricia going to college next fall?"

"She's been accepted at Southeast Missouri. How about you?"

"Oh, gosh, no." Casey held up both palms. "No college for me, thank you. I haven't got the brains for that. Raising horses is more my style."

Renee asked, "You still singing with that little band?"

"Nope. We broke up. Couldn't find anyplace to get a gig around here, plus Dad said it was keeping me up too late at night and even if I didn't want to go to college in September, I had to finish high school. He said the band was getting in the way."

Renee turned to Tess. "Casey's just like you, Tess. Singing all the time."

"Shh," Casey scolded. "She'll think I'm coming around here looking for her to help me get a break or something. I really just came to check on Mary. And to bring her this." She handed something to Renee. "It's a four-leaf clover. Found it out in the pasture. Give it to her and tell her Casey sends her love, okay?"

"Sure will, Casey. She'll appreciate it, I know."

"Well . . ." Casey stood a minute longer, then abruptly stuck out her hand to Tess. "Sure was nice to meet you, Miss McPhail . . . ah, Tess . . . Mac. I don't know what to call you."

"Around here everybody uses Tess. Out there"—Tess gestured at the rest of the world—"it's Mac. Take your pick."

"Mac, then." Casey smiled and released Tess's hand, stepping back. "There is one thing I'd like to ask you if I could. Since we go to the Methodist church where your mom goes—well, my dad directs the choir there—do you think you could come and sing with us one Sunday? It'd really be awesome. Tess McPhail and the Wintergreen First Methodist Church choir! We'd really have a packed house that day."

The idea of standing in the choir loft and being directed by Kenny Kronek was about as appealing as chewing glass.

"Let me think about it, okay?"

"Sure." Casey beamed straight at Tess. "Well, I better go. Nice to meetcha."

"Same here."

When she was gone, Tess remarked wryly, "Saint Kenny directs the church choir? Since when does he qualify?"

"He doesn't," Renee answered. "But when Mrs. Atherton got sick, there was nobody to take over, and Casey talked him into it. That was about six months ago, and nobody else has volunteered yet, so he's still directing."

Judy spoke up. "*Saint* Kenny?"

"Well, isn't he? Mother seems to have canonized him."

"He's very good to her."

"Very good to her! He might as well move right in. He plants her garden, fills her water softener, installs her new garage door. I'm surprised he didn't show up to do her hip-replacement surgery this morning. I mean, what is going on?"

Judy and Renee exchanged baffled glances.

"Maybe you'd better tell *us* what's going on," Renee responded. "The guy helps Mom. What's wrong with that?"

Tess stood caught in an unjustified bout of temper. How could she reveal that Kenny had set her off by ignoring her? If that didn't sound like a star with a bloated ego, what did?

"I send her money all the time. Plenty of money. What does she do with it? She could pay to have her garage door installed, and she could hire someone to mow her lawn, but instead she has Kenny Kronek do it. It just aggravates me, that's all. And you know what else hurts? The fact that I offered to buy her the house of her choice—a brand-new one—but she said no. For heaven's sake, have you taken a look at her kitchen cupboards lately? And her front steps are tilting, and the sidewalk is cracking apart. I send her nice clothes from really good stores, and she wears that lavender polyester slacks set that she probably bought fifteen years ago. I just don't understand her anymore."

When Tess quit speaking, a deep, thoughtful quiet spread through the room. Judy and Renee exchanged glances again before the latter spoke.

"She's getting old, Tess. She doesn't want change. She wants what's familiar. There's a lifetime of memories in that house. Why would she want to move away from it?"

"All right, I'll concede that she probably wouldn't want to leave the house, but couldn't she update it a little?"

"You know what your trouble is?" Judy said. "You haven't been around to see her aging. You come home once a year or so and demand that she be the same as she always was, only she's not. If she's happy, leave her alone."

Tess stared at Judy, then at Renee. "Is she right?"

"Basically. And while you're at it, let Kenny Kronek do what he wants for her," Renee added. "The truth is, he seems to be able to convince her to make changes when we can't. Jim offered—I don't know how many times—to install an automatic garage-door opener, but she always said no. Then one day she just announces that Kenny put one in for her. I don't pretend to understand, but I'm just grateful to have him around."

WHEN Tess and her sisters went into Mary's room for the last time that afternoon, Tess looked at her mother differently, trying to grasp the fact that she was aging, that at seventy-four she had a right to be getting a little feisty. Perhaps Judy was right. Perhaps coming home so seldom left Tess with the illusion that time was not marching on.

Renee pressed the four-leaf clover into Mary's hand. "That's from Casey Kronek. She came by to see how you are and said to give you this. She'll be back to see you tomorrow."

"Oh, isn't that nice. That Casey's a sweet girl."

"Listen, Mom." Tess took Mary's other hand. "I'm going to leave now, but I'll be back tomorrow."

"We're going, too," Judy and Renee said.

They all kissed her and left her looking drowsy and pale.

Outside, Tess took great gulps of the street air. It felt like she was being released, driving away, even in Mary's old Ford Tempo. The spring day was glorious. Tess took her time, stopping at a supermarket and buying herself some fresh vegetables, low-fat salad dressing, and boneless chicken breasts before heading back toward Wintergreen. Driving along the familiar roads, she found herself cataloguing her mixed feelings about being home again.

There was something to be said for living away from family. In Nashville she was clear of the daily reminders of her mother's health, of Judy's jealousy, and all the other petty irritations that had cropped up in the last twenty-four hours. Being here had made her aware of how different she was from the girl who'd left. Her values and priorities had changed. Her pace had changed. Was that necessarily bad? She didn't think so. What she had accomplished with her life had taken tremendous energy and commitment.

When she pulled up in the alley at six o'clock, Kenny Kronek was mowing her mother's backyard, dressed in blue jeans, a white V-neck undershirt, and a navy-and-red Cardinals baseball cap. He looked up but kept on mowing as she stopped in the alley and activated the garage door. When her mother's car was tucked away and her own car returned to the apron, Tess took her groceries and headed for the house. She and Kronek met head-on when she was halfway up the sidewalk. He stopped and switched the lawn mower motor to idle.

"How'd it go?" he asked, no smile on his mouth.

"Perfect," she snapped rudely. "No complications at all."

"Well, that's good news."

"I met your daughter today," she told him with surface civility. "She's quite refreshingly natural."

He reached down, picked up a little stick in front of the mower, and threw it away. "Meaning she smelled like horses, right?"

Had he been anyone else, Tess would have laughed. Since he was Kenny, she forcibly refrained. "Some. She asked me to come and sing with your church choir."

He gave her a quarter of a glance and mumbled as if cursing under his breath, then scratched the back of his head. "I told her not to bug you about it. I hope you don't think I put her up to it."

She remembered the crush he used to have on her in high school and said with enough sarcasm to nettle him, "Now, why would I think a thing like that?"

He squared the baseball cap on his head and gave her a disgusted assessment from beneath its visor. "I gotta get back to work." He turned up the engine till it pounded their eardrums.

She leaned closer and shouted above the roar, "You didn't have to mow this lawn, you know. I was going to call my nephew."

"No trouble," he shouted back.

"I'll be happy to pay you."

He gave her a look that cut her down to about the height of the grass. "Around here we don't pay each other for favors, Ms. McPhail."

"I was born around here, in case you've forgotten. So don't take that tone with me, Mr. Kronek!"

He let his gaze clip the edge of her face and offered, "Oh, excuse me . . . Mac, is it?"

"Tess will be fine, whenever you choose to come off your high horse long enough to speak to me."

"You know, you always did have an attitude."

"I do not have an attitude!"

He let out a snort and began pushing the mower away, calling back over his shoulder, "Look again, Mac." He could say Mac with such an insulting tone she wanted to run up behind him and trip him. Instead, she stormed into the house and slammed the grocery bag down, wondering when in the last eighteen years she'd been this riled.

To distract herself, she decided to call her producer, Jack Greaves, who informed her that Carla Niles was coming in to cut a new harmony track on "Tarnished Gold" and that he'd have it couriered to her tomorrow. While she was on the kitchen phone, a car pulled up and parked behind Kronek's garage—the same car as yesterday, a white Plymouth Neon. A woman got out and crossed the alley toward him. She was fortyish, wearing low-heeled pumps and a summer business suit of pale peach. As she approached him, he stopped mowing and moved a couple steps in her direction. Kenny jabbed a thumb toward Mary's house, and the woman glanced over briefly. Then she smiled and headed back across the alley while he returned to his mowing.

A half hour later Tess was washing a head of lettuce when she looked out the window and saw the woman, who had changed into slacks, carrying a tray out the back door to Kenny's picnic table. In a moment Casey followed with another tray. The woman hailed Kenny, who by this time had finished mowing Mary's yard and was halfway through with his own, and the three of them sat down to eat supper.

Who's that? Tess wondered. Tess caught herself and spun away from the window. Who cares, she thought as she put a chicken breast on to poach, then went into the living room to do what she'd been eager to do all day long. Composing seemed like play—always had. At times she found it ludicrous that she should be paid for doing something that gave her such absolute pleasure. Yet the royalties from her original songs brought in hundreds of thousands of dollars a year.

Armed with a small tape recorder, staff paper, and pencil, she sat down at the piano to work on the song idea she'd had last night.

> *One-way traffic crawlin' round a small-town square,*
> *Eighteen years've passed since she's been there,*
> *Been around the world, now she's coming back . . .*

The last line of the verse kept eluding her. Ideas came, but she discarded them one after another. She was wholly immersed in composing when a voice said, "Hey, Mac? It's me, Casey," bringing Tess around on the piano bench.

Casey stood jauntily in the middle of the room, smiling. Her stable gear was gone and in its place were clean blue jeans with a yellow cotton T-shirt tucked in around her slim waist.

"Heard you playing," she said.

"Working on a song that came into my head last night while I was in the bathtub."

"What's it about?"

"It's about what it feels like to come back here after being gone so long. The town, my mother, this house. How nothing changes."

"Can I hear it?"

Tess chuckled. "Well, I don't usually play my stuff for people until after it's copyrighted and recorded."

"Oh, you mean like I might steal it or something. Gee, that's a good one." Casey laughed. "Come on, let me hear it," she cajoled, flinging herself into an overstuffed chair and throwing a leg over its fat arm as if she were a comfortable old buddy.

Tess swung back to the piano, quite taken by the girl in spite of herself. There was a naturalness about Casey that fell just short of presumptuousness. The truth was, given Tess's busy life, she had few friends away from the music industry. This girl came on like one, and Tess bit.

"All right. This is what I've got so far."

She played the first three lines, then tried an optional fourth. It was easy to hear that it didn't work.

"Play it again," Casey said.

Tess played and sang one more time.

> *"One-way traffic crawlin' round a small-town square,*
> *Eighteen years've passed since she's been there,*
> *Been around the world, now she's coming back . . ."*

"Wider-eyed and noting what this small town lacks," Casey added in a corduroy contralto voice that was dead on tune. *"Can't return. Too much learned."*

The last two lines Casey had tacked on created a haunting afterthought. Tess picked it out on the keys, closing her eyes and holding the last chord as it dwindled into silence like lazy smoke around their heads.

The room remained silent for ten seconds.

Then Tess said, "Perfect."

She leaned forward and wrote the words and melody line on the staff paper. When she finished, she set the pencil down and said, "Let's do it again."

While they sang, Tess recognized a distinctively unique voice. It had a touch of grit and grime. It had a good musical ear behind it, but most important, a fearlessness. Not many seventeen-year-old girls Tess knew could sing side by side with someone of her renown without quailing. Casey did it with her leg still thrown over the chair arm and her eyes still closed.

When she opened them, the country-western star on the piano bench was looking back over her shoulder wearing a bemused expression. "So tell me, did you come in here to show me what you had?"

"Partly," the girl admitted.

"Well, I'm impressed. You could take the tread off of tires with all the gravel in that voice." Tess swung around and faced Casey. "I like it."

"Trouble is, it always sticks out."

"In a group like a church choir, you mean."

"Uh-huh. Oh, which reminds me. My dad didn't like me bothering you to sing with the choir. He said I'd been intrusive and ordered me to apologize. That's the real reason why I'm here. So I'm sorry. I just didn't stop to think." Casey shrugged. "You ought to be able to come home and move around town in peace without people bugging you the way they do everywhere else you go."

"That what your dad said?"

"Uh-huh."

Tess considered awhile. "That's a surprise." She got up. "Got some chicken poaching out here. I better go check it."

Casey followed her to the kitchen and leaned against the archway watching while Tess lifted the lid, poked the chicken breast, and found it tender. She turned off the burner and got her salad fixings out of the refrigerator.

"What's it like being up there in front of all those people?" Casey inquired. "I mean, it must be so awesome."

"It's the only thing I ever wanted to do. I love it."

"Yeah, I know what you mean. I've been singing since I was about three years old." As Tess put her food on the table, Casey pushed away from the doorway. "Guess I'd better let you eat."

"No. Sit and talk. I've got a piece of pecan pie I can give you."

"Mary's?"

"You bet."

"Hey, that sounds great."

When Tess made a motion to get it, Casey ordered, "You sit down and eat. I'll get it myself." She knew right where to find a plate, fork, and spatula.

"So what kind of place do you live in, in Nashville?" Casey asked as she brought the pie to the table.

"I've got a house of my own, but I'm only there about half the time. The rest of the time I'm playing concert dates."

"Is it bad being gone so much?"

"It was worse when I traveled by bus. It was like being marooned together, living in such close quarters with the same people day after day. But it's much nicer since I own my own plane."

"Your own plane? Wow!"

Tess chuckled at the girl's unbridled candor.

"So tell me what it's like when you're recording," Casey prompted.

Tess was still telling her when Kenny's voice came from outside the back door. "Casey, what are you still doing here bothering her?" Dark had fallen, and the kitchen lights were on.

Tess leaned forward to peer at him around the far doorway. "She's no bother. I asked her to stay."

Casey said, "We're talking, Dad, that's all."

Uninvited, he stepped into the back entrance. Pressing a hand on either side of the doorway, he poked his head into the room. "Casey, come on now. I told you to come straight home."

"Can I finish my pie first?" she said with strained patience.

To Tess he said, "You sure she's not bothering you?"

"Let her finish."

"All right. Ten minutes," he replied, then disappeared.

When the screen door closed behind him, Casey said, "I don't know why he's breathing down my neck so bad today. He never does that."

"What does your dad do?" Tess asked.

"He's a C.P.A. He's got his own business downtown just off the square, about three doors from the dress shop where Faith works."

"Faith?"

"Faith Oxbury, his girlfriend."

"She the one who was over there having supper tonight?"

"Mm-hmm." Casey licked her spoon. "She's over most nights for supper. They've been going together since forever."

Tess wondered how long forever meant, but she wasn't going to ask.

Casey set her spoon down and pushed back her plate. "Daddy and Faith have been going together so long that people kind of treat them like they're already married. They play bridge together and get invited to parties together. Heck, she even sends out Christmas cards with all of our names on them."

"Then why don't they get married?"

"I asked him once, and he said it's because she's a Catholic and if she married a divorced man, she couldn't receive the sacraments in her church anymore. But if you ask me, that's a pretty lame excuse not to marry a man you've been going with for eight years."

"Eight years. That's a long time."

"You know it. And I'll tell you something else. They'd like me to think there's nothing going on between them—I mean, she never stays overnight at our house, and he never stays overnight at hers. But if they think I buy that, they're stupider than they think I am. But you know what? Underneath it all I have to respect Dad for caring enough about my respect for him not to want to jeopardize it. So she comes over and fixes supper and stays till nine or so; then he walks her to the car and says good night. And on Sunday she goes to her church and he goes to ours. But at least we all get along. Faith is real nice to me."

Casey paused and took a deep breath. "Well, my ten minutes are up." She got up and took her dirty dishes to the sink, followed by Tess. When she'd run water onto her plate, she turned and said, "Thanks for letting me hear your song in progress and for the pie and for letting me ask you questions. Could I give you a hug?"

Tess had just set her own dishes down when she found herself hugged hard and hugging back.

While Tess was in Casey's clutches, the girl exclaimed, "Ooo, you're just super! And you grew up right over here, across the alley. I want to be just like you."

With that, the impetuous girl hit the door. " 'Night, Mac. Tell Mary I'll be up to see her tomorrow afternoon."

Chapter Four

♪ ♥ ♪ ♥ ♪

$O_{N THE}$ day following Mary's surgery, Tess arrived at her bedside at midmorning and found she missed the company of her sisters, who failed to show up as promised. It was difficult watching her mother clinging to a walker and struggling to stand upright.

A physical therapist named Virginia came in and raised Mary's legs several times, drawing soft moans.

"You'll be helping her with her therapy at home," the therapist told Tess. "Would you like to try it now?"

"No! I mean, you go ahead. I'll help tomorrow." The idea of being the one to cause her mother pain caused a lightness in Tess's stomach.

Midway through the day a nurse removed the oxygen prongs from Mary's nose, but the IV and catheter stayed, lashing her to the bed in her wrinkly regulation gown, with the split up the back.

When Judy showed up, around two p.m., Tess greeted her with overt enthusiasm, surprising even herself. Judy remained cool, waddling over to the bed to give her affection to Mary instead. "Hey, Mama, how you doing today?"

"Not so good, I'm afraid. Lots of pain."

"Well, you know how it was last time. If you can just hang in there for the first couple of days, it gets better really quick after that." Somehow, it seemed to Tess, her sisters knew all the right things to say, whereas she felt awkward consoling her mother. "Renee's taking a day off today," Judy told Mary. "She's got wedding stuff to do. Anybody else been up to visit?"

At that moment a cacophony of chatter approached from down the hall and three people entered the room at once: Casey, her father—bearing a box of chocolates—and a man in his mid-fifties, wearing a short-sleeved summer shirt with a clerical collar.

Mary smiled when she saw him. "Reverend Giddings."

"Mary," he said fondly, taking her hand.

"And Casey and Kenny. My goodness, this is nice."

They went to Mary and kissed her while Casey took the candy from her father's hand and laid the box on Mary's stomach. "Your favorites—very very extra-dark chocolates."

"Oh, my, yes, they are my favorites."

Casey oversaw the candy operation while Reverend Giddings passed along goodwill messages from members of his congregation.

In the general shifting of visitors, Kenny somehow ended up standing near Judy and Tess, at the foot of the bed. He glanced briefly at Tess and said, "Hello. How're you today?"

"Fine. A little tired. I'm not used to this schedule."

Mary said, "Girls, look. Dark chocolate. Would you like one?"

Tess answered, "No, thanks, Mom," but Judy moved away to pick one from the proffered box.

Kenny and Tess stood apart from the others.

"Casey was pretty excited when she came home last night. I suppose you know you lit a real fire under her."

"I think the fire was there before she came over to see me, so if you're upset about it—"

"Who says I'm upset about it?"

"Well, I understand you didn't like her singing with her band."

"Bunch of potheads and school dropouts, that's why. Heck, nothing short of a guillotine could keep Casey from singing."

"Do I hear my name over there?" Casey came over and joined them. "What are you two talking about?"

"About last night," Tess said.

Casey's natural ebullience spilled out once again. "Last night was too cool. I couldn't even sleep when I got home."

"I couldn't either. That song kept bothering me."

"You get a second verse down yet?"

"Mm . . ." Tess waggled a hand. "A bad one, maybe."

"I don't think you could write anything bad."

"Oh, listen, I've written some that were so bad my producer winced when he heard them."

"What if your producer likes a song and you don't?"

"Actually, that's happened. He asked me to listen to a demo one time that I thought was a real dud. But I agreed to give it a try, and in the end it turned out to be one of my best-selling singles ever."

"Which one?"

" 'Branded.' "

"Oh, I like that one."

Kenny stood back, listening. He was surprised by Tess's attention to Casey, given what he remembered of her in high school. Yesterday he had accused her of having an attitude, but it was nowhere in evidence with Casey.

Reverend Giddings approached Tess and extended his hand. "I don't believe I've ever had the pleasure of meeting you. I'm Sam Giddings. I've been minister at Wintergreen Methodist since Reverend Sperling retired."

"How do you do." Tess smiled at him. "Mother has talked about you."

"My wife and most of my congregation are big fans. People around here are mighty proud of your success, young lady, and I confess I'm among them."

"Why, thank you."

"Of course, Mary let it be known that you were coming home to take care of her. So this morning at breakfast my wife said to me, 'If you run into Mary's daughter at the hospital, see if you can get her to come and sing with the choir while she's here.' " He paused and glanced at Kenny.

"Reverend Giddings," Kenny began, "I'm sure that everywhere she goes, Miss McPhail gets requests like this, and I don't think we should bother her while she's home."

"I can't imagine why using her voice to praise the Lord would be such an imposition. The offer still stands, Ms. McPhail. I'm sure the congregation would be most grateful. Matter of fact, a week from

Sunday we're having our annual pledge drive. If you'd agree to sing that day, we'd have enough time for the church secretary to type it up in this Sunday's bulletin. Now, what do you say?"

Mary spoke up. "Well, of course she'll do it, won't you, Tess?"

Tess gaped haplessly at Reverend Giddings "Well . . . uh . . ." Her eyes connected with Kenny's. He looked as uncomfortable as she. She gave an exaggerated shrug, said, "Why not?" and let out a strained laugh that fooled no one.

Finally Reverend Giddings took his leave. Kenny and Casey left shortly thereafter, but the whole scene continued to rankle Tess even after she left the hospital.

She was still disgruntled when she got home. She washed some grapes and took a handful upstairs while she changed into a pair of cotton shorts, then went back downstairs. She was standing at the sink when she noticed the wilted tomato plants. Heck, she'd forgotten to water the garden yesterday.

Out she went and into the service door of the garage to search out a yellow plastic fan-shaped nozzle. At the house she screwed it onto the coiled hose and dragged the whole works across the narrow sidewalk to the garden. She had just started sprinkling when Kenny's porch door slammed and he came striding across his backyard toward her. Faith Oxbury's car was parked in front of his garage door, and he swerved around it.

"Just for the record," he said when he was ten feet from her, "I didn't have anything to do with Reverend Giddings's invitation."

She let her eyes shift over him once. He was frowning, standing a body length away from her. He had changed out of his suit and was wearing a white polo shirt and khaki pants—ultra tidy.

She moved farther away from him, dragging the hose and waving the nozzle above the carrots. "I believe you," she said, refusing to glance at him again.

He seemed nonplussed by her quick admission and stood momentarily disarmed before blurting out grumpily, "We practice on Tuesdays. If you intend to sing with us, you better sit in on next week's practice."

She closed the thumb switch on the sprinkler and threw it down on the grass. "Look!" She marched over to confront him at closer range. She rammed her hands on her hips and thrust her nose forward. "You've been mad at me since the moment you walked into my mother's house and saw me there. So do you want me to sing with your choir or don't you? 'Cause it's no skin off my nose if I do or I don't. But I don't intend to stand up in some choir loft and put up with your antagonism and your belittling attitude, so get rid of it, mister."

"You're a fine one to talk about belittling attitudes," he retorted with equal anger. "Yours stretches as far back as 1976, doesn't it?"

"Oh, so that's what this is about. How I treated you in high school."

"You were cruel. You made a mockery of people's feelings."

"Oh, and what about my feelings two days ago, when I came home? You walked into my mother's house and didn't even have the common courtesy to say hello to me."

"And what kind of common courtesy did you show me when we were in high school?"

"Oh, Kenny, grow up. That was years ago. People change."

"Oh, yeah, and you really did. Roaring in here with your forty-thousand-dollar car and your vanity license plates, wearing a shirt that says 'Boss.' Lady, you really impressed me."

"I wasn't out to impress you, *Kenneth*. The car is mine. I paid for it with my own money. Why shouldn't I drive it? And for your information, I bought the shirt at a Springsteen concert."

"Oh. Well, excuse me. I guess I was wrong about how you used to poke fun at me back in high school, too."

She gave him a short consideration and said, more calmly, "You carry a long grudge, Kenny."

"You deserve it, Tess," he replied, more calmly, too.

It was the first time he'd called her by her given name. She backed off a little. "All right, maybe I do, but did you have to be such a nerd?"

"See? Attitude. Didn't I tell you, you have an attitude?"

"Hey, tell me something. Do you still get nosebleeds?"

"No. Do you still send anonymous and insincere valentines to guys you think have crushes on you, just to watch them squirm?"

"I never sent you valentines."

"And I never had a crush on you. I hated you."

"Does your sweet little daughter know you harbor all this hidden viciousness?"

"No. But she knows all about yours. I've told her. How you teased me and set me up and wrote me notes starting, 'Dear Kenny Crow Neck,' and generally made my life miserable whenever you could."

"Yeah, and she still admires me, right?"

"That's right. So do you think you can haul your big ego over to church and give her some reason to?"

"If I do, are you going to treat me like an insect, or are you going to be nice?"

"I'll think about it."

"Uh-huh," she said dryly.

They eyed each other warily for a few seconds, but the air had definitely cleared. They suddenly realized they were sparring and enjoying it.

"Hey, you know what?" Tess said thoughtfully, tipping her head to one side a little.

"What?"

"For an ex-nerd, you sure are quick at repartee."

"Why, thank you, Tess. That's the nicest thing you've said to me since we were in rompers. I'm so relieved to know I've managed to elevate myself in your esteem."

They weren't actually grinning at each other, but they were tempted. It had been startlingly refreshing to air their grievances and see where it got them. They were still standing beside the garden, with the watering forgotten, when across the alley the porch door opened and Faith called, "Kenny, are you out here?"

"Better go," Tess said, smirking. "Your girlfriend is calling."

WHEN KENNY REACHED HIS porch, Faith was holding the door. "You were gone so long," she said. "I wondered where you went."

"Just talking to Tess." He went in ahead of her. "She thinks I sicced Giddings on her to get her to sing with the choir, and I wanted to set her straight."

"Oh." Faith let the door close against her backside while he stopped and waited for her. She was a woman of many averages—looks, shape, intelligence, style. She hardly ever showed anger, but hardly ever had cause, because they got along so well. She wore mostly dresses and slacks and always acted like a lady. The perfect role model for Casey, he thought, who tended to be tomboyish and in your face most of the time.

"I was rather hoping to meet her," Faith said.

"Listen, Faith, you wouldn't like her any more than I do."

"I don't see how she can be that bad, coming from a mother like Mary."

"Well, believe me, she is. She hasn't changed a bit."

In the kitchen Casey was waiting to pounce on him. "Daddy, why can't I go over and talk to Mac? You did."

"I'm not going to have you hanging around over there."

"I could just scream!" Casey stamped her foot. "When I graduate, I'm going to be out of here so fast I'll leave a vacuum. And you know where I'm going? Straight to Nashville."

"Fine. When you graduate, you can go wherever you want," he said calmly. "Tonight you're staying home."

"Arrr!" She turned on her heel and clumped upstairs. A minute later her guitar started whanging as loud as she could make it whang and she was singing at the top of her lungs.

He blew out a breath and muttered, "Teenagers."

Faith put her hand on Kenny's arm. "You have to put yourself in her place—that there's an honest-to-goodness Nashville star right across the alley and she's got to stay in this house as ordered. Just be careful, Kenny, that you don't rob her of an opportunity that could mean the world to her."

"You think I should let her go over there?"

"Maybe. Maybe not. Just make sure you make a fair judgment. Now I'm going upstairs and see if I can soothe some ruffled feathers." She patted his arm before leaving the room with her customary unflappability.

Upstairs she tapped on the closed door and asked, "Casey? May I come in?"

Casey stopped hammering her guitar. "I don't care."

Faith went in and shut the door. Casey sat on her desk chair, staring at her left thumbnail.

"You really want to be a singer like Tess McPhail, don't you?"

Casey looked up at Faith. "Do you think I'm crazy?"

"Not at all. And maybe I'm not the best judge, but I think you're good enough."

"But Daddy doesn't, does he?"

Faith moved into the room and sat on the edge of the bed. "Your dad might possibly be a little bit scared that you'll succeed. Did you ever think about that?"

"Why would he be scared of a thing like that?"

"Because it'll take you away from him. Because it's a hard lifestyle. Because a lot of musicians use drugs and lead wild and ruinous lives—or so we're told."

"But he knows what my music means to me."

"Mm-hmm," Faith said. "And you know what you mean to him."

Casey quieted, then bent forward. "Hey, Faith, can I ask you something?"

"Of course."

"When I'm gone, do you think you'll ever marry Daddy?"

"I don't know," Faith said, meeting Casey's eyes.

"But you and Daddy see each other every day. What would be different if you were married?"

"I know this won't make much sense to you, but your dad and I have the best of both worlds. We have companionship, but at the same time we have our independence. I actually like going home to my little house and having nobody to answer to but myself."

"Has Daddy ever asked you—to marry him, I mean?"

"Not for a long time."

"Oh." The room grew quiet as Casey sat studying Faith and trying to make sense of her relationship with Kenny.

"Well," Faith said, taking a deep breath, "I guess it's about time I was leaving. Take a long, leisurely bath, and when you're done, it'll all seem less crucial." She rose and stood beside Casey's chair, a hand on her shoulder. "As fathers go, he's a pretty good one."

Casey nodded, her gaze fixed on the floor.

"Want to have supper with us?" Faith invited nonchalantly.

That's what Casey liked about Faith. She understood that sometimes you had to be alone. "Naw. You go ahead without me."

Faith and Kenny ate alone that night. When she left for home, it was after eight thirty and already dark. Kenny walked her to her car. They went slowly, spiritlessly, into the spring night, their moods still flat because of his disagreement with Casey.

He opened her driver's door, and she turned before getting in. "I think you're going to have to let her try whatever it is she wants to try with her music."

He sighed, his eyes downcast.

"Well, I must go," Faith said. "Good night, dear." She kissed him on his cheek and got in the car. The headlights flashed across him, and he raised his hand in an absentminded farewell.

When Faith's taillights disappeared, Kenny's gaze wandered across the alley to Mary's house. The downstairs lights were off, and the single upstairs window below the roof peak was gold. Where Faith's departure had scarcely registered, the nearness of Tess McPhail smacked him with a sharp, masculine reaction. He stood looking up at her window, recalling the exchange they'd had in the backyard a few hours ago, wondering how she could still manage to do this to him after all these years. By the time that encounter in the yard had ended, they'd been flirting. Stupid, but that's exactly what they'd been doing. And why?

He'd made a well-adjusted life for himself and Casey. He had exactly what he wanted—a nice little business, a comfortable life, a circle of longtime friends, one very special friend in Faith. Then Tess came back, and things started changing. Casey was too starstruck and impressionable to be molded by a woman like Tess. And as for himself, he'd better start acting like the kind of guy Faith deserved.

THE next day, when Tess went out to start her car, she found a note stuck under the windshield wiper. "Mac," it said, "I've got a verse two that I think will work. Try it out."

> *Mama's in the home place, never changed a lick,*
> *House as worn and tattered as a derelict,*
> *Same old clock a-tickin' on the faded kitchen wall,*
> *Mama won't replace anything at all.*
>
> *Mama's fine.*
> *Can't change her mind.*

Tess stood in the alley reading the verse, singing it to herself.

She loved it. How surprising that a seventeen-year-old girl had the insight to come up with something this good.

She dialed her producer and said, "Jack, listen, I want you to save space on the album for one new song that I'm writing down here. It's not done yet, but it will be soon. I'm getting help from a high school girl who lives right across the alley, and you won't believe it, Jack, but it's good. She's good."

"A high school girl! Tess, have you lost your mind?"

"I know, I know, but this one's special. She's bright, and she's got talent to go with it. It's just one cut, okay? And if the song doesn't pan out, we'll use whatever you've got picked out from the demos."

He sighed. "All right, Tess. What's it called?"

" 'Small Town Girl.' I'll let you know the minute it's finished."

"Okay, Mac, you're the star. You know best."

MARY was progressing normally, which, in the case of hip replacement, meant slowly. By the third day her catheter had been removed, and when Tess arrived, a male aide and Virginia, the therapist, were helping Mary to her feet for her first attempt at using a walker.

When she had been swung around and tipped upright, she grew dizzy. Her eyes closed, and she gripped the arms supporting her.

"Take your time." Virginia gave her a minute, then said, "Okay? Do you feel nauseated?"

"I'm . . . okay," Mary answered breathlessly.

Tess was the worst possible nurse. Moving along beside her mother during her first hesitant steps with the walker was traumatic. Tess discovered she was holding her breath, glancing from Mary's white knuckles to her grim face to the sheen of tears the patient couldn't keep from her determined eyes. Tess was amazed by her mother's courage to face this pain a second time and chagrined with herself for her chickenheartedness.

Renee came later that morning and brought her daughter, Rachel, with her. "How ya doing today, Mama?" Renee said, bending over the bed and kissing her mother.

Rachel stepped close. "Hi, Grandma. Mom and I made you cookies. The chocolate ones rolled in powdered sugar you like so much."

"Rachel, darling. Top of the mountains?" Mary made an effort to push herself up to look at the cookies.

While Renee uncovered the tin, Rachel found a chance to greet her aunt. "Hi, Aunt Tess. I haven't seen you yet."

"Hi, Rachel. How are the wedding plans coming?"

"Perfect. I'm so glad you'll be here for it."

The longer Tess was home, the more she realized her sisters were probably right: She was out of touch with her family. She scarcely knew enough about Rachel to carry on a comfortable conversation.

Shortly after Renee and Rachel arrived, Faith Oxbury showed up, dressed in a pastel print dress, bearing a big vase of irises.

"Hello there," she said cheerfully from the doorway. "Is there anyone in here with a brand-new hip?"

"Faith," they all chorused. "Hello."

"Mary, dear, how are you? The nurses tell me that you've already taken a few steps." She set down the flowers and kissed the patient's cheek. Then she stood at the bedside squeezing both Mary's hands. "I'm so glad the worst part is over. I can't tell you how many times I thought of you day before yesterday."

"Oh, thank you, Faith. That means so much to me."

Faith said, "Mary, I haven't met your other daughter yet." She approached Tess and took both of her hands, as she'd done to Mary earlier. "I'm Faith Oxbury."

Tess squeezed back. "Hi, Faith. I'm Tess."

"And you're every bit as pretty as your pictures."

"Thank you."

"And as nice, if Casey can be believed. All we've heard around the house since you came home is Mac, Mac, Mac. You have that girl absolutely glowing."

"Well, I don't know why. I didn't do much."

"You respected her music. That was enough. I think you have a disciple for life." Faith released Tess's hands.

Tess liked Faith. There was nothing about her not to like. She was very genuine, charitable, kind to Mary, obviously a dear friend to the entire family, and more than likely a wonderful influence on Casey.

What bothered Tess was that she found herself analyzing Faith not in light of all this, but in light of the fact that she was, from all apparent evidence, Kenny Kronek's longtime paramour.

Chapter Five

♪ ♥ ♪ ♥ ♪

*A*T NINE o'clock that night Tess was just eating her supper—flatbread topped with herbed tomatoes and goat cheese. She was sitting at the kitchen table, barefoot, in her baseball cap and a huge white Garth Brooks T-shirt, turning the pages of a JC Penney catalogue that had arrived in her mother's mail that day. The radio on top of the refrigerator was tuned to KKLR in Poplar Bluff, and Trisha Yearwood was singing, "Thinkin' About You."

Out in front of Kenny's house Casey parked her pickup truck in its usual spot at the curb, walked around to the back-porch door, and called inside, "Hey, Dad, you home?" Getting no answer, she glanced across the alley. Mary's kitchen light was on and the back door open. The invitation proved too much for Casey.

She bounded up the back steps and put her forehead to the screen. "Hi, Mac. It's me, Casey."

Mac leaned forward and called, "Hey, Casey, come on in."

Casey went in. "Just got back from visiting your mom. Saw your lights on."

"How is she?"

"They got her up to walk while I was there." Casey winced as if watching Mary now. "Ouch."

"I know. But she's a tough one. Sit down. Want some flatbread?"

Casey picked up a wedge and took a bite. "What's this white stuff?"

"Goat cheese."

Casey stopped chewing and looked sickly. "Goat cheese?"

"Never tasted goat cheese?" Tess took another piece herself. "It's good."

"I bet." But Casey persevered and took a second bite. "It's not so bad if you keep at it. Can I have another one?"

"Sure, go ahead. I'll make more."

Tess got up to do so, but first she brought Casey a Coke and said, "Your second verse is good. I'm going to use it."

Casey looked stunned. "You're kidding!"

"No. Maybe you could come over and work on it some more tomorrow, see if we can finish it together. You know, when it's published, you'll have to take credit as one of the writers."

"Really? Me? Oh, Mac, are you serious?"

"Of course. I called my producer and told him to save one slot on the new album for it. The quicker we finish it, the better."

Casey let out a whoop as Tess brought more flatbread over to the table. While they ate, Tess mesmerized the girl with stories about going on tours and doing concerts with the big names.

Then Travis Tritt and Marty Stuart came on the radio with an oldie, "The Whiskey Ain't Workin' Anymore," and Tess and Casey yowled along like a couple of beer swillers in a bar.

That's how Kenny found them.

It was shortly after ten when he pulled into his garage. From clear out in the alley he could hear their voices. The lights glowed in Mary's kitchen as he crossed the backyard and stopped at the bottom of the steps.

They were bellowing fit to kill about needing one good honky-tonk angel as Kenny climbed the steps and peered inside. Casey was wearing jeans and her old cowboy boots; Tess, as far as he could see, wore nothing more than an oversize T-shirt. They were banging the tabletop with their drinks, and Mary's potted plant was quivering in time to the music.

The song ended, and they yowled and clapped as if they were coming off a dance floor.

Kenny knocked and called, "Is this a private party, or can anyone join in? I could hear you clear across the alley."

In an unusually happy and expansive mood Tess said, "Come on in, Kenny. We're just stretching our vocal cords."

He opened the door and went in, stopping just inside the kitchen doorway, surveying the two of them.

"Here." Tess hooked a chair with one foot and sent it scooting backward. "Pull up a chair."

He arranged himself on the chair across from her, recalling that he'd ordered Casey to stay away from here. Reprimands, however, were the furthest thing from his mind as he settled back.

Casey said, "Guess what, Dad. Mac likes the song I've been helping her write. She's going to record it on her next album, and she says I'll get credit as a co-writer."

"Really?" His gaze veered from his daughter to Tess.

"That is, if you have no objections," Tess added.

"Wouldn't do me much good if I did, would it?"

"Probably not."

Tess got up and got a can of Coca-Cola out of the refrigerator.

When she clapped the soda down in front of Kenny, his glance flicked up to her. "Thanks," he said. Her legs were bare, and a soiled spot on her shirt brought her down to mortal level, prompting a smile, which he concealed as he drank. For once Tess had removed her dangly silver-and-turquoise earrings. She looked better without them. Matter of fact, she looked a little too good to him all the way around tonight. He had to force his attention back to Casey, who went on talking.

"Mac and I are going to work on the song again tomorrow, Dad. Gol, I'm so excited. I can't believe this is happening." Without pausing for breath, Casey jumped up and announced, "I gotta use the bathroom, okay?"

She hurried away without waiting for an answer, leaving the other two sitting in the fluorescent-lit kitchen, trying to pretend disinterest in each other and carry on a neutral conversation.

Tess said, "You know, I was thinking. I really do want to sing with your church choir after all. You sure you don't care?"

He hid his surprise and answered, "No, I don't care."

"Practice on Tuesday, right?" she said.

"That's right. Seven p.m. Would you want to sing a solo?"

"That's up to you. I'm not after stealing your choir's thunder."

"My choir's not that good. No thunder to steal. If you want to do a solo, I'll pick out some music." Kenny cleared his throat. "So you met Faith today."

"Yes. She's very sweet."

"She said the same thing about you, actually."

"Don't believe her," Tess said with a grin.

"Don't worry," he replied, and though he tried to repress it, the barest grin also played on his lips.

"So what are you two? Engaged or what?" Tess asked.

"No. Friends."

"Oh, friends." She nodded as if giving that some thought. "For what? Eight years? Is that what Casey told me?"

"That's right."

"Mm. So what happened to Casey's mother?"

"She got tired of us and ran away to Paris."

"Got tired of you—just like that?"

"That's what she said."

"Ahh." She knitted her fingers together loosely and rested them beneath her chin. Finally she said, "But you and Casey are really close. I can tell that."

"I'd say so."

"And she's crazy about Faith. She told me so."

"Boy, you two have talked a lot. What else did she tell you?"

"That you don't want her to grow up and be like me."

He said nothing, only watched her steadily.

"It's understandable," she said. "The life doesn't leave much time for personal relationships."

"Meaning what? That you don't have a boyfriend?"

She considered before deciding she would answer him. "Yes, I do, as a matter of fact. He's on the road right now in Texas."

It was unclear why they were setting up boundaries. But before they had a chance to assess their motives, Casey returned, bringing back common sense. They kept it light after that, and Kenny and Casey left a short while later. On the back step Casey gave Tess another of her impulsive hugs.

"Thank you, Mac. You're making all my dreams come true."

"It's fun for me, too," Tess said, and it was true.

"See you tomorrow."

As Casey walked away with her father, Tess saw against the distant porch lights that the two were holding hands. She figured relatively few teenagers held their parent's hand anymore. Something within her was renewed, watching them walk away.

After they'd gone, Tess stood staring absently out the window, feeling the loneliness of being isolated from normality. She thought of her exchange with Kenny about Burt. Ah, well. . . . She sighed and turned from the window to go upstairs.

When she was settled down in bed, she lay awake thinking. She thought of Burt and herself, knowing it took more than a couple of days every now and then to forge anything meaningful.

There'd been more meaning in the brief time she'd spent tonight with Casey and Kenny than in any relationship she'd attempted in the last several years.

Oh, why think about it? But when she turned onto her stomach and tried to empty her mind so sleep could float in, it wasn't Burt she saw behind her closed eyelids but Kenny Kronek.

TESS and Casey finished the song on Saturday afternoon. They sang it together so many times that they had every lick and dip down pat in their harmonies. Their vocal qualities were totally different—Tess's resonant and soprano, Casey's gritty and alto, but the combination created an arresting blend.

When Casey left, Tess had a rough demo tape of their voices.

She called Jack Greaves and said, "The song is done. I'll express it to you on Monday. Pay attention to the voice that's singing harmony so you can tell me what you think of it."

After the call to Jack she hung around the kitchen feeling rootless. Saturday evening in a small town, and everybody had plans. Casey was off with her girlfriends. Renee and Jim were having dinner with their gourmet group. Judy . . . well, Tess didn't really want to be with Judy. So what was she going to do? Clean the house, since Mary was coming home tomorrow. It was a beautiful spring evening, however, and the prospect of housecleaning suddenly seemed like a gloomy occupation. She made herself a smoked-turkey-and-sprout sandwich and was standing by the kitchen sink eating it when she saw Kenny and Faith come out of his house and head for her car. They were all dressed up—she in a pink dress and he in a sport coat and tie. They were probably going out to supper. Tess wondered if he'd glance her way, but he didn't. The two of them drove away.

What was this heavy weight on Tess's chest? Disappointment? What in the world was wrong with her? Was she so caught up in being idolized that she needed to make a conquest of Kenny Kronek? Again?

Trying to drive the notion out of her mind, she dug into the housecleaning with a vengeance. She put clean sheets on her mother's bed, dusted, vacuumed, and scoured the bathroom. She tucked away any obstacles that might catch the leg of a walker. Then she found various recovery aids Mary had told her to dig out: a bath bench, a booster for the toilet seat, a long-handled sponge. It was already dark by the time she turned on the outside light and went into the yard to pick some bridal wreath and tulips. She put the flowers in a vase, threw away the awful yellowed plastic doily with the curled edges, and set the bouquet in its place on a pretty scalloped-edged plate she found in a high cupboard.

Bone-weary from the unaccustomed labor, Tess fell asleep on the sofa watching TV during the ten-o'clock news. When she woke up, it was deep night, and she stumbled upstairs groggily to fall into bed and sleep like a lumberjack till dawn.

She awakened sheerly amazed at what she'd done. The clock said six ten, and she felt fabulous. She bounded up and went out in the backyard to water her mother's garden.

This was a time of day Tess rarely saw. She stood on the back steps tightening the belt of a short jade satin kimono while enjoying the streaky explosion of colors in the eastern sky. Then she went to the faucet, uncoiled the hose, and dragged it across the crisp, wet grass to the garden, between the rows of beets and okra, where she set the oscillating sprinkler, then padded back to turn on the tap at the house.

She was standing beside the garden watching the sprinkler when she heard a door slam across the alley. She turned and looked.

Kenny stood on his back step sipping a mug of coffee. He was dressed as he'd been the day she'd taken her mother to the hospital—in gray sweatpants and a white T-shirt—only this time he was barefoot. He took a long pull from the mug, studying her with disconcerting directness. Finally he lifted a hand in silent greeting.

She raised hers, too, and felt a peculiar twist inside—a warning. Not Saint Kenny, she thought. Don't even think it.

But his watchfulness made her aware of her long bare legs and short silk wrap and the little she wore under it.

She turned back to the sprinkler, which wasn't quite in the right spot. She had to run out between the rows before she got it where she wanted it, high-stepping over the damp plants while Kenny watched. The oscillator came back and slapped cold water across her rump. She yelped once and might have heard him laugh—she wasn't sure. Maybe it was just her imagination.

Tess stood, waiting out two oscillations of the sprinkler to make sure it was covering the garden. Finally she made her way up the sidewalk, leaving wet footprints behind. She felt Kenny's eyes following, and reaching the top of the back steps, she turned to check. Sure enough, he stood as before, holding his coffee mug, not even pretending to disguise his interest. He did not move; did nothing more than watch her and make her heart dance as it had not in years.

Silly woman, she thought. But when she turned and went inside, her heart was still pounding.

TESS went to the ten-o'clock service at First Methodist that morning and heard Kenny's choir for the first time. They were passably good, and she could pick out Casey's voice as clearly as if she were singing alone. The Reverend Sam Giddings announced from the pulpit that Tess'd be singing with the choir next Sunday, and a good dozen people turned to smile at her. When the recessional hymn began, she piled into the aisle with everybody else, and people murmured kind remarks about how nice it was to have her back home. Some she knew; some she didn't. Judy's and Renee's families had gone to the earlier service, so Tess waited alone outside for Casey and Kenny.

They came out when the crowd was thinning, and though Tess caught sight of both of them, her gaze remained on Kenny. He came directly to her and spoke anxiously.

"Well, what did you think?"

"Very respectable. I enjoyed the music a lot. I'm looking forward to practice on Tuesday."

"Hi, Mac," Casey said, and they hugged. Then Casey drifted off, leaving Tess with Kenny.

"So you're going to bring Mary home today."

"I've got the pillows all loaded in the back seat of her car," Tess said, glancing at her watch. "I'd better be going. I can spring her anytime after noon."

There was a parking lot at the rear of the church. When she turned toward it, he turned with her and strolled along at her side, his hands in his trouser pockets. They went around the side of the building, their footsteps lagging. Kenny walked Tess to Mary's Ford and opened the driver's door for her. He did it without hurry—a man who performed courtesies for women without conscious thought. Tess got in, stuck the key in the ignition, glanced up, and said, "Thanks."

She started the engine. Much to her surprise she found herself reluctant to leave him.

He acted as if he felt the same. He gave the car door a push with both hands and said quietly, "See ya."

TESS found Mary bathed, dressed, and eager to leave.

"Hi, Mom," she said, kissing Mary's cheek. "This is the day, huh?"

"At last. You got my car downstairs?"

"Right by the door."

"Well then, let's bust me out."

When they pulled up in the alley at home, a surprise waited. Renee and Jim came out of the house waving hello and smiling. It was the first time Tess had seen Jim since she'd been home, and he had a bear hug for her. Then he leaned forward and looked through the open back door of the car. "Hi, Ma, how you doing in there? Need some help gettin' up those back steps?"

Tess got the walker from the trunk, and Mary maneuvered herself out of the car by degrees. As they reached the back steps, Kenny showed up, sprinting across the yards.

There was a flurry of greetings, and he said to Jim, "Just like last time?"

The two men took Mary's arms over their shoulders and lifted her up the steps and into the house. She ordered one of the girls to get her chair from the living room and put it in the kitchen, where she prepared to hold court.

Renee had brewed a pot of coffee, and Judy showed up with a German chocolate cake, and they all stayed to visit and snack. Judy's husband, Ed, was a quiet man who repaired appliances and largely took orders from his wife. He greeted Tess with a hug that was chary of body contact. Within twenty minutes all three of Judy and Ed's kids showed up, too, and around three o'clock the bride- and groom-to-be, Rachel and Brent.

It was small-town U.S.A., the traditional family-gathering at Grandma's house, and Tess could see how her mother reveled in it. When someone asked if they were wearing her out and should they leave, Mary said, "Don't you dare!" So they stayed.

The kitchen was crowded. Not everyone fit around the table. Kenny stood against the kitchen sink, and Tess stood with an arm propped against the living-room archway.

Conversations overlapped. The fourth pot of coffee got perked. A little while later Kenny set down his empty cup and maneuvered through the thicket of chairs and stopped right behind Tess.

She glanced back over her shoulder and inquired quietly, "Where's Casey this afternoon?"

"Out riding her horse."

"Horses and music," Tess observed. "Her two big things."

"You've got that right. Maybe you'd like to ride with her sometime while you're here."

"Sounds tempting. Maybe when Mama gets more steady on her feet. Speaking of Mama"—she turned her back against the archway and faced him—"I guess I've never properly thanked you for all you've done for her."

"No thanks necessary. Mary's a great gal."

"Faith's been awfully good to her, too."

"Yes . . . well, Faith is a good woman."

Of course Faith was a good woman. He wouldn't be tied up with her if she wasn't. Tess knew that much by now.

Just then Casey burst into the kitchen, still in her riding clothes. "Hey, y'all," she greeted. "What am I missing? Mary, you're home. Oh, cake. Yum! Judy, did you make this?"

She fit in as easily as Kenny did. She helped herself to cake and stood eating it and visiting with the cousins. Stuffing the last bite into her mouth, she said, "Hey, Mac, can we do our song for these guys?"

"What song?" somebody said, and the next thing they knew, they were all in the living room, Mary resting on the sofa. Tess and Casey shared the piano bench, with their backs to the group. But when they sang, everyone listened. And when they finished, everyone applauded. Except Judy. She had slipped away into the kitchen, where she was cleaning up the cups and saucers. Kenny remained with his shoulder to the wall, arms crossed, and the expression in his eyes was that of a man torn between celebration and suffocation as he watched and listened to Casey.

Everyone started talking at once, the hubbub full of surprise and praise. Kenny left the doorway and approached his daughter. He put a hand on her shoulder approvingly. "Is this what you've been working on behind your bedroom door when you were mad at me? Next thing I know, I'll be hearing you on the radio." He hugged her.

All he said to Tess was, "It's very good."

WHEN everyone was gone, Mary lay down on her bed to rest. Tess spent the time screening fan mail her secretary had forwarded to her and answering requests for autographed copies of her CDs. Every week at least a dozen fund-raisers wanted donations for their causes—city libraries, battered-women shelters, schools—and Tess sent a signed CD to every single one that sent her a plea.

Just as she finished, Mary woke up, complaining, "Why didn't you wake me? I missed the beginning of *60 Minutes*. I never miss *60 Minutes*."

"Well, you didn't tell me, Mama."

When Mary was settled on the sofa in front of the TV, she added, "And suppertime was at six, too. What are you making for supper?"

"Chicken breasts and rice."

"But I always fix potatoes with chicken."

"This chicken is different. I'm going to broil it."

"It gets dry that way. I like mine fried."

Tess sighed. "Do you want me to go to the store and buy you a piece of chicken so I can fry it?"

"Heavens, no. I wouldn't put you through all that trouble."

But when Mary sat down to supper, distaste was written all over her face.

During the meal Tess attempted to broach the subject of Judy's jealousy and how it hurt her, but Mary said, "Don't be silly. Judy's not jealous. She was in the kitchen washing up the dishes while all the rest of us were having fun."

So that's how it went at mealtime—always disagreements about what Tess chose to put on the table, always differing opinions when they tried to talk. The yellowed plastic doily reappeared in the middle of the table and stayed. Tess couldn't believe her mother had retrieved it from the garbage.

Starting on Monday they established a routine. Every day Tess helped her mother with physical therapy. Every day she watered the garden and did laundry and housecleaning and errands, none of which she enjoyed and with much of which Mary found fault. It became difficult to find a time when Tess could compose.

On Tuesday, Jack Greaves called and said, "The new song is a winner, and so is the other voice. Is it that high school girl's?"

"Yes. Her name is Casey Kronek. I thought you'd like her."

"So what's on your mind, Tess?"

"I'll let you know."

ON TUESDAY night choir practice started at seven thirty. An hour beforehand Tess bathed, washed her hair, dressed in a denim skirt and white shirt, and hooked a pair of silver disks in her ears. Tricia, Judy's daughter, had been commandeered into staying with her grandmother and arrived when Tess was putting the finishing touches on her makeup. She lounged against the bathroom doorway. "Wow, Aunt Tess," she said, "you look sensational. Going to a lot of trouble just for choir practice, aren't you?"

Tess checked the results in the mirror. "It's about maintaining an image. People expect you to look a certain way when they see you out in public."

It wasn't about that at all. It was about impressing Kenny Kronek, though Tess wasn't exactly admitting that to herself yet.

She walked out of the house and was halfway to the alley when the man himself came out of his house, heading in the same direction.

"Hiya," Tess said jauntily. She felt spunky and a little flirtatious and decided to test out her wiles on him. "I'm goin' to choir practice. Where you goin'?"

He caught her mood and squinted at the clear violet sky. "Full moon. Thought I'd go out and bite a couple necks."

"You all alone?"

"Yes, ma'am," he drawled.

"Where's Casey?"

"Gone already. She picks up her friends Brenda and Amy."

"Shame to take two cars when we're both going the same way. Wanna ride with me?"

He crossed the alley. "You bet."

Inside the Z, they both buckled up. She started the engine and shifted into reverse.

"Boy, this is nice. The car's incredible, Tess."

"Thanks."

"What'll she do?"

"I don't know. I've never opened 'er up." She tossed him a glance. "I wouldn't take you for a speeder."

"I'm not, really, but sometimes a person gets the urge. Specially when there's a full moon." He sent her an arch glance. "Moon can make you do all kinds of things you shouldn't."

He seemed like a totally different man tonight, as if he, too, had been anticipating this get-together. It was easier than ever to spar with him. "Hey, Kenny, know what? There's no full moon."

"Is that a fact? Must be something else that got into me, then."

She gave him a second, longer glance. He was watching her from the corner of his eye, everything about his pose flirtatious and teasing. His clothing was a surprise. He was wearing pressed khaki trousers and a short-sleeved shirt in a bunch of wild summer colors. He was freshly shaved and smelled good, too.

He eyed her openly. "So what happened to the huge earrings?"

"These were more reverent."

"Big improvement," he said.

"Thanks a lot," she said sarcastically.

"Hey, you know what? I read that about you, that you have a very cutting sense of humor."

"Oh, so you read about me, huh?"

"Why wouldn't I? Hometown girl. Mary's daughter."

"The bane of your youth."

"That, too."

They arrived at First Methodist, a red brick structure with a white bell tower. She parked at the curb, and they climbed the front steps together. He opened the heavy wooden door for her, and she entered the dimness of the vestibule. Steps curved up to the choir loft from Tess's right. She climbed them while Kenny switched on the lights. The church smelled exactly the way she remembered— of old wood and candle smoke.

Kenny came up beside her, looking down at the pews.

"We used to sit right down there." She pointed. "I remember coming to Sunday services when Daddy was still alive."

"I remember your dad. He used to call me sonny. 'Well, let me see if I've got any mail for you today, sonny,' he'd say when I was way too young to get any. Once when he came along the sidewalk with his great big leather mailbag, I was sitting there trying to get my chain back on my bike, and he stopped and fixed it for me. Do you think mailmen still do that today?"

She smiled up at him. "I doubt it."

It was a nice moment, standing there remembering.

A door opened below, followed by footsteps ascending the stairs. A boy appeared, tall, gangly, a red crew cut.

"Here's Josh," said Kenny. "Josh, come and meet Tess McPhail."

Josh was a senior, who played the organ and reacted with a blush when introduced to Tess. He escaped to unlock the key cover on the organ. Voices sounded below, and other choir members began arriving.

Casey and her friends made their appearance, and Tess had the extreme pleasure of being able to tell her, "I talked to my producer, Jack Greaves, and he likes the song and wants to include it on the album."

"Are you serious?"

"Absolutely. You're going to be a published songwriter—one who gets royalties."

The squeals of excitement might have been the slightest bit out of line in the church, but giving Casey the thrill of her life gave Tess one of her own.

Thirty-three people showed up for choir practice, and Kenny performed a simple introduction.

"I know you all recognize Tess McPhail, so make her feel comfortable by not asking her for her autograph tonight, okay?"

A ripple of laughter relaxed everyone, and they got to work. From the moment he raised his arms, Kenny became in all respects a leader, one who directed with animation and expressiveness. For Tess, being directed by him was not the trial she'd imagined when first asked. It was wholly pleasant. She'd been placed with the sopranos, who curved around on Kenny's right, while Casey stood with the altos, on his left. Sometimes when they were singing, Tess's and Kenny's glances caught, and she had the feeling that destiny had brought her home for much more than caring for Mary. It had brought her here for Casey. And for Kenny, too? Heavens, what in the world was she thinking? Yet every time she was with him, she saw a new facet of his personality, and what she saw she liked more and more.

He had chosen mostly familiar hymns for the choir. For Tess's solo he picked "Fairest Lord Jesus." The beautiful old traditional hymn crowned their practice with a sense of celebration that was still intact as the session ended and they said good night.

Everyone was gone by ten after nine. In the choir loft Kenny turned and met Tess's eyes across twenty feet of disarrayed chairs and music stands. Two inadequate ceiling lights hung by chains over the choir loft, tinting the hardwood floor gold.

"Thanks," he said.

"You're welcome."

They stood close, silence all around, captivated by each other but fighting it. He turned and headed for the organ, and she followed, giant-stepping down to the lowest level. He slid onto the bench and switched off the gooseneck light, then reached up for his own music, which lay askew on top of the organ. She came up behind him.

"Kenny, I have to talk to you about Casey," she said over his shoulder. "May I?" she asked, indicating the organ bench.

"Sure." He slid over, and she slipped onto the bench beside him, joining her hands in her lap. She took a moment, realizing that what she was about to say would have a major impact on his life as well as on his daughter's. She did not take it lightly.

"I want to take her to Nashville to sing harmony with me on 'Small Town Girl.' "

He sat so still she knew he didn't like it. He looked into her eyes and waited a long time before looking away.

"You understand what I'm talking about? A recording session on a major label."

"Yes, I understand."

"It's what she wants, and she's good enough."

"I know. I realized that Sunday afternoon."

She waited, but he said no more. She said, "Look, if you think I'd let anything bad happen to her, you're wrong. I'd be there. I'd look after her. I'd see to it that nobody took advantage of her."

"I know that, and I appreciate it. But what about her life?"

"You really think my life is so bad?"

"It's abnormal—half the time traveling, no husband, no kids."

"It's rewarding when it's what you love to do."

He allowed himself a small explosion prompted by frustration. "But it isn't what I want for her!"

She let his outburst fade away before challenging him quietly. "The choice isn't yours, Kenny."

Tormented, he stared her down before breaking. His shoulders slumped slightly as he admitted, "I know that."

She gave him time to think about it awhile. At length he spoke in a quiet voice, as if arguing with himself. "This is hard, you know. She's my only child. It's . . . it's hard letting go."

She laid her hand on his bare arm. "Of course it is."

He looked down at her hand, then covered it with his own, rubbing the back of it. Realizing what he was doing, he withdrew his hand, and she took hers back, too.

"When would she go?" he asked, meeting her eyes.

"As soon as school is out. She can stay at my house until she finds a place of her own. The album's scheduled to come out in September. We'd have to get into the studio in June so there'd be time for mixing and mastering and distribution."

He stared at her, thinking.

"I know lots of people in Nashville," she reassured him. "She won't have any trouble finding a job."

He hooked his hands over the edge of the bench, hunched his shoulders, and stared at his knees. She could almost read his mind.

"I suppose you're thinking, Why did Tess McPhail have to come back home?"

"Yeah," he said, "that's exactly what I'm thinking."

Finally he straightened up and said, "Come on." He slid off the bench. "Take me for a ride in your new car and make it up to me."

They walked downstairs together, and he turned off the lights in the vestibule, then shoved the heavy door open and let some night glow show the way down the steps to where her car waited.

They got in and slammed the doors. When she started the engine, she left her foot on the brake. "So where do you want to go?" she asked.

"Go on up to the stop sign at the highway and turn right."

While she pulled away from the curb, they both rolled their windows down and let the spring night rush around their heads. When necessary, he told her where to turn. She kept her speed around thirty-five so the night sounds could be heard—insects, gravel hitting the undercarriage, and the wind patting their ears.

"I thought you would be a speeder," he said.

"I think you have a lot of misconceptions about me."

"No more than you have about me."

"You might be right. Anyway, why hurry? It's nice to get away from the house for a while."

"Mary tells me you two don't get along so well."

She glanced over. "I think it's mainly age difference."

"My mother and I got that way, too, as she got older."

"It's funny, isn't it," she mused, "how they can test your patience with the smallest things. We argue all the time about what I'm going to cook for meals and how I'm going to cook it. You have to understand, I'm the world's worst cook to begin with."

"You don't like it?"

"Nuh-uh," she said with great passion.

Neither of them said anything more till he ordered, "Turn here."

They swung into a rutted driveway.

"Where are we?"

"At Dexter Hickey's, where Casey keeps her horse, Rowdy. Pull up next to that fence." She did, and killed the engine. They got out and sauntered toward a chest-high wooden fence. Inside the paddock a half-dozen horses stood close together. Roused from sleep, some lifted their heads. Out of the cluster one dark shape separated and moved lazily, head hanging, hooves plopping softly on the battered earth as he approached them.

Kenny waited, his arms crossed on the fence, till the horse arrived and blew softly at his elbow. Kenny laid a hand between the horse's eyes and said, "This is Rowdy."

"Hi, Rowdy," she said quietly, waiting, letting the horse take her scent. He reached out his enormous head to her hand.

Rowdy's nose was velvet beneath her hand. She thought he'd probably fallen asleep again, for he stood motionless, breathing evenly in heavy warm gusts against her palm.

Out of the blue she said something Kenny never expected, said it sincerely, so that one more barrier crumbled. "I can see, Kenny, that you're a very good dad."

He'd been right earlier: The moon made people do crazy things. But much as he wanted to kiss her, it wouldn't be wise. In fact, kissing her would be the height of folly, but he kept standing there thinking about it. The moon might have had its way if Rowdy hadn't whickered then and shaken his big head, startling them.

They drew back from the fence, and Tess said, "Do I have your permission to ask Casey, then?"

He expelled an uncertain breath before answering, "Yes."

And they returned to the car like two sensible people.

THEY reached town so fast she couldn't believe it, and when they pulled up in the alley, she shut off the engine, but neither of them moved. It was suddenly very quiet.

The silence underscored their changing attitudes toward each other and their marked reluctance to part. But both of their houses had lights on. Tess was supposed to give Tricia a ride home, and Kenny ought to go in and give Faith a good-night call.

"Well," he said, reaching for his door handle. He thought of how much she'd changed in the last few days. "Thanks for the ride."

"Anytime."

They got out of the car, slammed the doors, and stood in the warm night on either side of the Z.

He said over the car roof, "See you Sunday."

"Yeah, see you Sunday."

IN THE morning Tess called Jack Greaves and told him, "I'm going to ask Casey Kronek to sing backup on 'Small Town Girl.' Okay with you?"

"I think your voices are a perfect blend."

"Thanks, Jack. This means a lot to me."

That night at six forty-five, when Mary was settled before the TV, Tess went into the bathroom, freshened her lipstick, shook her hair, and crossed the alley to visit the Kronek house for the first time in well over eighteen years.

It was hot on Kenny's back step. She knocked and waited. Suddenly Casey appeared. "Hey, Mac, what a surprise." She threw open the door. "Come on in."

The aroma of baked pork chops warned Tess that they were still eating their supper. She followed Casey, nevertheless, and when they entered the kitchen, there sat Kenny and Faith at their meal, a picture of perfect domestic bliss.

Casey said, "Want a glass of iced tea?"

"Oh, no. I'm sorry. I thought you all would be done eating. I'll— I'll come back later."

Faith, unruffled, immediately said, "No, no. Please come in, Tess."

In her entire life Tess had never felt more of an impostor. She was sure Kenny could divine that part of her reason for coming here was curiosity.

Kenny recovered from his surprise and said politely, "Please sit down, Tess."

Casey made the point moot by putting a glass of iced tea at the empty place, then sitting back down and resuming her meal.

Tess sat and said, "Thanks, Casey." She decided since she had ruined their peaceful meal, she might as well go the rest of the way. "I really came over to talk to you."

Casey was cutting a pork chop. "Sure. What's up?"

"I want you to come to Nashville and sing background for me when I record 'Small Town Girl.' "

Casey's eyes grew big. The fork and knife fell from her fingers and clattered to her plate. "Oh, my Lord," she whispered.

Faith looked back and forth uncertainly between Tess and Casey and whispered, "Oh, my goodness."

Kenny set down his silverware silently, watching his daughter's eyes fill with tears. Without another word Casey went around the table to Tess, who rose and stepped into her embrace. It was more than an embrace. Something magnificent happened inside Tess while the girl hugged her. This must be what it feels like to be a mother, she thought, to have someone love you unconditionally and hold you up as a role model. Her heart was absolutely clubbing with happiness.

"You mean it, don't you?" Casey finally managed, stepping back to look into Tess's face.

"Yes, I mean it. I talked to your father about it last night, and he's agreed to let you come to Nashville and stay with me."

Casey turned to Kenny, amazed, her face streaming tears. "You did? Oh, Daddy, did you really? I love you so much!" She flung herself against him. "Thank you, thank you." She kissed him flat on the mouth. "Oh, my gosh, I can't believe it. I'm going to Nashville!" She grabbed Faith and kissed her. "I'm going to Nashville, Faith." Casey began bouncing around the room like a bumper car. "I've got to call Brenda and tell her. And Amy. No, wait a minute. I'd better sit down for a minute. My stomach feels funny." She dropped to her chair, shut her eyes, sucked in a breath.

Tess glanced over at Kenny, on her right. He was wearing a smile with the most bittersweet edge she had ever seen.

"Well," Tess said, filling the void, "I've certainly managed to ruin your supper, haven't I?"

"Ruin it," Casey yelped. "Are you kidding?"

Kenny pushed away his plate and said, "We can eat anytime."

Faith added, "That's for sure, but will you stay for some blueberry cobbler, Tess?"

Tess stayed for cobbler. Then Casey insisted Tess come up to her room and listen to a song she'd been working on with her guitar.

When Tess left a half hour later, via the kitchen, Kenny and Faith were just finishing up the supper dishes. "Well, guess I'll be getting back home. I've left Casey composing upstairs."

"I'll see you out," Kenny said.

The door slammed behind them, and he followed Tess toward the alley. "Well, it's done now," he said. "She's going to Nashville."

"If it's any consolation, I know how hard this is for you. I'll do my best for her, Kenny. I promise you."

They had reached the alley. When she turned to face him, she made sure there was plenty of space between them. He stood his distance, with his hands in his back pockets, as if in an effort to keep them off her.

"The two of you look like you're very well suited," Tess said.

"That what you came over for, to see how we're suited?"

She wasn't sure how to answer. "What if I said yes?"

"Then I'd probably ask what the hell you're after."

"And I'd probably answer, I don't know, Kenny. And that's the honest truth. I don't know."

He searched her eyes while the tension built between them. Finally Kenny released an immense gust of breath. "Why do I feel like I'm back on that school bus again?"

The time was getting long. Certainly, Faith would be wondering what was keeping him. But neither of them moved.

He whispered, "What are you trying to do to me, Tess?"

She took a decisive step backward. "I have to go," she said. "I'll stay on my side of the alley from now on. I'm sorry, Kenny."

Chapter Six

THE week waned. Casey came over after school, but Tess avoided Kenny and the backyard when she knew he was around. On Sunday, Mary announced she wanted to go to church and hear Tess sing. She'd been stuck in the house for a whole week, and it was time she got out.

Tess, dressed in a brick-colored silk skirt and blouse, was loading up Mary's wheelchair when Kenny came out of his house and called, "Wait. I'll help you with that." He was all dressed for church and looking hunky enough to set her heart racing.

"I thought you were gone already," Tess said as he lifted the chair into the trunk.

"No. I always leave at twenty to. Do you need any help getting her in the car?" he asked.

"No. She'll do it herself."

"All right, then. See you there." He slammed the trunk, avoiding her eyes, then headed for his garage.

Casey came flying out the back door, shouted "Hey, Mac" as she ran, and a minute later they were gone.

So, she thought. Mr. Iceman. He couldn't resist running out when he saw me, but he didn't like himself for doing it, so he took it out on me.

Twenty minutes later the choir was singing "Holy, Holy, Holy" while Kenny directed. It sent shivers up her spine. Their eyes met too often and locked too intently for them to remain aloof from one another. By the time she sang "Fairest Lord Jesus," he had removed his suit jacket and rolled up his white sleeves. Something happened between them when she sang her solo. Something irreversible.

In the vestibule after the service she was mobbed. Word had spread that she was singing here today, and the congregation had swelled beyond anything the church had ever seen. All Tess's family had come for the later service today, and she was touched by their show of support. Nieces, nephews, brothers-in-law, and sisters—everyone except Judy—had hugs and pride in their eyes.

Reverend Giddings approached and engaged Tess in a prolonged handclasp. "I cannot thank you enough, young lady. Splendid job." He released her hand and said to someone behind her, "Very nice job, Kenny, and a particularly fine choice of music." She had not known he was there, and turned toward him.

Though surrounded by a sea of familiar faces, Kenny and Tess became attuned only to each other.

"This was probably the best Sunday I've had since I started directing," he told Tess.

"Why?"

"You."

His directness loosened her resolve. "Something got me here." She laid a wrist across her heart. "It's how it used to be, when I was little—the music, my family, the familiar church. . . . I don't know. Something got you, too, didn't it?"

"Yes. Something got me, too." His tone was quiet. "I understand now more than ever why you've succeeded the way you have. You have charisma."

"You didn't seem to think so this morning when we met in the alley. I thought you were mad at me."

"It won't happen again." Without warning he took her in a quick embrace and kissed her temple. She had the sensation of his lips at her ear. "Thank you for singing today. I'll never forget it, Tess."

He had just set her free when Casey appeared and put an arm around each of them. "Hey, Mac, you want to go horseback riding this afternoon?"

Linked by the girl, they stood in a trio while Tess tried to hide the fact that she was rattled.

"Gosh, I don't know if I should leave Mama alone."

Casey spun away and nabbed the first family member she encountered. It was Renee.

"Hey, Renee, can somebody stay with your mama this afternoon so Tess can go horseback riding with me?"

"Sure, I can," Renee replied. "What time are you leaving?"

Apart from the others, Tess asked Kenny, "Are you going, too?"

He cleared his throat and answered, "No. Better not."

She hid her disappointment as Casey turned back to Tess, asking, "What time do you want to leave?"

"One o'clock. I need to be back in town by four or so."

The plan was set.

THEY took Casey's old pickup, which was so old it had rear wheel wells that stuck out like a bulldog's shoulders. But the radio worked, and they sang country songs all the way out to Dexter Hickey's.

The place looked different by daylight. The fence needed painting and the yard needed mowing, but the surrounding countryside was breathtaking. The ranch was framed by a great stretch of undulating grassland dotted by apple trees, with woods beyond.

Inside the stable, Dexter had left a mare named Sunflower for Tess, with instructions to turn her out after they were done riding.

When Sunflower and Rowdy were saddled, the women mounted up. In the sun the horses' hides gleamed as Casey led the way along the fence toward the rippling woods.

Casey turned in the saddle and asked, "How does it feel?"

"Like I'm going to hurt tomorrow. I'm not used to it."

"We'll take it slow at first."

When they reached a spread of buttercups, Casey asked, "Want to try trotting?"

"Why not."

She kicked Rowdy into a trot, and Sunflower followed suit. After fifty yards they picked up to an easy canter that took them up the rim of the valley into the woods, where Casey reined in and was waiting when Tess reached her and reined in, too.

"We'll let them rest for a while." Casey patted Rowdy's shoulder, then sat silently, looking up at the trees. Out of the blue she asked, "So what's going on between you and my dad?"

Tess did a poor job of hiding her surprise. "Nothing."

"I thought I caught some undercurrents at our table the other night, and on the church steps this morning he was hugging you."

"He was thanking me for singing today."

"Oh, is that all," Casey said dryly. She added, "Well, just in case something is going on, I want you to know it's perfectly okay with me." She was just turning her horse deeper into the woods when she glanced out toward the meadow and said, "Well, well, look who's coming."

Tess craned around in her saddle and saw Kenny riding toward them. He caught sight of them in the shade and kicked the bay into a canter. He rode like a man to whom doing so is second nature, dressed in blue jeans, a white T-shirt, and a straw hat.

Reaching them, he reined to a stop and said, "I changed my mind. It got lonesome at home." He barely had a glance for his daughter but studied Tess from beneath his hatbrim with eyes that gave away more than he wanted.

Casey was grinning. "I was just saying to Tess—"

"Casey!" Tess shot her a warning glare.

"Nothing," she finished, turning her horse up the trail. "Glad you came, Dad. We're taking it easy 'cause Tess isn't used to it."

They rode for another hour and a half, talking little, enjoying the beautiful spring day. Near four o'clock, when they were heading back toward the paddock, thunderheads had built up in the southwest and the breeze had cooled.

Kenny gave Tess a hand unsaddling Sunflower. She watched him carry the saddle through the door of the tack room and throw it over a sawhorse.

He turned and caught her staring. When he came back, he asked casually, "Want to ride back to town with me, Tess?"

She looked first at Casey, then at him. "Oh, I don't think—"

"It's okay," Casey put in. "Go with him. I'm in a hurry. I'm not even going to take time to curry Rowdy. I've got a date I gotta get ready for." She led Rowdy to the door and turned him out into the paddock, then came back, lifting a hand as she passed. "See you in the morning, Dad. I probably won't get in till after eleven."

"Okay. Be careful."

A minute later Tess and Kenny heard the sound of her truck rumbling away. They rubbed down their horses in silence; then he set down his brush and came to her. "That's good. I'll take her now." He led Sunflower and his own horse to the door, where he turned them out.

"Let's go."

Kenny drove with no particular hurry, the windows down and the wind blowing in. He glanced over. "You hungry?"

"Famished."

"How 'bout if a country boy from Wintergreen takes you out to dinner? I know just the place."

He took her to the Sonic Drive-in, and they parked under the long metal awning. The menu and speaker were on his side. He rested his elbow on the window ledge and looked the menu over. "What do you want?"

"Burger in a basket."

"All right." He pushed the call button and gave their order. When he finished, he angled himself in his corner and looked back at her. Thunder rumbled off toward the southwest, but they scarcely paid attention.

Finally Tess said, "Casey asked me today what's going on between you and me."

"What did you tell her?"

"The truth—nothing." She picked a piece of horsehair off her jeans. "Then she said it's okay if we start something."

They thought about it for a while before Tess said, "Of course, we both know that's not a good idea."

"Of course."

"After all, there's Faith. And I'm going back to Nashville in two weeks."

"Where you belong," he added.

"Where I belong."

They either had to give in and kiss each other or die wanting to. The carhop saved them from either catastrophe by delivering their tray.

"You know what?" Tess said when he was reaching for their food. "This is the first date I've had in two years, where I go out with a man and he buys me dinner and takes me home. I find I can't do that anymore."

"Too rich? Too famous?"

"Both. You don't know what people are after you for."

A blue pickup with three teenagers pulled in on their right. Kenny asked, "That what you think about me? That I'm after something?"

"No. I think you're just an accident."

"Oh, that's flattering."

"You know what I mean."

The burgers were juicy and delicious, and they gave up flirting to sink their teeth in, dipping their french fries in ketchup and munching pickles. As she finished hers, Tess wiped her mouth on a paper napkin and glanced at the blue pickup. "Oh-oh," she said, "I think I've been spotted." Three faces were smiling her way and gaping. "You all done?" Kenny jammed the rest of his burger in his mouth, and she said, "Let's go."

The rain began as they backed out of their parking spot and rolled up their windows. He switched on the wipers and turned onto Main Street. They drove around the town square, then headed north on Sycamore. When he turned into their alley, the trees were churning in the wind-whipped storm. He reached his own garage and would have driven inside, but she said, "Leave it out here. I like the storm."

With only a glance at her he complied, killing the lights, wipers, and engine. "You gonna run through this?" he said.

"No. I'll wait a minute."

More rain, more lightning, more thunder, and the two of them unable to think of more to say. Though it was only six p.m., the world was murky and obscure beneath the roiling clouds. Suddenly Tess's frustration boiled over. "Look, Kenny, this is ridiculous. I'm a full-grown adult, and I'm playing games with you like a kid. Just don't tell Faith I did this, all right?"

She reared up on one knee, dropped sideways, braced a hand on the driver's door, and kissed him. She caught him so off guard that he actually pulled back. When it ended, he had both hands around her ribs to keep her from falling completely against him.

She drew back a mere inch. His breath came fast, and his lips were open in surprise. She told him, "That's for the time I teased you on the school bus." His hands were warm through her T-shirt. "Consider this completely my doing," she added. "I absolve you from all guilt, my dear Saint Kenny. Thanks for a wonderful day."

She kissed him again, quickly, got out, and ran through the cold, driving rain to the house.

INSIDE the house Mary and Renee were watching *60 Minutes*. Tess came charging in the back door, dripping.

"About time you got here. We were getting worried," Renee said.

"Sorry. I should have called." Tess threw off her cap. "I went to the Sonic Drive-in with Kenny."

She sat on a step and pulled off her boots while Renee studied the top of her red hair. "With Kenny. Well."

Tess stood up and looked at Renee. "Hey, listen, are you in a hurry to get home, or could I talk to you for a minute?"

"I can stay a while longer."

They went upstairs, where Tess stripped off her wet clothes while Renee sat cross-legged on her old bed. "So what's going on?"

Tess threw on a cotton pullover, pulled the rubber band out of her hair, and sat at the vanity table combing her wet bangs. "It's bizarre," she told Renee. "You aren't going to believe it. I kissed Kenny about five minutes ago in his car. He wouldn't kiss me, so I finally kissed him. Pretty stupid, huh?"

"That's all? Just a kiss?"

"Yes. But Renee, something has happened to me in these couple weeks I've been home. I'm bumping into him all the time, and he turns out to be the nicest guy I've met in years, and he treats Mama like he's her son, and then I'm just crazy about that Casey, and I see what a good father Kenny is, and the next thing you know, I'm acting like a lovesick teenager. Renee, that's not like me."

Renee digested this for a moment. "You've got to be careful, Tess. You can't toy with people's feelings."

"I'm not toying."

"What's going to come of it? You'll head back to Nashville, and if you've spoiled what's between him and Faith, he'll end up the loser. Maybe you've lost sight of just how big a star you are and just how impressed a man could be with your attention."

"I've thought about that." Tess sighed. "You know what, Renee? Sometimes it can be mighty lonely being Tess McPhail."

Renee rose from the bed and approached her sister, placing her hands on Tess's shoulders. "You wanted me to talk some sense into you, well, here it is. For the rest of the time you're home, stay away from Kenny, okay?"

Tess nodded glumly.

Renee went on. "You know, Tess, there's one thing we're over-looking."

"What's that?"

"Kenny himself. If he's the kind of man I think he is, he'd never two-time Faith. You said yourself he refused to kiss you."

Tess thought for a moment, then said, "You're right. And you know what? That's one of the reasons I think so much of him."

Tess accepted Renee's admonition and took it to heart. She made a resolution that she would do everything in her power to avoid Kenny from now on.

IT HAD been over three weeks since Mary's surgery. She felt increasingly better. Feeling better, she seemed to argue less. Mary and Tess had finally had a meal with no clashes. Tess had found something that pleased them both—a taco salad, which they ate in front of the evening news. They were finishing up their meal when Tess said, "Mom, I've arranged a surprise for you."

"For me?" Mary said, surprised already.

"On Saturday morning at eight o'clock a hairdresser named Niki is coming to fix your hair for the wedding, and she'll do anything you want. Color it, perm it, cut it—anything."

Mary looked amazed. "Right here at home?"

"That's right."

"This Niki—she's not from Judy's shop?"

"No. Judy and her girls are doing all the bridal party that morn-ing, so they'll be busy. But Judy said Niki will do a good job. That's all right with you, then?"

"Well, sure." Mary continued to look amazed.

"And Mama, there's one other thing I wanted to ask you about. You know that pretty green silk trouser suit I sent you last year from Seattle? Have you worn it yet?"

"I tried it on."

"Why don't you wear it for the wedding? It would be perfect, since your legs have to be wrapped in those stockings all the time. What do you say, Mama?"

"I was going to wear this other pantsuit that I got last spring. It's perfectly good, and I've only worn it a few times."

Tess's first reaction was anger, and she got up and started stacking their dirty dishes, trying to swallow the lump of hurt in her throat. Then she changed her mind, set the dishes back down, and dropped to one knee beside Mary's chair. Taking Mary's hand in both of her own, she looked up into her mother's brown eyes. "Listen, Mama, I don't know how else to say this. I'm rich. It's a fact of life now. I'm very very rich, and it gives me great pleasure to send you things. But it hurts my feelings when you won't even try to use them."

"Oh, dear. . . . Well, I—I guess I never thought of that." Mary sat looking somber and somewhat stricken. Finally she glanced away, then back at her daughter.

"Well, since you're being honest, let me be honest, too. Sometimes when you send things, I think it's because you know you should come to see me yourself, but you're too busy to take the time. Maybe that's why I sometimes don't use them. Because if the truth be told, I'd rather have you than all the fancy presents in the world."

Mary's words stung sharply, for they were true, and Tess at last admitted it. She not only saw Mary less often than she should, she took issue with petty aggravations that love should overlook. Who knew how many more years Mary had?

"I'm sorry, Mama," Tess said softly. "I'll try to do better."

Mary reached out and put a hand on Tess's hair. "You know how proud I am of you, don't you, dear?"

Tess nodded with tears in her eyes.

"And I know what it took for you to get where you are. But Tess, we're your family, and you only get one of those."

"I know," Tess whispered, choked.

They remained in that tableau, each accepting what the other had said. They had not felt closer since Tess graduated from high school and loaded up her car to head for Nashville.

"Now I'll tell you what you do," Mary said. "You go in my closet and you find that pretty slacks suit that you sent me and get it ironed up for Saturday, and when this Niki finishes my hair, I'll put it on and do you girls proud at that wedding. How's that?"

Tess kissed her mother's cheek. "Thanks, Mama," she said.

THE weather on Saturday couldn't have been more ideal. Eighty-three degrees and sunny when Tess was getting dressed. She'd bought a new outfit—a midnight-blue sheath and matching sling-back faille pumps, with a faint peppering of miniature blue rhine-stones on the toes. At her neck she hung a platinum chain with a diamond-covered orb the size of a marble. On her ears were small sickle moons, also covered with real diamonds.

When she walked into Mary's bedroom, Mary stared.

"Something wrong?" Tess asked, glancing down.

"You've been running around here so long in your blue jeans and T-shirts that I forgot you're actually a big-time star. My Lord in heaven but you're beautiful, child."

"Well, what about you? Wait till we get that suit on you."

The suit was the color of light through a glass of crème de menthe. Getting it on Mary took some effort, but together they managed. When the trousers were in place and the jacket was buttoned, Tess said, "I want to put some mascara on you, okay? Come over here and sit down."

When Mary was seated before her mirror, Tess powdered her cheeks, brushed them with faint coral blusher, and used a little mascara and lipstick. Niki had done a commendable job, giving Mary a flattering hairstyle that took five years off her age. Her peachy gray hair lay in soft waves tipped up at the ends.

"Now earrings. I have just the perfect ones." Tess produced a small box of pale aqua, purchased in New York, and handed it to her mother. When Mary read the single word embossed on the cover, she lifted disbelieving eyes to Tess in the mirror.

"Tiffany? Oh, Tess, what have you gone and done?"

"Open it. Happy Mother's Day a little early."

Inside the aqua box was another, of black velvet. Mary lifted the lid to reveal a pair of teardrop earrings of emeralds surrounded by diamonds. "Oh, Tess."

Tess smiled at her in the mirror. "Go ahead, put them on."

Mary's hands trembled as she lifted the gems to her ears. When the earrings were in place, she stared at her reflection. She put a hand to her fluttering heart and whispered, "My word."

Tess bent down, putting her head beside her mother's, and they studied their reflections in the mirror. "You're beautiful, too, Mama."

"Thank you, Tess." Mary touched Tess's cheek lovingly.

"You're welcome. Now let's go knock 'em dead, eh, Ma? I'm going to put your wheelchair in the trunk. Wait till I come back before you use those crutches on the back steps, okay?"

"Okay."

Tess hauled the folded wheelchair down the steps and pushed it down the bumpy back sidewalk. She got Mary's car out, put hers away, opened her mother's trunk, and was getting ready to lift the wheelchair when Kenny opened his porch door and yelled, "Hey, Tess, wait. I'll give you a hand with that."

He strode down the length of his backyard in a navy pin-striped suit while she waited beside the car. He stowed the wheelchair and slammed the trunk.

"There." He turned, brushing his palms together. "Can't have you getting . . ." His eyes went down to her glistening toes and back up. He never did finish the sentence.

"Nice dress," he said quietly.

"Thanks. Nice suit."

He certainly hadn't bought his clothes in Wintergreen, nor had he any idea how his appearance made her blood rush. But he knew how to match a suit to his body, and he knew how to fix his gaze upon a woman in a way that made her aware of these things deep down.

"Well," she said, "I'd better get back up to the house. Mama is waiting."

"Does she need any help?"

"No, I don't think so."

In spite of her refusal, when she headed to the house, he followed. They reached the house, and Tess went inside while he waited on the step. Momentarily she reappeared, coming out first to hold the screen door open for Mary, who stumped over the threshold on crutches and paused, smiling, pleased.

From three steps below her, Kenny took one look and exclaimed, "Lord o' mercy, look at you!" His admiration was so genuine it made a blank of his face.

"Hi, Kenny," the old woman said girlishly. If she could have spun in a circle, she would have. "Tess took me over. What do you think?"

"I think if I were twenty years older, I'd fall head over heels in love. Come to think of it, I might anyway."

Mary looked like a woman reborn as she headed down the steps. Tess and Kenny escorted her to the car. He opened the back door and waited patiently while she fitted herself inside. He put the crutches on the floor and closed the door, then walked Tess around to the driver's side and opened the door for her.

He asked, "Will you be okay getting her into the church?"

"I'll be fine, thanks."

"Well, I'd better see if I can light a fire under Casey. See you later."

He slammed the door, and she admitted to herself that no matter what she'd promised Renee, she and Kenny were treading a fine line between common sense and a move that would create impending disorder in their lives. It seemed highly likely that before this night was out, they would set that disorder in motion.

Chapter Seven

♪ ♥ ♪ ♥ ♪

KENNY and Tess sat on the same side of the aisle, but she was ushered up front with the other family members. He was seated a few rows back, with Casey and Faith. The wedding was typical small-town: the organ was too loud, the singer projected in a piercing soprano, and the four-year-old ring bearer veered off the center

aisle when he saw his mother. Afterward Mary was part of the
receiving line in the vestibule, leaving Tess free to join the crowd
outside. The wind had come up to relieve the afternoon heat, and
great white cloud puffs scuttled along the blue backdrop. Everyone
stared at Tess, but not one soul approached.

Not until Casey came out of church. She made a beeline for Tess,
exclaiming, "Wow, you look awesome!"

When the last of the wedding guests spilled from church, Tess
caught sight of Kenny wheeling Mary down the ramp leading from
the side door of the vestibule. The bride and groom emerged, and
the church bells clamored overhead. Tess moved toward the parking lot, where she found Kenny standing beside Mary's car, waiting
for her. Mary was already installed in the back seat.

"Thanks for taking over my job."

"No problem."

Tess leaned down and smiled into the car window. "How you
doin', Mama? You getting tired?"

"Doing just fine, but I sure could use some supper. Wouldn't
mind if you'd get me to that reception before I faint dead away."

For a moment Kenny and Tess became an island. "I mean it,
Kenny. Thanks for seeing after Mama again and again." She
touched his sleeve, letting her hand trail down as she moved away.
Their fingers joined in passing; then Tess continued around the car.

The reception was held out in the country at Current River Cove,
the nicest reception hall in Ripley County. When the wedding party
arrived, a band was setting up in one corner, and their filler tape
amplified a mixed bag of country music across the hall.

Over two hundred guests milled and mingled, waiting for the
arrival of the bride and groom. Though most of them had kept their
distance from Tess on the church steps, the presence of cocktails
seemed to signal that it was now all right to approach. Nearly every
person asked her why she hadn't sung at the wedding and if she was
going to do so at the dance.

"No," she replied again and again. "I'm a guest here today. The
bride and the groom are the stars."

When the bride and groom arrived and dinner was served, Tess and Mary sat at a round table for eight, joined by Judy and Ed and Tricia. No sooner were they seated than Faith approached and asked, "Are these seats taken?"

"No," Judy answered. "Sit down. My other two kids were ushers, so they're seated at the head table."

"Oh, good. I'll go get Kenny." While she was gone, Casey arrived and took the chair right next to Tess. Faith returned with Kenny in tow, and the two of them took the remaining chairs.

Dinner turned out to be a tasty combination of chicken and herbed cheese rolled around asparagus and baked in puff pastry. The wine was excellent—a peppery pinot noir, which was passed around when the toasts began.

It was Faith who mentioned Mary's earrings and peered at them more closely. Mary divulged, "They're real. Tess gave them to me this afternoon."

Six people admired them. The seventh pursed her lips and nudged her husband's elbow. "Give me some more of that wine, Ed."

In the middle of the meal, Tricia brought up the fact that Tess was taking Casey to Nashville.

"Isn't she wonderful?" Casey beamed at Tess. "She's making all my dreams come true."

Mary had finished her second glass of wine and was looking well pleased with everything. Faith said, "I think it would be appropriate to make a toast to our up-and-coming star." They all raised their glasses—Judy, too, unable to do otherwise without looking like a jerk. But the moment the toast ended, she glared at her younger sister and escaped to the ladies' room.

Tess watched her go, laid down her napkin, and said calmly, "Excuse me, please. I have to talk to Judy."

Once inside the ladies' room, she locked the door. Judy had thrown her handbag on a counter and was stabbing at her hair.

Tess faced Judy's profile rather than her reflection in the mirror. "All right, Judy, let's talk."

"Leave me alone."

"No. Because I can't stand your jealousy anymore. I've been home for three weeks, and every time I've seen you, something has managed to get your goat."

"You love to throw it in our faces, don't you?" Judy accused. "Look at me, the rich, famous star coming back home to show the peons just how drudging their life is."

"That's not fair. I have never flaunted my fame or my money around you and you know it."

Judy glared at her younger sister. "Why don't you just go back where you came from?" she said venomously. "The rest of us can take care of Mama and do a lot better job of it, too." The lock clacked open, and the door slammed against the tile wall as Judy stormed out.

Tess stayed behind, struggling to compose herself. By the time she returned to the table, the band had started playing and Judy and Ed were gone. A moment later Renee arrived breathless from the dance floor. She looked particularly radiant in an apricot dress with a lace bodice. "What happened to Judy and Ed?" she inquired.

Tess confessed, "My fault. I got into it with Judy in the bathroom about you know what."

"So she stomped off home?"

"And took Ed and Tricia, too. I'm sorry, Renee."

"Hey, you know what?" Renee said. "It's Judy's problem, not ours. Now, listen. The bride and groom sent me over to talk to you. They're getting so many requests from their guests that they told me to ask if you'll sing just one song with the band. It would mean so much to them, Tess. Come on," Renee cajoled.

Tess glanced at the dance floor. Rachel and Brent were half dancing, watching Tess with hopeful expressions on their faces. Tess knew that if she sang, it would make their wedding the talk of the very limited social season in Ripley County.

"You sure it's all right with the band?"

"Are you kidding? What band wouldn't want to say they backed up Tess McPhail?"

"All right. Just one song."

Renee gave the bride and groom a thumbs-up, and they hugged in jubilation; then Rachel blew Tess a kiss and went to the foot of the stage and spoke to the lead guitarist.

At the next song break the band immediately announced, "Everyone knows we have a famous Nashville star with us tonight. She's the bride's aunt, and she's agreed to come up and do a song with us. Let's make her welcome. Tess McPhail!"

The crowd parted for her, and she went up on the stage with a confident stride, cuing the band on the way. "Can you give me 'Cattin' in G?"

The drummer said, "You got it, Mac," and gave them a four-beat cue on the rim of his snare.

When the rhythm broke and she grabbed the mike, she took two hundred hearts captive on the spot. She gave Wintergreen something to talk about for the next ten years, planting her glittering high heels as far apart as her straight dress would allow, keeping rhythm with her right knee and sending blue jets shooting from her sequins. She became one with her audience, giving them a performance filled with energy and rhythm. 'Cattin' had a rock beat and slightly naughty words. She used her hands and long flashing nails like a sorcerer to put her audience under her spell. She had an innate sense of drama and played the crowd like an actress, using eye contact and a hint of flirtatiousness to make each listener believe she was singing exclusively for her or him.

When the song ended, Renee yelled, "All right, sis!"

The bride and groom clapped while a general chant went up. "Mac! Mac! Mac!"

It pulsed through the room.

Taking her bow, Tess made sure she caught her mother's eye. Mary was applauding proudly. Then Tess thanked the band, gave a farewell flourish, replaced the mike on the stand, and went back to the table.

A bunch of Mary's friends came, and Mary found herself the center of attention, the mother of the girl who did good.

But nobody was going to ask the famous Tess McPhail to dance.

One song ended, another began, and Kenny came off the dance floor alone, snagged the chair next to Tess, and dropped onto it, facing her. He looked warm from dancing. He propped an elbow on the table and said, "Great wedding."

"You look like you're having fun. Where did you leave Faith?"

"Dancing with her brother-in-law. You're not dancing?"

"Nobody asked me."

He glanced around, let his eyes return to her, and said, "Well, we can't have that, can we? Would you like to dance?"

"I'd love it."

He took her hand and walked her onto the dance floor. The band was playing "The Chair" as she swung lightly into his arms.

"What's wrong with the guys around here anyway?"

"They get a little spooked by me. Happens all the time. You're a good dancer."

"Thanks. So are you."

He tightened his arm till their bodies brushed and her temple rested against his jaw. Tess thought about Renee's admonition to stay away from him. But it felt right.

When the song ended, they separated immediately, knowing people around them were probably gawking. Tess turned as if to lead the way off the floor, but he caught her hand and said, "Stay, Tess. One more."

She didn't bother saying yes, only moved up close to his side, hiding their joined hands until the next song started.

The tempo changed. The band played George Strait's "Adelina," and Tess and Kenny smiled and laughed a lot in celebration of how well they did together. When the song ended, they were flushed and hot, returning to Mary's table.

"Well, you two look like you've done that before."

"Not together," Tess said.

Mary's friends were gone, and her purse was resting on her lap. "I know it's early, but I'm afraid I've got to go home, Tess. I sure hate to take you away from the dance, but you can come back, can't you?"

"Of course I can. I'll take you right away."

Kenny said, "I'll come along and help."

Tess carefully refrained from looking at him.

"Oh, thank you, Kenny," Mary was saying. "That would be nice. This darn chair is so heavy."

"Just let me tell Faith I'm going, okay? Be right back."

IT TOOK fifteen minutes to drive back to town and another fifteen for Tess to help Mary get settled into bed. While she did, Kenny sat in the kitchen and waited patiently for Tess and the encounter they'd been anticipating all day.

She entered the kitchen, and he rose from his chair and spoke quietly. "Get her all settled down?"

"Yes."

He stepped back and let Tess lead the way outside. The backyard was dark. Even Kenny's backyard was dark. They had left in broad daylight, and nobody had thought to turn on the outside lights. Tess preceded him down the back steps, and he followed along the narrow sidewalk until they were halfway to the alley.

"Tess, wait," he said, and snagged her arm.

The single touch was all the invitation she needed. She swung about, swift and sure of what she wanted. He, too, knew what he wanted, and his arms were waiting to haul her flush against him; his lips were waiting to claim hers. They stood in the middle of the sidewalk and let the dark yard hide them. Their lips got wet and their breath got short and the back of her dress got twisted beneath his hands.

She doubled her arms around his neck, and he lifted her free of the earth, held her fast against him with the kiss still unbroken as he carried her across the grass to the blackest shadow, next to the back steps. There, beside the crickets and the hydrangea bushes, they kissed some more.

Then he dragged her backward with him onto the cool, soft turf. Her hair tumbled and covered his face, and he held it back as he rolled her over and lay half on top of her. They trod that delicate balance where indulgence and suppression vie for the upper hand, and when indulgence threatened to win, he fell to his back on the grass beside her. There they lay with cricket song pulsating in their ears.

It took a long time before either of them spoke. Finally he breathed, "Whoa."

"I'll say," she managed.

"What do we think we're doing?"

He continued looking at the stars. "I think they call it necking. It used to be popular back in the '50s."

She sat up and pushed her hair back. He sat up, too. She ran her hand down his sleeve and over the back of his hand and pushed her fingers between his.

"Hey, if we're going to do stuff like this, I've got a right to know. Do you and Faith sleep together?"

"Yes."

Her fingers stopped, and she sat very still. Then she stretched out on her back again and linked her hands at her waist. Gazing at the stars, she said, "Well, she's very lucky, I must say."

He stretched out on his side, propping his head with one fist, and laid his other hand in the center of her ribs. "Look," he said, "I'm not married to Faith. I've had this thing for you since high school, and I wasn't going to pass up the chance. We both knew this was coming."

"But she won't find out about it, will she?"

"No."

"It's just a crazy fling. Lots of people probably have crazy flings at weddings."

"Probably."

She emptied her mind and reached up to riffle her fingertips through the hair at his temple. She realized how much she missed having a man whose hair she could touch whenever she wanted to, who would kiss her and make her feel womanly and want her for more than her talent as a singer. She pulled his head down and whispered, "Kiss me some more."

He dipped his head and did as she asked. Minutes later he dragged his mouth away, drawing back to survey her face again.

"I think we have to get back to the dance now."

She sighed. "You're right."

He took her hand, pulled her to her feet, and they paused for one last lazy kiss. Then they shook their clothes back into place and turned toward the car.

As they drove back out to Current River Cove, they wondered about the future, when Tess would be back in Nashville and Kenny would resume his life with Faith. Would they look back upon this night and smile inwardly? They reached Current River Cove, and the car bounced as it entered the pitted gravel parking lot. She pulled up before the door.

"Aren't you coming in?" he asked.

"I think it's best if I go straight back. If anybody asks, just tell them I thought I should stay home with Mama."

"All right, then. When are you going back to Nashville?"

"Tuesday."

"Will I see you again?"

"I'm sure we'll run into each other in the alley."

Some wedding guests came out of the hall, laughing, heading right past them en route to the parking lot.

"I'd better be going," Tess said.

A light kiss seemed in order, but the wedding guests were close enough to see into the car.

"Well, it's been fun," Kenny said. "See ya, Tess."

He got out, and she watched him walk toward the building. When he opened the hall door, he stopped for a moment and looked back at her. She could hear the music from the band; then the door closed and he was gone. Back to Faith.

ON SUNDAY, Tess avoided Kenny by attending the earlier church service. In the afternoon she and Mary went to Renee's house, where the bride and groom opened their wedding gifts. They ended up staying for supper and got home late.

On Monday morning shortly after ten o'clock Tess's business manager, Dane Tully, called.

"Tess, I've been trying to call you all weekend."

"I was at my niece's wedding. What's wrong?"

"Papa John died. His funeral is tomorrow."

"Oh, no." Tess sank against the kitchen cabinet, fingers to her lips. Papa John Walpole was a sour-faced, sweethearted, leather-skinned old promoter who'd run a little dive called the Mudflats for over thirty years. It was said that in the last twenty, every successful recording artist coming out of Nashville, including Tess, played the Mudflats on the way to signing with a major label. Even now Tess went back and played the Mudflats whenever she had a night to spare—always gratis, always unadvertised.

She was stabbing at tears as she asked, "What happened?"

"A guy came in the back door when Papa John was counting the day's take, pointed a gun at his head, and demanded the money. Papa John told him to go piss up a rope."

Through her sniffles Tess let out a cough of laughter. "Sounds just like him. Oh, Dane, I can't believe he's dead."

"Neither can anybody in Nashville. He's being cremated, but there's a memorial service tomorrow at ten a.m., and everybody he ever helped is singing at it. Can you be here?"

"I've got to be."

She called Renee, who said, "Oh, Tess, I'm so sorry. Yes, go ahead and take off. If I'm not there by the time you leave, I'll be there shortly after. And don't worry about Mama."

Mary was dismayed. She'd planned on having Tess for one more day and grew twittery at her sudden announcement of departure. When Tess came downstairs for the last time, with her duffel and her oversize gray leather bag, Mary was waiting at the bottom, look-ing gloomy. The staples had been removed from her incision a week ago, and she had graduated from the crutches to canes, which gave her much more mobility. But she seemed rooted with sadness as Tess hugged her good-bye.

"You call the girls whenever you need anything. Promise?"

"I'm no baby. It's not me I'm worried about, it's you, driving all that way crying your eyes out."

"I'm not crying my eyes out. I'll be fine."

"You sure?" Mary stumped along behind Tess to the kitchen and took a sandwich bag off the counter. "Here. It's just pressed ham and cheese, but it might taste good on the road."

Couple hundred calories, Tess thought, recognizing that what she was taking along was a love sandwich, not a ham and cheese.

"Thanks, Mama. I'm sure it will. Listen, you don't need to come outside," Tess added.

"Of course I do."

Mary followed Tess onto the concrete stoop. There she stood, balancing on two aluminum canes while Tess loaded her car, put on her sunglasses, got in, and started the engine. She called through her open window, "Love you, Mama."

"Don't be gone so long this time."

"I won't."

Tess hit the gas pedal, backed into the alley, then roared away.

It was roughly one mile from her mother's house to downtown. Tess cried all the way—partly for the loving mother she'd left behind, partly for Papa John, and partly for herself because she was leaving Kenny Kronek.

The thought of driving away without bidding him good-bye caused an actual ache in her breast. She pulled up in front of his office, raised her sunglasses, checked her eyes in the mirror, and found she'd cried off all her mascara. Hiding behind her shades once more, she got out and stood for a moment studying his building. It had a gray wooden façade with a plate-glass door that said KENNETH KRONEK, C.P.A. and, on either side, a white window box filled with red geraniums. The geraniums looked like Faith's work.

She stepped inside, and there he was, working at a desk beyond an open doorway of a private office that stretched across the back half of the narrow building. Out front a small reception counter had been abandoned by his secretary, leaving him alone in the place.

He looked up, and his fingers stalled above the buttons of a calculator. She took her glasses off slowly and stared back at him while time froze. Finally he rolled his chair back, walked through the doorway, and stopped behind his secretary's empty chair.

"Hi," she said.

"Hi," he answered, and she could tell from the thick-throated syllable that her appearance had generated the same tumult within him that was going on within her. "What's wrong?"

"I have to go back to Nashville today. Something came up very suddenly."

"You've been crying."

"A little, yes, but I'm okay."

"Come into my office."

"No." She started rummaging in her purse, seeking a distraction from the awful stranglehold he seemed to have on her heart. "I just wanted you to know I was leaving so you can tell Casey. And I wanted to give you my card so that—"

He came around the desk and gripped her arm. "Come into my office, Tess."

He hauled her into his private domain, shut the door, and they stood facing each other. "What happened?"

"A man who got me started in this business was killed."

"Who?"

"His name was John Walpole. We called him Papa John."

"I'm sorry, Tess."

"Look, Kenny, I have to go," Tess said quietly, trying to keep her voice from breaking. "I just wanted you to tell Casey that I'm sorry I couldn't talk to her before I left, but here's my card. It's got my unlisted phone number on it, so she can call me anytime. And I just want you to know that when she comes down to Nashville, I'll take very good care of her. I'll always be there for her, so you don't have to worry, Kenny, honest."

She saw the pent-up emotion in his face, equal to that within her. Then she was in his arms—not kissing him, but drawn up against his chest in a painful good-bye.

"I'm going to miss you," he whispered.

Tess covered Kenny's lips with her hand. "This was just a . . . a crazy fling at a wedding reception. We both agreed, right?"

He reached up for her wrist and dragged her hand down, freeing his mouth. He held her hand over his hurting heart as they drank each other in, realizing no other ending was possible. "Yes," he whispered sadly, "we both agreed."

When they kissed, she was crying, and his chest hurt so badly he felt as if he had broken a rib.

She took a step back, and the contact broke, leaving his arms outstretched before they fell uselessly to his sides.

She opened his office door and looked back at him one more time before walking out of his life, back to her own.

Chapter Eight

SHE reached Nashville at quarter to five and wound her way toward Music Row, southeast of downtown. Home could wait. Right now she needed an infusion of what she had missed, the vitality and energy flowing from those twelve square blocks south of Division Street, where the business of record producing created the heartbeat of Music City. She felt invigorated as she approached her office. A larger-than-life-size likeness of Randy Travis welcomed her from a red brick wall. Tourists moved in and out of souvenir shops and climbed the ramp into the Country Music Hall of Fame. Along Music Square East and West, headquarters of industry-related businesses lined both sides of the street—recording studios, video-production companies, music-publishing companies, booking agencies.

Tess's office was located in a century-old Victorian house on Music Square West. Out front an oval brass plaque announced simply, WINTERGREEN ENTERPRISES. She had chosen the name to remind herself of how far she'd come.

Under the umbrella of Wintergreen Enterprises fell several companies that had each been born out of necessity or common sense: her music-publishing company, so that publishing-company royalties on her records could be collected by herself; her specialty clothing operation, which created custom-designed concert costumes not only for herself but for other recording artists as well; her printing company, which created posters, buttons, fan-club newsletters, and concert programs for her; and there was also the small fleet of jets she used and leased to others.

All of this remained secondary, however, to the phenomenally successful operation that kept Tess McPhail on top of the country charts. That operation scheduled roughly a hundred and twenty concerts a year, allowed her to co-produce her own albums and videos, and paid the salaries of over fifty permanent employees.

And Tess McPhail oversaw every aspect of it herself.

When she opened the door, Tess heard the hum of various conversations. She entered the central hall, where her receptionist sat at a desk with her back to the ornate stairwell.

"Hey, Jan, I'm back."

Jan Nash swiveled her chair slowly and broke into a smile.

"Hey, Mac, welcome back. We sure missed you."

Others heard Tess's voice and came out of various offices to offer much the same greeting. Soon Tess moved on to her own office, upstairs. It occupied the entire width of the rear and enjoyed the dappled green shade from four huge basswood trees outside. In a smaller, adjoining office her assistant, Kelly Mendoza, turned to smile when she saw her boss approaching through the connecting doorway.

"Mac, welcome back."

"It's good to be here."

Kelly said, "I'm sorry about Papa John."

"We all are. Do you have details about the memorial service?"

"Tomorrow morning, eleven a.m. at the Ryman, singers gathering one hour beforehand for a brief rehearsal."

"Good. What else?"

"Burt Sheer called, and Jack wants you to call him the minute you get in. Cathy Mack has five dress designs she wants you to look at, and Ralph wants to start concert rehearsals."

Kelly went with Tess into her office. "Oh, one other thing. Carla's seen a throat specialist. That problem with her voice is serious— some kind of thyroid thing. Looks like she'll be out of commission for a long time."

Concern crimped Tess's brow. Carla sang background on some of her recordings, and she was also supposed to go on this tour.

It became clear to Tess within an hour of her return that there was no place for Kenny in her life. Though at times over the past four weeks she'd questioned where she belonged, she had merely to face catching up with business to understand that her place here was fixed. There was no place in her life for any man.

Nevertheless, if one in particular phoned, she didn't want to miss his call.

"Kelly?"

"Yes?" Kelly appeared in the open doorway.

"Phone calls from either Casey Kronek or Kenny Kronek are to be put through to me immediately, no matter what, okay? Casey is a graduating senior from my hometown who'll be staying with me for a while in June. She's going to do the harmonies on one of my songs."

"Lucky girl," Kelly remarked.

"Talented girl," Tess replied. "She helped me write it."

Tess worked in the office till eight o'clock. As she headed home, she lowered the windows on the Z and breathed in the warm, humid southern air. It was one of those evenings when twilight refuses to hurry, and as her car climbed up Heathrow Boulevard, the oaks and elms spread like black chapel veils against a butter-yellow sky that thickened to peach at the tree caps. Two boys came coasting down the hill on bicycles, and she waited for them to pass her driveway before pulling in. It struck her that she knew neither of the boys; knew, in fact, no children in the neighborhood nor any of the homeowners.

Tess thought of the view out her mother's kitchen window and how she herself had watched the comings and goings at the house across the alley. So different here. So isolated by success.

Her towering living-room windows faced the street, and through them Tess saw that Maria had left a lamp on. The garage door rolled up at the touch of a button, and Tess noted to her surprise that Maria's little blue station wagon was still inside. She hauled her duffel bag through the back entry, calling, "Maria?"

"Miss Mac, welcome home." Maria was in the kitchen, topping off the water in a pitcher that held a bouquet of red zinnias.

Tess dropped her gear. "What are you still doing here?"

"Waiting for you. I'll take your things upstairs, Miss Mac."

"Thanks, Maria, but I can do it myself."

"Nonsense. Give me that."

Maria was Mexican, in her fifties, spindle-legged and bantam-size. She had no trouble wresting the duffel bag out of Tess's hand.

"All right, then," Tess conceded. "But your family will be expecting you."

"I told them I might be late. How is your Mama?"

"She's doing very well. Maria, thank you for staying."

Maria flapped a hand as if no thanks were needed, and the pair climbed an open stairway that curved up to the second story, where a C-shaped landing overlooked the living room. The guest suites lay to the right. Tess turned left into her own bedroom suite. Unlike at Mary's, everything was new, coordinated, all in neutrals, with only touches of pastel color here and there. Everything so perfect. Everything seen to for her.

Maria dropped Tess's bag onto a bench at the foot of the bed and went around the room lowering white pleated shades and closing the door to the balcony, which overlooked the pool.

"Thanks, Maria. You can go home now."

"I'll go home when I think I should," the woman said as she headed downstairs again. Tess smiled. Though she was used to living alone, she was remarkably happy to have the garrulous housekeeper here tonight. She went back through to the central balcony and stood looking down into the living room. It had sixteen-foot ceilings and was decorated in tones of white. A cream-colored grand piano—one of two in the house—stood at the foot of the immense front windows.

Tess washed her face, stripped off her jeans, and put on a one-piece cotton lounger, then returned to the kitchen, a tile-floored room with French doors set into a bay that jutted into a screened porch. Maria had set out a Caesar salad topped with grilled Cajun chicken and a cobalt-blue goblet of water on the distressed pine table. In the center of the table was the pitcher full of zinnias.

"Maria, bless your soul," Tess said, sitting down immediately and stabbing a forkful of crisp romaine.

"Looks like you put on a couple extra pounds," the housekeeper noted. "I'll get you back in shape in no time. I pressed your midnight-blue suit for the memorial service tomorrow. Too bad about Papa John."

"Thank you, Maria. Now, will you please go home?"

"Yes, Miss Mac, I believe I will. There's fresh-squeezed orange juice in the fridge and bagels in the drawer for morning."

When the back door closed, Tess was left in silence.

After she finished eating, she went up to take a whirlpool bath in the marble tub. While she was sitting in it with the jets on, the phones rang, and she answered the one on the wall by the tub.

"Hello?" she said, killing the jets.

"Hi, Mac. It's me, Casey."

"Oh, Casey." Joy sluiced through her, coupled with the realization of how lonely she'd been. "Hold on just a minute, will you?"

She got out of the tub, wrapped herself in thick white terry, and transferred to the bedside phone. "Casey? Listen, hon, I'm sorry I had to leave Wintergreen so suddenly without telling you."

"It's okay. Dad told me about your friend. I'm sorry, Mac."

"Yes, well, it's good to be back and keeping busy. It takes my mind off things."

"I hope it's okay that I called there—at your house, I mean."

"Of course. It's fine, Casey, anytime."

"Great. Well, listen, I just wanted to let you know I was thinking about you. I can't wait to come to Nashville. Now Dad wants to say something. Talk to you soon. Bye, Mac."

Before she could prepare for the impact of his voice, it came across the wire, subdued and hushed.

"Hi," he said—nothing more, only the single, lonesome word. It filled her heart with an amazing rush of emotion.

"Hi," she managed at last, feeling her senses reaching out to him even from two hundred and fifty miles away.

He said, "You got home okay?"

"Yes, just fine."

"I worried about you."

There were men who worried about her daily—her producer, her agent—but they were paid to. Nobody paid Kenny Kronek to worry about her. The very notion brought pressure to her throat.

"You mustn't worry about me, Kenny."

No reply came, then finally the sound of Kenny clearing his throat. "I'm looking out at your mother's house, and it seems like I should be able to walk over there and see you."

"Kenny, that's never going to happen—not . . . not like it did this past month."

"I know," he said so quiet and forlorn she could almost picture his chin on his chest. Yet another silence crawled by, filled with useless wishes.

"Well, listen," Tess said, "I'm bushed, and tomorrow's going to be rough, so I'd better say good night."

"Sure," he said, despondent. "Well, take care. I miss you."

"I miss you, too. Tell Casey good night."

When she hung up, she remained on the bed, heart-heavy, the phone on her stomach. Two tears rolled down, and she swiped at them with the tail end of her terry-cloth belt. She wondered if Faith had been at Kenny's house tonight. She sighed, tipped her head back against the wrought-iron headboard, and closed her eyes.

There were no answers, of course, only the enormity of her obligations, the silent luxury of her home, and the confusion in her heart.

THEY LAID PAPA JOHN TO rest but kept his memory alive—Tess McPhail and a list of mourners that read like the who's who of country music: Garth, Reba, and more.

Congregating with her peers again pointed out to Tess that she had been away too long. She had music to make, work to do—work she loved. She'd better get to it.

She did exactly that in the days that followed.

On her first full day back in the office she had an intense six-hour meeting with her business manager, Dane Tully, to go over everything that had happened since she'd been away. She met with her road manager, the producer of her upcoming tour, and the clothing designer to discuss the show in detail before rehearsals began. She and Jack Greaves met with record-label executives to discuss jacket photo, design, and release dates of individual singles from the album in progress. She had her quarterly meeting with her C.P.A. and her financial adviser. She signed over three hundred autographs on postcards and publicity photos for fans who had requested them by mail.

Concert rehearsals began.

She lost the five pounds she'd gained in Wintergreen. She made sure she called her mother every other night. She received a graduation announcement from Casey and put off answering it.

Burt called again, and she finally told him she couldn't see him anymore, that she'd met someone else. Then she put off answering Casey's invitation some more, afraid that someone might answer the phone and she'd get all soft and mushy about him.

SHE put off making that call until it absolutely could not be avoided. Casey would graduate on Friday night. On the preceding Tuesday night Tess was exhausted. It had been a lousy day. And when she picked up the phone to dial Casey's house at nine o'clock that night, Kenny answered, as she'd feared.

"Hello?"

Perhaps she was working too hard. For whatever reason, hearing Kenny's voice unglued her. Without the slightest warning she began to cry.

"Hello?" Kenny repeated, sharper. "Hello? Who is this?"

"Kenny, it's T-Tess," she managed.

"Tess, what's wrong?" he said, the change from irritation to concern immediate in his voice.

"N-nothing," she blubbered. Then, "Everything. I don't know. It's just been an awful day, that's all."

"Tess," he said soothingly. "Hey, come on, darlin', it'll feel better if you talk about it. I'm here. You can talk to me."

So she talked. She admitted to Kenny that her empire was getting to be more than she could handle without relinquishing personal control. But there were so many stories about superstars whose dominions had crumbled under mismanagement, undermining them to the point of ruin.

"I'm not going to let that happen to me," she vowed. "And the surest way to let it happen is to give over control to someone else. That's why I watch everything so carefully."

"You've got to learn to delegate," Kenny said. "Did you ever think that by not trusting your employees more, you undermine them?"

She knew he was right—knew, too, that most people wouldn't have had the temerity to say something like that to Tess McPhail, because of who she was. "How did you get so wise, Mr. Kronek?" she asked, feeling much better.

He chuckled. "By running a two-person office with such a grinding routine that the last time either one of us surprised the other was when my secretary came out of the bathroom with the hem of her skirt accidentally hooked up on the waistband of her panty hose."

Tess burst out laughing, igniting Kenny's laughter, and they spent some enjoyable time letting it pour forth across a couple hundred miles of telephone wire. When their mirth wound down, Tess released a huge breath. "Gosh, I feel so much better."

"Well, of course you do," he said smugly. "I'm good for you."

"You really are, Kenny. Too good." They enjoyed the thought for a few beats before she said, "I really called to talk to Casey. I got her graduation announcement and the invitation to the party on Saturday. Wish I could be there, but I'm afraid I can't."

"I wish you could be here, too."

Tess clamped a hand across her forehead. "Lord, I miss you, Kenny. I don't know, but I feel as if a piece of my heart stayed in Wintergreen when I left. Nothing's the same since I came back to Nashville, but I'd die without this, Kenny. This is my life. Yet I'm dying without you, too. I'm just so mixed up."

He said, "Maybe you love me, Tess. You ever think of that?"

"Yes, I have. But I'm not sure. It's too scary. And anyway, it's silly, because I'm here, you're there, you have your business, I have my career. Anybody with half a brain can see that what we've got here is a logistical stalemate. What do you say we wish each other good night and you put Casey on. We can talk about this another time."

"Fine," Kenny retorted. The phone clunked, and she heard him holler, "Hey, Casey, it's Tess."

Casey came on quickly, exuberant, a big smile in her voice. "Hey, woman! Less than a week and I'll be there."

"I know. Can't wait. I won't be able to get up there for your party on Saturday, though. I'm sorry, hon."

"Aw, shoot, I knew that," Casey said cheerfully, "but I wanted to send you an invitation anyway."

"I thought of something I can send you for a graduation gift though, but you'll have to keep it to yourself."

"What's that?"

"How would you like to hear the songs from my new album before anybody else outside of Nashville gets to hear them?"

"Oh, my gosh, Mac, are you serious? You're sending me that?"

"I can't wait to have you hear them, but you have to promise me you won't let anybody else hear the tape. Promise?"

"Not even Dad?" Casey sounded disappointed.

"Well, maybe your dad, but nobody else, okay?"

"You got my promise, Mac."

"All right, then. I'll see you next Monday, and you and I will celebrate your graduation when you get down here."

"Okay. Six days!"

"Six days. See you then."

Chapter Nine

♪ ♥ ♪ ♥ ♪

*I*T WAS a hot, bright afternoon when Casey was expected. Maria had the Memorial Day weekend off, so Tess had the house to herself. She found herself happy and anxious as she checked the house one last time. She had chosen the light blue suite for Casey. It had furniture of natural pine and on the bed a puffy coverlet of oversize blue-and-white checks. Tess gave the room a quick perusal. Then she turned on the sound system and two lights in the bedroom, just to give it that welcoming feel.

At two thirty a red Ford Bronco pulled into her driveway, and Casey got out. Tess threw open the front door. "Honey child, you made it!"

Casey catapulted into her arms, and after they hugged, Tess asked, "Where'd you get the Bronco?"

"Dad bought it for me for graduation. Can you believe it?"

"Very nice. Come on in and I'll show you the place; then we'll get your stuff unloaded and stashed in your room."

At her first sight of the living room Casey stopped and crooned in an amazed Missouri drawl, "Oh, my Looord, I've never seen anything so beautiful in my entire life. This is where you live?"

"This is where I live."

Casey followed Tess into the dining room, which had a ceiling that created the second-story balcony that overhung the living room. Then they went into the kitchen, through the French doors, and onto the screened porch, from where they looked down at the pool area, below. Next they checked out Tess's home office, then retraced their steps to the front of the house and went up the curving stairway to the second level.

In the open doorway of her own bedroom suite Casey halted and said, "You mean I get to stay *here?*"

"This is your room. And that's your bath."

"My own bathroom?" Casey entered as if it were a sanctuary, halting in the doorway, peering around at the marble tub and the long vanity. She said, "I wish Dad could see this. He wouldn't believe it." She roamed back into the bedroom and investigated the panel on the wall beside the bed. "What's this?"

"A sound system." The voice of Trisha Yearwood came softly through the speaker.

"So how come your new tape's not playing?"

"It can be, in a second."

"Well, put it on." As they clattered back downstairs, Casey said, "Hey, I really love your new album. Dad does, too. Thank you so much for sending it."

Tess started the tape, and Casey ordered, "Turn it up." They sang along while they went outside to empty the Bronco, while they hauled Casey's stuff upstairs, and while they hung her clothes in the closet. The tape finished, and Casey yelled, "Hey, run it again. I love it."

Tess was downstairs in the kitchen taking out some chicken enchiladas that Maria had left in the refrigerator. Casey bopped in and said, "What can I do?"

"Fix us some ice water."

The sound system was piped into the kitchen, too, and they sang along while they prepared the meal, then sat down to eat.

The lightning bolt struck Tess when she had half her enchilada still left: Casey knew every word to every song on the tape. She forgot all about the enchilada and fixed Casey with a stare.

"You know every word, don't you?"

"Yeah, I guess I do."

A bizarre, fortuitous, exciting idea had hit Tess, but it was too soon to pose it. Whoa, she told herself. Hold on. You haven't even heard her in the studio yet. But with Carla gone, Tess needed a replacement for the tour, which would begin in late June.

Frowning, Casey said, "What's wrong?"

Tess relaxed and answered, "Nothing. You're amazing, though, memorizing all those words so fast."

"Heck, I know the words to all your songs. I've been playing your albums since before there were CDs."

Tess decided to let the subject rest. "Come on," she said, rising. "You'd probably like a little time to kick back, maybe take a swim."

"A swim? Wow. That'd be great. I really should call Dad first, though. I promised him I would the minute I got in."

Casey dialed on the portable kitchen phone, and Tess listened while wiping off the tabletop. The conversation was the usual got-here-just-fine sort. Then Casey added, "Hey, Dad, you should see this place. It's like a palace. I have my own bathroom, and she's got a swimming pool. Gol, Dad, it's way too cool."

The conversation continued for a couple more minutes; then Casey said, "Yeah, she's right here. Hey, Mac, Dad wants to talk to you."

Tess took the phone from Casey's hand.

"Hi, Kenny," she said, trying to act unaffected. This was the first time they'd talked since they'd had the tiff on the phone.

"Hi, darlin'," he said, and her heart went kaboom with relief. "You still mad at me?"

"No."

"Well, that's better. My daughter likes your house. It sounds like *Lifestyles of the Rich and Famous* over there."

"I suppose it is. Pretty nice Bronco you bought this girl."

"She loaded it to the hilt. You know teenage girls."

Casey had wandered off into the living room, so Tess asked, "How you doing, Kenny? I mean, with her gone?"

He waited a beat before answering, "Worst day of my life."

She felt a surge of empathy. "I can imagine. Is Faith there?"

"No, not tonight. I was thinking I might go visit with Mary. Maybe see if she wants to play a hand of cribbage or something."

"Mama'd love that. Well, listen, I should go. Casey and I might take a swim or something. I'm sure she'll call you again tomorrow after the recording session and tell you all about it. I'll put her back on so you can say good-bye."

"Hey, Tess, wait," Kenny said. Casey was standing beside her waiting to reclaim the phone when he said without warning, "I love you."

Tess was so stunned she froze, staring at Casey while his words drove her heart into a backbeat. Just like that, when she was least expecting it—*I love you.* She stood gripping the phone, unable to respond with the same words. She struggled to come up with some fitting response.

"I think it's just the loneliness, Kenny."

"Is Casey listening?"

"Yes. She's standing right here."

"All right. Then I hope that next time you'll say it back."

Casey frowned at Tess and whispered, "What's wrong?"

"Nothing," she mumbled, handing over the phone.

It was harrowing trying to hide her overwrought emotions from Casey. They swam and looked forward to tomorrow, and Tess answered questions about what it was like in a recording studio. They retired near eleven, and only then, while Tess was lying wide-awake in her own bed, did she examine what Kenny had said. She drew his words, like polished stones, out of her memory, and she wondered if this was love, this underlying emptiness that marked each day spent without him, this feeling of jubilation upon hearing his voice at the other end of a telephone line.

Hey, Kenny, maybe I love you, too.

IT WAS quarter to two the next afternoon when they arrived at Sixteenth Avenue Sound, a converted bungalow not far from Music Row. Tess led Casey through a reception area and a room with sofas, tables, and chairs but no windows. Country music played softly from some unseen speakers.

"Come on," Tess said. "I'll introduce you to Jack."

Jack Greaves was already in the control room at the console. Beside him the sound engineer was deciding which of the fifty-six tracks he'd use, while the engineer's assistant sat nearby loading a tape machine. Through an immense window the recording studio was visible, where some studio musicians were warming up, playing riffs. A couple of the guys noticed Tess and gestured in greeting.

She leaned over, held a switch on the talk-back, and said, "Hey, guys."

Jack, a trim man of medium height, turned in his swivel chair. Though he smiled and kissed Tess's cheek and shook hands when introduced to Casey, it was clear he had business on his mind. As a record producer, he controlled the session, which was costing Tess plenty. He himself earned over thirty thousand dollars per project; the studio rental ran close to two thousand dollars a day; the sound engineer got eighty dollars an hour, his assistant twenty-five; the studio musicians five hundred dollars apiece for each three-hour session. Given that today they'd work for six hours, the cost of this session would run over ten thousand dollars.

Jack wasted little time. "You want one box or two, Tess?"

"One, I think. Might be easier for Casey the first time."

Casey whispered, "What's a box?"

"The recording booth. See?" Tess pointed through the window at a pair of doors leading to two tiny black-walled rooms. "Isolation booths to help keep the tracks from bleeding into one another. We can use one or two, but until we get used to each other, I figure it's better if we just use one. You sometimes get better synergy with close eye contact."

The musicians kept tuning, occasionally breaking into spontaneous warm-up music that might run for sixteen or twenty bars, then be broken up by laughter.

"What do you say? Should we look at the charts and give this demo tape a listen?" Jack asked.

The musicians came from the studio and crowded into the control room, and Casey beamed as she was introduced to all of them. The pianist passed out copies of the "charts"—a Nashville system that transcribed chords onto paper, creating a crib sheet for sessions players who sometimes were unable to read music. Casey looked while Tess gave a quick explanation. Keys were named. Numbers indicated how many lines would be done in that key. V indicated verse, C indicated chorus, and B meant bridge. It was like looking at the frame of a house before the siding was put on: The structure of the song was all there, waiting for the musicians to do it their way, with all the improvisation they pleased. The assistant engineer ran the demo tape, and it took less than half the song for the chart to make sense to Casey.

The demo ended, and the musicians voiced approval. "Hey, nice song. You two wrote this together? This thing is gonna cook."

"What key are we doing it in, Tess?"

"F," she answered.

Everybody wrote F on the top of their charts, and the guys took them back into the studio, where they sat listening to the demo tape a bunch of times while noodling around on their instruments, finding their own take on the song.

"Come on," Tess said finally, "let's go in." She led the way through the studio into one of the recording booths. It had two music stands and two mikes. A headset hung over each music stand.

The engineer said, "Let's do a sound check," and the women clamped the headsets on.

After several minutes of sound and flurry Jack Greaves said into the talk-back, "Okay, everybody, why don't we do a run-through?"

The drummer gave the standard downbeat, and the intro began. Tess watched Casey's face light up as the mix of instruments came through her headset, filling her head with full-bodied sound. *Wow,* she mouthed, wide-eyed, and Tess smiled as she began singing.

When Casey came in, it sounded sensational through the earphones. Their two very distinct vocal qualities blended like smooth chocolate and rough peanuts, coming out sweet to the ear, and Tess knew beyond a flicker of a doubt that she and Casey would do many many songs together. The girl was good. She had a natural feel for which words to sing and which to drop, which harmony note would sound best, when to crescendo, and when to hold back.

They finished their first run-through, and over the talk-back Jack said, "Sounding good, ladies. What would you think about running the last note of the second verse over onto Mick's solo for a couple beats, then fading?"

And so it went. The quality of the talent in the studio made the work inventive and mercurial as the song started coming together. After a second run-through, which sounded far smoother than the first, Jack said, "Okay, everybody, should we record one?"

After they completed the song and got it on tape, they all piled into the control room to give it a listen. Everybody in the room had a knee, a foot, a head, or a hand keeping time to the music.

The playback ended, and chatter broke out.

"It's solid."

"What we've got here is a fresh ballad with a heart."

"Nice way to start a career, Casey."

"Time to break bread," Greaves said. "We'll pick up again at seven o'clock."

While they were recording, a caterer had come in and set up food—grilled shrimp, rice pilaf, and a salad—on a large table in the lounge. The musicians loaded plates and sat around on the sofas, talking mostly about the song in progress.

Casey was so fired up she found it hard to sit. "This is way too incredible, Mac. I never had so much fun in my life."

Tess smiled and said, "Better eat something, Casey. We've got three more hours of work before we call it a night."

Jack barely ate. He remained in the control room working on the tracks they'd already recorded.

Tess left Casey visiting with the guys and went into the control room. "Can I talk to you a minute, Jack?"

"Sure," he said, turning from the control board.

"I want your opinion," Tess said. "It's about the tour. Carla's throat problem's not going to be straightened out anytime soon. I want to ask Casey to go on tour with me and sing backup vocals."

He considered for a moment, then said, "She's young."

"She's talented. And she knows my music. Jack, we were playing my old albums around the house yesterday, and she's got the backup cues cold on every one. Besides that, I like her, and we get along like two cats in a litter. What do you think?"

"I trust your instincts, Tess. I like the girl's voice."

Tess returned to the lounge to join the others. Then everyone went back to the studio for the evening session. They worked this way for two and a half hours, back and forth between the studio and the control room. Record it again. Listen again. Record. Listen. Record. Listen. Finally one run-through seemed to ignite a specific spark in everyone. They'd got it: They all felt it, and the charged atmosphere was palpable as the playback ended. After ten p.m. the last fixes were put on and Jack called the session over.

WHEN they got home, Casey's adrenaline was still pumping. She called her dad immediately on the kitchen phone while Tess leafed through the mail.

"Dad, it was so great. I mean, when I heard the sound coming through my earphones, it was like, wow! I mean, this really major rush, you know?" Casey went on and on while Tess moved out of the kitchen and into her office. After about ten minutes she heard Casey call, "Hey, Mac, Dad wants to talk to you."

Tess was in her office, so she answered there. "I wish you could've been there. She did great. Our voices are really good together."

He laughed. "I know. She told me—and told me and told me."

It was Tess's turn to laugh. Then she tipped her chair forward, elbows to the desktop. "Kenny, I'd like to try something. One of my backup singers has got a throat condition that's taking her out of commission for a while. I'd like Casey to go on concert tour with me starting at the end of June."

The line went silent. Then, "You're moving kind of fast with her, aren't you?"

"Yes," she admitted honestly. "But she knows every word of every song I've ever recorded, and not only that, she knows the background vocals to a T."

Silence passed again. After a long time he released a pent-up breath, then nothing.

"We open the concert tour in Anaheim on June twenty-eighth. Can you imagine your daughter singing in a place with eighteen thousand ticket holders filling the seats? I have this fantasy, Kenny," she went on. "It's of you, sitting in the front row for Casey's first public performance, then coming backstage to congratulate her and drink champagne with us. What do you think?"

"You've caught me so off guard here."

"Think about it. Maybe you can bring Mama, too. She just might come if she could travel with you and Faith."

"Faith, too? You want Faith to come?"

"Well, no, not especially, but how could I send tickets to you and not to her?"

"Tess, listen, it's . . . I don't know what to say."

"Say yes, Kenny, so I can ask her with your blessing."

"All right, then, yes. Lord, what am I saying?"

Tess smiled. "All right, then," she said with excitement in her voice. "Save June twenty-eighth, and I'll see you in Anaheim. And don't worry. I'm not going to let anything happen to Casey. I love that girl."

"Oh, you love her but not me?"

"I didn't say that. Good night, Kenny."

"Good night, Tess."

She was smiling as she hung up. And actually, she was pretty sure she loved him.

THE second day's session went the way Tess expected. Casey's voice blended with the two other backup singers so well that there was never a question she was the right choice. With the approval of Jack and her road-show producer, Ralph Thornleaf, Tess asked Casey the next morning if she wanted to go on tour, starting at the end of June. It was fun watching her face suffuse with shock.

"You're kidding," she said, dropping into a chair. "Me?"

"Yes, you."

And so began one of the busiest months of Tess's life. June was traditionally a wild month in Nashville anyway, kicking off with the Summer Lights Festival—a three-day street fair down by the capitol. Then came Fan Fair, an intense week when twenty-four thousand fans paid admission into the Tennessee State Fairgrounds to pay homage to their idols at close range, to shake their hands, and to have snapshots taken with them.

There were times during Fan Fair when Tess did ten radio interviews a day. There were also autographings at record stores, meetings with fan-club leaders from all over America, dinners with disc jockeys, and special get-togethers with managers of record shops.

It was a grueling week, but for Casey it was novel, exciting. She was getting a firsthand look at the hard work of being a country music star and deciding it was definitely what she wanted for herself.

When Fan Fair ended, concert rehearsals began.

Mac's stage show was an extravaganza of lights, costumes, and equipment, requiring a dozen semitrailers to haul it all and fifty employees to make it work. Everybody worked hard preparing for the tour, and Casey was no exception. Since time was tight and workdays long, she continued to live at Tess's house.

Casey called her father every night, and at the end of each conversation he asked to speak to Tess.

Tess told Kenny she'd ordered her road manager to set aside three tickets in the gold circle for him and Faith and her mama for the concert in Anaheim, even though Mary hadn't committed yet. Then she asked, "You're coming, aren't you?"

He paused a telltale beat before answering, "I'm coming."

"What about Faith?"

"I haven't asked Faith."

"Why?"

"I think you know, Tess," he said.

"I'm glad," she admitted. "I'll get you rooms at the Beverly Wilshire, where Casey and I will be staying. Kenny, I'm so happy."

"So am I," he said.

The days flew between then and the Anaheim concert. Tess spoke to her mother almost daily, trying to convince her to come with Kenny. Mary kept saying, "Well, I'll see how my hip feels. That's a long plane ride, you know."

She was still saying the same thing the day Tess headed for L.A. on her private Hawker Siddeley jet, taking Casey with her.

ON THE NIGHT BEFORE Kenny flew to L.A., he and Faith were scheduled to play cards. The bridge group met at Faith's house, and at ten o'clock she served warm peach pie à la mode. By ten forty-five everybody had left except Kenny. He was helping her clean the kitchen and put away the card table. He stuck the four metal chairs behind the coats in her entry closet and returned to the kitchen to find her storing away her good forks and spoons in a silverware chest.

"Kenny," she said, examining each fork before putting it in the velvet-lined box, "maybe we should talk about this mistake you're making."

"Mistake?"

"I wasn't born yesterday, Kenny. I know why you didn't ask me to come along to L.A. with you." She shut the chest and stood looking at him. "I could tell the minute you started to fall for her. But Kenny, think. What is she going to do with you when it's over?"

He thought for a moment and answered honestly, "I don't know."

His admission of guilt, coming so soon, quite stunned Faith. She had expected him to deny any involvement with Tess.

Faith said, "You're willing to give up everything we have to pursue this hopeless affair?"

"Everything we have? What do we have, Faith?"

"We have eight years of loyalty," she replied, sounding a little panicked. "At least, I've been loyal to *you*."

"And how many times have we talked about getting married and how many times have we both decided not to?"

"I thought you liked our situation the way it's been." She moved a step closer. "I don't want to lose you, Kenny. And that's what will happen if you go to L.A."

He showed a first hint of anger. "Faith, we've become a convenience for each other. We've been heading toward this day for eight years. I don't want to be a seventy-year-old man who's been dating you for half of his life."

She straightened her spine. "Well, I can see you're not going to change your mind."

"No," he said quietly. "I think I love her, Faith."

"Oh, don't be ridiculous," she retorted in the most disparaging voice she'd ever used on him.

"You think I'm ridiculous?"

"Believing a woman like that would fall in love with you? Doesn't that sound a little ridiculous, Kenny? And have you stopped to ask yourself why she's taken such a sudden interest in Casey? If she might be using Casey to get her hooks into you?" She paused a beat for effect. "So when she's done with you, she will be done with Casey, too."

He kept his anger under tight control. "You know, Faith, you and I have hardly ever had a fight, but you're really making me mad right now. So before I say something I'll regret, I'm getting out of here." He headed for the door, informing her over his shoulder, "I'm going to L.A. tomorrow, and I'll be there for three days. Maybe while I'm gone you should take your extra clothes out of my house and leave the spare key on the kitchen table."

She watched him in stupefaction as he broadsided her screen door with both hands and let it slam behind him.

"Kenny," she called, bolting after him. "Kenny, wait! Don't go."

"I have to, Faith," he called without turning back.

Chapter Ten

♪ ♥ ♪ ♥ ♪

THE Anaheim concert was scheduled to begin at eight p.m. At seven, backstage at Arrowhead looked like backstage at NASA—confusion to the untrained eye, order to the trained. Technicians darted everywhere, stretching cables and communicating on walkie-talkies. The curtains were closed. On the stage wings immense black speakers were piled like tall buildings, and everywhere in the dimness small red lights peppered the scene.

On stage right a corridor between the curtains led to a large windowless room completely curtained in white. Against one wall a long table held a bouquet of enormous white lilies. Also on the table were cold drinks on ice, a dozen kinds of finger foods, fruit, and hot coffee.

A half-dozen reporters milled in a corner. Two long white sofas were unoccupied, but near them stood the executives of the MCA record label and their spouses. A woman with a clipboard came in and glanced around and went back out, remaining just beyond the door. A different woman—younger, in a black leather dress, high black spiked heels, and a rhinestone belt slung low on her hips—approached the woman with the clipboard and said, "Hi."

The woman smiled. "Hi, Casey. Go right in."

The curtained walls were interrupted by a single door. Affixed to it was a small brass plaque that said MAC. Casey knocked and stuck her head inside.

"Okay if I come in?"

Tess was sitting at a dressing table having finishing touches put on her hair. Her face had been illumined by stage makeup—a thirty-five-minute application with brushes and a palette. The freckles were gone, covered by an alabaster base. The lip line was perfect—enlarged slightly and flattering. Her eyes, shaded and mascaraed, became vibrant with welcome as she caught sight of Casey in the mirror. "Of course. Hey, you look sensational."

"So do you."

Tess followed Casey with her eyes. "Scared?" she asked, smiling a little.

"Out of my mind."

Tess laughed, relieving a little of the tension. "That's all right. When you get on that stage, you forget all about it."

"I know. Hey, have you seen anything of Dad yet?"

"Not yet." *Where are you, Kenny? Where are you?*

"Do you think Mary will be with him?"

"I can't even guess. She absolutely refused to commit."

Finally Cathy, the makeup artist, said, "That's it for hair and makeup. Now for the suit." Tess got up, and Cathy went to pull a white satin trouser suit off a hanger. Tess dropped her dressing gown and stepped into the pants. They were trimmed with a strip of clear sequins down the outsides of both legs. The jacket was covered all over with clear sequins that glittered as she moved.

"Earrings," Cathy said, and handed Tess a pair made of white feathers dusted with the same iridescent sequins.

Then Cathy produced a pair of shoes that matched the suit. They, too, glittered when Tess walked.

The woman with the clipboard peeked in. "Twenty minutes," she said.

Twenty minutes. Where could he be? Then it seemed like everybody came in at once—the other backup singers, also dressed in black leather: "Just wanted to say break a leg, Mac." And Tess's publicist, who told her, "Got the press and a few people from MCA out here waiting whenever you're ready."

"Okay, be right there. Cathy, something's scratching my neck back there. Will you see what it is?"

Cathy was checking the neckline of her jacket when someone announced, "Somebody special to see you, Mac."

And into the dressing room walked Kenny with her mama.

It wasn't at all the way she'd imagined. She had wanted to be poised and smiling. Instead, she could only stand with her head down while Cathy snipped, able to see nothing but the black silk stripe on Kenny's tuxedo trousers next to Mama's green silk pant legs.

Cathy finally said, "Okay," and Tess was free.

She looked up and felt the impact all over. A full-body charge. A surge of joy and relief and promise. Then she was moving toward him—toward them. Mama first, she reminded herself.

"Mama, you came!"

"Kenny wouldn't have it any other way."

"And you look so pretty."

She was dimly aware of people stepping back while she embraced her mother, and of Kenny and Casey hugging, too. But all of this was secondary to the man she was dying to touch.

She gave him her hands at last.

"Hi, Tess," he said simply. But he nearly broke her knuckles, he was squeezing them so tightly. He lowered his head, and they gingerly touched cheeks, protecting her stage makeup, hair, and sequins.

"Thank you for bringing her," she whispered.

"Thank you for arranging it. You look beautiful."

"So do you. The tuxedo is smashing."

She stepped back dutifully and told him, "Someone will bring you back here afterward. Just wait in your seats."

"Time check, ten minutes," a voice warned, and she squeezed his hands and released them.

Kenny and Mary were ushered away, and Tess was taken into the anteroom, where the press and hierarchy from her record label were waiting for a five-minute audience. She shook every hand, beamed her famous smile, and wondered how in the world she'd be able to sing with this swollen feeling in her throat.

At her side someone spoke quietly. "Three minutes."

Her road-show producer, Ralph, always went with her right to the edge of the stage. As they reached the wings, Tess let her mind go blank, willing the tension away.

There was one last thing she had to do. She went out among the black-and-silver cubes, holding her band members at various heights, and reached up to the one where her three backup singers stood high above her. She squeezed Casey's hand and said, "Just like in Mama's living room, okay?" Then she gave Casey a wink and went back to stage right.

A calm, quiet voice advised, "Okay . . . anytime."

Tess took a huge breath. The drummer was waiting. He caught her nod, gave a tak-tak-tak on the rim of his snare, and out beyond the curtains the music rattled to life. The curtain lifted as a male voice boomed, "Ladies and gentlemen, America's leading lady of country music, Tess McPhail!"

Deafening applause surrounded her and carried her to center stage. Her cordless mike was waiting. She grabbed it and started giving these people what they'd paid to hear.

"All dressed up and howlin' on a Saturday night,
Creeping down the alley toward your back-porch light,
Gonna dress in satin,
Gonna go out cattin'
With you."

Tess could see nothing beyond the blinding footlights. But during rehearsal she'd marked the spot below the stage apron where Mary and Kenny would be sitting, and now she pointed a long copper fingernail at where he must be: *"With you."* Even though she couldn't see him, his presence fired her performance as never before.

The concert flowed seamlessly. When the band took over during the first costume change, Ralph Thornleaf was waiting in the wings to give her the thumbs-up. "You got 'em, kid. Dynamite!"

Cathy skinned her out of her white suit and zipped her into a green beaded gown. She put a quart bottle of cold Evian water into her hands, and Tess drank half of it, then climbed into a Stutz Bearcat that drove her onto the stage for the next sequence.

Midway through the show she introduced the band, saving Casey for last. She told the audience, "This little girl is from my hometown of Wintergreen, Missouri, and this is her first time ever onstage with me. We've been writing music together, and our first collaborative effort will be the title song on my new album in September. Won't you give her career a big send-off. Here's Casey Kronek!"

The audience responded with an enthusiastic ovation, and Tess saw the thrill in Casey's face. When the auditorium quieted, Tess moved close up to the footlights and spoke into her mike with an air of sincerity that silenced every rustle in the house.

"Tonight is very special for me because there are some people here I love." A spotlight hit row one on cue, and Tess saw Mary and Kenny for the first time since walking onstage. She let her eyes pause briefly on him before settling on her mother. "One stands out above all the rest. This lady sat on the front steps and let me serenade her when I was six. She bought me a piano when I was seven. And she watched me pack my suitcase and drive away to Nashville the very week I graduated from high school, without once letting me see the tears in her eyes. She always said, 'Honey, I know you can make it.' " Letting her gaze rest tenderly on Mary, Tess said, "Mama, won't you please stand up so these people can honor you."

Mary made an attempt to rise, but her hips were a little stiff, so Kenny graciously took her arm and helped her to her feet. She raised one hand and flapped it as if to say, All this fuss over an old woman. A ripple of laughter brought a down-home feeling to the fading applause. Tess let a beat pass.

"And beside her is someone else who is special to me. He's the proud father of Casey Kronek, and an old schoolmate of mine. Kenny, so glad you're here." To the audience she said, "Both Kenny and Mama know the genesis of this next song. They heard it performed for the first time in Mama's living room last spring, the very week that Casey and I wrote it. It's the title cut I just told you about. It's called 'Small Town Girl.' "

There had been special moments in Tess's career, songs that meant more than others. But singing this one in public for the first time truly was the emotional high of her life. The words seemed to run a thread through her and Casey and Mama and Kenny that bound them inexorably forever.

> *"One-way traffic crawlin' round the small-town square,*
> *Eighteen years've passed since she's been there,*
> *Been around the world, now she's coming back,*
> *Wider-eyed and noting what this small town lacks.*

> *"Can't return.*
> *Too much learned.*

> *"Mama's in the home place, never changed a lick,*
> *House as worn and tattered as a derelict,*
> *Same old clock a-tickin' on the faded kitchen wall,*
> *Mama won't replace anything at all.*

“*Mama's fine.*
Can't change her mind.

“*How we change*
As we grow.
Rearrange
What we know.

“*Heard a lot of talk about the boy next door,*
He's a part of yesteryear I see no more,
Circumstances took us eighteen years apart,
Took him just one night to soften up my heart.

“*Say good-bye.*
Mustn't cry.

“*Hometown girl departing on a one-way flight,*
Something deep inside her somehow set a-right,
Runs her tearful eyes across the faded kitchen wall,
Whispers, 'Mama, please don't change at all.'

“*Must return.*
There's more to learn.”

When the song ended, the audience response was thunderous. The remainder of the concert seemed almost anticlimactic. They did two encores, and when the curtain lowered and the houselights came up, Tess felt victorious. The adrenaline rush was still buzzing through her as guards escorted her to the same white-draped room where a hundred and twenty-five people had been invited for a champagne reception. Tess was taken straight through to her dressing room, where Cathy was waiting to remove her gown and replace it with a tailored trouser suit and silk blouse. She blotted Tess's hot face, ran a lipstick brush over her lips, and said, “All ready to meet your public.”

There were only two members of her public whom Tess was interested in tonight, and when she emerged, her eyes sought them out immediately. Mary was seated on one of the white sofas; Kenny was handing her a glass of champagne, while Casey was standing by with two plates of food.

Tess went straight to them.

"Hey, Mama," she greeted, and leaned over to kiss her mother.

"Oh, honey, here you are. Say, that was some concert. I'm sure glad Kenny made me come."

"So'm I." She slipped her arm around Kenny's waist and smiled up at him.

He looked into her eyes and said quietly, "I'm awestruck," in a way that excluded everyone else in the room. His low-key compliment was all she needed to gild the moment.

But there were people she simply had to pay attention to, and it was just past midnight before Tess's obligations had been fulfilled and the four finally walked out the stage door and got into the waiting stretch limousine. Tess sank down beside her mother, facing front, while the other two sat opposite, facing backward.

Casey was still wound up. She jabbered, making everyone laugh, and Kenny put an arm around her while they rode. Mary was soon nodding. Tess mostly let Casey do the talking, indulging herself in her absorption with Kenny. He stretched out one long leg, and his black tuxedo cuff deliberately touched her ankle. She rested her head back against the leather seat, connected to him by that tenuous link.

It was after one o'clock in the morning when they walked through the hotel lobby and took the elevator up to the fourth floor, where they unlocked Mary's room.

"Are you on this floor?" Mary asked Tess.

"No. Casey and I are up on sixth."

"And I'm right here across the hall from Mary," Kenny said. "But I'll walk you ladies up."

They bade Mary good night, and when her door closed, the three of them rode the elevator to the sixth floor, where they reached Tess's door first. Kenny kissed her cheek and thanked her. Next came a heartfelt hug from Casey, who said, "As long as I live, I'll never forget this night. Thank you again, Mac."

When Tess's door closed, Kenny walked Casey farther down the hall to her room, saw her inside, then took the elevator back down to four.

IN HIS room Kenny hung up his tuxedo jacket, removed his bow tie and cummerbund, washed his face, then sat down with a magazine. He'd give her ten minutes before going back up.

He lasted six before realizing he hadn't read a word. Tossing the magazine aside, he bolted from the chair and pocketed his key card on his way out the door.

When he rang Tess's doorbell, it was one twenty-seven a.m.—a bizarre hour to go courting, he thought.

The door opened, and there she stood, freshly showered, in bare feet and an oversize white robe, her damp hair rollicking around a scrubbed and shiny face.

She said very simply, "I thought you'd never get here," and he stepped inside, blindly swatting the door closed behind him. Their embrace was a collision, their first kiss a desperate thing—two starving people straining to make up for all the time apart.

"I thought I'd die before we could do this," she said within the satin folds of the kiss. "All those people . . ."

"And all I wanted to do was this." He found her mouth again and covered it, holding nothing back. His hands reached to untie her belt, but she caught his hand and looked into his eyes.

"I have to know first about you and Faith."

He said with neither smile nor regret, "I've asked her to take her things out of my house. It's all over between us."

"Really? All over?"

"I'd never lie to you, Tess. Not about that." Then he added, "Not about anything."

"I missed you so much," she told him.

"I missed you, too," he said.

Her forehead rested against his chin, and his breath beat against her uncombed hair. "Take me to bed, Kenny," she whispered.

He was struck by a broadside of awe, realizing who she used to be: the Tess from his past. Who she'd become: Mac, the superstar. And who he'd become: the man she wanted as fully as he wanted her.

He picked her up and headed for her bedroom, her arms coiled around his neck.

He was smiling as he reached their destination and released her on the foot of the bed. She lifted her hands to him, and they fell back in one swift motion, kissing tenderly, then not so tenderly as some primal force took control.

He knelt by her, and she reached up to touch the hair at his temple, feeling a compulsion to say to this man something she'd said to no other. "Let me say it now, Kenny. I love you."

She loved the look that overtook his face: joy and disbelief.

"Say it again, Tess."

"I love you," she repeated, with wonder seizing her soul.

He turned his face into her palm and kissed it.

"I love you, too," came his whisper, and together they finished what they'd started one dark spring night in a backyard on the grass beside some crickets.

LATER they lay in the lamplight, tired but unwilling to admit it, wanting to waste not a minute of this night. Their faces were close on a single pillow. She said, "Kenny Kronek, the boy next door. Whoever would have thought it?"

"Not me," he said with his eyes closed. "Not in a thousand years. Not with Tess McPhail."

"I'm just flesh and blood like anybody else."

"No. Not like anybody else." His eyes opened. "Not to me. I've loved you so long that I can't remember when I didn't."

"Oh, Kenny, I'm sorry I can't say the same thing back to you. But I only found out how wonderful you are this spring, and even then I resisted falling in love with you." Her fingertip trailed down to his lower lip and rubbed it softly.

"Why did you?"

"I don't know." She shrugged. "Scared, I guess."

"So are you saying you've never been in love before?"

"I didn't have time to fall in love. I had places to go, things to accomplish." She absently rubbed his chest. "It's a funny thing. I used to think my life was so full, and I never knew how I was fooling myself. I thought I had it all, till now."

They lay for a while feeling lucky and sated and very reluctant to part. They had tomorrow to spend together, but after that he'd have to go back to Wintergreen. And what then?

Kenny brought it up first. "How do you think it would work if we got married?"

She reacted without the least surprise.

"I don't know, but I've been thinking about it, too."

"That's all I've been thinking about, but there's a lot to work out."

"Where would we live?" she asked.

"In Nashville."

"And in Wintergreen?"

"What do you mean? We can't live in both places."

"Why not? We can afford it. We could use your house whenever we went back home to visit Mama. But what about your business?" she inquired.

"I'd sell it and take care of yours for you."

"You would?" She drew back and stared at him.

"It struck me one day when we were talking on the phone and you said how many things you have to keep tabs on. I thought, Hey, I could do that for her. Tess, I'm a C.P.A. Who better to see after your financial affairs?"

She sat up and looked at him in amazement. "You mean you'd do that? You'd actually give up your business to marry me?"

"Why, of course I would. Think about it. Everything I do all day long is something you pay somebody else to do. Why shouldn't I be doing it for you and making your life easier?"

She did think about it. It sounded too good to be true.

She said slowly, "But I'll confess to you that I don't want to have any kids of my own. My career is too important to me."

"Then Casey can be your kid. It's perfect." He kissed the top of her head, and his tired eyes closed.

Tess imagined Casey as her kid and loved the idea.

"I want you to see my house. It's really beautiful. When can you come and see it, Kenny?" Getting no answer, she discovered he'd drifted off to sleep. She smiled, reached across him, and turned out the light, then wriggled down and turned her backside against him. She closed her eyes and thought, *Now* I have everything.

In the morning Tess and Kenny ordered room service for four, then called Mary and Casey and invited them up to breakfast in Tess's suite.

At precisely ten the doorbell rang, and Kenny answered. "Hey, good morning," he greeted Mary and Casey jovially, kissing their cheeks as they came inside. "How did everybody sleep?"

Casey gave him a curious glance. "Gee, you're in a good mood this morning."

"You bet," he said, clapping his hands once and shutting the door.

More greetings and kisses were exchanged with Tess while they got Mary seated on the sofa.

"Sit down, honey," Kenny said. "Tess?" He pulled out a chair for her, then seated himself. "Who's for champagne?" he said, pulling a green bottle out of a silver wine cooler.

"Not me," Casey said. "It's ten o'clock in the morning."

"None for me either," Mary said. "I'll have coffee, though."

Kenny began filling everyone's cups, and Casey watched him curiously as he came to hers. "Dad, what's the matter with you? You know I don't drink coffee."

"Oh!" He stopped pouring and set the silver pot down. "Well, then drink your orange juice because Tess and I want to make a toast." He caught Tess's eye, giving her the go-ahead.

She lifted her champagne flute. "Mama . . . Casey . . . The toast is to all of us and to our future happiness. We called you down here to tell you that Kenny and I are going to get married."

Mary looked stunned, as if she'd drop her cup.

Casey exclaimed, "I knew it!"

"How did you know it?" Kenny said.

"Well, you've still got your tuxedo pants on, Dad," she said, leaping to her feet to hug him.

"Married?" Mary interjected belatedly. "But . . . but when did all this happen? I thought you two . . . Oh, my. . . . Oh, gracious." She started crying.

"Mama, what's wrong?"

"N-nothing. I'm just so happy." She covered her nose with a linen napkin. "You're really going to marry Kenny?"

"Yes, I am." Tess touched her mother's hand tenderly, and the two shared an awkward hug across the corner of the table.

Next, Casey threw a hug on Tess. "You guys," she said, growing emotional. "You sure know how to make a girl happy."

Then Mary said, "Kenny, come here," and put her arms up. He left his chair and went to hers and leaned down into her embrace. "Oh, Kenny," she whispered, but could say no more.

"I love her very much," he whispered. "Nearly as much as I love you."

It took a while before they got around to eating breakfast. Who could eat breakfast with happiness like this chasing everything mundane from the mind? They were two minutes into the meal when Casey stopped and said it for all of them.

"Hey, you know what? This is going to be absolutely perfect. I mean, all four of us as a family. It's like it was meant to be."

It certainly was, their smiles all said.

Meant to be.

THEY were married less than two months later in the church where she had sung in his choir. The wedding was scheduled for one o'clock on a Wednesday afternoon because the church was booked for all the weekend days that month and so was the bride.

It was a hot, late-summer, high-sky day. One hour before the ceremony was scheduled to begin, Mary was in her kitchen, all dressed, when she heard Tess and Renee coming down the stairs.

"Well, Mama, here I am," Tess announced from the doorway.

Mary turned and put a hand to her mouth.

"Oh, land. I think this is the happiest day of my life." She made a stirring motion. "Turn around. Let me see."

Tess turned a full circle, showing off her bridal dress. It was very simple, made of white linen, with cap sleeves, a square neck, and a stovepipe skirt. On her feet she wore white linen pumps, on her head a circlet of baby's breath. Her only jewelry was a tiny pair of sapphire ear studs matching the ring Kenny had given her: an emerald-cut sapphire surrounded by diamonds.

"Isn't she gorgeous?" Renee said, leaning against the doorway.

The bride was definitely the prettiest thing in that kitchen, which hadn't changed a whit. But the house was a cool seventy-two degrees because Tess had said, "Mama, if you want me to get married at First Methodist, you're going to have to let me put air-conditioning in that house, 'cause if you think I'm getting dressed in that attic in the middle of summer, you're wrong. I'll melt like an ice-cream cone, and you'll have to pour me into that church."

Everybody in town knew what was happening over at First Methodist. There would be lots of reporters there, and Tess had no desire to encounter her groom for the first time with shutters clicking from fifteen directions. So she and Kenny had made secret plans.

She took Mary's hands and said, "You understand, don't you, Mama? Kenny and I just want a few minutes alone together before we go to church."

"Well, of course. I'll get my purse; then I'm all ready to go."

While she went off to the bedroom, walking with scarcely a visible hitch, Tess and Renee exchanged a sentimental smile.

"Thanks so much for being with me this morning," Tess said.

"I wouldn't have missed it."

"All ready," Mary announced, returning. "Let's go, Renee, and leave these two to do whatever it is they want to do."

They went out, and the house grew quiet. In the alley the car doors slammed, an engine started, and then the car disappeared. Tess went to the window above the sink and looked out. Kenny's garage door was up, and inside she could see the tail end of a brand-new Mercedes she'd bought him for a wedding gift.

"Well, here goes," she whispered to herself, and turned to scan her mother's kitchen one last time. Doing so, she experienced an unexpected bolt of nostalgia and thought, Let it never change. Let me always come home and find it just this way, plastic doily and all.

Outside on the stoop, she paused and looked across the alley. It took less than five seconds before Kenny appeared on his back step, too, dressed in a gray tux with a cutaway jacket. Even from this distance his appearance made her heart race.

Two enchanted people in their wedding finery, initiating a ceremony of their own design, walked slowly down their respective steps to the alley, where they had met so many times during the weeks when they were falling in love.

He took her hands. "Hello. You look"—he searched for a word—"radiant."

"I feel radiant. And you look exquisite."

They smiled some; then he asked, "Are you ready?"

"Yes."

She dropped her gaze momentarily, composing her words, then looked up into his eyes.

"I, Tess McPhail, take you Kenneth Kronek . . ."

"I, Kenneth Kronek, take you Tess McPhail . . ."

"To be my beloved husband for the rest of my life."

"To be my beloved wife for the rest of my life."

"To love you as I love you today, renouncing all others."

"To love you as I love you today, renouncing all others."

"And we will share all that we will have—the joys and the sorrows, the work and the play, the worries and the wonders, and your daughter and my mother, and all the love and commitment it will take to see them through the years ahead."

They paused.

"I love you, Kenny."

"I love you, Tess."

He leaned down and kissed her lightly. When he straightened, they smiled.

"I feel as married as I'll ever feel," she said.

"So do I. Now let's go do it for everybody else."

IT WAS, to the surprise of many, one of the most modest weddings ever held at First Methodist. Some expected luminaries from the recording industry to sing at the ceremony. Instead, only the First Methodist choir sang, directed by a recovered Mrs. Atherton. Some expected an entire chorus line of attendants, but there were only two—Casey Kronek and Mary McPhail, each smiling fit to kill. And when the bride appeared, everyone craned around, supposing she'd be decked out in several thousand dollars' worth of wedding finery. Instead, she wore the simple white dress and the simpler ring of girlish flowers in her hair.

There was, at the Kronek-McPhail wedding, one element of glamour. Among the guests were a bunch of Tess's friends who had flown in from Nashville. Their names were household words, and their faces were recognized wherever they went. They were the crème de la crème of country music.

While their presence at the wedding was notable, the presence of another was even more notable. Faith had come. Kenny and Tess had decided that given how important she'd been in Kenny's life, she certainly should be asked.

She was every inch a lady, doing the proper thing as she came through the receiving line, taking Tess's hand and smiling. "Congratulations, Tess. You look lovely." She took Kenny's hand, too. "Kenny, I hope you and Tess will be very happy together."

The bride and groom rode in a white limo out to Current River Cove, where their reception was little different than hundreds of others that had been held there. The fried-chicken dinner was geared for down-home tastes. The dance, however, turned out to be the talk of the year. Tess's own band played, and a slew of Nashville stars got up and sang. In the middle of this spontaneous show Judy got huffy and stalked off to the ladies' room to fluff her hair and fume.

"Showing off all her famous friends," she hissed to two women who were in there freshening their lipstick. "It's sickening."

From the dance floor Tess saw her go and said to her new husband, "There goes Judy in one of her jealous snits."

He said, "You know what, darlin'? You're never going to change Judy. And you're not going to let her ruin your wedding day, are you?"

She flashed him an honest smile. "Absolutely not." Her sister Renee's sure, constant love counterbalanced Judy's jealousy.

And there, too, was Mama—flirting with country star Alan Jackson!

She was sitting at a table surrounded by her friends, who were all making a big fuss over him.

"Look at Mama," Tess said. "Six months ago I'd probably have apologized to Alan, but now I know she is what she is, and I love her."

She told Mary as much soon after that, when they went to wish her good-bye and sneak away without farewells to the crowd in general. Mary said, "Now, you kids come home soon as you can."

"We will, Mama," Tess said as they exchanged a kiss.

"Thanks, Mama," Kenny said, and made Mary all emotional, calling her that for the first time.

They found Casey and told her they were slipping away. She was driving Kenny's new car back to Nashville, so Kenny handed her the car keys and said, "Be careful with my new Mercedes."

She gave him a smooch on the cheek and said, "Be careful with my new mother." Then she added, "Bye, Mother Mac. Have a nice honeymoon."

Tess's private plane was waiting at the airport and flew them to Nashville, where her Z was waiting.

She gave Kenny a smirk and asked, "How'd you like to drive home?"

"Wow," he said drolly, accepting the keys, "this is really true love after all, then, isn't it?"

Some would have thought that a millionaire like Tess McPhail Kronek would choose to spend her wedding night in the fanciest bridal suite of the most exotic city in the world, but she'd spent enough time in hotels. Home was her idea of luxury.

When they reached her house, he carried her inside. They paused to kiss just inside the entry before he set her down. Maria had left walnut chicken breasts in brandy sauce ready to warm in the oven. A table for two was set with candles and a single white rose. In the living room they found some wedding gifts piled up on the piano bench, and upstairs the double doors to the master-bedroom suite stood open.

Kenny stopped in the doorway, holding Tess's hand.

"I can't believe I'm going to live here with you."

"Sometimes I can't believe it either."

"That we're this lucky, that we have all this."

"And love, too. It does seem a bit much, doesn't it?"

But it was theirs to accept, and they stepped inside to begin their life together.

Later, when they'd eaten and taken a swim in the pool and opened the pile of wedding gifts, they were sitting on the floor among the wrappings, with one small gift unopened.

"Mama said to open it last," Tess said.

"Well, go ahead," he said.

She began pulling at the Scotch tape. When the wrapping was off, she opened the end flap of a small cardboard box and tipped it till something slid out into her hand: a picture frame, and in it a photograph of Tess and Kenny at about ages two and four, eating watermelon on the back steps of Mary's house, their knees together, feet bare, toes hooked over the edge of the step, faces sunburned and dirty, as if they'd been hard at play just before the picture was taken.

"Oh," Tess said, a hand going to her lips and tears stinging her eyes as she turned the picture his way. "Oh, look."

He looked and got a lump in his throat, too.

She dusted the glass lovingly. "Do you suppose they planned this day back then, when they used to watch us play together?"

"Maybe they knew something we didn't."

They kissed, feeling magically fated to end up together.

"Let's go call Mama."

Kenny beamed and leaped to his feet. "Yeah, let's."

They took the picture along and went together to wake Mary and thank her and to tell her how happy they were. And then they simply had to call Casey, too, just to say good night and that they loved her.

When they finally went upstairs, they took the picture along and set it on their bedside stand, where it would be when they woke up in the morning.

And the morning after that and the morning after that.

And often, when they would look at it in the years ahead, one of them would say what Casey said that morning in the hotel: "It's like it was meant to be."

And the other one would smile.

For no other answer was necessary.

To the H

Dick Francis

Alexander Kinloch prefers painting peaceful, quiet scenes in his Scottish hillside cottage to the noisy complications of the world.

But complications keep calling him back.

Like his stepfather's sudden illness.

And a horse that must be hidden.

And missing family heirlooms sought by more than one pair of greedy hands.

So much for peace and quiet.

CHAPTER 1

DON'T think my stepfather much minded dying. That he almost took me with him wasn't really his fault.

My mother had sent me a postcard—"Perhaps I'd better tell you your stepfather has had a heart attack"—which I read in disbelief outside the remote Scottish post office where I went every two weeks to collect my letters. The postcard had lain there unread for approximately ten days.

Somewhat distractedly, though my stepfather and I were hardly intimate, I went back into the cluttered little shop and begged use of the telephone.

"You'll be reimbursing us as usual, Mr. Kinloch?"

"Of course."

Dour old Donald Cameron, nodding, lifted a flap of counter and allowed me through to his own jealously protected and wall-mounted instrument. The official public telephone, thoughtfully provided outside for the few surrounding inhabitants, survived vandalism for roughly thirty minutes each time it was mended, so old Donald was accustomed to extending to customers the courtesy of his own phone. Since he charged a fee for its use, I reckoned it was

Donald himself who regularly disabled the less profitable technology on his doorstep.

"Mother?" I said, connected to her in London. "This is Al."

"Alexander," she corrected automatically, not liking my abbreviation, "are you in Scotland?"

"I am, yes. What about the old man?"

"Your stepfather," she said reprovingly, "is resting."

"Er, *where* is he resting?" In hospital? In *peace?*

"In bed," she said.

"So he is alive."

"Of course he's alive."

"But your postcard . . ."

"There's nothing to panic about," she said calmly. "He had some chest pains and spent a week in the clinic for stabilization and tests, and now he is home with me, resting."

"Do you want me to come?" I asked. "Do you need any help?"

"He has a nurse," she said.

My mother's unvarying composure, I sometimes thought, stemmed from a genuine deficiency of emotion. I had never seen her cry, not even after her first husband, my father, had been killed in a shooting accident out on the moors. To me, at seventeen, his sudden loss had been devastating. My mother, dry-eyed, had told me to pull myself together.

A year later she had married Ivan George Westering, baronet, brewer, pillar of the British Jockey Club, my stepfather. He was not domineering, had been generous, even; but he disapproved of the way I lived. We were polite to each other.

"How ill is he?" I asked.

"You can come if you like. It's entirely up to you."

Despite the casual voice, it sounded closer to a plea than I was used to. "I'll arrive tomorrow," I said, making up my mind.

"If you're sure?" She betrayed no relief, no welcome.

"I'm sure."

"Very well."

I paid the phone call's ransom to Donald and returned to my

ancient four-wheel drive outside. It had good gears, good brakes, and little remaining color on its thin metal flanks. It contained, at that moment, food for two weeks, a big cylinder of butane gas, supplies of batteries and bottled water, and three brown cardboard boxes, parcel delivery, replenishing the tools of my trade.

I painted pictures. I lived in a broken-down, long-deserted shepherd's hut, known as a bothy, out on a windy Scottish mountainside, without electricity. My hair grew to my shoulders. I played the bagpipes. My many noble relations thought me weird.

Some are born weird; some achieve it; others have weirdness thrust upon them. I preferred solitude and paint to outthinking salmon and shooting for food; I had only half inherited the country skills and courtesies of my ancestors. I was the twenty-nine-year-old son of the (dead) fourth son of an earl, and I had no unearned wealth. I had three uncles, four aunts, and twenty-one cousins. Someone in such a large (and conventional) family had to be weird, and it seemed I'd been elected.

I didn't mind. Mad Alexander. Messes about with paints. Not even *oils,* my dear, but those frightfully common *acrylics.*

Acrylics, I said, were endlessly versatile and never faded. They outlived oils by furlongs.

I paid my uncle—the present earl, known as Himself—a painting a year as rent for the ruin I inhabited on his estate. The painting was done to his choice. He mostly asked for portraits of his horses or dogs. I quite liked to please him.

Outside the post office, on that cloudy, cold morning in September, I sat in my old jeep-type jalopy opening my letters. There were two checks that day for work delivered, which I dispatched to the bank, and an order from America for six more paintings. Ridiculous, mad Alexander, in his weird way, actually quietly prospered.

The paperwork done, I drove northward, first along a recognizable road, then up a long, rutted and indistinct track that led nowhere but to my home in the Monadhliath Mountains.

Whoever in the mists of time had first built my bothy had chosen its position well. It backed into an elbowed granite outcrop that sheltered it from the north and east; winter blizzards mostly leapfrogged over the top. In front lay a small stony plateau that on the far side dropped away steeply, giving me long views of valleys and rocky hills and of a main road far below. The only problem with the main road was that my dwelling was visible *from* it, so that too often I found strangers on my doorstep—hikers equipped with shorts, maps, walking boots, and endless energy. There was nowhere left in the world unpenetrated by inquisitive legs.

On the day of my mother's postcard I returned to find four of the nosy species poking around without inhibitions. Male. Blue, scarlet, orange backpacks. Glasses. English regional voices. Irritated by the invasion, I drove onto the plateau, stopped the engine, removed my keys from the ignition, and walked towards my front (and only) door.

The men ranged themselves into a ragged line ahead of me.

"There's no one in," one of them called. "It's all locked up."

I replied without heat, "What do you want?"

"Him as lives here," said another.

I felt the first tremble of something wrong. Their manner wasn't the awkwardness of trespassers caught in the act. They met my eyes not with apology, but with fierce concentration.

I stopped walking and said again, "What do you want?"

The first speaker said, "Where is it?"

I felt a strong primitive impulse to run. Instead, I said, "I don't know what you mean," and began retracing my steps towards the jeep, my back towards them.

I heard their heavy feet scrunching on the stony ground behind me but didn't truly believe in disaster until they clutched and spun me round and purposefully punched. I had a splintered view of intent, malevolent faces, of gray daylight reflecting on their incongruous glasses, of their bombarding fists as I doubled forwards over a debilitating pain in the abdomen. Neck chop. Jabs to the ribs. Classic pattern. Over and over. Thud, merciless thud. I swung at them in anger but fought an octopus. Bad news.

One of the men kept saying, "Where is it? Where is it?" I wondered vaguely if by "it" they meant money, of which I carried little. They were welcome to it, I thought groggily, if they would stop their attentions. I unintentionally dropped my bunch of keys, and a hand grabbed it up with triumph.

Somehow I ended with my back against the jeep—no further retreat. One of them snatched handfuls of my hair and banged my head against metal. I clawed blood down his cheek and got a head butt in return that went straight from my skull to my knees, buckling them like butter. I slid to the ground.

"Where is it?"

I didn't answer. Didn't move. Shut my eyes. Drifted.

"He's out," a voice said. "Fat lot of help you are."

I felt hands roughly searching my pockets. I lay still, not wholly conscious, no strength, no will.

After a time I heard, "Is he alive?"

"No thanks to you, but yes, he is. He's breathing."

"Chuck him over there."

"Over there" turned out to be the edge of the plateau, but I didn't realize it until I'd been dragged across the stones, lifted, and flung over. I went rolling inexorably down the steep mountain slope, bouncing from rock to rock, dimly aware of comprehensive pain. I slammed onto a larger rock and stopped, half on my side, half on my stomach. I felt pulverized. Dazed. Thought vanished.

Some sort of consciousness soon came crazily back, but memory took longer. Those hikers, I thought. I remembered their faces. I could draw them. They were demons in a dream.

I tried to move. A mistake. Give it time.

Those s.o.b.'s. Demons or not, their fists had been real. "Where is it?" had been real. In spite of everything, I ruefully smiled. Perhaps they hadn't known what they were actually looking for.

It occurred to me to wonder what time it was. I looked at my wrist, but my watch had gone.

Hell's teeth, I thought abruptly. Mother. Ivan. Heart attack. I was supposed to be going to London.

With fierce concentration I could move all my fingers and toes.

Anything more hurt too much. Wait. Lie still. Bloody stupid, being mugged on one's own doorstep. Embarrassing.

The ebb tide in my body finally turned. Movement could at last be achieved without breath-stopping spasms. All I had to do then was scrape myself off the mountain and go catch a train.

By immense good fortune I had broken no bones in my helter-skeltering fall. With an unstoical groan I raised myself to kneeling on my rock and looked up.

The edge of the plateau was alarmingly far above, hidden behind outcrops that could not be managed without climbing gear. Looking down was almost worse, though I understood at once where I was in relation to the bothy above. If I could traverse to the right without losing my footing, I would come eventually to an uneven path that meandered from the road below up to my home—the challenging, half-hidden ascent that probably brought the four hiker demons to my door. I certainly didn't want to meet them if they were on their way down. Hours had probably passed, though. I knew I had lain helpless for a long time. Realistically, that path was the only possible route.

I would never normally have attempted reaching it without an axe and crampons, but fear of a fall kept me stuck like glue to every protruding scrap of solid rock. Loose stones bounced away as I made the journey, digging in with my heels. Careful, *careful*.

When at last I reached the path, I sat on one of its rocky steps feeling weak, with my forearms on my knees, head hanging. The helpless rage of all victims shook in my gut. My physical state was shaming. Somehow I should have put up a better fight.

From where I sat, I could see most of the long path down to the road. No scarlet, orange, or blue backpacks moved on it anywhere. There was silence above me. With reluctant muscles and a fearful mind I got laboriously to my feet and began the climb.

No evil faces grinned over the plateau above. I crawled the last bit on hands and knees, and raised my head for a cautious look. The reason for the silence and the absence of attackers was immediately obvious: My jeep had gone.

Not only had I lost my transport but the door of my home stood wide-open, with heaps of my belongings spilling out of it—a chair, clothes, books, bedclothes. I walked wearily across the plateau and looked in at a sickening mess.

Like all who live purposefully alone, my actual household goods were few. Living without electricity, I owned none of the routinely stolen things like television, stereo, or computer, nor did I have a mobile phone. I did own a portable radio, but it was no grand affair. I had no antique silver. No Chippendale chairs.

What I did have was paint.

When I'd moved into the tumbledown building five and a half years earlier, I'd made only the center and largest of its three divisions habitable. About three yards by five, the small room had been given a new roof, a large double-glazed window, and rebuilt walls and flooring. Light, heat, and cooking were achieved with gas. Running water came from a small burn trickling through nearby rocks, and for a bathroom I had a weathered privy a short walk away. I'd meant at first to stay on the mountain only during the long northern summer days, but in the end, I'd stayed snug through a freezing January and February and had never since considered leaving.

Apart from a bed, a small table, a chest of drawers, and one comfortable chair, the whole room was taken up by three easels, stacked canvases, a wall of shelves, and a table covered with pots and tubes of paints and other essentials of my work.

Lack of space dictated order and overall tidiness, but so did the very nature of the acrylics themselves. They dried so fast when exposed to air that lids *had* to be replaced, tubes capped, brushes constantly rinsed clean. I kept buckets of water under the table and used tissues by the jeepload for keeping mess at bay.

The mess the four demons had made of all this was spectacularly awful.

I had left work in progress on all three easels. All three pictures were now facedown on the wood-block floor, saturated by the kicked-over buckets. My worktable lay on its side, brushes and paints spilling wide. Burst paint tubes had been squashed underfoot. My bed had been tipped over, chest of drawers ransacked, files and books pulled down from the shelves, every container emptied, sugar and coffee granules scattered in a filthy jumbled chaos.

I stood looking at the depressing damage and working out what to do. The clothes I was wearing were torn and dirty, and I'd been bleeding from many small scrapes and scratches. The bothy had been robbed of everything I could have raised money on. My wallet and watch had gone. My checkbook had been in the jeep.

I had said I would go to London. Well, so I would.

Mad Alexander. Might as well live up to the name.

I left the scene mostly as it was. I sorted out only the cleanest jeans, jersey, and shirt, and I changed into them out by the burn.

I ached deeply all over.

I walked to the privy; nothing to steal there, and they had left it alone. Of the two ruined flanks to my habitable room, one was now a carport with a roof of corrugated iron; the other, open to the skies, held the gas cylinders and trash cans. Let into one tumbledown wall were the remains of a fireplace with a small bread oven above. Perhaps the place had once been a kitchen. Nothing in these two side sections had been vandalized. Lucky, I suppose.

From the jumble on the main bothy floor I harvested a stick of charcoal and a sketch pad, and armed with such few essentials, I left home and set off down the wandering path to the road.

The Monadhliath Mountains, rising sharply to about three thousand feet, were bare of trees and starkly, unforgivingly gray. The steep path led down to heather-clad valley slopes and finally to the road. Up in the wild granite wilderness, life to me felt simple, complete, and austere. I could work there with concentration. The clutching "normal" life of the valley diminished my awareness of something elemental that I took from the Paleolithic silence and converted into paint; yet the canvases I sold for my bread and butter were usually full of color and lightheartedness and were, in fact, mostly pictures of golf.

By the time I reached the road, there was in the quality of light a hint of dusk hovering in the wings, getting ready to draw together the skirts of evening. As it was September, watch or no watch, I could pretty accurately guess at six thirty.

Though not a busy artery, the road had enough traffic for me to hitch a ride without much difficulty. The driver who stopped to pick up a long-haired, jeans-clad young male stranger was a fortyish woman. "Where do you want to go?" she asked.

"Just to Dalwhinnie railway station."

She gave me a sideways glance. "Have you banged your face?"

"Mm," I said. My ribs hurt, too.

She dropped me half a mile from the trains. Lights were going on everywhere when I reached the station, and I was glad of the minimum shelter of its bare ticket office, as the air temperature was dropping. Shivering, I made a collect telephone call.

A familiar Scots voice spluttered at the far end. "Yes, of course I'll pay for the call. . . . Is that really you, Al? What the heck are you doing at Dalwhinnie?"

"Catching the night train to London. The *Royal Highlander*."

"It doesn't go for hours."

"No. . . . What are you doing at this moment?"

"Getting ready to leave the office and drive home to Flora and a good dinner."

"Jed, I . . . I've been burgled," I said. "I need help."

He said briefly, "I'm on my way," and the line went quiet.

Jed Parlane was forty-six, a short, stocky Lowland Scot, and my uncle's factor, the man who managed the Kinloch Scottish estates. We had become the sort of friends that took goodwill from each other for granted. He would come. He was the only one I would have asked.

He came striding into Dalwhinnie station after his twelve-or-more-mile drive to reach me and stood foursquare in front of where I sat on a brown-painted bench against a wall.

"You've hurt your face," he announced. "And you're cold."

I stood up stiffly, the overall pain no doubt showing. I said, "Does the heater work in your car?"

He nodded without speaking, and I followed him outside. I sat in his front passenger seat while he restarted the engine and twiddled knobs to bring out hot air. I found myself unexpectedly shuddering from the physical relief.

"Okay," he said, switching on the car's internal light, "so what's happened? You're going to have a heck of a black eye. That left side of your forehead is all swollen." He stopped, uncertain. I was not, I guessed, my usual picture of glowing good health.

"I got head-butted," I said. "I got jumped on and bashed about and robbed, and don't laugh."

"I'm not laughing."

I told him about the four hill walkers and the devastation in the bothy. "The door isn't locked. They took my keys. So tomorrow maybe you'll take your own key there—"

"I'll take the police," he said firmly, and produced a notebook and pen and asked for a list of things missing.

"My jeep," I said gloomily, "and everything in it—food and stores. And from the bothy they took my binoculars and camera, my winter clothes, four finished paintings, and my golf clubs."

"*Al!*"

"Well, look on the bright side. My bagpipes are in Inverness having new bits fitted, and I've sent my passport away for renewal." I paused. "They took all my cash and my credit card, and they took my father's old gold watch. Anyway," I finished, "will you lend me a ticket to London?"

"I'll take you home to Flora and me. We'll give you a bed."

"No . . . but thanks."

"Why London?"

"Ivan Westering had a heart attack." I paused briefly, watching him assimilate the consequences. "You know my mother. She would never ask me to help her, but she didn't say *not* come, which was as good as an SOS, so I'm going."

"The police will want you to give a statement."

"The bothy is a statement. Will you lend me the fare?"

He said, "Yes, but—"

"Thanks, Jed." I fished the charcoal stick out of my shirt pocket and opened the sketchbook I still carried. "I'll draw them. It'll be better than just describing them."

He watched me start and, with a touch of awkwardness, said, "Were they looking for anything special?"

"One of them kept saying, 'Where is it?' "

Anxiously he said, "Did you tell them?"

"Of course not."

"If you'd told them, they might have stopped hitting you."

"Or they might have made sure I was dead before they left."

I drew the four men in a row, face on: boots, glasses, air of threat. "Anyway," I said, "they didn't say what they were looking for. They just said, 'Where is *it?*' so they might have been fishing for whatever I valued most, if you see what I mean?"

He nodded.

I drew the head of the "Where is it?" man, as I remembered him best, without glasses. "This is their leader. I'd say his accent was sloppy southeast England. Same with them all."

"Hard men?"

"They'd all done time in a boxing gym, I'd say. Short arm jabs, like at a punch bag." I swallowed. "I felt an utter fool."

"Al, that's illogical. No one could fight four at once."

"Fight? I couldn't even *connect.* I scratched one of their faces, though." I turned to a fresh page and drew again; his face came out with a clawed cheek, eyes glaring viciously.

I gave Jed the pad. He looked at the drawings, troubled and kind. "Come home with me," he repeated. "You look bad."

I shook my head. "I'll be all right by tomorrow."

He sighed heavily, went into the station, and returned with tickets. "I got you a sleeper for tonight and an open return. Ten-oh-one from here arrives at Euston at seven forty-three in the morning."

"Thanks, Jed."

He gave me cash from his pockets. "Phone me tomorrow."

I nodded.

He said, "They've put the heater on in the waiting room."

I shook his hand gratefully and waved him away home.

CHAPTER 2

EST to forget that night.

The face that looked back from an oblong of mirror as the train clattered into Euston was, I realized, going to appeal to my mother's fastidious standards even less than usual. The black eye was developing inexorably, my chin bristled, and a comb would be a good idea.

I righted what I could with the help of Jed's cash and a pharmacy in the terminus, but my mama predictably eyed me up and down with a pursed mouth before dispensing a minimum hug on her doorstep. "Really, Alexander. Haven't you *any* clothes free of paint?"

"Few."

"You look thin. You look . . . Well, you'd better come in."

I followed her into the prim, polished hallway of the architectural gem she and Ivan inhabited in the semicircle of Park Crescent by Regent's Park. As usual, she looked neat, pretty, feminine, and disciplined, with shining dark hair and a hand-span waist, and as usual, I wanted to tell her how much I loved her, but didn't, because she found such emotion excessive.

I'd grown tall, like my father, and had been taught by him from birth to look after the sweet-natured center of his devotion, to care for her and serve her and consider it not a duty but a delight. I remembered a childhood of gusty laughter from him and small pleased smiles from her, and he'd lived long enough for me to sense their joint bewilderment that the boy they'd carefully furnished with a good education and Highland skills, like shooting and fishing, was showing alarming signs of nonconformity.

At sixteen I'd said one day, "Dad, I don't want to go to university." (Heresy.) "I want to paint."

"A good hobby, Al," he'd said, frowning. He'd praised for years the ease with which I could draw, but he'd never taken it seriously.

"How's Ivan?" I asked my mother.

"Would you like coffee?" she said.

"Coffee, eggs, toast . . . anything."

I followed her down to the basement kitchen, where I cooked and ate a breakfast that worked a change for the better.

"Ivan?" I said.

She looked away as if refusing to hear the question and asked instead, "What's the matter with your eye?"

"I walked into . . . Well, it doesn't matter. Tell me about Ivan."

"I . . ." She looked uncharacteristically uncertain. "His doctors say he should slowly resume normal activities. But he won't."

After a pause I said, "Well, tell me."

There was then this subtle thing between us, that moment when the generations shift and the child becomes the parent.

I said, " 'James James Morrison Morrison Wetherby George Dupree . . .' "

She laughed and went on. " 'Took great care of his Mother, though he was only three.' "

I nodded. " 'James James said to his Mother, "Mother," he said, said he: "You must never go down to the end of the town, if you don't go down with me." ' "

"Oh, Alexander." A whole lifetime of restraint quivered in her voice, but the dammed-up feelings didn't break.

"Just tell me," I said.

A pause. Then she said, "He's so depressed, and I don't know how to deal with it. He lies in bed most of the time. He won't get dressed. He hardly eats, and Dr. Robbiston doesn't seem to be able to prescribe anything that will pull him out of it."

"Well, is his heart in a bad state?"

"They said there wasn't any need for bypasses or a pacemaker. He has to take pills, of course."

"Is he afraid he's going to die?"

My mother wrinkled her smooth forehead. "He just tells me not to worry."

"Shall I . . . um . . . go up and say hello?"

She glanced at the big kitchen clock. Five to nine. "His nurse is with him now," she said. "A male nurse. He doesn't really *need* a nurse, but he won't let him go. Wilfred, the nurse—I don't like him; he's too obsequious—sleeps on our top floor, and Ivan had an inter-com installed so he can call him if he has chest pains in the night."

"And does he have chest pains in the night?"

"I don't think so. But he did, of course, when he had the attack. He woke up with it at four in the morning, but at the time he thought it was only bad indigestion."

"Did he wake you?"

She shook her head. She and Ivan had always slept in adjoining but separate bedrooms. Not from absence of love; they simply pre-ferred it. "I went in to say good morning, as I always do," she said, "and he was sweating and pressing his chest with his fist."

"You should have got a message to me at once," I said. "You shouldn't have had to deal with all this by yourself."

"Patsy came. . . ."

Patsy was Ivan's daughter. Her chief and obsessive concern was to prevent Ivan's leaving his fortune and his brewery to my mother and not to herself. Ivan's assurances got nowhere, and Patsy's feel-ings for me, as my mother's potential heir, would have curdled sul-furic acid. I always smiled at her sweetly.

"What did Patsy do?" I asked.

"Ivan was in the clinic when she came here. She used the tele-phone." My mother stopped, amusement glimmering in her dark eyes. "She telephoned Oliver Grantchester."

Oliver Grantchester was Ivan's lawyer.

"How blatant was she?" I asked.

"Oh, straight to the jugular, darling." Patsy called everyone dar-ling. "She told Oliver," my mother said, smiling, "that if Ivan tried to change his will, she would contest it."

"And she meant you to hear."

"Naturally. And she was sugar candy all over the clinic. The loving daughter. She's good at it."

"And she said there was no need for you to bring me all the way from Scotland while she was there to look after things?"

"Oh dear. You know how *positive* she is."

"A tidal wave."

Civility was a curse, I often thought. Patsy needed someone to be brusquely rude about the way she bullied everyone with saccharine. At thirty-four she had a husband, three children, and a nanny, all anxiously twitching to please her.

"And of course," my mother said, "there's some sort of serious trouble at the brewery, and also, I think he's worried about the King Alfred cup."

I frowned. "Do you mean the race?" The King Alfred Gold Cup, sponsored by Ivan's brewery as a great advertisement for King Alfred Gold beer, was a splendid two-mile steeplechase run every October, a regular part now of the racing year.

"The race or the cup itself—I'm not sure."

At that inconclusive point the kitchen was abruptly invaded by two large middle-aged ladies who plodded down the outside iron steps from road level to basement and let themselves in. "Morning, Lady Westering," they said. They looked from my mother to me expectantly, awaiting an explanation as much as an introduction.

I said mildly, "I am Lady Westering's son. And you are?"

My mother said, "Edna and Lois. Edna cooks; Lois cleans."

Edna and Lois gave me stares in which disapproval sheltered sketchily behind a need to keep their jobs. Disapproval? I wondered if Patsy had been at work. Edna and Lois were both new since my last visit.

I said to my mother, "I'll go up now and see Ivan. I expect I'll find you upstairs in your living room." I gave Edna and Lois my most cheerful smile and found my mother following me gratefully up the stairs to the main floor, quiet now but grandly formal, with dining room and drawing room for entertaining.

"Don't tell me," I teased once we were out of the kitchen's earshot. "Patsy employed them."

She didn't deny it. "They're very efficient."

We went up to the next floor, where she and Ivan each had a bedroom, a bathroom, and a study. "Lois cleans very well." My mother sighed as we went into her study. "But she will *move* things. It's as if she moves them deliberately, just to prove she's dusted." Mother shifted two vases back to their familiar position on the mantel.

I went along to see Ivan, who was sitting palely in his study wearing a crimson robe and brown leather slippers.

"How are you feeling?" I asked, sitting in a chair opposite him and realizing with misgiving that he looked older, grayer, and thinner than he had on my last visit in the spring. Then, I now remembered, he had made an unexpected invitation for my advice, and I had been too full of doubt of his sincerity to listen properly to what he'd wanted. It had been something to do with his horses in training at Lambourn, and I'd had other reasons to avoid going there.

I repeated my question, "How are you feeling?"

He asked merely, "Why don't you cut your hair?"

"I don't know."

"Curls are girlish."

He had the short-cut shape that went with the businessman personality, with the baronetcy and membership of the Jockey Club. I knew him to be fair-minded and well respected, a middling man who had inherited a title and a large brewery and had done his best by both. "Is there anything I can do for you?" I said.

"Look after your mother" was what he said first.

"Yes, of course."

"I mean, after I've gone." His voice was quiet.

"You're going to live."

He said dryly, "You've had a word with God, have you?"

"Not yet."

"You wouldn't be so bad, Alexander, if you would come down off your mountain and rejoin the human race."

He had offered, when he'd married my mother, to take me into the business. The brewery, standing close outside Wantage, the ancient town of King Alfred's birth, supplied most of England with King Alfred Gold brew. But at eighteen I'd said no. I wasn't ungrateful, and I didn't dislike him. We were just entirely different.

He said, "Have you seen your uncle Robert during the last few days? I thought he might have wanted to see you."

My uncle Robert was the earl—"Himself." When he came to Scotland every August for the shooting and fishing and the Highland Games, he'd send for me. Although I knew from Jed that he was now in residence, I hadn't so far been summoned.

I said, "Anytime soon, I expect."

"I've asked him—" Ivan broke off. "He'll tell you himself."

I felt no curiosity. They had known each other for twenty years, drawn together by a fondness for owning racehorses. They both still had their steeplechasers trained in the same Lambourn yard.

Himself had approved of the match between Ivan and the widow of his youngest brother. At the wedding he'd told me to go to him if I ever needed help. Considering that he had five children and half a clan of nephews and nieces, I'd felt comforted in the loss of my father and secure. I had managed on my own, but I'd known he was *there*.

I said, "Mother thinks you may be worried about the Cup."

Ivan hesitated, then asked, "What about it?"

"She doesn't know if it's troubling you and making you feel worse. Is there something wrong with this year's race? Not enough entries?"

"Your dear mother," he deeply sighed. "Look after her."

She'd been right, I thought, about his depression. A malaise of the soul, outwardly discernible in weak movements of his hands and the lack of vigor in his voice. I didn't think there was much I could do to improve things if his own doctor couldn't.

As if on cue, a fifty-to-sixtyish, thin, mustached, busy-busy person hurried into the room announcing that as he was on his way to the clinic, he had called in to check on his patient. "How's things, Ivan?"

"Good of you to come, Keith."

Ivan drifted a limp hand in my direction. I stood up and was identified as "my stepson."

Dr. Keith Robbiston rose in my regard by giving me a sharp glance and a sharper question. "What have you been taking for that eye?"

"Aspirin." Euston station aspirin, actually.

"Huh." Scorn. "Are you taking any other drugs?"

"No."

"Try these." He produced a packet from a suit pocket, and I accepted it with gratitude. Ivan, mystified, asked what was going on.

His doctor briskly answered while at the same time producing from other pockets a stethoscope and blood-pressure monitor. "Your stepson can't move without pain."

"What?"

"You haven't noticed? No, I suppose not." To me he said, "The reduction and management of pain is my specialty. Pain can't be disguised. How did you get like this? Car crash?"

I said with a flicker of amusement, "Four thugs."

"Really?" He had bright eyes, very alert. "Bad luck."

"What are you talking about?" Ivan said.

I shook my head at Dr. Robbiston, and he checked his heart patient with no further comment on my own state.

"Well done, Ivan," he said cheerfully, whisking his aids out of sight. "The ticker's banging away like a baby's. Don't strain yourself, but do walk around a bit. How's your dear wife?"

"In her sitting room," I said.

"Great. Hang in there, Ivan." He departed as abruptly as he'd arrived.

I sat down again opposite Ivan and swallowed one of the tablets the doctor had given me. His assessment had been piercingly on target. Punch bags led a rotten life.

"He's a good doctor, really," Ivan told me defensively.

"The best," I agreed. "He makes house calls—a miracle."

Ivan frowned. "Patsy says he's hasty."

I said mildly, "Not everyone moves at the same speed."

Ivan took a tissue out of a flat box on the table beside him, blew his nose, then dropped the used tissue into a handy wastebasket.

He said, "Where would you hide something?"

I blinked.

"Well?" Ivan prompted.

"Er, it would depend what it was."

"Something of value."

"How big?"

He didn't directly answer, but I found what he said next more unusual than anything he'd said to me since I'd known him.

"You have a quirky mind, Alexander. Tell me a safe hiding place."

Safe.

"Um," I said, "who would be looking?"

"Everyone. After my death."

"You're not dying."

"Everyone dies."

"It's essential to tell *someone* where you've hidden something, otherwise it may be lost forever."

Ivan smiled. "I'm not telling you what it is. Not yet. Your uncle Robert says you know how to hide things."

That put me into a state of breathlessness. How could they? Those two well-intentioned men must have said something to someone somewhere that had got me beaten and thrown over a cliff. I shifted in undeniable pain in that civilized room.

"Ivan," I said, "put whatever it is in a bank vault and send a letter of instruction to your lawyers."

He shook his head.

Don't give anything to me to hide, I thought. Please don't. Let me off. I'm not hiding anything else.

"Suppose it's a horse," he said.

"What horse?"

He didn't say. He asked, "How would you hide a horse?"

"A racehorse?" I asked.

"Certainly."

"Then . . . in a racing stable."

"Not in an obscure barn, miles from anywhere?"

"Definitely not. Horses have to be fed. Regular visits to an obscure barn would be as good as a sign saying 'Treasure Here.'"

"Do you believe in hiding things where everyone can see them, but they don't realize what they're looking at?"

I said, "The snag with that is that in the end someone *does* understand what they're looking at."

"But you would still put a racehorse among others?"

"And move it often," I said.

"And the snag to that?"

"The snag," I said obligingly, "is that the horse can't be raced without disclosing its whereabouts. And if you didn't race the horse, you would waste its life and its value. In the end, it wouldn't be worth hiding."

Ivan sighed. "Any more snags?"

"Horses are as recognizable as people. They have faces."

"And legs . . ."

After a pause I said, "Do you want me to hide a horse?" and I thought, What am I saying? But in fact, I would do it because it might lighten his depression. I would do it for my mother.

The telephone on the table by his elbow rang, but he merely stared at it apathetically until it stopped. My mother appeared in the doorway to tell him that someone at the brewery wanted him.

"It's Tobias Tollright, dear. He sounds worried."

"I don't want to talk to him," Ivan said tiredly. "I'm ill. Let Alexander talk to him."

Both my mother and I thought the suggestion pointless, but I picked up the phone and explained who I was. "If you'll tell me what's the matter, I'll relay it to him for an answer."

"I am Tobias Tollright, a partner in a firm of chartered accountants. We audit the King Alfred Brewery accounts, and there are discrepancies. . . . Really, I must speak to Sir Ivan himself. It is *unethical* for me to speak to you instead of him."

"I do see that," I said. "Perhaps you'd better write to him."

"The matter is too urgent. Remind him it is illegal for a limited company to go on trading when it is bankrupt, and I fear that measures must be taken at once. Only he can authorize them."

"Well, Mr. Tollright, hold on while I explain."

"What is it?" my mother asked anxiously. Ivan didn't ask but looked deeply exhausted.

He knew.

I said to him, "There are things that only you can sign."

Ivan shook his head, and I went back to Tollright. "What if he gives me power of attorney to act for him in this matter?"

He hesitated. It might be a legal move, but he didn't like it.

I said, "Sir Ivan is still convalescing."

I couldn't say in front of Ivan that too much worry might kill him, but it seemed as if Tobias's mental cogs abruptly engaged in a higher gear. How soon, he asked, could he expect me?

"Tomorrow?" I suggested.

"This afternoon. Come to our main offices in Reading." He told me the address. "This matter is very urgent."

I lowered the receiver and spoke to Ivan. "I can sign things if you give me the authority. Is that what you really want?"

He said wearily, "I trust you."

"But this is . . . well, extreme trust."

Ivan simply flapped his hand. I said into the phone, "I'll see you as soon as I can."

I put down the receiver and told Ivan that such trust was unwise. He smiled faintly. "Your uncle said I could trust you with my life."

I did a double take. "*When* did he say that?"

"A few days ago. He'll tell you about it."

And *who else* had they told? Alexander can hide things. . . .

"Ivan," I said, "it's more solid if a power of attorney is signed and witnessed in front of a lawyer."

"Phone Oliver Grantchester. I'll talk to him."

Oliver Grantchester agreed to come to the house, but Ivan's gloom intensified. How on earth, I wondered, had a brewery as well known as King Alfred's tied itself in financial knots?

The phone call done, Ivan seemed grateful when a thin man in a short white cotton jacket came in from the next-door bedroom and told him respectfully that everything was clean and tidy for the day. The obsequious Wilfred, I presumed.

Ivan stood up, swaying unsteadily, and knocked the box of tissues from the table to the floor. I picked up the box, noticing that it had phone numbers written on its underside.

Seeing me looking at it, Ivan said, "That new cleaner keeps moving my notepad over onto the desk. It drives me mad. So I use the tissue box instead."

I helped him through to his bed, where he lay down. "Think I'll just rest until Oliver comes," he said.

I went back to his study and eased into a chair. Dr. Robbiston's tablet had diminished the acute stabs of muscular pain. I could no longer feel anything but a general soreness round my eye. Think of something else, I told myself. Think of how to hide a bankruptcy.

I was a *painter,* dammit. Not a fixer. Not a universal rock. I should cultivate an ability to say no.

My mother said, "You see? You see?"

I nodded. "I see a man who loves you."

"That's not . . ."

"That's what's the matter. He knows his brewery is in trouble, and the brewery is the base of his life. He may think he's failed you. He can't bear that." I paused. "He told me to look after you."

"But," she said, "I would live with him in poverty."

"You need to tell him. I know you find it hard to put feelings into words, but I think you should do it now."

"Perhaps—"

"No," I said. "I mean *now.* This minute. Go and put your arms round him. I think he's ashamed because of the brewery. He's a good man. He needs saving."

She gave me a wild look and walked into Ivan's bedroom as if not sure of her footing.

I sat in a sort of hiatus, waiting for the next buffet of fate and wishing that all I had to decide was whether to pick hooker's green or emerald for the grass at Pebble Beach's eighteenth hole. Golf was peaceful and well mannered and tested one's honesty. I painted the passions of golf as much as its physical scenery, and I'd learned it was the raw emotion, the conflict within the self, that sold the pictures.

The comparative peace came to an end with the arrival of Oliver Grantchester. He and I had met about twice over the years, neither of us showing regret that it hadn't been oftener. My presence in Ivan's study raised not a smile but a scowl, and he said not "Good morning," but "I thought you were in Scotland."

Ivan and my mother, hearing his voice, came through from the bedroom, and both gave him a friendly welcome. "Good of you to come," Ivan said, and took his customary chair.

"Anytime, Ivan," Grantchester said heavily. "You know that."

The lawyer's large gray-suited body and authoritative voice somehow made the study seem smaller. Perhaps fifty, he had a bald crown surrounded by graying dark hair and a large fleshy mouth with chins to match. I prompted no smile in him.

Grantchester said to Ivan, "You want to draw up a power of attorney? Wise of you, my old friend, in view of your health. I brought with me a basic document. A temporary power of attorney will smooth things over nicely until you're back to your old self."

Ivan meekly agreed.

"So who is to act for you?" Grantchester asked. "Patsy? Yes, your daughter will be eminently suitable."

Ivan cleared his throat. "No. Not Patsy. I'm giving the power of attorney to my stepson, here. Write Alexander Kinloch."

Grantchester looked utterly astounded and also angry.

"Alexander Robert Kinloch," Ivan repeated, and spelled out my last name so that there should be no mistake.

The lawyer said, "You *can't*. He's . . . *Look* at him."

"He has long hair," Ivan agreed. "All the same . . ."

"But your daughter. What will she say?"

What Patsy would say raised anxious lines on Ivan's forehead. He gave me a long look of doubt, and I looked back with calm, allowing the decision to be his alone. If Patsy got her busy fingers on his affairs, I thought, he would never get them back.

Ivan looked at my mother. "Vivienne, what do you think?"

She clearly felt, as I did, that he would have to make up his own mind. She said, "The choice is yours, my dear."

"I advise Patsy Benchmark," Grantchester said firmly.

Ivan dithered, where once he would have dominated. The brewery's predicament had knocked his certainties to pulp.

"Alexander," he said finally, "I want *you.*"

I nodded, giving him a tacit promise.

His lawyer wouldn't accept it without a struggle. He tried to persuade Ivan to change his decision, but Ivan wouldn't be budged. My name was typed on the document, and Grantchester told me, crossly, to sign it. Ivan, of course, signed it also.

"Make ten certified copies," Ivan said. "Also," he added tiredly, "I will write a letter to the company secretary making Alexander my alternate director, which will give him authority to act on my behalf in all business decisions at the brewery, not just my personal affairs."

"You can't!" Grantchester said explosively. "He knows nothing at all about business. He's . . . he's an *artist.*"

Ivan said obstinately, "I'll write the letter at once."

The lawyer scowled. "No good will come of it," he said.

CHAPTER 3

 Y MOTHER gave me her bank card for getting cash from machines, and I bought a train ticket to Reading, though I didn't, as she'd begged, acquire some "decent" clothes before arriving at the offices of Pierce, Tollright and Simmonds. Tobias Tollright looked me up and down, inspected the power of attorney and Ivan's letter, and telephoned my mother.

"This person who says he's your son," he asked her. "Would you please describe him."

He had his phone switched to conference, so I could hear her re-signed reply. "He's about six feet tall. Thin. He has chestnut hair, wavy, curling onto his shoulders. And, oh yes, he has a black eye."

Tobias thanked her and disconnected, his enthusiasm for my appearance still bumping along at zero.

"What is wrong," I asked, plunging in, "at the brewery?"

Once he'd come to terms with the way I looked, he proved both astute and helpful. In my turn I ignored his fussy little mannerism of digging round his teeth with a succession of wooden picks. After the first ten minutes we got on fine.

"Basically," he said, "the man in charge of the brewery's finances has milked the cow and done a bunk to Brazil or some such haven with no extradition treaties. Thus the brewery cannot meet its obligations. The creditors are restive, to put it mildly, and as audi-tor, I cannot give King Alfred an okay to continue trading."

More than enough, I thought, to give Ivan a heart attack.

I asked, "How much is missing?"

He smiled. "How big is a fog?"

"You mean, you don't know?"

"Our embezzler was the *finance director*. I warned Sir Ivan last year that I thought he had an open drain somewhere, but he didn't want to believe it. Now he's so ill, he still won't face it."

"So, what are your life-belt measures?"

He hesitated, picking at the teeth. "I would suggest," he said carefully, "that you call in an insolvency practitioner."

"A who?"

"Someone to negotiate for you. I can give you a name."

"And," I asked gratefully, "what will he do?"

"She. If she thinks the brewery can be saved, she'll set up a CVA. A CVA," he added patiently, "is a creditors' voluntary arrangement. In other words, she will call together a committee of creditors and ex-plain the scope of the losses. If she can persuade them that the brew-ery can go back to trading at a profit, they will work out a rate at which the debts can be paid off. Then, if they can produce a bud-get and a forecast that will satisfy me that the brewery has a viable future, I can sign the firm's accounts and it can continue to trade."

"Well"—I thought for a bit—"what are the chances?"

"Reasonable, but it depends on the creditors."

"And . . . er . . . who are they?"

"The usual. The bank. The Inland Revenue. The pension fund. The suppliers."

"The bank?"

"The finance director organized a line of credit for expansion. The money's gone. There's no expansion and nothing to service the loan. The bank will not honor any more checks."

"And the tax people?"

"The brewery hasn't paid its workers' compensation contributions for six months. The money's vanished. As for the pension fund—it's evaporated. The suppliers, in comparison, are small beer, if you'll excuse the dreadful pun."

"It sounds *hopeless*."

"I've known worse."

"What about the King Alfred Cup?"

"Ah. You might ask Sir Ivan where it is," he said.

"At Cheltenham," I said, puzzled. "They run it at Cheltenham a month on Saturday."

"Ah," he said again. "You're talking about the *race*?"

"Yes. What else?"

"The cup itself. The chalice. Medieval, I believe. It's extremely valuable," Tobias said. "But there is some doubt as to whether it belongs to the brewery or to Sir Ivan personally."

"Actually," I said, "I was wondering about the race itself, not the trophy. The race is part of the brewery's prestige. A sign of its success. Would the creditors agree to go ahead on the basis of keeping up public confidence? Canceling now, when the entries are already in, would send a massive message that the company's in a shaky state."

"You'll need to say all that to the committee."

"She—your insolvency angel—couldn't she say it?"

His gaze wandered from my hair to my paint-marked jeans, and I could see that he agreed. "You'll need to convince her." He smiled briefly. "You've convinced me. Incidentally, among the possible assets there is a *racehorse,* and it's unclear again whether it belongs to the brewery or to Sir Ivan himself. I'd be glad if you could clarify it."

How do you hide a horse? Ye gods.

"Its name is Golden Malt," Tobias added.

Ivan, I saw, wanted me to keep his horse hidden away from the clutches of bankruptcy. Ivan had given me the legal right to commit an illegal act.

"What are you thinking?" Tobias asked.

"Um, how will the brewery pay its workers this week? Will the bank cough up?"

"They say not. Not a penny more."

"Do I have to go to them on my knees?"

He said with compassion, "Yes."

It was by then Wednesday afternoon. Payroll day was Friday. On the Tollright telephone I engaged the services of the lady negotiator and also made an appointment with the bank for the following morning. Then I asked Tobias how much was needed to keep the ship afloat. He referred to the ledgers and told me a sum that made Ivan's heart attack seem a reasonable response.

"You can only do your best," Tobias observed. "It appears you've just been dumped into it up to the hilt."

I didn't know whether to wince or smile. In one particular way I'd been in jeopardy up to the hilt for the last five years. It had taken five years for the demons to arrive at my door.

For the next hour Tobias tracked with me through the past year's accounts, item by item. Then he produced papers for me to sign. I did my best to understand them but trusted a lot to his good faith. As Ivan had trusted his finance director, no doubt.

"Good luck with the bank tomorrow," Tobias said, sucking his toothpick. "Don't let them mug you."

They wouldn't be the first, I thought.

I CAUGHT the bus to Lambourn, and I spent some of my mother's cash on a new pair of jeans. In fractionally more respectable mode, therefore, I arrived on a Lambourn doorstep that I would have been happier to avoid.

My stepfather's horses—including Golden Malt—and also my uncle Robert "Himself's" horses were trained at the racing town of Lambourn by a young woman, Emily Jane Cox.

She said at the sight of me, "What are you doing here?"

"Slumming."

"I hate you, Alexander." The problem was that she didn't.

I had walked, feet metaphorically dragging, from the bus stop to the stable on Upper Lambourn Road. I had arrived as Emily was completing her evening rounds, checking on each of the fifty or so horses entrusted to her care. She loved the life. She loved the horses. She might once also have loved Alexander Kinloch, but she was not going to dump a busy career for solitude on a bare, cold mountain.

"If you love me," she'd said, "live in Lambourn."

I'd lived with her in Lambourn for nearly six months, once, and I'd painted nothing worth looking at.

"It doesn't matter," she'd consoled me early on. "Marry me and be content."

I had married her and eventually left her. She'd never used my name, but had become simply Mrs. Cox.

"What are you doing here?" she repeated.

"Er, my stepfather had a heart attack."

She frowned. "Yes. I read it in the papers. But he's all right, isn't he?"

"He's not well. . . . He asked me to look after his horses."

"You? You don't know all that much about horses." She shrugged. "But all right. You may as well set his mind at rest."

She turned and walked back across her stable yard. She had short dark hair and a figure that looked good in trousers. We were the same age and at twenty-three had married without doubts. I had admired—loved—her positive energy, but it had drained my own. I couldn't have forever bowed to her natural habit of command. We had met four times since I'd left, but never alone and never in Lambourn.

Ivan had three horses in training in Emily's yard—two unremarkable bays and one bright chestnut, Golden Malt. To my dismay he had noticeably good looks, two white socks and a bright white blaze down his nose—great presence as an advertisement for a brewery, not good for disappearing without a trace.

"He's entered for the King Alfred Gold Cup," Emily said with pride. "Ivan wants to win his own race."

"And will he?"

"Win? Let's say Golden Malt won't disgrace himself."

I said absently, "I'm sure he'll do fine."

"What's the matter with your eye?"

"I got mugged."

She nearly laughed but not quite. "Do you want a drink?"

"Good idea."

I followed her into her house, where she led the way through the kitchen and into the sitting room, where she entertained visiting owners and, it seemed, revenant husbands. As she hovered over a tray of bottles and glasses, I walked across the unchanged room, with its wool sofas and oak side tables, and stood before a painting she'd hung on the wall. I'd sent it as a peace offering after I'd left. It showed a view of windswept links with a silver slit of sea in the background, with gray, scudding clouds and two golfers doggedly trudging against the gale. In the foreground, where long, dry grass bent away from the wind, lay a small white ball, invisible to the players.

Emily said behind me, "One of my owners brought a friend with him a few weeks ago who recognized that painting from across the room. He turned out to be some sort of art critic. He'd seen a lot of your work. I said you always painted golf, and he said no, you painted the perseverance of the human spirit."

Lord, I thought, and I asked, "What was his name?"

"I can't remember. I didn't know I was going to see you so soon, did I?" She poured Campari and soda onto ice. "He was a round little man, and he went on about how you'd got those tiny red flecks into the stems of the dry grass in the foreground."

"Did he tell you how?"

She wrinkled her forehead. "No."

She handed me a glass and turned back to the picture. "So how did you get those tiny red flecks on the stalks?"

I said, "Well, first I painted the whole canvas bright cadmium red. You can still see faint streaks of red in the silver of the sea. Anyway, that grass . . . I overpainted that once with raw umber—dark yellowish brown—and on top of that I put mixtures of yellow ocher, and then I scratched through all the layers with a piece of metal comb."

"With *what?*"

"Comb. I scratched the metal teeth right down to the red. The scratches lean as if with the wind. They are the stalks."

She stared silently at the canvas that had hung on her wall for more than five years. "I didn't know," she said eventually.

"What didn't you know?"

"Why you left. Why you couldn't paint here."

"Em . . ." The old fond abbreviation arose naturally.

"You did try to tell me. I was too hurt to understand. And too young." She sighed. "Nothing's changed, has it?"

"Not really."

She smiled vividly, without pain. "For a marriage that lasted barely four months, ours wasn't so bad."

I felt a great and undeserved sense of release. I hadn't wanted to come to Lambourn again. I'd avoided it from guilt and unwillingness to risk stirring Emily to an ill will she had in fact never shown. Now, more than five tranquilizing years later, she said, "I wouldn't have given up training racehorses, not for anything. And you couldn't give up painting."

"No."

"So there we are. It's okay now between us, isn't it?"

"You're generous, Em."

She grinned. "I quite enjoy saintly forbearance. Do you want a divorce? Is that why you came here?"

Startled, I said, "No. Hadn't thought of it! Do you?"

"Actually, I find it useful sometimes to be able to mention a husband. But if you don't want a divorce, why did you come?"

"Ivan's horses. Ivan wants me to make Golden Malt disappear."

"What on earth are you talking about?"

In the kitchen, she made coffee as I explained about the brewery's financial predicament. "Ivan wants me to take the horse away so that it doesn't get sucked in and sold prematurely."

She frowned. "I can't let you take it."

"Well . . . yes, you can." I handed her a certified copy of the power of attorney explaining that it gave me authority to do as I thought best regarding Ivan's property.

She read it solemnly. "All right. What do you want to do?"

"To ride the horse away from here tomorrow morning, when the Downs are alive with horses going in all directions."

She stared. "First, he's not an easy ride. And second, where would you go?"

"If I tell you where, you'll be involved."

She thought it over. "You need me to tell the grooms not to worry when one of the horses goes missing."

I agreed. We drank the coffee, not talking.

"I like Ivan," Emily said finally. "If he wants the horse hidden, I'll help you. I have a friend, a woman, who offers good service."

"Is she within riding distance?"

"About eight miles across the Downs." She fetched a map from the office, spreading it out on the kitchen table and pointing. "Her yard is outside the village of Foxhill."

"I could find that," I said.

Emily looked doubtful but phoned her friend. "My yard's full," she said. "Could you take an overflow for a week or two? Keep him fit. He'll be racing later on. . . . You can? Good."

After some chitchat she put down the receiver. "There you are," she said. "One conjuring trick done to order."

"You're brilliant."

"Absolutely right. Where are you sleeping?"

"I'll find a room in Lambourn."

"Not unless you want to advertise your presence. You can sleep here, on a sofa, out of sight."

"How about," I said impulsively, "in your bed?"

"No."

I didn't try to persuade her. Instead, I borrowed her telephone for two calls—one to my mother to tell her I would be away for the night but hoped to have good news for Ivan the next day, and one to Jed Parlane in Scotland.

"How are you?" Jed said anxiously.

"Living at a flat-out gallop."

"I took the police to the bothy. What a mess. Himself wants to see you as soon as you return. When are you coming back?"

"With luck, on tomorrow night's *Highlander*. I'll let you know."

"Take care, then," he said. "So long."

Emily, deep in thought, said, as I put down the receiver, "I'll send my head groom out with the first lot, as usual, but I'll tell him not to take Golden Malt." She wrote, as she always did, a list of which groom would ride which horse when the first lot of horses pulled out for exercise at seven the next morning. She put her newly written list for the head groom in the message box outside the back door, then locked the doors against the night.

All so familiar. All so long ago.

She gave me two traveling rugs to keep warm on the sofa and said calmly, "Good night."

I put my arms around her tentatively. "Em?"

"No," she said.

I kissed her forehead, holding her close. "Em?"

"Oh," she said in exasperation, "all *right*."

SHE no longer slept in the big bedroom we'd shared, but in the old guest room. Her body to my touch was long known and long forgotten, like going back to an abandoned building.

I did what I knew she liked, and as ever, my own intense pleasure came in pleasing her. She was receptive.

"I've missed you," she said.

"I, too."

We slept peacefully side by side, and in the morning I'd almost forgotten I was there to steal a horse. I waited in the kitchen until the scrunching hooves outside had diminuendoed and Emily came in from the yard.

"I've saddled and bridled Golden Malt," she said. "For heaven's sake don't let him whip round and buck you off. The last thing I want is to have him loose on the Downs."

"I've been thinking about anonymity," I said. "Have you still got any of those nightcaps you put over their heads in cold weather? A nightcap would hide that white blaze down his nose."

She nodded, amused. "And you'd better borrow a helmet from the cloakroom and anything else you need."

I thanked her and went into the large cloakroom. I found some jodhpur boots to fit me and put on a shiny blue helmet and a pair of jockey's goggles—a fine disguise for a black eye.

Emily, still amused, said, "Do borrow one of those padded jackets. It's cold on the Downs these mornings."

I fetched a dark-colored jacket, and Emily gave me a leg up onto Golden Malt's back and frowned, filled with misgiving. "When did you last sit on a horse?" she asked.

"Er, some time ago." Golden Malt skittered around unhelpfully. It looked a long way down to the ground. "I'll phone you if anything goes wrong, and thanks, Em."

"Yes. . . . Go on, then. Bug off." She was smiling.

I'd reckoned that the first three hundred yards might be the most difficult, as I had to go along a public road to reach the track that led up to the Downs. But I was lucky. There were few cars, and I managed to steer a not-too-disgraceful course. I was just one of hundreds of Lambourn equine residents.

Golden Malt thought he knew where he was going. He tossed his head with pleasure and trotted jauntily eastward, up the rutted access to the downland. Solitude was rare. Strings of horses cluttered every skyline, and trainers' Land Rovers bumped busily in their wake. He began to fight when I turned him to the west at the top of the hill. He ran backwards; he turned in small circles; he obstinately refused to go where I tried to point his head.

I remembered suddenly that one day I'd stood beside Emily at a race meeting watching one of her horses refuse to go down to the start. The horse had cantered crabwise, turned in circles, ignored the instructions of the tough, experienced jockey on his back.

Across the years I heard Emily's furious comment, "Why doesn't the bloody fool get off and *lead* him?"

Oh, Em, I thought. My dear wife. Thank you.

I slid off the stubborn brute's back, took the reins, and *walked* westward, and as if his entire nature had done an abracadabra, Golden Malt ambled along peacefully beside me.

I could see glimpses of villages in the lower distances but no horses. When I'd walked about a mile, I tried riding again, and this time Golden Malt trotted docilely where I asked.

I crossed a footpath or two and skirted a few farms. Somewhere ahead lay the oldest path in Britain, the Ridgeway, which ran east to west. It was likely the Druids had walked it to Stonehenge.

When I finally reached it, I almost missed it, a simple rutted track. Shrugging, I turned left and trotted hopefully on. I had chosen a longer route than essential in order to avoid roads. As I didn't want to draw attention to myself, I considered the extra time and miles well spent. Eventually the path turned southwest and delivered me to Foxhill.

Emily's friend took my quiet arrival for granted. "We'll look after the old boy." She patted the chestnut neck with maternal fondness and nodded to me cheerfully as I left.

I thumbed a lift to Swindon, caught a train to Reading, and called on a powerful bank manager who wasn't expecting a padded jacket, jodhpur boots, and a blue riding helmet.

"Er . . ." he said.

"I'm sorry about the presentation, but I'm acting for my stepfather, Sir Ivan Westering, and this is not my normal world."

"I know Sir Ivan well," he said. "I'm sorry he's ill."

I handed him a certified copy of the power of attorney and Ivan's alternate director letter. He listened courteously to my plea for the brewery workers to receive their wages for this week, while the insolvency practitioner, Mrs. Morden, tried to put together a committee of creditors for a voluntary arrangement.

"I've already been approached by Mrs. Morden and Tobias Tollright. He told me you would come here on your knees."

"I'll kneel if you like."

"Hmph." The faintest of smiles twitched in his eye muscles. "All right. The wages checks will be honored for this week. Then we'll see." He stood up, holding out a smooth white hand. "A revelation doing business with you, Mr. Kinloch."

I shook his hand, breathing with relief on the way out.

My appointment with Mrs. Margaret Morden, fairy godmother to near-bankrupt Cinderellas, was next. Word had gone ahead of me, I gathered, as she knew at once who I was and welcomed me without blinking. The power of attorney was yet again carefully inspected and a copy of Ivan's letter taken.

Margaret Morden looked somewhere in the ageless forties and was not the severe businesswoman I'd expected. She was dressed not in a suit, but in a soft calf-length dress of pink-and-violet-printed silk. Involuntarily I smiled and, from her satisfied change of expression, realized that that was exactly the aim of her clothes—to encourage, to mediate, to persuade.

Her office was spacious, a cross between functional gray and leather-bound lawbooks, with six computer monitors ranged on one wall, all showing different information.

She sat down at her desk, brewery papers already spread out, and waved me to a chair. "We have here a serious situation—"

The serious situation was abruptly made worse by the door crashing open to admit a purposeful missile of a man, with a flustered secretary behind him, bleating, "I'm sorry, Mrs. Morden, I couldn't stop him."

The intruder, a thin fiftyish man with large glasses, pointed a sharp finger at my face. "You've no right to be here. *Out!*" Quivering with rage, he jerked the finger towards the door.

Mrs. Morden asked calmly, "And you are—"

"Madam," he said furiously, "in the absence of Sir Ivan, I am the brewery's acting chief executive officer. This wretched young man has no authority, and you will get rid of him."

Mrs. Morden asked noncommittally, "Your name?"

"Finch," he said sharply. "Desmond Finch."

"Ah, yes." She looked down at the papers. "It mentions you here. But I'm sorry, Mr. Finch. Mr. Kinloch has the undoubted right to act in Sir Ivan's stead."

She waved a hand towards the power of attorney on her desk. Finch snatched it up and tore the page across. "Sir Ivan's too ill to know what he's doing. *I* am in charge of the brewery's affairs."

Mrs. Morden invited my comment. "Mr. Kinloch?"

Ivan, I reflected, had deliberately bypassed Desmond Finch in giving me his trust, and I wondered why. If he had pointedly not passed his power to his second-in-command, then my obligation to my stepfather was absolute.

"Please continue with your work, Mrs. Morden," I said.

She smiled gently at Finch.

"I want this . . . this usurper out *now*," he said loudly. "At once. Mrs. Benchmark is adamant. He is trying to worm his way into Sir Ivan's fortune and cut out Mrs. Benchmark."

Mrs. Morden lifted her eyebrows in my direction.

"No," I said to Mrs. Morden. "The brewery will be Patsy's one day. Save it for her, not for me. And she won't thank *you*, Mr. Finch, if it goes down the tubes."

Finch gaped and made for the door, and then stopped dead and came back to accuse with venom, "Mrs. Benchmark says you have stolen the King Alfred gold cup and you're hiding it. If necessary, she will take it back by force."

Hell's teeth. *Where is it?*

The King Alfred gold cup. The *it* that the demons had been looking for. The *it* that I didn't have, not the *it* that I did have.

I said, "Was the cup kept in the brewery?" Finch didn't answer. "Don't you know?" I asked. "Has there been a rumpus, with police flourishing handcuffs? Or did Patsy just *tell* you I'd taken it? She does have a way of neutralizing people's common sense."

Desmond Finch made an exit as unheralded as his entry. When the air had settled after his departure, Mrs. Morden asked if I had a replacement copy of the power of attorney. I gave her one.

"I hope to bring together the brewery's creditors on Monday," she said. "Telephone me for a progress report."

"Thank you, Mrs. Morden."

"Margaret," she said. "Now, these depressing numbers . . ."

I WALKED back to Pierce, Tollright and Simmonds, where the auditor and I became Tobe and Al and went out for an early beer. I told him of Desmond Finch's visit, a tale that resulted in vicious chewing of a toothpick, but otherwise a diplomatic silence.

"Have you met him?" I asked, prompting.

"Oh yes. Quite often."

"What do you think of him?"

"Desmond Finch gets things done. He can't act without orders, but give him a program he understands, and he will unswervingly carry it out."

"You approve of him, then?"

He grinned. "I applaud his work. I can't stand the man."

I laughed. "Thank heavens for that."

We drank in harmony. I said, "What was Norman Quorn like?" Quorn was the finance director who had vanished with the cash. "You must have known him well."

"I thought I did. I'd worked with him for years." Tobias swallowed beer. "The last person, I would have thought, to do what he did. He was coming up to retirement. A meticulous accountant. We went through the firm's books together every year. Never a decimal out of place. I'd have bet my reputation on his honesty."

"He was saving everything up for the big one."

Tobias sighed. "When I told Sir Ivan about two weeks ago that the brewery was insolvent, he told me to keep it quiet. By then Quorn had already gone away. He was clever—I'll give him that."

"How did he actually steal so much?"

"He didn't go round to the bank with a sack, if that's what you mean. He did it the new-fashioned way, by electronic transfer, routing money all over the place via ABA numbers—those are international bank identification numbers—and by backing up the transactions with faxed authorizations bearing the right identifying codes. I believed I could follow any tracks, but I've lost him somewhere in Panama. It's a job for the serious fraud people, though Sir Ivan wants to hush up the whole thing and won't call them in."

We refilled the half-pints in suitable gloom.

I said tentatively, "Do you think Quorn could have stolen the King Alfred cup?"

"What?" He was astonished. "No. Not his style."

"Desmond Finch says that Patsy Benchmark—have you met Ivan's daughter?—is accusing *me* of having stolen the cup."

"I've met her," Tobias said. "The fact that no one seems to know where this priceless medieval goblet actually *is* does not mean that it's been stolen."

"I drink to clarity of mind."

He laughed. "You'd make a good auditor."

"A better slosher-on of paint."

WHEN I reached the house in Park Crescent, Dr. Robbiston was just leaving, and we spoke on the steps outside with my mother.

"How is Ivan?" I said.

The doctor glanced at my mother and said briefly, "He needs rest." His gaze switched intensely back to me. "Perhaps you can see he gets it." He flapped a hand in farewell and hurried off.

"What did he mean about rest?" I asked my mother.

She sighed. "Patsy is here. So is Surtees."

Surtees Benchmark was Patsy's husband. Tall and lean, he could waffle apologetically while he did you a bad turn, rather like his wife. He saw me through her eyes.

My mother and I went indoors. I could hear Patsy's voice upstairs. "I *insist,* Father. He's got to go."

As her voice was coming from Ivan's study, I went up there with my neat mother following.

Patsy saw my arrival with predictable rage. She too was tall and lean, and stunningly beautiful when she wanted to charm. Only those who knew her well looked at her warily.

"I have been telling Father," she said forcefully, "that he must revoke that stupid power of attorney and give it to *me*."

I said mildly, "He can, of course, do what he likes."

Ivan looked alarmingly pale and weak, sitting as ever in his dark red robe in his imposing chair. I went across to him, offering my arm and suggesting he should lie down on his bed.

"Leave him alone," Patsy said sharply.

"Lie down," Ivan said vaguely. "Good idea."

I helped him towards his bedroom, and short of physically attacking me, Patsy and Surtees couldn't stop me. But as I went past him, Surtees said spitefully, "Next time you'll *scream*."

My mother's eyes widened in surprise. Patsy's head snapped round towards her husband, and with scorn she shriveled him verbally. "Will you keep your silly mouth *shut*."

In Ivan's bedroom, my mother and I helped him into bed, where he relaxed gratefully, murmuring, "Vivienne . . . ."

"I'm here." She stroked his hand. "Go to sleep, my dear."

When he was breathing evenly, my mother and I went out into the study and found that Patsy and Surtees had gone.

"What did he mean, 'Next time you'll scream'?" she asked.

"I dread to think."

She looked doubtful and worried. "There's something about Surtees that isn't . . . Oh dear. That isn't *normal*."

"Dearest Ma," I said, teasing her, "almost no one is normal. Look at your son, for a start."

Her worry dissolved into a laugh and from there to visible happiness when, from the study phone, I told Jed Parlane that I would be staying down south for another twenty-four hours. I'd get to Dalwhinnie on Saturday morning.

Jed faintly protested. "Himself wants you back here as soon as possible."

"Tell him my mother needs me."

"So do the police."

"Too bad. See you, Jed."

IN THE morning I talked for much longer than usual with Ivan. He looked better. He still wore robe and slippers, but there was color in his face and clarity in his mind.

I told him what I'd learned over the past two days. He faced unwillingly the whole frightening extent of the plundering of the brewery and approved of the appointment of Margaret Morden.

"It's my own fault things got so bad," Ivan sighed. "But, you know, I couldn't believe that Norman Quorn would rob the firm. I've known him for years. . . . I *trusted* him."

His pain was more personal than financial, the treachery harder to bear than the actual loss. "I wish," he said, "that you would take over the brewery. I've always known you could do it."

"I'm sorry," I said inadequately. I didn't know why I couldn't take the offer. I did know it would result in meltdown.

He said with feeling, "I wish you were my son."

That silenced me completely. He looked as though he was surprised he had said it, but he let it stand. A silence grew.

In the end, I said tentatively, "Golden Malt . . ."

"My horse." His gaze sharpened on my face. "Did you hide it?"

"Did you mean me to?"

"Of course I did. I hoped you would. Where is he?"

"If you don't know, you can't tell." I paused. "Do you have any proof that you personally own him? Bill of sale?"

"No. I bought him as a foal for cash to help out a friend. He paid no tax on the gain." The phone rang at his elbow, and he gestured to me to answer it. I found Tobias at the other end, fluster in his voice.

"Al, I've had this man on the phone who says Sir Ivan has revoked your powers of attorney."

"What man?"

"A lawyer. Oliver Grantchester. He says he's in charge of Sir Ivan's affairs. He says the power of attorney was a mistake. Apparently, Patsy Benchmark got Sir Ivan to say so."

"Hold on," I said, "while I talk to my stepfather."

I explained the situation to Ivan. He picked up the receiver and said, "Mr. Tollright, I stand by every word I signed. My daughter misinformed Mr. Grantchester. Alexander acts for me in everything, and I give my trust to no one else. Clear?"

He gave me back the telephone, and I said to Tobias, "Okay?"

"Good grief, that woman is dangerous, Al."

"Mm. Tobe, do you know any good, honest, discreet private investigators?"

He chuckled. "Good, honest, and discreet . . . Got a pencil?"

There was a pencil on the table but no notepad. I turned over the box of tissues, in Ivan's fashion, and wrote the name and phone number of a firm in Reading. "Thanks, Tobe."

I disconnected and said to Ivan, "Patsy is also going around telling people I've stolen the King Alfred cup."

"But," he said, undisturbed, "you do have it, don't you?"

CHAPTER 4

FTER a moment of internal chill I said carefully, "Why do you think I have the cup?"

Ivan looked astonished but not yet alarmed. "Because I sent it to you, of course. You are good at hiding things, Robert said. I sent it to you to keep it safe."

Hell's teeth, I thought. *No.*

I said, "How? How did you send it to me?"

He frowned. "I gave it to Robert to give to you. That's to say, I told him where to find the damned cup and asked him to take it to you in Scotland. If you haven't got the cup, then Robert has."

I breathed slowly and deeply and said, "Who else knew you were sending the cup to me?"

"Who? No one else. What does it matter? Like the horse, the cup belongs to *me,* and I don't want to see it counted as a brewery asset and sold for a drop in the ocean."

"Bill of sale?" I suggested hopelessly.

"Don't be ridiculous."

"When did you ask Himself to take the cup to Scotland?"

"When? Last week, while I was in the clinic. Robert came to visit me, and it made sense to ask him to look after the cup, and he said he would, but better still, he would entrust it to you. I asked if he trusted you enough, and he said he would trust you with his life."

Hell, I thought, and asked, "Which day was that?"

"I can't possibly remember. Why do you think it matters?"

Next time you'll scream.

"Did you tell Patsy that I was looking after the cup?"

Ivan said, "I do wish you and Patsy could like each other."

"Yes, I'm sorry," I said, and it was true that I was. "She did, though, tell Desmond Finch that I'd stolen the cup, and he believes it and is spreading it about, which is unfortunate."

"Oh, Desmond," Ivan said indulgently. "Such a good man in so many ways. I rely on him, you know, to get things done."

"Yes," I said.

After a while Ivan said with weakness, "Patsy couldn't have been sweeter when I was in the clinic. I can't think how she thought you had *stolen* the cup. You must be mistaken about that."

"Don't worry about it," I said.

ARMED with generous cash from my mother, I trekked back by rail to Reading, to the firm of Young and Uttley, the investigators recommended by Tobias. An unprepossessing male voice on the telephone having given me a time and a place, I found a soulless box of an office—desks, filing cabinets, computers—with a man of about my age, dressed in jeans, black hard boots, a grubby singlet with cutout armholes, and a heavy black hip-slung belt shining with aggressive studs. He had an unshaved chin, close-cropped dark hair, and one dangling earring.

"Yeah?" he said when I went in. "Want something?"

"I'm looking for Young and Uttley. I telephoned."

"Yeah," said the voice I'd heard on the phone. "See. Young and Uttley are *partners*. That's their pictures on the wall, there. Which one do you want?"

He pointed to two glossy eight- by ten-inch photographs. Mr. Young and Mr. Uttley were, first, a sober, dark-suited man with a heavy mustache and a striped tie, and, second, a wholesome fellow in a blue jogging suit, carrying a football.

I turned away, smiling, and said to the skinhead watching me, "Those pictures are both you."

"Quick, aren't you?" he said tartly. "And Tobe warned me and all. What do you want done?"

"I want good, honest, and discreet—the discreet bit most of all. Then I want you to follow someone and find out if he's met, or knows where to find, four other people."

"Done," he said easily. "Who are they?"

I drew them for him in pencil—Surtees and each of my four attackers. I told him Surtees's name and address. I said I knew nothing about the others except their ability to punch.

"Are those four how you got that eye?"

"Yes. They robbed my house in Scotland, but they have southeast England voices."

I paid him a retainer for a week, gave him Jed's phone number, and told him to report. "What do I call you?" I asked.

"Young or Uttley, take your pick."

"Young and Utterly Outrageous, more like."

"You're so sharp you'll cut yourself."

I went grinning to the train.

I SPENT the later part of the afternoon shopping, accompanied by my long-suffering mother, who paid for everything.

Back at Park Crescent, I changed into some of the new clothes and left the riding gear for return to Emily. I told Ivan (having checked with Margaret Morden) that the brewery's creditors had agreed to meet on Monday. The three of us ate an Edna-cooked dinner; then I shook Ivan's hand, hugged my mother warmly, humped my bags and boxes along to Euston, boarded the *Royal Highlander,* and slept my way to Scotland.

Even the air at Dalwhinnie smelled different. Smelled like home. Cold. Fresh. A promise of mountains.

Jed Parlane was striding up and down to keep warm. He helped carry my clutter out to his car and asked how was I feeling.

"Good as new."

"The police want to interview you, of course."

"Sometime."

Jed drove me, as arranged, straight to Kinloch castle. The castle, like all ancient Scottish castles, had been constructed to keep out enemies. It was of thick, plain gray stone, with narrow windows that had once been arrow slots for archers. Built on a rise, it looked dour and inhospitable, even on sunny days.

My father had grown up there, and I'd played there as a child, but the castle itself no longer belonged to the Kinloch family. It was the property of Scotland, administered as a tourist attraction by a conservation organization. Himself, who had pronounced the heating bills too much for even the Kinloch coffers, had negotiated a retreat to a smaller, snugger home in what had once been the kitchen wing.

Himself would, on occasion, act as host to visiting monarchs in the castle's vast main dining hall, and it had been after one such grand evening, about six years earlier, that an enterprising band of burglars in the livery of footmen had borne away an irreplaceable gold-leafed eighteenth-century dinner service for fifty.

Less than a year later Himself had thought of a way of keeping safe the best-known and most priceless of the many Kinloch treasures— the jewel-encrusted solid-gold hilt of the ceremonial sword of Prince Charles Edward Stuart, Bonnie Prince Charlie.

The hilt was taken out of its thiefproof display case and replaced with a replica. Ever since, Himself had politely refused to tell the castle's administrators where to find the original. It belonged to *him,* he maintained, as it had been given personally by the prince to his ancestor, the Earl of Kinloch at the time, and had been handed down to him, the present earl, in the direct male line.

So had the castle, the administrators said. The hilt belonged to the nation.

Not so, Himself argued. The castle transfer documents had not included personal property and had specifically excluded the hilt.

There had been hot debates in newspapers and on television as to when, if ever, a gift to one man became the property of all.

Moreover, as Himself pointed out, the hilt had been given in appreciation for hospitality, horses, and provisions given to the prince and his retinue on their long retreat northward after a nearly successful campaign to win the English crown. The facts were well attested. The splendid hilt, as it was passed down the generations, had become known as the Honor of the Kinlochs, and Himself, though he had had to cede his castle, had finally won a declaration in the courts—still disputed—that the hilt belonged to *him.*

Since he had "disappeared" the hilt, the castle had been further robbed of a display of Highland artifacts: shields, claymores, and brooches. Himself, in residence in London at the time, had made sarcastic remarks about bureaucrats being hopeless custodians of treasures. Ill feeling flew like barbs. The castle's bruised administrators were now hell-bent on finding the hilt.

Under guise of rewiring and refurbishing the entire castle, they were inching with probes everywhere, determined to uncover the cache. All they had wrung out of Himself was a promise that the Honor of the Kinlochs had not left his property.

After Jed decanted me at the private-wing door, I went inside and found my uncle in his dining room, pouring coffee at the sideboard. He gave me, as always when we met after an interval, the salutation of my whole name, to which I replied with old and easy formality.

"Alexander."

"My lord."

He nodded, smiled faintly, and gestured. "Breakfast?"

"Thank you."

He took his cup over to the table. Two places had been laid, and he waved me to the free one. "That's for you," he said. "My wife stayed in London."

I sat and ate toast, and he asked me if I'd had a good journey.

"I slept all the way."

He was a tall man, broad without looking fat. At sixty-five he had gray hair, a strong nose, and guarded eyes. His mind was as tough and solid as an oak. If it was true that he'd told Ivan he would trust me with his life, then the reverse was also true.

He said, spreading marmalade, "Jed told me about the bothy."

He wanted me to tell him in detail what had happened, so I did, though with distaste. I told him also about Ivan giving me the powers of attorney and about my experiences in Reading.

Eventually I asked him calmly, "So do you have the King Alfred gold cup? Is it here?"

He answered broodingly, "I did tell Ivan you were good at hiding things."

"Mm." I paused. "Probably someone heard you."

"Good grief, Al."

I said, "I think it was the chalice, not the hilt, that those men were trying to find at the bothy. I also think they hadn't been told what they were looking for. They kept saying, 'Where is *it?*' " I sighed. "Anyway, I'd say now the 'it' was definitely the cup."

He said heavily, "Jed said they'd hurt you badly."

"That was Tuesday. Today's Saturday, and I'm fine."

He hesitated. "I still have to decide what to do with that damned lump of gold."

I did not make an offer to keep it safe. He listened to my silence. "I can't ask it of you, I suppose," he said.

Next time you'll scream. . . . There would be no next time.

"Patsy's saying I stole the cup from the brewery."

"That's nonsense! It was Ivan who took the cup out of the brewery, the day before his heart attack. He was feeling deeply upset by his auditor's warnings, and he was worried both about his people losing their jobs and about himself losing face—he takes his baronetcy and his membership of the Jockey Club seriously."

"But it wasn't his fault."

"He appointed Norman Quorn to be finance director. He says he no longer trusts his own judgment. So when he could see bankruptcy and disgrace ahead, he simply walked out with the cup. 'Sick at heart' was the phrase he used."

Poor Ivan. Poor sick heart.

I asked, "Did he take the cup back to Park Crescent?"

"No, and Ivan didn't want to leave a paper trail, so he left it—you'll laugh—in a cardboard box in the cloakroom of his club."

"Hell's teeth."

"I fetched it from his club. Brought the cup up here in my car. James and I drove up together. I didn't tell James what I'd got," Himself observed. "James doesn't understand the word 'secret.' "

James was his eldest son, his heir. A friendly fellow, liked to talk. Life, to my cousin, was mostly a lark.

My uncle and I left the dining room and walked outside, round the whole ancient complex, as he liked to do. He said, "Everyone refers to the King Alfred cup as priceless, but it isn't, of course. I wanted to get it valued. If Ivan wanted me to get you to look after it, I had to know its worth. But he said it was too well known. If I took it to a reputable valuer, he would end up losing it. I had to assure him I wouldn't take it to anyone that would recognize it."

"But," I said, "who else could give you a reliable estimate?"

He smiled. "This afternoon we'll find out."

THE valuer summoned to the castle was neither an auctioneer nor a jeweler, but a thin eighty-year-old woman, a retired lecturer in English from St. Andrews University, Dr. Zoë Lang, with a comet tail of distinguished qualifications after her name.

My uncle explained he had met her "at some function or other," and when she arrived, gushing but overwhelmingly intellectual, he introduced me vaguely as "Al, one of my nephews."

Dr. Lang gave me a strong, bony handshake. Himself made small talk and led the way into the dining room, where with gentle ceremony he sat his guest at the table.

"Al," he said to me, "there's a box in the sideboard, right-hand cupboard. Put it on the table, would you?"

I found and carried across a large brown cardboard box stuck all over with sticky tape, marked BOOKS. PROPERTY OF SIR I. WESTERING.

"Let's see what we've got," Himself instructed.

Dr. Lang looked politely interested. "I have to warn you again, Lord Kinloch," she said in her pure Scots voice, "that almost no significant works of goldsmith's art survive from the ninth century in England. I've kept your request private, as you asked, as the last thing you want, I'm sure, is ridicule."

"The last," Himself agreed gravely.

Dr. Zoë Lang had straight gray hair looped back into a loose bun on her neck. She wore glasses, lipstick, and clothes too large for her thin frame. Something about her, all the same, warned one not to think in terms of dry old spinster.

I ripped off the sticky tape, opened the box, and lifted out the books—old editions of Dickens. Underneath was a cloth drawstring bag enclosing another box, a twelve-inch cube of black leather with gold clasps. Between the clasps, stamped in small gold letters, were the words MAXIM, LONDON.

"Dr. Lang?" Himself said courteously, pushing the box to her.

Without flourish she opened it, then sat as still as marble.

"Well," she said finally, and again, "*Well . . .*"

Inside the box, supported by a white satin–covered cushion, the King Alfred gold cup lay on its side. I had never actually seen it, nor, from his expression, had my uncle. No wonder, I thought, that Ivan had wanted to keep that cup for his own.

The cup, bigger than I'd imagined, was a wide, round bowl on a sturdy neck with a spreading foot. The rim of the bowl was crenellated like many castles, and its sides glittered with red, blue, and green inlaid stones. Overall, it shone with the warm, unmistakable golden glow of twenty-two karats at least.

With reverence Dr. Lang lifted out the astonishing object and stood it on the polished wood table. It gleamed as if with inner light.

She cleared her throat. "King Alfred never saw this, of course. No, sad as I am to say it, this cup is modern."

"Modern?" Himself echoed, surprised.

"Certainly not medieval. Almost certainly Victorian—1860 or thereabouts. Very beautiful. But not old."

The cup had what looked like a pattern engraved right round the top, below the crenellations. Dr. Lang looked attentively at the patterns and smiled with obvious enjoyment. "The cup is engraved with a poem in Anglo-Saxon," she said. "But it's still Victorian. And I doubt if the stones are rubies and emeralds."

"Can you read the poem?" I asked.

"Of course. I taught Anglo-Saxon for years. Wonderful poetry." She fingered the engraving. "This is Bede's *Death Song*. Very famous. Bede died in 735, long before Alfred was born. In literal translation it says, 'Before that sudden journey, no one is wiser in thought than he needs to be, in considering, before his departure, what will be adjudged to his soul, of good or evil, after his death-day.' "

Her old voice held the echo of years of lecturing to students, the authority of confident scholarship. Bede's *Death Song*'s message was of taking stock of the good and evil one did on earth because hell after death was a certainty.

I took it for a certainty that Ivan knew what was engraved on his cup. He had judged and found himself culpable, and was harder on himself precisely because his standard for his own probity had been set so high. I wondered if he valued the cup more for what was inscribed on it than for its intrinsic worth.

"So how much," Himself was asking his expert, "should one insure this cup for?"

"Insure? You could weigh it and multiply by the current price of gold, or you could maintain that it is a valuable example of Victorian romanticism, or you could say it's worth dying for."

"Not that."

She nodded. "I don't think you could insure this cup for any more than its worth in gold."

Its weight in gold, even at five or more pounds, wouldn't go anywhere near saving the brewery.

"It's a great pity this remarkable chalice isn't a genuine ninth-century treasure," Dr. Lang said, "but of course, if it were, it would have been either stolen at once or lost when Henry the Eighth devastated the churches. Many old treasures were buried in the 1530s to keep them safe, and the buriers died without telling where the treasures were hidden. Alas, this cup wasn't around in the days of Henry the Eighth. I think the proper place for it now is in a museum."

She stopped.

Himself, who disagreed with her, thanked her warmly for her trouble and offered her wine or tea.

"What I would like," she said, "is to see the Kinloch hilt."

Himself blinked, then said, smiling, "We have had to bury it to keep it safe." He was making a joke of it, and she smiled tightly and settled for a sight of the copy.

We walked down the passage from the kitchen to the great hall, and Himself let us into the castle proper. The great hall's walls, thanks to the theft of the tapestries, were now grimly bare. The center table, where once fifty guests had dined in splendor, bore a thin film of dust. Without comment my uncle walked down the long room, with its high vaulted ceiling, until he came to the grilled glass display that had once held the true Honor of the Kinlochs.

The replica hilt lay on black velvet, and even though one knew it was not the real thing, it looked impressive.

"It is gold-plated," its owner said. "The red stones are spinel not ruby, the blue stones are lapis lazuli, and the green stones are peridots."

Dr. Zoë Lang studied it carefully and in silence. The hilt itself looked remarkably like the King Alfred gold cup, except that there were no crenellations and no engraving. There was instead the pommel—the grip that fitted into the palm of the hand—and instead of the circular foot, only the neck into which the snapped-off blade had been fastened. The sword had been made for Prince Charles in France and paid for by him personally in 1740.

Dr. Lang, with unexpected fervor, said, "I agree with the castle's custodians that the real Honor of the Kinlochs belongs to Scotland."

"Do you think so?" Himself asked jocularly. "I would defend my right of ownership . . ." He paused provocatively.

"Yes?" she prompted.

He smiled sweetly. "To the hilt."

"AL," HIMSELF asked thoughtfully as we walked back from seeing Zoë Lang out to her taxi, "how far would you actually go in defending the honor of the Kinlochs?"

"Up to and including the hilt?"

"I'm not joking, Al."

I glanced at his troubled face. "I don't know," I said.

"I don't ask for you to suffer to keep that thing safe. If they attack you again, tell them what they want to know."

We went peacefully into his house and into his dining room, where the King Alfred gold cup still lay on the table. I reenclosed the cup in its black cube and its drawstring bag, and replaced it in the cardboard box with the copies of Dickens on top. I restuck it all with the wide, sticky tape, and we put the box back in the sideboard, for the want of anywhere better.

"We can't leave it there forever," my uncle said. "Think of somewhere better for the cup, Al."

"I'll try."

At his own request I hadn't told him to the inch where to find the hilt, though he knew it was somewhere at the bothy. We had, as a precaution against us both inconveniently dying with our secret untold, entrusted Jed with the basic information.

Jed had never alluded to it since, except to say once that he felt overwhelmed by our faith in his loyalty.

Jed came back to the castle late in the afternoon, wanting to know if he could drive me home to the bothy.

"No," Himself said decisively. "Al will stay here tonight. Sit down, Jed. Get yourself a drink."

We were by then in the room my uncle considered his private

domain, a room with walls bearing stuffed fish and deer antlers. There were also three of my paintings of his racehorses.

Jed fixed a glass of whisky and water and sat down.

Himself, as usual, made the decisions. "I see Al seldom enough. He will stay here to please me, and on Monday morning you can take him to the bothy and the police station. I'll be fishing the Spey next week, and I have guests Monday, Tuesday, and Wednesday. James returns from sailing tomorrow. He'll be staying on here. His wife will take the children back to school. All clear, Jed?"

"Yes, sir."

Jed and he discussed estate affairs while I tried to imagine a good temporary home for Bede's *Death Song* engraved in gold.

I had asked Zoë Lang to read the poem aloud in Anglo-Saxon, and with joy she had done so, her love of the old language giving the words shape and meaning and new life. I couldn't understand a syllable, but the excitement, the *intoxication,* she said, was engendered by the rhythmic beat as much as by the vivid imagery of the words.

Himself and I had listened respectfully, and I thought of how much the outward appearance of age could color one's expectation of a person's character. I wanted to paint Zoë Lang as young, vibrant, fanatical, with the ghost of the way she looked now superimposed in thin gray lines, like age's cobwebs. I sensed a singular individual powerful entity that might have intensified with time, not faded. We were dealing with that inner woman and should not forget it.

If I underpainted thickly in Payne's gray mixed with titanium white, I thought, then brought the essential person to glowing life with strong bone structure in a faithful portrait, and then scratched down into the gray for the unthinkable future . . . then with a steady hand and a strong vision I might produce a statement of terrible truth. Or I might finish with a disaster fit only for the bin.

Hide the cup—my mind wandered back to the task in hand. I asked myself if I would have given up the cup if I'd known what the demon walkers were looking for. I thought quite likely not.

Mad, weird, ridiculous Alexander.

The problem with hiding anything in the castle was that Himself was rarely in residence, while the administrators were in and out all the time, actively hunting treasure. In the family's private wing lived a full-time caretaker and his wife, who eviscerated every cupboard in the name of spring cleaning. It seemed, then, the castle was out. The grounds were out also, thanks to an efficient gardener. So where?

Any thoughts I might have had about a peaceful evening were at that point blasted apart by the earthquake arrival of my friendly cousin James—who had listened to a gale-and-rain weather forecast and decided to run for port early—along with his boisterous family, who lived fortissimo at Indy car speed.

When the invasion stampeded upstairs to arrange bedrooms, James, red-haired and freckled, wandering by with gin and tonic in fist, asked amiably how the "old boy" was doing.

"Depressed," I said.

"Father says someone decamped with the brewery's nest egg."

"Nest egg, chickens, battery hens, the lot," I said.

"What a lark, eh? How are the daubs?"

"In abeyance," I said, and gave him a lightweight account of the trouble at the bothy.

"Good heavens!" He stared. "What rotten luck." His sympathy was genuine enough. "Did they take your pipes?"

"Luckily, they're in Inverness. The bag had sprung a leak."

Saturday evening passed in the chaos indigenous to James's family, and in the morning, when I went downstairs, I found Himself in the dining room looking around in bewilderment at an empty cardboard box, old faded copies of Dickens, and an empty black cube—all lying about on the floor. The sideboard door stood open. The King Alfred gold cup had gone.

There were squeals from the kitchen next door. Children's voices. Dazedly my uncle opened the connecting door, and I followed him into the large kitchen, where James was leaning against the sink, coffee mug in hand, indulgent smile in place.

His unruly children—two boys and a girl—scrambled around on the floor, all wearing large saucepans on their heads, handles pointing backwards. Spacewatch good guys, we were told. The King

Alfred cup also stood on the floor upside down. Himself bent down and picked it up.

"Hey," objected his elder grandson, "that's the galactic core of M.100, with all its Cepheid variables in those red stones. We have to keep it safe from the black-hole suction mob."

"I'm glad to hear it," his grandfather said dryly.

The boy—Andrew—was eleven and already rebellious, hard-eyed, and tough. He would one day succeed James as earl. James might be open to soft persuasion, but I wanted to know for sure about his son.

I said, "Andrew, if you had a favorite toy, something you really valued, and someone threatened to hurt you if you didn't give it to him, what would you do?"

He said promptly, "Bash his face in."

My uncle smiled as Andrew repeated stalwartly, "I'd bash his face in. Can we have the Cepheid monitor back?"

"No," Himself said. "You shouldn't have taken it out of its box."

"We were looking for something worth fighting for," Andrew said.

James said, "What is it, anyway? It can't be real gold."

Himself thrust the cup into my arms. "Put it away safely." To James he explained, "It's a racing trophy. I can't keep it for more than a year, and I need to give it back without dents in."

The explanation satisfied James entirely, and he told his children to look for a substitute galactic goody.

On impulse I asked James if he would like to spend some of the day playing golf. We both belonged to the local club, where I often walked after the elusive white ball.

He was pleased but said, "I thought your clubs were stolen."

"I might buy some new ones."

"Great, then."

He phoned the club and found us an afternoon slot. We drove over to the club in time for the pro shop to kit me out with clubs, shoes, gloves, balls, and umbrellas. Thus reequipped, James and I went out into the wind and rain, which had arrived as forecast.

"Will you paint this?" James asked.

"Yes, of course." My hands-on relationship with golf was essential to my work, I'd found.

"You're not really as weird as we all think, are you?"

I putted a ball to the rim of a hole, where it obstinately stopped. "I paint frustration," I said, and gave the ball a kick.

James laughed, and in good spirits we finished the eighteen holes and went back to the castle for the nineteenth.

James's children were in the dining room. The King Alfred cup, though still in its white satin nest, lay in full glorious view on the polished table under a chandelier's light.

"You didn't say we couldn't *look* at it," Andy said. "We couldn't find *anything else* worth fighting a space war for."

I said to James, "What about the hilt?"

"Oh yes." He thought it over. "But we'd only see the replica, and anyway, I can't let the children through into the castle proper."

"Let's ask Himself," I said.

We found him in his own room and asked, with the result that all of us—Himself, James, the children, and I—walked the length of the great hall and stood round the grilled glass cage, staring down at its floodlit treasure.

"That," Andrew decided, "would be worth fighting a galactic space war for. If it was real, of course. Where is the real one?"

His grandfather said, "We have to keep it safe from the black-hole suction mob."

Andy's face was an almost unpaintable mixture of glee and understanding. A boy worth fighting for, I thought.

Himself carefully didn't look at me once.

IT WAS still raining on Monday morning. James took his family to set off south, Himself left to meet his guests for fishing in the Spey River, and Jed arrived to pick me up and set my normal life on course.

He brought with him a replacement credit card and checkbook for me, and he'd heard from Inverness that my bagpipes were ready. He had freed one of the estate's Land Rovers for my temporary use, and he lent me a fully charged portable phone to put me in touch with events in London and Reading.

I said inadequately, "Thanks, Jed."

I went outdoors with him and found the boxes from London that I'd left in his car on Saturday already piled into the Land Rover. I'd taken into Himself's house only a few clothes, and I left with them in a heavy-duty duffel bag from the gun room.

Jed commented on my new clubs.

"Yes," I said, "but this time I'm storing my kit in the clubhouse."

Jed said, "Are you afraid the robbers will come back?"

I grinned. "Don't worry. This time I'll install a burglar alarm."

"There isn't any electricity."

"Cans on strings with stones in."

Jed shook his head. "You're mad."

"So they say."

He gave up. "The police are expecting you. Ask for Detective Sergeant Berrick. And take care, Al. I mean it."

"I will," I said.

We drove off together but parted at the estate gates. I headed for the bothy, stopping only to unload the new golf gear into a locker.

New keys to the bothy door opened my way into the same devastation that I'd left there six days earlier. With a sigh I dug out of the mess an unused plastic rubbish bag and filled it with the debris. My mattress and bedding were soaked and smelling from dirty paint water. My armchair, too, smelled revolting.

Bit by bit I stacked my ruined possessions in the dry carport. When I'd finished, I swept the floor and collected coffee, sugar, and sundry debris into a dustpan and gloomily looked at the paint-laden footprints on my wood-block floor.

I carted the boxes of new gear into the bothy and stacked everything on the bare springs of the bed. Then I locked the door and finally drove off in search of Detective Sergeant Berrick.

Within five minutes Berrick revealed himself as a typical good-hearted, aggressive Scot with a strong sense of justice. He told me not to expect to get my goods back.

I said, "I wonder if you might have luck with the paintings."

"What paintings?" He peered at a list. "Oh yes, here we are. Four paintings of scenes of golf courses." He looked up. "Is there any way we could recognize those pictures?"

"They had stickers on the back in the top-left-hand corner. Copyright stickers giving my name—Alexander—and this year's date."

"Stickers can be pulled off," he said.

"These stickers can't. The glue bonds with the canvas."

He gave a don't-bother-me stare but punched up my file on a computer and typed in the words "copyright stickers on backs." He shrugged. "You could put another sticker over the top."

"Yes, you could," I agreed. "But you might not know my name is printed in an ink that shows up in X rays."

He smiled. "Tricky, aren't you?"

"It's a wicked world," I said.

I next visited a shop that was a camper's heaven and acquired a sleeping bag and enough essentials to make living in the stripped bothy possible. Then I drove to Donald Cameron's post office for any letters for me and to stock up with food and gas.

"Will you be wanting to use my telephone?" old Donald asked hopefully. "There's something amiss with the one outside."

I bet there is, I thought. But to please the old beggar, I made one call, asking the bagpipe restorers if there was any chance of their delivering my pipes to Jed Parlane's house.

Old Donald practically snatched the receiver out of my hand and told the pipe people he would be going to Inverness on Wednesday and would collect my pipes for me personally. Donald, hanging up, beamed at me with expectation.

"How much?" I asked, and negotiated a minor king's ransom.

"Always at your service, Mr. Kinloch."

IT RAINED all the way up the muddy track to the bothy. Once there, I sat in the comparative comfort of the Land Rover and used Jed's portable phone.

I tried Tobias Tollright with trepidation. "Mrs. Morden wants to talk to you," he said. "She held the meeting of creditors."

"And that's good?"

"Encouraging."

I said, "Tobe . . ."

"What is it?"

"Young and Uttley."

Tobias laughed. "He's a genius. I wouldn't recommend him to everyone, but you're two of a kind. You both think sideways. You'll get on well together. Give him a chance."

"Did he tell you that I engaged him and why?"

"Er . . ." The guilt in his voice raised horrible doubts.

"So much for discretion."

Tobias said again, lightheartedly, "Give him a chance, Al."

It was too late, I thought ruefully, to do anything else.

I phoned Margaret Morden. She said in her crisp voice, "I laid out the figures. The creditors all needed smelling salts. But I've persuaded them to try to come up with solutions."

"Did you . . . did you ask the creditors about the race?"

"They see your point. They'll discuss it on Wednesday. Meanwhile, you may still sign for Sir Ivan. He is adamant it should be you and no one else."

"I'll do anything you need, and Margaret . . ."

"Yes?"

"What are you wearing today?"

She gasped and then laughed. "Coffee and cream."

"Soft and pretty?"

"It gets subliminal results."

"Appearances help."

"Indeed they do. . . ." Her voice tailed off hesitantly. "There's something odd, though, about the brewery's accounts."

Alarmed, I said, "What exactly is odd?"

"I don't know. I can't identify it. It's probably nothing."

"I trust your instincts."

She sighed. "Tobias Tollright drew up the accounts. He's very reliable. If there were anything incongruous, he would have noticed. I'll sleep on it. Solutions often come in the night."

I wished her useful dreams and sat on my Scottish mountainside in the rain-spattered Land Rover. I realized how little I knew and how much I relied on Tobe and Margaret and Young (or Uttley) for answers to questions I hadn't the knowledge to ask.

I wanted to paint. I could feel the compulsion.

Inside the bothy, there was an old familiar easel and new painting supplies from London. I would prepare a canvas for morning: Tack cotton duck onto a stretched frame. Prime with gesso to produce a good surface. Let it dry. Lay on the Payne's gray mixed with titanium white. Make working drawings.

First I phoned my mother.

Ivan was no worse, no better.

"The real trouble," she said, "is Surtees."

"What about him?"

"He is *paranoid*. Patsy is furious with him. Patsy is furious about *everything*. I do wish you would come back, Alexander. You're the only person she can't bully."

"Is she bullying Ivan?"

"Terribly. He told Oliver Grantchester he wants to write a codicil to his will, and now Patsy is demanding to know what Ivan wants a codicil for, and for once Ivan won't tell her, and oh *dear*, it's so bad for Ivan. She's at his elbow every minute."

"And Surtees? Why is he paranoid?"

"He says he's being followed everywhere by a skinhead."

I said weakly, *"What?"*

"I know. It's stupid. Patsy's livid with him. Ivan needs rest and quiet. Come back, Alexander. Please."

I wanted to paint, but the overt uncharacteristic plea was too much. I said, "I'll come back Wednesday night."

We said good-bye, and I phoned Jed.

He said, "All hell has broken loose at the castle."

"What sort of hell?"

"Young Andrew has run off with the King Alfred gold cup."

CHAPTER 5

 LAUGHED.

"I suppose it's quite funny," Jed said.

"What exactly happened?"

It seemed that soon after Himself and his guests returned to the castle, Dr. Zoë Lang had made an unheralded return visit, bringing an expert in precious stones. She couldn't rest, she said, while her evaluation of the King Alfred cup was incomplete.

Accordingly, all had gone into the dining room in the quest for truth. The cardboard box had been retrieved from the sideboard and the copies of Dickens removed. The black leather cube had been lifted out, gold clasps undone, and . . . nothing.

My cousin James, who had returned from seeing his family off to London, had instantly said he would tan the hide off his elder son, who had been fascinated by the cup. But the Spacewatch good guy could not at that moment be reached for questioning, as he was somewhere on the road back to boarding school with his mother.

Jed said, "When I called in to see Himself, I found this old lady rather rudely telling him he shouldn't be trusted to keep the Kinloch hilt safe if he couldn't guard things from his own grandson. Anyway, after she'd gone, he asked me to ask you if you thought he ought to worry about Andrew, so do you?"

"No."

Jed's sigh was half a chuckle. "I told Himself you had carried out of the castle one of those game bags from the gun room, and he beamed. But what's it all about? Is that cup worth a lot?"

"It depends where you stand," I said. "It's gold. If you're rich, it's just an expensive bauble. If you're a thief, it's worth murder. In between, you balance the greed against the risks."

On Tuesday morning a cold front swept the sky, dramatically clearing away the rain and leaving a pale blue cosmos with a yellowish tint of sunlight. The bothy faced west, which often gave me long mornings of near-perfect painting light.

On that Tuesday, on the gray-white underpainting, I lightly drew in pencil the head of a still young woman, with a face already strongly defined by character, intelligence, and purpose. I drew her not smiling, not disapproving, not arrogant, not self-conscious, but simply *being*. I then painted the whole head in light and dark intensities of ultramarine blue, mostly transparent. I worked dark shadows round the eyes and under the chin until I had a fairly complete monochrome portrait in blue on light gray. She looked as I thought Dr. Lang might have looked forty years earlier.

Brooding over my blue woman, I ate a sandwich and in the afternoon overpainted the background with browns and crimsons, glazing and rubbing the colors together until I had a rich background that receded from the eye, leaving the face itself startlingly near and clear.

That night I slept on the floor in the sleeping bag, and early on Wednesday I began overpainting flesh tones onto the blue bones, giving her strength and brain. By afternoon she was the young woman I saw in my mind.

I phoned Jed at the estate office. "Any news of Andrew and the cup?" I asked.

"The poor little guy swore he didn't take it. Himself believes him. Anyway, the thing seems to have vanished."

"Listen. I'm going back to London tonight. Can you meet me at Dalwhinnie station with a bedsheet?"

"Er . . ."

"I've been painting a picture that I really do *not* want stolen. Could you bring a sheet to wrap it in? Will you keep it safe for me?"

"Yes, of course, but what about . . . anything else?"

"No one will find anything else."

After barely a pause he said, "How about nine thirty?"

"Perfect."

Reliable as always, Jed brought a sheet to the station and drove away with my picture, my new climbing gear and paints and winter clothes (in a duffel bag), and also my bagpipes, newly ransomed from old Donald. And with minimum luggage I yet again rocked down the rails and hugged my mother before breakfast.

The Park Crescent house felt as claustrophobic as it had the previous week. I found Ivan, in robe and slippers, still looking exhausted in his armchair. He greeted me weakly.

"That woman wants you to phone," he said, pointing at the tissue box. On it I found Margaret Morden's number and phoned her.

"How did it go yesterday?" I asked.

"Quite well. Except that Patsy and that brewery manager, Desmond Finch, very nearly wrecked the negotiations by crashing the meeting. And she had her husband with her—he's a menace. I shouldn't say it, but if the brewery survives, it will be in *spite* of Mrs. Benchmark. How soon can you get to my office?"

"An hour and a half."

"Right," she said. "I'll clear the decks."

I sat with Ivan while he told me not to bother him with details (such as, would his brewery survive), but he stuck to *essentials* (namely, the safekeeping of his best horse and his gold cup).

"Bede's *Death Song*," I said casually, and watched astounded as my stepfather's eyes filled with tears.

"Look after your mother," he said.

"You are *not* going to die."

"I think so." He wiped the tears away and said, "I am adding a codicil to my will. Don't let anyone stop me."

"By 'anyone,' do you mean Patsy?"

"Patsy." He nodded. "And Surtees and Oliver."

"Oliver Grantchester? Your lawyer?"

"I asked him to come tomorrow, so please, Alexander . . ."

"I'll be here," I promised. "But if I were you, I would simply write down, here and now, what you want, and then get Wilfred and Lois to witness you signing. Then the codicil would be done, and you wouldn't have to endure any arguments tomorrow."

He saw the attraction of the peaceful path.

"And don't leave *me* anything," I said. "If you do, the codicil will be declared void, as Patsy will say I influenced you."

He smiled weakly. "You're as bossy as Patsy."

I fetched paper and a pen, and from across the room watched him write a scant half page. Then I sought out Wilfred and Lois, and Ivan himself asked them to witness his signing the simple legal document.

The witnesses themselves signed, and Ivan thanked them courteously, giving their service little weight. With luck, I thought, Lois wouldn't report within five minutes to Patsy.

When Wilfred and Lois had gone, I gave Ivan an envelope for his codicil. When he'd stuck down its flap, he signed his name and the date twice across the join. He held out the envelope for me.

"Look after it," he said.

"If you promise I'm not in it."

"You're not."

"Okay, then." I took it. Horse, cup, codicil, what else?

I WENT to Margaret Morden's office. She wore a wide-belted, soft printed wool dress of dark reds and blues, accentuating the fairness of her fine and flyaway hair. The creditors, she reported, had worked out a rate of payment that they would accept. Their terms were stringent but possible if sales held up. The creditors had also included the King Alfred Gold Cup race's expenses.

"Great," I said. "You're brilliant."

She smiled. "The receivables are enough to more than cover the running costs this week. The paychecks will be issued and honored. Once you sign the agreements, Tobias Tollright will okay the audit and the brewery will stay in business."

I stood up blindly, and she came to stand beside me. I put my arms round her silently and hugged her, and finally found voice enough to thank her in a more businesslike fashion.

On her desk she spread out the agreement papers and showed

me where to put my name, bringing in her secretary to witness every signature. I asked if protocol would stretch to a pub lunch for three—Margaret, Tobias, and me.

Margaret thought it might. Tobe agreed. Accordingly we sat round a small table in a dark, discreet corner and toasted the brewery's survival with a bottle of good Bordeaux.

I said to Margaret, "You mentioned something to me about a twitch of unease. Is it for our auditor's ears?"

Margaret considered Tobias and nodded. "He might help."

"What twitch of unease?" he asked.

"I looked at the accounts for the past five years," Margaret said tentatively, "and I just got a teeniest whiff that Norman Quorn may have done a trial run."

Tobias blinked. "A what?"

"Suppose," Margaret said, "that you were Norman Quorn and you wanted to retire with a pension big enough to give you all the luxuries you'd never had. And you know how easy it is now to send money whizzing round the world impersonally by wire. Then you open small banking accounts here and there, and every so often you move onwards to another bank. No one pays much notice, because the money never goes missing and comes safely home."

"Only one day it doesn't," Tobias said. "I lost him in Panama."

I WENT to see Young and Uttley.

Neither man was in the office, nor was the skinhead. I found a secretary at a computer—a young woman with dark curly hair, black tights, short black skirt, loose blue sweater, scarlet lips and fingernails.

"Can I help you?" she said, and went on working.

"Well . . ." I looked at her carefully. "You can tell me why the heck you made sure Surtees Benchmark saw you following him."

The busy fingers stilled. The bright eyes looked at my face, and the voice said in exasperation, "How do you *know?*"

"Eye sockets. I draw people. I look at their bones. Your eye sockets slant down. Also, your wrists are male. You should wear cuffs. So why did you let Surtees see you?"

"Let him? I made sure he did. I got him real worried, got him busy looking out for a skinhead."

"And," I suggested, "he then doesn't notice a secretary?"

"You got it."

"What did the secretary see?"

"Yon bonnie Surtees has a wife who keeps him on a throttling leash, but Wednesday afternoons the mister bolts into Guildford to consult his business colleague. Seems Surtees runs a stud farm that's half owned by his wife and half by the colleague. Yesterday Surtees drives round looking for the skinhead, and when he thinks it's safe, he steers not to any business office but to a house on the outskirts."

I sighed.

"Don't you want to hear about it?"

"Yes, but I'd rather he'd visited four thugs in a gym."

"Sorry about that. Anyway, yesterday Mr. Young paid a visit to the house at Guildford, and there's a poor little cow there that lets Surtees pay her for sex."

"Damn."

"Do you want me to carry on?"

"Yes. Also, see what you can find out about a goldsmith working in London in 1850 or 1860 called Maxim."

After a short stare he said, "Anything else?"

"How do you rate as a bodyguard?"

"That's extra." Extras, he said, would fall due at the end.

WHEN Ivan read, one by one, the creditors' agreements, his over-all reaction was one of relieved gloom.

When my mother came into his room, though, he lifted his head to her and smiled. She smiled back with the deep, understanding friendship of a strong marriage.

"Our boy," Ivan said—I was usually *your* boy—"has signed the brewery into chains and penury." He picked up a thick batch of paper. "But this," he said, "is our annual audit. Tobias Tollright has signed it. It is our passport to continue trading."

One could actually see his resolution trickling back.

"Well done, Alexander," he said.

I had expected, since he had written his codicil the day before, that he would have told his lawyer not to come. But it seemed he had forgotten, and Oliver Grantchester, with his loud voice, bulky frame, and room-filling presence, arrived punctually at ten o'clock.

Ivan gave an embarrassed apology, to which Grantchester didn't listen. He looked me up and down and told Ivan that they didn't need my presence. I might have gone, but at that moment Patsy arrived like a ship in full sail, Surtees floundering in her wake.

"You are not making any codicil, Father, unless I'm sure Alexander"—Patsy spat the word—"doesn't in any way benefit."

"My dear," Ivan told her, "I'm not writing any codicil this morning. None at all. I'm sorry I forgot to tell Oliver, but I wrote my codicil yesterday. We can just have some coffee."

Ivan was naïve if he thought coffee would quell a tempest.

"It's perfectly simple," Grantchester boomed. "You can tear up yesterday's codicil and write another one."

Ivan looked at me as if for help. "But I don't need to write another one," he said. "Do I?"

I shook my head.

The bombardment of voices went on. Ivan, upset, nevertheless held to his position.

"At least let me check it from the legal point of view," Grantchester said.

"No," Ivan said, regretfully polite.

Patsy said forcefully, "Alexander is manipulating you, Father."

Hunted and harried, Ivan looked at me with troubled indecision as the shouting continued.

They all resented me—Patsy, Surtees, Grantchester. Yet I'd done my best for the brewery, for Ivan, for my mother.

I looked at them one by one, and I smiled grimly. "I'm sick of the brewery," I said. "Ivan, let Patsy loose on the creditors. I don't give a hoot about the fact that she'll ruin her inheritance. Why should I care? The brewery is yours; it's rescued, basically. I'm a painter and I'm going back to my own work, and a heartfelt good-bye to you all."

Ivan said miserably, "Alexander . . ."

"For you," I said plainly, "I've taken risks, and I've begged and bargained to save your name. Because you sent me the chalice"—and I glanced at Patsy and Surtees, who stared as if transfixed—"I got beaten beyond a joke. And I've had enough."

My mother said, barely audibly, "Oh, *please,* Alexander."

Grantchester said, "Ivan tells us he gave you his codicil for safekeeping. He now sees that this was a mistake. So hand it over."

Into the silence that followed I said, "Ivan?"

His eyes looked strained. I understood the impossibility he faced. His faith in me was a disloyalty to his daughter—a disloyalty I had no right to coerce, even if I could.

"I'll get it," I said, letting him off. "It's upstairs."

I fetched the sealed envelope and put it into Ivan's hands.

"I'll take it," Grantchester said authoritatively.

Ivan shook his head. "I'll keep it, Oliver," he said. "Then I can tear it up if I change my mind."

I smiled into Ivan's troubled eyes and said I would be upstairs. Shaking my head to my mother's pleading eyes, I left the room.

They went on shouting downstairs, but finally the angry voices came out of Ivan's study and left by the front door. When all was quiet, I went out of my room and onto the stairs. Ivan was on the landing below me, looking up. He gestured towards his study, so I went down and followed him into his room, and sat opposite him.

My mother, looking as frail as her husband, stood beside Ivan.

He said to me, "Did you mean it, that you've had enough?"

In answer I asked, "Did you cancel the powers of attorney?"

"No, he didn't," my mother said. "Ivan, tell him. *Beg* him to go on acting for you." To me she said, "Don't leave us."

So small a thing, it seemed, to stay and field a few insults.

"What did you mean about being beaten?" Ivan said. "Keith Robbiston said you were hurt."

I told them about the robbers.

"Oh, my God," he said. "I've done so much harm."

"Nothing that isn't being put right," I said. "Ivan, if you just leave things, the brewery should be out of debt in three years."

My stepfather nodded with resolution. And how long, I morosely considered, would that resolution last?

The telephone rang. Ivan's hand asked me to answer it.

It was the Leicestershire police, wanting to speak with Sir Ivan. I explained that Sir Ivan wasn't well, and offered my services as his son. Well, near enough.

After a pause a different voice identified himself as Detective Chief Inspector Reynolds and inquired whether Sir Ivan knew anyone named Norman Quorn.

"Yes, he does."

The voice impersonally explained: The police had for two weeks been trying to identify a body that they now had reason to believe was that of a Mr. Norman Quorn. The chief inspector wanted Sir Ivan to assist in making an identification.

I said, "Doesn't he have any relations?"

"Only his sister, sir, and she is . . . *distressed.* The body is partly decomposed. The sister gave us Sir Ivan's name."

I thought briefly. "I'll tell my father. Give me a number to phone you back." He told me a number, which I wrote out of habit on the tissue box. "Five minutes," I said.

As emotionlessly as possible I gave Ivan the news.

"Norman!" he said disbelievingly. *"Dead?"*

"They want to know for sure. They ask you to go."

"I'll go with you," my mother said to Ivan.

I phoned the chief inspector, told him I would be driving, and wrote his directions on the bottom of the tissue box.

In the end, four of us went to Leicestershire in Ivan's Rover— Ivan and my mother in the back, with Wilfred sitting in the front beside me, a box of heart attack remedies on his lap. Fairly early in the afternoon we arrived at the mortuary in Leicester.

Detective Chief Inspector Reynolds met us, shook hands, and was impressed into solicitude by Wilfred's medical precautions. In the waiting room, a large weeping woman was being comforted by a policewoman. Reynolds indicated that he would take Ivan to see the body, but Ivan clutched my arm and wouldn't go without me. So, shrugging, Reynolds settled for taking me, too.

We were all issued disposable gowns. Dead bodies, it seemed, could infect the living. Then we went down a passage into a brightly lit room that smelled of disinfectant. On a high center table, under a white cover, lay a long, quiet shape.

Ivan's hand shook on my arm, but civic duty won the day. He looked steadily at the white face, revealed when a mortuary attendant pulled back one end of the covering sheet, and he said without wavering, "Yes, that's Norman Quorn."

"Thank you, sir."

I said, "What did he die of?"

There was a pause. The policeman looked assessingly at Ivan and came to a decision. "I'll take you back to your wife, sir." He offered Ivan his arm, neatly leaving me behind alone.

The mortuary attendant identified himself as the pathologist who had carried out the postmortem.

"So, what did he die of?" I asked.

"We're not sure. There are no obvious causes of death. No evidence of murder. He had been dead about two weeks when he was discovered in a dump. He had been placed there after death."

I frowned. "Was he simply ill? Heart attack? Stroke?"

"Quite likely, though there is an abnormality. . . ." He hesitated. "We showed it to his sister, and she fainted."

"I'm not his sister."

"No." He stripped back the sheet, showing the body's dark discoloration of decomposition. I thought it no wonder the sister had fainted, and hoped I wouldn't copy her.

"Look at his back," the pathologist said, and gripped the shoulder and half rolled the body towards him. There were about a dozen rows of dark marks in the flesh, and flecks of white.

"Those white bits," he said, "are his ribs."

I felt nauseous and swallowed.

The pathologist said, "Those dark marks are burns."

"Burns?"

"Yes. The skin and flesh have been burned away in a few places down to the ribs. He must have fallen onto something very hot when he died. Something like a grating. Any thoughts?"

My chief thought was how soon I could leave the mortuary.

I said, "Could he have died from the burns?"

"I don't think so. I would guess he had a stroke, fell unconscious on the fire, and died."

"Oh." I left the pathologist with relief and, stripping off the protective clothing, rejoined the group in the waiting room.

"Please tell us," I said to the chief inspector, "where exactly you found Mr. Quorn."

Instead of directly answering, he explained that the still weeping woman was Mr. Quorn's sister. My mother had taken over the role of comforter, although, true to form, she looked as if she would prefer saying, "Pull yourself together," to "There, there."

"Mr. Quorn," Reynolds told us, "was found by council workers who went to clear away a rubbish dump on a farmer's land. We made lengthy inquiries but drew a total blank. There are absolutely no indications of foul play, and unless any other facts turn up . . ."

He left the sentence unfinished. Neither Ivan nor my mother told him that the brewery's funds had vanished with Quorn, nor did I. Ivan would have to decide.

After returning to London, we spent the evening in discussion. Ivan was inclined to be glad that Norman hadn't after all run off with the money. "We misjudged him," he said. "My dear old friend—"

"Your dear old friend," I corrected regretfully, "certainly did transfer the money out of the brewery. I've seen copies of about six huge withdrawals he made just before he left. He did indeed send all the funds to destinations still unknown."

Ivan sighed. "If we tell the police that Norman stole the funds, would it affect the creditors' arrangements?"

"Well, the creditors do know he stole the funds. But they believe he skipped the country. They believe the money is with him, and it isn't."

"So?"

"So where is it?"

A long silence.

By ten in the evening Ivan had decided, in his law-abiding Jockey Club persona, that I should ask Margaret Morden whether Norman Quorn's death made any difference to the creditors, and that I should tell Reynolds that the now identified corpse had probably been an embezzler about to leave the country.

The next morning, at nine o'clock, I phoned Reynolds.

"Tell me on the phone," he said when I suggested meeting.

"Better face to face."

"I'm off duty at noon."

"I'll get there. Where?"

"Go to the mortuary. It's on my way home."

I refrained from observing that the mortuary was on everyone's way home, and managed to trace Margaret Morden to hers.

"It's Saturday," she said tartly. "It had better be important."

"The King Alfred Brewery's finance director has turned up, still in England, but dead."

"That *is* Saturday news. How did he die?"

"Stroke or heart attack, the pathologist thinks."

She thought briefly. "Phone me in the office on Monday. And tell Tobias. But if what's bothering you is the status of the creditors' agreements, my impression is that they will stand."

I hung up with a smile and drove to Leicester.

The chief inspector's reaction was as expected. "Why didn't you tell me this yesterday?"

"The brewery has hushed up the theft."

"The body," Reynolds said reflectively, "was dressed in suit, shirt, tie, underpants, socks, and shoes—all unremarkable." He shrugged. "It's possible Mr. Quorn died out of doors, in a garden. There were blades of mown grass in his clothes. That would jell with him falling back onto a barbecue of some sort."

"Hardly the right clothes for a barbecue."

He looked at me. "I'll complete my case notes with what you've told me, sir. I appreciate your help."

ON MONDAY I WENT BY TRAIN again to Reading and did the rounds of the offices.

"Quorn's dead!" Tobias exclaimed. "Then where's the money?"

I said, "I thought you might be able to work it out."

He chewed a toothpick and gave me his best blank outer stare, concealing furious activity within.

"I followed him to Panama," he said thoughtfully, then turned to one of his three computers. "Here we are. Wire transfer from the brewery to a bank in Guernsey—six transfers in one day to the same account. The Guernsey bank already had instructions to transfer the whole amount—multiple millions—to a bank in New York, which already held instructions to wire the money to a bank in Panama, and that bank cannot say where the money went from there."

"Can't or won't?" I asked.

"Quite likely both. These banks have unbreakable privacy laws. We only know the path to the Global Credit in Panama because Quorn had the ABA numbers on a paper and neglected to shred it."

"Remind me about ABA numbers."

"They identify all banks in the United States and the Caribbean. They're part of the Fedwire system," Tobias said. "There are three huge worldwide organizations dealing with the international transfer of funds. Fedwire—ABA included—is the Federal Reserve Bank's institution. They have nine-digit routing numbers, so any transfer with a nine-digit code is likely to have been seen to by Fedwire."

I sighed.

Tobias went on. "All the systems have identifying codes. The codes tell you the bank but not the account number, and it's against their law to pass that information on."

"Not to the police? Or the tax people?"

"Especially not to the police or tax people. They'd be out of business if they did that." Tobe smiled. "You're an infant, Al."

I acknowledged it. "But," I said, "what if the money just sits in Panama forever, now Norman Quorn is dead?"

"It may. Trillions in unclaimed accounts sit in banks all over the world, and you can bet the banks are in no hurry to look for heirs."

I left him pulverizing his toothpick and presented myself on Margaret's doorstep. I told her what I knew of Norman Quorn's exit.

"Poor man," she said.

"I wanted to ask you," I said, "about that possible trial run. Do you remember any of the trial's destinations?"

She frowned. Then, as Tobias had done, she consulted one of her row of computer faces and tapped in instructions.

"It's possible," she said finally, "that Quorn sent a small sum to a bank in the Bahamas, who forwarded it to a bank in Bermuda, who sent it back to Wantage. Half the information, like the actual account numbers, is missing. If the brewery's money is in either of those banks, which is doubtful, you won't find it."

"Thanks a bunch."

"Cheer up," she said. "First thing this morning I consulted your committee of creditors. The agreements they signed with you will remain unaltered by Norman Quorn's death."

CHAPTER 6

 WALKED to the office of Young and Uttley. The occupant that day wasn't a skinhead or a secretary, but a straightforward young man dressed as I was, in jeans, shirt, and sweater.

I smiled at him slowly. "Hello," I said. "What's your name?"

"Chris Young," he said. "I've done a bit of let-your-fingers-do-the-walking for you."

His accent was unchanged. The skinhead, the secretary, and Chris Young all spoke with the same voice.

"And?" I asked.

"There was a goldsmith by the name of Maxim working in London in the 1800s. Good name. Ritzy. Made fancy gold ornaments."

"Tobe promised me you were good," I said.

"Just good?"

"Brilliant. A genius, actually."

He grinned immodestly. "Tobe told me you were a walking brain and not to be put off by your good manners."

"I'll kill him."

"Tobe told me you were raised in a castle."

"It was cold."

"Yeah. I drew an orphanage. Warm."

We got on fine. I made a drawing of King Alfred's golden chalice, and he phoned back to his goldsmith informant with a detailed description. "Yeah, yeah, that's what I said, Anglo-Saxon verse. See what you can do." He put down the receiver.

"There's another thing," he said to me. "Your pal Surtees never goes near a boxing gym. He's as unfit as a leaking balloon."

"Suppose he uses a different name?"

Chris Young sighed. "He's not the gym type, I'm telling you."

Chris's telephone rang, and he answered. He listened and said "Thank you," wrote a few words on a notepad, and disconnected.

"Your chalice," he said, "was inscribed with something called Bede's *Death Song*. It was made in 1867, and it cost an arm and a leg because it was inlaid with emeralds, sapphires, and rubies."

"Real ones?" I exclaimed, surprised.

Chris consulted his notes. "Cabochon gems, imperfect." He looked up. "What does cabochon mean?"

"It means polished but uncut. No facets. Rounded, like pebbles." I paused. "They don't look real. They're big."

"You mean, you've actually seen this thing?"

"It's what I got bashed for. And you, I hope, are going to prevent anyone else from trying to bash that information out of me."

"Oh." He blinked. "Black eyes will cost you extra," he said.

We agreed that identifying my robbers took priority.

Ah, well.

RETURNING BY TRAIN TO PARK Crescent, I was met by my mother, who told me calmly that I should telephone Emily immediately.

"Golden Malt got loose."

Damnation, I thought, and phoned her.

"Golden Malt got loose on the Downs at Foxhill," she said. "He's not an easy ride, and he bucked off the exercise groom. He's found his way back *here*—don't ask me how. The thing is, Surtees called. He says the horse is Patsy's and he's coming to collect him."

I took a steadying breath. "The horse is Ivan's."

"Surtees says you've stolen the King Alfred cup and you'll steal Golden Malt. He's bringing a trailer to collect Golden Malt and take him to his stud farm for safekeeping."

I tried to organize scattered thoughts. "How did Surtees know you have the horse back?" I asked.

"I don't know. But all my lads know, too."

"I'll come as soon as I can. Don't let Surtees take Golden Malt."

She said despairingly, "But how do I stop him?"

"Let down his tires. Build a Great Wall. Anything."

I ran for a train and was lucky, catching a metro without waiting. At Didcot junction, a taxi driver hurried me to Lambourn. I had taken with me all my mother's cash, my own credit card and checks, and also a zipped bag containing Emily's helmet, padded jacket, and boots that my mother hadn't yet returned to her.

Helter-skelter though I went, Surtees had arrived first, with a horse trailer. He and Emily were out in the stable yard, Emily holding the horse by his bridle and arguing with Surtees. Her Land Rover stood in the driveway behind Surtees's trailer, effectively blocking his way out.

With reluctance I walked into the angry scene. Emily looked relieved to see me, Surtees furious.

"Good afternoon, Surtees," I said. "Having trouble?"

Surtees said with unthrottled rage, "Tell your wife to get out of my way. That horse is Patsy's, and I'm taking it."

I said, "It's Ivan's, and I'm looking after it. The horse is officially in training here. It can't race from your farm. You know the rules."

"The hell with the rules!"

Surtees, deciding that argument would get him nowhere, made a sudden American-football charge at me while my head was turned and, with his shoulder cannonballing into my stomach, knocked me over. He fell on top of me. I rolled over with him, scrambling for a weight advantage, trying to disconnect myself and stand up.

The whole situation was idiotic. Neither of us landed a decisive punch as Surtees clutched my hair and tried to bang my head on the ground.

I finally scrambled to my feet, dragging him with me. He tried a sweeping wide-armed clout to my head, which gave me a chance to both duck the blow and get hold of his clothes and fling him away from me, so that he overbalanced and, falling backwards, cracked his head against a stable wall.

It stunned him, and he slid to his knees.

I opened both halves of a vacant stall and, grabbing the groggy Surtees, half ran him, half flung him inside, closing both halves of the door and slapping home the bolts. Out of breath I went over to Emily, whose expression was a mixture of outrage and laughter.

"Now what?" she said.

"Now I bolt you into Golden Malt's stall so that none of this is your fault, and decamp with the horse."

She stared. "I did think you might ride this fellow away again," she said. "The saddle is over there, in his stall."

I found the saddle, which I carried back and fixed in place. There was a full net of hay in the stall also, and a head collar, which I carried out and threaded together with the zipped bag I'd brought, taking out the helmet but slinging the rest over the withers of the horse. Then I took the reins from Emily and walked with her to an empty stall. She went inside, and I bolted the lower half of the door.

"You'd better hurry," she said. "The grooms will arrive soon."

I kissed her over the stable door.

"Where will you go?"

"Who knows."

I kissed her again and finished bolting her into her temporary prison. Then I hauled myself onto Golden Malt and set off onto the Downs.

Golden Malt, to my relief, showed no reluctance to go along the familiar stretch of road. Even at four in the afternoon there were other horses around in the distance. Golden Malt whinnied loudly and received an echoing response from afar.

The problem was that I didn't know where to go. Surtees would send the police after me, so staying out of sight was the thing.

Golden Malt trotted happily the length of Mandown, his regular exercise ground. When I stopped at the far end and didn't turn back, he grew restive. Unwelcome though the thought had been, I'd accepted that we might have to stay out all night.

Shelter. The weather was fine, though chilly. It wasn't too cold for Golden Malt's survival, but four walls and water were essential. I needed the sort of shelter farmers built a distance from their home yards, providing walls and roofs against hail and gales, and troughs for their stock to drink from. There were two hours left until dark. It took me nearly that long to find a place Golden Malt would enter.

The first two such shelters I came to were both filthy inside, thick with droppings. More important, Golden Malt wouldn't drink the water, even though I cleaned out the troughs before refilling them from their taps. He turned his fastidious head away.

The third shelter I came to looked just as unappetizing, but Golden Malt walked into it amiably and then came out and drank from the trough. Much relieved, I waited until he'd drunk his fill and then walked back in with him. Exchanging the head collar for the bridle, I fastened the horse into his new quarters and positioned the hay net where he could eat when he wanted. I unsaddled him and finally took stock of my own situation.

By good luck, there was no strong wind that evening, although the temperature dropped with darkness. I unzipped the holdall and thankfully put on the padded jacket. Then I folded the holdall to make a cushion, propped the saddle against the wall, and reckoned I'd spent far worse hours in Scottish mountains.

After dark the clear sky blazed with depths of stars. I put my hands into the jacket pockets for warmth and slept sitting up. Soon after two o'clock (according to the luminous hands on the cheap watch I'd bought to replace my father's stolen gold one), I awoke from cold, and I walked around quietly to warm myself.

I drifted and dozed and woke again in the first gray promise of light. Golden Malt was pawing the ground, giving me the news that he had finished his hay. I took him outside for a drink. Deciding that grass would do for breakfast, he walked around, munching, while I thought of coffee and toast. Then I saddled him and, when the morning's first exercise strings would be peopling the landscape, heaved myself onto his back and set about completing the disappearing trick.

Not far ahead, I came to a road and walked the horse across. That done, I was free on the wide lands south of Wantage, seven miles away from Lambourn, to find a suitable string of horses to follow.

I was looking for a small string of no more than four or five, as I reckoned I would get a more hospitable reception from a small-scale trainer—and so it proved. Just when I thought I'd drawn a blank, I came across four horses plodding homewards, one of them being led by a groom on foot. I followed at a distance.

My leaders headed towards the heart of a village. On the far side the horses turned in between the peeling gates of a small stable yard. A motor horse van stood in the yard, with a trainer's name and phone number painted on it. I retraced Golden Malt's steps to a phone box we had passed in the village and called the trainer.

I was, I explained, an owner who was also an amateur jockey, and I needed to park my horse for a while. Could he help?

"Glad to," he said heartily, "and call me Phil."

He showed no less enthusiasm when I arrived on a good-looking thoroughbred, offering generous cash for its board and lodging. I would come to fetch my horse later that day, I told Phil, and at my request he phoned for a taxi for me.

Back in London, I met Ivan's and my mother's anxiety with perhaps more reassurance than I truly felt. Golden Malt, I said, was secure, but it might be better to move him right away. I asked Ivan to lend me his copy of *Horses in Training,* which gave the details of every licensed trainer in Britain, and I asked my mother to phone Emily and get her to go out shopping in Swindon and to phone us back from a public phone.

"But why?" my mother asked, puzzled.

"Emily's walls have ears, and Surtees is listening. And," I added, "please don't tell Emily I'm here."

My obliging parent looked disbelieving but talked to Emily, and forty-five minutes later Emily was calling from Swindon. I took down the number and jogged to the nearest outside line, and she wanted to know if all this cloak-and-dagger stuff was necessary.

"Just in case," I said. "What happened when I left?"

Emily almost laughed. "The grooms came for evening stables and let us out. Surtees was purple with fury and phoned the police, saying that you'd stolen Golden Malt. Fortunately, the police believed me when I said you had absolute authority to look after the horse, and I showed them the copy you gave me of the power of attorney. Surtees went practically berserk. I begged the police to stay until he had gone. They finally got him to drive his trailer away."

"He's a fool."

"He's pure poison. So take care, Al. You made him look stupid, and he'll never forgive you."

"Yes," I said. "I want to talk to you, though, about Golden Malt. He's safe, but it will be better if I move him again."

"Look up Jimmy Jenkins," Emily said. "He and I are good friends. I'll call and see what he says."

"Would the horse be able to race from there in your name?"

"Jimmy's a licensed trainer; no problem there. And I could inform the Jockey Club in advance. I can't see any difficulty. Give me ten minutes, and I'll phone you back."

I waited by the phone until Emily at last rang.

"It's all fixed," she said. "Jimmy's a hundred percent trustable, so I told him the whole situation. The horse will be cared for and exercised by Jimmy's sixteen-year-old daughter, who's already an amateur jockey and knows when to keep quiet."

Emily gave me directions to the village. Jimmy had said to look for a square white house with bronze flaming-torch gateposts.

"Okay."

"And I told Jimmy *not* to phone me. Do you really think my phone is bugged?"

"Don't take the risk."

I returned to Ivan's house, and to my mother's and stepfather's bemusement I told them in detail about the shenanigans in Emily's yard and my travels with Golden Malt.

I said, "Emily has arranged for a trainer friend to keep your horse fit so he can run in the King Alfred Gold Cup. If you agree with what we've planned, I'll transfer Golden Malt this afternoon. It would be only by bad luck that Surtees would discover where he is."

Ivan said slowly, "You've gone to a lot of trouble."

"Well, the horse is yours. You asked me to look after your affairs, so . . . er . . . I try."

"For your mother's sake." A statement, not a question.

"Yes, but for yours also." He looked at his hands and I couldn't read his thoughts, but I asked if I could borrow his car and he agreed.

Via the classified ads in *Horse and Hound* magazine and an up-to-date road map and the telephone, I arranged to meet a horse van in Phil's yard and there loaded Golden Malt for the last leg of his journey. The van driver followed Ivan's car as arranged, and I led him southeast until we arrived in a village that looked as if it had never seen a racehorse. But there, in the main street, stood a square white house with bronze flaming torches on the gateposts.

I went to ring the front doorbell, as instructed. A thin, middle-aged man opened the door. His handshake was strong. A pace behind him stood a short, fine-boned girl, whom he introduced as his daughter, saying she would drive through the village in the horse van and settle Golden Malt into his new home. He watched approvingly as she climbed into the high cab beside the driver for the journey, then reassured me of the horse's safe transit.

I drove back to London, having briefly checked on Golden Malt in his isolated splendor, Jimmy Jenkins's daughter tending him with years of experience showing. The hiding of Ivan's horse was, barring accidents, complete.

I returned to the house to learn that Patsy had spent the afternoon with Ivan, complaining that I had attacked Surtees and had brazenly stolen Golden Malt for my own illegal ends, such as holding him for ransom.

"Is my horse safe?" Ivan said judiciously.

"Yes."

"And a ransom?"

I said tiredly, "Don't be silly."

He actually laughed. "Patsy's my daughter and I love her, but I think she's wrong. I said once that I wished you were my son. I still do."

My mother embraced him with uncharacteristic delight, and he stroked her arm happily, content to have pleased her.

There was time for the three of us to eat dinner before I left for the night train. We drank wine in friendship, Ivan and I, and I did believe that Patsy could not henceforth sow doubts of me in his decent mind.

He insisted on returning to my care the unopened envelope containing the codicil to his will. "It will be safest with you, Alexander," he said. "And I've decided to tell you what's in it."

"You don't have to."

"I need to," he said, and told me.

I smiled and hugged him for the first time ever.

I hugged my mother, and went to Scotland.

To my surprise Jed was waiting at Dalwhinnie in the dawn. Himself had phoned my mother and learned that I was on the train, and he wanted me to go directly to the castle.

On the way Jed told me that I now had a new bed and armchair in the bothy, paid for by Himself, and my uncle would foot the bill unconditionally for any other things I needed.

"But he doesn't have to," I protested.

"If you ask me, he feels guilty. Let him atone."

As before, I found Himself in his dining room eating toast. He raised his big head at my entrance. "Alexander."

"My lord."

"Breakfast?" He waved a hand. There were three places laid, one used. James, I learned, had already gone out on the moors.

"He wants a round of golf," Himself said. "How about this afternoon? I've asked Jed to fix you up with wheels, and also with a portable telephone and extra batteries. It may not be to your liking for solitude, but please humor me in this." He looked at me and smiled. "You would no doubt die for me as your clan chief. You can suffer a portable telephone."

"Put like that . . ."

"You can go back to your damned paints tomorrow."

Resignedly I ate toast.

He wanted to know what I'd been doing in the south, prodding me for details. I told him about the codicil, about Patsy's chatty involvement with Oliver Grantchester, about the discovery of Norman Quorn's body, and about my fracas with Surtees.

"Several things emerge from all that," he said. "Surtees is a dangerous fool, and where is the brewery's money? And that woman," he said, meaning Patsy, "is a menace."

The two of us made a circuit outside the whole castle, as he liked to do, only to find on our return, outside the entrance, a small white car. It drew from him frowns and disgust.

"That bloody Lang woman! Why did I ever ask her here?"

Himself might rue the day, but I was fascinated to see her again. She and her eighty-year-old wrinkles climbed out of the car and stood stalwartly in our path.

"She has joined the conservationists who look after the castle," Himself said. "And you can guess what she's chiefly after."

"The hilt," I said.

"The hilt." He raised his voice as we approached the white car. "Good morning, Dr. Lang."

"Lord Kinloch." She shook his hand, then looked me briefly up and down, unsure of my name.

"My nephew," Himself said.

"Oh yes." She extended her hand and shook mine perfunctorily. "Lord Kinloch, I've come to discuss the Treasury of Scotland exhibition planned for the Edinburgh Festival next year."

Himself, with faultless courtesy, showed her into the grand drawing room and offered sherry. Dr. Lang accepted.

"Al?" he inquired.

"Not right now."

Himself took a polite tokenful.

"We must insist," Dr. Lang began crisply, "on taking charge of the Kinloch hilt. You can't hide it away forever."

Himself said, "Thieves grow more ingenious every year."

"You know my views," she told him crossly. "The hilt belongs to Scotland."

I could see that for each of them it was all hardening into a relentless battle of wills, a mortal duel fought over dry sherry in cut lead crystal.

I said to Zoë Lang, "Do you mind if I draw you?"

"*Draw* me?"

"Just a pencil sketch."

She looked astonished. "Whatever for?"

"He's an artist," Himself explained casually. "Al, if you want any paper, there's some in my room, in the desk drawers."

Gratefully I went to fetch some high-grade typing paper and a reasonable pencil, and returned to the drawing room.

She said, "Where do you want me to sit?"

I was grateful. "By the window, if you would."

I got her to sit where the light fell on her face at the same angle as I'd painted her, and I drew the face as it appeared now to my eyes, with folds and lines. It was accurate, and she didn't like it.

"You're cruel," she said.

I shook my head. "It's time that's cruel."

She sparred a little more with my uncle, then asked if King Alfred's chalice had turned up, as her friend was still waiting to put a value on its "glass ornaments."

"Not yet," Himself said unworriedly. "One of my family will no doubt have it safe."

She couldn't understand his carefree attitude, and it wasn't until after she had left that I told him the glass ornaments, if they were the original gems, were in fact genuine sapphires, emeralds, and rubies. "The cup," I said, "is almost certainly worth far more intrinsically than the hilt."

"You don't mean it! How do you know?"

"I had it traced to the firm that made it. It cost a fortune."

"Good grief. And young Andrew was playing with it on the kitchen floor! Does Ivan know where it is?"

"Not exactly," I said, and told him where to look.

"You're a rogue, Alexander."

JAMES beat me at golf.

"What did you say to Himself?" he asked. "Nothing but catching a twenty-pound salmon puts him in such a high mood."

"He's good to me."

"The sun shines out of you."

The difference between James and Patsy was that my cousin felt secure enough to make a joke of his father's occasional glance in my direction. James would inherit his father's title and estate. He had none of Patsy's devilish doubts sitting bleakly on his sunny shoulders.

As always, we went amicably round eighteen holes, laughing, helplessly incompetent, cousins in the simplest sense, family attitudes and loyalties taken for granted.

We pulled our golf bags along behind us on carts. If I was careful replacing my clubs each time, sliding them gently into the bag instead of ramming them home, it was because the handles rested not on the base of the bag, but in the bowl of the gray, cloth-wrapped shape within it—the jeweled gold treasure fashioned by Maxim in 1867.

I had bought a golf bag that could be taken apart at the bottom—for cleaning—and I had undone the necessary screws to take the bag apart and had lodged the cup inside. It fit there snugly.

We finished our round lightheartedly, and in the clubhouse, I wiped clean my woods and irons and stowed them upright in the bag in my locker, sentinels guarding the King Alfred gold cup. With amusement I returned with James to the castle.

BY MIDMORNING the next day my life in the bothy had taken shape again, and in greater comfort than before when it came to mattress and armchair. A rental truck stood outside my front door, the portable phone (with spare batteries) was working, and Zoë Lang's portrait stood unwrapped on the easel.

With a thankful feeling of coming home, I set out the paints I needed, feeling their texture on knife and brush, darkening the background, adding the shadows I had imagined in my travels, putting a glow on the skin and in the eyes. The woman lived on the canvas, as vital as I knew how to make her.

At five o'clock, when the quality of the light subtly changed, I washed the brushes and closed away the colors in their pots and tubes. Then I lit my lamp and cooked paella in contentment.

Early the next day I sat in front of the easel watching the slow change of light on that face, the growth of emerging personality taking place before me. When daylight was fully established, I tried to tap into that courage I was supposed to have. It was one thing to imagine, another to *do*.

While in London I had ransacked my mother's kitchen for a meat thermometer. This unlikely tool had a spike whose tip was sharp and abrasive. The spike was for sticking into joints of meat. The round dial from which it protruded measured the inner heat and the state of cooking—rare, medium, well done. It was scratchy and rigid. The dial gave it good grip. It was pretty well perfect.

So I had the tool. I had the light. I had the vision.

I held the pencil drawing beside the painting and started with the neck, seeing the outer shell of age as larger than the face within. I swept the sharp point across my careful painting, drawing the old Zoë in gray scratches, as if the flesh colors weren't anything but background. I was cravenly aware that a mistake couldn't be put right. It was a cold day, and I sweated.

By five o'clock the shape of Zoë Lang's old face was clearly established over the inner spirit. I stretched my cramped fingers, took the portable phone, and went for a walk outside.

Sitting on a granite boulder, looking down the valley, I phoned my mother. Ivan, she assured me, was at last shedding his depression. He had dressed. He was talking of not needing Wilfred any longer. She herself felt more settled and less anxious.

"Great," I said, and told her I would call her again on Sunday, the day after tomorrow.

"Take care of yourself, Alexander."

"You, too," I said.

The next day, with rigidly governed finger muscles, I worked on the painting until my arms and neck ached with tension. By late afternoon I had gone to the limit of what I could understand and show, and whatever the picture might be judged to lack, it was because the lack was in *me*. But that unchanging spirit of Zoë Lang looked out, present and past identical.

I COULDN'T sleep. Restlessly I got up at about four in the morning and, locking my door behind me, took my bagpipes up into the mountains, seeing my way by starlight, humbled by the distance of those flaming unvisited worlds.

I took up the pipes in the dawn and blew the bag full of air.

I never counted time up there on the granite heights. The gray dawn turned to a blue, sparkling day, and I reckoned I would go down to the bothy only when the lack of breakfast gave me a shove. Meanwhile, I played the pipes, filled with joy.

Too good to last, I supposed.

I was aware first of a buzzing noise that increasingly interfered with the drone of the pipes, and then a helicopter rose fast over the ridge of the mountain and flew overhead. I stopped playing. The helicopter swooped and clattered and dropped purposefully towards the bothy, finally settling onto the ground to one side of my parked truck.

The noise of the engine faded, and the rotor stopped. I watched motionless, in apprehension. If the four robbers had come, they wouldn't catch me up in the mountains, but they could again break into my house. They could destroy my painting.

The side door of the helicopter opened, and one man jumped out. A small figure, far below.

One. Not four.

He looked around him, then tried the door of the bothy. Something about the set of his shoulders brought recognition and floods of relief. Jed, I thought. It's Jed.

I played random notes on the chanter. In the clear, silent air Jed heard. He whirled and looked up and spotted me. He made huge circular movements with an arm, beckoning me down.

Not good news, I thought. Helicopters were extreme.

I went down to join him.

"Where have you been?" he demanded as soon as I was within earshot. "We've been trying to phone you for hours."

"What's happened?"

"It's Sir Ivan. . . . He's had another heart attack. He's dead."

I stood motionless. "No! He can't be dead. He was better."

"I'm sorry."

I hadn't thought I would care so much, but I found I cared very much indeed. "When?" I said. As if it mattered.

"Late yesterday. Your mother phoned Himself before six this morning. She said she'd been phoning you from five onwards."

I said blankly, "I'd better phone her at once."

"Himself said that Sir Ivan's daughter is now rerouting all calls, and she wouldn't let him get back to your mother. He says she has taken complete charge and is unreasonable. So he told me to find you by helicopter and fly you direct to Edinburgh to catch the first flight south."

We went into the bothy. Jed agreed to take the painting again, wrapped in its sheet, and also my pipes. I collected a few things into the duffel bag, and we locked the bothy door.

"Jed," I said awkwardly, aware of how much I owed him.

"Get going." He waved me away into the helicopter.

CHAPTER 7

Y MOTHER wept.

I held her tight while she shook with near-silent sobs, the grief deep and terrible. From lifelong habit, though, after the first revealing half hour, she stiffened her whole body, powdered her face, and presented, at least to the world, the outward semblance of serenity.

She told me that at bedtime the previous evening, she'd heard Ivan cry out, and she'd found him lying on the stairs in pain. He had been in his nightclothes. She didn't know why he had been downstairs. He seemed out of breath, as if he'd been *hurrying,* but why should he have been hurrying? It was after ten o'clock.

She said, "I loved him."

I squeezed my mother's hand. "I know."

She had been very frightened. They had given Wilfred the night off because Ivan had been so much better. She had put a tiny nitroglycerin tablet under Ivan's tongue, then miraculously reached Dr. Keith Robbiston at home. He would send an ambulance.

She had put a second pill under Ivan's tongue, but it hadn't stopped the pain. She had sat on the stairs, holding him.

The ambulancemen had been very quick, giving him an injection and oxygen, then carrying him to the London clinic. Dr. Robbiston had arrived and had driven my mother to the clinic.

A long, long pause.

"I wasn't with him when he died," she said.

I squeezed her hand again.

"What am I going to do?"

It was the unanswerable cry of all the bereaved.

The next day, Monday, Patsy swept in. She wasn't pleased to see me but seemed to realize my presence was inevitable.

She was brisk, decisive, the manager. Her grief for her father was chiefly expressed by a white tissue clutched valiantly, ready for stemming tears.

"Darling Father," she announced, "will be cremated"—she applied the tissue gently to her nose—"on Thursday at Cockfosters crematorium, at ten o'clock. I hope, Vivienne, that you don't mind the early hour? And of course, I've asked everyone to come here afterwards, and I've booked a caterer for drinks and a buffet lunch."

She went on talking about the arrangements, and my mother, who seemed mesmerized, simply said, "Thank you, Patsy."

My mother looked exhausted when Patsy left.

"She loved him," she said weakly, as if defending her.

We struggled through the next few days somehow. I cooked for my mother, shopped for her. We went one afternoon to see Ivan at the funeral home. He looked pale and peaceful.

For Thursday morning I engaged a car with a chauffeur to take the two of us to the crematorium and back again.

"All the brewery people are here," my mother murmured. They had come to Cockfosters in a chartered bus, we found, and were working extra hours to make up the time.

The racing people had come. Many bigwigs and owners. Several grooms from her stable accompanied Emily. Himself came with his countess, and James came with his pretty wife.

Patsy, with husband and children, received everyone graciously. My mother looked ethereal and shed no tears.

Chris Young showed up at my shoulder, dressed as the secretary, to guard my back against Surtees.

The grand drawing room at Park Crescent was packed afterwards with mourners. Tobias came, and Margaret Morden. I asked them both to linger for a while to discuss the brewery, and I was reminded triumphantly by Desmond Finch that all my powers of attorney had been canceled by Ivan's death.

Oliver Grantchester made his large presence felt, behaving rather as if Ivan had been his own personal achievement. "Of course Ivan regularly took my advice," I heard him saying.

I had invited Lois and Edna to join the gathering, but they stayed obstinately belowstairs. Wilfred spoke a few words to Patsy and descended to join them.

Emily eyed Chris with obvious speculation, wondering if the tall, leggy, dark-haired presence in black tights and short skirt was a serious girlfriend, in view of the glue that kept him ever and only a short pace away from my side.

Chris wore white, frilled shirt cuffs over his thick wrists, and a discreet white frill round his neck. He carried a small black purse. Tobias attempted to chat him up. They could hardly speak for laughing. "This is a *funeral,* for heaven's sake," I told them.

I wandered round the room, thanking people for coming, carrying a glass of champagne that I didn't drink. There was a woman standing apart in a corner, looking a little lost, so I drifted over.

"You have no champagne," I said. "Take mine. I haven't drunk any. I'll get some more."

"Oh, I couldn't." She took the glass, though, and sipped.

"I'm Lady Westering's son," I said.

"Yes, I know. I've seen you coming and going." Seeing my surprise, she added, "I'm Connie Hall, the caretaker next door. I've just popped in to pay my respects to Sir Ivan. Lady Westering invited me. Always so kind to me, both of them."

"Yes."

"Did Sir Ivan find what he was looking for?"

"Er . . ." I said. "What was he looking for?"

"Ever so distressed he was, the night he died."

She sensed in me the sudden acute sharpening of attention and began to look nervous.

"Mrs. Hall, please do tell me about the night he died."

"I was walking my little dog, you see, and when I got home, there was Sir Ivan in the road, and in his pajamas and robe, poor man, and frantic. *Frantic.*"

"Mrs. Hall," I said intensely, "what was he frantic *about?*"

"It was ever so unlike him, you see. I mean, scrabbling about in the plastic trash bags, tearing them open and looking inside. He was ever so *upset* and . . ." She stopped, herself distressed, and emptied her glass. I pivoted one hundred and eighty degrees, aware of Chris close behind me, and fielded his full glass of bubbles.

"Hey!" he objected.

"Get some more."

I turned back to Connie Hall and exchanged glasses.

"You'll get me tiddly," she said.

"What was Sir Ivan looking for?" I asked. "Did he tell you?" I waited, smiling vaguely, while she sipped.

"He said he was looking for an empty box." She frowned. "I asked what empty box, and he said Lois must have thrown it away. I *think* he said it was a tissue box."

Dear Lord, I thought. What had been written on it?

I said, "Have you told my mother about this?"

"No." She shook her head. "I didn't want to upset her."

"Well, thank you for telling me, Mrs. Hall."

I collected a plate of goodies for her and found her another Park Crescent neighbor to talk to, but later on I saw her talking to Patsy, and suspected she was telling her the same story. I felt a deep thrust of unease but wasn't quite sure why.

Surtees stood beside Patsy, listening, and when he saw me looking at him, he gave me a stare of such high-voltage malevolence that Chris said "Jeez" into my ear.

Himself also saw and, startled, asked, "Whatever did you do to deserve *that?*"

"Shut him into a stall in Emily's stable."

"A bad move."

The room gradually cleared until only those close to Ivan were left. There was to be no formal reading of his will, as its general provisions were well known—the brewery to Patsy, everything else to my mother for her lifetime, reverting to Patsy on her death. Oliver Grantchester, true to his loud-voiced, authoritative manner, took it as his natural province to orchestrate the semi–business meeting and cleared his throat noisily.

We all sat down: my mother, with me on one side and Emily on the other; Patsy and Surtees (scowling); Margaret Morden and Tobe; Himself (having sent his countess off with James and his wife); Desmond Finch (smirking); and, finally, Chris, beside me.

Chris crossed his legs, showing a stretch of thigh. Oliver stared at him with displeasure. Tobe put his face in his hands. His body shook.

Oliver said, "We all know that the powers of attorney that Ivan gave to Alexander expired with his death. Alexander has no authority now to conduct business for Ivan's estate."

I said mildly, "There's the codicil—"

Oliver interrupted. "Ivan may have written a codicil, but it can't be found. We can assume he tore it up."

"He didn't tear it up," I said. "Ivan gave it back to me again later, and I have brought it here today."

Both Patsy and Grantchester looked furiously disconcerted.

"Give it to me, then, and I'll read it out," Oliver said.

I hesitated. "I think," I said politely, "that I'll give it to Tobias to read out. If you don't mind, Tobe?"

He had, with difficulty, stopped laughing and said he would be of any service he could. I put a hand out towards Chris, who opened his black leather purse and took out the sealed envelope. Also in the purse were a scented handkerchief and a set of brass knuckles. It wasn't only Tobe who had trouble with giggles.

I took the envelope and crossed to Tobias. Soberly he examined it, reported on its secure state, and ripped it open.

He read the introduction. Then, "I bequeath my racehorses to Emily Jane Kinloch, known as Emily Jane Cox.

"I bequeath the chalice known as the King Alfred gold cup to my friend Robert, Earl of Kinloch."

Emily gasped, wide-eyed. Himself looked stricken dumb.

Tobias continued. "I appoint Alexander Kinloch, my stepson, my executor, in conjunction with my two executors already appointed— namely, Oliver Grantchester and Robert, Earl of Kinloch."

Patsy stood up, stiffly angry, and demanded, "What does that mean, appointing Alexander as executor?"

"It means," Himself told her neutrally, "that Alexander has a duty to help bring your father's estate to probate."

"Are you telling me he still has a say in the brewery's affairs?"

"Yes. Until your father's estate is wound up, he does."

Patsy stared. "He had no *right*. . . ."

"He had every right," Himself said. "Alexander will work with Mr. Grantchester and me to do the best we can for a good resolution to your father's affairs. Why do you not acknowledge that the continued existence of the brewery is thanks to Alexander?"

"Don't," I said, trying to stop him.

"You never stand up for yourself, Al." He shook his head at me.

Grantchester moved smoothly back to his intended agenda, accepting the codicil's provisions as fact. "The horse Golden Malt . . ." he began. "No one seems to know where the horse is."

Surtees stood up convulsively and pointed at me. "*He* knows where it is." He was shouting. "Make him tell you."

Himself said, "After probate the horse will belong to Emily. Until then, it can run in races by order of the executors."

Surtees obstinately shouted, "It belongs to the brewery. Alexander stole it. I'll see he goes to jail."

Even the lawyer began to lose patience with him. Grantchester said, "The executors can still authorize the horse to race if Mrs. Cox can comply with all racing regulations."

Well, bravo, I thought.

Surtees seethed.

Emily said sweetly that she was sure she could abide by all the regulations.

"Now," Grantchester said, "the chalice. Where is it?"

No one answered.

My mother said eventually, "Ivan never sent the real chalice to the races. A replica is given to the winning owner each year."

Desmond Finch made throat-clearing noises and reported that two replicas remained in Sir Ivan's office.

"The trophy's settled, then," Himself said cheerfully.

But Patsy told him with spite, "Your precious Alexander stole the real one. Make him give it back. And whatever my father said, the chalice belongs to the brewery. It belongs to *me*."

I didn't look at Patsy. I just wanted to go back to the mountains. It was like a physical ache.

Grantchester droned on. The executors would be doing this and that. Finally, Tobias broke up the session by apologizing to my mother that he had a plane to catch. He was off to Paris for the weekend. "I'll be back on Monday," he said to me.

When he had gone, Chris asked me what I wanted him to do.

"Follow Surtees," I said promptly.

Chris nodded and quietly left the room.

Emily appeared at my elbow. I said, "Has Surtees bothered you?"

She glanced at him where he stood across the room talking to Grantchester and stabbing the air with a vigorous forefinger. "He hasn't found the horse. He won't, either."

"The horse is yours now."

She blinked hard. "I liked Ivan."

It seemed natural to me to put my arms round her. She hugged me back, and I silently kissed her hair.

People gradually left. Himself, positively grinning, told me he would be in residence in his London home for the following ten days. Emily waved good-bye. Fussy Desmond Finch twittered away. Margaret Morden paid her respects. Oliver Grantchester ponderously closed his briefcase.

My mother asked, "Did you talk to Connie Hall?"

"Yes, I did."

She looked distressed. "Patsy told me what Connie said about Ivan searching the trash bags."

Patsy *would*. I said, "Mrs. Hall didn't want to upset you."

My mother said unhappily, "I think Patsy has gone down to the kitchen to talk to Lois about it."

"Let's go down, then," I suggested, and moved her with me. The caterers were packing up. We threaded a path through them and fetched up by Patsy's side in time to hear Lois saying, "Of course I threw the empty box away. What's wrong with *that?*"

"Didn't you check if anything was written on the bottom?"

"Of course not," Lois said scornfully.

"But you must have known my father wrote on the bottom of a tissue box all the time," Patsy said.

"Why should I know that?"

"You kept moving his notepad onto the desk out of his reach."

Patsy was right, of course, but predictably Lois inflated her lungs and stuck out her considerable frontage. "Sir Ivan never complained," she said, and tossed her head grandly.

My mother, looking exhausted, said soothingly, "Of course not, Lois." Turning to me, she said, "I think I'll go up to my sitting room, Alexander. Patsy, thank you, dear, for arranging everything so well. Ivan would have been so pleased."

She went desolately out of the kitchen. Lois slammed a few pots together. Patsy stalked away.

I started up the stairs to where my mother was bidding good-bye on the doorstep to Oliver Grantchester and, after him, to Patsy and Surtees. A taxi cruised past slowly on the road outside. Chris Young didn't look our way out the window, but I saw his profile clearly. Since the dustup in Emily's stable, Surtees hadn't often left home without a tail.

We went up to my mother's sitting room, followed by Edna, who had kindly brought some tea. Then my mother told me what I wanted to know without my asking.

"I can't bear it, Alexander. *I* would have looked for the box if he'd told me. But we'd kissed good night, and he didn't say anything about the box. He'd been so much better . . . calmer. We were truly *happy* that evening."

"Yes."

She drank her tea slowly and said, "What was written on the tissue box—I wrote it. And I don't remember what it was." The cup rattled in its saucer.

I kneeled beside her and waited until the inconsolable bout of grief subsided. She said finally, "Someone telephoned. It was a woman, and she wanted to speak to Ivan. He was dressing, and I said he would phone her back, so I wrote her phone number on the back of the box, like Ivan does. I told him, but"—she shook her head—"I didn't think it was important."

"And you don't know who she was?"

She frowned. "I remember that she said it was something to do with Leicestershire."

Leicestershire to me meant Norman Quorn. I said slowly, "Do you think it could possibly have been Norman's sister, whom we met in Leicestershire at that mortuary?"

"That poor woman! I don't know."

I couldn't remember her name. How could I find Norman Quorn's sister if I didn't know her name?

I called the brewery. No one even seemed to know he had had a sister. I phoned Detective Chief Inspector Reynolds. Off duty. I phoned the mortuary. All they could or would tell me was the name of the mortician to whom they had released the body of Norman Quorn. I phoned the mortician, asking who had arranged cremation and paid the bills. Sir Ivan Westering, I was told.

How like him, I thought.

I REACHED Chief Inspector Reynolds in the morning. He told me Norman Quorn's sister was a Mrs. Audrey Newton, widow, living at 4 Minton Terrace in Bloxham, Oxfordshire. Telephone number supplied.

I tried Audrey Newton's number and found her at home. And yes, nearly a week ago she had tried to talk to Sir Ivan Westering, but he hadn't called back. She had decided to give Sir Ivan something Norman had left with her.

"What thing?" I asked.

"A list. Very short. But Norman thought it important."

I asked if she would give the list to me instead.

After a pause she said, "I'll give it to Lady Westering. Ever so kind, she was, that day I had to identify Norman."

I said I would bring Lady Westering to her house.

My mother disliked the project.

"Please," I said. "And the drive will do you good."

I drove her out of London in Ivan's car to a large village not far from Banbury. Minton Terrace proved to be a row of small cottages with thatched roofs, and at Number Four the front door was opened by the rounded woman we'd met at the mortuary.

She nervously invited us in. She had set out sherry glasses and a plate of small cakes. Audrey Newton, plain and honest, was ashamed of the brother she had spent years admiring. It took a great deal of sherry drinking to bring her not just to give the list to my mother, but to explain how Norman had given it to *her.*

"I was over in Wantage, staying with him for a few days. I did that sometimes, you see. He was going to Spain on holiday, and he was going that day, and I was going to catch a bus home."

She paused. "He was going to go in a taxi to Didcot railway station, but someone, I think from the brewery, came to collect him first. We happened to be at the window when the car drew up." She frowned. "Norman wasn't pleased. I might almost say he was *frightened.* He said he'd better go, but all of a sudden he took an envelope out of his jacket pocket and pushed it into my hands and told me to keep it for him until he sent for it. It wasn't until after the cremation that I remembered the envelope and opened it. I wondered if it had anything to do with the brewery, if I should give it to Sir Ivan, as he had been so good to me, paying for the cremation and everything."

I sorted my way through the flood of words and said, "You still have the list, Mrs. Newton?"

"Yes." She crossed to a sideboard and took out an envelope, handing it to my mother. "I do hope I'm doing right. The brewery man telephoned about an hour ago, asking if Norman had left anything with me, and I said only a small list, nothing important, but he said he would send someone over for it this afternoon."

I looked at my watch. Twelve o'clock, noon. I asked my mother, "Did you tell anyone we were coming here?"

"Only Lois. I said we were going to see a lady in Bloxham and wouldn't be needing lunch."

I looked at her and at Audrey Newton. Neither woman had any understanding of the consequences of what they had just said.

"Mrs. Newton," I said, "the brewery told me they didn't know Norman Quorn *had* a sister."

She said, surprised, "But of course I'm known there. Norman sometimes used to take me to the directors' parties. Desmond Finch phoned me today. I've never liked him much. But he definitely knows me, even if no one else does."

I took the envelope from my mother and looked at the paper. It was a short list in two sections—one, a series of numbers; the other, a list of either personal or corporate names. A silence passed in which I did some very rapid thinking.

I said to Audrey Newton, "I think it would be a marvelous idea if you would go away for a lovely long weekend at the seaside." And I said to my mother, "And it would be marvelous if you would go with her, just for a few days."

My mother, astonished, said, "I don't want to go."

"I so seldom ask anything," I said. "I wouldn't ask this if it were not important." To Audrey Newton I said, "I'll pay for you to go to a super hotel if you would go upstairs now and pack what you would need for a few days."

She responded with an air of excitement and went upstairs.

My mother said, "What on earth is all this about?"

"Keeping you safe," I said flatly. "Just do it, Ma."

"I haven't any clothes!"

"Buy some."

"You're truly eccentric, Alexander."

"Just as well," I said.

I picked up my mobile phone and pressed the numbers of the pager Chris always carried. "This is Al. Phone me at once."

Barely thirty seconds later my mobile buzzed. "It's Chris."

"Can you do a chauffeur and car for three ladies?"

"No problem. When and where?"

"Like five minutes ago. Get the chauffeur to Emily Cox's stable in Lambourn. I'll meet you there."

"I'm on my way."

I was wearing a shirt under a sweater. I put the Quorn envelope in my shirt pocket and pulled my sweater down over it. "Have you a paper?" I said to my mother. "Anything I could draw on?"

She had in her purse a letter from a friend. I opened the envelope out flat and, with my mother's pen, had time to make nine small outline drawings of familiar people—Desmond Finch, Patsy, Surtees, Tobias included—before Audrey Newton came happily downstairs with a suitcase.

I showed her the page of small heads. "The person who came to pick up your brother—was it one of these?"

She looked and pointed firmly. "That one," she said.

"You're sure?"

"Positive."

"Let's go," I said, and we drove away, heading for Lambourn.

Emily was in her office, busy at paperwork when we arrived. Nothing I did surprised her anymore, she said. She agreed easily to my making lunch for her unexpected guests, but adamantly refused to join them in any flight. I persuaded her to go as far as her drawing room and there explained the explosive dangers of the situation.

"You're exaggerating," she objected.

"Well, I hope so."

"And anyway, I'm not afraid."

"But I am," I said. "Please, Em. I want you safe."

"What about my horses?"

"Phone your head groom later, using your portable phone."

"It's all mad." She breathed a long, capitulating sigh and went quickly out of the room.

She left me looking at the painting I had given her, which was not about an amateur game of golf in bad weather, but about the persistence of the human spirit. I took the Quorn envelope from my shirt pocket. I lifted the golf picture off its hook, turned it over, and slotted the envelope securely between the canvas and the frame. Then I hung the picture back on its hook and went out to see how lunch and life were passing in the kitchen.

My mother and Audrey were talking about how to pot cuttings from geraniums. I listened with the disjointed unreality perception of an alien. At any minute the brewery man might be breaking into the house in Bloxham.

A large car rolled up the drive. The chauffeur, in a dark blue suit and flat cap, climbed out, and I went to talk to him.

"Where am I going?" he said.

"Somewhere like Torbay. Find a good hotel with a sea view. It's my mother, my wife, and the sister of the man who stole the brewery's money. Hide them."

"Safe from Surtees?"

"And other thugs. What's your name today?"

"Uttley."

When I went back into the kitchen, Emily was giving instructions to the head groom on the telephone. She finished the details and hung up, not happy and not reassured.

"My dears," I said lightly, looking at all three women, "just have a good time."

My mother asked, "But why are we going?"

"Um, Emily knows. It's to do with hostages, and if that sounds a bit melodramatic, then it's better than being sorry. So go and enjoy yourselves, and don't tell *anyone* where you are."

"You might get your throat cut," Emily said nonchalantly, and although my mother and Audrey Newton looked suitably horrified, it seemed Emily's words did the trick.

I led them outside. "This is Mr. Uttley," I told them.

"Call me C.Y.," he said, and winking at me, he drove them cheerfully away.

I SAT in Ivan's car in a mall car park and tried to reach Margaret Morden by phone. She was at a meeting out of town, her office reported, and she would not be available until Monday. Tobias had said he was going to Paris, back in the office on Tuesday.

I hated weekends.

I sat indecisively, working out what to do next, when the mobile phone rang. It was Himself, surprisingly, inviting me to his London home for a drink.

I drove to Chesham Place, and Himself had a single malt ready. After a long silence he said, "What's on your mind, Al?"

"Well," I said, searching for an image, "it's as if there's a high wall with a path along each side of it, stretching into the distance, and I am on one side of the wall and Patsy and some others are on the other side, and we are all trying to go in the same direction to find the same pot of gold at the end. I can't see what they are doing and they can't see what I am doing, and the way forwards on both sides of the wall is difficult and full of potholes."

He listened, frowning.

I went on. "Yesterday, at the wake, Mrs. Connie Hall told me that on the night Ivan died, he was upset because he couldn't find a tissue box that had a phone number written on it. Mrs. Hall also told Patsy the same thing. So there we are, Patsy and I, one on each side of the wall, starting off together. My mother recalled having written the number on the box, and it was something to do with someone we met in Leicestershire. The woman we had met in Leicestershire was Norman Quorn's sister, but I didn't know her name, so I phoned the brewery and asked them for it, which was a very stupid mistake. It set an alarm bell jangling. *Why* did I suddenly want to know Norman Quorn's sister's name? It seemed that on Patsy's side of the wall, speculations began fizzing about."

Himself sat still, listening.

"This morning, when I took my mother to see Norman Quorn's sister, she said she had a list that her brother had given her and that she would give it to my mother. On the other side of the wall, which I can only guess at, someone decided to ask Norman Quorn's sister if her brother had given her anything to look after before he went on holiday, and she told them that yes, he had, but it was nothing very important, only some little list. In fact, I don't think the gold can be found without it.

"So here I am on my side of the wall, and on the other side they know I have the list. So if you want to know what's troubling me, it is how to find the treasure safely."

I sighed. "The problem is that the brewery will survive *without* that money, partly as a result of my own efforts. The coffers will fill again, and there's no guarantee that Patsy, or anyone else who finds the money, will use it to pay off the brewery's debts. Theoretically, after a year or two of prosperity, the brewery could be plundered again. That would be the end of the brewery because the creditors would not stand for it twice."

I shook my head. Himself poured more whisky.

I DECLINED my uncle's offer of a bed and stayed that night in one of the small hotels catering to London tourists. I ate a hamburger for dinner. I had with me the portable phone and spoke to Chris while I sat beside the fountains and bronze lions in Trafalgar Square.

"I'm back home," he said. "My passengers have nice sea-view rooms in the Redcliffe hotel in Paignton, in Devon, near Torbay. They all seemed quite happy. Anyway, what do you want done next?"

"You can charge me double time," I promised, "if you watch Surtees all weekend."

"Right," he said. "You're on."

Surtees's stud farm lay on the outskirts of a village south of Hungerford. Chris had assured me, laughing, that even if Surtees spent all his time looking out his front gate, he would seldom see the same person there. There were cyclists with baseball caps, housewives waiting for a bus, aged gentlemen walking dogs. Surtees never saw the skinhead or the secretary.

I tried to phone Margaret Morden at her home, but there was no reply. I tried again in the morning and reached her.

"It's Saturday," she objected.

"It's always Saturday."

"It had better be worth it."

"How about some numbers and names that Norman Quorn gave to his sister?"

She said, "Are you talking about routes and destinations?"

"I think so."

"Monday morning I will liaise with Tobias's office for an appointment, and I will rope in the big bank cheese. Say ten o'clock, Tuesday, at the bank? Will you bring the numbers?"

I agreed resignedly to what seemed to me an endless and endlessly dangerous delay. The weekend stretched ahead like a boring monochrome desert, so it was quite a relief when, early in the afternoon, Himself decided to give me a buzz.

"I have been talking to Patsy," my uncle said. "She phoned me, wanting to know if I knew where you were."

"What did you say?"

"I said you could be anywhere. She sounded quite different, Al. She sounded as if she had suddenly woken up. I told her that you had been working for her all along, at the brewery, and that she had misjudged you and been grossly unfair to you."

"What did she say?"

"She said she wanted to talk to you. Al, do talk to her. At least it would be a start. She said she would be at home all afternoon." He read her number out to me.

"I can't believe this," I said.

"Give her a chance," Himself pleaded. "It can't do any harm."

I said, "Any olive branch is worth the grasping." And ten minutes later I was talking to her.

She did sound quite different. She *apologized* for never seeing that I was no threat to her, and she was willing, if I was, to try to sort things out between us. Perhaps we could come to an understanding so that we don't fight all the time. Would I, she suggested diffidently, come by for a drink?

"Where?" I asked.

"Well . . . here, at home." She mentioned the name of the village. "Oh, Alexander, I just want to put things right."

I told her I would turn up for a drink at about six thirty, and then, disconnecting, I phoned Chris's pager. He called back.

I said, "Are you outside Surtees's house?"

"You betya."

"I have been invited for a drink."

"Belladonna? Aconite? Gin and toadstools?"

I sighed. "But if she is genuine . . ."

"She is never genuine, you said."

I was truly undecided. "I think I'll go," I said. "And take you with me. Is the 'secretary' handy?"

"In the car, zipped bag number five."

"I'll pick you up in the road at half past six."

I wondered if it was possible that Patsy had undergone a sea change. I had either to believe it or to fear a trap. But peace treaties had to start somewhere, after all. So, in the afternoon, I followed my road map and arrived in Patsy's village at dusk and came across a long, black-legged figure thumbing a lift.

I stopped beside him and he oozed into the car, wafting billows of expensive scent and doubling up with chuckles.

"Is anything happening?" I asked.

"Half an hour ago Surtees and his missus got into their car and drove down the road, and I followed. They turned into the gates of a house about half a mile away from here. They have got fairy lights all around the garden in the trees there, and cars outside. It looks as if it's some sort of party. So what do you want to do?"

"Try the house," I said.

I walked from the road to the front door, with Chris a step behind me, and rang the bell. A young woman opened it.

"Mrs. Benchmark is expecting you," she said when I introduced myself. "She says she is sorry, but when she was talking to you earlier, she forgot that she and Mr. Benchmark were going to a drinks party. It's through the village, past the pub; you can't miss it. It is all decorated with lights. Mrs. Benchmark asked me just to phone when you got here so that she can meet you when you arrive."

I thanked her, and Chris and I walked back to the car.

"What do you think?" I asked.

"A toss-up."

I tossed up mentally—heads you win, tails you lose—and lost.

CHAPTER 8

CHRIS and I drove along past the pub and came to the house with the lights. When we reached the driveway, which was full of cars, we parked in the roadway and climbed out, and Chris stumbled and broke the heel off one of his high-heeled patents.

He swore, stopped, and said he would break off the other one to level himself up. I laughed and set off towards the house a few steps ahead of him.

It was as if the bushes themselves erupted.

One moment I was walking unsuspectingly along and the next I was being enmeshed in ropes and nets and being dragged through some sort of rustic gate from the drive into a garden.

The garden, I was hazily aware, was lit by more festoons of fairy lights and by big multicolored bulbs; it was all strikingly theatrical, dramatically magnificent, a brilliant setting for a party.

No party that I'd been to before had started with one of the guests being tied to the trunk of a maple tree. At no party before had there been four familiar thugs as guests, one of them busy putting on boxing gloves. The only other guests were Patsy and Surtees and Oliver Grantchester. Surtees looked triumphant, Grantchester serious, and Patsy astounded.

I looked round the garden for possible exits and could see precious few. There was a lawn ringed with bushes, a flower bed, and an ornamental goldfish pond. There was a big house to the left, mostly dark. There was Oliver Grantchester.

Oliver Grantchester. The one crucial piece of information I hadn't learned was that he had a country place down the road from Patsy's house. Ivan's address book had given only Grantchester's address in London.

Audrey Newton had firmly pointed to Oliver Grantchester's sketched head as the person who had collected her brother on the day he left to go on vacation.

I'd known *who* would be looking for me but not *where*.

There weren't swear words bad enough to describe my stupidity. Patsy would never change. Why had I ever thought that she would? I'd *wanted* to believe. Serves me right.

Grantchester stood six feet away from me and said, "Where is the Kinloch hilt?"

I looked at him in bewilderment. I could think of no reason why he would want to know. He signaled to the wearer of the boxing gloves, who hit me low down in the abdomen, which hurt. Where the hell, I wondered, was my bodyguard?

Grantchester said, "Where is the King Alfred gold cup?"

Golf bag. Locker. Clubhouse. Scotland. Out of his grasp.

A bash in the ribs. Reverberations. Altogether too much and quite likely only the beginning.

Surtees strode to Grantchester's side and yelled, "Make him tell you where he's put the horse."

"Where's the horse?" Grantchester said.

I didn't tell him. Painful decision.

Surtees positively jumped up and down. "Hit him harder."

Oliver Grantchester hadn't the same priorities as Patsy's husband. He said to me, "Where's your mother?"

In Devon, I thought. Thank goodness.

Bash.

"Where's Emily Cox?"

Safe. Same thing.

Bash.

"Where is Norman Quorn's sister?"

I was by then fairly breathless. It would have been difficult to tell him even if I'd wanted to.

He stepped forwards to within three feet of me and with quiet intensity said, "Where's the list?"

The list. The point of all the battering.

He had never liked me. He had seen me always as a threat to his domination of Ivan. He had encouraged Patsy's obsessive suspicions of me. He hadn't wanted me looking into the brewery's affairs. He had been right to fear it.

His big body faced me now, with thunderous malevolence. He didn't care how much he hurt me. He was enjoying it. I saw the pleasure in his eyes. The full lips smiled.

"Tell me," he said. "Where's the list?"

The boxing gloves thudded here and there. Face, ribs, belly. Then the punch-bag practice stopped. Grantchester went away.

Patsy's face swam into view. "What list?" she said.

It made no sense. Surely she knew what list.

I would have said she looked worried. Horrified even. But she'd lured me there. "Why?" she said. "Why did Oliver ask where your mother and Emily are?"

I dredged up an answer. "How does he know they are not at home?" My face felt stiff. The rest just felt.

"Alexander," Patsy said in distress, "whatever Oliver wants, give it to him. This"—she gestured to the thugs—"is *awful*."

I agreed. I also couldn't believe she didn't know what her lawyer wanted. I was done believing Patsy. Finished. Grantchester was playing for millions, and boxing gloves were getting him nowhere. He returned from the direction of his house, pulling a barbecue cooker.

Oh God, I thought. Oh no.

Grantchester took the grill grid off the barbecue and poured a bottleful of lighter fuel over the charcoal briquettes. He struck a match and tossed it onto the fuel. Flame rushed upwards in a roaring plume. Satisfied, he settled the grill in place to get hot.

I could see the thugs' faces. They showed no surprise. *They've seen this before.*

They'd seen Norman Quorn burned in a garden, with grass cuttings in his clothes.

Patsy looked merely puzzled. So did Surtees.

The briquettes flamed, heating up quickly.

I would tell him. Enough was enough. My body already hurt abominably. Abstractions like the persistence of the human spirit might be all right for paintings but didn't apply here.

Grantchester waited with lip-licking anticipation while the heat built up. When the briquettes glowed a bright, searing red, he lifted the barred grill off the fire with tongs and dropped it flat on the lawn, where it sizzled and singed the grass.

"You'll lie on that if you don't tell me," he said. He was enjoying himself. "Where's the list?"

Cussed, rebellious, stubborn—I might be all those by nature, but I knew I would tell him. Defeat lay there at my feet, blackening the grass. Money was of no importance. The decision was a matter of will. Of pride, even. And such pride came too expensive. Tell him. . . . You have to.

"Where is it?" he said.

I meant to tell him. I tried to tell him. But I couldn't.

So I burned.

I COULD hear someone screaming, and I remembered Surtees promising, "Next time you'll scream," but it wasn't I, after all, who was screaming. It was Patsy.

"No. No. You can't. Oliver. Surtees. You can't do this. *Stop it.*"

The noise I made wasn't a scream. From deep inside it started low in my gut and ended like a growl in the throat, every nerve's message unified into one consuming elemental protest.

I could hear him repeating, "Where is it? Where is it?"

Irrelevant.

It all lasted not much more than a minute. Half a lifetime, condensed. I'd gone beyond speech when the scene blew apart.

With crashes and bangs and shrieking metal, a large bus smashed down the fence between the drive and the garden. Out of the bus and onto the lawn poured a half-drunk mob of football supporters, all dressed in orange scarves, with raucous shouting voices.

"Where's the beer, then? Where's the beer?"

The four thugs who'd been pinning down my arms and legs decided to quit and took their weight off me, so that I was blessedly able to roll off the grill. A pair of long legs in black tights appeared, with a familiar voice above me saying, "Jeez, Al."

The brightly lit garden went on filling with noise and orange scarves and demands for beer. Surrealism, I thought.

Chris poured a container of cold water over me, squatted down, and said, "Your sweater was *smoldering*. Al, are you okay?"

A goldfish flapped on the grass. Goldfish pond. Cold water. I made an attempt to crawl there, and Chris, seeing the point, hooked an arm under my armpit and hauled me the short distance. I lay down full-length in the cold pond, the relief enormous.

"Did bloody Surtees do this?" Chris demanded with fury.

"Bloody Grantchester."

He went away. There were more people in the garden. Policemen. Uniforms. Football fans scurrying about looking for free beer. I watched the police slapping handcuffs on everyone moving, including the four thugs, and I watched Patsy's bewilderment and Surtees's swings from glee to noncomprehension.

I heard one of the football crowd telling the police that it was a *girl*—a knockout—who had stolen the bus from outside the pub, a girl who had yelled that there was free beer at the party.

When they drifted away, Chris came back. "I caught Grantchester trying to sneak out through the garage," he said with satisfaction. "He'll be going nowhere for a while."

"Chris, get lost. The police are looking for you."

A shiny object, brass knuckles, splashed down into the water. Chris's hand briefly squeezed my shoulder; then his dark shape passed into the shadows.

The farce continued. A uniformed policeman told me to get out of the pond, and when I failed to obey, he clicked a pair of handcuffs on my wrists and walked off, deaf to protests.

A new voice said, "Get out of the pond." The voice held police authority. Just behind him stood Patsy.

"I don't know if he can," Patsy said. "They were hitting him."

"Who were?"

She looked over to where the handcuffed figures sat.

"And they burned him. On that grill thing, over there."

One of the policemen bent down to pick the grill up and snatched his hand away, cursing and sucking his fingers.

"Mrs. Benchmark, do you know this man?"

"Of course I know him." Patsy stared down at me. "He's . . . *he's my brother,*" she said.

It came nearer to breaking me up than all Grantchester's attentions. She saw that it did, and it made her cry.

Patsy, my implacable enemy, wept.

She brushed the tears away and told the policeman she would point out my attackers. When they moved off, their place was taken by Surtees, who had clearly enjoyed the earlier entertainment.

"Where's the horse?" he said. He sneered. His feet quivered. I thought he might kick my head.

I said with threat, "Surtees, any more from you and I'll tell Patsy where you go on Wednesdays. I'll tell her the address of the little house in Guildford and the name of the prostitute who lives there."

His mouth opened in horror. "How . . . I'll deny it."

I said, smiling, "I paid a skinhead to follow you. So you keep your hands to yourself as far as I'm concerned."

He looked sick and backed away from me, as if I'd touched him with the plague. Life had its sweet moments, after all.

No one had actually seen Oliver Grantchester being attacked in his garage. He was found, when he recovered consciousness, to be suffering from a blow to the back of the skull, a broken nose, a broken jaw, and extensive damage to his lower abdomen.

Whoever would do such a thing! Tut-tut.

The police put him in a prison hospital ward.

Patsy organized things, which she was good at. She organized me into a hospital that specialized in burns, with an elderly woman doctor able to deal with anything on a Saturday evening.

"Dear me," the doctor said. "Nasty." She wrapped me in burn-healing artificial skin and large bandages, and in her grandmotherly way inquired, "And a couple of cracked ribs, too, wouldn't you say?"

"I would."

She smiled. "I'll see that you sleep."

She drugged me out until six in the morning, when I phoned Chris's beeper and got his return call five minutes later.

"Where are you?" he demanded aggrievedly.

I told him and said, "Bring some clothes. Hospital gowns shouldn't be visited even on the damned."

He arrived to find me standing by the window. "To be frank," he said awkwardly, "I didn't expect you to be on your feet."

"More comfortable," I said. "That bus, if I may say, was brilliant."

He grinned. "Yes, it was, wasn't it?"

"Go on, then. Tell me all."

He dumped the bag with the clothes in it and came over to join me by the window, the familiar face alight with impishness.

"Those thugs that jumped you—there was no mistaking they were the ones I'd been looking for. And to be honest, Al, I couldn't handle four of them at once, on my own."

I nodded, understanding.

"So," Chris said, "I had to go for reinforcements. I ran down to the pub and telephoned the police that there was a riot going on. The barman told me that the house belonged to Mr. Oliver Grantchester. But the police didn't show up. So when this big busload of psychos in orange scarves invaded the bar, I went outside where half of them were still in the bus, and I yelled that there was free beer down the road, and I just got into the driver's seat and drove that damned jumbo straight through Grantchester's fence into the garden."

"It did the trick," I said, smiling.

"Yes, but meanwhile . . ."

"Best forgotten. What exactly did you do to Grantchester?"

"Kicked him a good many times." Chris laughed. "I'll work for you anytime," he said. "Attending to Grantchester will be extra."

AROUND MIDMORNING I HAD a visit from a Detective Inspector Vernon, whom I'd met, it transpired, in the garden. He joined me by the window. There were scudding clouds in the sky. A good day for mountains.

"Mrs. Benchmark says that Mr. Grantchester was instructing four other men to ill-treat you."

"You could put it like that," I agreed.

He was a bulky, short man, going gray, and seemed a down-to-earth and dogged investigator.

"Can you tell me why?" he said.

"You'll have to ask Mr. Grantchester."

"His lower jaw's badly broken. He can't speak."

Vernon asked me if I knew who had attacked him. I'd been in the pond, I said. As he knew. I said, however, that the same four thugs had battered me earlier in Scotland, and told him that I'd given a statement to the police there. I suggested he also talk to the Leicestershire police about people being burned on barbecue grills.

Vernon wrote everything down. If I had recovered enough, he said, he would appreciate it if I would attend his police station the following morning. They could send an unmarked car for me, he offered.

All I said was, "Okay."

The day passed somehow, and the night. Bruises blackened. The burns got inspected again. No sign of infection. Very lucky, I was told, considering the unsterile nature of goldfish ponds.

ON MONDAY morning I discharged myself from the hospital against their advice. I had too much to do, I said.

The unmarked police car came to transport me to Vernon's official stamping ground, where I was instantly invited to look through a window into a brightly lit room and to say if I'd seen any of the eight men at any earlier time in my life.

No problem. Numbers one, three, seven, and eight.

"They deny they touched you."

I gave Vernon a glowering come-off-it glare, then took a grip on my pain-driven temper and said, "Number three wore boxing

gloves and caused the damage you can see in my face. All four as-
sisted in compelling me to lie on that hot grill. All four also attacked
me in Scotland. I don't know their names, but I do know their faces."

It had seemed to me on other occasions that the great British
police force not only never apologized but also never saw the need
for it. But Inspector Vernon ushered me politely into a bare interview room and offered me coffee, which in his terms came into the
category of tender loving care.

"Mrs. Benchmark couldn't identify them," he observed.

I asked if he had talked to Berrick in Scotland or Reynolds in
Leicestershire. They had been off duty, he said.

Damn the weekends.

I asked to use a telephone and reached, miraculously, Keith
Robbiston. "Could I have a handful of your wipe-out pills?" I
asked. "I got bashed again."

"Oh . . . As bad as before?"

"Well, actually, worse. Cracked ribs and some burns."

He talked to Inspector Vernon and said my pills would be motor-
biked door to door within two hours. If nothing else, the doctor's
speed impressed the inspector. He went off to telephone outside.
When the coffee came, it was in a pot on a tray.

I sat and waited for unmeasurable time, thinking. When Vernon
returned, I told him that number seven in the lineup had been
wearing what looked like my father's gold watch, stolen from me
in Scotland. "Also," I said, "he didn't relish the burning."

"That won't excuse him."

"No, but if you could make it worth his while, he might tell you
what happened to a Norman Quorn."

The inspector didn't say, "Who?" He went quietly away. A uniformed constable brought me a sandwich lunch.

My pills arrived. Things got better.

After another couple of hours Vernon came back into the room,
sat down across the table, and told me that the following conversation was not taking place. Positively *not*. Understood?

"Okay," I said.

"First of all, can you identify your father's gold watch?"

"It has an engraving on the back, 'Alistair from Vivienne.' "

Inspector Vernon faintly smiled. In all the time I spent with him, it was the nearest he came to showing pleasure.

"Number seven may be known as Bernie, and Bernie, as you saw, is a worried man." He paused. "Can I trust you not to repeat this?"

I said dryly, "To the hilt. But," I added, "why all this cloak-and-dagger stuff?"

He spent a moment thinking, then said, "In Britain one isn't allowed to make bargains with people accused of crimes. One can't promise a light sentence in return for information. Also the business of what is and what isn't admissible evidence is a minefield."

"So I've heard."

"If you hadn't told me to ask Bernie questions about Norman Quorn, I wouldn't have thought of it. But Bernie split wide-open. The prosecution department will decide whether a trial should take place charging Grantchester with the manslaughter of Norman Quorn. At this point in such proceedings everyone gets very touchy about who knows what, in order not to jeopardize any useful testimony. It could compromise the case for you to have heard Bernie's confession. But I'll tell you what he said, although I shouldn't."

"You're safe."

"Bernie said that they—the four you call the thugs—all go to a gym in London, which Oliver Grantchester has been visiting for fitness sessions. He goes on the treadmill, lifts a few weights, and so on, but he isn't a boxer. So when he wanted a rough job done, he recruited your four thugs. Bernie was willing. The money was good, even though the job went wrong."

"Quorn died."

Vernon nodded. "Grantchester told them to turn up at his house in the country. He arrived with an older man, who was Norman Quorn. The four thugs tied the man to the same tree as they tied you. Grantchester lit the barbecue and told Quorn he would burn him if he didn't come across with some information."

Vernon paused, then went on. "Bernie didn't know what the

information was and still doesn't. Grantchester threw the hot grill onto the grass and told Quorn he would lie on it until he told him—Grantchester—what he wanted to know. Quorn said he would tell him at once, but Grantchester got the thugs to throw Quorn onto the grill anyway, and although he was screaming that he would tell, Grantchester wouldn't let him up and seemed to be enjoying it. When he did let him up, Quorn dropped dead."

Vernon stopped. I listened in fascinated horror.

"Grantchester was furious," Vernon said. "Quorn was dead, and he hadn't found out what he wanted to know. He got the thugs to put Quorn into the trunk of his car. Bernie doesn't know what Grantchester did with the body."

After a while I said, "Did you ask Bernie about Scotland?"

Vernon nodded. "Grantchester paid them again, to go to your house and beat you up until you gave them something. He didn't tell them what it was. You didn't give them anything, and Grantchester told them they should have made sure you were dead before they threw you down the mountain."

"Well, well," I said.

"Bernie says he complained that beating up people was one thing, but murder was another."

"Bernie is simple," I said.

"Just as well, from our point of view," Vernon said. "Anyway, the pay was good, so when Grantchester told them to turn up again at his house the day before yesterday, they did."

"Yes."

I listened without comment as Vernon gave me Bernie's version of the events of that afternoon. Finally he paused and looked at me. "Is Bernie's account of things accurate?"

"As far as I'm concerned, yes."

Vernon stood up and walked around the room twice, as if disturbed. "Mrs. Benchmark," he said, "called you her brother. But you're not, are you?"

"Her father was married to my mother. He died a week ago."

Vernon nodded. "Mrs. Benchmark is devastated by what happened in the garden. She doesn't understand it. The poor lady is very upset.

I again made no comment.

Vernon went to the door, opened it, and shouted to someone outside to bring tea. When he came back, he said, "We obtained a warrant yesterday to search Grantchester's house."

I asked if he'd found anything useful.

He didn't answer straightforwardly. He said, "Detective Sergeant Berrick in Scotland sent us faxes today of the drawings you did of the thugs the day they attacked you at your home. Bernie almost collapsed when we showed them to him. Your policeman also sent the list of things that were stolen from you. In Grantchester's house we found four paintings of golf courses."

"You didn't!"

Vernon nodded. "Your policeman said that the pictures had stickers on the backs, and if other stickers had been stuck over them, your name would still be visible under X ray. So this afternoon we x-rayed the stickers."

He smiled at me.

ON TUESDAY morning I went to the bank meeting in Reading and was shown into a private conference room where the area bank manager, Margaret Morden, and Tobias were already sitting round a table.

When I went in, they all stood up.

"Don't," I said awkwardly. "Am I late?"

"No," Tobe said.

They all sat. I took the one empty chair.

"Did you bring the list?" the bank man said.

I was wearing an open-necked white shirt with no tie and was carrying a jacket. I dug into a jacket pocket and handed Norman Quorn's envelope to Tobias.

They were staring at me.

"Sorry about the bruises," I said, making a gesture towards my face. "I got a bit clobbered again. Very careless."

Tobias said, "I've talked to Chris. He told me about . . . Grantchester's barbecue." Tobias had also, clearly, told the others. All of them were embarrassed. I, too. Very British.

"Well," I said, "can we find the money?"

They had no doubt of it. With an air of relief they passed around the piece of paper. It soon became apparent that although the numbers and names belonged to bank accounts, Quorn had been coy about setting down on paper which account referred to which bank. The list had been an aide-mémoire to himself. He had never meant anyone else to have to decipher it.

They each copied out the whole list. The information was so hot, each of them had brought a personal computer that was not connected to anything else and could not be hacked into from outside. The room grew silent except for the tapping of keys.

I waited without fret, moving stiffly on my chair, leaning forwards, resting my elbows on the table, taking shallow breaths, remembering. Body management, learned fast.

AT THE police station the previous afternoon, Inspector Vernon had told me that Ivan's car (the wheels I'd driven to the party) had been identified by Mrs. Benchmark and towed to the police station.

"Can I take it?" I had asked, surprised.

"If you think you're fit to drive."

Fit or not, I'd driven the car to Lambourn, found Emily's spare house key on its old familiar nail in the tack room, and spent the night lying facedown on her sofa, feeling shivery and sick.

In the morning I'd combed my hair, rinsed my mouth, and phoned Chris, who said he'd been trying without success to reach my mobile number. "The phone's in the car," I said. "I expect the battery's flat."

"For heaven's sake, charge it. Where are you? Are you all right?"

"Yes. I'm in Lambourn. Could you drive to Paignton and bring all three ladies here?"

"Chauffeur's togs coming up. Zipped bag nine."

We'd disconnected on a smile. Then I retrieved Quorn's list from the back of the golf picture and drove to the meeting in Reading.

BY LUNCHTIME THE EXPERTS had gotten nowhere nearer the end of the rainbow. We had sandwiches and drank coffee.

"The trouble is," the bank man told me, "that we have to match the account numbers on the list with both a name on the list and with a bank identification number that we already have. Then we have to send that combination to the bank in question. So far the nearest we have come is matching one account number to one bank. But we supplied the wrong name for the account, and the bank told us by return fax that as our inquiry is incomplete, they cannot answer it."

Tobias said, "I have been working on the belief that one of these numbers or names must mean something to the Global Credit in Panama, but they will not admit it."

"All banks are secretive," the big bank man said.

"Don't despair," Margaret said. "We'll find the money."

By the end of the afternoon, however, they were all looking cast down. They said they would think of a new strategy for the next day, carefully shredded every scrap of paper, and locked the list in the bank manager's private safe. I drove dispiritedly back to Lambourn.

Emily, my mother, and Audrey Newton had just arrived. Uttley was busy unloading suitcases from the trunk.

"We've had a lovely weekend," Audrey Newton said, beaming. "Thank you ever so much. You've bruised your face, dear."

"Walked into a door."

Emily took Audrey and my mother into the house, and Chris gave me an assessing inspection.

"You look lousy," he said. "Worse than Sunday."

"Thanks."

"Your bus-stealing Grantchester-immobilizing friend no longer exists," he assured me. "I dumped her today, bit by bit, in a succession of trash cans on my way to Devon."

"So wise."

"How do blond bubble curls grab you?"

"I wouldn't be seen dead with her."

"At least the lawyer didn't cauterize your sense of humor. Do you want anything else done?"

"Just take Audrey Newton home to Bloxham," I said.

"After that?"

We stared at each other.

"A friend for life," I suggested.

"I'll send my bill."

EMILY proposed that my mother and I stay the night in Lambourn and met with little resistance.

The telephone rang in the kitchen while we were sitting round the big table, and Emily picked it up. In a moment she held out the receiver in my direction. "It's Himself, looking for you."

I took the instrument and said, "My lord."

"Al, where have you been? I've had Patsy on the line all day. She sounds hysterical. She wants to talk to you. She says you signed yourself out of some hospital she put you in, and she won't tell me why she put you in hospital. What happened?"

"Er . . ." My mother and Emily could both hear what I said. "Can I come for a drink at six tomorrow evening?"

"Of course."

"Well, please don't tell Patsy where I am. Ask her if she'll meet me at two o'clock in the car park of the brewery's bank's head office in Reading. And tell her . . ." I paused. "Tell her thanks for the help." I put the phone down.

Emily said, astounded, "Patsy *helped* you?"

"Mm."

They would have to know, so I told them as unemotionally as possible about Oliver Grantchester. "He had either conspired with Norman Quorn to steal the brewery's money in the first place or tried to wrest it from him afterwards," I said. "I'm not sure which."

"Not *Oliver!*" my mother protested in total disbelief. "We've known him for years. Ivan trusted him."

I said, "Ivan trusted Norman Quorn. Both men were good at their jobs but fatally attracted by what looked like an easy path to a bucket of gold—and I'm not talking about the literal bucket of gold, the King Alfred gold cup, which Grantchester thought he could lay his hands on as a consolation when the serious prize slipped through his fingers. And Patsy has woken up to the fact that her dear darling avuncular Oliver has been trying his damnedest to rob *her,* as she now owns the brewery, complete with its losses."

My mother had her own concern. "You didn't really walk into a door, did you, Alexander?"

I smiled. "I walked into Grantchester's fist man. You'd think I'd know better."

"And no one took hostages," Emily said with much understanding.

I DROVE my mother to Reading in the morning and saw her onto the London train, promising to spend the evening and night in Park Crescent after my six-o'clock date with Himself.

Frail from grief, my calm and exquisite parent showed me in a single trembling hug on the railway platform how close we both were to being stretched too far. I understood suddenly that it was from her I had learned the way to hide fear and pain. It had been because of her ultracontrolled outer face, which I had all my life taken to be a deficiency of emotion.

"Ma," I said on Reading station, "I adore you."

"Alexander," she said, "don't be ridiculous."

IN THE bank Tobias, Margaret, and the big financial cheese were gloomily studying the electronic messages on the one fax machine they had left alive to receive them overnight.

Useful information from around the globe: zero.

The experts approached the problem from so-far-untried angles, but nothing worked. By lunchtime they were saying they couldn't dedicate more than that afternoon to the search, as they had other unbreakable commitments ahead.

When I asked if I could bring Patsy to the afternoon session, they said I could do anything I liked. But Tobias, chewing hard on a toothpick, asked if I remembered what had happened to me four days ago, on the one time I'd believed in her good faith.

I was leaning forwards, the morning's pills wearing off. I remembered, I said, and would rely on Tobe to defend me from the maiden.

I met her in the car park, as arranged. She wore a shirt, a cardigan, long skirt, flat shoes—wholesome, well groomed.

"Hello," I said.

"Alexander . . ."

She was unsure of herself. Awkward. I'd never seen her like that.

I explained that she should come into the bank with me and listen to the difficulties that had arisen in finding the brewery's millions. "For Ivan's sake, and for my mother's sake, I would have done anything to put things right," I said. "I've tried. I haven't managed it. I want the bank people to tell you that I am not trying to steal from you. I am trying to restore what Ivan built."

"Alexander . . ."

"I did believe on Saturday," I went on, "that you were sincerely offering a truce. I hope you didn't know exactly what you were beckoning me into. I know you tried to stop that little lark with the barbecue. . . . Anyway, will you come into the bank?"

She nodded speechlessly and went with me into the conference room, where, of course, her looks and natural charm immediately enslaved the bank man. He obligingly explained exactly how they were trying to find the missing millions by using the list.

"That list," she murmured. "That list?"

"Don't let her see it," Tobe said abruptly.

The bank man asked, "Why ever not?"

"Because of what it cost to bring it here. Al may sit at this table hour after hour pretending there's nothing the matter, but he's halfway to fainting most of the time."

"No," I objected.

"Yeah, yeah." He waved his toothpick in my direction. "It was Grantchester, I'll bet you, who got Patsy to inveigle you into that garden. He may be in the lockup at this moment, but he'll get out, and he may know a way of using this list that we haven't fathomed, and he may have told her what to look for, so don't let her see it."

There was an intense silence. Patsy slowly stood up.

"You are right. Oliver used me," she said. "But I didn't know anything about any list before Oliver tried to make Alexander give it to him. Don't show it to me. I don't want to see it." She looked directly at me and said, "I'm sorry."

I stood up also. She gave me a long look and went away.

AT THE end of an afternoon that produced nothing but baffling frustration, I drove to Chesham Place and told my uncle, over a tumblerful of single malt, that three clever financial brains had spent two whole working days trying to make sense of Norman Quorn's list of bank accounts and had failed.

"They'll succeed tomorrow," he said encouragingly.

I shook my head. "They've given up. They've got other things they have to do."

"You've done your best, Al."

I was sitting with forearms on knees, trying not to sound as spent as I felt. I told him about Patsy's visit to the bank and about her understanding of Grantchester's intention of robbing the brewery. "But the millions are lost," I said. "I'm glad Ivan didn't know."

After a while Himself asked, "What were you doing in hospital? Patsy wouldn't tell me."

"Sleeping, mostly."

"Al!"

"Well, it was Grantchester who sent the thugs to the bothy, thinking you'd given me the King Alfred gold cup to look after. He didn't tell them exactly what they were looking for, I suppose, because he was afraid they would steal it for themselves if they knew. Anyway, when he found out I had that damned list, he got the same thugs to persuade me to hand it over, but I didn't."

He looked aghast.

"Some of my ribs are cracked. Grantchester's in a police hospital ward. Patsy and I may come to that truce in the end."

MY MOTHER and I ate an Edna-cooked dinner, and afterwards I took a pill at bedtime and slept for hours. In the morning I phoned Tobe's office. He had gone away for the weekend.

"But it's only Thursday," I protested.

He would probably be back on Monday.

Damn him, I thought.

Margaret was "unavailable."

The big bank cheese had left me a message. "All the King Alfred Gold Cup race expenses will be honored by the bank, working closely with Mrs. Benchmark, who is now organizing everything for the day at Cheltenham."

Bully for Patsy. Big cheeses were putty in her hands.

I drifted through a quiet morning and in the afternoon drove to Lambourn, arriving in time for evening stables. Emily, in her natural element, walked confidently round her yard, instructing the lads, feeling horses' legs, patting necks, and delivering messages of love to the powerful creatures that rubbed their noses against her in response. I watched for some time before she realized I was there, and I vividly understood again how essential that life was to her well-being.

While I was still sitting in Ivan's car, a horse box drove into the yard and unloaded Golden Malt. He moved with liquid perfection, the arrogance of great thoroughbreds in every toss of his head.

Impossible not to be moved. I stood up out of the car. Emily, seeing me, came to stand beside me, and together we watched the horse being led a few times round the yard to loosen his leg muscles after the confines of his journey.

"He looks great," I said.

Emily nodded.

"And Saturday?"

"He won't disgrace himself." Her words were judicious but trembled with the hard-to-control excitement of any trainer who felt there was a chance of winning a big race.

We went into the house, where it proved impossible for her or me to do anything as ordinary as cooking dinner. I hadn't the energy, either. We ate bread and cheese.

At ten o'clock she went out into her stable yard to check that all her charges were happily settled for the night. I followed her and stood irresolutely looking up at the stars and the rising moon.

The clear sky and weak moonlight were millions of years old. The perspective of time could cool any fever if one gave it a chance. One could learn, perhaps, that failure was bearable. I had caused in myself more pain than I really knew how to deal with, and the fact that it had been for nothing had to be faced.

What I had done had been irrational.

I should have told Grantchester where to find the list. There was no saying, of course, that even if I had told him, he would have let me walk out of his garden untouched. That burning had been a gesture for nothing. Whatever information Norman Quorn had entrusted to his sister in that benighted envelope, it hadn't indicated what he'd done with the brewery's money.

I could admit to myself that I'd burned from pride.

Harder to accept that it had been pointless.

Essential to accept that it had been pointless and to go on from there. If I'd been in Scotland, I would have gone up into the mountains and let the wild pipes skirl out the raw sorrow.

CHAPTER 9

RIDAY morning, Lambourn, Emily's house.

I telephoned Margaret Morden. No, she said, no one had thought of any new way of finding the money.

"It was a false hope," I said. "Forget it. Give it up."

"Don't talk like that!"

"It's all right. Truly. Will you come to the races?"

"If you want me . . ."

"Of course we want you. Without you, there would be no race."

"Without *you.*"

"We're brilliant," I said, laughing.

"You do sound better."

"I promise you, I'm fine."

Out in the yard, life bustled along in the same old way, and by lunchtime I found myself falling into the same old role of general dogsbody, popping down to the village for such and such, collecting tack from repairs.

Emily and I ate dinner together and went to bed together. She lay in my arms and afterwards told me it broke her heart.

"What does?" I asked.

"Seeing you try to be a husband."

"But I am—"

"No." She kissed my shoulder above the bandages. "You know you don't belong here. Just come back sometimes. That'll do."

PATSY had organized the race day. The hundred or so commercial guests—creditors, suppliers—were given a big welcome, unlimited drinks, free race cards, lunch, tea. Cheltenham racecourse had extended to the King Alfred Brewery, in Ivan's memory, every red-carpet courtesy they could give to the chief sponsor of one of their top crowd-pulling early season afternoons. Patsy had the whole racecourse executive committee tumbling over themselves to please her. Her social gifts were priceless.

To Patsy had been allocated the sponsor's box in the grandstand, next best thing to the plush suite designed for crowned heads. She had organized a private family lunch there for my mother so that Ivan's widow could be both present and apart.

Having met my mother at the club entrance, I walked with her to the box. Patsy faultlessly welcomed her with kisses. Behind her stood Surtees, who would not meet my eyes.

"Hello, Surtees," I said, to be annoying.

He gave me a silent, frustrated look and took two paces backwards. What a grand change, I thought, from days gone by.

Patsy gave us a puzzled look and at one point later in the afternoon said, "What have you said to Surtees? If I mention you, he finds a reason for leaving the room. I don't understand it."

"Surtees and I," I said, "have come to an understanding."

"What about?"

"On my side, about his behavior in Oliver's garden."

"He didn't really mean what he said."

I clearly remembered Surtees urging the thugs to hit me harder. He'd meant it, all right.

I said, "For quite a while I believed it was Surtees who sent those thugs to Scotland to find the King Alfred gold cup."

It shook her. "But why?"

"Because he said, 'Next time you'll scream.' Because you were telling everyone that I'd stolen the cup. Surtees believed it."

"You wouldn't steal."

I listened to the certainty in her voice and asked, trying to suppress bitterness, "How long have you known that?"

Obliquely she told me the truth, revealing to me her own long years of unhappy fear. She said, "Ivan would have given you anything you asked for."

I said, "I would never have taken anything that was yours."

"I thought you would." She paused. "I did hate you."

She made no more admissions, nor any excuses; but in the garden she had called me her brother, and in the bank she had said, "I'm sorry." Perhaps, just perhaps, things had really changed.

WHEN Himself and his countess arrived to keep my mother company, I went down to the hospitality tent and found the mood upbeat, alcoholic, and forgiving. Margaret Morden, dressed in soft blue, greeted me with an embrace and said she knew nothing about horses but would back Golden Malt.

She followed my gaze across the tent to where Patsy was encouraging about everyone's future. "You know," I said to Margaret, "Patsy will make a great success of the brewery. She's a born manager."

"How can you possibly forgive her?"

"I didn't say I forgave her. I said she's a born manager."

"It was in your voice."

I smiled into the clever eyes. "Find out for me," I said, "whether Oliver Grantchester suggested the embezzlement or just stumbled across it and muscled in."

"I can tell you now. It was Grantchester's idea all along. Then Norman Quorn did some fancy footwork to keep the loot himself, and misjudged the strength and cruelty of his partner."

"How do you know?" I asked, entranced.

"That weasel Desmond Finch told me," Margaret said. "I leaned on him the tiniest bit, and he told me Quorn had practically cried on his shoulder. Still, I don't see how we can prove it unless Grantchester confesses. I think," she went on, "that Quorn must have said in all good faith to Ivan's trusted friend and lawyer, Oliver, how easy it would be in these days of electronic transfers to make oneself seriously rich. I think they worked it out together, maybe even as an academic exercise to begin with, and when the trial run succeeded, they did it in earnest. Then Quorn tried at the last minute to back out."

"He did steal the money," I said flatly. "He tried to cut his partner out."

She agreed bleakly. "They both did."

We drank champagne. Sweetish. Patsy was no spendthrift fool.

I sighed. "I wish Tobe could have been here today."

Margaret hesitated. "He couldn't bear that we hadn't been able to find the money with that list, when you suffered so much to bring it to us."

"Tell him not to be so soft."

She bent forwards and unexpectedly kissed my cheek. "Soft," she said, "is the last word I would apply to Alexander Kinloch."

WE STOOD in the parade ring with Emily, watching Golden Malt stride round, led by his groom. Emily's jockey joined us, dressed in Ivan's racing colors of gold and green blocks, gold cap.

Emily was all business. She told the jockey to be handy in fourth place and make his move after he'd rounded the last bend and straightened for the uphill run to the winning post.

"Don't forget," she said, "he's a great fighter uphill."

When the horses had gone out onto the track, we all joined my mother up in the sponsor's box. Dressed in black, she gazed out over the autumnal racecourse and yearned for her lost consort, for the steadfast man who had been all she needed as a companion. It was Ivan's race. Ivan's day. Nothing would comfort her.

Patsy arrived with Surtees. She was looking at her husband with the fresh cold eyes of disillusion. I would give that marriage another year at most, I thought.

Golden Malt looked splendid, but he faced no easy task. The Gold Cup race had drawn out nine of the best steeplechasers. Golden Malt was generally counted only fourth or fifth in the hierarchy.

White-knuckle time. Emily watched the start through race glasses, standing rock-still. It was one of those races when neither the fences nor the undulating curves sorted the runners out into a straggling line. All nine runners went round in a bunch, no one fell, the crowd on the grandstands yelled and drowned out the commentator, and Golden Malt came round the last bend in close fourth place and headed for glory up the hill.

Emily watched breathlessly. Himself was shouting. My mother clasped her hands over her heart. Patsy murmured, "Come *on . . .*"

Three horses crossed the line together.

One couldn't tell by eye which head had nodded forwards. We all went down to the unsaddling area for first, second, and third, and none could disguise the agony of the wait for the photograph.

When the result came, it was in the impersonal voice of the course announcer: "First, number five."

Number five: Golden Malt.

There was a lot of kissing. Patsy gave me an uncomplicated smile, with no acid. Emily's eyes outshone the stars.

Patsy had ordained that the trophy be presented to the winning owner by my mother, as Ivan's wife. So it happened that at the ceremony my mother presented the replica of the King Alfred gold cup to Emily, to universal cheers and a blaze of flashing cameras.

Ivan would have loved it.

W HEN MY MOTHER AND I WERE placidly breakfasting and reading congratulatory newspapers, my uncle Robert telephoned with a full head of steam.

"Whatever you're doing, stop doing it. I've had Jed on the line, foaming at the mouth. The conservationists have invaded the bothy with spades and pickaxes and are tearing everything apart, and Zoë Lang is there, the light of battle in her eyes. They are digging all round the bothy. Jed begs me to fly up there at once."

"Do you want me to come with you?"

"Of course I do," he bellowed. "Meet me at Heathrow."

I explained to my mother that I would have to go. Resignedly she told me to finish my toast. I laughed and hugged her, and found a taxi to Heathrow.

Himself was striding up and down, an awesome sight. We caught a flight to Edinburgh, where we were met by the helicopter pilot who had risked the bothy's plateau once before.

Our arrival alarmed a crowd at the bothy, who scattered outwards like ants. When the rotor stopped, the ants came back, led by Jed but with Zoë Lang close on his heels.

"How dare you?" Himself thundered to the fanatical lady.

She straightened, as if she would add inches to her stature. "This bothy," she insisted, "was given to the nation with the castle."

"It certainly was not," my uncle said furiously. "It comes under the heading of my private apartment."

No doubt the courts would decide, I thought, but meanwhile, the conservationists were making a mess of my home. There were holes in the ground everywhere. Beside each hole lay a little heap of empty Coke cans and other metal debris, which I'd buried to keep searchers busy. In the ruined section of bothy that held the trash bins, the corner with the old bread oven had been excavated and the oven left belly-up. In the carport end, the earth had more or less been plowed.

Staggered by the extent of the ruthless search, I went into my home to see what damage had been done inside.

To my surprise and relief, very little. The place looked tidy. Jed had brought back my pipes, and the picture, wrapped in its sheet, stood on the easel.

My mobile phone, which I now carried around out of habit, buzzed weakly in my hand. Because of the bad reception in the mountains, I could hear nothing in the receiver but a crackle.

I said loudly into the receiver, "Whoever you are, shout."

I heard an earful of crackle and one word, "Tobias."

I shouted unbelievingly, "Tobias?"

Crackle.

His faint voice said, "I've found it. I've found the money."

I couldn't believe it. I bellowed, "Where are you?"

Crackle. Crackle. "In Bogotá. In Colombia."

I still couldn't believe it. There was a sudden clearing of the static, and I could hear his voice plainly. "The money is all here. I found it by accident. The account here had three names on it, not just one or two. A person's name and two corporate names. I put them all on an application form by mistake, and it was like pressing a button. A door opened, and they are asking for my onwards directions. The money will be back in Reading next week."

"But I thought you went away for the weekend."

He laughed. "We were getting nowhere electronically. I went to Panama and the trail led to Bogotá."

"Tobe . . ."

"See you soon," he said.

The crackle came back. I switched off the telephone and felt my knees weakening.

After a while I took the sheet off the picture, and even to me the force of it filled the small room. The picture might not comfort, but one wouldn't forget it.

During the past few weeks I had painted that picture, the brewery's money had been found, and I had met Tobe and Margaret and Chris. I'd slept again with Emily and would stay married for as long as she wanted. I had come to a compact with Patsy.

There wasn't a great deal I would undo.

Shakily I went out of the bothy and walked to where Himself and

Zoë Lang were gesticulating at each other with none too gentle-manly fury. Himself stopped abruptly, alerted by my face.

"What is it?" he said.

"The money is found," I said.

"What money?" Zoë Lang demanded. But Himself didn't answer her. He stared at me alone, with the realization that what had been paid for had been miraculously delivered.

Zoë Lang, thinking that I had found some treasure or other within the bothy, strode off and disappeared inside.

"Tobias found the money in Bogotá," I said.

"Using the list?"

"Yes."

Himself's rejoicing was like my own—unexpressed except in the eyes, a matter of central warmth rather than triumphal whoops.

"Prince Charles Edward's hilt," he said, "is irrelevant."

We looked around at the determined searchers. None of them was now metal-detecting in the right place, but the prize had been within their reach. They had dug quite near it.

"Will they find it, Al?" my uncle asked.

"Would you mind it very much?"

"Of course I would. That woman would crow."

"If she perseveres long enough," I said, "she will. When I hid it, it was from burglars, not from a zealot with a mission. We could go away and not watch her gloat."

"Leave the battlefield!" He was outraged. "Defeat may be un-avoidable, but we will meet it with pride."

Spoken like a true Kinloch, I thought, and remembered bri-quettes flaming.

Zoë Lang came out of the bothy and walked towards us, still car-rying a metal detector—a long black stick with a white control box near the top and a flat white plate at the bottom. When she reached us, she ignored Himself and spoke with penetration to me alone.

"You will tell me the truth," she said in her old voice.

I made no reply.

She said, "I saw that picture. Did you paint it?"

"Yes."

"Is it you who has hidden the Kinloch hilt?"

"Yes."

"Is it here, in your bothy? And would I find it?"

I said, after a pause, "Yes . . . and yes."

My uncle's mouth opened in protest. Zoë Lang flicked him a glance and thrust the metal detector into his arms.

"You can keep the hilt," she said. "I'll look for it no longer."

Himself watched in bewilderment while she told one of her helpers to round up the searchers. "The hilt isn't here," she said. "We are going home."

We watched while they picked up their spades and pickaxes and metal detectors and drifted across to their minivan. When they'd gone, Zoë Lang said to Himself, "Don't you understand?"

"No, I frankly don't."

"He hasn't seen the picture," I said.

"Oh." She blinked. "What is it called?"

"Portrait of Zoë Lang."

A tear appeared in each of her eyes and ran down her wrinkled old cheeks. "I will not fight you," she said to me. "You have made me immortal."

HIMSELF looked long at the picture when Zoë Lang had driven away. "Mad Alexander, who messes about with paints . . ."

I smiled. "One has to be slightly mad to do almost anything, such as hiding a treasure."

"Yes," he said. "Where is it?"

"Well," I said, "when you gave me the hilt to hide, the first thing I thought about was metal detectors, because those things find gold easily. So I had to think of a hiding place safe from metal detectors, which is almost impossible unless you dig down six feet or more."

"So where is the hilt?"

"Everyone talks of buried treasure," I said, "so I didn't bury it." He stared.

I said, "The metal that most confuses a detector is aluminum foil.

So I wrapped the hilt in several layers of foil until it was a shapeless bundle about the size of a pillow. Then I took cotton duck—that's the stuff I paint the pictures on—and I primed it with coats of gesso to stiffen it and make it waterproof, and then I painted it with burnt-umber acrylic paint—a dark brown color and also waterproof."

"Go *on*," he said when I paused. "What then?"

"Then, all over the surface of the bundle, I superglued granite pieces." I waved a hand at the gray, stony ground of the plateau. "And then . . . Well, the more metal you offer to a detector, the more it gets confused, so I put the hilt bundle where it was more or less surrounded by metal. I glued it onto the mountain."

"You did *what?*"

"I glued it, granite to granite, and covered it with more granite pieces until you can't distinguish it by eye from the rock around it. I check it fairly often. It never moves."

He looked at the metal detector in his hands.

"Turn it upside-down," I said.

He did, waving the flat, round plate in the air. I switched it on and said formally, laughing, "My lord, follow me."

I walked not up onto the hill, as he obviously expected, but into my corrugated iron–topped carport.

The waving upside-down metal detector whined nonstop.

"If you go to the rear wall," I said, "and stand just there"—I pointed—"you will hear the indistinguishable noise of the Honor of the Kinlochs, which is up on the carport roof, where it joins the mountain. If you stand just there, the hilt of Prince Charles Edward Stuart's ceremonial sword will be straight above your head."

THE BURN MAN

...ING

Phillip Margolin

Up in flames . . .

That was how Peter Hale thought of his once promising law career. Nothing left but ashes. And no one to blame but himself.

So how could he hope, with his track record, to save a young man accused of a terrible crime?

If ever there was a trial by fire, this was going to be it.

Part One

1   ON THE day the gods chose for his destruction, Peter Hale ate his breakfast on the terrace of his condominium. The sun was just beginning its ascent above Portland, Oregon, and a blood-red aura surrounded the flat black silhouette of Mount Hood. A poet would have savored the sunrise for its beauty, but Peter enjoyed the advent of day for another reason. He believed that Galileo was wrong when he imagined the earth revolved around the sun. In his heart Peter knew that the sun revolved around him.

A crumb from his bran muffin fell onto Peter's gray Armani trousers. He flicked it off, then took a sip of the *caffè latte* he had brewed in the espresso machine that graced the marble counter of his designer kitchen. Peter pulled in a high five-figure salary as an associate at Hale, Greaves, Strobridge, Marquand and Bartlett. His salary at the law firm did not cover all his expenses, but he never had any trouble obtaining mortgages or car loans, since everyone knew he was the son of Richard Hale, one of the firm's founding partners and a past president of the Oregon State Bar. With all this, Peter was not a happy camper.

The living-room drapes moved. Peter looked over his shoulder. Priscilla padded across the terrace wearing only an oversized Trail-blazers T-shirt. She was a flight attendant with United. Peter had dated her on and off for a few months, but now Priscilla was talking about commitment and Peter was finding it difficult to avoid discussions of the dreaded C-word.

Priscilla bent down and kissed Peter on the cheek. Peter's head moved slightly, and she sensed the rebuff.

"Boy, are you a grouch this morning," Priscilla said.

"Yeah, well, I've got to get to court," he answered brusquely.

"How is the case going?"

"Great for my father. Not so good for me. Last night he informed me that he would be cross-examining all of the defendant's important witnesses and giving the closing argument."

"Oh, Peter, I'm so sorry. I know how much you've been counting on being lead counsel."

Peter shrugged. "I should have known better. My father just has to hog the glory."

When his father asked him if he wanted to work at Hale, Greaves, Peter had imagined a brief apprenticeship followed by a succession of major cases in which he would act as lead counsel, winning multimillion-dollar verdicts. It had taken four years to bring him to his senses. He had worked on *Elliot* v. *Northwest Maritime* from day one, and he knew more about the case than his father ever would. If his father would not let him be lead counsel in Elliot, he would seriously consider a new start with a new firm.

AT PRECISELY seven thirty a.m. Peter entered a small, windowless conference room on the fortieth floor of the Continental Trust Building. Here he and his father met before court every morning to review the witnesses who would testify that day. Peter's father still had the same massive build that helped him win second-team all-American honors in football in 1956. He practiced law the way he played sports—full steam ahead and take no prisoners. This morning he was striding back and forth in his shirtsleeves, a phone receiver plastered to his ear.

"When will you know?" he barked as Peter took several files from his attaché case. "No, damn it. That won't do. We're in the middle of the trial." Richard paused, listening intently. Then his craggy face turned scarlet with anger. "Look, Bill, I told you I needed the damn things two weeks ago. . . . Well, you better," Richard threatened, slamming down the phone.

"What's up?" Peter asked.

"Ned Schuster was in a car wreck," Richard answered. "He's supposed to testify today. Now Bill Ebling says they can't get the papers to court, because Schuster had the only copy."

Peter had no idea what his father was talking about. He glanced down at his files. There was one for each witness, and none were for a Ned Schuster. When he looked up, his father was leaning against the wall, his face as pale as chalk.

"Dad?" Peter asked, frightened. Richard grimaced in pain and began rubbing his breast with a clenched fist.

"Heart attack," Richard gasped as his knees sagged.

Peter raced around the conference table and caught him before he hit the floor.

"Help!" Peter screamed. A young woman stuck her head in the door. "Call 911, fast! My father is having a heart attack."

Richard's teeth were clenched, and his eyes were squeezed tight. "Hold on, Dad," Peter begged, holding his father's head in his lap. "The medics are coming."

Suddenly Richard's eyes opened, and he gasped, "Mistrial."

"Don't talk. Please, Dad. Save your strength."

Richard grabbed Peter's wrist. "Get . . . mistrial."

"Yes, I will," Peter promised just as two medics rushed into the room. The idea of Richard's dying sucked the air right out of Peter. His mother had died several years ago, but he saw his father as a mountain that would last forever. What if Richard didn't pull through? Then the medics were rushing out of the room with his father on a stretcher. Peter wanted to follow them to the hospital, but someone had to tell Mrs. Elliot what had happened and ask Judge Pruitt for a mistrial. Peter knew it would probably be hours before the doctors could tell him anything.

Peter stepped out of the conference room into the hall. It was empty. He was trembling and flushed. He went to the rest room and splashed cold water on his face. Then he looked at himself in the mirror. Peter had his father's intense blue eyes, but he also had his mother's smooth, high cheekbones. At five feet ten, one hundred and sixty pounds, he was slender and wiry with none of the bulk or height of his father.

When Peter had combed his brown blow-dried hair and straightened his tie, he felt back in control of himself. There was nothing he could do for his father now. Peter decided that he would quickly explain to the judge what had happened, then go to the hospital. Certainly, Pruitt would grant a mistrial under the circumstances.

The courthouse was only a few blocks away. As Peter rushed toward it, an unsettling thought suddenly occurred to him. Mrs. Elliot was suffering both physically and emotionally. If a mistrial was declared, she would have to suffer through a second trial. Peter paused inside the courthouse doors. Lawyers, litigants, policemen and clerks swirled around him, but he was oblivious to the crowd.

Did his father really want to abort the case when it was going so well? A lawyer's first duty was to his client. Why, then, had his father told him to ask for a mistrial? It took a moment for the answer to dawn on Peter. Richard Hale had no confidence in Peter's ability to take over the case.

Peter felt a sense of outrage. He squared his shoulders and strode toward the elevators. He would show his father just how good he was. He would win Elliot. Then he would place the multimillion-dollar judgment in front of Richard Hale.

ALVIN Pruitt ran his courtroom like a marine barracks. By the time Peter walked into court, he was ten minutes late, and the judge was furious. "I hope you have a good explanation for your tardiness, Mr. Hale."

"I do, sir. May I approach the bench?"

Pruitt frowned, then addressed the attorney representing Northwest Maritime and its driver. "Mr. Compton, you'd better get up here."

Peter paused at the plaintiff's table to say hello to his client. Nellie Elliot was a washed-out woman who had been worn down by poverty, the untimely death of her husband and the raising of five children, when life added a final insult by putting her in the path of a Northwest Maritime truck. Now she was a wheelchair-bound quadriplegic, and her lawsuit was worth millions.

"What's wrong?" Mrs. Elliot asked haltingly.

"I'll fill you in after I confer with the judge," Peter answered.

"Well?" Judge Pruitt asked impatiently.

"Your Honor," Peter said quietly, "my father had a heart attack just as we were leaving for court."

Lyle Compton looked stricken, and the judge's hard-bitten demeanor disappeared. Both men had known Richard Hale for more than twenty years and had the highest regard for him.

"Is he going to be all right?" Pruitt asked, genuinely concerned.

"I don't know."

"Well, I'll adjourn court, and we'll reconvene tomorrow so you can bring us up to date," the judge said.

"There's no reason to adjourn," Peter said, hoping he did not sound too anxious. "I won't be able to see my father for hours."

Judge Pruitt's brow furrowed. "You don't plan on continuing the trial, do you?" he asked.

"Oh, certainly. After all, our case is almost over, and it would be awfully hard for Mrs. Elliot to go through a second trial."

"Yes, but your father is lead counsel," the judge said.

Lyle Compton represented insurance companies for a living, but he was fair and sympathetic to plaintiffs. "Peter, it wouldn't be right to make you continue this case," he said. "Mrs. Elliot has a right to be represented by the best. If you move for a mistrial, I'm not going to object."

Peter kept control of his facial expression, but he was seething. That crack about Mrs. Elliot deserving the best . . . "I appreciate your concern, Mr. Compton, but I believe I know the ins and outs of Mrs. Elliot's lawsuit as well as my father. I'm prepared to continue."

"Is this what your client wants?" the judge asked.

"I haven't had an opportunity to confer with her."

Judge Pruitt looked troubled. "Well, why don't you take a few minutes to talk it over with Mrs. Elliot."

Peter felt a brief flash of elation. The trial was going to continue, and he was going to try it by himself.

"PLAINTIFF rests," Peter declared in a voice that conveyed to the jury the confidence he felt. His last two witnesses had been terrific, and Peter could not conceive of a juror who was not convinced that Nellie Elliot should be awarded millions to compensate her for the negligence of Northwest Maritime's driver.

"May I confer with Mr. Hale for a moment?" Lyle Compton asked Judge Pruitt.

"Why don't I send the jury out for lunch, Mr. Compton. As soon as you're finished talking to Mr. Hale, you can make any motions you may have. We'll start the defense case after lunch."

As he crossed the courtroom, Peter felt he was on top of the world. During a phone call to the hospital he had been assured that his father would make a full recovery, and he was on the brink of winning his first multimillion-dollar verdict.

"Peter," Compton said, "I'm prepared to recommend a settlement of one and a half million. I think that's a fair offer."

Peter's chest swelled. Compton was on the ropes, and he knew it. "Sorry, Lyle, but I don't think that's enough."

Compton looked down. "I probably shouldn't do this, but I don't want to take advantage of you. I feel compelled to tell you that you have problems with your case. Under the circumstances this is a very good offer."

Peter wanted to laugh in Compton's face. Problems with his case, indeed. "Lyle, I appreciate your concern, but it's no go."

As soon as the lawyers were back at their respective tables, Compton said, "I have a motion for the court."

"What is the basis for your motion?" Judge Pruitt asked.

"Your Honor, plaintiff's complaint alleges that Northwest Maritime is a corporation registered in the state of Oregon. It is in paragraph one of the complaint."

Peter looked down at the pleading that had been filed a year and a half before. Mrs. Elliot's complaint alleged that Northwest Maritime was a corporation doing business in Oregon, that a truck driven by one of its agents had caused her injury and that the driver was negligent in the way he drove.

"Our answer denied each and every allegation in the complaint," Compton went on. "When a defendant does that, it becomes plaintiff's duty to prove each and every allegation in the complaint. I submit that Mrs. Elliot has failed to prove the existence of the corporation. . . ."

Peter did not hear anything else. Suddenly he remembered Ned Schuster, the mystery witness who had been bringing the documents his father was so upset about. They must have been the documents that would prove Northwest Maritime was a corporation. That's why Richard had implored Peter to move for a mistrial.

"To dismiss the case against Northwest Maritime and grant a directed verdict for my client," Compton concluded.

Judge Pruitt looked very upset. He turned toward Peter, who was rereading the complaint as if, somehow, he could will the words to change. This point that Compton had raised was a technicality. Everyone knew Northwest Maritime was a corporation.

"Mr. Hale," the judge stated quietly, "I've been expecting this. The answer does deny the existence of the corporation. That does put the burden on you to prove your allegation."

"The . . . the driver, Mr. Hardesty. I believe he said . . ."

Judge Pruitt shook his head. "The question was never put to him."

"But Mrs. Elliot? What about her?" Peter asked pathetically. "If you dismiss the case against Northwest Maritime, only the driver will be left, and he doesn't have the money to pay for Mrs. Elliot's bills. You know Northwest Maritime is liable."

"Mr. Hale," Judge Pruitt said, "there is nothing I can do. If I deny Mr. Compton's motion, he will appeal, and the court of appeals will reverse me. My hands are tied."

Judge Pruitt turned toward Lyle Compton. "I'm granting your motion, Mr. Compton. A verdict will be directed for Northwest Maritime. The case against Mr. Hardesty will proceed."

Peter felt the wheels of Mrs. Elliot's wheelchair bumping against his chair. "What is it? What is it?" she asked, her voice trembling with fear. Everyone in the courtroom looked at Peter to hear the answer he would give to this poor crippled woman, who would not receive one cent for her anguish.

Peter could not speak. He could only sit, staring straight ahead, as his world went up in flames.

PETER staggered back to Hale, Greaves in a daze. Martin Strobridge was one of the state's most eloquent attorneys, but he was struck dumb by Peter's account of his attempt to try *Elliot* v. *Northwest Maritime*. When Strobridge recovered, he suspended Peter from all his duties until a committee reviewed his conduct.

Peter drove directly from his office to the hospital. He was allowed into the intensive care unit for only a few minutes. Richard's doctor assured Peter that his father's condition was not serious and he could go home in one week, but the shock of seeing his father hooked up to IV drips and blinking machinery was as great as the trauma of losing Elliot. The Richard Hale who stared at him with heavy-lidded eyes was old and frail. Peter made a few feeble attempts at conversation. Then he stumbled out of the room, grateful that the drugs his father had been given prevented him from thinking clearly enough to ask about the outcome of the Elliot case.

IN THE intervening days between his debacle and the inevitable summons to the Hale, Greaves offices, Peter hid in his apartment. Thankfully, Priscilla had flown off to some unknown destination, leaving him alone with his despair. Peter knew there would have to be some consequences for his actions, but he had created a fantasy in which he promised never to do anything so foolish again, and all was forgiven. On one of his visits to the hospital his father asked about Elliot, and Peter answered that everything was taken care of.

On the day he was finally summoned to his father's office, Peter knew immediately that someone had broken the news of his disgrace. The man who slumped behind the vast oak desk studied Peter with weary eyes. He had lost weight in the hospital, and his ruddy complexion was now pasty.

"Sit down, Peter," Richard said, indicating a high-backed leather chair. Peter sat.

After a moment Richard shook his head slowly and sadly. "You wanted to be lead counsel in a big case. That's why you did this, isn't it?"

Peter nodded.

"I know how much you resented me for denying you your chance, but I could not permit it." Richard sighed. He looked defeated. "I've tried to fool myself about you, Peter, but what you've done has forced me to face the truth. You are a highly intelligent young man, but you are lazy and self-centered, and you have never lived up to your potential. You didn't apply yourself in high school, so I had to use my pull to get you into a good university, where you partied for four years, achieving grades that were so low that I had to call in every chip I could find to get you into law school. Then I did the same thing to get you a job with this firm, hoping against hope that you would finally change into a responsible adult.

"This case was Mrs. Elliot's life. Your arrogance and your thoughtlessness have deprived that poor woman of the money she needs for medical care and for her children, and the saddest thing for me, as your father, is that I don't believe you care."

"Dad, I . . ." Peter started, but Richard shook his head.

"Naturally, under the circumstances, you can no longer remain here. As a favor to me, the firm will give you the option of resigning. That, however, is the last favor you will ever get from me."

Richard leaned forward. "It pains me to say this, but I must be blunt with you for your own good. I hope and pray that I'm doing the right thing. First, I've changed my will to disinherit you. Second, I will never give you another penny. From now on, you must live according to what you earn."

The words hit Peter like a hammer. Not one more penny, Richard had said. How would he meet his payments on the condo? How would he pay his debts? And the will. Disinherited.

"Dad, you can't do this. You can't cut me out of your life."

"No, I can't. I'm going to give you one last chance to make something of yourself."

Peter collapsed with relief. "Anything, Dad."

"If you can prove to me that you are a responsible adult, I will reconsider my decision to disinherit you. To that end, I've spoken to an old friend, Amos Geary. Amos and I played football together at Oregon State, and we were once partners. He has a practice in Whitaker, a small town in eastern Oregon, and a contract to provide indigent defense. His associate just quit. He's willing to give you the job. It pays seventeen thousand to start."

Peter could not believe his ears. He'd been to Whitaker to take depositions two years earlier. There were five streets in downtown Whitaker. When the wind blew, you couldn't see the buildings for the dust. If it wasn't for the college, there wouldn't be any life there at all.

"I won't do it," Peter said. He stood up. He'd had enough. "You call yourself a father. You were never a father to me. Mom raised me. You put in appearances and made rules. And it sure is no surprise to me that you think I'm a failure. You let me know how little you thought of me every chance you had. My grades were never good enough. I never put out enough at sports. Well, I'll show you. I'll get a job with another firm. I'll make partner, and to hell with Hale, Greaves."

Richard listened to Peter's tirade calmly. When Peter was through, Richard asked, "What firm will give you a job after the stunt you pulled? They all know what you did. You're the talk of the Portland legal community."

Peter's bravado disappeared. What his father said was true.

"You may not believe me," Richard said, "but I do love you. You have no idea how it hurts me to cast you out, my only child. But I have to do it for your sake. Go to Whitaker. Learn to stand on your own two feet and live within your means. Learn how to be a good lawyer. Learn to be a man."

2

THE sun was a blistering disk that baked the vast expanse of wasteland east of Whitaker. The young Oregon state trooper was grateful for his Stetson and fervently wished for a breeze that would cool him down and create a cloud of swirling dust thick enough to obscure what lay among the sagebrush halfway down the gully. When Dr. Guisti's vehicle appeared, the trooper was intentionally standing with his back to the young woman's body. The desert creatures had feasted on her, the elements had had their way with her, and something else had been at her. Some person whom the trooper had trouble thinking of as human.

A group of students on a geology field trip had found the body. They huddled together while members of the Major Crime Team took their statements. The Major Crime Team consisted of a detective from the small Oregon State Police office headquartered in Whitaker, the Whitaker County sheriff, a member of the Whitaker Police Department and police from neighboring Blaine and Cayuse counties. The team had designated Detective Jason Dagget of the Oregon State Police as the officer in charge.

Dagget had summoned Dr. Harold Guisti, who had practiced family medicine in Whitaker for thirty years and was contracted to perform autopsies in Whitaker, Blaine and Cayuse counties. The doctor's battered Range Rover bounced to a stop in front of Dagget, and Dr. Guisti stepped out.

"Where's she at?" Guisti asked.

"In the gully. We think she was killed somewhere else and dumped down there. She's naked, but there are no clothes. She was butchered, Harold. Plain and simple."

There had been another body discovered in an outcropping of rock two months earlier, naked and butchered. Guisti believed the weapon was a hatchet of some kind. He was hoping he would not come to the same conclusion when he examined this young female, because he did not want to think about what that would mean for the people of Whitaker, Cayuse and Blaine counties.

SURROUNDING the city of Whitaker was farmland made green by irrigation systems that tapped into the Camas River, but beyond the farms hot, dusty winds blew tumbleweeds across vast flatlands. As Peter drove, he felt his spirit burning up and crumbling slowly to gray ash, and he entered Whitaker as empty as the arid land that encircled it.

Peter spent his first night in Whitaker at the Riverview Motel, which was clean and quiet and actually had a view of the river. After breakfast he walked from the motel to the offices of Amos Geary. He was exhausted from tossing and turning all night as his emotions shifted from boiling rage at the injustices of life to fear that he might have lost forever the love of his father.

The walk took Peter through Wishing Well Park, which ran the length of the town between High Street and the Camas River. There was a wistful beauty in the slow-moving Camas, but Peter found the town as dry and uninteresting as the wasteland that surrounded it.

City center started at High and First, where the courthouse stood. Peter turned up First Street to Main. Running parallel to Main Street was Broad Street. Elm, the street farthest from the river, started commercial, then curved through a pleasant, tree-shaded, residential section until it arrived at the campus of Whitaker State College.

On both sides of Main were old two- and three-story brick buildings. Peter glanced up and saw AMOS J. GEARY, ATTORNEY-AT-LAW painted in flaking gold letters on a second-floor window. Peter found a narrow doorway between a beauty salon and a coffee shop and climbed to the second floor.

The hall at the top of the stairs was dark and musty. Geary's name and profession were painted on a door to the left of the stairwell. Inside, a middle-aged woman with hennaed hair was sitting behind a desk working at a word processor. She looked up and stared at Peter through glasses with thick black plastic rims.

"I'm Peter Hale. I've an appointment with Mr. Geary for nine."

The woman eyed him suspiciously. "You're the young man who's going to work here, aren't you?"

"Yes, ma'am."

"Well, take a seat. Mr. Geary's not in just yet. But he'll be along any minute. He has court at ten." She went back to her work.

Peter sat on a couch made of cracked red imitation leather and picked up a nine-month-old magazine. He had just finished skimming it when the door to the law office opened.

Amos Geary's face was a beet-red matrix of busted blood vessels. What was left of his unkempt hair was a dingy gray, and he had a shaggy walrus mustache. Geary was as tall as Peter's father and looked twice as heavy. His stomach sagged over his belt, and the buttons on his shirt looked as if they were about to pop. He was wearing an awful aquamarine tie spotted with stains that matched those on his rumpled brown suit.

Geary studied the young man from the open doorway. "Peter Hale, I presume?" He extended his right hand, and Peter gave it a light touch. "How was the drive?"

"Fine," Peter responded, flinching slightly as Geary's alcohol-and-mouthwash-drenched breath hit him full in the face.

"Don't forget you have court at ten," the secretary reminded Geary.

"Okay, Clara," Geary answered, turning his back on Peter and trudging down a hall.

"Follow me," Geary called over his shoulder. Peter trailed his new boss to a poorly lit office that stank of stale smoke. On one wall, among the diplomas and certificates attesting to Geary's admission to various state and federal bars, was a photo of the 1956 Oregon State football team. Geary caught Peter looking at it.

"I'm in the front, kneeling down. Your father's behind me on the right. I opened holes for him for four years, and I've got cleat marks on my back to prove it," Geary said with a brusque laugh.

Peter forced a smile. Then he noticed a framed law degree on the wall. "You went to Harvard?" he said, trying not to sound incredulous.

"Class of '59. Does that surprise you?"

"Well . . . Uh, no," Peter said, flushing because Geary had read him so easily.

"It should. A Harvard man stuck out here in the boonies. But then, you're stuck here with me, aren't you?"

This time Peter flushed from anger.

Geary slumped onto his desk chair. "Your father told me everything when he asked me to hire you. To be honest, I was against it. Not because I was unsympathetic to Dick's attempts to save your soul. I just didn't want to put my practice at risk."

"Then why did you agree to hire me?" Peter asked resentfully.

Geary leaned back and studied Peter without rancor. "I owe your father a great debt. Supervising your stay in purgatory will take a little off the top. But I made it clear that I'll drop you like a hot coal if you screw up. Now, let me tell you the facts of life. I write wills; I handle divorces. Then there's crime. About fifteen years ago the state decided to contract out indigent defense, and I was firstest with the mostest. I've had the contract for Whitaker, Blaine and Cayuse counties ever since, and I aim to keep it. That's where you come in. You're gonna become the Perry Mason of Whitaker County."

Peter was gripped by deep depression. He had not gone to law school to muck around in the swamp called criminal law. "I hope my father didn't misrepresent my qualifications, Mr. Geary," he said hesitantly. "I've never handled a criminal case."

"Peter, we're not talking crime of the century. We're talking shoplifts, driving while stupid. Your dad told me about some of the cases you've handled. I'd say that you're probably one of the most experienced attorneys in town. Read through the case files on your desk. If you have any questions, try not to bother me with them. I'm very busy." Geary grinned maliciously. "Welcome to the real world, son."

WHITAKER State College was founded as an agricultural school in 1942 but had since developed a decent liberal arts program. The older, ivy-covered brick buildings surrounded a quadrangle at the center of the campus. A school of business, the football stadium, an athletic facility and a block of two-story brick dormitories were among the newer-looking buildings that spread out from the hub.

Shortly before ten p.m., evening classes ended, and the faculty and off-campus students emptied into a large parking area. Christopher Mammon drove a dull green Chevy when he did not want to attract attention. Tonight the Chevy was parked as inconspicuously as possible on the edge of the lot because there were two kilos of cocaine in Ziploc bags under the driver's seat.

The Chevy was a normal-sized car, but Mammon was so massive that there was barely room in the front seat for Kevin Booth's flabby two hundred pounds. Booth looked over his shoulder through the rear window, as he had several times since Mammon parked. "Where is she? She said nine forty-five."

"Relax, man." Mammon's eyes were closed. He sounded bored.

Booth could not believe how calm Mammon was with this much dope in the car. "If this deal gets blown, Rafael is gonna be really pissed," Booth said. He could not decide who scared him more, Mammon or the slender man with the lifeless eyes who supplied Booth with cocaine.

"That's why you should be glad I'm dealing with your buddy this time."

"But what if the girl doesn't show?"

"She'll be here." Mammon lifted his huge head from the head-rest. "She knows what would happen to her if she let me down."

Booth imagined the things Mammon would do to punish the blonde if she crossed them. Then he imagined what Rafael might do to him if the sale did not go through. One of Rafael's mules had dropped off the two kilos at Booth's house early this evening. Booth's part in the transaction was turning over the cocaine to Mammon and then giving the thirty thousand the girl was bring-ing to another of Rafael's mules. Objectively, Booth was only a go-between, but Booth had vouched for Mammon.

"What if she goes to the cops?" Booth asked anxiously.

Mammon sighed. He switched on the dome light. Then he took a mirror and a razor blade from the map holder on the driver's door and handed them to Booth. Mammon opened one of the Ziploc bags and dipped a slender coke spoon into the bag. He held the spoon over the mirror. "If you promise to shut up, Kevin, I'll let you have a little nose candy."

Booth leaned forward greedily as the white powder cascaded onto the mirror. Booth separated the small mound of powder into several thin lines, rolled a ten-dollar bill tight, inserted it into his nostril, then sucked up the coke and leaned back to enjoy the rush. Mammon returned the razor blade and the mirror to the map holder and turned off the dome light. He started to close his eyes when a voice next to his left ear said, "Freeze," and he found him-self staring into the barrel of a gun.

PETER spent his second morning in Whitaker looking for a place to live. After lunch he went to the office. As soon as he opened the door, the secretary thrust a case file at him.

"Mr. Geary will be out all day. He wants you to interview this man at the jail. It's a block from the courthouse."

Peter opened the file. On the right side was an order appointing Amos Geary to represent Christopher Eugene Mammon. Beneath the order was a complaint filed by the district attorney charging Mammon with possession of cocaine.

Peter cleared his throat. "Uh, Clara, what exactly am I supposed to do with Mr. Mammon?"

"How am I supposed to know? I just do the typing here, Mr. Hale. Didn't they teach you what to do in law school?"

THE narrow concrete interview room in the Whitaker jail was about the length of a dog run. Peter sat on a metal folding chair in front of a rickety wooden table, nervously waiting to meet his first criminal client. He stood when the door opened. A guard stepped aside, and all the light from the hall was obliterated by the man who filled the doorway.

"Knock when you want me," the guard said.

Peter heard the lock on the thick metal door snap shut, trapping him inside with Christopher Mammon. Peter was used to large men. His father was large; Amos Geary was large. But Christopher Mammon was bizarre. Curly black hair hung down over his high, flat forehead and cascaded over his massive shoulders. A short-sleeved orange jumpsuit was stretched taut across his gargantuan chest. Peter could see snake and panther tattoos rippling along Mammon's forearms and biceps whenever he moved. His cold blue eyes were narrow and focused, like a predator's.

"Good afternoon, Mr. Mammon. I'm Peter Hale, the attorney the court appointed to represent you," Peter said, holding out one of Amos Geary's business cards.

Mammon examined the card, then examined Peter. "If you're my lawyer, why isn't your name on this card?"

"Well, actually, the court appointed Amos Geary. He'll represent you if we go to trial. I work with him. Mr. Geary is away this afternoon. He wanted me to conduct the first interview. Why don't you sit down and we can get started."

Peter sat down and took out a pen. Mammon remained standing. Clara had placed an interview form in the file. "There's some background information I'll need."

"Can I see that?" Mammon asked, pointing at the form.

Peter handed the form to Mammon, who ripped it into tiny pieces.

"If Geary's my lawyer, I'll talk to Geary and not some flunky."

It suddenly occurred to Peter there was only a flimsy wooden table separating him from a very dangerous wild animal. "Yes, well, I'm an experienced attorney, and anything you tell me is confidential," Peter told Mammon.

"Just how experienced are you, Peter?" Mammon asked.

"I've been a lawyer for four years."

"And how many criminal cases have you handled?"

"Well, none, but I've tried many complex legal matters—"

Mammon leaned across the table until his face was inches from Peter's. "You just lied to me, didn't you, Peter?"

Peter turned pale. All he could manage was, "I . . . I . . ."

Mammon held him with his eyes for a moment. Then he went to the door and pounded on it. The locks snapped open, and Mammon walked out of the room.

PETER'S only other visit to Whitaker had been spent humiliating and browbeating a local attorney and his client. After the deposition Peter had celebrated at the Stallion, a bar popular with the students at Whitaker State, where he met a nurse named Rhonda something, whom he fascinated with his description of the devastation visited on his adversary. Since the Stallion provided the only good memory Peter had of Whitaker, it was here that he ran as soon as he escaped the jail.

What am I going to do? Peter asked himself as he started on his second Jack Daniel's. He could not endure another encounter with a Mammon-like individual. But what was his alternative? Being a lawyer was all Peter knew, and no one except Amos Geary would offer him a job after the Elliot fiasco.

"Peter Hale?" A tall, solidly built man in a business suit was staring down at him. "Steve Mancini," the man said. "We went to law school together."

"Right!" Peter said, breaking into a smile.

"Mind if I sit down?" Mancini asked as he slid into the booth.

"Not at all. What are you drinking?"

"No, no. It's on me. I'm half owner of this joint." He signaled for a waitress.

"You live in Whitaker?" Peter asked incredulously.

"And practice law here. But what are you doing in town? I thought you worked at your father's firm. Are you out on a case?"

"Uh, yes and no," Peter said. There was no way he was going to tell Mancini the truth, but what could he say?

"There you are," a woman said, and Peter looked over his shoulder into the hazel eyes of a beautiful brunette. Standing next to her was a rugged-looking man with the broad shoulders and thick forearms of a laborer. He had curly black hair, a bushy mustache, and he was grinning widely at Steve.

Mancini stood and kissed the woman; then he took her hand. "Pete, this is my fiancée, Donna Harmon, and her brother, Gary."

A law school memory of Steve Mancini and a pretty blond wife made Peter frown for a moment, but he caught himself and said, "Hey, congratulations. When is the wedding?"

"In a few weeks," Mancini answered as he ushered Donna into the booth and sat beside her. Gary slid in next to Peter.

"Do you have my football tickets?" Gary asked Mancini.

"Here they are, buddy," Mancini said, pulling out an envelope.

Gary's face lit up, and he started to grab for the tickets.

"What do you say first, Gary?" Donna asked gently.

Gary looked confused for a second, and Peter examined him more closely. The guy looked normal, but he was acting like a kid. It dawned on Peter that Gary was retarded.

Gary's face broke into a grin, and he said, "Thanks, Steve."

"Hey, guy, you're welcome." Mancini gave Gary the tickets. "So, Pete," he asked, "what brings you to Whitaker?"

Peter had hoped that Mancini had forgotten the question, but the arrival of Donna and Gary Harmon had given him time to invent an answer. "I'm working for Amos Geary."

"Geary?" Mancini's face registered disapproval. "I thought you were aiming for a partnership in a megafirm."

"Yeah. That's what I thought. I was working in my father's firm.

But I got tired of the rat race, and Dad's an old friend of Amos."

Mancini forced a smile.

"How did you get to Whitaker?" Peter asked.

"Didn't you see the trophy case when you walked in?"

"Well, no, I . . ."

"Then check it out when you leave. In my senior year I quarter-backed the Stallions to the NCAA Division Two title, Whitaker State's only national championship in any sport. In this town I'm an immortal. After graduation most of the class gravitated to the big city, but I've got a great practice here. I'm big in the chamber of commerce, and," Mancini added, puffing up his chest, "my ship may soon be sailing into the dock."

"Oh?"

"Yeah. The city of Bend has the inside track on the next Winter Olympics. I'm involved with some guys who are building condos there."

"Have you found a place to live?" Donna asked.

Peter shook his head. "I'm still at the Riverview Motel."

"We can't have that," Donna said, turning to her fiancé. "Can't you help him, Steve?"

"I think so. I own a few rental properties."

"I've got my own house," Gary said proudly.

"Gary just moved into his own home, and he's working as a janitor at the college," Donna explained. "It's his first job."

"Oh, yeah," Peter said, trying to be sociable. "Do you like it?"

Gary frowned and considered his answer. "It's hard, but Mr. Ness says I'm doing good. He says I work real hard."

"Well, that's great," Peter replied lamely.

"I think I might have a place for you," Mancini said. "It's furnished and only three quarters of a mile from town, not too far from my house." He took out a business card and wrote an address on it.

Donna looked at her watch. "We should go. Mom's expecting us."

"It was good seeing you," Mancini told Peter. "Give me a call after you look at the house."

Mancini followed Donna and her brother out of the bar, and Peter ordered a pitcher of beer and a burger with everything. He felt better. At least he knew someone in town.

When he finished eating, he suddenly remembered the last name of the nurse he had spent the evening with the last time he had been in Whitaker. It was Kates. Rhonda Kates. He decided to go back to the motel and give her a call.

On the way out, Peter looked in the trophy case. There was Mancini's helmet and cleats, a program from the championship game and a photo of Mancini. Fame and fortune, Peter thought wistfully. Steve Mancini seemed to have it all.

ON FRIDAY morning of his second week in town, Peter awoke in the house he was renting from Steve Mancini. He dressed for court and ate breakfast in his postage stamp–size kitchen. Then he walked to the courthouse to watch Amos Geary handle the preliminary hearing in Christopher Mammon's case. So far Geary had not let Peter handle anything by himself, but Peter was starting to realize that criminal law was not that difficult.

Criminal complaints in felony cases were lodged in the district court, but only a circuit court had jurisdiction to try a felony. There were two ways to change the jurisdiction of a felony case to the circuit court: A grand jury could meet in secret and hand down an indictment, or, as in this case, a district court judge could hold a preliminary hearing in open court and order the case bound over to circuit court.

The four-story courthouse was the tallest building in Whitaker, and it stood at the end of High Street across from Wishing Well Park. Peter walked up to the second-floor courtroom and found Steve Mancini standing in the hall talking to the cutest thing Peter had seen since moving to Whitaker. Peter figured her for five two at most. She had curly red hair, freckles that made her look like a high schooler and a body that was definitely not adolescent.

Mancini waved Peter over. "You're here to help Amos with the prelim, aren't you?"

"Yeah. He wanted me to sit in," Peter said.

"Then you should meet Becky O'Shay, Whitaker's most vicious prosecutor and deputy D.A. Becky, this is Peter Hale."

"Pleased to meet you, Peter," O'Shay said. She extended a tiny, delicate hand.

"Are you involved in this case?" Peter asked Mancini.

"I'm representing Kevin Booth, the codefendant."

O'Shay entered the courtroom and walked to the prosecution table. When Peter tore his eyes from her, he saw Christopher Mammon sitting with Amos Geary at the defense table. To Mammon's right was Kevin Booth. Mancini's client was a mess. His jumpsuit sagged on him, his dirty black hair was uncombed, and pimples dotted his pale skin. The contrast between Booth and Christopher Mammon was amazing. Mammon looked as if he were going to fall asleep, while Booth could not keep his hands still. Peter edged behind Mammon and Geary and sat at the end of the table.

The bailiff rapped his gavel, and district court judge Brett Staley, a balding man with thick glasses, ascended to the bench. Becky O'Shay told Judge Staley that Earl Ridgely, the D.A., was on vacation and she was handling the preliminary hearing. Then she called her first witness, Jeffrey Loudhawk.

A dark-complexioned man with straight black hair was sworn in. He was wearing the uniform of a Whitaker State campus security guard. After some preliminary questions O'Shay asked Loudhawk if he had seen either of the defendants on the evening of May 22.

"Yes, ma'am. I saw both of them. I was patrolling around ten o'clock when I noticed the defendants seated in a car at the far end of the parking lot."

"What was it that attracted you to these two gentlemen?"

"The dome light came on, and I was able to see into the car. When I came closer, I saw a rolled ten-dollar bill in Mr. Booth's right nostril. I know, from my narcotics training, that addicts use rolled bills as straws to assist them in snorting cocaine."

"What did you do then?"

"I radioed for assistance. Ron Turnbull, a fellow security guard, arrived, and we approached the car. I went to Mr. Booth's side, and Officer Turnbull went to the driver's side."

"Mr. Mammon was driving?"

"Yes, ma'am."

"What happened next?"

"Officer Turnbull told Mr. Mammon to freeze, and I did the same with Mr. Booth. I looked across Mr. Booth and saw a transparent plastic Ziploc bag filled with a white powder halfway under Mr. Mammon's seat on the driver's side."

"Did you see anything else associated with narcotics use?"

"Yes, ma'am. I saw a mirror in a map holder on the driver's side. I know, again from my training, that users of cocaine will prepare the drug on a mirror before snorting it."

"What happened after you saw the powder and the mirror?"

"I asked Mr. Booth what the powder was. He said he didn't know. I accused him of snorting cocaine, and he denied it. I placed both men under arrest and radioed the Whitaker police for assistance. When the police arrived, I turned over the prisoners, two bags of cocaine, the mirror and the rolled bill."

"Nothing further."

Geary asked a few perfunctory questions of the witness, but his heart was not in it. Then it was Steve Mancini's turn.

"Officer Loudhawk, how far from Mr. Mammon's car were you when you saw Mr. Booth with the bill in his nose?"

"It's hard to say. About six car lengths."

"Out of curiosity, was a test administered to Mr. Booth to determine whether or not there was cocaine present in his blood?"

"Not that I know of."

"No further questions."

Miles Baker, a chemist with the Oregon State Police, explained how he determined that the substance in the two bags was cocaine. Geary did not cross-examine.

"Mr. Baker," Mancini said, "several other items were turned over to you, including a ten-dollar bill and a mirror. Did you test the bill and the mirror for traces of cocaine?"

"No, I did not."

"Thank you. No further questions."

"The state rests," O'Shay said.

"Any witnesses for the defense?" the judge asked.

Geary shook his head.

"No witnesses, Your Honor," Mancini said, "but I have a motion for the court. The state has accused Mr. Booth of possession of a controlled substance. Now, there was a controlled substance under Mr. Mammon's seat in a car registered to Mr. Mammon, but there was no evidence connecting Mr. Booth with that controlled substance. Officer Loudhawk never said he saw Mr. Booth with cocaine, and nothing was done to determine whether Mr. Booth had ingested cocaine, although this could have been accomplished with a simple blood test. I move for dismissal of the charges against Mr. Booth."

Judge Staley frowned. "What do you have to say to Mr. Mancini's argument, Miss O'Shay?"

Peter gazed at the prosecutor. He was certain she would respond with a brilliant argument. Instead, all she managed was, "Mr. Mancini is being ridiculous, Your Honor. It's obvious that Mr. Booth was snorting cocaine. He had the bill up his nose."

"That's not illegal conduct in this state, no matter how disgusting it may be. No, I have to grant Mr. Mancini's motion."

Peter studied Christopher Mammon, expecting him to go insane with rage because his codefendant was free, but he sat passively as Judge Staley addressed Steve Mancini's client.

"Mr. Booth, don't think you have fooled me one bit. I know full well you possessed and used cocaine on the evening of your arrest, but one of our most fundamental rules of criminal procedure is that the state must prove its case with evidence, not conjecture. So I am going to dismiss the case against you. But you better not come before me again, young man, or I will make certain that you go to prison for a long, long time."

AMOS GEARY TOOK A LONG drag on a cigarette and trudged toward his office. "What did you learn this morning, Mr. Hale?" the old lawyer wheezed.

"Uh, well, I saw how a preliminary hearing works."

Geary shook his head. "You saw an aberration. Ninety-nine times out of one hundred the judge binds over the defendant. I don't know what got into Brett this morning."

"Steve was pretty amazing. I didn't know he was that good."

"You know Mancini?"

"We went to law school together."

"Watch yourself. Mancini's an opportunist. Has he suggested that you invest in Mountain View?"

"Is that the condominium deal?"

Geary nodded. "He's tried to get every lawyer in town to invest, except me. He knows I don't have any money."

"Steve seems to think those condos will make him rich."

"Oh, they will. *If* Bend is awarded the Winter Olympics. I just hope he doesn't sucker Jesse Harmon into putting up some money."

The name sounded vaguely familiar. "Who is Jesse Harmon?"

"He's one of the most successful farmers in the county. Mancini wasn't divorced more than a month when he put a move on Donna Harmon, Jesse's daughter."

They walked on together in silence. Peter was not surprised that Geary was trashing Steve, especially after the way Mancini had shown him up in court.

Peter's thoughts turned to Becky O'Shay. He wondered if she was seeing anyone. "How long has Becky been a prosecutor?"

Geary stopped in mid-stride, then shook his head in disgust. "Forget it. Stay away from Rebecca O'Shay."

"What's wrong with her?"

"Did you see that Tom Cruise movie *Interview with the Vampire*?"

"Sure. Great flick."

"Remember the little girl vampire?"

"Yes."

"Rebecca O'Shay was the model."

Part Two

3 HIS mouth was dry, and he could barely breathe. She was so beautiful—a goddess with long blond hair. He wanted to close his eyes and stop his ears to make time move faster, to bring her to the moment where she would take off her clothes.

He heard a sound on the path that went past the girls' dormitory. Instantly he was down, hidden by the bushes. Two girls passed, chatting. When they were gone, he rose up slowly, until his eyes were level with the sill.

Where was she? He could not see her. Then the bathroom door opened, and his heart stopped. Her jeans were off. She was tossing them onto the bed. Her legs were bare. She walked to the chest of drawers and took out a shorty nightgown.

He had been here so long, waiting forever, worshipping her while she studied. Praying so hard to see her naked. And now, as he peeked into the room, she began unbuttoning her blouse slowly. The moment was now. Now!

Suddenly a deep voice said, "Well, well. What have we got here?" and fear and shame engulfed him.

RHONDA Kates was dying to see the romantic comedy playing at the Whitaker Cinema, so she and Peter caught the early show, then ate dinner at an Italian restaurant on Elm. Rhonda lived just on the other side of the campus near the hospital. It was a beautiful June evening, and they walked the mile or so to the theater and back. Rhonda had to get up early, so Peter only stayed for a while. He was on his way home when he heard a commotion. A small crowd was watching two men struggle in the bushes under a window of the women's dormitory. Peter pushed his way to the front and saw Jeffrey Loudhawk, the campus security guard who had testified at the preliminary hearing, wrestling with a man who was wailing incoherently. Loudhawk jerked the man around, and Peter recognized Gary Harmon.

"What's going on?" Peter asked just as Gary made it halfway to his knees. Loudhawk was a large, muscular man, but it took all his strength to bring Gary back down to the ground.

"Gary, don't fight. You'll only get hurt," Peter said.

"You know this guy?" Loudhawk gasped.

"He's Gary Harmon. What'd he do?"

"I caught him peeping in a girl's room."

"Don't tell Mama," Gary pleaded, his voice rising.

"You're Jeffrey Loudhawk, right?" Peter asked. "I heard you testify at that prelim the other day. The drug bust."

"Right."

"I don't suppose you could cut Gary any slack? He's retarded. I'm sure he didn't mean anything by what he did."

"It's not my call. I radioed for backup before I arrested him. You'll have to work it out with the Whitaker police."

"Could you wait to write this up until I talk to them? Gary works at the college. If you report him, it will cost him his job."

"It should," Loudhawk answered indignantly.

"Well, yeah. Normally. But he's slow. Like a kid."

Loudhawk took a hard look at his prisoner, who was weeping and moaning. "Okay. I'll wait to see what the police say."

Peter rushed home, then drove to the police station. When he arrived, Gary was being interrogated. Peter told the officer at the desk that he was Gary's lawyer, and he was escorted back to the interrogation room. The door was opened by Sergeant Dennis Downes, a jovial young officer who wore his hair in a crew cut. He was rolypoly, which made some people believe he was soft, and he always smiled, which led some people to think he was dumb. Downes did not try to dispel either impression. As a policeman, he found it was an advantage to have people underestimate him.

The only furniture in the interrogation room was a long wooden table and a few straight-backed chairs. A large two-way mirror covered a section of one wall. Gary Harmon was seated at the table across from a second uniformed officer.

Downes dismissed the other officer. When the door closed, Downes asked, "Just what is your interest in this, Mr. Hale?"

"I'm a friend of Steve Mancini. We went to law school together. Steve is engaged to Gary's sister. I just happened to be on campus when Gary was arrested, and I recognized him."

"Well, Gary here is lucky he has you as a friend. I should throw the book at him, but I'm gonna let him go. Gary's folks are well respected. I sure don't want to embarrass them." Downes turned his attention to Gary. "And you shouldn't either. You hear me?"

"Yes, sir, Sergeant Downes. I'm real sorry." Gary's eyes watered. "I'll never, never do that again. I promise."

Downes turned to Peter. "You better have a talk with this boy. If this happens again, he'll be seeing the inside of a cell."

GARY opened the front door of his tiny cottage and turned on the lights. The living room was neat. He cleaned it every day.

"You want a Coke?" Gary asked, as his mother had taught him.

"Sure," Peter answered. In the kitchen he found a "To Do" list taped to the refrigerator door.

"Your mom write that up?" Peter asked, pointing to the list.

"Yeah. Mama didn't want me to forget nothing important." Gary suddenly thought of something. "Are you gonna tell my mom what I done?"

Gary seemed pretty contrite. It looked as though Downes had done a good job of scaring him.

"I should tell your folks, but I'm not going to." Peter took a sip of his drink. "How would you feel if you found some guy peeping in your sister's window? You wouldn't want that, would you?"

"No." Gary hung his head.

"You have to think about things like that."

"I will, honest."

Peter finished his drink. "I'm going now. We both have work in the morning, and we need our sleep. Do I have your word that this won't happen again?"

"Never. I swear."

After Peter drove away, Gary put the soda cans in the garbage. He checked the "To Do" list and was pleased to see he had done everything he was supposed to.

GARY Harmon always felt important when he went to the Stallion because Steve Mancini was one of the owners. The bartenders, the waiters and the waitresses knew Steve was his friend, and they treated him well. This Friday night Gary felt even more special than usual because Steve and Donna were getting married tomorrow and he was the best man. Arnie Block, one of the bartenders, had given him a free drink and so had several other people. In fact, Gary was drunk when he spotted Kevin Booth, who was frantically scanning the crowded tables for Christopher Mammon, who had ordered Kevin to meet him at the Stallion at ten thirty.

Gary and Kevin Booth were both graduates of Eisenhower High. Gary remembered Booth as one of the few students who would talk to him, forgetting that it was because Gary was one of the few students that Booth could bully.

"Hey, Kevin," Gary yelled over the music of a raucous band. Booth stopped. "It's me, Gary Harmon."

Booth had no time to waste on Gary, but all the tables were taken, and he had no idea how long Mammon would be.

"How's it going?" Booth said, sitting down.

"It's going great! Do you know Steve Mancini?"

"Sure. He's my lawyer. Why?"

"Steve is my friend. He's gonna marry my sister tomorrow."

"Congratulations, man," Booth said. He looked toward the door just as Mammon walked in. Kevin stood up and waved him over.

"Hey, my man," Mammon said, clapping Booth on the shoulder as he sat down. "Who's your friend?"

"Oh, this is Gary Harmon, a guy I knew in high school."

"It's nice meeting your friends, Kevin," Mammon said sarcastically, "but we have business to discuss."

"Do you know Steve Mancini?" Gary asked with a big smile. "He's marrying my sister tomorrow. I'm gonna be the best man."

"Why should I care?" Mammon snapped.

"It's okay, Chris," Booth said nervously. Then he whispered, "Gary's a retard. He don't mean anything."

Mammon thought about that for a moment. He had to get rid of Harmon, and he had an idea.

Mammon whispered in Gary's ear, "Look over my shoulder at the blonde at the end of the bar near the door."

Gary turned slowly. A slender woman with straight shoulder-length blond hair, wearing tight jeans and a Whitaker State T-shirt with a rearing stallion on it, was talking to a short brunette.

"Gary, that woman has been giving you the eye since I sat down."

"Nah," Gary said nervously. "It wouldn't be me."

"Kevin, did you notice that blonde giving Gary the eye?"

"Yeah, Gary," Booth said enthusiastically. "She's hot for you."

Mammon put his arm around Gary's shoulder. "You do know how to pick up girls, don't you?"

"Sure," Gary answered, too embarrassed to tell the truth.

"Then you know you have to go down there and ask her if she wants a beer. Now, she'll say no at first. You insist, though. Women like guys who won't take no for an answer. Be forceful."

Mammon gave Gary a push toward the bar. Gary walked over slowly. He was sick with worry, but he could not disgrace himself by turning back.

There was an empty space next to the blonde. Gary stood there for a moment, but the girl did not seem to notice him. Finally he tapped her on the shoulder. The girl stopped in midsentence and turned toward him.

"Can—can I get you a beer?" Gary managed.

The girl flashed a smile. "No thanks," she answered, making it clear that she didn't like being hit on. She turned back to her friend. Gary remembered what Chris said about being persistent. He tapped the girl's shoulder again, a little harder.

The girl turned around. She looked angry. "What do you want?"

"I like you, and I want to buy you a beer."

"Thank you, but I'm talking to someone, okay?"

"Ch-Chris said you want me to buy you a beer." Gary pointed toward the table where Mammon and Booth were doubled up with laughter. The girl saw them and figured out what was going on.

"Go tell your friends they were wrong and leave me alone."

"You—you don't like me?" Gary asked, hurt and confused.

"Are you an idiot?" the girl asked. "Didn't I just tell you—"

Gary's hand shot out and grabbed the girl's T-shirt. "I ain't no idiot," he yelled. "Don't call me no names."

The girl staggered backward. "Let me go," she screamed as she tried to pull out of Gary's grip. Gary yanked her toward him.

Arnie Block, the closest bartender, turned when he heard the girl scream. At the end of the bar farthest from the front door, another attractive blonde in a Whitaker State T-shirt and jeans was sitting across from Dave Thorne, the other bartender. The girl was wearing a silver medallion around her neck. It had a cross embossed on it. The girl fingered the medallion while she sipped a beer. Thorne was working on a drink order when Arnie shouted to him.

"Dave, call Steve. Tell him to get over here."

Dave grabbed the phone on the shelf behind him and made the call. When he hung up, he noticed that the blonde with the medallion was watching two men who were walking toward the back door that led into the rear parking area. One of the men was big and flabby. The other looked like a professional wrestler. The girl looked very frightened, but Thorne had no time to think about her, because Gary was shaking the other girl by both shoulders.

"Say I ain't no idiot," Gary screamed, "or I'll kill you."

Arnie Block reached across the bar and grabbed Gary around the neck. "Let her go, Gary. Can't you see she's scared?"

Gary looked at the girl. She was near tears and very frightened. Gary released her, and she staggered against the bar.

Dave Thorne pushed through the crowd. "I called for Steve," he said. "You'll be lucky if you don't get arrested."

Gary's eyes widened as he remembered what would happen to him if he was arrested again. He would go to jail, and it would be in the paper. Mama would read it, and it would kill her.

"Dave," Block said, turning away from Gary, "take care of this lady. Make sure she's all right."

When Block turned back, Gary was streaking for the door.

Dave Thorne took the blonde and her friend to an empty booth. Arnie brought over a glass of brandy just as Steve Mancini walked in. "What happened?" Mancini asked the bartender.

"Gary got a little out of hand with that girl," Arnie said, pointing. "He took off as soon as I said you were coming over."

"I'm gonna talk to her," Mancini told Block. He walked over to the booth. "I'm Steve Mancini, one of the owners. Are you all right, Miss . . . ?"

"Nix. Karen Nix. I'm just shaken up." She shook her head. "He just went crazy. He threatened to kill me. I'm calling the cops as soon as I find out who that creep is."

"I wish you wouldn't," Steve said. "He's my fiancée's brother. Normally he's a sweet kid, but he's retarded, and—"

Nix's hand flew to her mouth. "Oh no. I feel terrible. He wanted to buy me a drink. I told him not to bother me, but he persisted. Then I called him an idiot. That's when he went crazy."

"That explains it," Mancini said. "Gary is very sensitive about his intelligence."

"I feel awful."

"Don't. You had no way of knowing, and Gary should have known better, but he's like a little kid—"

"You don't have to say any more. I'm not going to call the police."

"Thanks a lot, Karen." Mancini looked at his watch. "Look, if it's all right, I'll leave now. I have some work at my office. You've been very understanding. Not everyone would be."

At the other end of the Stallion, Dave Thorne was making up a drink order for a waitress. The blonde with the medallion was no longer on her stool. Thorne assumed she had left, but he turned around to give the waitress her order and saw the blonde walking out of the front door behind Steve Mancini.

CHRIS Mammon led Kevin Booth out of the bar while Gary was screaming at Karen Nix. The muffled music from the bar rumbled in the night air. Fear tightened Booth's gut when Mammon stopped in the darkest part of the parking lot.

"It's great seeing you out, Chris," Booth said, trying to sound sincere. "What's your lawyer think will happen now?"

"Geary's an old drunk, but he seems to know his stuff. He's not too encouraging, though."

"That's too bad. So, what did you want to talk about?"

"We have a problem. Rafael wants his thirty thousand dollars."

Thirty thousand was the amount that Mammon was supposed to pay for the two kilos of cocaine the police seized.

"That's not my problem," Booth answered nervously. "You made the deal with Rafael."

"I agree with you, but Vargas sees it differently. He says you set up the deal, so you're responsible for the money."

"That's not fair. I introduced you as a favor. You still have the money you were going to use to buy the dope. Give it to him."

"No can do. See, I represent people. These people put up the money, but they won't pay it over unless they get cocaine for it."

"Well, I don't have thirty thousand. And I shouldn't have to come up with money your people owe. I'll tell that to Rafael."

"I wouldn't do that. He was very angry with you, Kevin. He said to tell you not to call him unless you had the money."

Booth knew Rafael Vargas well enough to know that he was only rational part of the time and that he was very violent all of the time. If Rafael said don't call, Booth was not going to risk it.

"There is a solution to our problem," Mammon said. "My people are still interested in buying a very large shipment from Vargas. I'm too hot to be involved, so I thought up a plan that helps my people and helps you make it up to Rafael."

A wave of nausea passed over Booth. Mammon was a bully. Since he arrived in Whitaker six months ago, Booth had never seen him do anything for anyone without an ulterior motive.

"I don't want to be involved, Chris. You heard what that judge said he'd do if I was arrested again. The cops are gonna be watching me. I don't want to go to jail."

Mammon stared hard at Booth. "There are worse things than jail, Kevin. Besides, you don't have a choice. I've already assured Vargas that he can count on you."

"Aw, man. Call him back."

Mammon placed a hand on Booth's shoulder near his neck and applied a bit of pressure. "You do as you're told." Mammon squeezed a little harder. Booth dropped to his knees. He tried to pry Mammon's hand off, but the iron fingers would not budge. Booth twitched and wriggled in pain.

Mammon released Booth, and he tumbled onto the asphalt. Then he reached down and pulled Booth to his feet as easily as if he were a child. "I'm sorry I had to do that, but I'd rather hurt you a little now than have to hurt you a lot later. Now, do I have your promise that you'll be a good boy?"

"Sure, Chris. What—what do I have to do?"

"Just sit tight. You'll be contacted soon. I don't think it's a good idea for us to be seen together from now on, so don't call me or try to see me."

Mammon started toward his car. But he stopped just as a man walked by the far end of the Stallion heading toward the side parking lot. A light at the far end of the building illuminated a slender blonde in a Whitaker T-shirt and jeans. She called to the man and headed toward the lot. Mammon squinted. He knew that girl. He wondered what she was doing.

TWO stone pillars at the end of High Street marked the main entrance to Wishing Well Park. A wide path led to the wishing well, which had been built as a memorial to the men of Whitaker County who had given their lives in the Vietnam War. From the wishing well, the park expanded into a recreational area with a marina, baseball diamonds, a playground and a series of hiking trails.

It was only one mile from Oscar Watts's house to the wishing well, but the two-mile round-trip of alternate jogging and walking was pure agony. Oscar worked as a bookkeeper at the JC Penney on Broad. Though his doctor was always chiding him about his weight, Oscar loved to eat, and he didn't really need to be physically fit to add up columns of numbers. Then Oscar had a stroke, and now, each morning, instead of consuming stacks of his wife's fabulous maple-syrup-and-butter-soaked hotcakes, Oscar struggled along the hiking trails of Wishing Well Park.

He was one hundred yards from the well when he spotted the object at its base. He was fifty yards away when he realized it might be human. Could that be a woman? It was hard to tell. The person was curled around the base of the well—as if sleeping, Oscar thought hopefully as he crept forward.

At twenty-five yards Oscar started to make out the dark stains that had soaked into the long blond hair and puddled at the base of the well. He wondered if he should call a cop now or take a closer look. Oscar decided to check things out. It was a long time before he thought about food again.

EARL Ridgely was a slender man with thinning straw-colored hair, tortoiseshell glasses and a thick mustache. He was at the tail end of his second term as county D.A. A spot on the circuit court bench would be opening up soon. It could be his first step up a ladder that he hoped would end at the Oregon Supreme Court.

As Ridgely approached the perimeter set up by the forensic experts, a young policeman was holding up for Sergeant Dennis Downes's inspection a thin metal chain at the end of which dangled a medallion.

"Should I bag this?" the officer asked. "I found it in the bushes by the entrance."

"Better do it," Downes decided, even though the bushes were a distance from the wishing well.

Downes had been selected by the Major Crime Team to be the officer in charge because the crime was within the Whitaker city limits. The team was composed of the same men who had viewed the body found several weeks ago in a gully at the border of Whitaker County. The cases were sufficiently similar to put every one of these seasoned professionals on edge.

"Morning, Dennis," the D.A. said. "Any idea who she is?"

"Not yet, but she's got to be from the college. Looks the age, and she's wearing a Whitaker T-shirt."

"Then let's get her picture on TV and ask the *Clarion* to run it on the front page of the afternoon edition."

Downes jerked his head toward the body. "Like that?" he asked.

"Of course not. Have King make a sketch."

Ridgely had taken only one quick look at the corpse, but it was enough to leave him light-headed. The girl's skull had been split, and her long blond hair was drenched with blood. Her face had been lacerated by chopping blows.

Ridgely spotted Dr. Guisti bending over the body. Guisti straightened up when he saw the D.A. approaching.

"Was the murder weapon a hatchet?" Ridgely asked when they could not be heard.

"I'm not certain, but there are enough similarities between this crime, the murder in the gully and the murder in Blaine for me to say they are either the work of the same person or a good copycat."

"Any signs of sexual activity?" Ridgely asked. The first two women had been raped before they were killed.

"I won't know until I examine her, but I'm guessing no. The other women were naked. She's got her clothes on. The first two were murdered in a location different from where they were found. I'm guessing the killer abducted and held them for a while but fouled up the abduction here and had to kill her."

"I don't like this one bit, Harold. What you're telling me is that we've got a serial killer in Whitaker County."

THE MANCINI-HARMON wedding reception was held in the dining room of the Whitaker Elks Club. A long table stocked with food stood against one wall next to the bar. A band played in front of a large dance floor on the opposite side of the hall. Peter was refreshing his drink at the bar when a finger poked him in the back.

Peter turned too quickly, and a splash of gin and tonic slopped over the lip of his glass. He looked down and found Becky O'Shay smiling at him.

"Don't you know better than to sneak up on a person like that?" Peter asked, annoyed that he'd been made to look foolish.

"Just practicing what I was taught in law school," answered Becky. Peter laughed. O'Shay was just too cute to stay mad at.

"Are you a friend of the bride or the groom?" Peter asked.

"Steve. How about you?"

"Steve. We went to law school together."

"He tells me you worked at Hale, Greaves before moving to Whitaker. Isn't Whitaker a little dull after the big city?"

"Dull is what I wanted after four years in the rat race," Peter answered tersely, keeping to the story he told everyone. "What else did Steve say about me?"

"I said you were a pervert and an incurable womanizer," Mancini answered, draping an arm across Peter's shoulder. "How are you two getting along? Had enough food, enough booze?"

Mancini looked dashing in his tux, but his eyes were bloodshot, and his speech was a little slurred.

"Congratulations, Steve," O'Shay told the groom.

"You're a lucky guy," Peter added. "Donna looks great."

"I think so," Mancini said.

"What have you got planned?" Peter asked.

"Portland tonight and Sunday. Then a week in Hawaii."

"I could live with that," Peter said.

"I need it. I've been breaking my chops on Mountain View."

"Your condo deal."

"Yeah." Mancini flashed a smile that looked a little forced. He took a Scotch from the bartender and swallowed half of it.

"You need an associate to take some of the pressure off you. Why don't you put Donna through law school?" O'Shay joked.

"Donna? A lawyer?" Mancini answered derisively. "Not a chance. Besides, she's going to be too busy with the little Mancinis to have much time for anything else."

"What's this about little Mancinis?" asked Donna. She looked radiant in white.

"I was just telling Peter and Becky about our plans," Mancini said as he gave Donna a kiss. Donna blushed with pride.

The newlyweds wandered off.

"They make a great couple, don't they?" Peter said.

"They sure do," O'Shay answered without enthusiasm. Then she added, "I hope Donna's doing the driving to Portland."

GARY took two more shrimps from one of the silver platters on the table, then wandered down the line and put another chicken leg on his plate. He remembered his part as best man in the ceremony, and he smiled. When Steve drove him to the church this morning, he told Gary that he looked handsome in his tuxedo. Gary looked around to see if any girl was looking at him like she thought he was handsome. He did not see any, but he did hear a lady with gray hair tell another lady about a body that had been found by the wishing well. Gary walked over to listen.

"Eric thinks this killing might be connected to the girl found in the gully and the one murdered in Blaine," the gray-haired lady said.

"Oh no."

"Eric saw the body. He said it was awful. The killer used a hatchet."

"I remember when you could walk anywhere in town, any time of day," the other woman said.

"That girl was at the Stallion last night," Gary said.

The two women looked at Gary. He smiled, proud to know something they did not.

"Hey, Gary, you look great," said a big, balding man. Gary recognized Eric Polk, a Whitaker policeman. "Hon, we got to go,"

Eric said. "It's one thirty, and we're expected at the kids' at two."

Wilma Polk looked at her watch. "I had no idea. I'm going to have to leave, Mabel. It's Kenny's third birthday."

"Is that grandson of yours three already?" Mabel Dawes asked.

"Looks five, he's that big," Eric said proudly.

MARJORIE Dooling's shoulders shook convulsively each time she sobbed into her boyfriend's shoulder. Tommy Berger tried to comfort her. Dennis Downes waited patiently. He understood Marjorie's shock at viewing Sandra Whiley's body, because he had experienced the same feeling that morning in the park.

"I'm sorry," Marjorie apologized, trying hard to stop her tears.

"You take your time," said Downes. "Want some water?"

Marjorie nodded, and Downes poured some from a pitcher.

"I'll be okay," Marjorie managed after taking a few sips.

"What made you call the police?" Downes asked.

"I saw the sketch in the *Clarion*. It looked so much like Sandy."

Downes nodded. "You two share a dorm room?"

"No. We live in a boardinghouse near the campus."

"Did you worry when Sandy didn't come home last night?"

"We, uh, spent the night at my place," Tommy answered.

"When was the last time you saw her?"

"About ten thirty," Tommy said. "We all went to the Stallion."

"Tommy and I wanted to leave. We offered to drop her off at the house, because we came in Tommy's car, but she wanted to stay." Marjorie's eyes teared again. "Sergeant Downes, I was wondering. When they found Sandy, was she wearing a necklace?"

"Why do you ask?"

"Sandy always wore a medallion around her neck. A crusader's cross. It would be for her mom. I know she'll want it. Sandy's grandma gave it to her, and it was her lucky piece."

Sandy Whiley wasn't wearing anything around her neck when she was found, but it seemed to Downes that one of the officers had retrieved something resembling the jewelry Dooling had described. He would check on it later. For now, the medallion was evidence.

BUSINESS WAS SLOW AT THE Stallion at four in the afternoon. Dennis Downes spotted Arnie Block and Dave Thorne chatting behind the bar. They stopped talking when he sat down.

"Hi, Sergeant," Block said. "The usual?"

"Not today, Arnie. Were you and Dave on duty last night?"

"Yeah. We were both here."

Downes took out a photo of Sandra Whiley that Marjorie Dooling had given him. "Remember seeing this girl in here?"

Arnie studied the photo. "She looks familiar."

Thorne frowned. "It could be . . . Yeah, I'm sure. See that medallion around her neck? She was playing with it at the bar. It's definitely her. Hey, she's not the girl they found by the well?"

Downes nodded.

"A couple of customers were talking about that earlier. We thought it might be the other one, the one Gary Harmon was hassling."

"What happened?"

"Gary tried to hit on her," Arnie said. "She shot him down, and he didn't take it too well. He grabbed her T-shirt and yelled in her face."

"What kind of T-shirt?" Downes asked, remembering the way Whiley was dressed.

"Uh, a Whitaker State one."

"And you thought Gary might have killed her?" Downes asked.

"Not really," Block said. "Gary just gets excited sometimes. I mean, he did threaten to kill her, but no one took him seriously."

4

DENNIS Downes was normally an easygoing guy, but the possibility of busting the serial killer had him on edge. Seated next to him in their patrol car was Bob Patrick, whom everyone called Pat. His face was narrow and pockmarked, and his eyes were close-set, making him look scary and mean, which was why Downes had brought him along. Patrick was as psyched up as his partner.

"Dennis, I think you're onto something here," Patrick said as Downes drove toward Gary Harmon's house.

"It's got to be him," Downes responded confidently. "I talked to Karen Nix at her dorm around six. She and Whiley are the same type. Blond, long hair, slender. And they were both wearing jeans and that same Whitaker T-shirt. The way I see it, Harmon fights with Nix. He stays mad like a little kid would; then he gets a weapon and waits outside the Stallion. Out walks a blonde—only it's the wrong one. He follows her, waits for his chance . . ."

"And kills her, just like he threatened."

"There's something else. A few weeks ago Harmon was arrested for peeping a coed's room at the dorm. I got him out of that scrape," Downes said as he parked outside Gary's house. "We can play on that, but I might need some help. That's why I brought along the meanest guy on the force."

Patrick smiled. He knew exactly what Downes wanted. They had played this game before.

It was seven thirty when Downes rang the bell. Gary opened the door. He was barefoot and wearing jeans and a Whitaker football team T-shirt.

"Hi, Gary, remember me?" Downes asked with a smile. "I'm here because I need your help. Can I come in?"

Gary remembered his manners and stepped aside. Downes led Patrick inside.

"Nice place you got here," Downes commented.

"Thank you. Do you want to sit down?" he asked, acting just the way his mom told him to when company called.

"Sure," Downes said, lowering himself onto the sofa.

Gary sat opposite the burly police officer. The officer with the mean face made Gary uncomfortable by moving out of Gary's line of vision and standing behind his armchair.

"Have you heard about the girl who was murdered in Wishing Well Park?" Downes asked.

Gary nodded. Downes handed him a snapshot of Sandra Whiley.

"We're talking to anyone who might have seen this woman last night. Did you see her?"

"I don't think so. I don't remember too much what happened. I was drinking a lot."

"You were at the Stallion yesterday evening, weren't you?"

Gary's heart rate increased. They were here about that girl. The one he yelled at. "Yeah," he said.

"Did you try to pick up a girl at the bar?" Downes prodded.

"I . . . I might have."

Downes lifted his head and made eye contact with Patrick.

"Look, Harmon," Patrick barked, "we know you attacked a girl at the bar, so can the b.s."

Gary's head swiveled around. Patrick loomed over him. He looked as if he might hit Gary.

"Calm down, Officer Patrick," Downes said firmly. "Sorry about that, Gary, but we did talk to some witnesses, and they told us about the argument you had with a girl."

Gary hung his head. "I got a little mad. I shouldn't of."

"What made you mad?"

"I don't know," Gary mumbled. He didn't know what to say.

Downes let him sit for a while; then he said, "Why don't we continue talking at the station. Is that all right with you?"

Gary looked panicky. "You ain't gonna arrest me?"

Downes laughed. "Arrest you? What gave you that idea? I want your help, that's all. You do want to help me, don't you, Gary?"

Gary wrung his hands. Reluctantly he nodded his head.

"Terrific! Why don't you get dressed and we can go."

Gary went to his bedroom, and Downes followed him. The first thing he saw were the Stallions football posters and memorabilia.

"You really are a Stallions fan," Downes said while Gary put on his sneakers.

"Yeah," Gary said, brightening. "We're going all the way."

"I sure hope so. I never miss a game."

"Steve bought me season tickets."

"He's a nice guy, a good citizen, just like you."

Gary felt proud that the sergeant thought he was like Steve. He didn't feel so scared now that he understood that he was just being a good citizen and helping the police solve a murder.

"Say, there's one more thing," Downes said. "Would you mind letting us look around your place? I'd appreciate that."

"Look around?"

"We always look around when we're investigating a case, Gary."

"I guess it's okay."

"That's great," Downes told him, beaming with good fellowship as he fished a piece of paper out of his pocket and handed it and a pen to Gary. "Why don't you read this and put your John Hancock at the bottom where I've put the X."

"What is it?"

"A consent-to-search form. It's just routine."

Gary looked at the form. He could read, but it took a lot of effort. After a minute of struggling, he got tired and signed. Behind Gary, Bob Patrick smiled. Everything was going according to plan.

"CAN I get you something to drink?" Sergeant Downes asked as soon as Gary was seated in the interrogation room. Gary was thirsty, but he shook his head. He did not want to be left alone with the mean policeman.

"Okay, then," Downes said, taking a seat across from Gary. "I don't want to keep you long, so why don't we get down to it. What happened between you and that girl at the Stallion? She probably didn't treat you right is what I'm guessing."

"She wouldn't let me buy her a drink, and she told me to go away. Then she . . . she said I was stupid," Gary blurted out.

"Well, that girl had no cause to do that." Downes leaned across the table. "Gary," he asked in a low, sympathetic tone, "what did you do when you got mad at Karen Nix?"

"I . . . I guess I grabbed her."

"What's all this 'guess' stuff?" Patrick snapped angrily. "Either you did or you didn't."

"Relax, Pat," Downes said. "I'm conducting this interview." He turned back to Gary. "I know this is hard for you, but we need your help to catch the killer. So tell me what you said to Karen Nix when you grabbed her."

"I . . . I guess I said something like I would kill her."

"What did you do after you left the bar?" Downes asked.

"I went to see Steve, but he wasn't home."

"What did you do then?"

"I went to the Ponderosa."

Downes's pulse rate jumped. The Ponderosa was a workingman's bar near the Riverview Motel. It was a few blocks from Sandra Whiley's boardinghouse. If Whiley was walking back to her place along High Street and Gary was walking toward the Ponderosa from Steve Mancini's house, they could have met.

"How did you get to the Ponderosa, Gary?"

"I walked down High."

"So you went by the park?" Downes leaned forward. "This is real important, Gary. Did you see anything going on in the park?"

Gary's brow furrowed. Then his face broke into a wide grin. "I did see something. I seen a guy and this girl. They were hugging."

"Where did you see this?"

"By the big park entrance, near where you go down to the wishing well, only closer to the street."

"What did the man look like? How tall was he?"

"I'm not sure. It was dark. He was leaning on her. You know. Hugging her. Leaning down."

"Gary, this is important. Think real hard. Could the girl have been Sandy? Could the man be the murderer?"

Gary looked apologetic. "They was just hugging, Sergeant Downes. I'm sorry, but they was just hugging."

DOWNES and Patrick stepped into the hall, leaving Gary in the interrogation room. "What do you think?" Downes asked.

"I don't know. What about you?"

Downes shook his head. "He seems too dumb to lie, but he's admitted to being at the park right around the time of the murder, and he threatened to kill a girl who looks a lot like Whiley."

"I think we need to get a D.A. in on this," Patrick said.

Downes frowned. Earl Ridgely had instructed Downes to call him if there was a break in the case, but Ridgely might insist on getting Gary a lawyer, and that would be that.

Becky O'Shay would never suggest getting Harmon a lawyer, but she would try to take the credit if Harmon confessed. Still, she wouldn't interfere with the interrogation.

"I'm gonna find Becky O'Shay," Downes said. "That will give you some time to soften up Gary."

"How do you want me to work it?" Patrick asked.

Downes thought for a moment. Then he got an idea. "Why don't you try the black light."

"I don't know, Dennis. It's trickery. It could taint the whole confession if we get one."

"No, it won't. Let me tell you how I'd do it."

GARY looked up anxiously when the door to the interrogation room opened. His anxiety increased when Bob Patrick entered.

"Hi, Gary," Patrick said pleasantly. "I brought you a drink."

Before entering the room, Patrick had dusted a can of Coke with detection powder. Although invisible to the naked eye, the powder would look orange under ultraviolet light.

Gary took the Coke with his right hand and drank it greedily. Patrick sat down next to Gary and placed a flashlight where Gary could see it. Then Patrick took several crime scene photographs of Sandra Whiley and laid them next to the flashlight.

Gary took one look at the photos and turned his eyes away. "I don't like them p-pictures."

"Is it the blood that bothers you?"

"Y-yes."

"Most of the killers I've interviewed couldn't look at their victim's blood," Patrick lied. There had been only two homicides in Whitaker County since he had been on the force, and he had never interviewed any of the prisoners. Patrick gathered up the pictures and put them away. He tapped the flashlight. "Know what this is?"

Gary shook his head.

"It's a blood machine, a light that can pick up the smallest drop of blood on a killer's hands. Most murderers think that you can wash off the blood of a victim, but you can't."

Patrick paused. "Now, you say you didn't kill that girl. Well, I'm open-minded." Patrick picked up the flashlight and pointed it at Gary. "Why don't you stick out your hands and we can settle this right now."

Gary wrapped both hands around the Coke can.

"What's the matter, Gary? You aren't worried about what the blood machine might show, are you?"

"N-no."

"Then open your hands and hold them palm up."

Gary put the can down. Very slowly he extended his hands toward Patrick. Patrick switched on the flashlight and directed the ultraviolet beam at Gary's palms. Large iridescent orange splotches appeared on both hands. Gary stared at them in horror.

DENNIS Downes and Becky O'Shay conferenced in the small room on the other side of the two-way mirror. Through the glass Becky could see Gary Harmon huddled on his chair, casting frightened looks at Bob Patrick.

"I called Don Bosco from county mental health, and he's going to see if he has anything on Gary," Downes said.

"Good idea," Becky agreed. "I definitely think you're onto something. Were the victim in the gully and the victim in Blaine blond?"

"One was, and the girl he peeped on at the college was blond."

"All right!" Becky exclaimed.

"What about the absence of blood on his clothing and in the house?" Downes asked.

"Let the criminalists run their tests. If they don't come up with anything, we can worry about it then. Harmon may have done something as simple as getting rid of his bloody clothes. You know, it might not be a bad idea to have Don Bosco sit in here with me.

The observations of a trained psychologist could be useful at trial."

"Okay. I'm gonna start taping the conversation. You'll be able to hear everything we say in here once I switch on the intercom."

Downes left to get a tape recorder. Becky was really excited. Her plans did not include a long stay in Whitaker. She would gain experience here, then try to land a job in the prestigious U.S. Attorney's office. Then she'd go on to a big firm where she could make some real money. If she could claim credit for breaking a case involving a serial killer, she might not have long to wait before she was on her way.

"WHAT happened with the black light?" Downes asked Patrick. They were in the hall outside the interrogation room.

"Gary freaked. He started moaning and wringing his hands."

"Did he admit to anything?"

"No. But he's pretty scared. If he's going to crack, it'll be now."

Gary stood up when Dennis Downes preceded Bob Patrick into the room. "Can I go home now?" Gary pleaded.

"I have just a few more questions to ask you." Downes held up the tape recorder. "My memory ain't what it used to be," he said, "and this gadget saves me from having to write everything down. Do you mind if I tape-record our conversation?"

"No."

"Great. Before we get started, I'm going to read you your rights."

"What are you doing that for?" Patrick asked angrily. "This punk's just gonna hide behind a lawyer's skirts."

Downes jumped up. "I've had enough out of you, Officer Patrick. Gary has nothing to hide. If he does want a lawyer, that's his right."

Gary watched Bob Patrick flush with anger, then storm out. Gary felt so relieved that he sagged on his chair. "I don't like him," he said.

Downes leaned forward and told Gary in a confidential tone, "I don't either. The guy has no respect for a good citizen like you. You'd never hide behind a lawyer, would you?"

"No." Gary shook his head vigorously.

Downes proceeded to tell Gary that he had a right to remain

silent and could have a lawyer present during questioning. Gary said he understood his rights but wanted to talk anyway.

"I want to help catch the guy who killed that girl," Gary said.

"That's great." Downes had Gary talk about the incident at the Stallion again, so it would be on the tape. He drew his chair a little closer. "Gary, I want to go back to something you told me that I think is really important. Remember you said you saw a man and woman at the entrance to Wishing Well Park? I want you to think about that couple again."

Gary thought real hard. He shook his head. "I just remember they was hugging, Sergeant Downes."

Downes seemed frustrated. Then he thought of something. "Gary, have you ever heard of the subconscious mind?"

"I think so," Gary answered hesitantly.

"Right now you're hearing and seeing me with the conscious mind. But you can still tell me about those two at the park. See, you have a subconscious mind that stores stuff when you aren't thinking about it. The trick in police work is to help a witness unlock his subconscious mind so he can remember things he thinks he's forgotten. I want you to close your eyes and get real loose, because I think there's a good chance you saw Sandy and her killer when you walked by Wishing Well Park."

Gary did as he was told. The two men sat in silence for a few minutes, until Gary opened his eyes.

"It's no use. All I see is them two hugging."

"Hmm," Downes said thoughtfully. "You know, Gary, if those two weren't Sandy and her killer, they probably were hugging, but what if it was Sandy and the murderer?"

"You mean they wouldn't be hugging?"

"I didn't say that. I don't want to put words in your mouth. What I'm saying is that the mind can play tricks. For instance, there are other things that look like hugging. What they were really doing could be registered in your subconscious mind. Now relax, Gary. Close your eyes and picture that night."

"I'll try," Gary said, closing his eyes.

"Okay. Now, maybe this will help. Think about what you were wearing. What do you see?"

"Uh, I think it was jeans and a short-sleeved shirt."

Downes tried not to show his excitement. "Have you done anything to those jeans since you wore them?"

"Oh, yeah. I have to wash them when they're dirty. Every Saturday is washday, and I washed everything in the hamper right when I got up, because I was going to the wedding."

Downes's heart sank. Whiley had been murdered Friday night or early Saturday morning. If there was blood on Gary's jeans and shirt, it was gone now. Out loud, Downes said, "Okay, you're doing great. You're walking by the park. Now what do you see?"

Gary's features contorted with effort. Then his eyes opened. "It's no good. I didn't see anything new."

"Not a thing?" Downes said, sounding disappointed.

"Can I try again?" Gary asked. He wanted to help. He closed his eyes and tried to relax. There were the two stone pillars and the path between them. And on the path were the boy and the girl. He was holding her, leaning down, which meant he was taller. And she was . . . what? Gary slowed time in his mind, trying hard to see. "She's leaning back, pushing him away."

"Is it Sandy?" Downes asked excitedly.

"I can't say for sure."

"You know what might help? Why don't you picture a movie screen in your head and watch what's happening on it. That way you can slow down the movie to make it easier to see."

"That's what I done," Gary said proudly. "Slowed everything down."

"Well, I'll be. You know, Gary, you might be a natural at this stuff."

Gary blushed at the compliment. "I just want to get this guy."

"I know you do, so let's see if you can be sure if it's Sandy."

"Okay," Gary said. This time as he approached the park entrance, the scene slowed to a crawl and the two people started to appear. He strained to see if the woman's features were the same as . . . as those in the photograph of Sandra Whiley that Sergeant Downes had shown him.

"I can see them. She's kind of turning, and he grabs her. By the shirt. And she whips around, and I think they're probably hanging on to each other, kinda . . . you know."

"Was it her, Gary? Was it Sandy? Slow the picture. Make it lighter on the screen. You can do it, Gary. What do you say?"

"I'm . . . I think . . ."

"Go ahead. Say it."

"I'm sure it's her. The one that got killed. And . . . that's the murderer too, because he jerked her back. They weren't hugging."

"Did you see anything shiny, Gary? We know there was a weapon. So look at his right hand. It would probably be there."

Gary concentrated real hard, running the picture forward and backward while Downes waited quietly.

"What have you got, Gary?"

Gary's eyes opened. "Nothing more," he answered groggily.

"But you know it's the killer and Sandy?"

Gary nodded. "I could see she was scared."

AN HOUR and a half later Dennis Downes was frustrated and Gary Harmon looked exhausted. The remains of a greasy hamburger, an empty can of Coke and several paper containers for coffee littered the tabletop. They had been over and over Gary's walk by the entrance to Wishing Well Park, and Gary still would not give any more details.

Downes was thinking of giving up when an idea occurred to him. "Have you seen people on TV who can predict the future or read minds?"

Gary nodded. He was beat. All he wanted to do was sleep.

"Those people are called psychics, and some of them help the police. You give them an object that belonged to a murdered person, and they can project their supernatural mind into the mind of the killer through this object and find a missing body or see who did the killing through the victim's eyes. I suspect you have a very developed supernatural mind. I want you to use it to help me."

"Gee, Sergeant, I've never done anything like that," Gary said.

Downes stood and stretched. "We're gonna need something of Sandy's for this. You sit here while I get it."

Downes left the interrogation room and went next door. Sitting next to Becky O'Shay was Don Bosco, a short, squat man dressed in tan chinos and a short-sleeved shirt.

"What was that all about?" Bosco asked.

Downes explained his plan. "What do you think, Becky?"

"I think he's covering up. You've got him admitting he saw the murder. We need to have him slip up on a detail that will prove he committed the murder. I say, go for it."

"Do you see any problems, Don?" Downes asked.

Bosco looked troubled. "I think it could get risky. He's awfully tired. He's going to be susceptible to suggestion. You have to be very careful not to lead him."

GARY held the picture of Sandra Whiley in one hand and her crusader's cross in the other. His head was swimming.

"Okay, Gary, close your eyes and relax. I'm going to teach you a trick you can do with that cross. It's called projection transfer. That's Sandy's cross. I want you to project your supernatural mind into that cross and tell me what Sandy saw."

Gary let his mind run loose. "I'm starting to see them more . . . along. You know, after I walked by," Gary said in a voice heavy with fatigue. "She . . . she's . . . He's holding her."

"Like she's trying to get away?" Downes asked, suddenly excited.

"Yeah. It seems like she slapped him."

"Sandy fought back?"

"Uh-huh. And then . . . his right hand was going down. Like he was hitting her."

"This is what we want, Gary. Now we know she hit him and he hits her with his right hand. What is he using? Look at his right hand and tell me what you see."

Gary concentrated as hard as he could. What would it be? Then he remembered what the two women said at the wedding about the girl's face being chopped up. What was it they said the killer used? "He chopped her up with a . . . a hatchet."

Downes's heart leaped. He took the picture of Sandy from Gary's right hand and replaced it with a ruler from a drawer.

"Gary, you are unbelievable. I've never seen anyone with your powers. Now, with your supernatural mind, you can transfer this ruler to the hatchet. I'm gonna stand, and so are you. I'm gonna be Sandy, and you're gonna let that hatchet lead you to strike like the killer did. Let it flow, Gary. First hit. Where was it?"

Gary brought his arm up sluggishly. "Top of the head," he said as his arm slowly descended.

"This is great. Then what?"

Gary saw it all. His arm swung sideways. "Another to the right side. And another." Gary's arm rose and fell. Then he stopped.

"Okay. The killer took the hatchet away. Where is it now?"

"He . . . he threw it away."

"Where, Gary? Help us find it."

Gary's head wobbled. He wet his lips. "He's running to a dark place because he's scared."

"Someplace dark? But where? Come on, Gary."

"I'm trying, Sergeant, but he's too far from Sandy to see him."

"Where is Sandy?"

"By the well."

"Okay. One last try at something. Why did the killer murder Sandy? Do you know why he did it?"

Gary thought about the girl at the dorm and the girl at the Stallion and how he wanted them to love him. "He wanted Sandy to be nice to him, but she said no, and he got mad."

"Like you got mad at Karen Nix?"

"Yeah. Can I go home now?"

"Not just yet. Gary, I'm gonna be honest with you. We have a problem here. The problem of how you know so much about Sandy's murder."

"I seen it with my powers."

"But that wouldn't explain one thing. Bob Patrick told me what he saw on your hands. What did you see, Gary?"

"B-blood."

"Why do you think you saw blood? Where did it come from?"

Gary understood what Downes was suggesting, and he started to squirm. "Oh no, Sergeant. I couldn't of done that."

"Do you know what you just said, Gary? You said 'couldn't.' Why didn't you say, flat out, that you did not kill Sandy?"

"I—I don't know."

"You were drunk that night, weren't you? You told me that you don't remember everything clearly."

Gary looked at Downes with pleading eyes and asked, "Do—do you think I killed that girl?"

"I don't know, Gary. But you'd know in your heart if you did it. Even if you couldn't remember with your conscious mind, because you were so drunk, your subconscious mind would know."

"I—I couldn't have done that," Gary said desperately. "No, no, I couldn't. Could I?"

"I don't know, Gary. Why don't we talk about that."

5

PETER was wrenched out of bed by the ringing of the phone.

"Pete, it's Steve Mancini."

"Steve? Aren't you on your honeymoon?"

"I was. Donna and I are on our way back. Gary's been charged with murder, Pete. It's that girl at the wishing well."

"What?"

"I won't be back in Whitaker until eleven or so. He needs a lawyer right away. The cops will make mincemeat out of him."

"Steve, I'm very sympathetic, but I'm not your man. I've been handling criminal cases for . . . what? Two months?"

"I'm not asking you to take the case. I just want you to make certain that Gary doesn't do anything stupid before I talk to him. You're the only one I can trust to do this the right way."

"What do you want me to tell Gary?" Peter asked.

"You'll do it?"

"Yeah, yeah. Come on. Brief me." It was the least Pete could do for one of the few people in Whitaker he could call a friend.

PETER stood when Gary stumbled into the room where Peter's abortive interview with Christopher Mammon had taken place. In the weak rays of dawn Gary's face seemed drained of color, and there were dark circles under his eyes.

"I'm Peter Hale, Gary. I helped you out when you were arrested at the college. Do you remember me?"

Gary nodded.

"Why don't you sit down." Peter indicated the folding chair on the other side of the wooden table. Gary shuffled forward.

"Are they treating you all right?" Peter asked.

Gary nodded. "When can I go home? Can you get me out?"

"I'm not going to be your lawyer, Gary. Steve asked me to help out until he comes back. He's driving here from Portland right now. I'm sure he'll come see you."

"Sergeant Downes said I was helping to catch the killer. He said I was a good detective. Why won't he let me go?"

"You're charged with a pretty serious crime." Gary looked sad. In an effort to distract him Peter asked, "How long did you talk to the police? An hour? Two hours?"

"It was a really long time. I got sleepy."

"Why do the police think you killed Sandra Whiley? Did you tell Sergeant Downes you killed her?"

"No. I just seen the girl killed."

"You saw the murder?"

"Part with my eyes and part with my mind."

"What do you mean, you saw part of it with your mind?"

"I got these supernatural powers. I never knew I had 'em, but the sergeant showed me how to use them to see who killed Sandy."

"How much of the evening can you remember when you don't use your powers?"

Gary looked sheepish. "I don't remember a lot of it too well. Everyone was buying me drinks because of the wedding."

"I'm going to ask you a serious question, and I want you to try real hard to answer it. Is it possible that you killed that girl, but you don't remember because you were drinking?"

"I . . . I couldn't have killed that girl," Gary said uncertainly.

"Then how do you know so much about the murder? I don't buy this superpower stuff. Be honest with me. Did you do it?"

Gary swallowed. He was chewing his lip and looking around the narrow room as if trying to find a way out. There were tears in his eyes. "I don't want to talk about that no more. I didn't do nothing bad. I want Mama. I want to go home."

AT EIGHT o'clock Sunday morning Becky O'Shay called District Attorney Earl Ridgely at home and asked him to meet her at his office. When he arrived at nine thirty, Becky was waiting.

"We got him," Becky said excitedly as soon as her boss walked in. "The man who killed Sandra Whiley. We nailed him."

"Who is it?" Ridgely asked.

"Gary Harmon."

"Not Jesse and Alice's boy?"

Becky nodded. Ridgely walked slowly to his chair and sat down. He felt sick. "I've known Gary since he was born. He's mildly retarded."

"I know. It's terrible. But there's no doubt he did it."

"What's your evidence?"

Becky started with the peeping incident, then moved to the attack on Karen Nix and Gary's threat to kill her. "Nix and Whiley look alike. We think Nix was the intended victim, and Harmon attacked Whiley by mistake. Besides, he gave Dennis details about the murder that only the killer would know."

Ridgely sat lost in thought. After a moment he said, "There's no way I can prosecute Gary Harmon. I know the family too well."

O'Shay had been hoping he would reach this decision. She'd been worried that he would want to prosecute Harmon himself.

"I can ask the Attorney General for assistance," he went on. "They provide help to small counties in major cases."

Becky knew it was now or never. She pulled her chair up to the desk and leaned toward Ridgely. "Earl, I can do this. You know I'm good. I'm running a ninety-five-percent conviction rate."

Ridgely could not think of a reason to deny O'Shay the case. "Harmon is yours," he said.

"Thank you. I'll never forget this."

"Before you prosecute Gary, I want you to be certain he's the right man."

"Definitely." O'Shay paused. She looked a little nervous when she asked, "What about the death penalty?"

Ridgely paled. "I can't answer for the same reason I can't try the case. If you ask for the death penalty, it must be your decision."

Becky nodded solemnly. She had decided she was going for the death penalty. A lot of doors would open for a lawyer who was tough enough to successfully prosecute a death case.

STEVE Mancini's office was in a single-story building five blocks from the courthouse. It was furnished with cheap wood paneling, a large imitation Persian rug and a battleship-size desk. A month ago Peter would have thought the office pretentious, but serving time in Amos Geary's rattrap had dulled his senses.

"How's Gary holding up?" Mancini asked when Peter was seated.

"Not too well. Uh, just how slow is Gary?"

"He's retarded, but he got through high school, and he can work. Why?"

"Dennis Downes conned him into talking about the case by convincing him he has supernatural powers."

Mancini looked puzzled. "I know Dennis. He's a good guy. I can't see him taking advantage of Gary like that."

"I don't care how nice Downes has been in the past. This sounds like a trick to take advantage of someone who's not too bright. You better check it out."

Mancini looked uncomfortable. "I've got a problem, Pete. There's no way I can be lead counsel in this case. Think of what it would do to my marriage if I lost. Donna loves that kid. She'd never forgive me."

"I see what you mean. You're going to have to bring in someone from Portland to handle a case like this."

Mancini shook his head. "Whitaker juries won't take to an outsider. No, Pete. I was thinking of you."

"Me?" Peter laughed uneasily. "You've got to be kidding. I'm as much of an outsider as any other Portland lawyer."

Mancini looked Peter in the eye. "If you win, you'll be the most famous lawyer in this part of the state."

"That would be great, Steve. But I'd only be famous if I won. A murder case is out of my league."

"Don't be ridiculous. It's not as complex as some of the stuff you handled at Hale, Greaves. Besides, I'll help you."

Mancini had Peter thinking. He had second-chaired several major cases with his father, and he had tried a number of smaller matters that were much tougher than any criminal case.

"Don't tell me you can't use the money," Mancini said. "You'd have to ask for at least a hundred grand."

"Do the Harmons have that kind of dough?"

"Jesse Harmon is worth a lot, and he doesn't spend a nickel he doesn't have to, but he'd clean out his savings for Gary."

"What about Amos?" Peter asked, suddenly remembering his boss. "We're up to our eyeballs in court-appointed stuff."

"Forget Amos. I can't believe a guy like you is saddled with that old drunk." Mancini leaned forward in his chair. "When Mountain View gets going, I'll have to spend a lot of time with the project. I could use a partner right now, but there hasn't been a lawyer in the three counties I'd let near one of my files until you came along."

Peter's heart was beating fast. Amos Geary was in Cayuse County all week trying a robbery case. "It sounds tempting," Peter said, "but I really should think about this."

"Pete, I hate to pressure you, but the Harmons are here now. They're in the conference room waiting to meet you."

For a nanosecond it occurred to Peter that Gary could die if he screwed up the case, but he banished this pang of conscience.

Peter had no intention of spending his life trying traffic cases for peanuts. Steve Mancini had confidence in Peter's abilities, and he was handing Peter the chance of a lifetime. Besides, with Steve as his partner, Gary would have a great defense.

"Let's do it!" Peter said.

Mancini grinned at him. "That was the smartest decision you ever made. Let's meet your new clients."

Jesse Harmon was pacing the floor of the conference room when Steve opened the door. Harmon's fifty-nine years showed in his thatch of white hair and in his weather-beaten face. He was barrel-chested and broad-shouldered from years of farmwork. Donna was sitting next to Alice Harmon, a tall, rawboned woman with more gray than brown in her hair.

"I've got good news," Mancini said enthusiastically as soon as the introductions were made. "Pete's going to take the case."

Jesse and Alice Harmon's faces showed none of Steve Mancini's excitement. They were drawn with worry. "Steve tells us you've got lots of experience in these cases," Jesse said.

Before Peter could answer, Mancini said, "Pete's spent the last four years with the most prestigious firm in Portland working with its top litigator, who just happens to be his father. You might say Pete's got high-level litigation in his genes."

"Did that firm handle criminal cases?" Jesse asked, ignoring Steve's attempt to skirt the issue of Peter's experience.

"Jesse," Mancini interjected, his expression turning somber, "there is something that Peter and I know about Gary that we've kept from you. A few weeks ago Gary was arrested when he was caught peeping in a window at the girls' dormitory while a young woman was undressing."

Alice's hand flew to her mouth, and Donna said, "Oh, my."

"Pete just happened to be walking across campus when this happened. He calmed down campus security and convinced the police that Gary should not be charged. Gary trusts him. And, in a case like this, trust is essential."

Peter was concerned that Jesse Harmon would become suspicious if Steve kept speaking up for him. "Mr. and Mrs. Harmon," he said, "I want you to know I am convinced that the police took advantage of Gary's mental handicap to trick him into confessing to something he never did. What the police have done to Gary is wrong, and I intend to do something about it."

Jesse Harmon's features softened. "We appreciate your concern for our boy, and we'd be grateful if you would help him out."

6 KEVIN Booth lived six miles outside of Whitaker at the end of a gravel road in a single-bedroom house that was little better than a shack. Booth's nearest neighbor was half a mile away. The view was brown flatlands and desolation, broken only by the wavering outline of another shack, abandoned long ago.

Booth had staggered in around one and collapsed on his unmade bed. He was in such a deep sleep that the pounding on his front door did not arouse him immediately. When the din finally penetrated, he jerked awake, upsetting the lamp on his end table.

"One minute," he called out, but the pounding continued.

Booth pulled on his jeans, then slipped into his sneakers and staggered into the front room.

"Who is it?" he called through the door.

"Rafael Vargas," said a voice with a faint trace of Spain.

"Open the door," a deeper voice commanded.

Refusing would have been useless. Booth opened the door. The first man through it, Carlos, the bodyguard, wore a suit jacket over a tight black T-shirt that stretched over corded muscles. When he moved, the jacket flapped back to reveal the butt of a large handgun. A jagged scar cut across his cheek, and his eyes were wild.

Rafael Vargas was lean and wiry. His smile revealed even white teeth. Over his upper lip was a pencil-thin mustache.

"Did Chris explain what we want from you?" Vargas asked.

"Yeah," Booth answered quickly. "Uh, look, Mr. Vargas," he said, "I told Chris I didn't think I was right for this."

Carlos took a threatening step forward. Vargas held up his hand. "Look, amigo," he said, "Chris is hot. DEA is gonna have him under surveillance. He's smart enough to know that."

"I was arrested with Chris. They probably suspect me too."

"DEA forgot you the minute you left the courtroom. Kevin, wheels are in motion. It's too late to stop them from turning. I've got twenty kilos of cocaine in a van parked out front. All you have to do is hold it for a few days."

"Twenty . . . Mr. Vargas, I really don't want—"

"There is nothing to worry about. We don't plan to leave it here for very long," Vargas said. "Let's go to the van."

Vargas and Carlos followed Booth outside. There was no moon and no light in the yard except for the van's headlights. Vargas found a flashlight in the glove compartment, while Carlos opened the back of the van, revealing two large plastic garbage bags.

"Take them out," Carlos commanded.

Booth grabbed the bags by their necks and pulled them out. As soon as he started for the garage, lights flooded the yard.

"Freeze! Federal agents!" shouted a man in a dark blue windbreaker. Stenciled on the back in yellow was DEA. Vargas started to run, but two armed men appeared from the side of the garage. Carlos held his hands out. Booth froze.

"Drop the bags," commanded the man in the windbreaker.

Booth complied instantly. Rough hands frisked him; then his arms were wrenched behind him and metal cuffs were snapped on his wrists. Booth found himself standing next to Vargas. Vargas turned to Booth and whispered, "You are a dead man."

MANCINI shook his head. "This is going to be tough, Kevin. With a case this big, I'll need twenty thousand up front."

"Twenty . . . Last time you only charged seventy-five hundred."

"Last time we were in state court and you weren't caught with twenty kilos of snow. Fighting the feds is expensive."

"I don't have twenty thousand dollars," Booth said desperately.

"Where did you get the dough last time?"

"Chris Mammon lent it to me."

"Well?" Mancini said. "From what you've told me, you're in this scrape because of Mammon. Ask him to go your fee."

"I already called him. He won't talk to me."

Mancini sighed. "I want to help you, Kevin, but I can't work for free. Not on a case this big." He looked at his watch. "Hey, I'm going to have to break this off. I'm due in court."

"Wait a minute. You can't just walk out on me." Booth grabbed him by the arm. "I'll—I'll tell the cops about you."

Mancini did not move his arm. Instead, he turned until his face was inches from Booth's. "What exactly will you tell them?"

The former quarterback's biceps felt like steel through his suit jacket, and Booth knew he had made a mistake. "You—you know," Booth stuttered.

"Let go of my arm, Kevin," Mancini said softly.

Booth released Mancini's arm.

"Never threaten me again, Kevin. But if you feel compelled to talk, remember that two can play that game. Would you like me to visit Vargas and confirm his suspicions about you?"

Booth sank back on his chair, shaking with terror.

REPORTERS from the *Clarion*, several other eastern Oregon papers and the local TV station were waiting for Peter outside the courtroom where Gary was to be arraigned. Peter made a brief statement expressing his total belief in his client's innocence.

Donna and her parents were sitting with Steve Mancini in the front row of spectator seats. Peter stopped briefly to say hello, then walked through the low wooden gate that separated the spectators from the court. Becky O'Shay called the case.

A guard brought Gary into the courtroom. He was used to his status as a prisoner by now and looked more confused than afraid. The clerk presented Peter and Gary with copies of an indictment charging Gary with aggravated murder, which carried the death penalty. The judge explained the charge and his rights to Gary, then asked what plea he wanted to enter. Peter told him to say, "Not guilty," and Gary said the words in a nervous whisper. Peter and Becky discussed scheduling with the judge for a few minutes; then the arraignment was over.

As soon as Gary was led out, Peter asked O'Shay, "Where's Earl? I thought . . . You're going to prosecute?"

O'Shay smiled. "Come up to my office, and I'll give you the discovery."

PETER was so excited about the prospect of being the lead counsel in a major case that he had not given much thought to whether Gary killed Sandra Whiley. He had little basis for forming an opinion until he read the police reports.

When he returned to his office, Peter dumped the stack of police reports and the box of tapes O'Shay had given him onto his desk and hunted up a tape recorder so he could hear Gary's interrogation. As he listened, Peter's mood changed from excitement to confusion to concern. Something was not right. Peter could see that Gary knew a lot about the murder, but it sounded to Peter as if Sergeant Downes had tricked Gary into making many of the statements that were incriminating.

SEVERAL hours after the arraignment a guard let Gary into the attorney-client interview room at the jail.

"Gary, why don't you sit down and we'll take that first step toward getting you out of here." Gary sat down obediently on the other side of the table.

Peter pointed to several tape cassettes and the stack of police reports he had reviewed. "I've read a summary of the statement you made to Sergeant Downes, and I've listened to a few of the tapes of your interrogation. I want you to tell me again how you know so much about this murder."

"It's my powers."

Peter shifted uncomfortably on the metal chair as he searched for the words he wanted to say. Gary watched him hopefully. Peter had thought a lot about the fame and fortune Gary's case could bring him, but very little about Gary Harmon. At first he was even put off by his client. But Peter found Gary's childlike dependence on him endearing as well as flattering. After the way he had been treated at Hale, Greaves, it was nice being appreciated.

Peter looked at Gary. "I'm your friend, Gary. Do you trust me?"

"Yeah."

"And you know if I say something that hurts your feelings, I'm saying it because I have to in order to save you?"

Gary nodded.

"Okay. Do you understand that you aren't as smart as some other people?"

Gary flushed, but he nodded.

"Do mean people play tricks on you sometimes?"

"Yeah. I don't like them mean people. They hurt my feelings."

"Gary, Sergeant Downes played a trick on you. He said you have supernatural powers, but you don't."

Gary's expression was blank for a moment. Then his brow furrowed. "How did I see the murder if I don't have powers?"

"There are only two explanations I can think of, Gary. Either you murdered Sandra Whiley . . ."

"Oh no, Mr. Hale. I couldn't do that."

"Or you made up what you said."

"No. I didn't make it up. I seen it."

"Sergeant Downes told you to imagine what you saw in your head. That's all it was, Gary. Your imagination."

"But it seemed so real."

"Do me a favor. Close your eyes."

Gary obeyed Peter's request.

"Now imagine this room and imagine it's winter." Peter waited a few seconds. "Can you see snow on the window? Is it cold?"

"Yeah." Gary's eyes opened. He wore a look of puzzlement.

"Do you understand what Sergeant Downes did to you?"

"I know I seen two people in the park when I passed by."

"Can you swear you saw Sandra Whiley?"

Gary shook his head. He looked dejected.

Peter's heart went out to him. "This is our job, then, Gary. To find out what you really saw and what you made up. But it's going to be a hard job. Will you work with me? Will you help me?"

"Yes, I will, Mr. Hale. I'll try real hard."

IT WAS almost five o'clock when Peter left the jail. Working with Gary was exhausting. He was so open to suggestion that Peter had to watch every word, and he could never be certain if Gary really understood him or was nodding to be polite.

As he walked up the stairs to Geary's office, Peter checked his watch. He was going to Steve's house after dinner to discuss strategy. There were all sorts of technical defenses, like diminished capacity, but after today's session with Gary, Peter was wondering if they shouldn't dispense with them and go with a straight not guilty on the grounds that Gary did not commit the crime.

The hatchet used to kill Sandra Whiley screamed premeditation. Who walks around with a hatchet? No, the killer planned his moves. Peter had a hard time picturing Gary Harmon planning breakfast.

"Mr. Geary wants to speak to you," Clara said as soon as Peter opened the office door. "He's at the Bunkhouse Motel in Cayuse County. Said to have you call the minute you walked in."

Peter wondered if Geary knew he was on the case already. He had hoped for more time to cement his position as Gary's attorney before having to confront his boss.

"Mr. Geary," Peter said as soon as he was put through by the motel clerk, "Clara said you wanted to talk to me."

"Yes. Yes, I do. I was sitting in Judge Gilroy's chambers after court, and he jokingly offered me condolences on getting stuck with the Harmon case. I told him I didn't know what he was talking about. The judge said Judge Kuffel had phoned him, and he thought Kuffel said that my young associate had appeared at the arraignment for Mr. Harmon. That isn't true, is it, Peter?"

"Well, uh, yes, it is. But you don't have to worry. This isn't a court appointment. The Harmons are going to pay us one hundred thousand dollars and expenses."

There was silence on the line for a moment. When Geary spoke again, he sounded as if he was fighting to keep himself under control. "Peter, I want you to call Jesse Harmon and tell him you made a mistake when you accepted his son's case without consulting me. Then you march down to Judge Kuffel's office and resign as quickly as you can."

"But Mr. Geary . . ."

"No buts, Peter. You and this office are off the Harmon case as of now. Do you understand me?"

"Well, no, I don't. I just brought in a one-hundred-thousand-dollar fee, and you're acting like I did something wrong."

"You did do something wrong, Peter," Geary said. "First, you took this case without consulting me, your boss. Second, our firm has a contract to represent indigent defendants in three counties. In order to honor my part of the contract I need to have you available to represent the indigent accused. Third, and most important, if you screw up, Gary Harmon will have lethal chemicals injected into his veins. And you will screw up, Peter. Are you so shallow that you want to risk Gary Harmon's life for money?"

"I resent the implications that I took this case for the money."

"I don't give a damn what you resent," Geary shouted. "You either march down to the courthouse and resign the minute I hang up or clear out of your office." The line went dead.

Peter hung up and slumped in his chair. What was he going to do? If he didn't resign from Gary's case, his last chance to get back in his father's good graces would be gone. But if he did resign, he'd lose a golden opportunity to make a name for himself.

Peter remembered Steve Mancini's advice: "Forget Amos." Mancini was right. With one hundred thousand dollars he could forget about a lot of people. And there was the partnership waiting. When Peter thought about it, the choice wasn't all that hard.

"WHAT are you going to do?" Steve asked when Peter finished recounting his conversation with Geary. They were seated on the couch in Mancini's living room. Donna was in the kitchen brewing coffee and slicing a coffee cake.

"I know what I'd like to do, but I have one huge practical problem. If I stay on as Gary's lawyer, I've got to clear out of my office."

"That's no problem at all. I have an extra office at my place you can rent. You'd have a receptionist, and you can pay one of my secretaries by the hour to type your stuff."

"That's terrific." Peter smiled bravely, but his insides were churning with fear.

"Now that we've got that settled, let's get to work," Steve said.

"I want you to read this report." Peter handed a thick, stapled stack of paper to Mancini. "It's a summary of Downes's interrogation. Then I want you to listen to sections of some tapes. They'll give you some idea of what's going on."

Donna came out of the kitchen carrying a tray. She gave Peter and her husband cups of coffee and slices of cake. Then she sat on the couch next to Steve and listened as Dennis Downes explained to Gary the marvelous powers he possessed.

"Are Gary's statements the reason he was arrested?" Donna asked Peter when the tapes were finished.

"They're a big part of it."

"But that's so unfair. Doesn't the fact that Downes lied to Gary mean anything?"

"I seem to remember reading cases in law school that held that a confession elicited by deceit won't hold up," Peter said.

"Maybe I can help find them," Donna volunteered. "When I was studying to be a legal secretary, I took a course on how to do legal research."

"I can use all the help I can get," Peter said.

Mancini frowned. "When would you fit it in, honey? You're pretty busy at work."

"I could do the research after work or on the weekend. Please, Steve. I want to do something to help Gary."

"Well . . . I guess if it's okay with Pete . . ."

Donna leaned over and kissed her husband on the cheek. Then she started back to the kitchen. "I'll let you two get back to work while I clean up. And Peter, let me know what you want me to do."

"You did okay, Steve. Donna's terrific."

"Why thanks," Mancini answered. "But don't count on Donna for much help. She's a good legal secretary, but legal research?" Mancini flashed Peter a patronizing smile.

"She seems pretty sharp to me," Peter said, surprised to hear his friend put down his wife. "Let's see what she can do."

"Sure," Mancini said. "Now back to the confession. We should list possible attacks on it. I noticed that Don Bosco observed a lot of the questioning. Why don't I see what he has to say."

"Good idea. And I'm going to need a good investigator."

Mancini thought for a moment. "There's a guy I've used, Barney Pullen. He works as a mechanic at his brother's garage, but he used to be a cop. You might see if he's available."

Peter jotted down the name. "Becky included a police report about the peeping incident," he said. "I think she is going to try and have the evidence admitted. What can we do about that?"

"We have to file a motion to keep that out. The jurors are going to believe Gary's a pervert if they hear it."

"I agree. And there's something else." Peter handed Mancini a stack of police reports. "I'm hoping these reports are in here by mistake. If they're not, Gary may be in big trouble."

Mancini skimmed the first report. His features clouded. "Becky can't think Gary was also involved in these cases."

"She must. Why would she give me reports about the murders of two other women if she didn't think Gary committed them?"

7

THE prisoners in the Whitaker jail were allowed an hour a day to exercise in the yard. Gary leaned against the chain-link fence and watched several prisoners pumping iron. He wasn't feeling so good. The meeting with Peter Hale had left him confused. If he didn't have supernatural powers, how did he know so much about the murder?

"Hey, Gary?" a familiar voice said. Gary turned and saw Kevin Booth. He finally had a friend to talk to.

"Hi, Kevin! Are you arrested too? What did you do?" Gary asked with concern.

"I screwed up big time. Federal stuff."

Just as he said this, Booth noticed Rafael Vargas sitting in the bleachers near the bodybuilders. Not far away, his bodyguard, Carlos, was working out with weights the size of car tires. Booth looked away quickly.

"So, man," Booth said, "I read about you. You're a media star. Front page! Murder! That's heavy."

"I didn't do anything to that girl," Gary said. "I just seen it."

"Seen what?"

"My lawyer doesn't want me to talk about the case to anyone."

An idea suddenly occurred to Booth. He shot a quick look at Vargas. When he turned back to Gary, he was wearing an ingratiating smile. "Your lawyers probably don't want you talking to someone you don't know. But I'm your friend, right? We've been buddies since high school."

"Oh, sure," Gary agreed. Kevin Booth was a friend. So Gary proceeded to tell him everything about his case.

IT WAS late afternoon when Steve Mancini returned to his office. He picked up his message slips at the reception desk and glanced through them as he walked down the hall. One was from Harold Prescott. Mancini closed his office door. As he dialed Whitaker Savings and Loan, he said a little prayer.

The U.S. Olympic ski team trained near Bend, Oregon. Three years ago the state of Oregon had launched a campaign to bring the Olympics to Bend. Shortly after, Mancini had joined a group of investors to form Mountain View, Inc. Harold Prescott had engineered a construction loan at his bank. The loan was used to start work on a ski lodge and the first condo units, but the weather, labor problems and escalating costs had eaten up most of the money. The loan was due soon. Mountain View was trying to get a long-term loan to pay off the construction loan and complete the first phase of the project. If the project failed, Mancini would be ruined.

"I'm afraid I have bad news, Steve," Prescott said as soon as they were connected. "The committee met this afternoon. It voted against authorizing the loan."

Mancini felt sick. "What's the problem?" he asked desperately.

"The problem is that there's no assurance Bend will get the Games. The committee was unwilling to take the risk."

"Harold, I don't know who you've been talking to. Roger Dunn told me his sources say we've got a terrific shot. Once the announcement is made, those condos will sell like hotcakes."

"That wasn't the only problem. There aren't enough liquid assets in your group. Most of the land is only optioned. The feeling was that there wasn't enough hard equity in the project."

The rest of the conversation went by in a dull hum. Mancini responded automatically as a sharp throbbing pain filled his head. All he could think about was his financial ruin.

Mancini told his secretary to hold his calls. Then he took a glass and a half-filled bottle of Scotch out of his bottom drawer. He poured a stiff drink, downed it and poured another.

"DONNA Harmon is here to see you, Mr. Hale," Clara said over the intercom.

"Send her in," Peter answered, relieved not to be told that Amos Geary was on the line.

Donna looked excited when she came in the door. "I think I found some good cases about tricking people into confessing," she said, thrusting a manila envelope at Peter.

"Sit down. Let me take a look."

"There's a great sentence in *Miranda* versus *Arizona*," Donna said. The famous U.S. Supreme Court case had established the rule that police had to warn suspects about their constitutional rights to remain silent and to have counsel before being questioned. "It says that even a voluntary waiver of your rights is no good if the accused was threatened, tricked or cajoled into giving the waiver. And look at this University of Pennsylvania *Law Review* article about 'Police Trickery in Inducing Confessions.' "

"You're pretty good," Peter said with genuine admiration after he skimmed the material. "This will really help."

"You think so?" Donna asked hopefully. Her features clouded. "Have you talked to Gary?" she asked.

"Not since yesterday. He's doing pretty well, under the circumstances. You really love your brother, don't you?"

"I love him very much. We all do. When Gary was small, he was always running and laughing. It wasn't until he was older that we realized how dreadfully slow he was. It was something we knew but never admitted. Then one day Mom told us what Gary's teacher had said about a special class with other 'slow learners.' Mom said that Gary was God's child, like everybody else, and that was all she was interested in. That shaped Gary's life. We never made him feel like a freak or demanded less than he could accomplish."

Donna took a deep breath and stood, embarrassed by her display of emotion. "I—I'd better go. I have to shop for dinner."

"Thanks for the cases."

"I hope they help," Donna said as she left the office.

Peter closed the door behind Donna and wandered back to his desk. It occurred to him that he should talk to someone with a little experience in this area in order to get some idea of what he was getting into.

Peter looked up the phone number for the Oregon Criminal Defense Lawyers Association. The secretary at the OCDLA gave him the name of Sam Levine, a Eugene attorney.

"So this is your first death case," Levine said after Peter explained why he was calling. "I remember my first. I'd tried about seven, eight murder cases, and I thought I was a hotshot." Levine chuckled. "I had no idea what I was getting myself into."

"Why is that?" Peter asked nervously.

"No other case is like a death case. They're unique. You have to prepare for two trials from the get-go. The first trial is on guilt and innocence. If your guy is convicted, there is a whole second trial on what penalty he should receive.

"With your usual case, you don't think about sentencing until your client is convicted. With a capital case, you have to assume he's going to be convicted even if you're personally convinced you're going to win, because the penalty phase starts almost immediately after a conviction in front of the same jury that found your client guilty, and you won't have time to prepare for that if you wait until the last minute."

Peter asked question after question and felt more and more insecure with each answer. After three quarters of an hour Peter said, "Thanks. I really appreciate the time you've taken."

"You'll learn that there's a real fraternity among death penalty lawyers. I always call other attorneys for help. You've got to. With a death case, you have to be perfect. If you make one small mistake, the state eats your client."

"STEVE, I'M HOME," DONNA shouted cheerfully as she deposited her groceries on the counter next to the sink. She called Steve's name again as she walked down the hall to the living room. Donna was startled to see her husband sitting silently by the fireplace.

"Why didn't you answer me?" she asked, still smiling. But the smile faded as her husband looked up at her. Mancini's eyes were bloodshot, and his clothing was rumpled. He was holding a drink, and it was obvious that it wasn't his first.

"Do you know what time it is?"

"I lost track of time. I was meeting with Peter about some research I did in Gary's case. I'm sorry if I'm late."

"Is that supposed to make everything better? I bust my chops all day, and all I ask is that you have my dinner ready when I get home."

Mancini stood up slowly and walked over to Donna. The muscles in his neck stood out, and his face was flushed. For the first time since she'd known him, Donna was frightened of her husband.

Mancini stopped in front of her. "Now let's get one thing straight here. You are not a lawyer. You're a secretary and my wife. You work from eight to five; then you get home. Is that clear?"

Donna was so hurt it was hard for her to speak. Tears welled up. "I—I said I'm sorry. I appreciate how hard you work."

"I would like less appreciation," Steve said between clenched teeth, "and some food. Do you think you can manage that?"

"You're not being fair. I was trying to help Gary. I—"

"What did I just say?" Mancini shouted.

The first blow was backhand and rattled her teeth. The second was openhanded and sent her stumbling backward. Donna gaped at her husband, unable to accept what was happening, even though she could see Steve's fist moving toward her. The blow struck her in the solar plexus, driving all the air from her. Donna sank to her knees. Mouth open, she sucked in air. She could not breathe, and she thought she would die. Then her lungs filled, and a sob escaped from her. Donna rolled over and saw her husband put on his jacket. By the time she could speak, he was gone.

WHEN DONNA AWOKE THE next morning, it was to the scent of roses. She sat up to find the bed, the floor and the furniture covered by roses of every color and her husband sitting in a corner of the room watching her.

Steve was unshaven. His clothes appeared to have been slept in. There was no anger in him. Only contrition. He walked over and knelt by the side of the bed. "I have no excuse for what I did to you. All I can do is pray for your forgiveness."

Steve seemed so chastened that Donna let him try to explain his savage attack.

"I'd been drinking. I started in the afternoon and never stopped." Mancini paused and took a deep breath before continuing. There were tears in his eyes. "The bank turned down the Mountain View loan. I didn't know what to do," he sobbed. "We could be ruined. I was so full of anger and so afraid, but I should never have taken it out on you. Please, Donna, I don't want to lose you."

Kneeling by the bed, his head down, framed in the bouquets of roses, Steve looked like a little boy. Donna reached out and touched his cheek. "I'm sorry about the loan," she said, "but we'll pull through. You have your practice, and you have me."

Steve looked at Donna with gratitude. "I should have known you'd stand by me. But I was so depressed. I wanted Mountain View to succeed so much. But now"—Mancini shook his head slowly—"I don't think we can make it. I'm tapped out, and I can't think of any place to turn for money."

"Maybe," Donna said, "I could talk to my father."

"Oh no, Donna. I couldn't ask you to do that."

"How much do you need?"

"I'd have to talk to my partners," Mancini answered excitedly. "If we could buy some of the property instead of having it on option, we might get Whitaker Savings to rethink the loan."

Mancini stood up and sat next to Donna on the bed. They fell into each other's arms. "I don't deserve you, Donna. What I did can't be excused. I swear I will never, ever hurt you again."

"I DON'T THINK THIS IS important," Eric Polk told Sergeant Downes, "but I figured better safe than sorry, so I had Wilma come in."

Eric was also on the Whitaker police force, but he was not working on the Harmon case. Wilma was his wife.

"So, what do you have for me?" Downes asked her.

Wilma Polk was a heavyset woman in her mid-fifties with curly gray hair and a round, pleasant face. "It's probably nothing. I'd even forgotten about it until Eric said something about Donna Harmon's wedding reception. Mabel Dawes and I were talking about the murder because Eric had been at the scene that morning. Gary was nearby, and he must have overheard us. He came over and said he had seen the girl at the Stallion the night before."

"How did Gary seem? Was he nervous, excited?"

"Maybe a little excited, but we all were."

"Okay," Downes said, smiling. "Thanks for dropping by."

Eric Polk escorted his wife out of Downes's office. Downes looked at his watch. It was time for a break. He decided to dictate a report for the D.A., then go out for coffee. He was finishing the dictation when the phone rang. It was Becky O'Shay.

"Dennis, I just received a call from the jail. One of the prisoners claims Gary Harmon confessed to him. I want you to come along with me. If this pans out, I'll treat you to lunch."

"THE last time, you escaped justice by a nose, Mr. Booth," Becky O'Shay said with a smirk, "but your luck seems to have run out. I understand you have something for us."

"Yeah. What I want to know is what I get in return."

"What do you want?"

Booth licked his lips. "I want witness protection. I want to go somewhere Rafael Vargas and Chris Mammon can't get me."

O'Shay turned to Dennis Downes. "Can we transfer Mr. Booth to the jail in Stark?"

"We've done that before. They got a nice modern security wing."

"So, Mr. Booth?" O'Shay asked.

"What about my deal? If I talk, what do I get?"

"Let me explain something to you. The first thing Peter Hale will ask you on cross-examination is what reward you're getting for your testimony. If you can say that you are testifying as a service to humanity, it will make you much more believable."

"You want me to testify for nothing?"

"I didn't say that. But if you want to be a good citizen and help me out, I'll be very receptive to any pleas for assistance you might make after Harmon's trial."

Booth didn't trust O'Shay, but he realized he had no choice. "Gary confessed to me. He told me he done it."

"Why would he do that?"

"I've known Gary since high school. He thinks I'm his friend. He's so dumb, it was easy. At first he denied doin' it, but I told him it took guts to commit murder. I built him up. Soon I had him bragging about how good it felt to snuff Whiley."

"That's interesting, but how do we know you're not making up this whole story? You have a lot of motivation to lie."

Booth looked wild-eyed. "I ain't lying. This is the truth."

"Maybe, but I only have your word for that. Unless you can give me something concrete, something that proves Harmon killed Sandra Whiley, your testimony will be useless."

Booth put his hands to his head. He closed his eyes and shifted on his seat. Suddenly his face lit up. "I got it," he said. "I got something solid. Something that will prove I'm not lying."

PETER watched Clara leave Amos Geary's office from the coffee shop across the street. Geary had left half an hour before. Peter gave it fifteen minutes more to be certain Clara would not return before scurrying across to the law office.

He had brought an empty carton with him. He set it on the desk and was filling it with personal items when he looked up to find Amos Geary watching him from the doorway.

"He-hello, Mr. Geary," Peter said with an uneasy smile.

Geary shook his head sadly. "You are some piece of work. How are you going to defend a man's life when you don't even have the guts to leave my office in broad daylight?"

"I . . . Uh, I was, uh, going to drop in tomorrow to, uh, thank you for—" Peter started, but Geary cut him off.

"You really don't have any pride, do you?" Geary asked. "Where are you sneaking off to?"

"I'm not sneaking anywhere. I'm moving to Steve Mancini's offices." Peter's voice quivered a little.

Geary nodded. "You and Mancini should get along just fine."

Peter straightened up. "I, uh, I really do appreciate the chance you gave me. I learned a lot these past weeks."

"You didn't learn a thing, Peter. You're the same sorry case you were when you cheated that poor woman in Portland. If you continue with this farce and Gary is executed, you will be as much a murderer as the s.o.b. who killed that poor girl in the park."

Part Three

8

THERE were no fancy decorations in the Whitaker County circuit court. The county could not afford them. So the spectators benches were hard, the judge's dais was unadorned, and the only dashes of color were in the flags of Oregon and the United States that flanked Judge Harry Kuffel's high-backed chair.

"The state calls Don Bosco, Your Honor," Becky O'Shay said.

As the psychologist walked to the front of the packed courtroom to take the oath, Judge Kuffel sneaked a look at the clock. It was four thirty. He was about ready to recess for the night.

"Will this be your last witness?"

"Yes, Your Honor."

"Very well."

Peter had been relieved when Steve Mancini volunteered to handle the pretrial hearing. He knew very little about the law of confessions and was only too glad to let Mancini do the research, write the brief and examine the witnesses.

Bosco explained his credentials and gave the court a brief outline of his duties as director of mental health for the county.

"Mr. Bosco," O'Shay asked, "were you summoned to the police station on the evening of Sandra Whiley's murder?"

"I was. It was sometime between nine and ten."

"Where did you go when you arrived at the station?"

"Into a small room next to the room where Mr. Harmon was being questioned. There was a two-way mirror and an intercom that let me hear what was said."

"How much of Mr. Harmon's interrogation did you hear?"

"Several hours. Maybe five."

"Did Sergeant Downes make any promises in exchange for Mr. Harmon's cooperation?"

"No."

"Did you ever hear Sergeant Downes threaten the defendant?"

"No."

"Did it sound like Mr. Harmon was being coerced into talking to Sergeant Downes?"

Bosco hesitated and looked at Steve Mancini. Peter caught the look, but Mancini did not react at all. "No," Bosco said.

Becky O'Shay smiled at the witness. "No further questions."

"Mr. Mancini?" Judge Kuffel asked.

"No questions."

Bosco frowned. He stood slowly, as if trying to give Mancini time to act. Mancini only smiled at him, and Bosco walked out of the courtroom.

Peter leaned over to Steve. "I think he wanted to say something. Why didn't you follow up?"

"I already interviewed Bosco. He can't help us," Steve said.

"Do you have any rebuttal witnesses, Mr. Mancini?" Judge Kuffel asked.

"No, sir."

"Then we'll recess for the day, and I'll hear argument in the morning." Judge Kuffel left the bench.

Becky O'Shay intercepted the two defense attorneys. "Drop by my office before you leave the courthouse," she said.

"What's up?" Peter asked the deputy D.A. when they were all in her office. O'Shay handed Peter copies of a police report.

"We received this information last week, but we've been checking it out. Now that I've decided to use this witness, I'm obligated to give you his statement."

The two defense lawyers read the police report. Mancini chuckled. "You're not serious about using Kevin as a witness, are you? You can't believe a thing Kevin says. You know he's just trying to weasel out of this federal drug bust."

"I'm dead serious," Becky answered.

"WE'VE got a problem," Steve Mancini told Peter as soon as they were outside the courthouse. "I've got to get off Gary's case. I've got a conflict of interest. I can't represent a client if another client is going to be a key witness against him."

"Hang on, Steve. How am I supposed to try this case alone?"

"Hey, if you don't think you can do it, you can resign."

But Peter knew that resigning was not an option. He had cut himself off from his father and quit his job. Without the Harmons' retainer he would be dead broke. A victory for Gary Harmon was his only way out of the hole he'd dug for himself.

"No. I can't let Gary down," Peter said.

Mancini clapped Peter on the back. "That's what I wanted to hear. Besides, this might even work out better for you in the long run. When you win, you won't have to share the credit."

"I HAVE something I wanted to mention," Becky O'Shay said. It was the next day. She and Peter were seated in Judge Kuffel's chambers. "We recently interviewed an inmate at the jail who claimed that the defendant confessed to him."

"Did you notify the defense?" the judge asked.

"Oh yes. Mr. Booth is awaiting trial on a serious drug charge and has a reason to try to ingratiate himself with our office, so I asked him for some corroboration for his story. We just got it."

O'Shay handed Peter and the judge a copy of a document.

"What's this?" Peter asked as soon as he scanned it.

"It's a report from the FBI laboratory in Washington, D.C. We sent them a hatchet we found in a storm drain on the Whitaker campus. It was right where Mr. Harmon told Kevin Booth he threw it after he hacked Whiley to death. The handle was wiped clean of fingerprints, but Sandra Whiley's blood and hair are on the blade."

When Peter found his voice, he said, "I move to have this evidence suppressed. This is a violation of the discovery statutes. This should have been revealed to us as soon as it was discovered so we could have our own experts test the blood and hair."

O'Shay smiled sweetly at Peter. "The statutes only require the prosecution to reveal the existence of evidence we intend to introduce at trial. I had no intention of introducing this hatchet until I was certain it had some connection with this case. After all, Peter, Kevin Booth is a criminal. We weren't sure he was telling the truth about your client's confession. Until now, that is."

"MOVE it, Booth," the guard commanded as Kevin Booth lathered up for the second time. "This ain't a resort." A minute later the guard cut off Booth's hot water. "I warned you. Now finish up. We got other guests in this hotel."

Booth dodged in and out of the freezing water until all the soap was off. His clean clothes were in his cell at the other end of the security tank. He wrapped as much of his shivering body as he could in a towel and hunched his shoulders as he walked.

Booth hated his new situation. The security block was for prisoners who could not be allowed to live in the normal jail population: escape risks, homosexuals, ultraviolent prisoners and informants.

Booth hated them all, but he was going to have to stay in this mad-house if he expected to live long enough to trade Gary Harmon's freedom for his own.

Booth's cell contained a sink, a toilet and two bunks, but he was the sole occupant. As soon as the guard saw that his prisoner was inside, he closed the moving bars electronically. The guard never entered the security block unless there was an emergency.

"How you doin', Kevin?" a voice asked as Booth was getting dressed. Booth looked through the bars. The prisoner who had spoken to him was a slender young man with pale skin and a blond crew cut. Booth noticed the swastika tattoo on his right forearm at the same time he noticed the milk container concealed under his bath towel. The young man kept his easy smile as he tossed the contents of the milk container over Booth's naked body. Lighter fluid, Booth thought as a lit match followed the liquid through the bars and transformed him into a human torch.

PETER ran as fast as he could along the jogging trails in Wishing Well Park, pushing himself to exhaustion in the hope that his brain would be too busy working on his oxygen supply to concern itself with Gary Harmon. But Peter's brain would not cooperate.

What troubled him was the possibility that Gary might be guilty. Gary would not state unequivocally that he did not kill Sandra Whiley. Did he kill Whiley and repress the memory, or was he simply lying? Peter could not believe Gary was capable of sustaining a lie long. But if Gary had not killed Whiley, how was he able to tell Dennis Downes that the killer used a hatchet and how was he able to tell Kevin Booth where to find it?

Peter reached his house depressed and exhausted. He had barely caught his breath when the phone rang.

"Mr. Hale?" a shaky voice asked.

"Gary? You sound upset. Has something happened?"

"I said I had to talk to you. I said I wanted to call my lawyer."

"That's good, Gary. You did just what I told you to do if you were in trouble. Are you in trouble?"

"They say I burned up Kevin. I didn't. Please tell them I didn't."

"Calm down, Gary. Who says you burned someone?"

"That lady lawyer and Sergeant Downes."

"Are Sergeant Downes and Becky O'Shay with you?"

"Yeah."

"Put Ms. O'Shay on the phone."

As soon as O'Shay took the phone, Peter said, "What's going on? Why are you questioning Gary?"

"Kevin Booth was set on fire in his cell in the Stark jail," O'Shay answered, her rage barely under control. "Unfortunately for your client, Booth's still alive."

"You don't think Gary was involved, do you?" Peter asked. "He's not bright enough to plan something like that."

"We'll soon find out. Sergeant Downes and I are going to question him."

"I can't let you do that. You two shouldn't be anywhere near Gary without my permission. Now get him back to his cell immediately, and don't ask him any questions. If I find you have, I'll move for a mistrial. You know what you're doing isn't ethical." But O'Shay had already hung up.

PETER was at the office on Sunday afternoon when he heard the front door open. He walked into the corridor and saw Steve Mancini checking his messages at the reception desk.

"Am I glad to see you," Peter said.

For a moment Mancini looked as if he was not happy to see Peter. Then he smiled. "How's the trial going?"

"We've got our jury, and Becky's putting on her first witness on Monday. Can we talk? I need your advice."

Mancini looked at his watch. "I'm really pressed for time. But—" He clapped Peter on the back and started for his office.

During the next half hour Peter brought Mancini up to date on the torching of Kevin Booth. "The D.A. wants Gary Harmon to be involved. The feds would love to hear that it was someone in Vargas's organization. But there's no evidence now connecting anyone other than the man who set Booth on fire." There was also the discovery of the hatchet.

When he finished, Mancini said, "There's no way Gary was involved with setting Booth on fire. He doesn't have the brains to think up a scheme like that. This sounds more like something Rafael Vargas would do. Have you talked to Becky about a plea? You should look into it after these new developments."

"A plea? You don't think Gary is guilty, do you?"

"I don't know what to think. I wouldn't have believed he was a Peeping Tom. And look at the way he jumped on that girl in the Stallion. Gary doesn't think the way we do. He's impulsive."

"Gee, Steve, I don't know. . . ."

"I'm not saying you should plead him out, just explore the possibility with Becky. From what you tell me, the case isn't going all that well. You don't want to see Gary executed, do you?"

"I've got to think about this." Peter stood up. "Oh, one other thing. This investigator Barney Pullen—he doesn't seem to be doing anything. I've only received a few reports, and they weren't worth much. I'm worried. It's too late to switch investigators. By the time a new one was up to speed, the trial would be over."

"You're right. Look, why don't you let me give Barney a call."

"That would be great."

Peter went back to his office. He was depressed about Gary's chances, but he was not going to seek a plea just yet.

ON THE first day of testimony Becky O'Shay led off with Karen Nix, who told the jury about Gary's attack and his threat to kill her. Marjorie Dooling testified that Sandra Whiley had been at the Stallion on the evening of the fight. After Dooling described how Whiley was dressed, the bloodstained clothing was introduced into evidence, and a photograph of the jeans and the Whitaker State T-shirt Nix was wearing was shown to the jurors so they could compare the similarities between her clothing and the victim's.

Arnie Block, the bartender, gave his account of the fight and told about Gary's flight from the bar. The other barman, Dave Thorne, established that Whiley left the Stallion around eleven twenty, about twenty minutes after Gary ran outside.

On the second day Oscar Watts told the jury about discovering Whiley's body. Then several police officers described the crime scene investigation and the gathering of evidence.

On the morning of the trial's third day Becky O'Shay called Harold Guisti. As the hall door opened to admit the doctor, Peter's attention was momentarily diverted by Christopher Mammon, who was watching from a seat in the back. Peter could not imagine why the gargantuan drug dealer would be interested in Gary's case, but he did not have time to worry about it.

After establishing Dr. Guisti's credentials, O'Shay asked him to describe what he found when he performed an autopsy on Sandra Whiley.

"I found eight cutting or chopping wounds on the body. Seven of them were located on the head. The eighth was located on the top of the left hand and was consistent with a defensive wound."

"Do you have an opinion, Dr. Guisti, as to the type of instrument that might have been used to inflict these wounds?"

"I do. Either an axe or a hatchet would cause such wounds."

O'Shay reached into a large cardboard box. "Dr. Guisti, I hand you what has been marked as State's Exhibit Twenty-three. Could the wounds on the victim have been inflicted with this exhibit?"

Dr. Guisti opened the plastic evidence bag. It contained a small hatchet. "The blows could have been inflicted by this weapon."

"Thank you," O'Shay said, taking the hatchet from the doctor and returning it to the bag. She placed the hatchet on the rail of the jury box and turned back to the witness. Several jurors had trouble moving their eyes away from the weapon.

"Dr. Guisti, do you have an opinion as to the cause of death?"

"Yes. I think the eventual cause of death was hemorrhaging caused by the wounds I have described."

"Do you have an opinion as to whether the blow to the top of the skull was the first blow struck to the head?"

"In my opinion it was."

O'Shay turned the witness over to Peter.

"Dr. Guisti, what side of the head were the wounds on?"

"One was to the top of the head, as I said. One blow was to the right eye. The rest were to the left side of the head."

"Thank you, Doctor. I have no further questions."

BARNEY Pullen had a beer gut, a bushy beard and a don't-mess-with-me attitude. He had worked as a cop in Eugene, Oregon. Pullen wasn't exactly fired, but he didn't exactly quit the force either. The affair was murky, and Pullen moved to Whitaker, where he worked in his brother's body shop.

One day Pullen was assigned the job of figuring out what caused the knocking sound in Steve Mancini's Cadillac. In between discussions of car engines Pullen mentioned his police background. Mancini needed an investigator with a knowledge of cars for a personal injury case, and Pullen had done spot investigation for him ever since.

Pullen was bent under the hood of an old Buick when Peter entered the garage during the lunch recess. "Afternoon, Mr. Hale," he said, wiping his hands on a greasy rag.

"Good afternoon, Barney. I've had trouble reaching you, so I thought I'd drop by to see how the investigation's been going."

Barney shook his head ruefully. "It's slow. I've been talking to lots of people, but nobody seems to know anything helpful."

"Who have you talked to?"

"Uh, well, I don't have my notes right here. Family, of course. I do have a lot of good information for you for the penalty phase from the mother, the father and Steve's wife. Lots of good stuff."

Peter recalled receiving several poorly typed reports rife with misspellings. "I have the family interviews, but that's all. What about Kevin Booth? Have you found out anything I can use there?"

"Not yet. His father split a long time ago, and the mother died last year. She was an alcoholic."

"Did you talk to Booth's neighbors, run a rap sheet?"

"Rap sheet's the first thing I thought of. That arrest for drugs he beat is the only thing I could find. There aren't any neighbors. Booth lives way out of town."

"Barney, you have to get moving. If you don't come up with something soon, we'll be facing a penalty phase for sure."

"I'm gonna get on it, Mr. Hale. Soon as I'm done with this car."

AFTER a fast dinner Peter went to his new office in Steve Mancini's building and completed his preparations for the next day of trial. It was a little after eight thirty when he opened the front door of his house. The phone was ringing.

"Mr. Hale?" an unfamiliar voice asked.

"Yes. Who is this?"

"Don Bosco, director of mental health for the county. I know I shouldn't be disturbing you at home, but I've been wondering since that pretrial hearing why no one from the defense asked me any questions on cross and why you haven't gotten in touch with me about my trial testimony."

"Do you know something that might help Gary?"

"Didn't Steve Mancini tell you that I believe Harmon was inadvertently hypnotized by Dennis Downes during the interrogation?"

Peter blinked. "No. He never told me anything about hypnotism."

"You're kidding me. That really surprises me. I told Miss O'Shay that she shouldn't be using Harmon's statements to convict him, but she won't listen to me."

"And you also told Steve Mancini about this?"

"I told him over a month ago. I thought you'd be interested."

Peter was dazed. Gary's statements were the basis for the state's case. "Can we get together tonight? This is very important."

"Okay. There's an all-night restaurant near the turnoff to the interstate. The Jolly Roger. I'll be there in half an hour."

"HOW'D you get involved in this case?" Peter asked as soon as he and Don Bosco were seated in a booth with two cups of coffee.

"Downes called me. He wanted me to check my records to see if we had anything on Harmon's mental health history."

"Did you find anything?"

"No. I thought it was important enough to tell him in person, so I went over to the station house. When I arrived, Becky O'Shay asked me to watch the interrogation with her through a two-way mirror. She wanted my take on Harmon."

"Was there anything unusual about the way Gary was responding to Downes?"

"I didn't like the way Dennis conducted the interview. I even told him to be careful, but he didn't pay any attention. He and Becky seemed too excited about cracking the case."

"What was the problem?"

Bosco took a sip of coffee. "The first thing I noticed was all the leading. You know, asking a question that suggests the answer. I mean, Dennis was feeding him everything. Harmon was exhausted by the end, and the more tired you are, the more open you are to suggestion. In my opinion, most of what Harmon said is worthless. Especially the last third or so of the interview. I think Downes induced a trance state, and anything Harmon said then, well . . . Dennis wouldn't have to do it intentionally. He could have hypnotized Harmon without either of them knowing."

"Explain that to me."

"Hypnosis isn't all that mysterious. All you're really doing when you induce a trance is getting a person relaxed and focused enough to block out exterior influences so they can go into a quiet inner space. We all do that when we drop off to sleep at night or when we're so engrossed in a book that we don't hear someone ask us a question. Dennis helped Harmon along when he told him to shut his eyes and imagine he was watching events on a movie screen. That's a common technique that hypnotists use when they're trying to induce a trance."

"What would be the consequences of Gary being in a trance?"

"The big problem is reliability. It would be difficult, if not impossible, to tell what Harmon was really remembering and what he was repeating as a result of Downes's suggestions, or just plain making up. See, a person in a trance is not only wide open to suggestion, they also fantasize in order to please the questioner or to fill in gaps in their memory."

"And you didn't warn Sergeant Downes or Becky about this?"

Bosco looked embarrassed. "I mentioned it to both of them, but I really didn't catch on to what was happening until I'd been there awhile. By then the questioning was pretty far along. I guess I should have been more forceful, but most of the harm had already been done."

PETER drove directly to Steve Mancini's house. At first Bosco's information elated him. Then he realized how much Steve had cost them by failing to use the information at the pretrial hearing.

Peter rang Steve's doorbell at a little before eleven. As soon as Steve opened the door, Peter asked, "Why didn't you tell me about Don Bosco?"

Mancini looked confused. Donna walked out of the living room. She was wearing a bathrobe over a nightgown. Mancini glanced at his wife, then back to Peter. When he answered, he sounded nervous. "We're getting ready to go to bed, Pete. Can't this wait until tomorrow?"

"You know it can't. If Gary was in some kind of trance when he was questioned by Downes, the interrogation was no good. Don Bosco called me at home because he was surprised that you never brought that out during the hearing on the motion to suppress. He was also surprised that you never told me about your conversation with him. Quite frankly, Steve, so am I."

"I didn't tell you about the conversation, because I didn't buy into what Bosco said. You heard the tape. Downes didn't say anything about trying to hypnotize Gary."

Peter looked astonished. "What Downes did or did not say is irrelevant. We have a witness who would have testified that Gary was hypnotized during the most important part of his interrogation. Didn't you know that there is a statute that forbids the use of hypnotized testimony unless the most stringent precautions are taken? We could have gotten the whole thing thrown out."

"Did you know about this and keep it from Peter?" Donna asked her husband.

Mancini turned on Donna. "I can handle this, thank you. Bring us some coffee. Come on, Pete. Let's discuss this calmly."

"It's hard to be calm when I find out that you messed up on the single most important issue in the case."

Steve looked concerned, but calm. "I can see why you're upset. I'm upset too. Let's sit down and talk this out."

Peter walked into the living room and sat down on the couch. "I just don't understand this, Steve. I can't believe you didn't see the significance of what Bosco told you."

"It's true. I thought the issues were whether Downes gave Gary his Miranda rights and whether he coerced him into talking."

"Isn't there anything you can do?" Donna asked as she lowered a serving tray onto the coffee table.

"There might be," Peter said cautiously. "A defendant can always argue to a jury that they should not accept a defendant's statements because they are involuntary."

"If Gary was hypnotized, he wouldn't be responsible for what he told Downes!" Mancini said. "That's great thinking, Pete."

"Yeah, but I've got to convince the jury that Gary was hypnotized. That may mean hiring experts, and that's expensive." Peter looked at Donna. "Can your folks afford it?"

"Don't worry about the money, Peter," Donna said. "If my folks can't do it, Steve and I will pay."

Peter did not see Mancini's sudden anger, but Donna did. She was shocked by its intensity, and she remembered what happened the last time he was angry with her.

"I think we should all get some rest," Mancini said quickly. "Don't forget you have to be in court tomorrow."

"You're right," Peter said as he stood up. He suddenly realized how much the day's events had taken out of him.

As soon as the door closed, Mancini returned to the living room. Donna was bent over the coffee table gathering up the cups and the creamer.

"What was that about our paying for Gary's experts?" Mancini demanded angrily. "Gary made his own mess. We cannot afford to bail him out. Didn't you understand a thing I said about Mountain View? I'll bet you haven't even talked to your father about helping with it."

"I haven't had the chance." Donna straightened up with the tray in her hands.

"That's great. You can't take the time to help your own husband, and you expect me to spend my money on some shrink."

"Gary is my brother."

"That's right, Donna. He's your brother. Not mine."

Steve's cruel reply shocked Donna. "We wouldn't need the money for experts if you hadn't made a mistake," she said angrily.

The openhanded slap spun Donna's head to the right, and the tray went flying. Donna watched the cups and spraying cream sail away as Steve grabbed her robe and flung her to the ground.

"Damn!" Steve screamed. As she hit the floor, he gave her two strong kicks to her ribs.

Then, as swiftly as it started, the assault stopped. As Donna started to crawl away, Steve dropped next to her on the floor. Donna curled into a ball with her hands protecting her head.

"No, baby, no. You don't have to be afraid. I'm sorry. Please."

Donna looked up, and Mancini saw the blood. The blow to Donna's face had split her lip. "Oh no! What have I done?"

Mancini jumped up and sprinted to the bathroom. He ran cold water over a towel. When he returned, the front door was open. Donna was gone. Mancini raced out of the house. The car was parked in front. He looked right and left. Where was she? Without the car she couldn't get far. He ran inside and grabbed the car keys. He would find her. He had to find her.

DONNA waited for the car to drive away before pulling herself to her feet, hanging on to the bushes behind which she had been hiding. A sharp pain in her ribs doubled her over. She gritted her teeth and eased into a standing position.

Her parents' house was too far to walk. Besides, they were worrying so much about Gary that she could not let them know that her marriage was failing.

Then she thought of Peter. He lived nearby. She could keep to backyards, and Steve would not see her. Donna wanted to run, but the pain in her ribs was so intense that she had to walk hunched over.

A dog barked, and Donna tensed. She kept moving. "Just a few more blocks," she repeated over and over until, moments later, she was ringing Peter's doorbell.

When Peter opened his door, he took one look at her tearstained and bleeding face and brought her inside. "What happened to you?" he asked. Then Donna was sobbing in his arms.

Peter led her to the living room. She clung to him. As he lowered her to the couch, she spasmed and gripped her side. "He hit me. Steve hit me."

"Steve?" Peter repeated. "Has—has he done this before?"

Donna managed a nod. She got her crying under control. "It's been a nightmare, Peter. He's so kind to me, so loving. Then all of a sudden . . . I can't take it anymore."

Donna was too exhausted to go on. Peter stared at her. Her hair was in disarray, and her robe was open. She was wearing a short nightgown because of the heat. Peter could not help noticing her slim, tanned legs. "How badly are you hurt?" he asked.

"He kicked me in the ribs. It really hurts if I move quickly."

"I'll drive you to a hospital."

"No! No hospital. They'd have to report Steve."

Peter thought for a moment. "I have a friend. A nurse. Rhonda Kates. She works at the hospital. Let me call her. I'll explain what happened. Maybe she can check you out to make sure you don't have any internal injuries."

Peter made the call, and Rhonda told him to bring Donna to her place immediately. Donna could spend the night with her.

"Let's get going," Peter said as soon as he hung up.

"Thank you, Peter. You're a good friend."

9

"MR. HALE," Judge Kuffel said, "I've given a lot of thought to the matter of testimony about the peeping incident and evidence concerning the other two murders. I will permit the state to introduce evidence concerning the peeping incident. It is relevant to the state's theory that Mr. Harmon had an obsession with women with physical characteristics very similar to the victim."

It had been two thirty in the morning when Peter returned home after leaving Donna with Rhonda Kates. He was exhausted, but he sat forward to hear the judge's ruling on the other murders. He had battled hard to keep any reference to them out of the trial.

"Miss O'Shay, you have made a persuasive argument that the murder of Sandra Whiley is part of a series of murders, but I am not going to permit you to put that theory to the jury. First, there is no evidence connecting Mr. Harmon to the other killings. Second, there are substantial differences between the cases. The other women were sexually assaulted and—"

"Your Honor," Becky interrupted, "Wishing Well Park is a public place. We believe Mr. Harmon was frightened away by other individuals before he could have sex with Miss Whiley."

"Your theory may be correct, but I have to make my ruling based on the evidence."

"There's the hatchet," O'Shay argued. "The weapon is a trademark of this killer. It is very unusual."

"Not in a farming community, Ms. O'Shay. Without something more, I must bar you from mentioning the other murders."

The judge's ruling snapped Peter out of his funk. He was concerned about the introduction of evidence about the peeping incident, but if the judge had let O'Shay argue that Gary was a serial killer, there was no way Peter could win an acquittal.

"Do you have an update on Kevin Booth's condition?" the judge asked.

"I spoke with Mr. Booth's surgeon this morning," O'Shay said. "Mr. Booth cannot be transported to Whitaker without endangering the success of the skin grafts. However, he will be able to testify in his hospital room in Portland by Monday if the court is agreeable."

"I object, Your Honor," Peter said. "Booth's testimony is crucial to the state's case. If the jury sees him in a hospital room, it's going to generate a lot of sympathy. Booth has been burned to a crisp. I'm going to look like an ogre if I go after him. And what happens to Mr. Harmon's right of confrontation if Booth's doctor says I shouldn't excite Booth?"

"Your concerns are valid, Mr. Hale, but it seems to me that they are theoretical. It may be that you will be able to carry on a vigorous cross of the witness without any medical problems occurring. Of course, we could have a mistrial or Mr. Booth's testimony may be struck if you are foreclosed from examining Booth, but that's a risk the state runs.

"As to the prejudice caused by Booth's appearance, I will instruct the jurors not to let sympathy affect their decision. Now we'll take a short recess. Then I'll have the clerk bring in the jury."

Judge Kuffel left the bench, and Steve Mancini walked to Peter's side. There were dark circles under his eyes, and it was obvious that he had not slept last night either.

"I really screwed up, didn't I?"

"What's done is done," Peter answered. "I'll just have to call Bosco as a witness and hope that the jury buys his theory."

Mancini hesitated. Then he said, "Donna left me."

"What!" Peter responded, hoping he looked suitably surprised.

"We had a fight after you went home. I feel really bad. I love her so much." Mancini's voice caught, and Peter was afraid he was going to cry.

"Hey, it'll work out. She loves you too. She'll come back."

"I hope so, Pete. I can't stand being away from her. If you run into Donna, tell her I love her, will you? Ask her to call me. I'm sure everything would be all right if we could just talk."

"You bet," Peter said, but he did not mean it. He felt terrible about deceiving his friend, but he remembered Donna's pain and terror too vividly to help Mancini find his wife.

DURING the rest of the morning session, witnesses told the jury about the peeping incident. Becky O'Shay started the afternoon session by calling Sergeant Downes to the stand. Downes testified about the history of his investigation and the evidence that led him to Gary Harmon. Becky introduced the tapes of Gary's five-hour interrogation into evidence and supplied everyone with a transcript. Then she played a two-hour edited version of it to the jury. The day ended with a recitation by Downes of his part in finding the hatchet in a storm drain.

After court Peter went to his office to finish the work on his cross-examination of Sergeant Downes. Fortunately, Mancini was not in the building. Peter felt a little guilty about helping Donna hide from her husband and was troubled by his part in the Mancinis' marital problems. He should never have barged into their house, throwing accusations at his friend in front of Donna. He had made it sound as if Steve was intentionally sabotaging Gary's case. He decided that he owed it to Steve to tell Donna how sorry he seemed in court.

As soon as he wrapped up his work, Peter drove across town to Rhonda Kates's apartment, near the hospital. Donna looked apprehensive when she opened the door, but the look turned into a smile of relief, and she ushered him in. She was wearing shorts and a green tank top that belonged to Rhonda.

"You all alone?" Peter asked.

"Rhonda has an evening shift at the hospital."

"How are your ribs?"

"Still sore, but nothing's broken. It could have been worse."

They sat down in the living room. "I was too upset to thank you last night," Donna said. "Some men wouldn't have wanted to get involved. Especially with the wife of a friend."

"I like both of you, and I . . . Well, I really find it hard to believe that Steve hit you like that. Actually, he talked to me today at the courthouse. He's a mess. I think he's really sorry for what he did."

"Sorry isn't good enough. I am not going to be Steve's punching bag." They sat quietly for a moment. Donna looked attractive even with her split lip and bruises, and the cruel reminders of Steve's beating made Peter want to protect her. Then Donna asked, "How did the trial go today?"

Peter told her about Judge Kuffel's decision to allow testimony concerning the peeping incident but to keep out evidence of the other murders.

"Give Gary my love," Donna said. "Tell him I have to go out of town for a few days, so he won't wonder why I'm not in court." She paused. "Is Gary going to be convicted?"

Peter's first thought was to assure Donna that he would win Gary's case, but he found that he could not lie to her. "I don't know, Donna. I wish I could assure you that he'll be okay, but I just don't know."

PETER began his cross-examination of Dennis Downes by asking, "Are you aware that Gary Harmon is mildly retarded?"

"Well, I knew he wasn't a scholar."

"That's obviously true," Peter said, "because you would have had some trouble convincing a scholar that he had supernatural powers. In fact, you had a pretty easy time convincing Gary that he had psychic powers, didn't you?"

"I guess."

"That's because he trusted you, didn't he, Sergeant?"

"I suppose he did."

"After all, when he was arrested for peeping at that girl at the college, you fixed it so he wasn't charged."

"I did."

"You must not have felt Gary was very dangerous, or you wouldn't have let him go, would you?"

Downes suddenly saw where Peter had led him. He hesitated before answering, "No."

"Let's discuss Gary's supernatural powers, Sergeant. Until you came up with that idea, didn't Gary insist that he knew nothing about the murder of Sandra Whiley?"

"No. He said he saw her and the killer by the park entrance."

"That's not really accurate, is it?" Peter asked. He handed the witness a transcript of the interrogation. Sticking out of several pages were numbered labels. "Let me direct your attention to the page labeled number one. What Gary told you initially was that he had seen a man and a woman hugging in the park, did he not?"

"I guess he did."

"He had no idea who they were?"

Downes scanned the page, then agreed.

"In fact, it took you a long time to convince Gary that he had seen Sandra Whiley in the park."

"I didn't convince him of anything."

"Oh, didn't you? Look at number five. What is Mr. Harmon's response when you tell him, 'There's a good chance you saw Sandy and her killer when you walked by Wishing Well Park'?"

Downes scanned the page until he found the question and answer. "He said, 'All I see is them two hugging.'"

"And at nine, when you tell him to relax and let it come, doesn't Mr. Harmon tell you, 'It's no good. I didn't see anything new'? And at ten, what does he say when you ask, 'Is it Sandy?'"

"He says, 'I can't say for sure.'"

"That's right. Now look again at ten. I'm quoting. 'You know, Gary, you might be a natural at this stuff.' And Gary says, 'I just want to get this guy.' Isn't it true that you told him to guess at what happened in the park?"

"They were pretty good guesses."

"Oh, really? Like the guesses about where the blows fell on Miss Whiley's head?"

"That was accurate. He described where the wounds were."

"Let's look at twenty-two. Read that to the jury, if you please."

"I said, 'Let it flow, Gary. First hit. Where was it?' and he said, 'Top of the head,' which is where the first hit was."

"Go on."

"I said, 'This is great. Then what?' and he started swinging his arm and said, 'Another to the right side. And another.' "

"Stop there, Sergeant. Are you aware that Dr. Guisti testified that the killer struck his blows to the left side of the head?"

"Yes, but . . ."

"Yes or no?"

"Yes."

Peter did not let the jury see how elated he felt. "How long did the interrogation last?"

"About seven hours."

"So there are two hours that are not on the tape? It was during that part of the interrogation that you had Officer Robert Patrick play a little trick on Mr. Harmon, wasn't it?"

"I don't understand the question."

"What is a black light, Sergeant?"

Downes colored. "A, uh, black light is like a flashlight, but it shoots out an ultraviolet light beam."

"Did you have Officer Patrick dust a Coke can with an invisible powder that shows up orange under ultraviolet light?"

"Yes."

"After Gary handled the can, did Officer Patrick, on your orders, shine the black light on Gary's hands?"

"Yes," Downes answered uncomfortably.

"Did Officer Patrick then tell him that the orange splotches on his hands were the blood of Sandra Whiley?"

"Yes."

"That was a lie, wasn't it?"

Downes looked as if he was going to say something else at first, but ended by simply agreeing.

"Where did you learn your projection-transfer technique?"

"Nowhere," Downes answered proudly. "I made it up."

"Are you aware that the technique you used on Mr. Harmon is identical to that used by hypnotists to induce a trance?"

"I don't know what technique a hypnotist would use."

"Whether you knew or not, isn't it true that you led Mr. Harmon to give those answers that you wanted to hear?"

"No, sir, that's not true."

"Sergeant Downes, did you not lead Mr. Harmon to say that the man was holding a weapon after Mr. Harmon repeatedly told you that he had not seen a weapon in the man's hand?"

"Gary brought up the hatchet."

"Look at marker twenty-nine. Read the top lines, please."

"I ask, 'Did you see anything shiny, Gary?' "

"You were the first person to use the word shiny, weren't you?"

"Yes," Downes said after a moment's hesitation.

"And it is you who mentioned that the weapon would probably be in the killer's right hand?"

"I . . . I may have mentioned that first."

"You put those words in Mr. Harmon's mouth."

"No, sir. I just asked questions, and he supplied the answers."

"Only some of them were your answers, weren't they? Nothing further, Your Honor," Peter said before O'Shay could object.

"I only have a few questions, Sergeant," the deputy district attorney said. "Mr. Hale pointed out that the defendant described the hatchet wounds as being on Miss Whiley's right side, whereas they were actually on the left. When Mr. Harmon was describing these wounds, was he also demonstrating the strikes?"

"Yes. I gave him a ruler and told him to act out the blows."

"Were the defendant's actions consistent with what he said?"

"No, ma'am. See, Mr. Harmon had that ruler in his right hand, and he was saying the blows were landing on my right side, but really, with me facing him, it was on the left side of my face."

Peter understood with sickening clarity that he had lost one of his major points.

"Now, Mr. Hale asked you if you led the defendant to say that the man in the park had a weapon. Did you ever suggest that the weapon used was a hatchet?"

"No, ma'am. When I was talking to Gary, we didn't know what was used, other than it was a sharp-bladed instrument."

"Who first said that the murder weapon was a hatchet?"

"Gary. The defendant."

"And lo and behold, the murder weapon did turn out to be a hatchet, didn't it, Sergeant?"

"Yes, ma'am. Much to my surprise, it certainly did."

DR. LEONARD Farber, Kevin Booth's physician, had thinning brown hair, clear blue eyes and an easy smile. While he walked with Becky O'Shay, Farber explained that his patient had recovered enough to be moved to a regular hospital room. He had arranged for Booth to be temporarily placed in a room big enough for the judge, the court reporter, the attorneys and the jury.

"We're set for two, right?" Farber asked.

"You should probably be here at one forty-five. Just in case the judge or Harmon's attorney has any questions."

"See you then," Farber said, and he headed back to his office.

A policeman stationed outside Booth's door opened it as soon as he checked Becky's ID. Booth was sitting up in bed. O'Shay kept her poise, though the sight of him made her feel light-headed. His face was covered with silver sulfadiazine, a white, greasy cream. The right side looked normal, but bright red circles and blobs of healing outer skin covered the left side. Booth's hospital gown bulged in numerous places where bandages covered the skin grafts.

"How are you feeling, Mr. Booth?" O'Shay asked as she sat next to the bed.

"Bad," Booth rasped. He had breathed in smoke from the bedding that burned in his cell. Booth's pain medication had also been withheld so he would be clearheaded for his testimony.

"You'll feel better when you're through testifying and I let the U.S. Attorney know how much I appreciate your help."

O'Shay could see that Booth was frightened.

"Don't worry, Kevin. You'll do fine. I'm here to tell you the questions I'm going to ask, so you won't be surprised by them. Okay?"

Booth nodded, and for the next half hour O'Shay went through her direct examination with him. By the end of that time Booth seemed to flag, so O'Shay decided to wind up their meeting.

"That was great, Kevin. I wanted to go over one more thing; then I'll let you get some rest. You told me that Harmon said that Sandra Whiley wore a silver medallion on a chain around her neck. Did Harmon ever mention anything else about this necklace, something that only the killer would know?"

"What . . . would he . . . have said?"

"The necklace was found in some bushes near the entrance to the park. We think the killer tore it off of her neck while they were struggling. Did Harmon ever mention anything about that?"

"I . . . I'm not sure."

"Try and remember. Don't make up anything. But it would be important, if Harmon did say it." O'Shay stood up. "I'll come by before everyone else arrives, and you can tell me if you remember anything."

PETER Hale and Becky O'Shay sat on either side of Judge Kuffel on the left side of Booth's bed. Behind them, against the wall, sat the jurors. Dr. Farber and the court reporter sat on the right side of the bed. Gary sat behind Peter. Two guards stood against the wall. Another policeman was stationed outside the room.

The jurors seemed uneasy so close to a person who had been horribly burned.

"Mr. Booth, are you feeling well enough to talk to the jury?" Becky O'Shay asked with unctuous concern.

Booth nodded. It had been agreed that he could respond with a nod or shake of the head when the answer was yes or no.

"Okay. Now, after your arrest on various charges relating to narcotics, were you placed in the Whitaker County Jail?"

Again Booth nodded.

"Was Gary Harmon in the same jail?"

Booth's head turned slowly until he was staring directly at Gary. "Yes," Booth rasped.

"How long have you known Mr. Harmon?"

"High . . . school. Six . . . seven years."

"Describe your relationship with Mr. Harmon."

"Gary . . . was my . . . friend."

"Did you talk to Mr. Harmon in jail?"

Booth nodded.

"Did he ever discuss his case?"

Booth nodded.

"Tell the jury how that happened."

Booth took a deep breath. "First time I saw Gary in yard, he seemed . . . glad to see me. Excited. When I asked about murder, he said he didn't . . . didn't kill girl."

Booth paused and sipped from a straw in a water bottle. "Next day he told me the truth. He said . . . he killed her."

"Did he just come out and confess?"

"No. He was upset. I told him he didn't have to be afraid. If . . . he wanted to get something . . . off chest."

"Tell the jury the defendant's description of the murder."

"Gary tried to get date with . . . girl at Stallion. She said no. Gary . . . kept after her. She called him stupid. . . . Made him angry. Gary grabbed her. Yelled at her. Gary said he . . . ran away. Still mad. Ran to his . . . house. Got hatchet. On his way back to Stallion he saw girl. Thought she was . . . girl from bar."

"Where did he see her?"

"Near entrance to . . . Wishing Well Park."

"What did he say he did after spotting this woman?"

"He grabbed her. They struggled. She had . . . necklace. Gary grabbed her . . . by the necklace. It came off. She broke away."

"Then what happened?"

"Gary . . . ran after her. Caught her. Killed her."

"Did he say how many times he struck her or where?"

Booth shook his head.

"What happened after he hit Miss Whiley with the hatchet?"

"He saw he killed the wrong one. He was scared. Ran away."

"What did the defendant do with the hatchet?"

"Put it in storm drain . . . near college."

"Did he ever express remorse for killing Sandra Whiley?"

"He was sorry."

"Sorry?"

Booth looked at the jury. "Sorry he killed the wrong girl."

"Was anyone else present during these conversations between Mr. Harmon and yourself?" Peter Hale asked after a recess.

Booth shook his head.

"So the jury has only your word that he made this confession."

Booth did not answer.

"You stand to benefit greatly from your testimony, don't you?"

"I don't . . . understand."

"Well, you were arrested holding two garbage bags containing a total of twenty kilos of cocaine, weren't you?"

Booth ran his tongue across his lips, then nodded.

"Which means you will most likely be sentenced to more than ten years in prison if you are convicted?"

"Yes."

"Did Ms. O'Shay tell you about that sentence?"

The question caught Booth off guard, and he could not help looking at the prosecutor. "Don't . . . remember."

"Why don't you tell the jury about the deal you're going to receive for testifying."

"No deal."

"Are you telling this jury that you're not going to receive any benefit from the prosecutor for testifying against Gary Harmon?"

"Your Honor," Becky said quickly, "Mr. Booth has already said that he is testifying without any promise of assistance."

Peter could not believe this. "Do you want this jury to believe that you are testifying out of the goodness of your heart?"

"Didn't want to," Booth managed. "Gary is my friend. But . . . that girl. To kill her like that. What if Gary was free . . . and killed again? Couldn't have that . . . on conscience."

"Did it bother your conscience when you lied to Mr. Harmon by telling him that Karen Nix wanted to go out with him?"

"Not me. Chris Mammon told Gary . . . about girl."

"You enjoyed tricking and teasing Mr. Harmon, didn't you?"

"No," Booth rasped, but he did not sound convincing.

"And you have no trouble lying to this jury about what Gary said to you to save yourself from a prison sentence?"

"Objection," O'Shay shouted.

"Sustained," Judge Kuffel said.

"Then I have no further questions, Your Honor."

PETER replayed Kevin Booth's testimony over and over during the five-hour ride from Portland to Whitaker, and he always came to the same conclusion. His cross-examination of Booth had been as disheartening as his cross-examination of Dennis Downes. Neither witness had been broken.

He considered going to the office and working on the case, but he was too depressed and tired. He thought about going home, but he did not want to be alone. Finally, he decided to visit Donna, and he felt better immediately.

Rhonda Kates opened the door when he knocked. Peter smiled warmly. "Hi, Rhonda. Is Donna here?"

"She's freshening up. Donna's moving back to her folks' house. I was going to drive her."

"I'll do it. I have some stuff to go over about the trial."

The bathroom door opened, and Donna walked out. She looked surprised to see Peter. Then the look changed to a smile.

"Rhonda tells me you're going to your folks."

Donna sobered. "I'm sick of hiding. I didn't do anything wrong. Steve did. My brother is on trial for his life, and Steve is not going to keep me from being in court to support him."

"Are you going to tell your folks what happened?" Peter asked.

"Yes. I've decided that I have no reason to feel ashamed."

"Good for you. If you want me to, I'll take you to the farm. I can fill you in on the case while we're driving."

Donna hugged Rhonda and thanked her for putting her up.

As soon as they were on the road, Peter recounted Booth's testimony. "What scares me is that he seemed to be telling the truth. And he was so pathetic. He could hardly talk."

"Didn't your investigator find anything useful?"

"Pullen has been a disaster."

"I thought he was supposed to be good."

"That's what Steve said, but his reports are useless. He's been working at his brother's body shop instead of on the case."

The road to the Harmon farm followed the river. Donna had lapsed into silence, so Peter rolled down the driver's window and enjoyed the rich summer air until she said, "I've lived in Whitaker my whole life. Why don't you let me help. If we go to a penalty phase, I can line up a million witnesses with good things to say about Gary."

"You've never done any investigation. You need training."

"I can't do worse than Pullen, from what you've said, and I might do a lot better."

Peter dropped Donna off at the Harmons' and headed back to town. The phone was ringing when he walked into his house.

"Is this Peter Hale, the lawyer who's defending that guy who's supposed to have killed the girl in the park?"

"Right. Who's this?"

"Zack Howell. I'm a student. I go to Whitaker. I, uh, read your ad in the *Clarion* asking anyone who was near Wishing Well Park when Sandy Whiley was murdered to call you. I talked it over with Jessie, my girlfriend, and she said we had to call."

"You were near the park on the evening of the murder?"

"Yeah, we were."

10

A REPORTER from the *Clarion* spotted Donna and her parents in the corridor outside Judge Kuffel's courtroom and asked Jesse for a comment. While her father talked to the reporter, Donna took a step back, hoping she would be left alone.

"Hi, Donna."

She turned. Steve was standing next to her. Fear froze her. "I don't want to talk to you, Steve. Please go away."

"You have every right to be angry. I just wanted to find out how you're doing."

"I'm doing fine, now that you can't hit me."

Mancini looked down. He seemed contrite. "You don't deserve what I did. I'm . . . I don't know what I am. But I still love you and I feel sick about what I've done to our marriage. I just want to know if we have a chance."

"I don't know if we do," Donna answered.

Jesse Harmon turned away from the reporter and saw Steve. He flushed with anger and took a step forward.

Donna put a hand on his arm. "It's all right, Dad."

Jesse glowered at Mancini but held his tongue. "Let's go, Donna," he said. Donna followed her parents into the courtroom.

Peter and Gary were already at their counsel table. Peter walked over to the bar of the court and motioned toward Donna. "I thought over your idea about investigating for me. There are a few things I'd like you to do. We can talk about it tonight."

"Oh, Peter," Donna said excitedly, "that would be great."

The bailiff called the court to order, and Becky O'Shay recalled Dennis Downes to the stand.

"I have one more matter I want to discuss with you, Sergeant Downes." O'Shay handed Downes a plastic evidence bag. "Do you recognize this item marked State's Exhibit Seventy-six?"

"Yes. It's a crusader's cross on a chain."

"Who owned this necklace?"

"Sandra Whiley. She was last seen wearing it by one of the bartenders at the Stallion shortly before she left the bar."

"Where was the necklace found?"

"In a bush near the entrance to Wishing Well Park. The clasp had been broken in a manner consistent with the necklace having been jerked off of the victim's neck."

"How many people knew that Miss Whiley was not wearing the necklace when she was found?"

"Not many. The police at the scene. The medical examiner."

"What conclusion would you draw if you learned that Gary Harmon told someone that Sandra Whiley's killer had ripped a necklace from her just before he murdered her?"

Peter objected, and Judge Kuffel sustained his objection, but Downes's answer did not matter. The jury was going to wonder how Gary could possibly have known that Sandra Whiley's crusader's cross had been ripped from her neck just before she was killed. Peter was wondering about that too when Becky O'Shay told the judge that the state was resting its case.

DURING the morning session of court Peter called the policemen who searched Gary's house to establish that no blood had been found on Gary's clothes. He also called the bartender from the Ponderosa, who testified that he saw Gary around midnight on the evening of the murder and did not notice any blood on his clothes.

"I remember that clear as day," the bartender said. "The Mariners game was over, and I glanced at my watch. It was eleven fifty-three, eleven fifty-four. I was switching the channel when the Harmon kid came in."

Then Peter called Elmore Brock. "How are you employed, Mr. Brock?" he asked.

"I'm the school psychologist at Eisenhower High School."

"Tell the jury your educational and professional background."

"I graduated from Portland State University with a B.A. in psychology, and I obtained a master's degree in special education from the University of Oregon. I spent one year in Portland at the Allen Center, a treatment facility with programs for preschool through adolescence. When the school psychologist position at Eisenhower High opened up six years ago, I applied for it. I've been there ever since."

"Did you know Gary Harmon when he was a student there?"

"Yes, I did," Brock said, turning toward Gary and smiling.

"What is Gary's IQ?"

"Somewhere between sixty-five and seventy."

"What is the IQ of an average, normal person?"

"One hundred. Most college students have IQs in the range of one hundred and twenty."

"Mr. Brock, what is the difference between Gary and someone with an average IQ?"

"Gary's speech is slower and less distinct. His vocabulary is significantly smaller. His coordination and fine motor skills are also more awkward and less developed. He doesn't have the ability to plan very far into the future, and the plans he does make are vague and may be unrealistic."

"What classes did Gary take in school?"

"Special education classes designed to give Gary living skills and vocational skills. He trained to be a janitor, and he worked at the college with the janitorial staff while in high school."

"Do children with Gary's handicap tend to fight?"

"No. To the contrary. Mentally handicapped children tend to shy away from fights, even if they are big and strong like Gary."

"Was Gary mean or aggressive while at Eisenhower?"

"Definitely not. He was usually docile and very sensitive to other people's feelings. Let me give you an example. Gary loves football. I remember one game where a teammate was injured. Mentally handicapped kids have feelings like everyone else, but they have a harder time controlling them. I remember Gary being in tears while the coaches attended to this kid."

"Were you surprised to learn Gary was charged with murder?"

"Yes, I was. Nothing I know about Gary would have prepared me for this. Just the idea of Gary inflicting that kind of pain on another person is inconsistent with his personality."

"No further questions."

Becky O'Shay smiled warmly at Elmore Brock. "It's Mr. Brock, not Dr. Brock?" she asked sweetly.

"Yes."

"So, *Mr.* Brock, you don't have a Ph.D.?"

"No."

"In fact, you are not a licensed psychologist, are you?"

"No."

"A licensed psychologist has to take national written exams and an oral examination given to him by the Oregon State Board of Psychologist Examiners, but you didn't do that, did you?"

Brock flushed. "No," he answered.

"Now, I believe you said that someone like Mr. Harmon would have poor coordination?"

"Yes."

"Didn't he earn a varsity letter in football his senior year?"

Brock started to say something, then choked it back. "Yes."

"I'd like to ask you about some things the defendant can do. For instance, can Gary Harmon lie?"

"Well, yes. Gary could learn how to lie."

"If he murdered a young girl, would he be frightened?"

"Yes."

"So if Mr. Harmon committed a particularly bloody and violent murder, fear might spur him to lie?"

"Yes."

"Now, you told a touching story about the defendant weeping when he saw a teammate injured during a football game. Then I believe you testified that he wept because mentally handicapped people have a harder time controlling their feelings."

Brock saw the trap into which he had fallen, but he had no choice but to respond affirmatively.

"Mr. Brock, if someone with an IQ of sixty-five to seventy was drinking and very frightened because he had just butchered a young girl with a hatchet while in an uncontrollable rage, might he not block out the memory of what he had done?"

"That's . . . that's possible."

"You said that planning is more difficult for someone with Mr. Harmon's IQ. But he could plan a killing, couldn't he?"

"What type of killing are you talking about?"

"Let's say he was told that a woman at a bar wanted to go out with him. When Mr. Harmon asks the woman if she wants a beer, she not only rejects him but insults his intelligence. Let's further that Mr. Harmon physically assaults this woman. My question is whether Mr. Harmon is intelligent enough to make a plan that involves going to his house to obtain a weapon, returning to the area of the bar, following a woman from the bar, killing her and getting rid of the murder weapon."

"He . . . he could carry out that plan."

O'Shay smiled. "Thank you. I have no further questions."

"Mr. Brock, you aren't a Ph.D., but you are a specialist in dealing with the mentally handicapped, are you not?" Peter asked.

"Yes. That's where my training lies."

"Ms. O'Shay pointed out that Gary was on the varsity football team at Eisenhower. Tell the jury about that."

"Gary went out for the team in ninth grade. The coach let him work out with the other boys, but learning all but the simplest plays was beyond him. Every once in a while, if the team was really behind or really ahead, the coach let him go in for a play or two. They gave him a varsity letter because he tried so hard, not because he did the things the other kids did."

"I have two final questions, Mr. Brock. How easy would it be to fool Gary into believing that he had supernatural powers that would enable him to project himself into the mind of a dead woman and see how she was killed?"

"It would be very easy. Gary wants very much to please people. He would do or say anything for approval."

"What effect would there be on Gary if the person questioning him was a policeman?"

"That would have a big effect. Someone with Gary's IQ will follow people in authority without question."

AFTER lunch Peter called Don Bosco, who voiced his opinion that Dennis Downes had unwittingly placed Gary in a trance state during the interrogation, thus making many of Gary's statements unreliable. Bosco pointed out sections of the transcript where answers from Gary had echoed suggestions made by Downes.

"Mr. Bosco," O'Shay said when it was her turn, "you weren't at the park when the murder was committed, were you?"

"No."

"So you don't know whether Gary Harmon committed this murder and was telling Sergeant Downes about an incident he remembers or whether he was making up a story?"

"That's true."

"Would one way of telling whether the defendant was making up what he told the officer be to see if he knew things about Sandra Whiley's murder that were not common knowledge?"

"Yes."

"Thank you. No further questions."

Peter had saved his next witness for late in the day, so his testimony would be the last thing the jurors heard.

"Mr. Harmon calls Zachary Howell," Peter said.

"Mr. Howell," Peter asked when the young man took the stand, "are you a freshman at Whitaker State College?"

"Yes, sir."

"Do you have a girlfriend, Mr. Howell?"

"Yes. Her name is Jessie Freeman."

"Do you remember what you were doing on the evening that Sandra Whiley was murdered?"

"Jessie and I went to a late movie. Afterward we went to Wishing Well Park, and, uh, we were in the park for a while."

"When did you start to leave the park?"

"A little before eleven thirty."

"How can you be certain of the time?"

"We were going white-water rafting the next day, and we had to get up early, so I looked at my watch to see what time it was."

"What path did you take to get out of Wishing Well Park?"

"We walked along the river until we reached the wishing well. Then we left through the main entrance."

"Did you see a dead body next to the well?"

"No, sir."

"Would you have noticed a body?"

"Yes, sir. Jessie made a wish at the well and threw in a penny."

"Do you know what Jessie wished for?"

"Yes, sir." Howell smiled.

"Tell the jury how you figured out Jessie's wish."

"When we reached the stone pillars, Jessie kissed me."

"And did you kiss her back?"

"Yes, sir."

"What happened then?"

"Jessie was holding on to my hand, and she swung away from me and said, 'See, wishes do come true.' "

"She swung away," Peter repeated. "And why do you remember all this so well, Mr. Howell?"

"Sandy, the girl who was murdered, was in one of my classes. Everyone was talking about it the next day when we got back from rafting. I realized that we must have been right where the murder took place, right before it happened. That really scared me."

"Mr. Howell, how long did it take between the time you decided to leave the park at a little before eleven thirty and the time you actually left the park?"

"I'd say no more than five minutes."

"So, it was around eleven thirty-five when you were at the entrance to the park?"

"Yes."

"How was Jessie dressed?"

"Jeans and a T-shirt."

"Mr. Howell, are you taller or shorter than Jessie?"

"Taller. She's only about five four, five five."

"One last question. What is the color of Jessie Freeman's hair and does she wear it short or long?"

"Jessie's hair is blond. She has long blond hair."

"ARE you telling me you didn't know a thing about this witness?" Becky O'Shay shouted at Dennis Downes. "Our whole case depends on the theory that Harmon made up his story about two people kissing at the entrance to Wishing Well Park. Now we've got two cute teenagers smooching at the pillars at eleven thirty-five. He is taller than she is, just as Harmon said. She swings away from him, just as Harmon said. And the girl has blond hair and was wearing jeans and a T-shirt, just like Sandra Whiley. Finally, we have Harmon at the Ponderosa without a drop of blood on him at midnight. The case is falling apart."

Downes shrugged. "I don't know what to tell you. No one knew about Howell until he called Hale. It's just a bad break."

O'Shay sank onto her chair. "I'm sorry I yelled, Dennis. I'm just tired. You go and interview Howell for me. See if you can get me something I can use on cross. Call me at home if you do."

Downes left, and O'Shay stared at the stacks of police reports that covered her desk. She had read through them countless times, but she vowed to go through them again in hopes of finding anything that would help her deal with Zack Howell's testimony.

Becky missed it her first time through. In fact, she did not put it all together until she caught sight of that afternoon's edition of the *Clarion* lying unread on top of her filing cabinet.

Becky sat up, openmouthed. She rummaged through the police reports until she found the one she wanted. Then she placed several calls. The people she spoke to confirmed her conclusion. Zack Howell and Jessie Freeman may have been kissing at the entrance to Wishing Well Park at eleven thirty-five, but Gary Harmon had murdered Sandra Whiley, and Becky could prove it.

THE next day Peter rested the defense case, and Becky O'Shay called Dennis Downes as her first rebuttal witness.

"Sergeant, you are aware that Dr. Guisti places Sandra Whiley's time of death sometime between eleven thirty p.m. and two thirty a.m.?"

"Yes, ma'am."

"And the body was discovered early on Saturday morning?"

"Yes."

"When was the identification made?"

"After four that afternoon. We couldn't find a wallet or purse, so it took a while."

"How did you discover the identity of the victim?"

"Marjorie Dooling, Miss Whiley's roommate, saw a sketch of the victim in the afternoon edition of the *Clarion* and came down to the station house."

"No further questions."

"Any cross, Mr. Hale?" Judge Kuffel asked.

Peter had no idea why Becky had asked Downes about the time of the identification, so he shook his head.

"The state calls Martin Renzler."

Martin Renzler was tall and slender with a studious look.

"How are you employed, Mr. Renzler?"

"I'm the managing editor of the Whitaker *Clarion.*"

"On the morning of the day that Sandra Whiley's body was found, did you receive a request from the Whitaker police?"

"Yes. Sergeant Downes asked if the paper would publish an artist's sketch of the murdered woman, because the police could not establish her identity. We ran the sketch on the front page."

"When does the paper hit the streets?"

"The earliest it would have been out is two thirty p.m."

"Nothing further," O'Shay said.

Something Peter had read in a police report began to nag him.

"The state calls Harry Diets."

An overweight, thirtyish man was sworn in. O'Shay established that he was the manager of KLPN, the local television station. Diets had also been contacted by Dennis Downes.

"Mr. Diets, did you broadcast the sketch of the murdered girl?"

"We did. We made it part of a special bulletin at three p.m."

O'Shay called her next witness. As Wilma Polk walked to the witness stand, Peter remembered her statement to the police. The reason she, Diets, Renzler and Downes had been called to testify dawned on Peter. As she testified to her recollections of the Harmon-Mancini wedding reception, he felt a sick, swirling feeling in the pit of his stomach.

"Did you discuss the murder with Mabel Dawes, a friend of yours, at the wedding reception?"

"Yes, I did."

"Tell the jury what happened while you were talking to her."

"We were at the food table. Gary Harmon walked over. He told us that the girl had been at the Stallion that night."

"Do you remember when this conversation took place?"

"Oh yes," Polk answered. "It was one thirty. Eric said we had to hurry because we were due at my daughter's house at two. I looked at my watch. Eric said it was one thirty, and that was exactly what my watch said."

THE first job Peter gave Donna was to use a stopwatch while tracing the possible paths Gary could have followed on the evening of the murder. While she was making a list of the routes she would have to walk, she noticed that she would be near the house where Sandra Whiley had lived with Marjorie Dooling.

The boardinghouse was a yellow two-story Victorian with white trim. A middle-aged woman answered the doorbell.

"Good afternoon," Donna said. "Is Marjorie Dooling in?"

"I believe so. Who should I tell her is calling?"

Donna identified herself, and the landlady went upstairs. A few minutes later she descended, followed by a girl wearing a T-shirt and cutoff jeans. Her brown hair was cut short. Donna recognized Marjorie Dooling because she had seen her testify.

"Ms. Dooling, I'm an investigator working for Peter Hale. I'd like to ask you a few questions about your friend Sandra."

"All right. Come on up to my room. But can you make it quick? I'm studying for a test."

Dooling's apartment consisted of a large living room, a bathroom and two bedrooms. Dooling sat on an old couch. In front of her was a low coffee table covered with textbooks. Donna sat in one of the two armchairs.

"Do you miss Sandra?"

"We weren't close, but she was nice. I guess I do miss her."

"Did she date?"

"A little."

"Could she have been killed by someone she dated?"

"I only met a few of the guys she dated. None of them seemed like the type who would . . . You know."

"Did anything unusual happen around the time she was killed?"

Dooling looked a little nervous. Then she sighed. "I guess it can't hurt now, and I already told the D.A. that Sandy used drugs. Cocaine. I think she was seeing someone who turned her on to it. She was staying in her room a lot and skipping classes."

"Was this around the time of her death?"

"Actually, around then I began thinking she was trying to quit. She was acting different. She seemed scared of something too. She was locking the door and not going out at night."

"Was she scared of anyone in particular?"

Dooling hesitated. "There was a guy. I only saw him once from the upstairs window. He came to pick her up. He stayed in his car."

Donna asked her some more questions about Whiley's interests, her courses and her personal life. When Donna noticed that Dooling was glancing at the clock, she stood up.

"Thanks for talking to me. I'm sorry I bothered you, but this has been helpful." Donna handed Dooling the business card of the lawyer for whom she worked with her name handwritten on it. "If you remember anything else, please give me a call."

THE guard closed the door to the interview room, and Gary sat down across from Peter. There was a dull smile on Gary's face. He was totally oblivious to the havoc that had been wreaked on their case by Wilma Polk's testimony.

"I want you to listen up, Gary. I have a very important question for you, and I want you to think before you answer it."

"Sure." Gary sat up straight and stopped smiling.

"Sandy was murdered between eleven thirty on Friday night and two thirty on Saturday morning. You got that?"

"Uh-huh," Gary answered with a nod.

"Good. When Sandy's body was found early Saturday, she didn't have any identification on her. No one knew her name. So the police asked the newspaper and the TV to show her picture and ask for help in finding out who she was. Are you following me?"

"Yeah, Pete. They didn't know Sandy's name."

"Right. Good. Okay. Now the newspaper came out around two thirty in the afternoon, and the TV showed Sandy's picture at three. Sandy's roommate told the police Sandy's name around four. Two thirty in the afternoon is the earliest anyone could have known who Sandy was, because that's when the paper came out with her picture. Now, here's my question, Gary. Mrs. Polk says that at one thirty, at the wedding reception, you told her the dead girl was at the Stallion on Friday evening. If no one else knew who was killed at one thirty, how did you know the girl had been at the Stallion?"

Gary thought hard for a moment. He looked confused. "I don't know. How did I do it, Pete? How did I know who that girl was?"

THE Harmons lived in a white two-story colonial farmhouse. Donna ushered Peter into the large front room. Jesse and Alice were out. As soon as they were seated, Peter related the testimony that established that Gary knew the victim had been at the Stallion before anyone else knew her identity. Donna looked more and more troubled as he spoke.

"Where was Gary before he went to the Stallion Friday night?"

"With us. Mom cooked a meal for Steve and the family. Steve had to leave early to work on his cases so he could go on our honeymoon. He gave Gary a lift into town."

"Did Steve tell you where he dropped off Gary?"

"I think it was at home. Gary must have walked to the Stallion on his own. It's not that far from his house."

"When did you see him next?"

"When he and Steve arrived at the church. Steve picked up Gary and drove him over. I asked him to do it in case Gary was having any trouble with his tuxedo."

Peter thought for a minute. "Did Gary say anything to you at the church or the reception that relates to the murder?"

"Gary did say there were police cars at the park. You pass it on the way to the church. I remember that he was excited."

Peter shook his head. "Donna, I don't think Gary killed Whiley, but I don't think I can save him. I . . . I probably shouldn't have taken the case in the first place. Amos Geary was right. He said I would screw it up, and I have."

"That's not true. You've done a wonderful job."

Donna was so trusting. Peter felt sick. "There's something I have to tell you. It's about why I came to Whitaker. I . . . I didn't choose to leave Hale, Greaves. I was fired. I was helping out in a big personal injury case my father was trying." Peter told her about his father's heart attack and how he'd lied to the judge so he could finish the trial.

"The case was so easy it took a real genius to screw it up, but I did, and . . . and this poor woman . . . You should have seen her, Donna. I destroyed any hope she and her kids had."

"You're being too hard on yourself."

Peter looked directly at her. "When I took your brother's case, I didn't even think about him. All I was thinking about was how famous I'd be if I won."

"You care for him now, though, don't you?" Donna asked.

"I do. I admire Gary. I don't think he would ever intentionally hurt anyone. He thinks about the feelings of other people. When he has to do a job, he tries to do his very best. He's not like me at all, and I wish I could be a little more like him."

Donna reached up and touched Peter's cheek. "I don't know what kind of person you were in Portland. I just know you now."

Peter wanted to take Donna in his arms, but he couldn't take advantage of her when she was so vulnerable. For a moment they sat on the couch in an awkward silence; then Donna said, "I paced off those distances for you this afternoon."

"Great," Peter answered. "What did you find out?"

"I started at the Stallion and walked to Gary's house. It's a little over three quarters of a mile, and it took me about twelve minutes. Then I went back to the bar and continued to the park entrance. It's a quarter mile from the Stallion to the entrance, so it took me sixteen minutes to walk from the house to the park."

"That means Gary got home at about eleven twelve if he left the Stallion at eleven and walked straight home."

"He could have run or walked faster than I did."

Peter worked the numbers in his head. "Damn. It could still work out. If he leaves his house around eleven twelve, follows Whiley and gets to the park around eleven thirty-six . . . If Howell and his girlfriend left the park around eleven thirty-five and Whiley passed by a little after . . ."

"I've been thinking about that, Peter. If it's only a quarter mile from the Stallion to the main park entrance, it would only take about three minutes to walk. If Whiley left the bar around eleven twenty, she should have reached the park before those kids."

"You're right! That would put her there around eleven twenty-five. But Zack Howell said that Jessie Freeman made a wish at the well around eleven thirty and the body wasn't there. Where was Sandra Whiley between eleven twenty, when she left the Stallion, and eleven thirty-five, when Howell and Freeman left the park?" Peter shook his head. "Tell me about the rest of your results. Did you go from the park to the storm drain where the hatchet was found and back to the Ponderosa?"

"Yes. The storm drain is near the campus. We're talking a little under two miles. Even if Gary ran it in a seven-minute mile, there's no way he could kill Whiley after eleven thirty-five, ditch the hatchet and make it to the Ponderosa by midnight."

"So he'd have to hide the hatchet somewhere before going to the Ponderosa, then pick it up later. That sounds a little complicated for someone of Gary's intelligence."

Peter stood up. He looked depressed. "I've got to go back to the office. You keep working on character witnesses for the penalty phase. I hope we don't need them, but I'm afraid we will."

THEY came for Gary just as the sun was setting. The reporters were waiting on the courthouse steps. When the car doors opened, the mob pressed in, jabbing at Gary with microphones and screaming questions. The sheriff's deputies cleared a path as Gary, handcuffed, struggled out of the car. He looked for a friendly face and saw Peter pushing through the crowd.

"What did they say?" Gary asked.

"I don't know. They have to read the verdict in court. The jurors are waiting in the jury room."

"Are Mom and Dad here?" Gary asked as they took the elevator up to the courtroom, surrounded by sheriff's deputies.

"Yes. I called them first thing. Donna is with them."

The guards escorted Peter and Gary to the defense table. As they took off Gary's handcuffs, a stir in the back of the courtroom signaled Becky O'Shay's entrance. She looked grim and avoided eye contact with Peter and his client. Moments later the door to the jury room opened, and the jurors went to their seats.

Everyone stood when Judge Kuffel entered the courtroom. When he was seated, the judge turned toward the jury box. "Ladies and gentlemen, have you reached a verdict?"

Ernest Clayfield, a farmer, stood slowly. He held a folded sheet of paper. "We have," Clayfield answered grimly.

"Please hand your verdict to the bailiff."

The bailiff took the verdict form and gave it to the judge. Kuffel unfolded it and read it once. Then he looked at Gary.

"Will the defendant please stand," he said in a subdued voice. Gary jumped up, but Peter felt dizzy from tension, and his legs were weak. It took an effort to get to his feet.

"The verdict reads as follows," Judge Kuffel said. " 'We the jury find the defendant guilty as charged.' "

There was silence for a moment; then Peter heard Alice Harmon moan as Donna softly cried out, "No." A babble of voices filled the air. Judge Kuffel gaveled for silence. Peter touched Gary's shoulder and then slumped down in his seat.

"What happened?" Gary asked Peter.

"They found you guilty. They think you killed that girl."

Gary looked stunned. He stared at the judge. The guards started forward. "I didn't do it," Gary said.

"Please sit down, Mr. Harmon," the judge said.

"I didn't hurt that girl," Gary cried out, his voice breaking.

"Mr. Harmon," the judge repeated as the guards drew closer.

Peter stood and placed a hand on Gary's shoulder. Behind him he could hear Donna's sobs.

"I wanna go home. I want my mama. I don't like that jail."

Peter wrapped his arms around Gary and held him. Gary's body shook as he wailed like a confused and frightened child.

Part Four

11   JUDGE Kuffel set the start of the penalty phase of the trial for a week from Monday, which gave Peter very little time to recover from the trial. On Sunday he woke from a restless sleep. After a shower and breakfast he went to the office.

Peter had no plan to save Gary. He had been through the police reports and witness statements several times. The only thing new were Donna's neatly typed investigative reports. Peter went through them without enthusiasm until Donna's summary of her interview with Marjorie Dooling triggered a memory.

PETER located Dooling in the college library, where she sat studying at a large table. He took the seat across from her.

"Miss Dooling, my name is Peter Hale." He handed her a business card. "I represent Gary Harmon. You were kind enough to talk to my investigator the other day, and there was one small item in her report that I wanted to clear up."

"One question. But that's all. I have a test tomorrow."

Peter showed Dooling the section of Donna's report where she had mentioned the man who came to the house to pick up Sandy. "You said you thought Sandy was frightened of him."

"She was real nervous all day. When he honked the horn for her, she seemed scared to me."

"Can you remember him? His hair color, his size?"

Dooling started to shake her head. Then something occurred to her. "I only saw him from the second-floor window, and he was in his car. But when Sandy came out of the door, his arm was resting on the car window. He was wearing a short-sleeved T-shirt, and I could see part of his biceps and his forearm. They were really big, like a weight lifter's, and they were covered by tattoos. I think I saw snakes and a panther."

PETER drove back to his office in a fog. Sandra Whiley knew, and was afraid of, Christopher Mammon. Mammon had the opportunity to commit the crime. He left the Stallion around the time that Whiley did. If Peter could show that a monster like Mammon had a reason to harm Whiley, Gary Harmon would cease to be the only viable suspect in her murder.

As Peter parked in front of Mancini's building, he remembered Amos Geary telling him to read Mammon's file before the preliminary hearing, but Peter had only given it a cursory glance. Now he wished he had been more thorough. However, Steve Mancini had represented Kevin Booth in the case involving the Whitaker State bust. He would also have the police reports.

All of the closed files in the office were in a large room behind the secretarial station. Peter found Booth's file and read through the police reports, but discovered nothing helpful until he found two reports that looked different from the others. They had not been written by the police, but by agents of the DEA, the federal Drug Enforcement Administration.

The first report detailed the activities of an unnamed confidential, reliable informant, or CRI, who had been busted with cocaine and had agreed to work off the case by setting up Kevin Booth. The CRI was to purchase increasingly larger amounts of cocaine from

Booth until Booth was unable to supply the demand and had to agree to put the CRI in touch with his supplier.

The second report detailed the arrest of Booth and Mammon on the Whitaker campus, but it contained information about the arrest that was new to Peter. The CRI was supposed to be bringing thirty thousand dollars to Booth for two kilos of cocaine. It appeared that the arrest had been totally unexpected, and neither the DEA nor the Whitaker police had wanted it to occur.

Peter was certain he had never seen either of the DEA reports in Geary's file. Why would Mancini have them, but not Geary? A thought occurred to him, and he felt himself grow cold. What if Sandra Whiley was working off an arrest for cocaine and had betrayed Christopher Mammon to the DEA? That would give Mammon a huge motive for murder.

As Peter was putting the reports back in the file, he spotted a telephone message slip that Mancini had clipped into the folder. The slip was dated the day before the preliminary hearing.

The message was from Becky O'Shay. She wanted Steve to call as soon as he came in so they could discuss a deal in the Booth case. Peter wondered what the deal had been. Obviously it had fallen through, because Booth had not pleaded guilty.

Peter was about to leave the file room when another thought struck him. Becky O'Shay must have given Steve the DEA reports. If Whiley was the CRI, and Becky knew it but kept it a secret, Peter could file a motion for a new trial. But first he had to find out if Sandra Whiley was the CRI, and Peter thought he knew how he could do that.

"I DON'T know, Peter. I could get in a lot of trouble," Rhonda Kates said. "Why don't you just tell the district attorney that you need to talk to Booth. Don't they have to let you talk to witnesses?"

"They do. But I have to sneak into Booth's room, because I think the D.A. has done something illegal. Look, all you've got to do is get the guard away from Booth's door. I only have one question to ask him. I'll be in and out."

"This is a lot to ask."

"Rhonda, Donna's brother may be innocent. If Kevin Booth says what I think he will, I may be able to set Gary's verdict aside and give the police the real killer. If I don't get in to see Booth, Gary will probably be on death row by the end of next week."

KEVIN Booth had been moved to the Whitaker hospital two days before. A guard sat in front of his door. Peter waited in an alcove and watched as Rhonda told the guard that there was an urgent call for him at the nurses station farthest from Booth's room. As soon as the policeman got up, Peter slipped into Booth's room.

"Hi, Mr. Booth. I'm Peter Hale, Gary Harmon's lawyer," Peter said with what he hoped was a winning smile.

"I thought the case was over." Booth's speech was normal now.

"It is. Actually, I had a question about the Whitaker State bust. The one you beat. Chris Mammon still has to go to trial on it."

"I don't give a damn about Mammon."

Peter thought fast. "Your answer could really hurt his case. But I've got to know if he's telling us the truth. If he's not, he could end up serving a long prison term."

"What do you want to know?" Booth asked, interested now.

"You remember when you were busted at Whitaker State. Was Sandra Whiley bringing you thirty thousand dollars or three thousand? It will make a big difference at sentencing. Mammon claims that she was only bringing three thousand and that he didn't know how much cocaine was in the bags."

Booth snorted. "Mammon's lying. He knew exactly how much dope was in the bags. And he knew how much dough Whiley was bringing because he told her to bring the thirty grand."

"Was Mammon aware that Whiley was working for the feds?"

"Not before we got busted. But after, I said she must have turned us in. Chris was furious. He was gonna check it out."

"That's what we heard," Peter said solemnly.

Suddenly Booth laughed. "If Whiley was working for the feds, there's gonna be a lot of nervous people in this burg."

"Why's that?"

"She never had much money, so she had to earn her snow by making deliveries. She could name a lot of names."

"Like who?"

"Mr. Football, for one. It would serve him right, the way he left me hanging as soon as I said I didn't have any money."

"Who are you talking about?"

Before Booth could answer, the guard walked in and saw Peter. "Who are you, and what are you doing in here?"

"I'm an attorney," Peter said with righteous indignation. "This man is a witness in the Harmon case."

"Yeah, well, sneaking in here on my watch is going to get you hauled in." He turned to the doorway. "Nurse, call the station house. Tell them we have a situation here."

DENNIS Downes had no idea whether Peter's shenanigans were legal or illegal. As soon as he learned what Peter had done, he called Becky O'Shay. O'Shay told Downes she would be at the station in a few minutes.

"Just what do you think you're doing, Hale?" O'Shay demanded as the door to the interrogation room closed behind her.

"My duty under the Constitution of the United States."

"Bull. That man is my witness, and he's in protective custody. You are in big trouble. You're looking at a bar complaint."

"Do you think what I did was as bad as hiding the fact that your victim, Miss Whiley, was bringing the thirty thousand dollars to Mammon and Booth on the evening of their arrest? Or as bad as concealing from me that she was working with the cops, a fact that Mammon suspected and that drove him into a murderous rage, thus making him a very viable suspect in Miss Whiley's murder?"

"What—what are you talking about?" O'Shay stuttered. "Mammon didn't kill Whiley. Your client did."

"We'll see about that. I think it's time to go to Judge Kuffel."

For a brief second O'Shay looked panicky. Then she sat down

across from Peter and, in a reasonable tone, said, "Listen, Peter, I shouldn't have gotten so angry. I know the pressure you've been under. But I can tell you that you're barking up the wrong tree."

"I've seen the DEA reports you sent to Steve Mancini."

"What are you talking about?"

"The reports that mention the CRI who was involved with the drug deal at Whitaker State."

"I didn't send any DEA reports to Steve Mancini. I think you're confused, Peter. If Whiley was working with the government, I would have been told." O'Shay stood and headed for the door.

"Are you going to tell Downes to let me go?"

"As soon as I'm certain that you haven't broken any laws."

The police held Peter for two more hours; then they let him go. While he was in custody, it occurred to Peter that he should make a copy of the DEA reports to show to the judge when he filed his motion for a new trial.

He arrived at the office a little after eight and went directly to the file room. He took out the envelope with the police reports and shuffled through them twice before realizing that someone had removed the DEA reports.

Peter's first reaction was anger at Becky O'Shay. She must have kept him in custody long enough to send someone to retrieve the reports. But fortunately, there was someone else who knew about the documents. Peter walked to his office and dialed Mancini.

"Steve, something has happened," he said as soon as Mancini picked up. "I found out that Sandra Whiley was involved with the drug deal where Mammon and Booth were arrested. I think she was working with the police and Mammon found out. It gives him a terrific motive to kill her."

"That's incredible. How did you work that out?"

"I hope you're not mad, but after I learned about the relationship between Mammon and Whiley, I looked in your file on Booth. I should have called you first, but I was too excited."

"That's okay. The file is confidential, but Gary's life is at stake."

"Thanks, Steve. Anyway, I found two reports in your file from the DEA," Peter went on. Then he told Steve about his discovery that the reports had been removed from the file. "Becky must have had someone break in here and remove them," Peter concluded, "but she forgot that you've seen the reports. You can confirm their existence. Kuffel is going to have to give Gary a new trial once he determines that Becky failed to turn over evidence that points to another suspect."

"Pete, I honestly don't remember seeing any reports from the DEA in the discovery I received from Becky."

Peter hung up in a daze. If Mancini could not remember the reports, he had nothing. Then Peter recalled the last thing Kevin Booth said before the guard burst into Booth's hospital room. Something about several people in Whitaker having to worry if Whiley named names. The only person he'd had time to mention was Mr. Football, who had dropped Booth when he found out Booth did not have any money.

Peter walked to the front door of the law office and inspected it. He did the same with every other door into the building. None showed signs of forced entry. Whoever took the DEA reports had a key. Could Steve have taken the reports? Suddenly Peter recalled Steve's failure to tell him about his interview with Don Bosco. It was Steve who suggested that Gary plead guilty. Mancini had given him the name of the incompetent Barney Pullen. Peter had assumed that Steve Mancini was his ally, but now it appeared that Mancini had a hidden agenda. And Peter suspected it included saddling Gary with the lawyer least qualified to handle his case.

PETER parked his car at the edge of the dirt drive next to Amos Geary's house. Like its owner, it was broken down and aging. Weeds had overgrown the yard; the paint was peeling and faded. One of the steps leading to the porch was cracked, and Peter stumbled over it. When he looked up, he found Geary, dressed in a bathrobe and pajamas, looking down at him with contempt.

"Hale, you are pathetic. Can't you even walk up a flight of stairs without making a mess of it? What are you doing here?"

"I'm in trouble."

"I'm not interested." Geary turned to go inside.

"Wait!" Peter shouted. "It's not me. It's Gary. Gary Harmon. That poor guy is in jail for a murder he didn't commit."

Geary looked at Peter over his shoulder. "Whose fault is that?"

"Mine! There, I said it. Are you happy? I'm everything you said I was. I'm a self-centered, shallow idiot, and I'm asking for your help because I don't have what it takes to save Gary."

"Come inside. It's too cold to talk on the porch."

The interior of Geary's house was in as much disorder as the exterior. The living-room couch sagged when Peter sat on it.

"You want a drink?" Geary asked.

"Actually, yes."

Geary shuffled out of the room and returned with a fifth of Johnnie Walker and two glasses. He poured and handed one of the glasses to Peter. "Talk," he said after taking a sip.

Peter started at the beginning. He explained how Steve Mancini had manipulated him into taking Gary's case and his suspicions about the ways Mancini had sabotaged it. Finally, he told Geary about the day's incidents, ending with his suspicion that the missing reports had been removed by Steve Mancini.

"That's quite a story," Geary said. "The way I understand it, with the DEA reports missing and Mancini and O'Shay denying their existence, you have no evidence at all to support your story."

"That's true."

"Then why do you think I can help you?"

This was the hard part. Peter took a deep breath. "When I learned the reports were missing, I decided to go to the source. I called the DEA office in Portland, and I was put through to the agent in charge, Guy Price. I told him everything, and I told him how important it was to get copies of the reports so I could go to Judge Kuffel and ask him to reopen the case." Peter paused, remembering one of the most depressing moments in his day. "He told me that he couldn't confirm or deny any ongoing investigation."

"You still haven't told me how you think I can help you."

"I almost gave up. Then I remembered there was one person I knew who had enough clout to make someone like Price talk."

"I hope you don't mean me?" Geary asked incredulously.

"No, Mr. Geary. I . . . I came here tonight to ask you to please call my father and ask him to talk to me."

12

PETER had not slept well, and the five-hour drive from Whitaker should have exhausted him, but he was floating by the time he saw the skyline of downtown Portland. He was home, and he was welcome once again in his father's house.

The night before, Amos Geary had talked to Richard Hale on the phone in his den while Peter waited nervously in the living room. Finally Geary told Peter his father wanted to talk to him.

"Dad?" Peter said, in a voice choked with emotion.

"I'd like you to tell me everything from the beginning, Peter," Richard had responded. It was as if there had never been an Elliot case or the intervening months of exile.

The office of the U.S. Attorney for Oregon was in downtown Portland, a few blocks from his father's office. When Peter entered the lobby, a little after five, Richard was standing off to one side. "Thanks for doing this for me," Peter said.

Richard smiled. "You're my son," he answered simply. Then he turned toward the elevators.

The elevator doors opened into a reception area. Richard announced their presence to a receptionist. Minutes later a tall, well-dressed woman walked into the waiting area.

Katherine Hickox owed her appointment as U.S. Attorney to Richard Hale. Richard had quietly touted her to Oregon's U.S. Senators and had made a phone call to a high-ranking official in the Justice Department. So, it was no surprise when Hickox agreed to meet with Peter's father at five thirty and to make certain that Guy Price attended the meeting.

"Richard," she said, offering him her hand.

Richard took it, then motioned Peter forward. "This is my son, Peter. He's just driven in from Whitaker."

"It's nice meeting you," Hickox said warmly. "Let's go back to my office. Guy is waiting for us there."

Hickox led them to a corner office with a panoramic view of the city. When they entered, a short, muscular man in a brown sport coat stood up. After she made the introductions, Hickox sat down behind a large oak desk, and Price sat beside it.

"Why don't you tell us why you're here," Hickox suggested.

"Mr. Price," Richard said, looking directly at the DEA agent, "my son called you from Whitaker yesterday."

When Richard called Hickox to set up the meeting, he had not mentioned that his son would be accompanying him. Price suddenly made the connection. He did not looked pleased.

Richard gave a summary of the facts surrounding Gary Harmon's case and the reasons for Peter's suspicions. Then he said, "I'm here to ask Mr. Price to tell Peter if Sandra Whiley was working for the DEA in a case involving a very dangerous and violent drug dealer named Christopher Mammon. If she was, Peter can try to avert a miscarriage of justice."

Price looked uncomfortable. "I told your son that I can't discuss ongoing investigations, even to confirm or deny them. That's still my position. I wish you'd called me before having your son drive all the way here from Whitaker for nothing."

"I understand your official position, Mr. Price. What you need to understand is the effect of following it. If Whiley was working for the DEA and the district attorney concealed this fact from Peter, she is guilty of a gross violation of the discovery rules. If she conspired to have the reports destroyed to prevent Peter from proving her misconduct, she may be guilty of a crime."

"Mr. Hale, if this D.A. is violating some law, you should take it up with the judge who's trying the case."

In a level tone Richard said, "If I find out that you're aware that Sandra Whiley was an informant for the DEA and you kept quiet about it, knowing it could cost a young man his life, I will personally make sure that you wish you were never born."

Price's eyes widened and he leaped to his feet.

"Guy!" Hickox said. Price remained standing but restrained himself. The U.S. Attorney turned to Richard. "I won't have you threatening Guy in my office, Richard."

"You're quite right," Richard said. "I apologize, Mr. Price. I'm certain that you'll do the right thing if you discover that an obstruction of justice is occurring in Whitaker."

Price glared at Richard but held his tongue.

"Thank you for meeting with Peter and me, Katherine."

"Let me show you out," Hickox answered stiffly.

As soon as they were out of Price's hearing, Hickox said, "How dare you pull a stunt like that?"

Peter's father looked directly at Hickox. "You are the chief law-enforcement officer for the United States in this district. Something dirty may be going on in your bailiwick. Mr. Price may be clean, but he can find out if someone else is dirty, and he can make certain Peter gets a copy of those reports. I've known you a long time, Katherine, and I know you'll do what is right."

When the elevator doors closed, leaving Peter and his father alone, Peter exhaled with relief. "Dad, are you sure you know what you're doing? Price is a really powerful person."

Richard turned to Peter with a wry smile. "It's because Price is so powerful that I called him out. As soon as we left the room, I bet he started thinking about what type of person would have the nerve to dress him down like I did. And Katherine is going to tell him as soon as he asks her, which should be right about now."

"Dad, thanks. You put yourself out for me."

"I haven't done a thing. You're the one who's going the extra mile for a client, and I'm very proud of you."

Peter's chest swelled, and he felt a lump in his throat. His father had just given him the best present he had ever received.

PETER WAS EXHAUSTED BUT happy when he pulled into his driveway the next evening. Over dinner he and his father had not talked about the future, but it was obvious that they had one together. Not right away. Peter still had a lot to prove to Richard, but the wall between them had come down.

As soon as he entered his house, the phone rang. "Peter Hale?" The voice was indistinct, as if the speaker was trying to disguise it.

"Yes?"

"I'm only going to say this once, so pay close attention. If you want the truth about Christopher Mammon and Sandra Whiley, take the highway east. Eight point three miles from the Welcome to Whitaker sign there's a dirt road on the right. Drive down it until you come to a barn. I'll be waiting. If you're not here by ten thirty, I'll be gone. And come alone, or I won't show."

THE flatlands was a desolate stretch of cracked brown earth that began a few miles east of Whitaker. It was not a place to visit in the dead of night.

Peter set his odometer as soon as he passed the WELCOME TO WHITAKER sign. When it read eight point one, he slowed down and strained toward the side of the highway. The turnoff was more of a dirt track than a road, and he almost missed it. After a while on the narrow, rutted trail, Peter's headlights settled on the shape of an abandoned barn.

Peter kept the lights on and the motor running. He took a flashlight from the glove compartment and stepped out of the car. A wind ripped across the flat, dry ground and knifed through him. He zippered his windbreaker tight around his neck and took a few steps toward the barn. No shapes emerged; no lights flickered in its dark recesses.

"Have any trouble finding this place?"

Peter spun toward the voice, reflexively raising the flashlight like a weapon. Suddenly a blur became a vague shape, and Christopher Mammon stepped out of the darkness. "I hear you've been telling people that I killed Sandra Whiley."

Peter took a step back. Could he get into the car and lock the doors before Mammon got to him?

"Not smart," Mammon continued. "Everyone else thinks Gary Harmon murdered Whiley. If I did kill her, you'd be the only one who suspected it. It would be in my best interest to lure you to an isolated spot like this and get rid of you."

Mammon took a step forward. There was something small and black in his hand. Peter's next step brought him hard against the side of the car. Mammon raised his hand and pointed the object at Peter. Oh, Lord, Peter thought, don't let me die now. I'm not even thirty. Then part of the object dropped down, revealing something shiny.

"Relax," Mammon said. "I'm not going to kill you. I'm a cop."

It took a moment for the words to register. About the same time it took for Peter to recognize the object in Mammon's hand as a leather case for a badge. Peter sagged against his car.

"Now listen up," Mammon said. "If you want to learn the truth about what happened to Sandra Whiley, I need a guarantee that you will never, ever tell anyone about this meeting. As soon as we finish talking, I'm leaving this continent. No one at DEA will acknowledge my existence. You won't find a trace of me in any files."

"I . . . I've got no choice, then."

"That's right. And there's something else you should know. You and your father really ticked off a couple of people. I've got instructions from the top to stay as far away from you as I can."

"Then why are you doing this?"

Mammon took a breath. "It's Gary. If it wasn't for me, he wouldn't be in this fix. I was hoping he'd be acquitted. But now . . . If he was executed, I would be to blame."

"What do you mean?"

"Kevin Booth lived in Seattle for a while. He got to know Rafael Vargas, who runs cocaine in the area for a Colombian cartel. Kevin picked up pin money acting as a mule. When he moved back to Whitaker last year, Vargas asked him to set up a network.

"Eight or nine months ago Whiley was busted on her way to deliver cocaine to a customer of Booth. The locals had no idea who

Booth worked for. Whiley spilled everything. The Whitaker cops called the state police, who knew we were trying to find a way into the organization Vargas works for. I've been in deep cover for two years building a background and trying to make contacts. I was transferred here to get close to Booth and force him into a position where he had to introduce me to Vargas."

"Did Whiley know who you were?"

"No. We couldn't risk that. She thought I was working for organized crime. The night Booth and I were arrested at Whitaker State, I was waiting for Whiley to bring me thirty thousand dollars to pay for the two kilos of coke that were found in the car. Our arrest was bad luck, and it came at a really bad time. I had to stay credible in Vargas's eyes, so it was arranged for Booth to win his preliminary hearing and for me to lose mine."

"What do you mean, it was arranged for Booth to win?"

"That whole thing was a hoax. O'Shay was contacted by the Justice Department and asked to throw the prelim. And she did."

Peter was stunned. "Who was in on the fix?"

"O'Shay, Mancini and the judge."

"What about Earl Ridgely?"

"He was out of town for the week, and O'Shay was asked to keep the whole thing from him. He's too much of a straight arrow to go along with fixing a court case. She told the judge that she had Ridgely's approval, but that was a lie. Ridgely still doesn't know why Booth won his prelim. Even Booth didn't know.

"The night of the murder I was meeting Booth to convince him to take over my part in our plan to bring down Vargas. The plan worked. We not only caught him red-handed with twenty kilos of cocaine but we have evidence that implicates him in the importation and sale of a lot more. Vargas knows he's facing life without parole. We hoped he would cave and give us a way to get to the next level in the cartel. He broke three days ago."

Mammon paused. He looked embarrassed. "When I arrived at the Stallion on the night of the murder, Harmon was sitting with Booth. I had to get rid of him, so I told him Karen Nix had the hots for him. I'm the one who caused his argument with Nix and got him convicted for a crime he didn't commit."

"How can you be so certain that Gary is innocent?"

"I know who killed Whiley."

"Who is it?" Peter asked anxiously.

"While Gary was arguing with Nix, I went outside and talked with Booth. While we were talking, I saw Whiley follow a man to his car. They argued over something; then they drove off together. The man was a customer of Booth. Someone to whom Whiley had delivered cocaine. Steve Mancini."

"Oh, my Lord," Peter said. Everything made sense now. Whiley must have threatened Steve. Mancini could not afford a scandal with Mountain View's finances hanging in the balance. When Gary was arrested, it was a godsend, and Mancini did his best to make certain that Gary would be convicted.

"You've got to testify for Gary."

"No. I'm leaving for South America tomorrow. If I stay and testify, my cover will be destroyed. I'm close to being accepted by the cartel. If Mancini is going to be caught, you have to do it."

"How am I going to prove any of this?"

"I don't know, Hale, but I hope to God you can."

"You have problems," Geary agreed the next morning after Peter finished telling him about the meeting at the U.S. Attorney's office, his encounter with Mammon and about Steve Mancini.

Peter sighed. "The penalty phase starts in a few days. There's got to be some way to show that Whiley was the CRI."

Peter noticed that Geary had a faraway look in his eyes and the hint of a smile on his lips. Suddenly Geary chuckled. "Rebecca messed up. Come on, think. There's a witness who can bury O'Shay."

Peter went over everything he knew while Geary watched his struggle with glee. Finally Peter gave up.

"Listen up, then, and I'll tell you how we're going to bust this case wide open."

EARL RIDGELY LOOKED surprised when he walked into the chambers of district court judge Brett Staley with Becky O'Shay and saw Peter Hale and Amos Geary sitting next to the judge's desk.

"What's up, Brett?" Ridgely asked.

"Why don't you and Miss O'Shay sit down and let Mr. Hale explain," the judge replied.

"On Sunday, I made a very unsettling discovery, Mr. Ridgely," Peter said. "I learned that Miss O'Shay has been withholding evidence that casts the whole Harmon case in a different light."

"Earl, this is a crock," O'Shay said. "What really happened on Sunday is that Mr. Hale snuck into Booth's room at the hospital and was arrested. I'm preparing a bar complaint."

"Why don't we hear what Peter has to say, Becky," Ridgely said. O'Shay started to protest. Then it suddenly dawned on her why they were meeting in Judge Staley's chambers instead of Judge Kuffel's, and she turned pale.

"Becky has known for several months that Sandra Whiley was working as an informant for the DEA in a case involving Christopher Mammon, Kevin Booth and Rafael Vargas," Peter said.

"Is this true?" Ridgely asked her.

"Earl, this is nonsense," O'Shay answered angrily.

"I suppose I'd also be crazy to suggest that you fixed the Booth-Mammon preliminary hearing?" Peter said. "I'm sure your boss will be interested in knowing that you told Judge Staley that he knew all about your deal with the Justice Department."

"What deal?" Ridgely asked.

Judge Staley answered. "Miss O'Shay told me that you had approved a plan that involved my dismissal of Booth's case so that a federal undercover operation would not be endangered."

"I what!"

"Earl, there was no time to track you down," O'Shay said.

"Will someone explain what's going on here?" Ridgely asked.

"The feds were monitoring a drug deal that was supposed to go down on the Whitaker State campus," Peter said. "The deal was being used to help an undercover agent infiltrate a Colombian drug cartel. Then the campus security guards screwed everything up by arresting Booth and Mammon.

"The feds wanted Booth back on the street, so they concocted this plan to fix Booth's prelim. Becky lied to Judge Staley and said she'd cleared everything with you.

"When Gary was arrested for Whiley's murder, Becky knew Whiley was an informant. She'd been briefed by the DEA, and she even sent Steve Mancini two DEA reports about the Whitaker State case. I found out about the reports, and she convinced Steve to destroy them. She knew Judge Kuffel would have to throw out Gary's conviction if he learned about her cover-up."

"I don't believe this," Ridgely said incredulously.

Peter looked directly at O'Shay. He was about to bluff, and he hoped O'Shay could not tell how scared he was that he had guessed wrong. "Why would Steve destroy the DEA reports for you, Becky? Why would you trust him to do that instead of running to me with evidence that would win Gary a new trial? You knew that Steve had a reason to want Gary convicted. You knew that Steve had to obey you or risk exposure. You knew that he was with Sandra Whiley right before she was murdered."

"Is this true?" Ridgely demanded.

"What does all this matter?" O'Shay implored Ridgely. "Harmon's guilty. How did he know that the victim had been at the Stallion hours before anyone knew Whiley's identity?"

"I talked with Gary before I set up this meeting," Peter said. "The morning the body was found was the morning Steve was married. He drove Gary to the church. They passed by the park and saw the police cars. Gary was excited by all the activity. He probably asked Steve about it. I'm betting Steve slipped and said some girl who'd been at the Stallion last night had been murdered.

"I also spoke to Wilma Polk. Her husband was at the crime scene. He told her that the man who killed Whiley chopped her up with a hatchet. Mrs. Polk told her friend when they were at the reception following the wedding. Mrs. Polk remembers Gary standing next to her and listening to what she said.

"And the placement of the blows. Before Bob Patrick tricked Gary with the black light, he showed him several crime scene photos of Whiley's head wounds. There are explanations for a lot of the evidence that incriminates Gary, but you weren't interested in the truth, were you, Becky?"

"I . . . I thought it was Gary. I still do. I didn't know that Steve was with Whiley that night until I debriefed Booth. He saw them together at the Stallion."

"And you told Booth to keep his mouth shut," Peter said.

"I couldn't tell you. The jury would never have convicted if it knew about Whiley being an informant and Steve being with her right before she was killed. There would have been too many other suspects. And Steve swore he didn't kill her."

"You still don't understand what you've done, do you?" Peter asked, amazed by O'Shay's continued defiance. "How could you blind yourself to the possibility that Steve killed Whiley when it was right in front of you? How could you . . ."

Suddenly Peter knew why O'Shay had shielded Steve. "Did Steve swear he was innocent while you two were having sex?"

Becky's eyes widened. "What are you talking about?"

"Are you denying that you've been sleeping with him? Did you keep quiet about Mancini because he threatened to expose you?"

"No, no. It wasn't like that. As soon as Kevin Booth told me he had seen Steve with Whiley at the Stallion, I confronted Steve. He swore he was innocent. Then he reminded me of . . . of something I should have remembered. Steve and I . . . we've been together off and on since I moved to Whitaker. And, well . . . We'd planned to spend the evening before his wedding together."

"What!" Peter said.

"You don't think Steve married Donna Harmon for love, do you?" O'Shay said scornfully. "He was worried about Mountain View, and he figured Jesse Harmon would come through with a sizable investment once he was married to Jesse's daughter."

"That son of a . . ." Peter began.

Geary put a restraining hand on his arm. "You were telling us how you knew Mr. Mancini was innocent, Miss O'Shay," Geary prodded.

"Steve was with me the night Whiley was killed. He showed up around midnight. Later I confronted him about Booth seeing him with Whiley. He admitted it. He said Whiley was at the Stallion. When he left, she cornered him in the parking lot saying she had to leave town. She was scared of Mammon. She thought he suspected her of setting him up at Whitaker State and would kill her.

"She was making a scene, so Steve told her to get in his car. They drove around for a while. She demanded money from Steve so she could run away. She said if he didn't give it to her, she would tell everyone he was using cocaine. Steve told her he had some money at his office. He didn't want to be seen with her, so he dropped her at the entrance to Wishing Well Park and said he'd meet her at the well."

"When did he say he dropped off Whiley?" Peter asked.

"Eleven fifty. He checked his watch because he was supposed to come to my place around midnight."

Peter controlled his excitement. The bartender at the Ponderosa had testified that Gary came into the bar at eleven fifty-three or eleven fifty-four. If everyone's times were accurate, it would be impossible for Gary to be the killer.

"What did Steve say happened next?"

"He said he went to his office, picked up every penny he could find, which was about three thousand dollars in cash, and went right back to the park. Steve said he parked on a side street and walked over. He saw someone running away from the well. At first he thought it was Whiley. Then he saw her body."

"And . . . and you kept this to yourself?" Earl Ridgely asked. "You made that poor boy and his family go through a trial for murder when you knew he wasn't guilty?"

"I didn't know that. I still think Gary committed the murder."

"How could you?" Ridgely demanded. "Whiley was blackmailing Mancini. He was at the park with her at the time of the killing."

"I'm sure he didn't kill her, Earl. I remembered the suit he was wearing when he came to my house. I'd seen him in it earlier in the day. It was the same suit and tie. The killer would have had blood all over him, and there wasn't a drop of blood on Steve."

THE Harmons sat in the front row of the courtroom. Steve Mancini sat in a row behind them on the other side of the room. A deputy had served him a subpoena while he was eating breakfast. Mancini wondered why Earl Ridgely was sitting alone at the prosecution table. He was not aware that Becky O'Shay was in jail charged with tampering with a witness and official misconduct.

Gary Harmon looked desperate when the guards led him into Judge Kuffel's courtroom. "Please get me out of jail, Pete," he begged as soon as he was seated between Peter and Amos Geary. "I'm scared there. I just want to go home."

"Well, you might be doing just that, Gary. So calm down."

Judge Kuffel emerged from chambers carrying the motion for a new trial that Peter had hastily prepared. He looked perplexed. "You're joining in this motion, Mr. Ridgely?" the judge asked.

"Yes, Your Honor. In light of certain matters that have come to my attention, I believe that the interests of justice require the court to set aside the guilty verdict against Mr. Harmon."

"Very well. Call your first witness."

Peter called Kevin Booth to the stand. Yesterday afternoon, after meeting in Judge Staley's chambers, Earl Ridgely, Peter Hale, Amos Geary and a detective from the state police had interviewed Booth at the hospital. Now Booth was brought into court in a wheelchair and allowed to testify from it.

"Mr. Booth," Peter said, after the witness was sworn in, "you have already testified in the case of *State* versus *Harmon*. Was the testimony that you gave in Portland truthful testimony?"

"One second here, Mr. Hale," Judge Kuffel said. "You're asking this man if he committed perjury. If he says he lied, he's admitting to a crime."

"That's true, Your Honor. But Mr. Booth is also testifying under a grant of immunity from prosecution for any false testimony given in Mr. Harmon's case."

"Very well. Proceed."

"Mr. Booth, I repeat, did you testify truthfully in this case?"

"No."

"When you discussed his case with Gary at the Whitaker jail, did he ever tell you that he murdered Sandra Whiley?"

"No. He said he didn't do it."

"Why did you lie about what Mr. Harmon told you?"

"I was scared I'd go to prison on my federal drug charge, so I had to make a deal. It was my only way out."

"The prosecutor in Mr. Harmon's case is Rebecca O'Shay. Did Ms. O'Shay instruct you to conceal from the defense certain information that would have cast doubt on Mr. Harmon's guilt?"

"Yeah. Whiley was a cokehead, and she bought from me. She didn't have a lot of money, so sometimes she had to work off her debt. On the evening I was busted with Chris Mammon, Whiley was late bringing thirty thousand dollars to the meet. When we were arrested, Mammon thought Whiley set us up. He told me he was going to kill her if he found out it was true."

"And you told Ms. O'Shay about the threat?"

"Yeah. I thought she'd be interested, but she said Harmon did it, and I wasn't to tell anyone that Mammon knew Whiley."

"Did Ms. O'Shay tell you to keep quiet about anything else?"

"Yeah. I told her I saw Steve Mancini drive off with Sandra Whiley from the Stallion on the evening that Whiley was killed."

Donna put her hand over her mouth. Mancini looked around nervously. He started to stand, but stopped when he noticed the armed guards stationed inside the courtroom doors.

"What happened when you told this to Ms. O'Shay?"

"She said I'd better forget about it."

"Did Mancini know Whiley before the evening of the murder?"

"Sure. Mancini bought cocaine from me. Whiley delivered it to him at his office and his house a few times."

"No further questions, Mr. Booth. Your Honor, we call Steve Mancini."

Mancini hesitated, then walked unsteadily to the witness-box.

"On the evening that Sandra Whiley was murdered, did you drive away from the Stallion tavern with her?" Peter asked.

"I'm . . . I want to speak to a lawyer," Mancini said.

Peter knew this would happen, and he did not object. Mancini started to stand up. Ridgely signaled to two police officers. "I have a warrant for your arrest, Mr. Mancini," Ridgely said.

Steve froze. "Hey, Earl, this isn't true. I didn't kill her."

Ridgely ignored him. "Bring Mr. Mancini to the jail," he told the officers. "See he's read his Miranda rights and is allowed to call an attorney." Mancini was led out of the courtroom.

"May Mr. Harmon be released into the custody of his parents, Your Honor?" Peter asked.

"That would be unusual. He's been convicted of murder."

Earl Ridgely stood and addressed the court. "Rebecca O'Shay is not present today, because she is under arrest. Ms. O'Shay intentionally concealed crucial evidence from the defense. Evidence which casts grave doubt on Mr. Harmon's guilt. I feel that justice will be served best by releasing Mr. Harmon into the custody of his parents while I sort everything out."

"Very well," Judge Kuffel said. "Mr. Harmon, I am ordering your release to the custody of your parents. You will have to follow certain conditions, which I will devise after consultation with counsel. Do you follow what I'm saying?"

Gary looked uncertain. He turned to Peter.

"He's sending you home, Gary," Peter said.

Gary's mouth formed into a wide smile. "I'm going home?" he asked, as if he could not believe it.

Peter could not help smiling back. "Yeah, you're going home."

"WILL you have another piece, Peter?" Alice Harmon asked.

"If I eat one more slice of your apple pie, I'll explode."

"I believe I can fit in another piece," Amos Geary said.

"Gary, hand me Amos's plate, please," Alice told her son. When Gary picked up the plate, his back was to Alice Harmon, and he did not see how his mother beamed.

Donna stood up and turned to Peter. "I'm going to get some fresh air. Do you want to join me?"

Donna opened the screen door and led Peter into the front yard. It was mid-September, the sun was almost down, and the night air was nippy. Donna wrapped her arms around herself as they strolled.

"It's so great having Gary home," Donna said. "You can't believe the change in Mom and Dad."

"It's not over yet," Peter cautioned. "We still have to get the charges dismissed."

"Who do you think killed Sandra Whiley?" Donna asked when they reached the large oak that shaded the front lawn.

"I don't know. It would be great if I did prove who killed Sandra Whiley, but as long as I can convince Earl that he should set Gary free, I've done my job."

"What about Mammon? I heard that he's disappeared."

"Mammon is definitely not the killer."

"How can you be so certain?"

"In order to tell you, I'd have to break a promise I made. Just trust me. I know it's not Mammon."

"If Mammon isn't guilty, then Steve probably is."

"I guess that's true," Peter answered thoughtfully. "We just learned that his first wife left him because he also beat her, so he clearly has a propensity for violence. The problem with the case against Steve is Becky O'Shay's evidence." Peter caught himself. "I'm sorry . . ." he started, but Donna shook her head.

"Don't be. I'm glad I found out that he was with her on the night before our wedding. It relieves me of any lingering doubts I may have had about Steve."

They walked on in silence until Donna asked, "Will you be moving back to Portland when you've wrapped up Gary's case?"

"No. I was really thoughtless leaving Amos shorthanded, so I'm going back to work for him tomorrow."

"I'm glad you'll be around," Donna said, looking into Peter's eyes.

Peter reached out and took her hand. "There's another reason

I'm sticking around Whitaker. I don't know if this is the right time to say this. You're going through so much right now."

"We don't have to rush, Peter. Now that you're staying, we can take our time. Let's just see how things work out. Okay?"

Then Donna kissed him. It was a soft kiss, but it stunned Peter. Donna rested her head on his shoulder, and they held each other in the dark. Peter had never made a commitment to a woman before. Even thinking about it was a little scary. But he had done some pretty amazing things since arriving in Whitaker.

"YOU look pretty satisfied with yourself," Amos Geary said when they were on their way back to town in Peter's car.

"What do you mean?" Peter asked self-consciously. He had been reliving his kiss with Donna.

"She's not someone to play with. If you're not serious about Donna, don't start anything."

"Hey, Amos, give me some credit, will you," Peter protested.

"Given your track record, I decided to be blunt."

They drove on in silence for a while. Peter drifted back to thoughts of love, but Geary was thinking about something else. After a while he let out a long breath.

"What?" Peter asked.

"I was thinking about that poor girl. The police have lost so much time that I don't think they'll ever catch Whiley's killer."

"I haven't ruled out Steve. It's pretty unlikely, but Ridgely should check Steve's alibi for the time when those other two women were killed. The person who killed Whiley probably killed them too."

"I'll say one thing—whoever committed those murders is one sick s.o.b."

Suddenly Peter pulled the car over to the side of the road. Geary was thrown forward, but he caught the dashboard with his hands. "What the devil is wrong with you?" Geary shouted.

Peter turned slowly. He looked pale. "The hatchet. I didn't even think. . . . We've got to go to the office and look up something in Mammon's file."

"What are you talking about?"

"I'll explain on the way," Peter said.

"Is THIS where we turn?" Peter asked.

Geary studied a map of the Whitaker area. "Okay. This is the road that was listed in the police report in Mammon's file."

Peter drove a mile up an unpaved dirt track. There was a full moon, and they soon saw the object of their search. Peter stopped in front of the dilapidated house.

Peter tried the door. It wasn't locked. He had brought along a flashlight, but Geary flipped on a switch, and he didn't need it.

"Looks like the electricity is still paid up," Geary commented.

"Whew! What's that smell?"

Both men winced as a sour and fetid odor assailed them. Flies buzzed around rotting pizza crusts and decomposing cheese. Unwashed clothes lay in clumps on the couch.

"Let's search it fast, so we can get out of here," Geary said.

They split up, Peter taking the bedroom and bathroom and Geary searching the living room and kitchen.

"Anything?" Peter asked.

"Not a thing," Geary answered when they both finished.

"I was so sure." Peter walked outside. Geary turned out the lights and shut the door. Peter was at the car when he froze.

"What's that?" he asked. Another house could barely be made out in the moonlight.

The two men turned on their flashlights and walked a dusty quarter mile. It was not until they reached the shack that they could tell it was deserted, but there was a padlock on the door.

"What do we do now?" Peter asked.

Geary raised his foot and kicked the door with all the force of his near three hundred pounds. The rotting door splintered and gave. An odor, different and more foul than the one they had smelled in the other house, assailed Peter when he went in.

"Oh, my God!" he whispered when the flashlight beam found the bloodstained mattress pushed up against the far wall. He moved his beam around the floor and gagged when he realized that almost every square inch was encrusted with dried blood.

"Peter," Amos called. Peter looked at the corner of the room that Geary's beam was illuminating. He saw piles of women's clothes, a purse and two wallets.

"What do you want to bet that one of those wallets belongs to Sandra Whiley?" Geary asked.

"Let's get out of here and call the police."

KEVIN Booth was asleep when Earl Ridgely entered his hospital room followed by members of the Major Crime Team. He stirred when the nurse turned on the lights, then sat up.

"What's going on?" Booth asked, rubbing his eyes.

"I have a few questions for you, Kevin," Ridgely said.

"It's three in the morning. Can't this wait?"

"No." Ridgely pulled a chair next to Booth's bed. "But I promise not to take up too much of your time. First, though, I'm going to give you your Miranda rights."

"What is this?" Booth asked when Ridgely was through.

"Can you explain why Sandra Whiley's wallet and the clothing of Emily Curran and Diane Fetter were found in a shack less than a quarter mile from your house and why the floor of the shack was covered with blood?"

"What . . . what shack? I don't know what you think you've got, but you've got nothing connecting me to no murders."

"Actually," Ridgely said, "we've got quite a lot. For instance, Curran and Fetter both had a lot of cocaine in their system when they died. I think you lured them to your house with promises of free drugs, got them high, then raped and killed them. I also think you made one monumental error. Peter Hale explained it to me. It's so obvious that I feel stupid for missing it.

"It was after you decided to trade testimony against Gary Harmon for a deal that would keep you out of prison. You tricked Gary into telling you all of the details of Whiley's murder that he told the police. But that wasn't enough for Becky O'Shay. She needed corroboration, so you told her something that only the killer would know. You told her where to find the hatchet you used to murder Curran, Fetter and Whiley. The hatchet you threw in the storm drain because you were afraid that Mancini might have seen you running from the murder scene.

"Gary Harmon couldn't have told you where the murder weapon was hidden. It was impossible for him to have killed Whiley. He was at the Ponderosa when the murder occurred."

Booth stared wide-eyed at Ridgely. "I want a lawyer," he said.

Ridgely nodded. "I think you're wise to ask for one, Mr. Booth, because if anyone needs a lawyer right now, you do."

EPILOGUE

THE scoreboard on top of Stallion Stadium showed that there were fifty-eight seconds remaining in the game between the Whitaker Stallions and Boise State, with Whitaker leading by a touchdown. Peter figured that fifty-eight seconds was about as long as he could take the frozen rain that had turned the last game of the season into a mud-wrestling contest. Donna huddled against him, just as miserable as he was. Gary was on his feet screaming with each play, transported by the very real possibility that the undefeated Whitaker Stallions might go all the way.

Many things had happened in the three months since the dramatic termination of the charges against Gary Harmon. Kevin Booth had not held out for long, confessing to the murders of Sandra Whiley, Emily Curran and Diane Fetter. To escape the death penalty, he cut a deal that would keep him in prison for the rest of his life.

Booth told Earl Ridgely that he had watched from his pickup truck as Whiley and Mancini argued. Then he followed them as they drove aimlessly through Whitaker. Whiley had haunted Booth's fantasies since she began buying cocaine from him. He also suspected Whiley of betraying him and longed to make her suffer. When Mancini dropped Whiley off at Wishing Well Park, Booth had taken his hatchet from the pickup and followed her with the idea of taking her to his shack to torture and rape her, but Whiley had fought Booth and had paid with her life.

As soon as Steve Mancini was certain that he would not be prosecuted for killing Whiley, he confessed his attempts to cover up his involvement with Whiley on the night of the murder. His motive in sabotaging Gary's case was simple cowardice. He feared an arrest for Whiley's murder, and, with the Mountain View project on the verge of destruction, he could not afford a scandal involving his use of cocaine.

"As soon as this game ends, we're heading for my place and a gallon of hot toddies," Peter managed to chatter to Donna.

"We'll have to figure a way to get Gary out of the stadium. He always wants to run down on the field and shake hands with the players."

The whistle blew, and Gary's face lit up. "All the way, all the way," he shrieked as his fists pummeled the air. Then he was scrambling down the icy grandstand and streaking onto the field.

"It looks like the only good thing that husband of yours did was to get Gary these season tickets," Peter joked as he and Donna cautiously made their way out of the stands.

"Soon-to-be ex-husband. Judge Kuffel is hearing the divorce next week. At least Steve had the grace not to contest it."

"He's got a lot more on his mind than the divorce. Ridgely has agreed to dismiss the criminal charges if he resigns from the bar. I hear he's going to leave town."

Donna and Peter found shelter near the concession stand where they always waited for Gary after a game. Peter bought two cups of hot coffee. They drank in silence for a few minutes, savoring the warmth of the steaming hot liquid. After a bit Peter decided it was time to talk about something he had been meaning to say all day but had not had the courage to bring up.

"Dad called last night. He asked me to come back to Hale, Greaves. I guess all is forgiven. I told him my answer depended on the answer to another question."

"What question?"

"Well, uh, my practice is going pretty good. I've picked up a lot of business because of Gary's case. Personal injury and retained criminal stuff. But there would be a bigger reason to stick around if you'd marry me when your divorce is final."

Donna blinked; then her eyes filled with tears and she threw her arms around Peter.

"Does that mean yes?" Peter asked as he broke out laughing.

Before Donna could respond, Gary came running toward them. He was holding a muddy jersey. "Look!" he shouted. "The coach said I could keep it. He said I'm lucky. He said the Stallions couldn't win without me."

"That's great, Gary," Donna managed.

"We did it, Pete. We went all the way."

"Let's get you home," Donna said to Gary as they started toward the parking lot. She had to shout to be heard over the blaring horns and raucous shouts of the jubilant Stallions rooters.

"Hey," Peter shouted, "what about my proposal?"

"We're going all the way," Gary shouted at a group of boisterous students.

"My sentiments exactly," Donna told Peter Hale.

ABOUT THE AUTHORS

PHOTO: FULGONI

KEN FOLLETT

After three historical sagas Ken Follett eagerly embraced the change of pace provided by a contemporary thriller. He welcomed the chance to explore a thoroughly modern woman as his heroine. "Jeannie is very strong-willed," he said from his home in London. "This sometimes makes her unpopular, but when she is in real trouble, it saves her." *The Third Twin* is Ken Follett's tenth best seller and the eighth to appear in these pages.

LAVYRLE SPENCER

A lifelong love of music—she plays the bass guitar—gave LaVyrle Spencer the inspiration for her latest novel. To get the details right, she interviewed country music star Reba McEntire and even sat in on a recording session. When the story had taken shape, Spencer had another idea: "I thought it would be fun to have a theme song to tie in with the book." So she composed one, and will sing it on the audio version of *Small Town Girl*. Does a new career beckon? Nashville, watch out!

DICK FRANCIS

To the Hilt is, amazingly, Dick Francis's thirty-fifth novel in as many years. He first took up the pen after a 1957 riding accident ended his youthful career as a steeplechase jockey. He found success with a racing column for England's *Sunday Express* and soon applied his knowledge of track life to fiction. In 1996 he was named Grand Master by the Mystery Writers of America; his recent best seller, *Come to Grief,* also won an Edgar award—his third—for best mystery novel of the year.

PHILLIP MARGOLIN

"Some of the events in *The Burning Man* are similar to incidents that actually occurred in a case that I handled many years ago," says Phillip M. Margolin, a criminal defense attorney in Portland, Oregon. But, he adds, the "book is peopled by characters I invented for the purpose of entertaining my readers." His previous legal thrillers include *After Dark* and the best seller *Gone, But Not Forgotten.* Margolin and his wife, Doreen, have two children.

The volumes in this series are issued
every two to three months. The typical volume
contains four outstanding books in condensed
form. None of the selections in any volume has
appeared in *Reader's Digest* itself. Any reader
may receive this service by writing
The Reader's Digest Association, Inc.,
Pleasantville, N.Y. 10570
or by calling 800-234-9000.

ACKNOWLEDGMENTS

Pages 154–155 (photo): Robert Milazzo. Page 155: cross-stitch design © Denis M. Williamson.
Pages 288–289 (background plaid): courtesy of Perthshire
Tourist Board; horse race photo: Ed Byrne.
Page 303, lines 19–25: from "Disobedience" by A. A. Milne, from *When We Were Very Young*
by A. A. Milne. Illustrations by E. H. Shepard. Copyright © 1924 by E. P. Dutton,
renewed 1952 by A. A. Milne. Used by permission of Dutton Children's Books,
a division of Penguin Books USA, Inc.
Page 339, lines 16–18: from English translation of "Bede's Death Song" from *The Earliest English
Poems*, Penguin Books, Third Edition, 1991. Translation by Michael Alexander.
Pages 424–425 (background photo): Charles Orrico/SuperStock. Page 425 (inset): SuperStock.